MW00528201

HERITAGE OF CYADOR

Tor Books by L. E. Modesitt, Jr.

The Saga of Recluce

The Magic of Recluce
The Towers of the Sunset
The Magic Engineer
The Order War
The Death of Chaos
Fall of Angels
The Chaos Balance
The White Order
Colors of Chaos
Magi'i of Cyador
Scion of Cyador
Wellspring of Chaos
Ordermaster
Natural Ordermage
Mage-Guard of Hamor
Arms-Commander
Cyador's Heirs
Heritage of Cyador

The Corean Chronicles

Legacies
Darknesses
Scepters
Alector's Choice
Cadmian's Choice
Soarer's Choice
The Lord-Protector's Daughter
Lady-Protector

The Imager Portfolio

Imager
Imager's Challenge
Imager's Intrigue
Scholar
Princeps
Imager's Battalion
Antiagon Fire
Rex Regis
Madness in Solidar (forthcoming)

The Spellsong Cycle

The Soprano Sorceress
The Spellsong War
Darksong Rising
The Shadow Sorceress
Shadowsinger

The Ecolitan Matter

Empire & Ecolitan (comprising *The Ecolitan Operation* and *The Ecologic Secession*)
Ecolitan Prime (comprising *The Ecologic Envoy* and *The Ecolitan Enigma*)
The Forever Hero (comprising *Dawn for a Distant Earth, The Silent Warrior,* and *In Endless Twilight*)

Timegod's World (comprising *Timediver's Dawn* and *The Timegod*)

The Ghost Books

Of Tangible Ghosts
The Ghost of the Revelator
Ghost of the White Nights
Ghost of Columbia (comprising *Of Tangible Ghosts* and *The Ghost of the Revelator*)

The Hammer of Darkness
The Green Progression
The Parafaith War
Adiamante
Gravity Dreams
The Octagonal Raven
Archform: Beauty
The Ethos Effect
Flash
The Eternity Artifact
The Elysium Commission
Viewpoints Critical
Haze
Empress of Eternity
The One-Eyed Man

L. E. Modesitt, Jr.

HERITAGE OF CYADOR

A Tom Doherty Associates Book / New York

This is a work of fiction. All of the characters, organizations, and events portrayed in this novel are either products of the author's imagination or are used fictitiously.

HERITAGE OF CYADOR

Maps by Ellisa Mitchell

A Tor Book
Published by Tom Doherty Associates, LLC
175 Fifth Avenue
New York, NY 10010

www.tor-forge.com

The Library of Congress Cataloging-in-Publication Data is available upon request.

ISBN 978-0-7653-7613-8 (hardcover)
ISBN 978-1-4668-6101-5 (e-book)

First Edition: November 2014

Printed in the United States of America

0 9 8 7 6 5 4 3 2 1

To David,

for taking a chance more than thirty years ago . . .

and sticking with me the whole way

Characters

Lephi	Emperor of Cyador (Deceased)
Mairena	Empress of Cyador (Deceased)
Kiedron	Duke of Cigoerne, Son of Lephi and Mairena
Xeranya	Healer and Consort of Kiedron
Emerya	Healer, Daughter of Lephi and Mairena
Jhalet	Commander, Mirror Lancers
Chaen	Majer, Second-in-Command, Mirror Lancers
Altyrn	Majer [stipended], former Commander of Mirror Lancers
Maeroja	Consort of Altyrn
Rojana	Daughter of Maeroja and Altyrn
Lephi	Eldest Son of Kiedron and Xeryana
Lerial	Second Son of Kiedron and Xeranya
Ryalah	Daughter of Kiedron and Xeranya
Amaira	Daughter of Emerya
Atroyan	Duke of Afrit
Haesychya	Atroyan's Consort; their children are Kyedra, Traeyen, and Natroyor
Rhamuel	Arms-Commander of Afrit, brother of Atroyan
Khesyn	Duke of Heldya
Casseon	Duke of Merowey
Tyrsalyn	Third Magus of Cyador, First Magus of Cigoerne
Saltaryn	Magus, former Tutor of Lerial
Apollyn	Magus
Veraan	Former Captain, Mirror Lancers, head of Myrapol House
Aenslem	Merchanter of Afrit, father of Haesychya

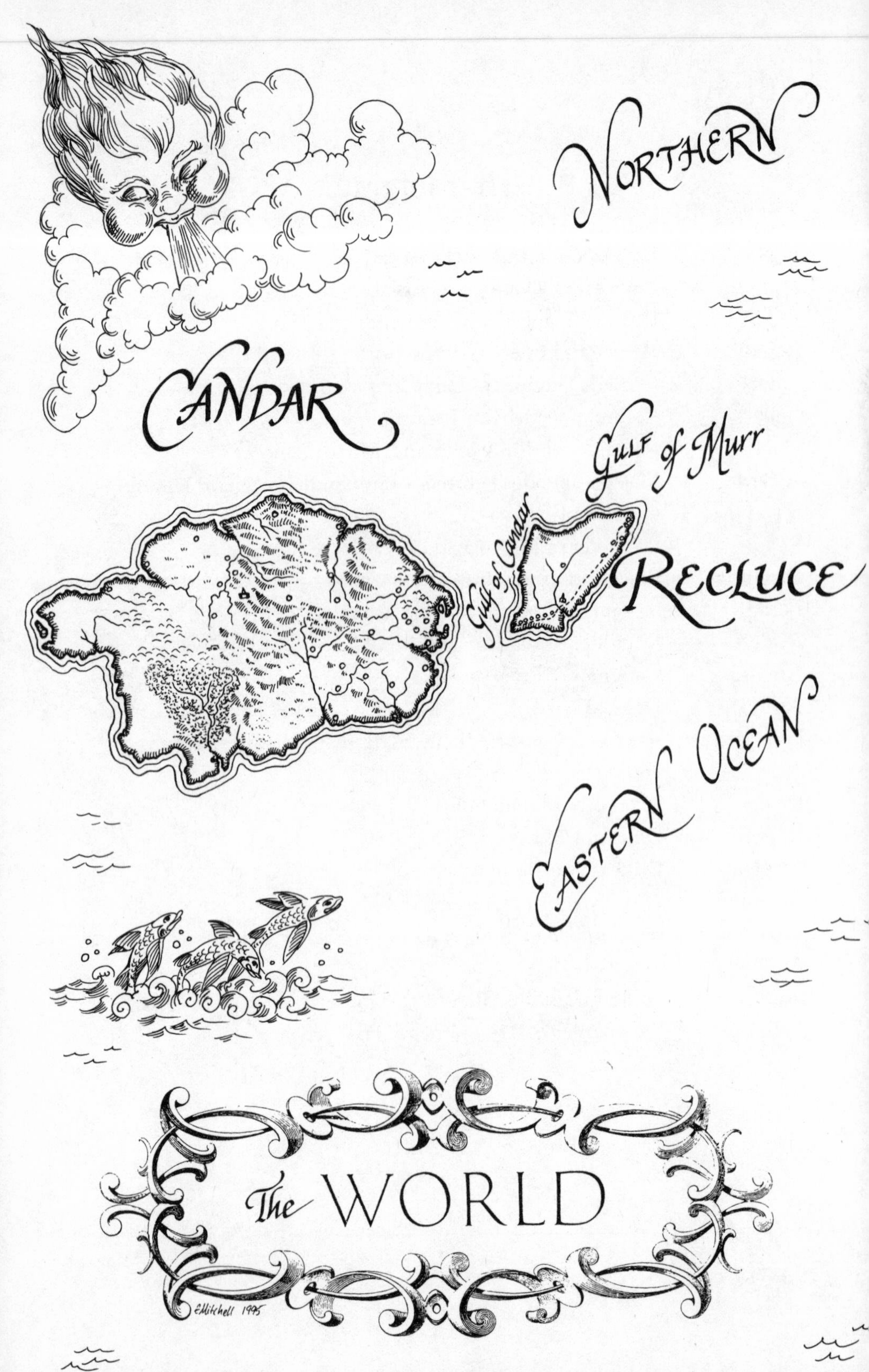
Northern
Candar
Gulf of Murr
Gulf of Candar
Recluce
Eastern Ocean
The WORLD
EMitchell 1995

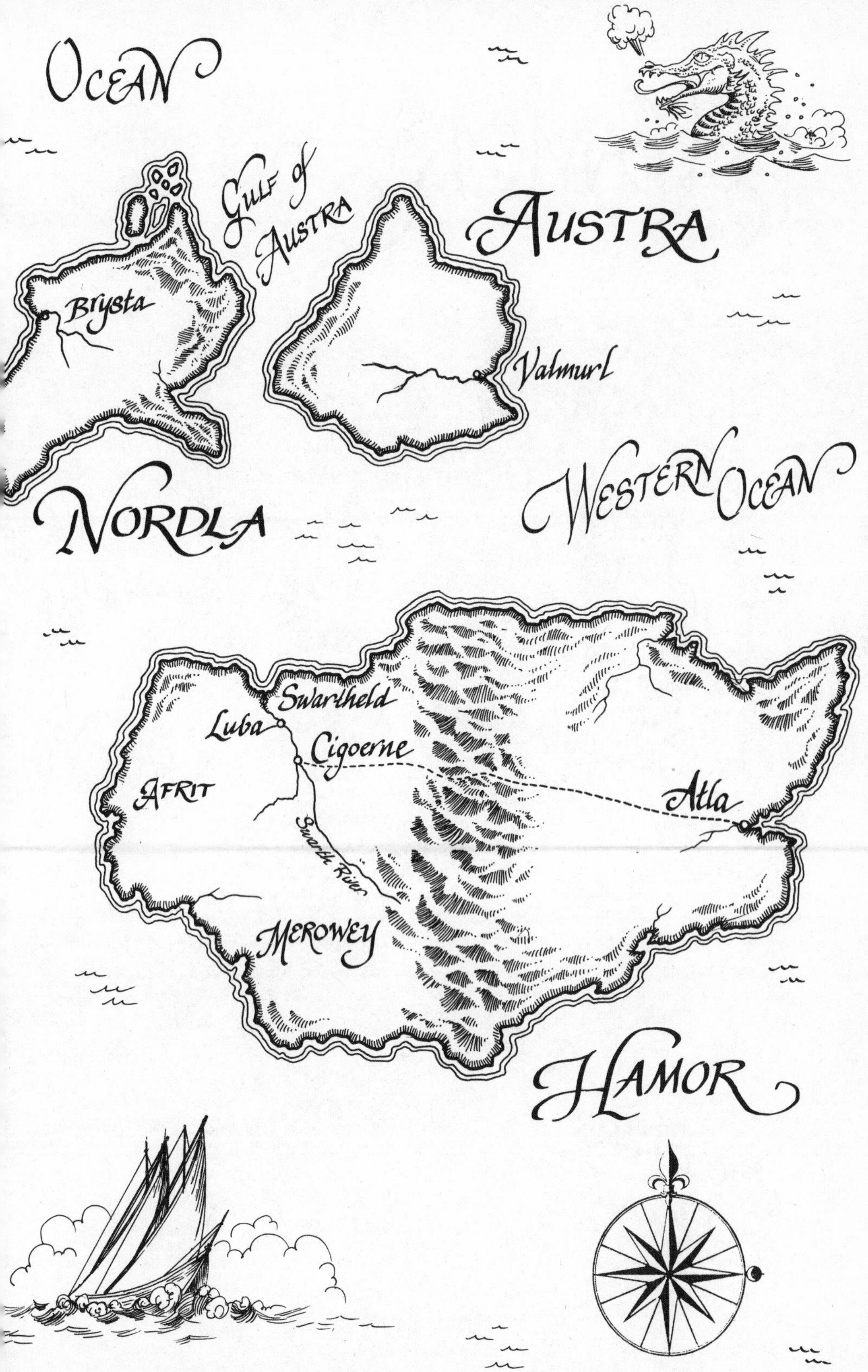

Ocean

Gulf of Austra

Austra

Brysta

Valmurl

Nordla

Western Ocean

Swartheld

Luba

Cigoerne

Afrit

Atla

Swarth River

Merowey

Hamor

HAMOR
Dolari
Northpoint
Swartheld
Luba
Guasyra
Cigoerne
Heldya
Highpoin
Quarries
SWARTH RIVER
Westyr
CLYAN RIVER
Jabuti
Clyanaka
Alsenyi
Kysha
MEROWEY
Dawhut
AWHUT RIVER
Elmari
Nubyat
Sastak
SOUTHERN
OCEAN

Eastern Ocean
N
W
E
S
Sanclar
Midpoint
Great Highway
Atla
Heldyn Mountains
Sylpa
Plyath
Elisa Mitchell 2007

HERITAGE OF CYADOR

PROLOGUE

From the low rise where he has reined up, the Mirror Lancer undercaptain glances eastward to the Swarth River, slightly more than five hundred yards away, its waters far lower than usual in the hot afternoon, an afternoon more like late summer or early harvest. Then his eyes turn westward, taking in the open lands, whose grass is dry and brown and barely calf high. More to the north are the few scattered plots that have brought forth little enough from the drought-plagued past harvest. Less than a kay behind him, beside the small stream that flows down the middle of the swale between the rolling rises, is a scattering of cots and hastily built shelters—structures thrown together by the people of Ensenla after they had fled the town of the same name, a town less than two kays north of where he waits, a town burned to the ground early that morning and now marked only by trails of smoke rising into the silver-hazed green-blue sky. Roughly fifty yards in front of him is a single post, stained a faded green. There is another such post a quarter kay to the east, overlooking the river, and another a quarter kay to the west, and that line of posts extends a good ten kays west of the river, perhaps farther, since the undercaptain has not measured the precise distance they extend in the three eightdays since he arrived to patrol the area.

The undercaptain studies the lay of the land, and the approach to the rise, knowing that a full battalion of Afritan Guards rides toward him and Eighth Company. They are less than half a kay to the north, just out of sight on the dirt road that has linked the burned-out town to the Cigoernean hamlet of Penecca for the past twenty years.

The undercaptain continues to reach out to the skies, frowning as he does. Still . . . there is enough moisture there to continue to create the clouds he would prefer but does not need.

"Ser?" asks the senior squad leader.

"Five companies. They're riding up the slope just on the other side of the border. They'll want us to stand aside so that they can slaughter the people who fled. We can't let them do that."

"Strange that the duke isn't here, ser."

The undercaptain knows that the senior squad leader is suggesting a withdrawal might be in order. "It's better that he isn't."

"Begging your pardon, ser . . ."

"The blood won't be on his hands." The undercaptain is being obscure, but he also knows that obscurity will serve him and the duke far better than clarity in the matter.

The Afritan battalion appears at the north side of the top of the rise perhaps two hundred yards from the undercaptain and the senior squad leader. The Afritans continue forward until the lead riders are within fifty yards of the border post, and the line of five companies abreast comes to a halt. All five companies re-form into a five-man front, then dress their ranks, and even their files.

An armsman carrying a white banner bordered in the dull crimson of Afrit rides forward, stopping just short of the border post.

The undercaptain motions for him to proceed, even as he separates order and chaos in the air above the rise, watching as the cloud above expands and darkens slightly.

The Afritan rides forward, reining up ten yards short of the Mirror Lancer undercaptain.

Neither speaks, but the undercaptain gestures.

The lancer clears his throat, then begins. "Majer Ehraam is pursuing traitors who have rebelled against His Mightiness Duke Atroyan. He would appreciate your not impeding his duty."

"These are the lands of Duke Kiedron. While we understand the majer's desire to do what he perceives as his duty, our duty is not to allow the armsmen of another land to murder and ride down those who have fled to Cigoerne for refuge."

"I am commanded to inform you, Undercaptain, that you and your men will be treated as allies of those who are traitors if you stand in the majer's way."

"Might I ask if Arms-Commander Rhamuel accompanies the field commander?"

The Afritan armsman does not answer.

"Surely, you must know," prompts the undercaptain.

"The majer has the authority of His Mightiness."

The undercaptain nods. "You may inform the majer that we will not harm him or his men so long as he does not cross the border into Cigoerne. My Mirror Lancers are posted a hundred yards south of that border."

"The majer must insist on the right to bring traitors to justice."

"He has the right to bring them to justice in Afrit, not in Cigoerne. That is the rule in all lands, and that is the agreement between Duke Kiedron and Duke Atroyan. We will enforce that right by force of arms if necessary."

"The majer has declared that he will pass."

"If the majer crosses the border with his battalion, we will enforce our right to protect ourselves."

"Then . . . the majer says you will suffer the consequences."

"So will he and all his men." The undercaptain glances at the small but thickening cloud that has gathered partly above him and mainly over the center of the rise to the north of where Eighth Company has reined up, arms ready.

Abruptly, the Afritan armsman turns and rides back to the massed formation.

The undercaptain waits.

"Ser . . . ?" ventures the senior squad leader.

"Have the squads hold their positions. I'll give the order if we need to attack."

"Yes, ser."

While the senior squad leader relays the order, the undercaptain concentrates, extending his order-senses and beginning to create order-lines as parallel as he can make them to the dancing chaos within the small thundercloud overhead, a cloud that darkens moment by moment as raindrops begin to fall across the top of the rise.

A trumpet triplet sounds, and the Afritan battalion starts forward at a fast walk. Carefully and precisely, the undercaptain eases apart order and chaos in both the air above the advancing Afritans and in the ground below them. The Afritan riders break into a canter as they pass the faded green boundary post.

As he senses, with what he thinks of as brilliant light, the interplay between a deeper level of order and chaos, an interplay within all things, the undercaptain begins to separate small bits of order and chaos in the ground under the mounted mass of Afritan riders. Seemingly just before, but in fact, a calculated time before that point where his separations would unleash massive power, he limits the separation, and creates a quadruple ten-line order coil with the power going into a shielded circle around the Afritans.

HSSSST!!!!

Lightnings flare from ground and sky in a pattern that crisscrosses men and their mounts, galvanizes blades with such force that they are ripped from the hands of men who do not even feel their death. Thunder with the force of mighty winds slams into everything within that fiery circle, and the charred fragments of men and mounts are thrown to the ground, consumed almost totally by flame, and then covered with fine ash that is all that remains of the browned grass of harvest.

The undercaptain shudders in his saddle as a wave of silver gray flows over him, a wave unseen by any but him. His eyes blur, and tears stream down his cheeks. His head feels as though it is being pounded with a wooden mallet. He squints, enough to sharpen his blurred vision so that he can make out what lies before him on the top of the rise.

All that remains of a battalion of mounted Afritan armsmen is a circle of ash and blackened ground some two hundred yards across.

The senior squad leader gapes, then looks to the undercaptain, his mouth open, but wordless.

"The skies and storms favor Cigoerne," says the officer. After a long silence, he adds, "Have Second Squad continue the patrol. The other squads will return to our camp. We need to tell the people of Ensenla that it is safe to reclaim what they can from their old town. They're entitled to it. They've little enough left to their names."

"Yes, ser."

The rain is already beginning to let up as the undercaptain and the bulk of Eighth Company begin their return to the temporary camp and post in Ensenla, a post that the undercaptain knows full well will soon become a large and permanent base for protecting the northern border of the duchy.

I

Lerial looks up from the half-written report before him, thinking, *Saltaryn, if you only knew how all your efforts to improve my writing with precise statements are being corroded by the requirements of being post captain.* Then he concentrates on the words he has just written.

> . . . the Afritan Guard continues to patrol the top of the ridge one kay north of Ensenla. They occasionally stray across the marked boundary. They do not stay on the south side of the boundary for long, and they refrain from crossing when a Mirror Lancer force larger or roughly equivalent to the Afritan force is present . . .

He shakes his head. *They're not quite taunting us, but what can you do?* At the same time, he worries about what he writes, because he had earlier sensed, not that much after dawn, a number of riders leaving the Afritan Guard post to the north, and now he waits for his scouts to return and report.

Lerial glances from the dispatch he is writing, the required summary of Eighth and Eleventh Companies' evolutions and other events occurring over the previous eightday, to the dispatch he had received two eightdays earlier.

> *From:* Jhalet, Commander, Mirror Lancers
> *To:* Lerial, Captain, Ensenla Post
> *Date:* Third Twoday of Winter, 593 A.F.
> *Subject:* Border Patrols
>
> Please find attached a map of the border between Afrit and Cigoerne, as agreed to by Duke Kiedron and Duke Atroyan. These borders are to be respected. Duke Kiedron has affirmed that no Mirror Lancer company is to cross them, even under extreme provocation. All officers and squad leaders are to be familiar with the borders and to conduct patrols in such a fashion that no Mirror Lancer evolution can be taken as provocative or as an encroachment upon Afritan lands.

> Duke Atroyan has issued a similar proclamation to the Afritan Guard. Should the Guard inadvertently trespass, all Mirror Lancer squads and/or companies should offer the Guard the opportunity to retreat before resorting to arms. That opportunity need not be offered should any Afritan force commence hostile actions on the lands of Cigoerne.
>
> If such hostile action is commenced on the lands of Cigoerne by Afritan or other forces, whatever response may be necessary shall be determined by the officer or squad leader in command of the Mirror Lancer force so attacked. In no case, however, shall a Mirror Lancer force knowingly enter the lands of Afrit. The sole exception to this directive is that a company commander or more senior officer may commission a force to recover Mirror Lancers carried into Afritan territory.
>
> Any attacks by Afritan forces are to be reported expeditiously to Mirror Lancer headquarters, as are any border crossings for the purpose of recovering personnel. Such reports must contain the time, the location, and the complete scope of forces, both Mirror Lancer and others, involved in the action.

Lerial returns his attention to his own report and continues to write. A third of a glass later, he signs the report and eases it aside to let the ink dry before folding and sealing it for dispatch. He considers all that has happened over the past four years—and all that has not—ever since the people of Ensenla all fled Afrit over less than an eightday and subsequently rebuilt the town, or much of it, in the duchy of Cigoerne . . . and then demanded the right to continue to till their lands and tend their flocks on their ancestral hills.

Duke Atroyan's response had been quick . . . and disastrous for the Afritan Guard. Lerial shakes his head, recalling the events that followed. Thankfully, over the last four years, he has not been required to use such force. The upside of the "effect" of such a storm has been that Duke Atroyan could suggest that the deceased field commander had been unwise to attack in such weather . . . and lay the blame there, with no word about the fact that the duke himself had ordered the attack while his brother, the arms-commander of Afrit, had been either inspecting the ironworks at Luba or ill with a severe flux . . . at least that is what Lerial has gathered over the years, from listening and from veiled hints from his aunt Emerya, who has her own sources. But the downside of letting a freak storm take most of the blame for the deaths of over five hundred men is that at least some officers in the Afritan Guard are wagering that such a freak storm is unlikely to occur again . . . and they are tired of being restrained from pursuing the growing numbers of refugees who have fled to Cigoerne, many of whom have been skilled crafters. Nor has Duke Atroyan grown more patient as time has passed . . . which is why Commander Jhalet issued the order that rests on Lerial's desk. It is also why Lerial has insisted on training one squad from each company to use horn bows similar to those used by the Verdyn Lancers—even if it took some pressure by his sire to get permission for that . . . and well over a year of training.

Lerial has no desire to unleash the power of unbinding linked order and chaos again . . . and he has been fortunate in not having to do so. *But how long will you be able to refrain?*

Cigoerne has grown to almost half again its size in five years, and places like Penecca, the "new" Ensenla, and Teilyn, as well as others that had been barely more that hamlets or small towns, now are far more than that, and the factors in Cigoerne have added two more river piers to handle the trade from all over Hamor, and even from Candar and Austra.

A rap on the study door breaks through his momentary musing. "Yes?"

"Captain, the watch reports the scouts are at the crossroads."

"Thank you. I'll be out in a moment."

Lerial checks the dispatch, thinks about folding and sealing it, then snorts softly. *No point in doing that until you hear what the scouts have discovered . . . or not.* He rises and leaves the study, stepping into the small anteroom of the Ensenla Post headquarters building and walking to the duty desk.

"Ser." The duty ranker looks up.

"I'll have something later for a dispatch rider. Let the duty squad know."

"Yes, ser."

"Thank you." Lerial then walks out into the cold wind blowing out of the southwest and stands waiting for the scouts to ride into the post and report. He does not wait long.

The two Mirror Lancers in their greens and heavy riding jackets—and gray gloves—rein up outside the headquarters building. Both have red faces from the cold and wind. "Tie your mounts. You can report where it's warmer." Lerial smiles. He can recall every winter he has spent in Ensenla, and how much he appreciated the few days of leave spent at the palace in Cigoerne.

Once the three are seated in his study, Lerial nods to Vominen, the former Verdyn Lancer who transferred to the Mirror Lancers as soon as he could, even before the Verdyn Lancers became Mirror Lancers and ceased to exist as a separate force. "You look like something has happened." It's not that the scout looks that way, but that Lerial can sense the patterns of order and chaos that flow around him, and the turbulence of those patterns is suggestive.

"Ser . . . almost all of the Afritan Guard pulled out of the north Ensenla post just after dawn this morning."

"How do you know?" Lerial grins. "Or did you sneak over there?"

"Wouldn't call it sneaking, ser. Just rode over and asked one of the herders. Besides, there was no one about, and they do the same when they can."

"And?"

"I rode almost to the gates. They're barred. No one's in the watchtower. No smoke from the chimneys. No smoke in midwinter, ser?" Vominen shakes his head.

"What did you see, Naedar?"

"Same as Vominen, ser. One of the herder boys said they took three wagons, too."

Lerial nods slowly.

After another third of a glass with the two scouts, Lerial feels they have told him everything they can recall, and he dismisses them. He looks to the dispatch he had written earlier. *You'll need to rewrite that and send it off immediately.*

Why . . . why in the name of the Rational Stars would Rhamuel pull three companies of guards from Ensenla when for the past two years those guards have been patrolling the border and looking for any excuse to provoke the Mirror Lancers into a skirmish?

Lerial can think of only two reasons—a crisis in Swartheld, even an armed uprising, since Duke Atroyan has been far from the most effective ruler of Afrit, or an attack on Afrit, most likely on Luba or even Swartheld itself, by the forces of Duke Khesyn of Heldya. Either of those events would be far worse for Cigoerne than another Afritan attack on Ensenla or anywhere else along Cigoerne's northern border.

Could there be other reasons? Quite possibly, although Lerial has no idea what they might be, only that it's unlikely that they would be any better than the alternatives that he already suspects are the reasons for the Afritan withdrawal.

II

By fourday morning, just before muster, Lerial has still heard nothing from headquarters, not that he expected a dispatch in the morning, but he had thought there might have been one on threeday afternoon. He'd even sent lancers to check the lone pier that serves Ensenla, and the scouts had talked to more of the Afritan herders and growers, but none of them knew anything more than Lerial and the scouts. A delay in response from the commander means nothing in itself, but Ensenla post is less than a day's ride north of Cigoerne—though a fast ride to make in that time—and Lerial sent out the dispatch on oneday.

There's no helping that, he thinks as he steps out of headquarters to receive the morning reports. Both officers are waiting on the narrow porch.

"Eleventh Company stands ready, ser," reports Undercaptain Strauxyn.

"Eighth Company stands ready, ser," reports Senior Squad Leader Fheldar, who handles the muster for Lerial, since Lerial is both Eighth Company captain and post commander.

"Good." Since Eleventh Company is the duty company for the day, Lerial turns to Strauxyn. "Keep up the scouting runs on the Afritan post . . . and to the west, just in case the withdrawal was some sort of feint. If anything changes, let me know. Keep someone posted at the pier as well."

"Yes, ser."

At the inquiring looks from the two, Lerial shakes his head. "You'd have already heard if we'd gotten a dispatch from the commander. He may not know anything more than we do." *In fact, he might not even have known what we know.* Lerial understands the need for following the chain of command, but there are times when not following it might result in better information . . . and sooner, and this might be one of those times, since it is just possible that either his father or his aunt might have information that would be useful.

"Yes, ser," replies Fheldar blandly.

Lerial manages not to smile, knowing exactly what Fheldar's blandness signifies. At the same time, having served under Phortyn, the previous commander of the Mirror Lancers, Lerial would far rather have the not terribly imaginative, and very honest and loyal, Jhalet in that position. "I'll be riding out on my own inspection in half a glass, Strauxyn. If you'd have four rankers . . ."

"Yes, ser."

It is closer to a third of a glass later when Lerial rides out through the post gates on the brown gelding that has been his primary mount for almost six years, accompanied by four lancers. The post stands on high ground to the west of Ensenla, ground not quite so high as that of the rise along which the border between Cigoerne and Afrit runs, but with a swale between it and the border rise.

As always, but especially when he leaves the post, Lerial has created an order-shield that will repel chaos-bolts and iron weapons—and linked it to his belt knife. Even after five years of trying, for reasons he cannot fathom he has been unable to create shields directly linked to himself, and that could pose a problem at times, because the linked shields have a tendency to fade, unless renewed, roughly two glasses after being created. He can create momentarily larger shields, enough to protect a company, for a short time, but holding them for any longer than a tenth of a glass quickly exhausts him.

You should count yourself fortunate, he reminds himself. And he should, because his father, for all his Magi'i bloodline, has no ability to shield himself at all, and his brother Lephi's shields, although based on chaos rather than order, are far weaker than Lerial's.

Lerial turns the gelding onto the main road from the post through the town and to the river pier. Less than half a kay from the post gates is a dwelling under construction, its walls of sun-dried mud bricks that will be covered with a mud plaster when the house is completed and roofed and then whitewashed with numerous coats until the walls are almost a shimmering white. The walls of the older dwellings, not that any are more than four years old, are beginning to take on a faint pinkish shade from the reddish dust that is all too prevalent in summer.

As he rides into the center of the town, and across the small square, he sees that the small walled and roofed terrace of the inn on the south side of the square is vacant, as it usually is in winter, but that two men watch from the narrow front porch.

"Good morning, Captain!" calls Carlyat, the taller of the two, and the son of Harush, who owns the inn and tavern.

"The same to you," returns Lerial cheerfully.

Carlyat grins and shakes head.

Beyond the square are a handful of crafters' shops, and the only chandlery north of the city proper of Cigoerne. More than once when he was young, Lerial had questioned his father about why the city that held the palace and the duchy itself were both called Cigoerne, and the answer was invariably the same: "Because that is the way it has to be."

Now . . . it doesn't have to be that way, but the habit is so ingrained that it's unlikely to change, at least not anytime soon. Beyond the crafters' shops is the single factorage in Ensenla, and it is, given the herders, a wool factorage that sits almost at the foot of the single brick and stone pier extending some twenty yards from the shore out into the gray-blue water, which also holds a touch of brown. At the moment, no craft are tied there, as is usually the case. Lerial glances across the river toward the marshes on the far side, but he sees no fishermen or bird hunters there, nor any flatboats or trading craft.

While he has never measured the width of the river, it is more than half a kay across when it reaches Swartheld, according to Emerya, and from Lerial's own best judgment it is not that much narrower at Ensenla or even Cigoerne, although it narrows considerably upstream of Cigoerne. That, he does recall from the few journeys he had taken with his father when he was much younger.

After a short time, he turns the gelding away from the pier and rides north along the river road, which quickly turns into little more than a trail, well before it reaches the faded green post that marks the boundary between the two duchies. He takes his time as he heads west along the border. Almost three glasses after he set out, Lerial rides back into Ensenla Post, his winter jacket loosened because the sun and the still air have made the day almost pleasant. He has seen no sign of any Afritan troopers or raiders . . . and he has been able to sense no bodies of men within more than five kays of Ensenla . . . and that worries him.

He is still worrying, sitting behind his desk and looking at maps, two glasses later when the duty ranker calls out, "Ser! There's a dispatch rider coming through the gates."

Lerial does not quite bolt to his feet, but he is waiting by the duty desk as a dispatch rider he does not recognize hurries into headquarters.

"Captain Lerial, ser?"

Lerial nods. "Yes?"

"These are for you, ser." The rider hands over two sealed dispatches and a small leather pouch. "They're from Commander Jhalet, ser."

"Thank you."

"My pleasure, ser."

"If you'd arrange for food . . ." Lerial looks to the duty ranker.

"Yes, ser."

Lerial turns and takes the dispatch and pouch back into his small study, closing the door behind himself. Then he breaks the seal and unfolds the first dispatch, a single sheet, and begins to read.

The message is brief, and the key sentence is simple and direct: "In view of your service and ability to keep the north border secure, you are hereby promoted to Overcaptain, effective immediately." The signature at the bottom is that of Commander Jhalet.

The small pouch that has come with the dispatch contains the insignia of an overcaptain.

The unexpected promotion troubles Lerial greatly, because in the normal course of events he would not have been considered for promotion for roughly another year and a half, and also because his older brother Lephi has been an overcaptain for less than a year, having spent the full five years as a captain.

Lerial looks at the second dispatch, then opens it. The substance of that dispatch, also from Jhalet—and, unlike the first, written in the commander's own hand—is equally brief and direct.

> You are hereby temporarily recalled to Mirror Lancer headquarters for consultation, to leave no later than fiveday morning and to make deliberate speed. Undercaptain Strauxyn will act as temporary post commander in your absence.

The two dispatches could easily have been written on a single sheet, but Jhalet had not done so, most likely because a duplicate of the promotion dispatch would be in Lerial's files, and that means that the recall dispatch is not something that Jhalet wishes to share with anyone at the moment.

An early promotion and a recall for consultations, whatever that means? Lerial has grave doubts that it means anything good. The only question is how bad the trouble is and where.

III

Just after first light on fiveday, Lerial rides south from Ensenla, accompanied by half a squad from Eighth Company. While the river road is not paved until it is within five kays of the city of Cigoerne, it has been traveled so much over the past ten years, with sand added periodically, that the mixed sand and clay is packed hard. Duke Kiedron had also insisted that the road be set on the highest relatively level surfaces and that all bridges be wide enough for a least a wagon and a horse side by side.

Even making good speed, Lerial does not catch sight of the city until the second glass of the afternoon, when he reaches the north side of the rise that holds, on its southern end, the Hall of Healing, where he had spent so many days learning what he could from his aunt. The reddish sandstone building, surrounded by its sandstone walls, looks no different to him, but to the west of the hall stretches a good half kay's worth of smaller dwellings that over the past five years have crept northward from the boulevard that links the hall with the palace. Every time that Lerial returns to the city, he is surprised at the additional growth.

As he and the lancers ride past the Hall of Healing, heading south on the paved avenue that runs along the river toward the Mirror Lancer headquarters, Lerial wonders if he should stop briefly, then shakes his head. He will certainly see Emerya at the palace later that afternoon . . . and the dispatch conveyed urgency.

South of the hall, but north of the River Square, are the factorages of the larger merchanters in Cigoerne. Not only are they busier than he recalls, but he could swear that there are more factorages, and that some new ones have been built, taking the place of smaller factorages or perhaps crafters' shops.

There is also a new, longer stone pier south of the two piers that had projected from the stone levee walls protecting the city for almost as long as Lerial could remember—and all three piers have rivercraft of various sorts tied there. There are no Lancer sailing craft, either. At that, he frowns . . . and looks farther south along the river, but the buildings flanking the avenue block his view. Extending his order-senses, he discovers another pier, several hundred yards north of the Mirror Lancer headquarters compound. *So much trading that they had to add a pier for the river patrols?*

Before long, he and the rankers near headquarters. Even from the River Avenue, Lerial can see the white-edged black draping on the headquarters' gateposts. *Who died?* It cannot be Jhalet, unless it happened in the last day, and that would be unlikely. Nor would it be anyone from his family . . . again, unless it has happened in the last few glasses. *Majer Chaen?* Lerial hopes not, but then, he wouldn't like it to be any of those whose names have passed through his thoughts.

He rides more slowly up the stone causeway toward the gates, trying to think over who it might have been.

"Welcome to headquarters, Captain, oh . . . excuse me, ser, Overcaptain," calls out the ranker posted on the east side of the headquarters compound gate.

"Thank you." Lerial gestures at the white-edged black drape on each of the gateposts. "Not Commander Jhalet?" "

"No, ser. Not him. It was the majer . . . I mean Commander Altyrn. We heard late last night."

The ranker's clearly regretful words go through Lerial like a lance of ice. *Altyrn? The majer . . . the man who has made all that you have done possible. The man who taught you blade skills, who worked you until you understood what work truly was . . . and who gave you the sabre you still carry . . . telling you that he was restoring your own heritage . . .*

"Ser . . . ?"

Lerial manages to rein up the gelding, but cannot speak for a moment. "I'm sorry. I had no idea . . ."

"No one did, ser."

"Do you know . . . ?"

"No, ser. Commander Jhalet might."

"Thank you." Lerial rides directly to the hexagonal stone headquarters building, still trying to grapple with the idea of Altyrn's death. The majer—

that was always the way Lerial thought of him—had been anything but young. Lerial had never known his actual age, but he'd been close to the age of his Grandmere Mairena. Another thought strikes him. *Could that be why you're being recalled to Cigoerne?* No, that couldn't be, not when headquarters had only heard of the majer's death late the night before.

Outside the headquarters building, he reins up, then turns to Dhoraat, the First Squad leader. "Have the horses watered and rested, but don't unsaddle them until you hear from me. We may be quartering here or at the palace. I won't know until I talk to the commander." *Assuming he's here . . . but he should be . . . with Altyrn's death, especially.* Even as he thinks those thoughts, Lerial knows that they make little logical sense.

"Yes, ser."

Lerial dismounts and hands the gelding's reins to the nearest ranker, then walks into headquarters, taking off his lancer's visor cap and tucking it under his arm as he crosses the anteroom.

The young ranker at the duty desk snaps to his feet. "Ser! The commander said you're to go right in."

"Thank you." Lerial steps around the desk and pushes the door, already slightly ajar, open, enters the study, and closes it behind himself.

Jhalet rises easily from behind the table desk. Lerial again notices how, over the past five years, the commander's once jet-black hair has gained more and more strands of silver white, and his face has hardened somewhat, but he smiles pleasantly enough. "You made good time, Overcaptain."

"We left at first light. Your dispatch suggested urgency." Before Jhalet can reply, Lerial goes on. "Majer Altyrn? Do you know . . . ?"

Jhalet shakes his head. "We got word from the palace lancers last night." He gestures toward the chairs in front of the desk, then seats himself. "All we know is that he died at his villa."

"If his death isn't the reason I've been recalled . . ." Lerial seats himself, if slightly forward on the straight-backed armless chair. "Your dispatch did stress urgency."

"That's because your father the duke believes we face an urgent situation. I would prefer not to say more, but let him explain. He has requested that we both join him at the palace as soon as possible after you arrived."

"I did not have my mount unsaddled, nor those of the rankers who accompanied me. We can leave as soon as you wish."

"There is a mount standing by . . . and a half squad to accompany me back." Jhalet offers a wry smile. "I have no doubt that you and your men will be quartered at the palace. We can leave now." The commander rises.

Lerial is grateful not to sit longer and does so as well. "Before we go . . . how are matters in the southeast?"

"At Sudstrym Post? With the Heldyans?" Jhalet smiles. "Very quiet since midfall. Even the Meroweyan traders report fewer encounters with raiders or overzealous tariff inspectors."

Lerial nods, but given the way Jhalet has spoken, his words do not totally reassure Lerial, except that they mean that Lephi has not been in any great danger . . . so far. Lerial also knows that can change almost in moments, even for an heir of Cyador who is of the Magi'i.

Jhalet slips on his Lancer riding jacket and picks up his visor cap, and he and Lerial leave the study. In less than a tenth of a glass they and a full squad of rankers—the ten from Eighth Company and ten from headquarters—are riding northwest on the paved boulevard that connects the Lancer compound with the Square of the Magi'i and the walled ducal palace that stands on the west side of the square. Half a glass later, they ride through the palace gates, also draped in white-edged black mourning cloth, and then to the north courtyard and the entrance in the middle of the north wing.

As they dismount, a comparatively small and wiry undercaptain steps forward. "Welcome back, ser. And congratulations."

The man looks familiar, black-haired, brown-eyed, with a swarthy complexion and deeply tanned skin, but it takes Lerial a moment to place him. "Kusyl! What are you doing here?"

"The Lancers out west had enough of me." Kusyl grins. "Commander said I deserved a pleasant tour heading up a new company here. These days, half of what I do is work with the newer men, bring them up to the level of the others."

Lerial wonders just how many new companies are being formed.

"Now that I've got the whole company working well"—Kusyl shrugs—"the commander will send us to one of the border problem areas." He grins again. "Might even be Ensenla."

"That would be fine with me. Did you have any trouble with Duke Casseon?"

"Not a sign of his armsmen. They've left handling the grassland raiders to us. They just kill 'em if they enter his lands and attack his growers. Not many of them left anymore, not since they discovered that Casseon had no use for them and they had much shorter lives if they came north."

"We need to talk, but not now. We've been summoned."

"We . . . ?" Kusyl's eyes take in the officer behind Lerial. He smiles good-naturedly, if wryly. "Good afternoon, Commander. Might I ask how long before you'll be needing the mounts?"

"That depends on the duke. Those who came with Lord Lerial will be quartered here. The others will return with me."

"Yes, ser."

Once Lerial and Jhalet are past the Lancer guards and walking down the corridor toward the duke's main-floor study, the commander laughs softly. "He's even better for this post than I thought."

"He's good in the field, too. Very good."

"He'll be promoted to captain next season." Jhalet shakes his head. "And then I'll likely hear from Magus Apollyn, indirectly of course, about the degradation of the proud heritage of the Mirror Lancers."

"Magus Apollyn?" Then Lerial remembers. "Veraan's father. Is he still angry about that?"

"Still? He was never just angry. He was furious about Veraan's dismissal, and his fury likely hasn't ever abated. Veraan's really the one in charge of Myrapol House now. They say he's quite effective as a merchanter . . . even worked out an arrangement with a big merchanting house in Swartheld. Alaphyn, or Alapyrt, something like that."

Lerial nods, deciding against saying more, although his own recollections of Veraan are anything but pleasant, and those date back to well before the incident when Veraan tried to use an unblunted blade in sparring against Captain Woelyt—although Woelyt had still been an undercaptain then. Jhalet had cashiered Veraan. *But then, Veraan's slimy enough to succeed as a trader . . . for a while, anyway.*

The guard outside the study sees the two coming and raps on the door, announcing, "Lord Lerial and Commander Jhalet, ser." Then, presumably in response to Duke Kiedron, he opens the door and steps back, then closes it behind them.

Kiedron is standing by the widow that looks into the central palace courtyard, but faces the study door. "Lerial . . . Commander." He smiles warmly, but only for a moment, then gestures to the small circular conference table at one end of the study.

Lerial looks at his father. Kiedron's dark brown hair is thinning on top. Elsewhere, especially on the sides, where it is remains thick, the brown is shot with gray, when a year earlier there had been no sign of either. There are dark circles under his eyes. His broad shoulders seem to slump just a touch, and for the first time the duke looks his age, and that is surprising for Lerial, because, until now, Kiedron has looked younger than the years he has lived.

Just to make sure that something is not terribly wrong, as Lerial moves toward the table he immediately extends his order-senses, although he knows his mother and his aunt, as healers, surely would have noticed something amiss. There is no sign of rampant body chaos or illness, only the feeling of slightly weaker order that creeps up on all people as they age.

Has he changed that much? Or did you always just see him as strong and vital, almost indestructible? Lerial seats himself as the other two do, then waits for either Jhalet or his father to speak.

"You summoned us, ser," Jhalet says quietly.

"I did." Kiedron looks to his son. "I asked Commander Jhalet not to talk about this with anyone until we talked over matters. Duke Khesyn is moving armsmen to Vyada . . ."

Vyada . . . just across the river and south of Luba. Lerial nods and waits for his father to continue.

". . . and he has already gathered a number of flatboats there."

"Might I ask how you came to know this, ser?"

"Both indirectly and directly. The formal and direct notice came from Atroyan himself, or at least in a dispatch purportedly signed and sealed by him . . ."

Lerial doesn't like the slight emphasis on the word "purportedly."

". . . but the information appears to be accurate from what various traders have reported and from other sources. The dispatch from Atroyan suggests that it might be to our benefit to send a force to Luba for joint friendly maneuvers." Kiedron smiles pleasantly, although Lerial can sense from the chaos-order flows around him that he is not so composed as he appears.

"Do you think Atroyan is ill," asks Lerial, "and that someone, such as Rhamuel, is using his seal to obtain the assistance that Atroyan would never request? Or is this a ploy to trap and destroy at least several companies of our lancers?"

"Those are good questions," replies the duke. "We know that Khesyn is sending armsmen to Vyada. We don't know why. The dispatch from Swartheld came by a fast sail-galley."

"That means that whoever dispatched it did so with the approval of someone high in Atroyan's counsels," suggests Jhalet.

"There is also the fact that the Afritans have abandoned their Ensenla post and withdrawn all the Afritan Guards stationed there," Lerial points out.

"That strikes me as offering no risk at all to Atroyan," Jhalet points out. "He knows we won't invade."

"If he is threatened by Khesyn, that would be the first place from which he would withdraw the Afritan Guards," Kiedron replies. "He knows that we know that. So that offers no evidence as to whether his dispatch is genuine or a ploy and trap." He looks to Lerial.

"I think *someone* in Swartheld is very concerned, and I would suspect it is not the duke."

Jhalet turns his eyes on Lerial but does not speak.

"Why do you say that?" asks Kiedron.

"Because when we know that Arms-Commander Rhamuel has been in command of the Afritan Guards, they have not attacked us. Only when he has not been in command have we been attacked. They have taunted us time and time again on the northern border but always retreated before we could come close to attacking. That would seem to me, at least from the perspective of a captain who only patrolled the border, that Rhamuel has been having the Guards act as aggressively as possible without provoking an actual fight. That means that Atroyan is the one who wants to attack, and that he has been restrained by his brother. They built a new post in old Ensenla . . . but they've pulled out? That, just in my opinion, suggests great need for those troops, but I have my doubts that even Rhamuel could pull them unless the need is very great or Atroyan is indisposed . . . if not both."

"That may be," replies Jhalet. "If it is, what happens if you dispatch a force, and Atroyan recovers and declares that we are invading Afrit? Or someone else takes power?"

"We would have to dispatch that force in such a way and under such a commander that it would be unwise for the Afritans to attack, regardless of who controls Swartheld." Kiedron looks to his son.

Lerial understands immediately. "What forces would you wish I take? And what gifts will you proffer?"

"You are one of the heirs . . ." Jhalet draws out the words.

"My father is strong and healthy, and so is my brother, and I am not the principal heir."

"There is also the fact that Lerial speaks perfect Hamorian, and any officer who is assigned to this duty must be able to understand it well enough to know what is not being said." Kiedron holds up his hand to forestall any more discussion. "Commander, I would like you to come up with a plan for how the Mirror Lancers could support a force moving north along the river to Luba. I would also like to hear any reservations you might have, and the reasons for those reservations. Likewise, of any advantages such a plan might create. Lerial and I will discuss the other matters such an evolution might affect. We will meet tomorrow morning at eighth glass."

Jhalet inclines his head. "Yes, ser."

"Tomorrow morning, at eighth glass," says Kiedron firmly. Then he stands.

Lerial and Jhalet immediately rise.

Once the commander leaves the study, Kiedron turns to Lerial. "Your mother and the girls would like to see you, but there is something else you need to attend to."

"Ser?"

"I assume you heard about Majer Altyrn."

"Yes, ser. I wanted to know more, but Commander Jhalet couldn't tell me."

"Maeroja is here. She brought the news. She is waiting for you in the small south salon."

Lerial understands. His mother has never fully approved of Altyrn's consort, and his father has given Maeroja the use of the salon as far from her as possible . . . and the one about which Xeranya cannot complain.

"She has indicated she wishes to speak to you first. I'm certain she'll tell you what you need to know," adds Kiedron. "All of us, including Maeroja, will be having refreshments in the main salon at fifth glass."

"Did she come alone?"

"Captain Shastan sent half a squad of lancers as her escort. None of the majer's daughters accompanied her." Kiedron glances toward the door.

"Yes, ser." Lerial nods and then leaves the study. As he walks along the main front corridor toward the south wing of the palace, he wonders exactly why Maeroja wishes to see him . . . and why she does not wish to speak of the majer to anyone before Lerial.

He pauses outside the closed door to the small salon, then opens it and steps inside, easing the door closed before he moves forward.

Maeroja rises immediately from the dark green velvet armchair in which she has been sitting, setting aside a folder. From what Lerial sees and senses, she looks no older than the last time he saw her, almost five years earlier when he returned from Verdheln, and just as striking. Her hair remains a shining jet black, her skin lightly tanned, and her blue eyes intense and penetrating . . . but upon closer scrutiny when he steps toward her, he can see that her eyes are slightly bloodshot and that there are dark circles under them. Her smile remains warm, but . . . there is sadness in it as well. She wears a pale blue blouse, with a dark blue vest and trousers, and a mourning scarf of white-bordered black.

"Lady," Lerial offers gently.

"You do persist, don't you?" she murmurs softly.

"You were, are, and always will be a lady," he replies with a smile. "Grant me the wisdom to see that."

"You've grown . . . even more."

"I would hope so. Otherwise, I wouldn't be following the majer's teachings." He gestures. "Please sit down. The last days have to have been tiring for you."

"And not for you? There's still road dust on your boots."

"I did ride in this afternoon, but I had to meet with Father and Commander Jhalet. Father didn't tell me you were here until after the meeting."

"He and . . . Altyrn . . . always had their priorities."

As do you. Lerial inclines his head momentarily, then picks up one of the straight-backed chairs, sets it on the carpet directly facing Maeroja, and after she reseats herself sits down. "I didn't hear until I rode into Lancer headquarters. I asked about the mourning drape, and the gate guards told me, but no one could tell me more than that."

"He wanted it that way. I owed him that . . . and much more than I could ever repay."

"I think not, Lady. You gave him love and respect that no one else could have done." *Especially given your past, a very illustrious past that you have kept well shrouded.*

Maeroja opens her mouth as if to protest, then smiles softly, ironically. "I won't insult you by protesting . . . but he deserved that."

"He deserved more than that."

"We don't often get what we deserve, especially those who are very good . . . or very evil."

"No . . . we don't. That was something I learned from him, among many other lessons."

"Unlike most, you did learn. He was proud of you, you know?"

"I wanted him to think well of me and what I did, Lady . . . and the way in which I did what had to be done. I don't think he always totally approved, but I tried to stay within the scope of what he taught." Lerial isn't about to point out Altyrn's often utter ruthlessness in his quest to assure the future of what he believed to be the best of the heritage of Cyador, especially since Maeroja must already know that.

"He knew that." Maeroja leans forward, reaches for the folder she had been reading, and extracts a sealed sheet. "He wrote this some time ago, last harvest . . ."

"Was he ailing then?"

Maeroja shakes her head. "He was never ailing. He came to bed, very tired. He held me, and then went to sleep." Her voice catches, and she swallows. "I think he knew. I told you once, you might recall . . ."

"That he had a sense, a certainty about some things. I remember."

"You would." Maeroja's smile is gentle, but sad. "He told me what was in the letter, but I did not read it. It is for you, and you alone. He said you would understand."

Lerial takes the letter. On the outside is his name, written in a precise but slightly ornate script. He looks up. "I would read it now, with you here."

"If you read it to yourself . . ."

Lerial nods. After a moment, he breaks the seal and begins to read.

> Dear Lerial—
> There is a time for all things, and a way to end them. It is fitting that, since the beginning of my life was never quiet, the ending will be. What you will and must do is also fitting. What I task you with, and it is a task and not a request, is to assure that the heirs of the Malachite Throne do not perish, that they do not stoop to petty bargains for a peace that will not last, and that their heritage will shine on when the City of Light is long forgotten. This does not mean you are to re-create Cyad or Cy-

ador. That time is past. It does mean that what was best of that time should live on through you and what you do.

Lerial lowers the letter slightly. *Why me? Why not Lephi? What did he know that he never said?*

. . . You will likely not understand fully the burden I have placed on you for some time to come, much as you may think you have. Then I could be deceiving myself. That becomes easier, even necessary, when one has great hopes for another.

If one chooses power over good, then that power will fail in time, as it did in Cyador. If one chooses good over power, then evil will triumph because there will not be strength to oppose it. Finally, it is not good to be merciful, if that mercy will doom others in even greater numbers. All this, you know. Knowing what to do, regardless of what others including sages say, is not the most difficult task. Doing what needs to be done for good to survive is far harder. Good only needs to survive, not triumph.

Those words strike Lerial—*Good only needs to survive, not triumph.* Then he looks at Maeroja and nods.

Before he can continue, she speaks. "Your expressions when you read the letter . . . Some of them were like his. You are more alike than you know."

Once Lerial would have protested that, and certainly he still would likely have rejected that observation from anyone but Maeroja.

. . . As for the blade you bear, I am fairly sure that it belonged to one of the great ones, possibly even Lorn himself, although I cannot be certain. I am absolutely certain that it is and should be yours. Call this the certainty of an ancient Lancer.

Use it to balance good and power.

At the bottom, there is a single ornate "A." At that moment, Lerial realizes that he has never seen the majer's handwriting before . . . and most likely never will again.

After a long moment, he refolds the letter and slips it inside his riding jacket. "Thank you."

"I only did what he asked."

"You have always done more than that, I think." *As he did for you.*

Another silence follows before he asks, "How are Rojana and the girls?" As the words leave his lips, he realizes the meaning of the way he has inquired, and he blocks a self-amused smile.

"All three are fine. Rojana can handle Kinaar quite well in my absence . . . if not quite so well as she thinks. She has taken over the brewery and is expanding production."

"Because she detests the shimmersilk worms and will do anything else?"

"There is some truth to that."

Lerial does let himself smile. "She is quite a young woman."

"She is."

"One other thing . . ." Lerial pauses.

"Yes?" The hint of a smile appears at the corners of her mouth.

"Father said you would be joining us for refreshments and dinner at fifth glass. I would be greatly disappointed if you were not there. So, I think—"

"You don't have to say it. I understand, and you're right."

"I know it may not be easy . . ."

Her laugh is soft, short . . . and bitter.

"I will see you then?"

"You will."

Lerial rises and inclines his head. "Thank you . . . again."

"You're more than welcome." Her words are warm, anything but perfunctory.

After leaving the small salon, and wanting to be alone, he walks back to his own chambers, rooms he has not occupied in more than a season, and for less than two eightdays over the past several years. There, he rereads the letter.

Use it to balance good and power. Good only needs to survive, not triumph. Lerial thinks he understands what the majer was suggesting, but he decides not to pursue that line of thought. *Not yet.* One of the other lessons he has learned from the majer is that matters are often not what they first seem, and when one has a chance to wait and reflect, it is often better. *But then, sometimes you don't get that choice.*

At a fifth before fifth glass, he makes his way down to the main salon. Emerya and the two girls are the only ones there.

Ryalah runs to him and throws her arms around his waist. "You're here!"

Lerial realizes, belatedly, that she has indeed grown . . . and so has Amaira, who now stands almost as tall as her mother. "I am indeed."

"How long?" Ryalah releases him and steps back.

"I don't know . . . but not too long." Lerial looks to Amaira. "You're looking very good."

"Thank you, Uncle Lerial." Amaira's smile is still shy and sweet, although Lerial can sense a certain strength in the flow of order and chaos around her, and a definite darkening of the order she holds, suggesting that, like her mother, she will be a strong healer. He can also see that her black hair holds hints of a reddish tinge, something he does not recall, either with her or anyone else.

Last, he turns to Emerya, whose hair is now close to entirely silver, a shade not unbecoming to her. "It's always good to see you." He steps toward her and adds in a lower voice, "We need to talk later."

She nods. "Your mother will be here, but only when your father arrives."

"I wouldn't have expected it otherwise. You've told the girls we'll be having company at dinner?"

"I did. I told them that Maeroja's consort had just died, and that they need to be very kind because he was a special man, and she loved him very much." Emerya smiles, although the smile is for her daughter and niece.

"Isn't she special, too?" asks Ryalah.

Behind the younger girl, Amaira nods.

"She is," replies Lerial.

The palace bells are striking fifth glass when Maeroja enters the salon, the mourning scarf draped more widely across her shoulders.

Even before she has taken three steps into the chamber, Kiedron and Xeranya follow her.

"I'm so glad you could join us," offers Xeranya as Maeroja turns to face the couple.

"I do so appreciate your courtesy and kindness," replies Maeroja.

Lerial translates those words to mean his mother's courtesy and his father's kindness.

"We could do no less for you, given all that you have done for Lerial and all the majer did for me," replies Kiedron.

Lerial senses that his father's voice has almost caught. That surprises him, but he adds, "I cannot say how much I appreciate how at home you both made me feel."

"What will you have?" asks Kiedron, stepping toward the refreshments table.

"The lager, if you please."

"I'd be more than pleased," replies the duke cheerfully.

Lerial turns to his mother.

"The white wine, thank you."

As Lerial moves to the refreshments table, Emerya eases over to Maeroja and begins to speak. "It's been years since we've talked, and I was hoping we'd have a chance . . ."

The interplay confirms to Lerial that dinner will be polite, punctuated by the attempts of Emerya, his father, and himself to bring warmth to the formality that will continue to be exuded by his mother.

IV

Dinner goes exactly as Lerial has expected—formal, with underlying tension, and with Kiedron, Lerial, and Emerya being as warm and cheerful as possible. When it is over, Emerya ushers the girls off to bed, and Lerial escorts Maeroja back to her quarters in the south wing of the palace. He can sense Maeroja's relief as soon as they are away from the dining chamber and walking along the main front corridor.

"I'm sorry," he says quietly.

"It's not your fault. There are some things that must be, and it's a small price to pay for years of happiness."

"But it's hard to pay after a loss."

"That's when it's most important," Maeroja murmurs softly. "Wasn't it hard for you to talk to Elder Klerryt?"

Lerial is momentarily surprised, but realizes that the majer would certainly have told his consort. "Yes . . . but I wasn't in love with Alaynara."

"You knew exactly what I meant about what happened in Verdheln five years ago, Lerial. That should tell you something."

He laughs softly, barely above a murmur. "I should never dispute you, Lady."

"Do not make me more than I am. Do not do that to anyone . . . but do not make them less, either."

Those were the majer's words. He is still considering that when Maeroja speaks again.

"I will be leaving before sunrise tomorrow so that we can make Teilyn in a single day. I cannot keep Captain Shastan's lancers any longer."

"Nor would you, knowing what you know."

"I do not know exactly what he wrote, Lerial, but I will add my own words. Do not make foolish sacrifices for others. Very few sacrifices of self are worth that price, because one who lives and strives can keep making the land a better place. Accomplishments end with death."

"The majer said that it was better to have the enemy make the gallant sacrifices."

"Sometimes, one must let friends or others close to one make the sacrifices." She smiles wryly. "That can also become a rationalization for using others without care. It is far better to avoid useless sacrifices or those which gain little or sacrificing others in the same fashion. Most sacrifices are unnecessary and can be avoided. Too often those who send others into avoidable danger call their deaths necessary sacrifices. They usually are not. In the end, you will do what you feel you must." She stops outside the door. "Thank you for walking with me."

"Thank you for letting me. Do take care on the ride back . . . and give my best to your daughters."

Maeroja offers the smile he has found so enigmatic. "I will." Then she opens the chamber door and slips inside, closing it behind her.

Lerial can hear the latch bolt click into place. He turns and begins to walk back toward Emerya's chambers—her new chambers, a sitting room with two bedrooms off it, reflecting how Amaira has grown.

When he reaches his aunt's second-level quarters, he raps gently.

"You can come in, Lerial."

Lerial does, closing the door quietly. He does not see anyone, nor does he order-sense anyone. Then, abruptly, Emerya is seated before a small hearth in which a low fire burns. "I've never been able to detect your concealments."

"One of my few magely talents. And a vanity."

He takes the chair across from her. "Is Amaira asleep?"

"She's likely reading, but the door is solid. How are you doing?" she asks.

"Better . . . now." He shakes his head. "How can Mother be so cold, so hostile to Maeroja? She just lost her consort, and he was a man who gave everything for us, especially for Father and for me."

"Don't you think she must have her reasons?"

"I suppose she must, but what did Maeroja ever do to her? Maeroja consorted Altyrn, and they were happy together. I can't imagine that Mother's sister would have been happy with Altyrn. She wasn't even happy in Cigoerne, from what you told me."

"Lerial . . . there's more that I haven't told you. Your mother believes she lost her sister because Altyrn spurned Zanobya. Zanobya would have consorted Altyrn. She was taken with him, but she couldn't bear staying in Cigoerne when he turned her down. He was gentle about it, but . . ."

Lerial can't help but think about Altyrn's reaction when Lerial had distanced himself from Rojana.

"So . . . Zanobya fled to Swartheld. She died there in childbirth three years later. She might have lived had she given birth here. Xeranya never saw her again. Your mother blames Maeroja."

"Why didn't you tell me that?"

"Your mother asked me never to mention it. Your father asked that I honor that request. I would ask that you never reveal that I have told you . . . but you should know. Your mother loved Zanobya dearly."

Lerial conceals a wince. *What else could Emerya do?* Then he frowns. "But the majer couldn't have met Maeroja until after Zanobya fled, could he?"

"No, he didn't, but that doesn't matter. Altyrn did so much for your father that Xeranya dared not blame him. And then, after he helped you so much . . . Blaming Maeroja was so much easier."

Lerial can understand his mother's feelings of loss and grief, but not why she feels she must blame Maeroja. Yet it is more than clear what she feels and that those feelings will never change. "You've been writing Rhamuel for years, haven't you?"

"You've just come to that conclusion?" Emerya offers an amused smile.

"I've thought so ever since I left for Verdheln, but I never said anything. Is Atroyan . . . not particularly stable?"

"That's one way of saying it. He is always charming and witty, but he thinks that everyone is plotting against him."

"Including his brothers?"

"Especially Mykel, his youngest brother . . . and that is absurd."

"Why?"

"I'd prefer to leave it at that, Lerial."

"So Rhamuel has been keeping Atroyan out of trouble . . . mostly?"

"He tries. He's not always successful. Every so often there's some field-grade officer who gets to the duke when Rhamuel isn't around and persuades the duke to do something unwise. Then, too, Rhamuel isn't as wise as he could be. He's balanced and has common sense, but not too much imagination."

"But he's charming and gentle with women?"

"Of course."

Lerial waits.

"I did what I had to . . . Kiedron and your mother needed all the help they could get."

Lerial can sense something behind the black mist of order. *Sadness . . . or something even more painful?* "And it was unlikely that Rhamuel would ever be allowed a consort in Swartheld?"

Emerya nods.

"Does Amaira . . . ?"

"She knows. She also knows that she can say nothing. I write him, always about *my* daughter, should others read the letters, and convey what other information he needs to know. In a veiled and fluttering feminine fashion . . ."

Lerial doubts that Emerya has ever been a fluttery female.

". . . and your father and I discuss that. In turn, he sends me cheerful letters with gossip and odd bits of information."

"Enough that you can learn what you and father need to know."

"Not always . . . but usually."

"Do you think that Khesyn is really planning to attack Afrit . . . somewhere?"

"I'm afraid I do, Lerial. He's made far more raids on Afrit than on Cigoerne. We don't talk about it, but it's clear from what I hear and from what the traders report."

"And we can't afford to have Afrit fall?"

"What do you think?"

"About the same as you and Father feel, I suspect. Khesyn holding even Luba would destroy us both in time." Lerial pauses. "But how much can we trust Atroyan . . . or Rhamuel?"

"Atroyan not at all, and Rhamuel only to the extent that something benefits him and he cannot hurt you."

Lerial is tempted to ask again how she could have done what she did . . . but she has already answered him.

Her eyes fix on him. "You have already done things that are necessary . . . I can see that. Destiny exacts a heavy price. What else do you want to know?"

"You've told me all I need to know."

She shakes her head. "All you want to know, and all I can tell you, perhaps, but not all you need to know."

He smiles in return. "You're right."

"If there's nothing else . . ."

"Not now."

Emerya rises. "Then . . . good night, Lerial."

He stands. "Good night."

As he walks along the corridor toward the steps up to his chambers, he thinks over what she has said. Some of what he has learned are things he has long suspected, but what he has not fully realized is the various prices so many have paid to create and strengthen the duchy . . . to continue the good traditions of the Malachite Throne, as Maeroja and Altyrn might have put it. Given all that, Altyrn's use of the Verdyn war—and Lerial himself—to strengthen the duchy in the west, the cold-blooded poisoning of Dechund to put an end to the captain's treachery and plotting . . . and likely much more about which Lerial knows nothing.

Lerial shakes his head.

And yet . . . what else could any of them do, faced with the destruction of all that they held dear?

Are you any better . . . given what you have already done?

V

Lerial sleeps well enough, but wakes early on sixday, thinking about what Emerya has said, and pondering over what she has left out that he knows too little about to ask the right questions. In turn, he still wonders about just how close—or distant—she and Rhamuel may be, although he certainly has the impression that they have not seen each other since she returned to Cigoerne after healing him and accompanying him back to Swartheld.

Early as he is dressed and in the breakfast room, seemingly within moments of the time he has seated himself, his father, mother, and sister join him, followed shortly by Emerya and Amaira.

"We thought we should have breakfast together," his mother announces. "A family breakfast."

Meaning that dinner last night was not at all a family affair. That realization saddens Lerial, particularly since Altyrn and Maeroja had certainly made him a part of their family when he had lived at Kinaar and worked and studied under the majer.

"You have to go back soon, don't you?" asks Ryalah.

"Yes." Lerial takes a swallow of lager, looking away from Kiedron, who happily takes a deep draught of bitter greenberry juice.

"In the next day or so," adds Kiedron.

"There is one other matter we have not discussed, Lerial," says Xeranya, smiling.

"Yes?" he replies as warmly as he can, given that something about her words and expression makes him wary.

"You're twenty-two . . . almost twenty-three . . ."

"That's true." Lerial takes a mouthful of egg toast and waits for the other boot to drop.

"You might wonder why we haven't talked about consorting lately . . ."

That is a subject that Lerial is more than happy has not been brought up, but he replies, "I had noticed that."

"Duke Casseon and Duke Khesyn have been reluctant to make any commitments, especially where Lephi is concerned. Atroyan has said nothing . . ."

"Why don't they want to consort their daughters—" questions Ryalah loudly.

Xeranya looks hard at her daughter. "Ryalah . . ."

"Yes, Mother." Ryalah looks down at her egg toast.

"Or nieces," adds Lerial quickly, and turning to his sister, "to Lephi or me? Because Cigoerne is the smallest duchy in all of Hamor."

"What about Atla?" asks Ryalah.

"Atla's not a duchy. It's mostly desert and grassland, and there's not much of worth there. The Tourlegyn clans share it—sort of, except they fight among each other as much as share, and there hasn't been a leader from the same clan in hundreds of years."

"I *know* that. I even know that some of the Tourlegyn clans live in Heldya. But why isn't Atla a duchy?"

"Because they fight so much that no one clan has ever really ruled."

"Ryalah," says Xeranya coolly, "would you like to finish your breakfast? Or go without?"

Ryalah takes a bite of egg toast.

"As I was saying," Xeranya continues, "if you should encounter either Duke Atroyan or Arms-Commander Rhamuel, it would be most helpful if you inquired as to the health of the duke's daughter."

"Kyedra? The one I met years and years ago?"

"She is his only daughter," replies Xeranya.

"I will." Lerial takes another swallow of lager, followed by a mouthful of egg toast. "What about Casseon? Does he have any daughters?"

"His oldest is about Amaira's age," says Emerya. "Khesyn's sole daughter is around my age, and she has, I've heard, a daughter a year or so younger than you, Lerial. His eldest son has two boys. The youngest is about Lephi's age, maybe a year or two older."

From what he is hearing, Lerial almost wishes he had not asked.

Xeranya glances at Amaira and then to Ryalah. "Girls, it's time to finish your breakfast. You can go to the courtyard until it's time for your lessons."

Lerial takes the quiet time while the girls eat to finish his own breakfast, suspecting that he would rather not be caught with a mouthful of food during whatever is coming after the girls leave the breakfast room.

Once Ryalah and Amaira have departed, Kiedron clears his throat. "You all realize that Lerial will have to be the one to head the force we send to Luba."

"What about Lephi?" asks Emerya politely.

"Lerial is better suited to this." Kiedron glances at Xeranya, then continues. "Because of what happened in Verdheln . . . and Ensenla, Lerial has more experience in avoiding great losses if he must deal with overwhelming forces. There is also the considerable problem of timing. Lerial can reach Luba almost in the time it would take Lephi to get to Cigoerne, and that doesn't include the time for the fastest dispatch rider to get to Sudstrym. I doubt we can afford almost an additional two eightdays."

Lerial can sense that, while his father is telling the truth, if exaggerating the time for dispatch riders, it is likely that there are other things he is not saying at all, but what those might be, Lerial has no idea.

"Should you go?" asks Emerya.

Lerial knows that those are not questions Emerya would normally ask. *Why is she doing it?* After just an instant's thought, he realizes just why. *Father asked her to.*

"If I go . . . then there is too much temptation for Khesyn to attack with an even larger force at Luba, and there is too great a risk that even I could not save Atroyan. I suspect that is exactly what Khesyn hopes for. With Lephi at Sudstrym, Cigoerne is much less vulnerable."

"That is if you remain in Cigoerne . . . or near it," concludes Emerya.

"I still don't like it," says Xeranya. "How will Lephi get any experience in dealing with Atroyan?"

"He'll be getting more experience in dealing with Khesyn's forces, and they're going to be the far greater danger in the future." Kiedron looks to Lerial. "Because of the timing, you'll need to take Eighth and Eleventh Company. You can also take Kusyl's Twenty-third Company. You've worked with him before. That will give you three companies. Commander Jhalet can pull together enough lancers to protect the palace, until another new company can be formed and trained."

"Are we spread that thin?" Lerial has his doubts.

"We've been forced to place more than fifteen companies along the Swarth to deal with Heldyan raiders," admits Kiedron. "There are another ten companies across the northern border west of Ensenla, and that doesn't count the fifteen companies of Verdyn Lancers keeping Casseon in check, nor the various outposts throughout the duchy. We can likely pull some of the northern companies now, but that will take time."

Almost fifty companies . . . and they're not enough? When we had less than twenty six years ago? And you feel you can only spare three companies to aid Atroyan? Three companies—not enough to weaken Cigoerne if you lose—and enough to strike fear into both Khesyn and Atroyan if you win. That assumes that there will be any fighting at all, and it's possible that there will not be . . . but then again.

"Khesyn has been raising armsmen for ten years now, and that doesn't count what he pays the raiders to attack us."

Lerial nods. He had no idea matters are that dire.

Little more is said other than pleasantries, few as they are, for the remainder of breakfast, and, as he stands and leaves, Lerial ponders over the clearly scripted exchange between Emerya and his father. Why had his father felt it necessary? Did his mother really want Lephi . . . or even his father . . . to go to Luba?

Lerial suspects she had . . . and that bothers him. Still, his father has brought up the issue before most of the family, and Lerial has no doubts that he is being sent because he is the most expendable, and because sending an heir, even the most junior, allows his father not to commit more Mirror Lancers. His father also expects him to use his order-chaos skills, if discreetly.

After deciding to wait in the north courtyard until Commander Jhalet arrives, Lerial makes his way into the early-morning sunshine there.

"Lerial!" Ryalah runs toward him, then stops and walks the last yards much more sedately, allowing Amaira to join her. "Why did Mother get so angry? I just asked."

"I still think it's awful that no one wants to consort you," adds Amaira shyly. "Why can't you consort Rojana?"

"What gave you that idea?" asks Lerial, half amused and half concerned . . . and wondering where Amaira came up with that idea.

"When she and her father and mother visited the palace last year. We talked, both of us. She talked a lot about you."

They visited last year . . . and no one told me? "They were here?"

"Just for a day," replies Amaira. "I thought you knew."

"Perhaps Father mentioned it, and it just skipped my mind."

"Rojana's very nice," says Ryalah.

"She's very intelligent and very attractive," Lerial admits. "But it wouldn't be a good thing for her to consort me."

"So you'll have to consort whoever Father says?"

"Most likely."

"That's awful."

"It's necessary. So will you, when you're older."

Ryalah grimaces. "What if I don't like him?"

"You shouldn't worry about that now. It'll be years before you're old enough."

"What about Amaira?"

"That's up to Aunt Emerya."

"You mean she doesn't have to, and I do? That's not fair." Ryalah looks to her cousin.

"Sometimes, life isn't fair . . ." With the thought of fairness, Lerial thinks about Emerya . . . and Maeroja, or Korlyn, or Alaynara, or even the lancer who died on Lerial's first riding expedition with Altyrn.

"It should be," declares Ryalah.

"People are the ones who can make life fair," says Amaira.

Your mother said that, didn't she? Lerial is certain of that, especially now that Amaira has taken to accompanying her mother to the Hall of Healing, but he only says, "That's true, and sometimes it's very hard to be fair to everyone at the same time." He can order-sense riders coming into the palace courtyard and smiles at the two. "I have to go meet with Father and Commander Jhalet. I'll see you later."

"You won't go until you do?" asks Ryalah.

"No . . . I won't."

Lerial walks briskly to his father's study, nods to the guard, and enters.

Kiedron looks up from behind his desk. "Is the commander here?"

"There are lancers in the courtyard. I imagine he'll be here shortly."

"You didn't greet him?"

"I heard them enter," Lerial lies. "I was in the center courtyard. So I came here."

Kiedron frowns momentarily, then nods.

Several moments later, the guard opens the study door, and Commander Jhalet enters. Kiedron rises, and he and Lerial move to the circular conference table, where the three seat themselves.

"Have you discovered anything new?" asks Kiedron.

"The Heldyans have stepped up attacks along the Swarth, and there appear to be more troopers moving to Amaershyn."

"Then we'll need to pull some of the companies from the northern border with Afrit and use them to reinforce Sudstrym."

"What if that's what Khesyn intends?" asks Jhalet.

"I'm certain that he wants us to be reluctant to do so. That way he can overmatch the forces already there and either create great damage or inflict great losses. That will ensure that the reinforcements will be overmatched . . . and he will do the same thing again."

Jhalet's brow furrows. "If that is so . . . can we afford to send any companies north to assist Atroyan?"

"If we assist Atroyan, we won't need as many companies in the north. Not for a time. I'd wager that other Afritan Guard companies in addition to those in Ensenla have been recalled. Leave the company in Tirminya, but call in the other seven."

The commander frowns.

"Lerial will be taking Eighth and Eleventh Company from Ensenla. Also Twenty-third Company from the palace. You can detail some headquarters squads here until you can raise another company."

"Begging your pardon, ser . . . but three companies . . ."

"Duke Atroyan cannot very well object to three companies being commanded by Lord Lerial . . . either for being a threat . . . or not being a proper response to his request. And with the companies from the north, that should provide you with adequate lancers to deal with the Heldyans." After a deliberate pause, Kiedron adds, "Should it not?"

"Yes, ser . . . . But do you trust Duke Atroyan?"

"Only to act in his obvious self-interest. It is not in his interest to destroy three Mirror Lancer companies, especially when it is likely to cost him at least twice as many companies of his own. Nor is it in his interest to undertake actions that could result in Lord Lerial's death at his hands or those of his Guards."

"That much is true."

"Good! Then we are agreed. You will have orders for Undercaptain Kusyl shortly and three supply wagons ready to accompany Twenty-third Company at dawn tomorrow. And you'll have two squads here at the palace by then." Kiedron pauses. "You probably ought to send a squad to hold Ensenla Post as well in the absence of Eighth and Eleventh Company."

"Yes, ser."

Kiedron rises from the table and bestows a warm smile on the commander. "Excellent! I'll walk with you to the courtyard." As he moves toward the door, he looks back and gives Lerial a glance that indicates he should remain in the study.

While he waits for his father to return, Lerial considers the possibilities. Even with further thought, he doesn't like any of them.

"What do you think?" are the first words from Kiedron's mouth when he returns to the study.

"There's one possibility you overlooked," ventures Lerial.

"Only one?"

Lerial ignores the jocular question and says, "Atroyan could place me and my companies in a position where Khesyn's forces could accomplish what he dares not."

"I'm sure that's exactly what he'll attempt, hoping that you'll die a glorious death while wiping out most of Khesyn's forces and thereby saving him. And that's what you must avoid."

"You're asking—"

"That's something you can do. Lephi can't. He doesn't think the way you do." He pauses, then goes on. "There are risks in everything, but there are also great opportunities. If you succeed in Afrit and Lephi succeeds in beating back the Heldyans along the Swarth, then that tells all of Hamor that you are both capable and to be feared and respected. It also makes it clear to Khesyn that attacking either Afrit or Cigoerne is not in his interest."

"And you expect him to stop being what he is?"

Kiedron shakes his head. "I cannot guess what he will do, but if he is wise, he will turn his attentions to the east, or to the south . . . east of the river. He could gain great territory and some riches and goods with far less cost. And I'd rather have a ruler who ostensibly believes in the God of the Balance than deal with the Tourlegyns and their Chaos Demon. He shrugs. "We don't have the men or the wealth to do that, and we'd have to cross his territory or Casseon's even to try. It will be a strain to send you off with fifty golds for what you may have to purchase."

"If we succeed . . ."

"When you succeed." Kiedron smiles. "Go on."

"When we succeed, that will show how weak Atroyan is . . . and how much he needs us."

Kiedron nods.

"You've had that in mind all along, haven't you?"

Kiedron smiles wryly. "I have, but it was your grandmere who pointed out that possibility. She saw it first."

Grandmere. Of course.

Kiedron looks at Lerial. "There is one thing I want to be very clear about. You can lose almost all your force—if you have to—but I do not want you to make a needless sacrifice of yourself. It is not necessary, and it is anything but wise. We are so outnumbered that no one will think less of you if you have to withdraw, provided you inflict substantial casualties upon any who attack you and your forces."

Lerial cannot help but wonder if Maeroja and his father have talked about him, but, given the edginess that her name brings up, he does not ask, because it does not matter in this case. Both Maeroja and his father share the same view, and that suggests that they're likely right. *Except . . . all those lancers trust you, and that means you have to bring most of them back or, before long, you won't be followed with any great loyalty.* And Lerial suspects his father knows that as well.

"I trust you understand, Lerial."

"Yes, ser." *I understand exactly what you want.*

VI

After Lerial mounts up in the dim light before dawn on sevenday, he checks the dispatch pouch once more to make certain that he has the "request" from Atroyan inside it as well as his father's response authorizing one Overcaptain Lerial, his son, to act in reply to Atroyan's communiqué . . . and, of course, the golds hidden in slots in his belt. Then he rides to the north entrance to the palace where Emerya and the girls stand, the only ones to see him off.

Ryalah looks up at her brother. "Be careful."

"I'll be as careful as I can. You, too." Lerial offers a smile, then looks to Emerya.

"The more charming anyone is, the less you should trust them."

"Honesty doesn't require charm?" he quips back.

"Desperate rulers in debt can't afford honesty." Emerya reaches up and hands Lerial a small object heavily wrapped in cloth. "You'll know what to do with this when the time comes."

He takes the object, seemingly oval beneath the cloth padding and not even quite the size of his hand, then slips it into the inside pocket of his jacket. He glances toward Amaira and then back to Emerya, raising his eyebrows, knowing that the metal oval must hold a miniature portrait of her daughter.

His aunt nods.

"I'll make certain. Is there anything else?"

"Nothing else that I haven't already told you."

Lerial looks to Amaira. "Take care."

"I always do. Mother insists on it."

Lerial offers a last smile, then turns the gelding back toward Twenty-third Company, almost formed up, with the three supply wagons in the rear.

"Twenty-third Company mounted and ready, ser," declares Kusyl as Lerial reins up beside him.

"Then let's head out."

"Yes, ser." Kusyl calls out, "Company! Forward!"

Once the company has left the palace gates and is riding smoothly on the boulevard that leads toward the Hall of Healing, the two officers riding side by side behind two outriders ten yards ahead of them and the main body, Lerial turns to Kusyl. "Tell me more about the company, if you would."

"Better than any new companies, and some old ones, a lot better than what we had to do in Verdheln. Four solid squad leaders. Maylat—he's Third Squad—might be a touch too solid, if you know what I mean."

"He'll carry out any order just the way you order it?"

"If he has doubts . . . yes, ser."

"What else?" prompts Lerial.

"We've got maybe two or three rankers with some fighting experience in each squad. That's helped."

"But they're usually not the brightest ones?"

"Half of each, I'd say."

"How long have you been working them?"

"A couple of eightdays less than a season."

"How are they doing?"

"Half as well as your company, if that."

"You've never seen Eighth Company."

"Don't have to. You were in Verdheld. I saw what you did there with troopers as green as saplings."

"I was almost as green."

"Begging your pardon, ser . . . you weren't. Young . . . but never green. You spent years learning from the majer."

Not years . . . a year at most, even if it felt like years.

"Also heard watertalk about what you did at Ensenla four years back."

"You can't believe all you hear," replies Lerial with a genial laugh.

"No, ser. That's not so with you. Have to figure you did a lot more than anyone knows. It was that way in Verdheln, and you're likely better at keeping things quiet."

"It's usually better that way."

"Most times. Not always."

Lerial nods. "I'd agree to that."

They ride almost another third of a glass before Kusyl speaks again. "Tell me, ser. Is this going to be as bad as Verdheln?"

"How can you say something like that?" Lerial laughs. "Didn't we win a great victory there?"

Kusyl grins. "Except we lost every battle except the last two . . . and pretty near half our lancers. That's the kind of victory every old lancer dreads."

"I have no idea, except that it won't be good. We're supposed to help Atroyan and keep Khesyn from even thinking about taking Luba when he's been eying it and Afrit for years."

"Worse than Verdheln, then." The not-quite-wizened undercaptain gives a theatrical groan. After a moment, he asks, "Why Luba . . . and not Swartheld?"

"The ironworks, I'd guess. Also, taking Luba would split Afrit in two, if not so much in terms of people, and there's a paved highway from Luba to Swartheld that Khesyn could use. If Khesyn can take and hold Luba, that would make things more difficult for us, too, because he'd control both sides of the river there, and we'd lose access to the traders who come upriver from Swartheld, especially the outland traders."

"You're not making this old lancer feel any younger, ser."

"You're not that old, Kusyl."

"Maybe not, ser, but we'd all like to get older."

Lerial can definitely agree with that, but he says, "Tell me more about Twenty-third Company. Start with more about your squad leaders."

"I can do that. First Squad leader is Elsyor. Quiet type. Thinks things through. Better with a blade than a lance . . ."

Lerial listens intently.

VII

By midafternoon on sixday, Lerial is more concerned than ever about what faces them in Luba. They have followed the river road for five days since leaving Ensenla, except, after the first two days, the road cannot truly be called a river road, as it has moved farther and farther from the river, presumably to avoid the sandy desert-like ground along the river that is periodically interrupted with marshy areas. They have come across no towns to speak of, just poor hamlet after poor hamlet, set amid browned and overgrazed grasslands, and scattered plots too small to be proper fields set next to creeks, with triangle-pole waterlifts . . . and not even proper irrigation ditches, let alone canals. Almost all the dwellings are of wind-worn mud brick with branch and reed-grass roofs.

Lerial has not loitered, nor has he pressed, since he does not wish to tire the horses, because, while they have brought a score of spare mounts, that number would only suffice for less than a squad. One of the scouts always rides with a parley banner in his lance holder at all times. Even after seeing the green-edged white banner—a narrow cloth triangle a yard in length and half that in width next to the staff, if tapering to a point—no one has come close to them, although Lerial has kept his forces well clear of the local people, except when they ride through a hamlet. At those times, every shutter and door is closed, and the only animal Lerial ever sees is an occasional scrawny cat. Away from the hamlets, there are few tracks in the road, scarcely surprising, since the land is largely sere, brown, and dusty. Dust is everywhere, rising into clouds when the wind picks up, at times so thick that Lerial can see scarcely more than a score of yards, so that he must rely on his order-sensing to determine what lies ahead. All he can smell is dust, and it sifts into his uniform and down into his boots.

Now there is but the slightest hint of a breeze. Even so, that is enough that fine dust drifts across the road. From where he rides at the head of Eighth Company, Lerial scans the gentle slope that leads to the crest of a rise perhaps two kays away. If his maps are correct, before long, they should be nearing Guasyra—the only large town between Cigoerne and Luba. Still, he has his doubts about the maps, a doubt that Altyrn instilled in him.

Hard to believe he's gone.

He forces his thoughts from that and studies the bent brown grasses and the dust that coats them, then shakes his head. *How can people live here? Then, not many do.* At those thoughts, he recalls what his grandmere had told him about the original lands she had purchased from Atroyan's sire, lands so dusty and dry that the old duke had little compunction in selling them . . . or little enough that the golds outweighed his concerns. *Was Cigoerne like this then?* He looks north once more and frowns, because he sees dust beyond the crest of the road. He immediately extends his order-senses . . . and discovers a squad of men riding toward them.

"There's an Afritan Guard squad riding toward us. Ready arms!" he orders. "Pass it back, Fheldar. Send a messenger to the undercaptains."

"Yes, ser."

Lerial concentrates on the riders he can sense, but not see. He can discern only eleven, with no others farther north. Absently, he wonders if the Afritans have been waiting for them . . . or if the riders represent a force stationed in Guasyra and he and his companies have been sighted by a routine patrol. *Does it matter?* After a moment, he answers himself. *Probably not.*

Before long the road dust becomes a hazy brown mist over the rise ahead, and then riders appear, moving at a fast walk. Lerial squints to make out the numbers, but there are still just eleven, and his order-senses reveal no others nearby. He also can barely sense the Afritan Guard post some four kays to the north, but gains a feeling that it is close to being empty.

When the oncoming riders, all wearing the dull crimson uniforms of the Afritan Guard, are less than a hundred yards away, Lerial calls a halt, then renews his own shields, linked as always to the ordered iron of the knife he received from the High Council of Verdheln. Absently, he wishes he had figured a better way to maintain his shields, but even after five years and discreet inquiries to Saltaryn and other Magi'i he has not found a more effective way of maintaining strong shields without that link to some form of iron, not without continually concentrating on maintaining them.

"They don't look too happy, ser," murmurs Fheldar.

"In their boots, would you be?"

The senior squad leader's laugh is more of a snort.

Before long, the hard-faced undercaptain, older and clearly a former ranker, reins up some five yards from Lerial. "Parley banner? A hundred kays into Afrit? Isn't that stretching things, Overcaptain?"

"No," replies Lerial pleasantly. "We're here at Duke Atroyan's request."

"It would be helpful if you had some way of proving that . . ."

Lerial can sense no surprise, almost as if the undercaptain has expected them but has to fulfill an unpleasant duty. "We can do that." Lerial extracts the two documents from the dispatch case fastened to his saddle, then turns to Fheldar. "If you'd have someone convey these . . ." Lerial could do that himself, perfectly safely, but that would reveal too much, besides compromising his position.

"Lystr, forward," orders Fheldar.

A heavyset but young-faced ranker eases his mount forward, up beside the senior squad leader, to whom Lerial has handed the documents. In turn, Fheldar passes them to Lystr.

"Convey these to the Afritan undercaptain. Let him read them, and then return them." Fheldar speaks loudly enough—his words in Hamorian, since most rankers, even in the Mirror Lancers, are more comfortable speaking it, rather than Cyadoran—that his words carry to the undercaptain.

"Yes, ser." Lystr nods, then urges his mount forward, halting beside the Afritan officer and tendering the documents.

The hard-faced undercaptain reads both, slowly, as if he has to struggle with the words, and then finally looks up. "It looks like the duke's seal." He stares at Lerial. "But it would, wouldn't it?"

"It would," admits Lerial, "but why in the world would we be more than a hundred kays from our border with only three companies if it weren't real?"

"That does pose an interesting problem."

"The other problem," adds Lerial, "is that you've already sent most of your forces to Luba, and you couldn't stop us if you wanted to. And, if you try, you'll lose men that Duke Atroyan desperately needs, while denying him our assistance."

"You don't know about my forces."

"But I do. You have an outpost a little more than three kays north of here, just out of sight. It's largely empty, since I'd judge you have two squads at most—the one with you and possibly one you left there, if that. What forces you have are still here because the duke or his arms-commander doesn't want to give the people the idea that they've been totally abandoned."

"You're Overcaptain Lerial, ser?" The undercaptain obviously doesn't wish to dispute Lerial's observations.

"I am."

"Welcome to Afrit. I'd prefer that you take over our post for the night. It's quite a nice post. We'll ride to Luba and inform the duke of your arrival. The other squad will remain at the post. We'll also pass the word to the hamlets along the way to expect you."

Lerial can sense none of the chaos that usually accompanies lies, but he still frowns.

"It's simple, Overcaptain. First, you're here at the duke's invitation. Even if you weren't, we couldn't fight you. You pointed that out. I still would like to protect the people, and I'm willing to wager that if you have a place where you feel safer and have provisions, then both you and the townspeople will feel better." A sardonic smile follows. "Besides, I was ordered to make the offer."

"We accept your offer with thanks."

The undercaptain nods and returns the documents to Lystr, who accepts them and rides back to Fheldar, who takes them back.

"The guards at the post will be expecting you." With that, the undercaptain turns his mount. In moments, the Afritans are riding north, the hooves of their mounts raising dust once more.

"Friendly sort, ser," observes Fheldar dryly.

"I don't know as I blame him." Lerial's brief smile fades. "We'll wait a bit and let the dust settle." One of the great advantages of having officers with him who were once rankers is that all of them speak Hamorian, while quite a number of Mirror Lancer officers, especially those from a Magi'i background, speak Hamorian poorly and often with a thick accent. That his father assigned Kusyl was anything but coincidental, Lerial suspects.

After perhaps a tenth of a glass, Lerial and his forces set out again and before long reach the crest of the road. At that moment, Lerial's mouth almost drops open, because the valley below him is green—or as green as is likely at the end of winter—with orchard after orchard, the trees set in neat rows. While the Guard post is but two kays ahead, the town proper is much farther, perhaps another five kays, and appears to sit on the north side of a small river—the Rynn, according to his map. Canals and ditches extend southward from the Rynn out across the wide and low valley. Then, roughly three kays to the west, the trees and green end at the base of low hills that look just like the near-barren lands through which Lerial and his companies have been riding. Beyond the hills lie low but rocky mountains.

Why hasn't Atroyan done the same thing farther to the south? It's not as though the Swarth is a tiny stream that would be exhausted by a few more canals. *Or is the land beside the Swarth so sandy that it makes little sense? Or don't the traders and merchanters in Swartheld care?*

Lerial pushes aside all the questions that flood through his thoughts and keeps using his order-senses to make certain that there are no surprises hidden in the orchards that begin beyond the bottom of the gentle incline. He finds no hidden forces with his senses, nor does he see anyone near the road. He does cross two bridges over irrigation canals that serve the olive orchards to the west of the road before he and Eighth Company reach the Afritan Guard post. The post stands in the middle of a dusty and largely grassless area roughly a quarter kay on a side, its front walls less than thirty yards west of the road. Those walls are little more than two yards high and are covered with a plaster that might once have been a glistening white, but which has faded and eroded enough that it is more tannish than white. In places the mud bricks forming the walls are clearly visible. The timber gates are open, drawn back. The end of each gate rests on several bricks, suggesting that the gates themselves are tired and would sag to the packed clay of the courtyard.

A young and worried-looking guard stands on each side of the post entrance as Lerial and Eighth Company ride through. Lerial surveys the post, with its stables set against the south wall, and another set of buildings extending from the north wall, all of them showing a certain lack of repair. Nowhere is there any paving in the open courtyard in the middle of the walls and buildings. The windows he sees have shutters of worn wood that has not been painted or recently oiled, nor do any appear to be glazed, and there are drifts of dust in the corners where buildings join the walls.

A single figure in a crimson uniform, presumably a senior squad leader, stands in front of a long building whose rear wall is also the rear wall of the post. When Lerial reins up, he says, "Welcome to Guasyra Post, Overcaptain, ser."

"Thank you."

Lerial smiles politely. If Guasyra is a "nice" post, he shudders inside to think what a post that isn't nice might be. Still, any hospitality is better than none.

VIII

On sevenday morning, Lerial is a bit surprised when it takes his force a good glass to reach the center of Guasyra, not because the road is rutted and blocked, but because the Afritan Guard post is more than four kays south of the town. The second surprise is the almost total lack of interest in the Mirror Lancers—except from several small boys who stare at the lancers from behind a porch railing on the north side of the town, which seems as though it might be a third the size of Cigoerne.

North of Guasyra are rocky hills that are closer to small mountains, and the road winds back and forth so much so that it takes the three companies almost two glasses to reach the low pass and then descend—a distance that might be less than three kays from point to point. As the road finally straightens, Lerial can make out a triangle of roads below, standing out amid the browned grass and the scattered fields and orchards. Near the bottom of the incline the road splits, with one fork heading northwest and the other northeast, but perhaps three or four kays north another and wider road running east to west connects both forks, so that the three roads create a triangle. Beyond where the western road disappears over a low rise, Lerial can see a haze of what appears to be smoke. To the east, at the edge of what appears to be the Swarth River, he can make out what must be the city of Luba, and there is only a faint blurring of the air above and around the city. He can barely see two large wagons on the east-west road, both heading east.

After another half glass, the Cigoernean force reaches the bottom of the long incline and turns onto the northeast fork. Lerial loosens his riding jacket. Somehow, the air is far warmer in the valley than it had been in Guasyra or on the top of the rocky rise. *But spring is still four eightdays away.* He tends to forget how much warmer it gets the farther north one travels.

They ride another three kays before the northeast fork joins the east-west road and continue on for another kay or so before entering an area where there are more fields and orchards and almost no meadows or grasslands—and where there are irrigation ditches that appear to branch off an actual canal from the Swarth River. Lerial can sense riders moving in his direction, but says nothing, since the numbers indicate only a squad.

"Riders headed this way, ser!" calls out Naedar, one of the Eighth Company scouts. "Look to be Afritan Guards."

A third of a glass more riding, just past the first roadstone—inscribed LUBA 2K—that Lerial has seen in Afrit, brings him and his forces to another fork in the road. There a squad of Afritan Guards has reined up.

An officer rides forward and halts his mount a few yards short of Lerial. "Lord Lerial . . . or is it Overcaptain?" His words are in halting Cyadoran.

For a moment, Lerial does not recognize the insignia, but then he realizes that the officer greeting him is a subcommander, a rank that does not exist and never has in the Mirror Lancers, even in Cyador.

"Overcaptain, if you please." Lerial replies in Hamorian.

"That does make matters simpler," replies the graying officer, switching back to Hamorian.

"It's also accurate. I've spent the last six years in the Mirror Lancers." *Or close enough.*

"So I've heard."

How much else have he and the other officers heard?

The subcommander smiles. "By the way, I'm Drusyn. Arms-Commander Rhamuel sent us to escort you to the staging area."

"Staging area? That sounds like you've mustered more than a few companies here."

"Twenty so far . . . officially. The arms-commander says with your three we'll have more than five battalions."

For just an instance, Lerial is puzzled by the figures that don't add up. Then he grins. "I'm afraid that he's thinking of my father."

"From what we've seen, it doesn't seem to matter which of you is in command." Drusyn delivers the words wryly. "Your presence alone is likely to give Khesyn some pause." After the slightest hesitation, he goes on. "We can talk later. The arms-commander would like to meet with you once you have your men settled. Oh . . . and I have to say that your Hamorian is absolutely perfect."

"Speaking Hamorian well is something my grandmere insisted upon."

"You'll find that will be more helpful than you know."

Because other senior officers would think you're a barbarian if you don't speak well. Lerial finds that amusing, given that some of the senior Magi'i in Cigoerne still believe that Hamorian is a totally barbarous tongue.

"I take it that Duke Atroyan remains in Swartheld at present."

"He does."

Lerial can sense that there is more that the subcommander is not saying . . . and likely not to offer even if asked, at least not at the moment. He also wonders about the proper time to present the miniature portrait of Amaira to Rhamuel, and if he will be able to meet with the arms-commander privately enough to slip him the portrait of his daughter. "Where are we headed?"

"The staging area is set on the duke's lands south of Luba, right on the river. It's at the end of the causeway that serves as a river road. This road goes there directly. That way we don't have to ride through Luba." A twisted smile follows those words. "It's better that way."

Lerial immediately worries about being directed away from the city itself, but he can sense no falsehoods or evasions . . . and no shields. That worries him. *You'd better be ready for anything.* He renews and reinforces his own shields, nodding politely. "If you would lead . . ."

"Of course." Drusyn nods, then turns his mount, and starts down the more southern of the two roads, followed by the squad of Afritan Guards.

For all of Lerial's concerns, he can sense nothing out of the ordinary for the roughly three kays that they ride before approaching a gray stone wall, with stone gateposts three yards high. The stone wall stretches a half kay in each direction before coming to a corner surmounted by a low stone tower. The walls extend eastward to the Swarth River, from what Lerial can sense. There is also another set of gates on the north wall that front the causeway that Drusyn has mentioned. The grilled iron gates in the middle of the west wall are swung open, but four Afritan Guards man them, two by each post. The guards do not move as the Afritans ride through, followed by Lerial's three companies and the three wagons that bring up the rear. The lane beyond the gates is stone-paved, the first paved way Lerial has seen since entering Afrit almost an eightday before.

Once through the gates, Lerial can not only sense but see a structure more than twice the size of the palace in Cigoerne, if not even larger, surrounded by a score of outbuildings, all of gray stone. In the southwest corner of the walled compound is a hill, and upon it a round tower, rising higher than the main building. For a moment, Lerial is puzzled; then he nods. *A water tower.* To the south of the seasonal or regional palace, for that is what it must be, or something similar, are rows upon rows of tents, and south of the tents are railed corrals, filled with mounts.

Just what sort of attack does Rhamuel anticipate? What if Khesyn actually intends to attack Swartheld itself from Estheld? Or does Rhamuel have forces mustered in both places? The last possibility may be why Rhamuel—and Lerial is fairly certainly it was Rhamuel, using his brother's seal—requested aid from Cigoerne. *You'll find out sooner or later.*

Lerial's speculations are cut short as Drusyn rides back along the paved lane and then turns his mount to ride alongside Lerial. "The arms-commander has bivouacked your forces beside the south gate. That's a bit separate from ours, but he thought it might be best that way."

"South gate? Does it lead anywhere?"

"Just into the hunting park, but there's a road beside the wall that goes all the way to the west gate, and then to the north gate."

"That's very thoughtful on his part." Lerial understands. Rhamuel doesn't want him to feel that his forces would be trapped. He turns in the saddle. "Fheldar . . . would you have the word passed to Undercaptain Kusyl and Undercaptain Strauxyn about the quartering arrangements."

"Yes, ser."

Before long, Lerial and the Cigoernean companies are riding down a cleared space in the middle of the rows of tents.

"The long tents are for your men—twenty-five pallets to each tent," says Drusyn. "We weren't certain whether you had twenty or twenty-five men to a squad. The smaller tent is for your company officers. The arms-commander has quarters for you and the other senior officers in the country house . . . at your discretion, of course."

"I'll be the only one staying at the country house. Otherwise, it will be hard to meet with the other senior officers . . . besides you, of course."

"There are more than a few who would like to meet you. It's been years since anything like that has happened."

"I did meet a squad leader some six years ago, north of Tirminya," comments Lerial. "Never any officers."

"It's said that Duke Kiedron insists that most of his junior officers be promoted from the senior rankers."

"Quite a number are, but there's no requirement for that. Not that many young men of altage or Magi'i birth survived the fall of Cyador."

"Altage . . . ?"

"Families with a tradition of service as officers in the Mirror Lancers. Quite a number of the junior officers are the sons of former squad leaders. From your question, I would guess that many of your officers come from families who are well established in one fashion or another . . . but that's just a guess on my part." Lerial smiles apologetically.

"That's generally true, but the arms-commander has suggested to the senior officers that we should keep our eyes open for squad leaders who have the potential to be good officers, and I have several undercaptains in my battalion who came to rank that way."

"And you have one of the more effective battalions?"

Drusyn laughs. "I'd like to think so . . . but doesn't every commander?"

"Of course," replies Lerial with a wide grin.

"It's been said that you have a wider range of experience in combat than most other senior officers in the Mirror Lancers . . ."

Lerial represses a knowing smile. He has been wondering when the probing questions might begin. "A wider range . . . that's a polite way of saying that I've had a greater opportunity to make more mistakes in different places . . . and that's certainly true. I was fortunate to serve under Majer Altyrn in the Verdyn rebellion, and I learned a great deal from him, more than I can ever repay." *And that is definitely true.* "He died just two eightdays ago . . . I don't know if word has reached Afrit."

Drusyn shakes his head. "Everyone in Hamor knew of him and his exploits. I never met him, although I was a junior undercaptain when . . . when the duke began to build Cigoerne."

"And you had your doubts about the wisdom of the duke's sire in selling lands to my grandmere?"

"I did. So, I understand, did a number of others." The subcommander shrugs. "There's nothing more dangerous for a junior officer to be right and say anything after something has already been decided. Even then, I knew that."

"It's even more dangerous for senior officers," replies Lerial dryly. *Or junior heirs.*

"There is that. I often thought that might have been why Commander Orekyn asked to be stipended. He died rather suddenly after that. The arms-commander—well, he wasn't arms-commander then—he was rather upset at that . . . or so it's said. I didn't know him then." Drusyn's words are blandly spoken.

"Those things happen. Sometimes, it's for the best." Lerial could speak to that in the case of Majer Phortyn. He refrains. "Too often, it's not."

Drusyn gestures ahead. "Here are your tents and corrals." There are fifteen tents set within fifty yards of the south wall, if east of all the corrals. The nearer corrals are empty.

Lerial surveys the heavy canvas tents. *If this is a trap . . .* He manages not to shake his head. The tents appear spacious and sturdy, far better than a mere bivouac. Given the preparations for his arrival, it's most unlikely that Rhamuel intends direct treachery, which suggests Atroyan is truly desperate . . . or will employ indirect treachery, in letting Lerial and his forces face overwhelming odds against Khesyn's forces. *Or both.* "They look far better than most places we've bivouacked . . . and better than most field quarters."

"We think so." Drusyn reins up. "The arms-commander believes in looking after his men."

There is something behind those words, but Lerial cannot decipher what it might be as he halts the gelding. "That's the sign of a good commander."

"There are barrels of feed by the corrals . . . the blue tents are the ranker mess tents, the crimson one for the company officers . . ."

Lerial listens as the subcommander outlines the supplies and situation.

When Drusyn finishes with those details, he looks to Lerial and says, "I'll ride back later to see how you and your men are faring and escort you over to the country house to get you settled before you meet with the arms-commander."

"Thank you. We do appreciate it."

"We appreciate your willingness to ride so far to assist us."

Even with the tents awaiting them, along with several barrels of fresh water—which Lerial inspects with his order-senses—it takes him almost a glass and a half before he is satisfied. Then he meets again with Fheldar, Strauxyn, and Kusyl.

"For some necessary reasons, I'll be staying in what the subcommander calls the 'country house.' I need to meet the other senior officers, and I'm supposed to meet with Arms-Commander Rhamuel before the evening senior officers' mess. As the senior company officer among you, Kusyl will be in command in my absence . . ." While that is standard, because Kusyl has not been a part of Lerial's command recently Lerial wants to emphasize that. He has barely finished going over what he expects should anything not go as anticipated when he sees Drusyn riding toward them. He remounts the gelding and rides to join the subcommander.

"The tents are quite solid," Lerial says as he joins Drusyn.

The subcommander laughs. "They were created for a festival two years ago. The arms-commander stored them. They're too heavy for real field use, but they have come in useful here."

"What sort of festival?"

"I've forgotten the official name. It was a forest frolic or some such."

Lerial decides against pursuing that and instead studies Atroyan's country home, which sits on a raised knoll facing the Swarth River and rises three levels, although most likely the knoll was raised around the lower foundation. There are two wings extending from the central building, which looks to have been constructed around a center square. Those wings are parallel to the river, and comparatively narrow.

The two ride to a smaller side entrance to the north wing, with Drusyn taking the outer circular lane that curves around the paved plaza before the high pillared receiving portico before the main section of the small palace. As soon as the two officers rein up, a crimson-liveried footman hurries out, looking to Lerial and then to the subcommander.

"I trust Lord Lerial's quarters are ready?"

"Yes, ser." The footman turns to Lerial. "Will you be needing your mount soon, ser?"

"I may."

"The ostlers can have him back here in less than a third of a glass," says Drusyn quietly.

"I likely won't need him that soon." Lerial smiles cheerfully.

"Just let one of us know, ser." The footman gestures, and a young stableboy in gray hurries from where he has been standing in the shadows of the entrance.

"I will see you later." Drusyn nods, then turns his mount and rides back toward the troopers' tents, again riding around the entry plaza.

Lerial would have been happy to carry his kit bag, but he understands the formalities and the need to let the young footman carry it inside the north wing and up a modestly wide staircase to the second level.

The chamber to which the crimson-liveried footman escorts him contains a wide double bed with an age-darkened golden oak bedstead and matching armoire, bedside tables, and writing desk, with even a weapons rack. There is a small washroom and jakes, and a tap for water. Emerya had mentioned that there was running water in the Palace of Light, but this is the first time Lerial has encountered it—*except water running in a stream.* Still, he makes good use of it, not only washing up, but using a damp cloth to rub away the dust and dirt on his uniforms.

He even has some time to look out the wide center window across the river toward Vyada, but outside of the tops of buildings, he can see nothing, and no sign of where Khesyn may have posted armsmen. Then there is a knock on the door.

"Lord Lerial, ser?"

"Yes?" Lerial walks to the door and opens it to see an Afritan Guard standing there, a man perhaps a year or so younger than Lerial himself.

"I'm to escort you to the arms-commander, ser."

"Just a moment." Lerial retrieves his father's response to Atroyan's "invitation" before returning. As he walks down the corridor beside the ranker, he says nothing for a few moments, then asks, "Are you attached to his staff or part of the household here?"

"His staff, ser."

"Who are the senior officers who report to him? I'd rather not offend anyone by not knowing what everyone else does."

"Yes, ser. I can understand that. Commander Sammyl is his chief of staff. Subcommander Valatyr is in charge of evolutions. Subcommander Klassyn runs logistics. Majer Prenyl and Captain Waell are assigned to the staff, but I don't know their duties. I'm sorry, ser, but I've only been on the staff for an eightday. Oh . . . and the two battalion commanders are Subcommander Drusyn and Subcommander Ascaar."

"Thank you. That will be a help." Lerial can't help but wonder why Drusyn greeted him, rather than the staff subcommanders, or even the majer or the captain, neither of whom would have been considered a slight. Another thought strikes him. "The Afritan Guards don't have submajers, do they? I've never heard that rank mentioned."

"No, ser. Not that I've ever heard, ser."

The corridor ends at a staircase just short of what has to be the wall to the center section of the massive dwelling. *So that those quartered in the wings cannot reach family quarters directly?* Lerial follows the ranker to the main level and then through a set of heavy double doors guarded by two rankers who scarcely blink as the two walk into the center section of the building. The wider marble-floored corridor on the other side leads to a large central hall. From that center hall, Lerial sees the main entry to his left and another entry to a central garden courtyard down another corridor to his right. His guide takes him to a doorway on the south side of the main hall, where another guard is posted.

"Lord Lerial is here to see the arms-commander," announces the junior ranker.

The guard raps on the door. "Lord Lerial, ser."

After a moment, the guard opens the door. "You may go in, ser."

Lerial steps through the door and finds himself in a small—small for the size of the dwelling—study no more than fifteen cubits by ten, containing little more than a small circular table with six chairs around it and a table desk set out from the south wall with a chair behind it . . . and several file chests.

Rhamuel stands, and then moves from behind the table desk toward Lerial. The arms-commander is not as tall as Lerial remembers from the one time they had met, but that was when Lerial had been only ten. The arms-commander is in fact several digits shorter than Lerial himself. His skin is perhaps a shade darker than that of Amaira, and his eyes are the same warm brown. "Welcome to Lubana, Lerial." He speaks Cyadoran with a heavy accent, but smiles. "You're rather taller than the last time we met, but you've the same red hair."

"It has been a while, ser," Lerial responds in Hamorian.

" 'Rhamuel' while we're alone, please." This time, the arms-commander speaks in Hamorian.

"I'll try. You've been the arms-commander of Afrit for as long as I can remember." Lerial extends the document. "This is the official acceptance of Duke Atroyan's invitation."

Rhamuel takes the parchment and scans it quickly, then nods.

Lerial takes that moment to survey the study more thoroughly, but finds nothing of a personal nature that might reveal more about the arms-commander, although the lack of clutter and papers reveals much in itself.

"This is a bit small, but it's mine." Rhamuel motions toward the table, then takes one of the chairs and seats himself, setting the document on the table. "I prefer not to intrude upon my brother's spaces whenever possible."

Should you take the opening? Lerial decides to. "I understand that all too well." He offers a wry smile as he sits. "Also having an older brother."

"You and I—and your aunt—have that similarity and a few others in life and position," says Rhamuel pleasantly.

"Being the younger sibling, so to speak," replies Lerial.

"There is that."

"Speaking of similarities—" Lerial slides the cloth-wrapped miniature from his riding jacket, using a slight concealment to blur it, should there be eyes in the walls, so to speak, although he can sense no one near but the guard, then slips the miniature into the older man's hand. "—there are more than a few."

Rhamuel takes the miniature and slides it inside his tunic, then nods. "We should talk about them sometime. How was the ride from Cigoerne?"

"Most uneventful, thankfully, and the undercaptain of the Guard in Guasyra was most helpful."

"He should have been. He was briefed that you might arrive. One never knows, though. One's invitations are not always accepted." Rhamuel glances to the document on the table. "Especially in spare but elegant words backed by valuable forces and an experienced commander."

"And one never knows in what fashion any invitation might be reciprocated," replies Lerial. "My father would prefer that you and your brother hold Afrit, particularly since Duke Khesyn has been a continuing irritation to Cigoerne."

"I had thought that might be so." Rhamuel pauses. "I understand that your brother is an overcaptain as well . . . and that he has been dealing with Heldyan . . . incursions."

"He is; he has, and he is senior to me." *If only by a few seasons.*

Rhamuel nods once more. "How might your aunt be? As I am certain you have heard, I owe some injuries to your sire's skill as a Mirror Lancer commander and my life and future to her healing abilities."

"She is well. She heads the Hall of Healing in Cigoerne, and she is even more skilled now. She and my mother have trained a number of healers."

Rhamuel nods. "They are reputed to be the greatest healers in Hamor. The trait must run in the blood. It is also said that you can do some field healing."

Where did he hear that? From Emerya? Why would she reveal that? Because she thinks it will somehow help you? "I have some skills in that, but I am far less skilled than she is." He pauses but briefly before asking, "Can you tell me how many companies Duke Khesyn has gathered . . . and what might be likely?"

"By fiveday, he had twenty-five companies mustered south of Vyada, and far more than fifteen in Estheld, perhaps as many as five battalions. That means we cannot move the ten battalions in Swartheld, and Commander Nythalt would prefer even more companies there." Rhamuel shakes his head. "Even six battalions should be enough to defend against forces that have almost a kay of open water to cross, but . . . for obvious reasons, the duke would prefer not to allow any more Guard forces to move from Swartheld to Luba. That is another reason why your companies are most welcome."

"I'd heard that Duke Khesyn has been gathering flatboats in Vyada."

"He has. He does not have enough . . . yet. He could embark half his forces and cross downstream in the dark . . ."

"And then use the same flatboats again a few days later."

Rhamuel nods. "We'll have to see."

Lerial suspects that, if Duke Khesyn intends to attack, he will use some variation on what Rhamuel has suggested.

"I was sorry to hear of Majer Altyrn's death. Some would say that, with your sire, and your Grandmere, he made Cigoerne what it has become."

Clearly Drusyn has reported to Rhamuel—unless Emerya had dispatched a letter with a trader almost as soon as Lerial had left Cigoerne . . . and that is possible. "He was a great man, although few know all of his accomplishments, especially those not having to do with arms or tactics."

"I had not heard . . ."

Lerial decides against saying too much, but replies, "He understood canals and irrigation systems, with watergates, and he even created a brewery and a brickworks. He was a superb tactician . . . but I'm certain you know that . . ."

Rhamuel offers a wry smile. "That skill I know all too well." He stands. "We will have to talk more, but I'm expecting Commander Sammyl momentarily with new information about Khesyn's forces."

Lerial rises. "I look forward to that. It is good to see you again."

"I would hope that you will join me and the senior officers for dinner." Rhamuel smiles, this time warmly, and adds, "And for all meals."

"I wouldn't miss it . . . once I make certain my men are fed and comfortable."

"You should have time for that. In camp, and this is camp for those purposes, the rankers are fed at fourth glass, and the junior and senior officers at sixth glass."

"Might I ask where the senior officers' mess is?"

"Oh . . . the private dining room here in country house."

Country house. And what exactly might the duke's palace in Swartheld look like, or his summer palace, wherever that might be? "Thank you."

"If you arrive early, we have refreshments in the salon across the entry hall here. Most officers manage to squeeze in a half glass before dinner."

In other words, no later than half past fifth glass. "I should be able to manage that." *As if there's any real choice.*

Rhamuel is still smiling pleasantly when Lerial leaves, somewhat puzzled by Rhamuel's warmth and apparent lack of deception. *At least, there's little sign of the chaos and order disruption that usually reveals deception.* But then, Rhamuel has said very little, in fact nothing, that Lerial essentially does not know. Saying nothing may withhold information, but it is not providing false information.

Lerial has to wait a time for the stableboy to return with the gelding—who has been well curried—but he does get back to his companies to see that his men are indeed being fed, and fed well, and that nothing seems amiss.

Less than a glass later, after his return to the country house, he crosses the main hall from the north entrance and makes his way toward the unguarded doorway across from Rhamuel's study. When he steps inside, he immediately surveys the salon, taking a quick count—eleven other officers, seated in various places.

A servitor in crimson and gray immediately steps forward.

"What would you prefer, ser?"

"Light or amber lager."

"Very good, ser." The servitor slips away.

"You must be Overcaptain Lerial."

Lerial turns to find himself facing a black-haired officer wearing the same insignia as Drusyn wears, except the device is silver rather than bronze. "Commander Sammyl . . . perhaps?"

The commander smiles. "Who described me?"

"No one. The only commander anyone mentioned was you. So . . ." Lerial shrugs.

"We need to talk." Sammyl guides Lerial to a pair of armchairs separated from the settees and chairs in the middle of the salon.

Lerial seats himself, accepts a beaker of lager from the servitor, who swiftly withdraws, and waits for the commander to speak.

"I have to say that I'm surprised that Duke Kiedron decided to support Duke Atroyan . . . although I do believe such is in his interests." Sammyl's black eyes focus on Lerial.

"My father, to my knowledge, has always put the interests of Cigoerne above personal feelings." *Even in dealing with family.* "So did my grandmere."

The commander nods. "Your presence would suggest that in regards to your father. I have only heard stories about the empress, but those suggest a rather . . . powerful personality."

"I saw most of that in retrospect. She was unfailingly kind, if firm, in dealing with me."

"Your presence does present . . . certain challenges."

Lerial decides to let silence respond for him, although he nods and then waits, punctuating the silence with a sip of the amber lager . . . better than many he has tasted, but not quite so good as that brewed at Kinaar by the majer, although it had taken Lerial years to appreciate that.

"Some five years ago, a certain Mirror Lancer undercaptain destroyed, and that is, from what can be determined, an accurate summary of what occurred, an entire battalion of Afritan Guards dispatched directly by Duke Atroyan. This has not been mentioned often, but it has not been forgotten either."

"As I recall, Commander, never has a Mirror Lancer force ever entered Afritan territory, except now, and that has only been by the invitation of the duke." *Or his seal.*

"That is true," admits Sammyl, "but it still poses a certain difficulty."

"Because some officers might feel a certain concern? They shouldn't, not unless they intend the Mirror Lancers or Cigoerne harm . . . and act on that intent."

"I thought you might say something like that. Still . . . it is good to hear those words. No one of your lineage has ever, to my knowledge, broken their word . . . unlike some other rulers."

Lerial has the feeling that Sammyl is not alluding to just Khesyn and Casseon. "My father has stressed the importance of keeping one's word, regardless of the costs." *And the majer emphasized the great danger in making threats.*

"Subcommander Drusyn has expressed an interest in working with you, in any instance where he would require forces additional to his battalion. Would that be satisfactory to you?"

"If it is acceptable to you and to the arms-commander," replies Lerial, hoping his initial judgment of the subcommander is accurate.

"Good. It may not come to that, but . . ."

"Do you have any idea where Khesyn might first attack?"

"It's unlikely to be anywhere but here. My best judgment is that he will attack here in order to take Luba, gain complete control of the river, and then move north until he can bring his forces at Estheld across and attack Swartheld."

"Does he have that massive a force? What about white wizards or mages?"

"He has gained the support of several war leaders of the western Tourlegyn clans. It's likely he's promised them spoils. The Tourlegyns love spoils and pillaging. He is also known to have mages and white wizards, but how many . . . and how talented . . . who knows?"

"Might I ask about your forces?"

Sammyl smiles wryly. "Afrit has never been endowed with many with chaos or healing talents. So few that most are jealously guarded by the merchanters who pay them handsomely."

Atroyan can't command their use against invaders? That raises some disturbing concerns, but not ones that Lerial can afford to mention. Not at present.

"As I am sure you understand," Sammyl continues, "Khesyn is likely to have the tacit support of Duke Casseon. Your presence here will likely reinforce that support."

Wonderful! Casseon's support of Khesyn can't be considered unexpected after the Verdyn rebellion. Even as he thinks that, Lerial is also aware that all the other officers are keeping well away from the two of them, not that he wouldn't have done exactly the same thing in their boots. "I doubt that he will commit armsmen."

"Not unless we are unsuccessful."

Lerial shakes his head. "He won't even then. He wants Verdheln back, and he wants Cigoerne destroyed."

"You may be right about that, but . . ."

"That will happen if Afrit falls . . . and that is why we are here."

"I'm glad we're both clear on that." Sammyl shifts his weight in the armchair. "I just thought we might have a few words." He stands. "Oh . . . one other thing. If you want your uniforms cleaned, bring them to the room at the foot of the stairs in the morning."

"Thank you. I appreciate your courtesy and your directness, ser." Lerial rises as well.

"A few last things. First, senior officers staff meeting every morning at seventh glass. Breakfast is after sixth glass, when you can get there. Second, as Lord Lerial, you'll be seated to the arms-commander's right at the mess at the evening meals."

"I would trust, that in his absence, you would stand in for him," Lerial replies. "Or the most senior Afritan Guard officer present."

Sammyl smiles, warmly, but ironically. "It appears as though we are in agreement in many matters."

Lerial nods. *Most matters . . . at present.*

Once Sammyl has slipped away, Drusyn appears, beaker in hand. "I see you received the commander's welcome chat."

"Something like that." Lerial notes that, unless the subcommander has refilled the beaker, he has drunk very little. "Details, his general observations on Khesyn and Casseon, and where I'm to sit at the mess."

"Unlike some senior officers, he is good with both details and larger matters."

While Drusyn's words are pleasant, Lerial understands the caution behind them. "I understand that can be a rare combination."

"Very rare." The dryness of that reply might have turned grapes to raisins instantly.

A bell chimes softly.

Lerial looks to the older officer.

Drusyn nods.

The two follow the other officers from the salon directly toward the courtyard. The private dining chamber is through the last door on the right before the center courtyard. Lerial does find himself seated at Rhamuel's right, even though all the officers in the entire mess officially outrank him. Although the rank of overcaptain doesn't exist in the Afritan Guard, he supposes he ranks as a majer, but that would still put him at the bottom of the table.

Once everyone is seated, Rhamuel lifts his goblet. "I'd like to offer a toast to Lord Lerial, who arrived this afternoon with three companies of Mirror Lancers. Welcome!"

After what Sammyl said in the salon and what Lerial did not hear or overhear in the salon, Lerial suspects that the meal will be more than passable and that the conversation, at least near him, will be both polite and not terribly revealing.

IX

When Lerial awakes on eightday morning well before sixth glass, he reflects on the evening before, from the dinner in the private dining room that had been every bit as polite and unrevealing as he had expected, to his subsequent walk back through the de facto avenue in the middle of the tents to meet again with his officers, and his return to the "country house." The fact that nothing untoward has occurred is almost more disturbing than if it had.

He washes and dresses and then heads for the private dining room, hoping, even on eightday, to see if he can talk to other officers on a more personal and less formal basis. On the way down, he notes the room where a ranker waits, and sees other uniforms there. Comparatively early as he arrives, there are already three officers in the dining chamber. One is Drusyn, seated next to Subcommander Ascaar, and the third, sitting slightly apart from the pair near the other end of the table, may be Subcommander Valatyr, by process of elimination, because Lerial does not recognize the man, and Valatyr had not been at the evening mess. *But there might be another senior officer . . .*

Drusyn immediately motions.

Lerial takes the chair beside him and across from Ascaar, offering a friendly "Good morning" to both.

"You may not think so after morning meetings every day for a season," says Ascaar.

"Ascaar doesn't care much for mornings." Drusyn grins.

"Demons know why I put up with you in the morning." Ascaar's grumble is more genial than gruff.

"Because you need a friendly voice to cheer you up."

"Ser?" offers the servitor standing almost at Lerial's shoulder. "Juice or lager?"

"Lager . . . please," Lerial says.

"Man after my own heart," declares Ascaar. "How did you find your quarters?"

"More than adequate, but it's a long walk to my companies."

The two subcommanders exchange a quick glance, but neither speaks as the servitor arrives with a platter and a beaker of lager. On the platter are eggs, seemingly scrambled with a cheese so pungent Lerial can immediately smell it, along with some yellow peppers. There are thin strips of meat, fried crisply—mutton, Lerial suspects—and a small loaf of whitish bread. He takes a swallow of the lager, then says pleasantly, "I'm assuming that each of you commands two battalions, but I don't know your command structure."

"That's right," replies Drusyn. "Majers command battalions, subcommanders two to three battalions, and commanders four or more battalions. There have been exceptions."

"Does anyone know exactly how many companies Khesyn has in Vyada?"

"Word is twenty-five." Drusyn frowns. "I'd wager more than that. No offense . . ." He pauses as if unsure exactly how to address Lerial.

" 'Lerial' here. 'Overcaptain' in the field."

"No offense, Lerial," adds Drusyn, "but the arms-commander wouldn't have been able to persuade the duke to invite you to join us if we weren't outnumbered."

"The arms-commander told me that Khesyn also has more than fifteen companies held at Estheld, possibly five battalions."

"Frig . . ." mutters Ascaar. "No wonder Rhamuel can't pry any of the other companies from Swartheld . . . as if Khesyn would risk crossing almost a kay of water in flatboats . . . and some merchanters might help the duke."

Might? That definitely concerns Lerial.

Drusyn glances around, then murmurs in a low voice, "The duke doesn't want to be more indebted to them."

"Whereas he feels Cigoerne might . . . just might . . . feel indebted for other reasons . . . or unwilling to exact repayment for helping him out?" asks Lerial lightly, if also quietly.

Drusyn laughs softly. "There might be something to that, but we won't know that until after it doesn't matter. One way or the other."

Lerial takes a bite of the eggs, discovering that they taste better than they smell, followed by one of the mutton strips, which tastes exactly like mutton fried and heavily peppered. The bread is warm and slightly doughy.

"I take it that one of the reasons you were sent," says Ascaar dryly, "is to limit the number of companies your sire felt he had to commit."

"You can see why Ascaar isn't on the arms-commander's staff proper," adds Drusyn.

"And why he must be a very good field commander?" returns Lerial as soon as he swallows.

"He is. He doesn't like to admit it," replies Drusyn.

"And so are you."

"Why might you say that?" There is a hint of a smile around the corners of Drusyn's mouth.

"Because you're in command of battalions where it's most likely that Khesyn will attack." *And it's far more important that whoever commands the forces left in Swartheld be loyal to Rhamuel than be the best commander.*

"That brings up the other reasons why you were sent," says Drusyn.

"He's the most effective field commander Duke Kiedron has," interjects the subcommander sitting several chairs away.

Lerial hopes the two subcommanders with whom he is sitting don't catch the slightest stress on the word "effective."

"Thank you, Commander," replies Drusyn.

Ascaar merely looks at Drusyn and shakes his head, then murmurs, "Valatyr knows everything."

"How long . . . ?"

"Have I been a Mirror Lancer? Close to seven years."

"You don't look that old."

"I'm not," Lerial admits. "I'll be twenty-three just after the turn of summer."

The two exchange glances.

"He killed his first raider when he was sixteen," interjects Valatyr. "He destroyed more than three battalions in the last battle of the Verdyn rebellion. He wouldn't have told you that, and neither of you needs to know more."

Lerial understands fully why Valatyr has offered his last words. Obviously Rhamuel knows who the undercaptain was who also destroyed a full battalion of Afritan Guards at Ensenla . . . and would prefer that information remain unknown.

Ascaar tries to stifle a grin as he looks at Drusyn and says in a low voice, "You had to know."

"Your sire obviously didn't pamper you," says Drusyn dryly.

"He didn't pamper either of us . . . and he's never indulged himself." Before either subcommander can say more, Lerial asks, "What is the routine here?

Is there an area where I could have my companies practice maneuvers—starting tomorrow? The horses need some rest."

"The grasslands southwest of the hunting park are open for maneuvers," answers Drusyn. "We have to get approval from Subcommander Valatyr. That's just so we don't interfere with each other and the arms-commander knows who's doing what."

"The routine?"

"It's up to each commander to keep his forces ready in whatever manner he sees fit."

"What about archers?"

"We each have a company. Each battalion has four companies of lancers that can double as mounted foot, and one company of archers who can do the same." Ascaar looks to Lerial.

"My companies are lancers, who can attack with either lances or sabres, or be mounted foot. Two of the companies have one squad that can double as mounted archers." Lerial pauses, then goes on. "The Meroweyans had companies of heavy foot and used a shield wall for advances against archers and even lancers. Do you have any heavy foot, or does Duke Khesyn?"

"We have two companies. They're in Swartheld. They're more suited to defending a city, according to Commander Nythalt."

"He's the commander in charge in Swartheld?"

Both subcommanders nod.

Lerial takes several more bites of his breakfast, and a swallow of lager.

"Do you have any other questions?" asks Drusyn.

"How many companies or battalions are still in Swartheld?"

"Ten battalions I've heard tell. No one's said. Anything else?"

"Well . . ." Lerial grins. "There is one. Exactly where are the ironworks? The city didn't look much like there were any there."

Ascaar smiles in return. "There aren't. The ironworks are more than ten kays to the west, at the end of the west road."

"The wide east-west road?" asks Lerial.

Ascaar nods. "They mine it and smelt it there, and pound it into rough plate. The plate comes here. Some is sent downriver to Swartheld. Most is smithed here."

"I just wondered, because everyone talks about the ironworks at Luba."

"There's really not a town there. Most of the heavy work at the works is done by lawbreakers."

That makes a certain sense to Lerial, since the irrigation ditches in Cigoerne are dredged by lawbreakers and new canals dug in the same fashion.

As Valatyr rises and leaves the dining room, Ascaar glances in his direction, then back to Lerial. "It won't be that long until the morning meeting, not if you want a quick word with your company officers. Commander Sammyl is prompt."

"I told them not to expect me this morning until after the senior officers' meeting. That won't be a problem, not with the horses needing rest. They know where to find me."

"They always do," comments Drusyn, "especially when you'd prefer not to be found."

Ascaar nods.

Before long, the three make their way to the salon.

The chairs and settees have been rearranged into three rows, facing away from the doorway. Lerial settles himself at the left end of the second row in a simple armless chair with a seat upholstered in slightly faded dull crimson, beside Subcommander Klassyn. "Good morning, Commander."

"Good morning, Lord Lerial. I trust all is well with you and your men."

"Everything seems to be settled. I imagine you have your hands full, though."

"Full, but not overfull. That will happen when another two battalions arrive."

"Are they expected soon?"

"They're not expected at all, but I keep working to see what I can do if they show up. If I don't, they'll arrive tomorrow." Klassyn glances toward the north end of the salon, where the chief of staff appears.

All the officers stand.

"As you were." As Lerial and the others reseat themselves, Commander Sammyl takes a position facing the seated senior officers and clears his throat. "Good morning. There's nothing new to report on the Heldyan forces. There are no indications of more forces arriving in Vyada." He glances toward Klassyn, who shakes his head, and then toward Valatyr, who does the same. "Then I'll go over the day's evolutions. Overcaptain Lerial, if it is agreeable to you, I thought that Subcommander Valatyr might accompany you and one of our squads and give you a thorough orientation of this side of the river—before you have to join us in fighting here."

"I'd very much appreciate that, ser."

"Good."

"Now . . . Subcommander Ascaar . . . you have the river patrols south of Lubana."

"Yes, ser."

"What do you have to report?"

"No change, ser. Riders in uniform on the east shore, but never more than a squad at a time. Three more large flatboats passed our patrols. They were empty and stayed close to the other shore. They tied up with the others at the new piers south of Vyada."

"Nothing else?"

"No, ser."

"Subcommander Drusyn?"

"It's much the same on the east shore north of Vyada. Squad-sized patrols and sometimes lone riders. There haven't been any flatboats going downstream. Late yesterday afternoon, there was a sail-galley that arrived from the north and docked at the new piers. It had the banner of Duke Khesyn. There weren't any armsmen to greet the galley. That usually means that there was a message from the duke."

"Suggesting that he is still in Estheld, you think?"

"He's either there, ser, or wants us to think he is. I couldn't say which from what my scouts saw."

"Is there anything else? No? Good. Dismissed to duties."

Everyone stands once more, while the commander leaves the salon.

Then, as most of the other officers follow, Commander Valatyr walks over to Lerial.

"Thank you for your comments earlier this morning."

"You know why I made them, I trust?" Valatyr's smile is somehow both wintry and wry, matching a countenance that seems stern when he is not smiling.

"I'd judge so. In the interests of harmony."

Valatyr nods. "Quite so. Would you prefer to see the river area south of Lubana first or the area north first? We'll provide a mount so that yours can rest."

Although Lerial has brought some spare mounts, he merely nods. "Thank you. I'd prefer to see the area where we'd be most likely to fight, possibly downstream of Khesyn's new piers, but since I don't know the location of those piers . . ." He offers an apologetic shrug.

"The piers are about a kay south of Lubana, on the south side of a wide bend in the river. With the current, they could land on our side less than half a kay south of here."

"At the edge of the hunting park?"

"More like the middle of the park. It's . . . extensive."

"Also . . . if I could drop off some uniforms to be cleaned and if we could stop for a moment so that I could brief my officers?"

"Naturally. I took the liberty of having the mounts brought to the north entrance." Valatyr gestures, and the two leave the salon.

Waiting outside the salon are Captain Waell and several rankers, presumably to return the salon to its primary function.

Valatyr does not speak as the two cross the main hall to the north corridor and then continue to the north wing. Lerial hurries up to his chambers and reclaims the soiled uniforms. By the time he has dropped them off and made his way out the north entrance, Valatyr, a half squad of Afritan Guards, and Lerial's gelding are waiting.

"It's unlikely we'll run into trouble, but one never knows," the subcommander declares as he mounts.

True enough. Lerial nods, then rides beside the older officer as they circle around the circular entrance plaza toward the south. When they reach the Cigoernean area, Lerial reins up short of the officers' tent, but he barely dismounts before Strauxyn, Kusyl, and Fheldar appear.

"Good morning, ser."

"Good morning. This won't take long. I've just come from the senior officers' meeting, and I'll be getting a tour of the areas where we might be called to fight . . ." Lerial quickly goes over not only what Commander Sammyl has said, but also some additional information about the current location of Heldyan forces. Then he lays out what he wants from the men for the day, including blade practice. Even so, he is finished in less than a third of a glass, and is back in the saddle.

One of the Afritan Guards opens the southern gate, and Valatyr leads the way through the gate, then immediately turns left, heading eastward toward the Swarth River, which has to be a half kay away.

A brisk wind, neither warm nor cool, sweeps out of the south, but given the hazy sky, the sun does not provide that much warmth, and Lerial is glad for his riding jacket. He studies the hunting park to his right, which seems to be a mixture of a woodlot with long-needled pines, well-trimmed groups of bushes and olive trees here and there at random, with browned grass covering the ground in most places, except around the bases of some of the pines.

"What sort of game does the duke hunt here?" he finally asks Valatyr.

"I don't know that the duke has ever hunted here. His sire liked to hunt the small gazelles, it's said. I've only seen a few. They're fast and very wary."

"How much of the edge of the river between Lubana and the point opposite Khesyn's new piers is marsh, and how much is open water?"

"You'll see. There's open water immediately east of Lubana. That's because Duke Natroyan had the marshes dredged away back to where there was bedrock. That's where he built the east wall."

"Natroyan?"

"Duke Atroyan's grandsire."

At the east end of the south wall there is another corner tower, and Valatyr reins up and points to the north. "You can see what he did."

Lerial can indeed. The east wall of Lubana is the riverbank, although stone riprap perhaps three yards in width extends from the base of the wall then drops another two yards to the water's surface. The marshes begin less than twenty yards south of the corner tower, largely rushes and reeds with only small patches of open water, and extend a good thirty to fifty yards out into the river. A graveled lane, with a low hedgerow—trimmed to a height of two yards—separating the lane from the park proper heads south along the western edge of the reed marshes, and Valatyr gestures. "The lane has been well maintained."

"It looks like parts of the marsh were filled to make sure the lane is straight."

"Duke Natroyan's doing. Even then, when Heldya was far less strong, he wanted roads along the river."

"All of the good roads along the Swarth were his doing?"

"Most of them," Valatyr admits, turning his mount.

Lerial eases the mare alongside Valatyr. "You were a battalion commander once, I take it."

"For a time."

"Where, might I ask?"

"Here. Drusyn was my successor."

"Does that mean that Ascaar's forces are normally posted somewhere between Luba and Swartheld?"

"They are. At Shaelt. It's a small river city, perhaps twice the size of Luba. It's about seventy kays north."

Lerial nods, his eyes taking in the marshes to the east and to the south. He can see the gradual turning of the river more toward the south and southwest, and his maps show that it actually flows from the west to the east before returning to its general flow from the southeast to the northwest, much as it does near Cigoerne, except the shift is larger there. Before long, the lane swings to the southwest, and the reed marshes give way to a shallow backwater. Across the grayish water he can see Vyada. At first, he has to wonder if it is as large as others have said, but then he realizes that the buildings and dwellings on the other side seem smaller because the Swarth is wider than at Cigoerne or Ensenla, close to three-quarters of a kay.

"The new piers are farther west." Valatyr points. "There. Just below the point of that bluff that extends into the river."

"I'd say they're almost two kays from here."

"That's about right."

Lerial studies the river. The current doesn't look that strong. *It's usually not as fast where the land around the river is flat and the river is wide . . . but that would make crossing it here easier and possible in a shorter distance.* His eyes go to the hunting park to his right. The ground is more open, with fewer trees than closer to the south gate. "If they landed here at night, they could make it to the main road without getting much nearer to Lubana."

"They could. That's why we have scouts posted there." Valatyr points ahead to what appears to be a small timber house on piles set between the lane and the river. "They wouldn't do that. They'd attack us. They might even wait for us to attack them."

"To defeat and destroy the duke's forces . . . and then begin to take and occupy every town and city along the river as they move toward Swartheld."

"That's my opinion. The arms-commander's, too." Valatyr makes a gesture to the rankers following them, but keeps riding until they are a good fifty yards ahead.

Lerial checks and reinforces his shields, but says nothing, doubting he will be attacked, but wondering what the subcommander might have to say that he does not wish overheard.

Valatyr reins up and looks appraisingly at Lerial for several moments before he finally speaks. "You know you're not anything like anyone pictured."

"I couldn't say. I've never thought about it."

"I should have said, 'Anyone but the arms-commander.' He did say right after you arrived that you were close to what he expected."

"That's not surprising. He has good sources in Cigoerne."

For a moment, Valatyr is silent, as if Lerial has offered an unexpected comment. Then he smiles, faintly. "You know his sources?"

"At least one of them."

"And your sire does as well?"

"Of course. It's to our interest that he receives accurate information." Lerial shrugs, although he knows his next words must be carefully chosen. "To my knowledge, neither of us has ever said a word to a source about their communications, or even hinted that we knew." That is stretching matters slightly so far as Lerial is concerned, and more than that for his father, yet certainly his words do reflect the underlying truth.

Valatyr frowns for a moment. "Begging your pardon, Lord Lerial, but I have great difficulty in accepting that."

"I can understand that, but what I said is true and reflects everything I know."

"Yet you conceal all that you are."

"Conceal, not lie. I certainly am not denying anything to you. I know as well as you do that, should Khesyn attack, I will not be able to conceal whatever abilities I may have. No officer can do that and survive." *Either the enemy or his commander.*

"Why are *you* here?"

"Because Cigoerne cannot afford to have Afrit fall to Duke Khesyn."

"Then why did your sire not send a greater force?"

"Because, had he done that, Khesyn would have attacked Cigoerne instead of Afrit. He might still."

"And you will make the difference?" The subcommander's voice is only faintly ironic.

"I have pledged to do all that I can." *Without giving up your own life . . . and trying not to lose your entire command.*

Valatyr's laugh is both harsh and soft. Then he shakes his head. "Come. Let me show you the rest of this end of the hunting park, and the various lanes and roads."

Once more Lerial nods. He can sense that that his very presence in Afrit has unsettled the other officer, and that the subcommander is disturbed, but that he has not lied. All that reinforces the concerns that Emerya had once suggested about Afrit's weaknesses. *And you're supposed to do something about that . . . with merely three companies?*

Almost two glasses later, Valatyr and Lerial return to the "country house" and the salon, where they have a lager and some slices of bread and cheese before setting out again.

As the two ride toward the north entrance to Lubana, whose iron-grille gates are closed and guarded by at least a half a squad of Afritan troopers, Valatyr says, "We'll just follow the river road north until we get to the hills and the north bluff. You can tour Luba proper on your own later."

Three of the Afritan Guards hurry forward and swing open the heavy gates, then close them behind the two officers and the half squad of rankers escorting them. The lane beyond the gates is paved and extends due north for another kay through well-tended fields and pastures before it intersects the wide road that heads westward to the ironworks and eastward to Luba proper, seemingly less than a half kay away, assuming that the rows of houses that begin just ahead represent the town boundary.

Valatyr turns his mount eastward. "We'll take the river road."

The river road is almost exactly a half kay away, as it should be, reflects Lerial, given the dimensions of the wall surrounding Lubana, and the riders turn north on it, not that it extends south into the duke's estate, although there is a narrow lane south along the river, but access is blocked by a gate set in a short stretch of wall, and a longer hedgerow extending westward.

There is a low rough-stone wall, no more than a yard high, perhaps two yards east of the road, and beyond it is a narrow strip of marshes and reeds.

For the first several blocks after they enter Luba, there are only small houses on the west side of the road, mostly of mud brick, with walls almost up to the road forming courtyards. From the trees Lerial can see, there are apparently walled gardens behind even the meanest and smallest of dwellings.

Just ahead Lerial spies a stone bridge over a canal.

"That's the first canal. You'll find cafés and shops beyond it . . . and the southern trading piers on the river side."

Because it is eightday, many of the shops are shuttered, but most, generally with quarters above or behind them, do not look all that different from those in Cigoerne, except that a number are clearly older, with weathered wood and fading paint. The chandlery, directly across from the pair of river piers, at which only a single flatboat is tied, boasts new—and newly oiled—shutters and front door and has otherwise been recently refurbished, at least on the outside. It is open, as evidenced by a man entering as Lerial rides past, and two others standing under the roof of the narrow front porch and talking. Only one of the pair even glances in Lerial's direction.

"The market square is just ahead. It won't be quite as busy as on sevenday, but there will likely be some carts and peddlers there." Valatyr laughs. "I've never seen a day when someone wasn't here. Drusyn says there's always someone here."

That reminds Lerial of a question he'd meant to ask. "Are Drusyn's battalions stationed at Lubana?"

"Just one of them. The other is split up. He has four companies at Guasyra, and one north of here at Haal. The barracks buildings will hold two battalions, but except at times like this, they're half empty. Ascaar's forces are usually more spread out, all across the western woods and hills."

The river road runs through the middle of the paved market square, actually an oblong running north some hundred yards and perhaps twenty-five east to west. Many of the worn red stones are cracked, and in a few places, missing entirely. Lerial makes a rough and quick count of the small stalls and wagons scattered almost at random and comes up with some thirty sellers. He also uses his order-senses to try to pick up some of the comments from those in the square.

". . . looks like a Mirror Lancer type . . ."

". . . never thought I'd see that . . ."

". . . duke must be worried . . ."

". . . not enough brains left to be worried . . . his brother's the one worried . . ."

". . . three for the bag . . . not a copper less . . ."

". . . sshh . . . high-ranking types . . ."

". . . ignore 'em . . . never stop to buy anything . . ."

". . . one in the strange uniform . . . younger than most . . ."

". . . any potatoes not winter-soft . . . ?"

Lerial wonders about the potatoes . . . cool sand in a root cellar should prevent softness.

Beyond the market square is a second canal, and immediately to the north of it and west of the river road, Lerial notes an area of much larger dwellings—also set on larger pieces of property with higher walls surrounding the mansions, mansions at least in comparison with anything else he has seen in Luba. "The more affluent merchants and others live just north of this next canal?"

"So I've heard," replies Valatyr. "I can't say that I've met any of them."

"Are you usually posted in Swartheld?"

"Most of the time, but I go where the arms-commander wants me."

"I've never been to Swartheld, but it must be filled with wealthy traders."

Valatyr laughs. "More than you can believe, and they all want something, either to sell the Guard something or a favor for some relative."

"Do you get many young officers from the merchanters?"

"Some. Usually second or third sons. Often from smaller merchanters. They're usually very good or very bad."

"And the ones from the wealthiest families are generally the very worst—except for the one that's outstanding?"

"You're obviously familiar with that problem."

"I've seen it." *And Magi'i sons can be even worse.*

Even before they approach the third canal, Lerial can smell the odors rising from the water. He glances toward Valatyr.

"It does smell," replies the subcommander to Lerial's quizzical look. "All the smiths—blacksmiths, tinsmiths, silversmiths, coppersmiths—must be located along the north canal. Most people live on the canals or lands upstream of here . . . for obvious reasons."

Lerial represses a frown. He has not thought Cigoerne particularly advanced, especially after his aunt's comments about all that she and his father lost when Cyad fell, but his grandmere and father had insisted that all factoring or smithing wastes be carted to the disposal ponds west of the city, ponds ringed with special lilies, or to a dryland gully to the northwest. Nightsoil also has to be collected, although it can be used to fertilize fields that grow fodder.

"You look skeptical," observes Valatyr.

"We don't have enough smiths for their waste to fill an entire canal," Lerial temporizes.

"I'm sure that those who live near here wished that were true here."

Roughly a third of a kay beyond the third canal, the dwellings come to an end. They continue riding, but to the west of the road is a gentle rise half covered with brown grass, with sandy ground between the patches of grass. Lerial can sense more rises farther west, but has the impression that they have even less grass. Ahead the road angles to the northwest as it climbs the west end of a bluff that the river curves eastward around before seemingly returning to its north-northwesterly course.

Valatyr finally reins up short of where the road steepens. "You can see how steep the incline is between the road and the river from here north. It's at least that steep for a good fifteen kays. That's why Khesyn will attack somewhere between the south end of the hunting park and here. That is, if he chooses to attack here at all."

"Could he just be mustering forces from the south here before sending them downstream for an attack on Shaelt or Swartheld?"

"That's possible. That's why there are battalions being held in both places. But we can't afford to lose the ironworks, either, and that would certainly happen if we didn't have forces here."

"I can see that." *And you'd have the dark angels' time if they ever got a sizable force established on this side of the river.*

"Now that you've seen what there is to see of Luba by the river, so to speak, we'll head back." Valatyr turns his mount.

So does Lerial.

X

The remainder of eightday goes without event, as do oneday, twoday, and threeday. On all of those days Lerial takes his companies to the grasslands southwest of the hunting park and conducts maneuvers. He also uses some of that time to study the land and the area farther south along the river, and insists that Fheldar and the undercaptains do as well. While he sees several more empty flatboats arriving, and Subcommander Drusyn and Valatyr report that at the morning meeting of the senior officers on threeday, the Heldyan piers south of Vyada remain filled with apparently empty flatboats.

Although he has not pressed the issue, Lerial feels that Fheldar and the undercaptains need a tour of Luba and the area north of Lubana. Before the morning meeting on fourday, Lerial meets with Fheldar and his officers and arranges for arms practice for the rankers, under their squad leaders for the day. Then, after the morning meeting on fourday, he approaches Commander Sammyl.

"What is it, Overcaptain?"

"You were kind enough to arrange for Subcommander Valatyr to give me a tour of the area around Lubana, and I've familiarized my officers with everything south of the estate. While I would not wish to intrude on any of your officers' time, I would like to familiarize them with Luba itself and the ground immediately north of the city." Lerial offers an apologetic smile before continuing. "I fear, however, if Mirror Lancer officers and rankers ride unaccompanied through Luba, this might create some misapprehensions. So I would like to request the presence of four Afritan Guard rankers to accompany us."

Sammyl smiles. "That would be most appropriate and easy enough to arrange."

Less than half a glass later, Lerial, Kusyl, Strauxyn, Fheldar, four Mirror Lancer rankers, and four Afritan Guards ride out through the north gate of Lubana, with Lerial leading the officers and Fheldar, followed by the Afritan Guards, with the Mirror Lancers bringing up the rear.

Lerial says very little on the ride along the river road, past the piers and market square, all the way to where the road swings inland and begins its climb over and around the bluff. Once there, he turns the gelding west, and leads his group up the grassy rise to the crest, where he reins up. As he has suspected, the eastern slope of the next rise presents more reddish sand than grass. So he turns south and rides along the crest until he nears the line of dwellings and small plots that mark the northern edge of Luba, finding his way to a narrow lane that leads south.

Seemingly within moments after Lerial re-enters the small city, the stench becomes far more pronounced, close to unbearable in the still air, cool as it is, and Lerial wonders just what it must be like in the heat of summer. He leads his group on a wandering ride through the city, slowly leaving the stench behind and heading generally westward until they eventually reach the road to the ironworks. Rather than head eastward, Lerial heads west, studying the canals and ditches and the irrigated plots and olive orchards that are everywhere, continuing until the road intersects the side road that leads to the west gate of Lubana.

As he rides back through the gate slightly before second glass in the afternoon, Lerial considers what he has learned from his ride north from

Cigoerne . . . and from his tours around the Luba area. Luba itself is markedly smaller than Cigoerne, less than half its size, not nearly so neat or well kept, and definitely smells much worse. There seem to be more hamlets in Afrit than in Cigoerne, but of all those Lerial has seen, Guasyra and Luba are the only ones that appear prosperous. *But then, it could just be that everywhere prosperous is north of here . . . and that's why Rhamuel doesn't much care about southeastern Afrit.*

A glass later, Lerial is busy watching lancers spar, occasionally offering advice to the squad leaders, and despite the coolness having to open his riding jacket. *Just how warm will Luba be by spring, let alone summer?*

By the time he enters the officers' mess in the private dining room that evening, Lerial cannot help but wonder, even more, exactly what Duke Khesyn has in mind. Are the boats tied up at Vyada a decoy? If they aren't, how long will it be before Khesyn attacks? And why would he attack where Rhamuel has amassed so many troopers? *Because he wants to destroy Atroyan's Afritan Guard in order to make conquest of Afrit easier? Or because it's easier to cross the river here?*

After the opening toast by Rhamuel, this time to "patient officers," Lerial quietly asks just those questions once the arms-commander has been served—some sort of sliced beef in a cream cheese sauce over sliced boiled potatoes, with turnips on the side.

Rhamuel smiles, looking up from his platter. "You're not terribly interested in dinner, are you?"

"I'll eat it, ser, but I've been watching and thinking . . ."

"So have we all."

"And being patient doesn't necessarily bring one answers."

"Sometimes insisting on an answer brings the one least appreciated."

Lerial laughs softly. "And sometimes waiting does."

Rhamuel shakes his head, obviously amused, then takes a sip of the hearty red wine he prefers before speaking. "Khesyn has two objectives. The first is to decimate, if not destroy, the Afritan Guard. The second is to conquer Afrit. If he can achieve the second without achieving the first, he will. My task is to make certain that he has to attempt the first before doing anything else."

"And because Swartheld is the key to Afrit, you have more guards there and in Shaelt than is commonly known. The guards here are to stop his forces from gaining this side of the river where there are roads that lead to Shaelt and Swartheld."

Rhamuel nods. "We should have brandy—or better lager—in my study after dinner."

"I'd be honored."

The arms-commander smiles, ironically. "Perhaps."

That suggests that while Lerial may be honored, he won't necessarily be pleased. He returns the smile. "Your lager is good. If your private stock is better, it must be quite good."

"It's excellent, if I do say so. You haven't mentioned much about Cigoerne, you know."

"Well . . . since the last time you were there—"

"The only time," interjects Rhamuel mildly.

". . . it has grown a great deal. There are more piers on the river, and the dwellings now extend as far north as the Hall of Healing all the way as far west as the palace . . ."

For the remainder of the meal, after Lerial finishes providing Rhamuel with a description of how Cigoerne has changed, he replies politely and tries to listen to what others are saying. One set of comments, which he can barely make out, even with his order-senses, comes from the bottom of the table between Majer Waell and Majer Sethwyn, whom Lerial knows only by sight and name.

". . . understand that Natroyor was ailing . . ."

"He's all right now. That's what I heard."

"Good . . . don't need something like that now . . . still wonder . . . not coincidence . . . not after what happened to the duke's eldest . . ."

Lerial refrains from frowning. *Did something happen to Kyedra?* He tries to pick up more, but the conversation turns to speculations on what types of troopers Khesyn might bring to an attack on Lubana . . . or anywhere in Afrit.

"How did your ride through Luba go," inquires Sammyl politely.

"It was very instructive. We spent a bit more time in the north. I wanted to look over the rises and swales north of the third canal. We came back through the town and then used the ironworks road to return to the west gate."

"How does Luba compare to Cigoerne?"

"It's smaller, but it has more smiths and metalworkers than Cigoerne does. I'd judge that Cigoerne has more factors and traders, but that makes sense. Swartheld would seem to be the trading center for Afrit, not Luba . . ."

As he talks, Lerial tries not to reveal anything most likely not already known to Rhamuel.

After the last goblets of wine and the last beakers of lager are finished, Rhamuel rises, then nods to Lerial, who stands and walks with the arms-commander from the private dining room through the main hall to Rhamuel's study . . . and then to the small conference table, on which is a silver tray holding a goblet and a beaker and two pitchers, one likely of white wine and the other of lager.

Rhamuel seats himself, as does Lerial. "I presume you know why I've not invited you here before."

"To make it appear as though my presence is strictly a necessity and not to show favoritism . . . or to cause excessive prying that might reveal certain things."

"There is that. I also wanted you to see matters as any officer might . . . although we both know that you are anything but any officer. Your father knows that great rewards do not come without great risks." The older man pours himself a goblet of the white wine.

For a moment, Lerial wonders what Rhamuel means. Then he smiles pleasantly. "He did not place all those risks before me." *Altyrn did.*

"Then you are a greater gambler than I thought."

Lerial reaches for the pitcher of lager, scanning it with his order-senses as he lifts it, but he can feel none of the chaos that might suggest poison; not that he suspects such, but he is trying to make that a habit, especially when he is the only one drinking from a pitcher or other vessel. As he half fills the beaker, he replies, "I don't seek risks. I try to do only what is necessary."

"That can be the greatest risk of all."

Lerial smiles again, more broadly. "You are more familiar with that than I am."

Rhamuel returns the smile. "What questions would you ask of me?"

"Before we talk about what you might have in mind," *or not,* "ser, I did have one question that has little to do with Duke Khesyn and my presence here. I overheard someone talking about something that had happened to the duke's eldest child, and I hadn't heard anything about Kyedra." Lerial smiles apologetically. "I suppose I'm interested because she's the only one of the duke's children I ever met, and that was over ten years ago."

Rhamuel frowns. "Kyedra? There's nothing . . ." Then he shakes his head. "They must have been talking about his elder son. That was Traeyen.

He had a rare blood flux. There was some sort of chaos in his body. Not even the best healers in Afrit could do anything. He died. That was last fall, though."

"I hadn't heard anything about that. I don't think anyone in Cigoerne knows . . . and there was something about Natroyor . . ."

"Contrary to your words, Lerial, those matters may have a great deal to do with you, me, and Duke Atroyan. "

"You're suggesting that his younger son is also ill . . . or frail?"

"At times, there is little difference."

"He has no other sons?"

Rhamuel shakes his head.

From that gesture, Lerial gains the impression that other children are unlikely. "Yet neither you nor your brother . . ."

"You know I can have no sons, not under the laws of Afrit. Nor can Mykel, not that his interests lie there."

Not only does what Rhamuel has disclosed suggest even more reasons for Duke Khesyn's interests in Afrit, but there are definite implications. *Should you press?* "What can I do to help you?"

Rhamuel laughs, softly, but with a bitter edge. "You are more of a gambler than you realize . . . or better at disguising it."

Lerial waits.

"You may be able to help Afrit. Or you may be able to help me. Or yourself. Or none. You will, I think, know what must be done when the choice is before you." After a moment, Rhamuel adds, "I would ask that you never aid Khesyn, but since that is so against your interests and those of your sire and your people, I trust I should not have to ask that."

Neatly done . . . asking without asking.

"You asked about what Khesyn will do. There will be an attack. It will come soon. If we repulse it without many casualties, or if we inflict massive casualties, Khesyn will withdraw. That has been his pattern."

"Then why do you need me . . ." Lerial shakes his head. *Of course!*

"I think you understand."

"What better way than to smooth over past differences? In a fashion that even those who are less than charitably inclined cannot but accept?"

Rhamuel nods. "And there is also the possibility that Khesyn may attack again."

"Would you like me to tell you about my family, especially about those you did not meet or spend much time with when you were in Cigoerne—my brother, my younger sister, my aunt, and her daughter?"

"That would be helpful, especially if the duke calls upon me to advise him on such matters. That has happened, upon occasion, if less often in recent years."

"You may recall that my brother Lephi is two years older. As an overcaptain he is in command of two companies posted to Sudstrym—that's a newer post just across the river from Amaershyn . . ." Lerial goes on with obvious information about his parents and Ryalah, and then his aunt Emerya . . . "remains as the head of healing at the Healing Hall in Cigoerne. She was the one who first instructed me in field healing. She has one daughter. That is Amaira. She has brown hair and brown eyes, much like you, and she is warm and has a good sense of humor." Lerial almost mentions that Amaira is deeply grounded in order, but decides against that because it would raise too many questions about how he would know and what else he knows. "She's very intelligent, and she is quietly strong, but sensitive. She's been very good for my sister Ryalah and far more patient with her than I'd have been likely to be in the same circumstance. Her mother thinks she might have the talent for being a healer, and she's been spending time at the Hall of Healing . . ."

When Lerial finishes, Rhamuel nods and smiles, almost sadly. "That's quite a family you have, even the girls."

"Ryalah has been a challenge now and then . . . Amaira, never, not that I can recall. She's very thoughtful. She should make a good healer, but that's something that only time will tell."

"Like a good officer."

Lerial laughs. "I think my father despaired of my ever being a decent officer, let alone a good one."

"I'm afraid my father felt the same way," Rhamuel says pleasantly.

When he finally leaves the study, more than a glass later, after more general conversation, what puzzles Lerial most is why Rhamuel hadn't requested that Emerya come to Swartheld. *Or had Atroyan forbidden him to do so? Or had Grandmere? Or is there more going on?* He almost laughs at the last thought. One thing he has learned is that there is always more happening than is known by most.

He is halfway across the main hall and headed for the staircase to the north wing when a figure slips from the less well-lighted corner near the archway leading to the north wing.

"You're carrying a concerned expression. After leaving the arms-commander's study, that doesn't bode well." Drusyn smiles pleasantly.

"Does anything about what Khesyn may plan bode well?" Lerial replies dryly. "What I learned was that Khesyn will attack, probably sooner than later, and our success will depend almost entirely on how few casualties we take and how many we inflict on his forces." He pauses for just an instant and adds sardonically, "Just as in any battle or war."

Drusyn laughs. "That's all?"

"Of course not. He detailed why most precisely, then asked about my family and how Cigoerne had changed since he visited it years ago. I told him what he seemed to want to know. Then he bid me good evening . . . and here I am."

"He never does anything without a purpose."

"I got that impression. One purpose was to impress on me the importance of quickly destroying any attacking force. Another purpose was likely to find out more about how Cigoerne has changed over the years, at least from my perspective, and he will doubtless compare what I said to what he has learned from traders, factors, and others."

"That is the way he works." Drusyn pauses. "Well . . . good evening."

"Good evening to you. I'll see you in the morning. As usual." With a smile, Lerial turns and makes his way up the stairs to the second level.

XI

An insistent rapping on his door, well before dawn, awakes Lerial on twoday morning, the last twoday of winter, not that winter is that cold as far north as Lubana is, and he struggles out of bed. "Yes?"

"The arms-commander wants all senior officers in the salon in the next third of a glass, ser."

"Thank you. I'll be there." *The Heldyans must be attacking. Why else would he want us all there so far before dawn?* Lerial's ability to use his order-senses means he doesn't have to light the lamp in order to dress, although he needs light to read something or locate a very small object. He does light the lamp, using a touch of chaos rather than fumbling for a striker, when it comes to washing and quickly shaving. He is ready fairly quickly and makes his way from his quarters toward the staircase.

There, he pauses to wait for Ascaar, who appears more discomfited and rumpled than usual in the morning, then says, "A Heldyan attack, you think?"

"If it's anything worse, I don't want to know," growls the Afritan battalion commander as they descend to the main level of the so-called country home.

In the dimness of the main hall, its cavernous expanse lit but by two lamps, Lerial sees Drusyn waiting by the salon door.

The graying subcommander smiles cheerfully.

"Don't say a word," says Ascaar gruffly. "Too early for cheer."

Drusyn just shakes his head and accompanies the two into the salon, where Majer Prenyl stands by the dark widow that overlooks the front plaza. Subcommander Klassyn waits by one of the settees, as does Valatyr. Before any can exchange greetings, the majer says, "Arms-Commander, ser!"

Lerial and the others remain standing as Sammyl and Rhamuel stride into the salon and past them. Sammyl stops beside Valatyr.

Rhamuel moves to the end of the chamber. "You all can sit down. Not that you'll be here that long." He waits for a moment, as Lerial and the officers who had been standing seat themselves, then continues. "The lookouts to the south have reported lamps and torches on the Vyada piers. It would appear that the Heldyans are loading many, if not all, of the flatboats. We can't tell where they intend to go. For all we know, they could be headed all the way to Estheld or Swartheld . . . or they could land south of Lubana. My best judgment is that they will attempt to land the flatboats in a number of places near Luba in order to prevent us from massing our forces in any single spot. I could be wrong, but we will proceed on that assumption." The dark-haired arms-commander pauses and his eyes sweep across the officers present. "Subcommander Drusyn, you will be responsible for stopping any incursion immediately south of Lubana. Subcommander Ascaar, you will deal with any landing north of Lubana. Overcaptain Lerial, for the moment, you will remain ready to reinforce either of the other forces . . . or to deal with a third possible point of attack, if there is such, once we can determine that. I will keep you informed as we know more. Because it will likely be a glass before the first flatboat leaves the piers, I've ordered the immediate dispatch of field rations to all companies, and officers' rations are already in the dining room. Take a moment to eat something before you head out to your officers and men. It will likely be a long day." He pauses again. "That is all." With a quick nod that is just short of being brusque, Rhamuel turns and leaves the salon.

Lerial looks to Drusyn. "Do you think they'll really land where you're being dispatched?"

"Who knows? They'll do their best to do what we don't expect. Wouldn't you? What do you think?"

"What the arms-commander does—that, if they attack, they'll attack in more than one place."

The two walk from the salon without saying more, through the hall and into the private dining room. "Officers' rations" turn out to be a full breakfast set at each place, with a healthy helping of egg toast, ham strips, and a small loaf of bread for each officer. Lerial sits between Ascaar and Drusyn, since seating by rank is only at the evening mess, and pours himself a lager from one of the pitchers.

"What do you think?" Lerial asks Ascaar after taking several mouthfuls of the egg toast, sweetened by a dark berry syrup, followed by some lager.

"Duke Khesyn's been wanting to conquer Afrit for years, if not longer. Figures he has to do it soon."

"Why soon?" asks Drusyn.

"Duke Kiedron gets stronger every year. I'd wager Khesyn didn't think that he'd send forces to support the arms-commander. Even if Khesyn did think that might happen, every year that passes means Cigoerne will be able to back Afrit more." Ascaar looks to Lerial. "You don't have a choice, do you?"

"No," Lerial admits. "For all the trouble we've had between us and Afrit, it's been nothing," *not since Ensenla, anyway,* "compared to the difficulties we've had with Casseon and Khesyn."

Drusyn frowns.

"Casseon sent more than forty companies against Verdheln, and there are usually close to a score of raids by Heldyans every year. Khesyn claims they're raiders over whom he has no control, but we've captured arms that look like the same kind of blades used by his armsmen." Lerial takes another bite of egg toast and then a ham strip, not quite as crisp as he would have preferred.

"Don't hear much about that," admits Ascaar. "And the bastard claims to follow the God of the Balance."

"There's no way we would, I imagine," comments Drusyn. "And when did any ruler really follow faith if it wasn't in his interest?"

Ascaar snorts.

"Just as there's no way we'd hear about Khesyn building up armsmen in Estheld," returns Lerial, before eating the last of the barely warm egg toast.

Drusyn rises. "Need to be off."

Lerial nods. "Best of fortune."

"Appreciate it." Drusyn does not look back.

Lerial finishes the egg toast and the ham strips, then swallows more lager. He and Ascaar get up almost together, but the older officer just gives a quick smile and nods before he turns and heads for the door.

After slipping one of the small loaves left in the dining room into his riding jacket, Lerial also departs, hurrying back to his quarters, where he recovers his sabre and visor cap, then makes his way down to the main level and out the doors into a dimness barely lightened by faint glow on the eastern horizon. His gelding is saddled and tied to the railing outside. It is cool enough that when the gelding snorts, Lerial can make out his breath. He mounts quickly and turns the gelding south. As he rides toward his companies, he tries to sense any Heldyan forces beyond the walls of Lubana, but can find none within the range of his abilities.

He has no more than reined up and dismounted at the Cigoernean tents than Fheldar, Strauxyn, and Kusyl hurry toward him.

"Ser . . . there's word . . ." begins Fheldar.

"That the Heldyans may be attacking. They're loading flatboats with troopers. The Afritan Guards are being positioned to the south of the hunting park and closer to Luba. We're being held back to see where else they may attack. The Afritans are sending rations. Have they arrived?"

"Not yet, ser."

"We're likely last because everyone else will be moving out before us. Have your men eat as soon as the rations arrive. Fheldar . . . we'll send Vominen and Gherst out through the south gate. Have them take positions just south of the southeast corner tower of Lubana. That way, they can survey the river and the riverbank—and marshes—to the south, as well as the eastern wall of Lubana itself."

"Yes, ser."

"Do you know where we'll be fighting?" asks Kusyl.

"No." Lerial pauses. "Just an idea. We may not be going all that far."

"Ser?"

"We'll have to see. Just make sure everyone gets fed . . . and quickly."

Less than a third of a glass later, the rankers are all eating bread, cold mutton slices, and cheese, washing it down with watered ale. Lerial is using his order-senses to scan the river, but can only discover a half score of flatboats barely leaving the piers at Vyada, although he has the feeling that more will be pushing off before long.

Another half glass passes, and the cloudless eastern sky has turned to greenish gray before the first group of flatboats nears the western shore of the river a good kay south of Lubana, where Drusyn's forces are already marshaled and waiting. A second, and larger, group of boats has departed the piers and looks to be headed farther downstream. Lerial cannot tell exactly where that might be, but it is clear they are not reinforcing the boats beginning to ground on the shore south of the hunting park because they are almost even with those boats and remain in midriver.

"Ser . . . ?" prompts Kusyl.

"There's another group of boats headed downstream. I can't tell where." Lerial pauses. "I'm going to join the scouts."

In little more than moments, Lerial and the fourth squad of Eighth Company ride through the south gate and then east toward the river. He can sense that there are more than twenty flatboats in the second Heldyan contingent. By the time he and Fourth Squad reach the southeast corner of the walls, where the graveled lane continues north at the foot of the east wall, and a similar lane continues southward between the hedgerow at the east edge of the hunting park and the marshes, the first rays of sunlight appear, almost directly in Lerial's eyes. Lerial has to squint to make out the dark shapes of the flatboats against the low light. Still, from what he can tell from eyes and senses, the flatboats appear to be too close to the center of the river to land south of Lubana proper.

Even as he is thinking that, he can sense and see, if barely, that the lead boats are angling nearer to the shore. While Lerial has his doubts as to whether the approaching flatboats will actually attack Lubana itself, it is clear that they will at the very least pass close to the walls. He turns in the saddle. "Gherst, here are my orders to Fheldar and the undercaptains. All archers on the wall, on each side of the midwall tower. All other company elements to join us here immediately. All companies with lances, except for the archers."

"Yes, ser."

Another quarter glass passes, and Lerial's archers are in position on the walls. Kusyl's Twenty-third Company is riding north along the lane under the wall to take a position near the northeast corner of the walls. Lerial watches as the flatboats reach a point no more than two hundred yards south of him. They remain barely within accurate range of his archers, if definitely nearer the Afritan shore, clearly aiming for a landfall somewhere near Luba, most likely on the northern edge of the city, Lerial would guess. He can sense continuing activity on the Vyada piers, suggesting another force to come, but little beyond that.

The flatboats continue down the Swarth past Lubana.

"Now, what, ser?" asks Fheldar.

"We do what all good lancers have to do," Lerial replies dryly. "We wait."

He continues to monitor the pending attack to the south, because, from what he can tell, the flatboats have not actually landed, but appear to be standing offshore. From the occasional flash of muted silver he senses, it appears as though the Afritans and Heldyans are exchanging volleys of arrows. It could even be that the Heldyans are using heavy crossbows mounted on the flatboats.

Another and larger group of flatboats pulls away from the piers at Vyada, moving across the river more swiftly than the previous grouping. Within a fraction of a glass, it is clear to Lerial that the third group of flatboats is aimed at Lubana, or if not, at a point very close.

Lerial thinks about positioning Eighth Company along the midsection of the wall, then shakes his head. *Too easy to be trapped with nowhere to go.* At the same time, the ramparts at the top of the wall are barely wide enough for a single lancer, and there are only a few sets of steps to the top of the wall, those few on the inner side. At three yards in height, the walls were clearly built for privacy and to deter casual intruders, not to withstand any prolonged armed assault.

"Undercaptain Strauxyn!"

"Yes, sir."

"Take Eleventh Company back inside the wall. Take a position at least fifty yards back of the wall. Your task will be to deal with any intruders who might scale the wall and enter Lubana. Wait for them to clear the wall and then attack with lances."

"Yes, ser."

"It may not come to that," Lerial adds after seeing a hint of puzzlement on the undercaptain's face, "but I won't put a company between a wall and the river with archers on flatboats approaching. If they have five or ten companies on those boats and ladders as well, some will likely get over the wall."

Strauxyn nods. "Yes, ser." He turns his mount.

Lerial continues to watch the oncoming flatboats, as well to sense what is happening at the southern end of the hunting park and farther downstream, where the flatboats that had passed Lubana are massing somewhere just offshore beyond the third canal. To the south, four or five flatboats have landed, and a Heldyan shield wall, with pikes protruding, has formed on a narrower spit of firm land that apparently mitigates against attacks from the side as it advances. *You'll definitely need lances against a shield wall.*

The flatboats nearing Lubana are far closer to the shore, almost as if some plan to land in the marshes south of the walls. *Of course they do. They've got archers that we can't attack easily.* While Lerial's personal shields, those close to his body, will protect him against most weapons, at least those made of iron or iron-tipped, he has never been able to project that type of barrier shield more than a few yards—except momentarily, and that will not suffice against continuous volleys of arrows.

"Fheldar, pull the squads back to where the hedgerow and those trees provide some cover. I'm thinking the Heldyans will stop in the reeds and try to clear the area with archers. I'll stay here." Lerial is glad he doesn't have to explain to the grizzled senior squad leader, who has politely suggested that he has no interest in being an undercaptain, even though he handles many of those duties.

"Yes, ser."

For the moment, Lerial doesn't have to worry about Twenty-third Company, since the Heldyan archers, if that is what the attackers have in mind, cannot reach the middle of the wall, let alone the northeast corner, beyond which Kusyl's men are formed up.

He continues to watch, and before long the first of the flatboats halt in the marshes less than a hundred yards south of the wall tower and little more than a hundred and fifty yards from Eighth Company, although the hedgerow west of the lane assures that any archers cannot fire directly at the lancers, if indeed they even know Eighth Company is there.

Lerial pauses for just an instant to check what has happened to the south. He can't help but frown, because the Heldyans appear to be withdrawing. *They pushed their way ashore . . . and they're withdrawing?* There's nothing he can do about that, and certainly Drusyn can send more accurate information to the arms-commander just as quickly as Lerial can.

While there might be archers on the flatboats, no arrows are loosed at Lerial, who is most likely the only visible target, and, after a time, the flatboats move away from the reeds, and let the current carry them toward the wall. Lerial watches as the first of the flatboats nears. In the front and on the shore side is a wall of shields. Below and behind the shields he can sense the archers he had felt would be there.

He can sense no chaos around the nearer flatboats, nor does he feel the chaotic mist that usually means a white wizard or chaos-mage hiding behind a shield of sorts. At the same time, he recalls something that Saltaryn had told him years ago—that water, especially large bodies of water, tends to mask concentrations of both order and chaos . . . and make using either more difficult. Still . . . shouldn't he sense something?

The six flatboats with the archers swing away from the shore and the narrow lane in front of the wall, and another line of flatboats, a good seven or eight of them, begins to angle toward him.

Frig! Lerial raises a concealment around himself and urges the gelding toward the middle of the wall. Far too late, he can see the plan of attack on the part of the Heldyans. He just hopes he can reach a point where his archers can see him and take his orders, because there isn't time to send an order around the walls and through the south gate.

The boats seem to move almost as fast as he and the gelding do. At least, when he reins up just short of the midwall tower, the boatmen are throwing out anchors, slowing and then halting the shielded flatboats holding the Heldyan archers.

"Lancer archers!" Lerial releases the concealment and uses order to amplify his voice. At least he hopes it does. "Target the Heldyan archers offshore!"

He has barely finished the command when arrows arch from the shielded flatboats toward the wall. Then . . . moments later, just as Mirror Lancer shafts begin to fly at the Heldyan archers, a chaos-blast arcs from one of the boats amid the flatboats holding the archers.

Lerial snaps a triple five-line order-coil out to redirect the chaos back at the Heldyan white wizard, but the wizard's shields hold, and the redirected chaos-bolt slams into the water on the west side of the boat, raising a cloud of steam.

At the same time, Lerial can sense something well beneath the water and the ground, which begins to shake. Then, just to the south of him, less than ten yards away, the masonry of the wall begins to shake . . . then sags, before dropping into a pile of rubble perhaps a yard high, if that, as if the earth or rock beneath has been removed and the wall dropped into the gap. With the collapse come yells and screams as the handful of archers on that section of the wall are thrown in one direction or the other.

An earth-mage? Or one who can use chaos below ground?

Another chaos-bolt arcs toward the wall, and Lerial redirects it. Again, the wizard's shields hold, and more steam rises. With it come screams from the boats, and Lerial realizes that steam and boiling water must have splashed some of the Heldyans.

Another earth rumble shakes Lerial, and a second section of wall crumbles, to the south of the first, throwing more Lancer archers back into Lubana or forward onto the lane. The first of the second wave of boats grounds just south of the gap in the estate wall, and shield-bearing armsmen with bright blades jump from the square prow of the flatboat.

For a moment, Lerial just watches, trying to think what he can do that will not cause more harm to the remaining archers and lancers of Eleventh Company.

He can't raise lightnings, not out of water.

Think!

Steam? Lots of steam? He concentrates on breaking apart the wood of the flatboats, separating order and chaos within the wood of the flatboat grounded near the wall. Then the one that holds the chaos-wizard—and possibly the earth-wizard. As he can feel the buildup of chaos-order separation, he creates a momentarily larger shield, hoping it will hold just long enough.

WHUUUMPT!

The force of the explosion, despite his shields, nearly rips him out of his saddle, and a wave of heat washes around him. His own shields contract tightly, and he can barely hold them, and the knife to which they are linked feels as though it is burning through its leather sheath and searing his hip.

He forces himself forward in the saddle, but can see nothing through the mist that seems everywhere. His order-chaos senses reveal nothing, either.

Then, slowly, a cooler wind blows from the south, and he begins to be able to make out the tangled mess in the river. Of the eight flatboats with armsmen, there is no sign of three. Behind them are two hulks, one half-buried in the river mud, the second turning in the current. Lerial can finally sense some things, those within a hundred yards or so, but he can only locate three of the shield-ringed boats, and they are already moving with the current well out into the river, as are the last three boats with armsmen.

Lerial continues to watch for several moments, realizing to his horror that the flatboats that survived his efforts are joining those that had abandoned the attack on the south end of the hunting park and another group of flatboats . . . and look to be moving toward the city piers at Luba.

He glances around, then sees a ranker riding toward him from Eighth Company, clearly sent by the resourceful Fheldar. He only has to wait a few moments.

"Ser?"

"Tell the senior squad leader to have Eighth Company join me. We're headed to Luba with Twenty-third Company."

"Yes, ser!" The ranker turns and heads back south, but he has to pick his way around the rubble of the fallen wall. Lerial rides south just enough to reach the collapsed section of the wall, where he reins up.

"Undercaptain!" He boosts his voice, although it turns out that he does not need to because Strauxyn is already riding forward.

"Yes, ser?"

"Hold this position as well as you can. The Heldyans are attacking farther downstream."

"Yes, ser."

Lerial turns the gelding and then gallops toward the northeast tower. He reins up short of Kusyl. "The Heldyans are heading for the piers. Take Twenty-third Company and stop them. Eighth Company is coming, but we won't reach the piers in time if we wait for them. But . . . don't . . ."

"Don't strain the mounts?" asks the undercaptain with a grin.

"Exactly."

"We'll take care of the bastards."

Lerial watches as Kusyl and his three squads ride north, knowing that the boats and Twenty-third Company will arrive at close to the same time. Eighth Company takes a bit longer than Lerial would have liked to reach him, because the company can get through the rubble of the fallen wall only single-file. From what he can sense, Ascaar is engaged in trying to repulse the Heldyan landing north of Luba proper, a landing likely designed just to keep the Afritan forces from blocking the coming attack on the town itself.

Lerial rides forward to meet Fheldar. "Send a messenger to the main dwelling. Have him report that the Heldyans are attacking Luba proper and that two of our companies are responding."

"Yes, ser."

Lerial realizes he should have done that earlier, but by the time he'd thought of it, he had no one to send. "We need to move to back up Kusyl. Have the squads re-form on the move."

It takes less than a quarter glass before Eighth Company nears the southernmost pier. Even before that, Lerial can sense that two factors have helped his outnumbered Twenty-third Company contain the attackers. First, the stone riverwall and the dredged area north and south of the piers have kept the flatboats from grounding, and has required them to try to anchor to keep from going farther downstream. Second, climbing out of the boats onto the river wall and the piers has slowed the formation of the shield wall and pikes. Clearly, Kusyl used lances to repulse and slow the shieldmen before the Heldyans could position their pikes.

Even so, Kusyl and his men are giving ground to a widening shield wall and the pikemen behind the shields as they push off the pier and onto the river road.

Lerial does not hesitate, but again separates order and chaos, this time targeting sections of the flatboats below the waterline.

FHWHUSSSH!!!

Geysers of superheated water erupt, and steam and hot mist cover the more than thirty flatboats in and around the Luban piers, jammed so close that they almost form a continuous surface. The screams are mercifully short. Lerial winces as the silver-gray mist of multiple deaths flows shoreward and across him, a mist that only a mage or wizard—or a healer—could sense.

"Eighth Company! Halt!" Lerial order-boosts his voice. "Twenty-third Company! Withdraw! Withdraw now!"

The moment that Kusyl's men effect a separation of more than ten yards, Lerial acts, although he can only create a small line of order-chaos separations along the river road. Still, separating the underlying chaos and order in the stone is far easier than doing so in wood surrounded by water. The lightnings that crisscross the area are enough to take out or injure perhaps half of the Heldyans, and leave pikes and shields strewn here and there.

"Lancers! Charge!"

Lerial, sabre out, leads Eighth Company into an attack from the south, although he holds back just enough to let the points of the lances of the first rank strike the shields before he reaches them. One of the shieldmen pushed off balance by a lance tries to thrust his shield, but Lerial lets the gelding turn the shield, and then slashes a backcut across the man's neck. Then he is among footmen with small shields and blades. After that, he loses track of exactly what he does with the sabre, except that his head throbs more and more with each use of the blade.

A quarter of a glass later, he has trouble seeing, between the flashes of light in his eyes and the throbbing in his head, but by then almost all of the disoriented Heldyans are either dead, disarmed, or surrendering. Lerial just takes a position on the river road, flanked by two rankers, doubtless detailed by Fheldar, and watches as the two companies round up the few handfuls of able-bodied captives. For a stretch of over a hundred yards the paved road is cracked and crazed with black lines, and more than a hundred bodies lie scattered, all wearing the bluish-gray and black of Heldya.

He has to squint to make out what has happened to the north, but it appears, again, that the Heldyans have withdrawn, since the flatboats are all in the river away from the shore. Either that or they have abandoned their armsmen, but Lerial feels that is unlikely, although he could not prove that, and, at the moment, he cannot order-sense farther than a score of yards.

In time, Fheldar and Kusyl approach and rein up. Kusyl gestures to the senior squad leader.

"Ser," reports Fheldar, "two dead, five wounded. That doesn't include the archers in Third Squad. What about the prisoners?"

"We'll march them back to Lubana. The arms-commander can decide what to do with them." Lerial looks to Kusyl.

"Three dead, eight wounded."

"Very well handled, both of you."

Kusyl glances down at the black marks and cracks in the paving. "The duke may have a few repairs to make."

"Better his repairs than our rankers." Lerial clears his throat. "Get the prisoners moving. We don't want to stay here. Oh . . . and send another messenger to the arms-commander or Commander Sammyl. Inform him that we're returning with Heldyan prisoners."

"Yes, ser."

Lerial hopes that the Afritan forces have fared better, or at least not too much worse, but he has doubts about that. He also worries about the purpose of the attacks. *If they weren't that serious about attacking, why attack at all?* Except . . . the Heldyans had seemed most intent on attacking Luba proper. *Why? To show weakness in Afrit? Or to make sure that Rhamuel has to keep forces in the south?*

Before he turns the gelding, he takes a last look at the remaining Heldyan flatboats, all continuing downstream.

XII

Once the Eighth and Twenty-third Companies enter the grounds at Lubana, and Lerial's recovering order-senses tell him that there are no other Heldyan forces near, he immediately rides to where Strauxyn's Eleventh Company waits.

"Ser! No other attacks here," Strauxyn immediately reports.

"Casualties?"

"We lost three archers, and had five wounded when the wall collapsed. Eighth Company's Third Squad lost two and had four wounded."

Ten men dead, and twenty-two wounded. That is the most Mirror Lancers lost on a single day in more than five years. *And those numbers will seem like nothing if Afrit and Cigoerne end up in a full war with Heldya.*

"The wounded?"

"One likely won't make it; the others should."

Lerial understands—some will not make it without healing aid. "Where are they?"

"In one of the tents in our area, ser."

"Thank you."

Lerial is turning his mount from Strauxyn to return to the tent area where Eighth and Twenty-third Companies are returning when he sees Commander Sammyl riding toward him. He looks back to the undercaptain. "Wait for a moment, until I see what the commander has to say."

"Yes, ser."

Lerial reins up once and waits.

The commander rides within two yards of Lerial before halting. "I don't believe you had orders to attack the Heldyans, Overcaptain, especially at Luba." Sammyl's voice is even. "It also might be difficult to explain the damage to the wall to the duke."

Lerial forces a smile. "It would have been harder to explain the loss of the entire wall. A Heldyan earth-mage was starting to demolish all the stonework when we stopped him. Nor would I have wished to explain to either Duke Atroyan or my sire why we did nothing when the Heldyans were about to attack and destroy the center of Luba. Since I received no orders, I did what I thought necessary."

"The arms-commander would like to speak to you."

"Where?"

"In his study."

"I'll be there shortly."

"He did say as soon as possible."

"I'll be there shortly, Commander." Lerial's eyes are cold as he looks directly at the commander.

"I would hope so, Lord Lerial." Sammyl turns his mount.

Once Sammyl is well away, Lerial says to Strauxyn, "I'll be with the wounded. Have your men remain here, but stand down for now."

"Yes, ser."

Lerial rides to the Cigoernean tent area, knowing he does not have enough strength to heal twenty-two men. Still . . . there may be some he can tend enough so that he can do more later, when he is stronger. He recalls, belatedly, the loaf in his saddlebags and takes it out, beginning to eat dry mouthful after mouthful and taking swigs of watered lager from his water bottle when necessary. By the time he reaches the tents holding the wounded, he feels somewhat better, and the flashes across his eyes have almost ceased. The throbbing in his skull is muted, but definitely remains.

He eases into the first tent, where those lancers trained as field healers are splinting bones and cleaning wounds. He walks toward the first five men, all with broken legs or arms, or both, splinted earlier, indicating that they were among the archers under whom the wall collapsed. He stops beside the fourth man, touching his shoulder lightly, and easing the smallest bit of order into a small pocket of wound chaos deep inside his leg bone. *With luck . . .*

"That's a bad pair of breaks, lancer, but you'll be fine."

The next three men have various breaks, one in his foot, another of his forearm, and the third of his collarbone, but those breaks are clean. He forces a cheerful smile as he nears the last archer. Even from yards away, he can sense there is nothing he can do. The man is moaning softly, likely because he has not the breath to scream. His chest is partly crushed, and bloody spittle oozes from his mouth. Lerial touches his forearm lightly, then moves on.

He can only offer some healing to three more of the recently arrived wounded before his vision blurs and he begins to feel weak. After that he walks to the gelding, where he takes several swallows of watered lager before mounting and riding toward the duke's country house, still accompanied by two Eighth Company rankers. Ignoring protocol, he reins up at the main entrance and dismounts, handing the gelding's reins to one of the rankers.

His steps are slow as he walks to the center door.

One of the Afritan Guards, in a crimson dress uniform, steps forward. "Ser . . ."

Lerial looks at the ranker, who steps back, then walks to the door and opens it. Once inside, he makes his way to Rhamuel's study.

The guard posted there opens the study door. "He's expecting you, ser."

"Thank you." Lerial walks into the immaculate study, belatedly aware of the streaks of blood on the sleeves of his uniform jacket and on his green trousers.

Rhamuel stands from where he has been seated at the conference table, on which is a single map. Belatedly, both Valatyr and Sammyl stand as well. The arms-commander says quietly, "I'll send for you when I'm done."

Valatyr nods to Rhamuel, then moves toward Lerial, nodding and offering a quick smile as he passes. Sammyl does not move.

"Later, Commander," Rhamuel says quietly.

Sammyl stiffens, then nods, and walks swiftly from the study, not only avoiding Lerial, but not even looking in Lerial's direction.

Rhamuel gestures to the table, then reseats himself.

Lerial as much as sinks into the chair as seats himself.

"Commander Sammyl observed that you appeared reluctant to hasten here." Rhamuel's voice is pleasant.

"I needed to check on my wounded," Lerial replies.

"You and your family are most assiduous in that."

"It is necessary. We need as many officers and rankers as possible. We have far fewer people than any other duchy in Hamor."

"I thought that might be the case. I told my orderly to bring some lager and biscuits once you arrived. While we wait for them, I won't ask questions. I will tell you what seems to have happened. You doubtless know some of it." A crooked smile appears and then vanishes. "The first attackers landed on a spur of land south of the hunting park. They formed behind a shield wall, advanced some, repulsed an attack by Subcommander Drusyn's halberdmen, then withdrew. The second attack went past Lubana and landed downstream and north of Luba. The Heldyans had several companies on the road before Subcommander Ascaar's forces arrived and were able to push them back to the river, but they fought hard and withdrew largely in good order. You presumably know about the third and fourth attacks."

Rhamuel motions, and a ranker moves from the study door to the conference table, setting a silver tray between Lerial and the arms-commander. On it are a single beaker, a pitcher, and a platter of what look to be butter biscuits. The ranker immediately bows and departs.

"Please help yourself."

Lerial does, if not before using his order-senses to check the pitcher and the platter for the chaos that might reveal poison or the like, first half filling the beaker and taking a long swallow, and then taking a biscuit and eating it. He takes a second welcome swallow of lager and looks at Rhamuel. "I was aware of the third and fourth attacks."

"You acted without orders, the commander tells me."

"I did. It seemed foolish to wait for orders when the Heldyans were destroying the duke's property and killing my rankers. As for the fourth attack, I didn't think the duke would mind the effort to keep his people from being slaughtered, particularly since Subcommander Ascaar had his hands full, Subcommander Drusyn was too far away to reach the piers, and since I'd left a company to hold the breach in the wall against no known Heldyan attackers."

"You acted rather effectively." Rhamuel smiles. "More so than I even expected."

"I just used some misdirection, and their mages, or wizards, did the rest."

The arms-commander nods.

Lerial shrugs, deciding the less he says, the better. When Rhamuel does not speak, he adds, "I have to say that I worry about all those armsmen headed downriver."

"So do I, but I would appreciate your not saying much about that for the next day or so."

Lerial nods in return, then takes another biscuit, and another swallow of the lager, both of which seem to be helping his vision and his throbbing head.

"You can heal some, I understand."

"A little," Lerial replies. "That was what I was doing before I came here. I could only do a little. Perhaps more . . . later."

"I thought that might be delaying you. Healing must run in the blood."

"That's possible. My aunt and my mother are both healers, as I told you earlier. It's too early to tell how good a healer Amaira will be, but it's clear she has some ability."

After a silence, Rhamuel says, "So far as I have been able to determine, the only mages with the Heldyan forces were those with the armsmen who attacked Lubana. Do you know anything other than that?"

Lerial shakes his head. "There were two mages with that force. One was a chaos-wizard, and the other was an earth-mage. At least, the ground shook before the wall collapsed." He pauses briefly. "Commander Sammyl told me you have no mages, although there are some in Swartheld."

"A very few. My great-grandsire was less than fond of mages, and their services do not come cheaply. He also blamed the Great Fire on them, although I doubt they were the cause. So we must do what we can without mages. You say that you couldn't tell more than you did about Khesyn's mages?"

Lerial does not press the fact that Rhamuel has not really addressed the matter. "That was the only thing I felt—that and the chaos-blasts. I'm assuming that there were two mages, because I've never heard of those talents being held by the same magus . . . and if they were, I don't know that Khesyn would hazard that talented a wizard on an almost casual attack." Lerial uses the word "casual" in hopes of drawing out Rhamuel.

"What makes you think it was casual?"

"The fact that they really didn't pursue it. Once they ran into trouble, they left. The attackers who landed north of Luba had to be forced back. At least, it looked that way from the piers." As he finishes those words, Lerial realizes that what he has said is only half true. The hunting-park attack was casual, but he doesn't know that about the attack on Lubana, not since he destroyed most of the attackers.

Rhamuel shakes his head. "All four attacks were designed with a deliberate purpose in mind."

A deliberate purpose? What about two . . . or three? "Which was?"

"What do you think it was?" counters Rhamuel.

"To embarrass you, in order to have you replaced."

Rhamuel laughs, if ruefully. "That's certainly the first thing that crossed my mind, but I wonder if I'm taking that too personally."

Given what appears to be happening in Swartheld? Lerial smiles. "It also could be to make sure you keep at least a battalion or two of Afritan Guards in the south to weaken your defenses of Swartheld."

"That is also possible."

Lerial nods and waits.

"You know," Rhamuel says casually, "my brother is rather fond of Lubana. I've never understood why, but he is. I'd much prefer the hunting lodge at Chaendyl—that's in the wooded hills west of Swartheld—or even the villa at Lake Reomer."

"Thank you," says Lerial, giving a double meaning to the words, "I wouldn't have known where either of those are."

"I thought not." The arms-commander purses his lips. "I shouldn't keep you longer, and I do need to go over a few matters with Sammyl and Subcommander Valatyr."

"I wouldn't want to keep you from that," Lerial replies. "I did appreciate the lager and the biscuits . . . very much."

"I thought you might, and you're very welcome."

As Lerial leaves the study, he recognizes, once more, that even the arms-commander of Afrit must watch every word, even in the privacy of his own spaces. But he is indeed grateful for the refreshments, since he feels strong enough to go back and do some healing on at least another wounded ranker or two, possibly three.

XIII

Four of the wounded lancers die before midnight on twoday. Although Lerial's efforts at healing seem to be working with those he has been able to help, and while those with less chaos in their wounds and broken bones also appear to be improving—at least, they were when he left, late in the evening—Lerial is still worrying in the gray dawn light as he goes to meet with his officers . . . well before breakfast and the morning meeting that will follow, and which he dreads. He knows that he did not handle the battle before the wall well. He should have gathered all his forces within the wall, let the wall take the brunt of the initial attack, and then struck back with his own abilities. He is more pleased with the second battle, although his timing could have been better.

For all the maneuvers you've conducted, and the handful of skirmishes with raiders, you haven't fought a pitched battle in almost five years. That thought does not console him. Nor does the fact that he and his men likely would have taken far higher casualties, or even been slaughtered, without his order-chaos abilities. *Maybe not Kusyl's company, no thanks to you.*

The tents holding the various Afritan Guard companies are largely quiet as he walks down the open space that serves as an avenue of sorts. Two Afritan rankers, handling guard duties, nod politely and step back. Lerial returns the nod and continues on, trying to use his order senses to see what they may say to each other.

". . . the one . . . tell by the red hair . . ."

". . . rode out of the rubble and killed all the Heldyan bastards?"

". . . same . . . doesn't pay to cross Mirror Lancers . . ."

Lerial only wishes that were true. Duke Khesyn has been crossing Cigoerne for years, what with his raids and his occasional attempts to block river trade.

When he reaches the Cigoernean tents, Fheldar and the two undercaptains are waiting.

"How are the wounded?" Lerial asks immediately.

"There are some . . ." begins Strauxyn.

"Let me deal with them first. Come along." Lerial leads the way to the tent holding most of the wounded, where Kusyl points out a young ranker from Twenty-third Company.

"Nothing that I can see," says Kusyl. "Just . . . something."

Lerial studies the young man, who feels warmer than he should, with both eyes and order-senses, the latter likely to be more accurate in the grayness before dawn. There is more wound chaos than there should be in the wound—a thrust into the upper chest, at an angle, not even to the bone. Lerial can sense a small object there, surrounded by wound chaos.

Can you use order, maybe with a touch of chaos, to get that out? His brow is covered with sweat within several moments, but he finally removes part of the dressing and uses the tip of his belt knife, touched with order. The knife, a pulse of order, and the tiniest touch of chaos result in a narrow sliver of something that feels ugly on the tip of the knife, and some pus on the skin around the wound.

"Have them clean the skin with clear spirits and re-dress the wound." Lerial follows Strauxyn to the end of the tent to a ranker moaning in his sleep. His left leg and forearm are splinted.

"He seems to be moaning more than the others . . ."

Lerial uses his order-senses to probe gently, then shakes his head. "He should be all right. Broken bones, especially where he has them, can be very painful."

He applies a touch of order to two other wounded rankers, then leaves the tent, followed by the other three, and makes his way to the officers' tent. Once there, he asks, "What have you heard, if anything?"

"Not much," replies Kusyl. "None of the junior officers know any more than we do. I've had my squad leaders asking some of the Afritan squad leaders. They took more casualties than we did. Well . . . their lead companies did. Some of the companies that were at the hunting park didn't even fight before the Heldyans backed off."

"The ones that met the Heldyans north of us all fought," adds Fheldar. "All took casualties. Maybe one, two men in ten."

Two battalions, ten companies—that's more than a hundred casualties, perhaps two hundred. Lerial frowns. That suggests that Luba was indeed a target, rather than a feint. *But why? The ironworks are more than ten kays away. Or does that just confirm that the attacks were made to put Rhamuel at a disadvantage . . . as he intimated? And with whom? It has to be with more than his brother . . . doesn't it?* "It appears as though we had the fewest casualties."

"Some of the Afritans noticed that, too," comments Fheldar. "And we fought two times."

"Keep listening. I'll be back after the senior officers' meeting and let you know what I find out. Is there anything else?"

The three exchange glances. Finally, Kusyl speaks. "Not that we haven't talked about."

"Then I'll see you later." Lerial walks swiftly back to Atroyan's country house, but does not overhear any comments pertaining to himself or the Mirror Lancers.

He slips into the private dining room, somewhat surprised that Majer Prenyl is the only officer there, and takes a seat at one end of the table.

Prenyl immediately rises and walks over. "Ser?"

"Yes?" replies Lerial pleasantly, wondering why Prenyl is addressing him and what adverse news the majer might be about to convey.

"Ah . . . I just wanted to say that . . . some of us . . . we appreciate that you came to Lubana." The major offers an embarrassed smile. "The Heldyans might not appreciate your presence, but some of us more junior officers do."

"Thank you. I'm glad we were able to help. I don't think any of us want Duke Khesyn on this side of the river."

"No, ser." Prenyl smiles again. "That's all, ser. I won't be keeping you."

Abruptly. Lerial understands. "Thank you very much."

"Not at all, ser."

After the majer retreats, Lerial nods, wondering exactly what words Sammyl will be using to minimize or otherwise imply less than favorable behavior on the part of the Mirror Lancers . . . or their commander.

Ascaar sits down across from Lerial. "Saw you out early this morning."

"I was checking on the wounded."

"You didn't have that many, did you?"

"Not as you did, I hear, but we only have three companies, not ten. On a man-for-man basis, it's likely not much different."

"Hadn't thought of that." Ascaar takes a swallow of lager, then adds, "Your three companies took out more Heldyans than our twenty."

"We were fortunate." Lerial is tempted to confess some stupidity, but refrains, instead eating more of the warmish eggs scrambled with ham chunks. As he does, he sees Drusyn enter the officers' mess and sit down with Subcommander Klassyn. Shortly, Sammyl and Valatyr enter and sit together, and Captain Waell joins Prenyl.

"I don't much believe in fortune." Ascaar offers a sly smile. "Except as an ally to keep others from realizing you're more skillful than they are."

"There are times when any ally is welcome."

"You were welcome, and then some, yesterday. I saw those boats coming in to the piers, but we couldn't get there. Appreciate it. When the Heldyans saw they'd lost any chance of reinforcements, they backed off."

While Lerial has his doubts that the Heldyan withdrawal was entirely because of his effectiveness, he merely says, "I'm glad we could get there in time. It was a close thing."

"Close doesn't matter . . . not unless it's close on the wrong side."

Ascaar's words are so sardonic that Lerial smiles in appreciation.

The two finish and leave the private dining room, just behind Majer Prenyl, and make their way to the salon, where they wait by one of the wide windows.

"Beats me as to why the duke's sire ever built this place here," offers Ascaar. "His consort didn't like it, even died in childbirth right here when she bore the arms-commander's younger brother. The present duke hasn't been here in years, but I hear he always talks about how much he likes Lubana. Every once in a while, the arms-commander mentions it, too."

Lerial nods.

Before long, Drusyn and Klassyn appear, and then Valatyr, although none of the others make a move to join Ascaar and Lerial.

The officers all stiffen as Commander Sammyl enters the salon, although Sammyl immediately orders, "As you were. Take your seats."

By the time Sammyl reaches the end of the salon and turns, all the officers are seated and waiting. The commander offers a bleak smile. "Yesterday was interesting. I don't like interesting days. Neither does the arms-commander. For your information, and so that everyone understands . . ." Sammyl pauses. "The verified Heldyan casualties consist of three hundred and twelve dead, sixty wounded, and one hundred prisoners. The prisoners were largely captured by Overcaptain Lerial's companies. One disturbing matter is that at least one company, possibly more, of the attackers was made up of Tourlegyn warriors . . . even if they wore Heldyan blue. The number of Heldyans and Tourlegyns killed in the chaos-explosions here at Lubana and at the piers of Luba cannot be determined. The lookouts report that more than fifteen flatboats were destroyed, and most boats carried fifty armsmen. Those are, of course, estimates. The Heldyan death toll is likely less than that because a good three boats' worth of advance troopers had vacated the boats at Luba before the explosions."

Captain Waell glances toward Lerial, his eyes wide.

"Given the high death toll among the Heldyan attackers, the arms-commander has determined that an increased risk to Swartheld and the cities and towns north of here exists." Sammyl pauses and takes a breath, as if for emphasis. "Therefore, Subcommander Drusyn and his battalions will depart for Swartheld on fiveday, saving the wounded, who will recover here.

One of Subcommander Ascaar's battalions—Sixteenth—will remain at Lubana, under Majer Chorazt, while the subcommander and Fifteenth Battalion will depart Lubana to return to Shaelt on sixday, again saving the wounded."

Trust Sammyl to place the blame for danger on you. Despite that thought, Lerial maintains a pleasant expression, if not a smiling one.

"Whether Overcaptain Lerial's companies will remain here is a matter being considered by the arms-commander, and, of course, is at the sufferance of Duke Kiedron. At present, scouts and lookouts have determined that only three flatboats remain at the piers in Vyada." Sammyl pauses, then asks, "Do any of you have anything to add to what I've said? Or any questions?"

When none of the other officers speak, Lerial smiles and says, "The only observation I might make is that there were no mounts whatever on any of the flatboats we encountered. Perhaps I am not well acquainted with Heldyan tactics as practiced north of Cigoerne, but in the south most Heldyan incursions have included some mounted units. I was wondering if either Subcommander Drusyn or Subcommander Ascaar encountered any mounted forces or saw any horses."

"An interesting observation, Overcaptain." Sammyl glances at Drusyn.

"We did not encounter any mounted units," replies Drusyn. "They did not disembark all their flatboats. There may have been horses on some."

"Every last Heldyan got off the boats, and those that survived got back on," says Ascaar flatly. "Not a horse in sight."

"Thank you, subcommanders," Sammyl says so quickly that Lerial could not have replied, even had he been so minded, which he is not. "Now . . . I will be meeting separately with the battalion commanders shortly . . ." For the next quarter glass, Sammyl goes over such matters as possible changes to battalion departures from Lubana should the weather change, arrangements for the wounded once they recover or must be invalided out of service, and arrangements for rations for travel north.

Finally, he smiles and says, "If there is nothing else, you all may return to your duties."

Lerial rises with the other officers, but does not hurry to leave the salon. Neither does Ascaar, and the two walk out together, leaving the salon empty, except for Captain Waell, who, as usual, directs a pair of rankers in rearranging the chairs and settees.

Lerial notices that Sammyl and Valatyr are headed toward the private dining room, and he wonders what they might be discussing. So, as he and Ascaar reach the stairs to the upper levels on the north wing, he pauses. "Go ahead. I'll see you later."

"Later it will be. Much later," says Ascaar. "It appears as though I have more to do than I'd thought." The older officer starts up the white marble steps.

"Don't we always?"

Ascaar laughs.

Lerial turns and heads back toward the main hall, pausing by an alcove that is mostly shadowed. When he is sure no one is around, he raises a concealment and then walks as quietly as he can toward the private dining chamber, slipping through the open archway and moving toward the far end of the table where Sammyl and Valatyr are sitting. Valatyr is seated so that he can observe the archway, but the subcommander shows no sign of having penetrated Lerial's concealment.

". . . you think of the overcaptain's observation?" asks Sammyl.

"He's very observant," returns Valatyr.

"His observation was meant to suggest something."

"You mean that the Heldyans had no intention of invading us at Luba? Just causing destruction? He was just pointing out the obvious."

"That's one way of looking at it."

Valatyr seems to shrug, although, since Lerial cannot make out facial expressions when he is using a concealment, that is a guess.

"You don't want to say much, Subcommander."

"No, ser. I dislike guessing about the intentions of those I do not know. Especially when they are more powerful than they appear. He might well be a mage."

Sammyl's snort is more than audible. "Of course he's a mage. What else would he be? That whole family is descended from the Magi'i of Cyador. His father isn't much of one, though, and the overcaptain can't be too powerful, or he wouldn't be an officer on point . . . so to speak. He does have some ability as a field healer, but probably not much more. You'll notice Kiedron didn't send his eldest."

"I wouldn't send the heir, either."

"Nor would I, but Kiedron sent the overcaptain to Verdheln when he was sixteen or seventeen. If that demon-cursed Altyrn hadn't been with him, there would be only one heir to Cigoerne, and our problems would be much fewer."

Why would that be? What do you have to do with Afrit's problems? Even as those thoughts cross Lerial's mind, he realizes how much easier matters might be for Duke Atroyan if one heir had vanished years earlier.

"And Casseon wouldn't be scared of his own shadow," adds Valatyr.

"He doesn't have anything to fear now that the majer's safely dead."

"Except that Altyrn trained and disciplined so many Verdyn Lancers that it would be a waste of armsmen for him to try to reclaim Verdheln."

"For now. For now. Times change . . . and we'll have to help them change." After a moment, Sammyl speaks again. "You're certain that Majer Chorazt is the best commander to leave here?"

"He's good enough to be a battalion commander. He's loyal. He'll do anything to stop any Heldyan raiders, and he follows orders."

"Good. Would that . . ."

Lerial gains the impression that Sammyl offers a minute shake of his head.

"I'll convey that to the arms-commander, and I'll see if he's decided what else might be necessary." After another pause, the commander adds, "No, he hasn't said. He keeps his own counsel, and sometimes . . . sometimes . . . you understand?"

"Yes, ser."

Lerial is afraid he understands as well, but he eases himself into a corner and waits until the two leave the dining chamber before he follows, still holding the concealment.

XIV

For the remainder of threeday, Lerial busies himself with two main tasks: healing his wounded, as he can, and dealing with the mundane aspects of commanding three companies, from arranging for horses to be reshod and saddles to be repaired, to looking over the captured Heldyan weapons and gear, as well as arranging for the distribution of the coppers and silvers taken from the dead attackers.

All the time, one question remains unanswered. *Now that the Heldyans have been repulsed . . . what do you do now?* In theory, Lerial could claim his duties and responsibilities have been fulfilled and arrange for a return to Cigoerne. He hears nothing from Sammyl or the arms-commander, and since Rhamuel does not come to the officers' mess on threeday evening, Lerial cannot even bring up the question indirectly. He does not want to press immediately for a meeting with the arms-commander, much as he would like to, feeling that, since his men and wounded, not to mention the horses, need time to recover, there is little to be gained by pressing and conceivably more to be lost by making the first move.

Nothing changes on fourday, a warm and blustery day that suggests spring is around the corner, except that it appears that all the wounded who have survived thus far will recover and will likely be able to return to full duty, if not for a season or so.

Breakfast and the senior officers meeting on fiveday are both uneventful, and Sammyl makes no reference at all to Lerial or his companies. After leaving the meeting and bidding a rather quiet Drusyn an uneventful ride to Swartheld, Lerial has turned to head out to report on events to his officers when a ranker approaches.

"Lord Lerial, ser?"

"Yes?"

"The arms-commander would like a word with you, ser . . . at your immediate convenience."

Lerial withholds a smile at the oxymoronic terminology of "immediate convenience" and says, "Of course. Lead on." He follows the ranker across the entry hall.

The guard outside Rhamuel's private study nods politely to Lerial. "Ser, please go in." He opens the door.

"Thank you." Lerial smiles and enters, noticing how quickly and quietly the door closes behind him.

The arms-commander stands from behind the conference table, on which rests a large silver tray with what appear to be the remnants of his breakfast. "Please join me."

"Thank you." Lerial slips into the seat across from Rhamuel.

"How are your men?"

"The wounded who survived the first two nights all look as though as though they will recover completely. Given time, anyway."

"And you?"

"I'm healthy enough." Lerial isn't about to admit how much the battles and the subsequent healing have drained him.

"You still look tired."

"The healing takes effort," Lerial admits, feeling that won't reveal much.

"You accounted for the most Heldyan casualties, you know?" Rhamuel offers.

"I'll take your word for that," replies Lerial. "I didn't see what happened anywhere else."

He isn't about to admit to the fact that he can sense what occurs beyond what he can see, if not in nearly the detail as with his eyes.

"Take it." The arms-commander's voice is dry. "Your success creates a slight problem for both of us."

Lerial nods politely, fearing he knows what is coming next. "Commander Sammyl seemed almost displeased with our response to the Heldyan attacks."

"The commander worries about the comparative effectiveness of the Afritan Guard. He has for some time."

"I sense his concerns, but the duchy of Cigoerne has no desire to fight with Afrit. We never have wanted such a conflict."

"I, especially, understand that." Rhamuel pauses and presents a faint smile. "The duke insisted on the commander as my chief of staff. He puts great faith in him."

"I can see that he must."

"I believe you do. Like some of your more distant predecessors, you have talents beyond the obvious, much as you try to keep them very much unobvious. I presume you would prefer that they remain less obvious."

Lerial manages a soft laugh. "You're presuming I have such talents."

"I'm presuming nothing." Rhamuel's voice is even. "I have not mentioned this to any, but I watched the Heldyan attack on the eastern wall from the midwall tower. My closeness to such a violent attack made Subcommander Valatyr very uneasy."

"That would concern any officer in his position." *Especially if my thoughts about your brother are correct.* "What about Commander Sammyl?"

"He was less concerned."

Because he serves your brother?

"I think it would be in both our interests for you to accompany me back to Swartheld to be thanked personally by the duke. He will be informed only that you repulsed two of the four attacks on Luba." Rhamuel holds up his hand. "There is no need to mention any specifics of how you managed to do so."

Both our interests? Perhaps. "Wouldn't my bringing three companies to Swartheld be viewed as . . . excessive?"

"Not at all. That is what is in my interest. If your companies escort me and my personal squad, then I can leave without further weakening the Afritan Guard in place here." Rhamuel smiles. "We will not announce this until after Subcommander Ascaar departs tomorrow."

"What about Commander Sammyl?"

"He is accompanying Subcommander Drusyn, and he believes I will accompany Ascaar. Commander Klassyn will accompany him, as Valatyr and my personal squad will accompany us. Sammyl does not like being in Luba, and so long as he is assured I will return shortly, he will be pleased. He will also wish to brief the duke."

"To be the first to brief him?"

"Of course."

"You think this was just the first battle of the attack against Afrit?"

"In one way or another. When and where the next attack will come is another matter. But if another attack comes soon, I would like to have you in Swartheld. Even if it does not, your presence will do much to improve relations between Afrit and Cigoerne."

Again, Lerial suspects he knows what Rhamuel means but does not wish to say, and the implications suggest that he may have no choice but to escort the arms-commander. The fact that Rhamuel is willing to place himself in Lerial's hands, so to speak, also suggests the gravity of the situation.

"There is also the problem of the Tourlegyns."

"Oh?"

"The fact that there were a number in the Heldyan forces suggests that Duke Khesyn has reached some sort of . . . accommodation with them. That is not the best of news. They love to fight."

"And fighting us means they don't fight Heldya?"

"That was my thought. We will see. It is something to keep in mind."

"What do you want from me?" asks Lerial.

"Your presence, that of your Mirror Lancers, and your best judgment about what will benefit Cigoerne . . . and your heritage."

The last three words bother Lerial, because they imply far more than the first three desires expressed by Rhamuel. "My heritage?"

"A man with your background can be present and act with what he thinks is his best judgment and be mistaken. If he is also true to his heritage that is far less likely."

"What about your heritage?"

Rhamuel laughs. "I would trust your heritage far more than mine. That is another reason why I would like you to see Swartheld, whether or not Khesyn attacks or refrains."

"You make Swartheld sound so inviting."

"I'm being honest, or as honest as I dare. I would say that your presence is necessary for your sake and for that of your heritage."

"And if I don't find it so?"

"You may leave. I have no intention of forcing you to remain, only to have you see Swartheld and meet my brother the duke . . . and a few others."

Lerial offers a wry grin. "How can I refuse such an invitation?"

Rhamuel smiles in return. "You can't. Or you shouldn't."

"I'll need to send back some of my rankers, perhaps with a few of the riding wounded, with a dispatch detailing my acceptance of your invitation."

"I can spare a squad to escort them to Ensenla."

"That would be helpful."

Rhamuel nods, and Lerial knows there is nothing else that needs to be said.

When Lerial leaves the country house, he can see Drusyn's battalions of Afritan Guards already formed up and beginning to ride out of Lubana. He makes out a banner he has not seen before and wonders if that signifies Sammyl's presence or just that of a battalion overcommander. He can't say that he is unhappy to see Sammyl depart, but he has his doubts about what impressions Sammyl will convey of him and the Mirror Lancers. *But then, that is exactly why you're going to escort Rhamuel and why Sammyl isn't being told that Lerial will be coming to Swartheld.*

As he walks toward the Cigoernean encampment, another fact strikes Lerial. In a way, his own heritage and that of Rhamuel have been entwined for years. *You just haven't thought of it in that way. But does Rhamuel?*

Even when he reaches the officers' tent where his officers wait, Lerial doesn't have an answer for that question.

"What is it, ser?" asks Kusyl. "You have that look."

"We may be in Afrit for a time."

"Another frigging Heldyan attack?"

"Not yet." Lerial smiles wryly. "We've been invited to escort the arms-commander back to Swartheld . . . and he wants the duke to thank me personally for our supporting them." He holds up a hand. "For the moment, you're not to tell the men or the squad leaders anything except that we'll be here for a few more days, and especially don't say anything but that to anyone else, either." While Rhamuel has not specifically asked for that silence, Lerial feels that, at present, some caution is wise, especially from what he has seen of Sammyl, and even possibly Drusyn.

Strauxyn and Kusyl exchange glances. Fheldar shakes his head. Then all three look to Lerial.

"I could refuse . . . but I don't think that would be a good idea."

"Ser?" asks Strauxyn after a moment.

"Think about it. Duke Khesyn wants to rule all of Hamor, and Duke Casseon still hasn't forgotten what we did to him in Verdheln."

"So we really don't want to piss off Duke Atroyan, do we?" says Kusyl. "Frig!"

Lerial has no doubt that the two undercaptains would say more with even less complimentary language if they knew what he suspects. "We'll leave on sevenday. We can send some of the riding wounded back to Ensenla with our letters and dispatches, along with the other wounded. The arms-commander will provide an escort squad that far."

"That's even worse," comments Kusyl. "He's got something even tougher in mind for us."

"Most likely," agrees Lerial. "But if we don't stay allied against Khesyn . . ."

"Fragging mess," mutters Kusyl.

Absolutely. Lerial shrugs . . . and then smiles. "We might as well go over what we'll need."

XV

Only a handful of senior officers remain in the private dining room on sixday morning—Lerial, Ascaar, Valatyr, Klassyn, and Majer Waell.

As they near finishing their meal, Lerial says to Ascaar, "I wish you and Subcommander Klassyn a pleasant and uneventful ride to Shaelt."

"With the arms-commander accompanying us, one hopes for an uneventful journey even more than a pleasant one."

Rhamuel hasn't told him? Or have I been deceived? Lerial manages just to nod, but also feels glad that he has told his officers to say nothing about when the Mirror Lancers will be departing and what their plans may be.

"You will be leaving shortly, I presume." Ascaar's voice is cheerful, at least as close to cheerful as it ever is in the early morning.

"Tomorrow or eightday," replies Lerial. "I don't want to hurry the wounded." *What else can you say?* His eyes go to Valatyr, but the operations commander's face betrays nothing, one way or the other.

"Can most of them ride? I know you have some wagons, but . . ." Ascaar's voice shows honest concern.

"Those that survived have broken arms and slashes, mostly. Three have broken legs, but with three wagons . . . we should be able to manage." Lerial actually plans to send one wagon back to Ensenla with the wounded.

"Sounds as though you'll manage."

"So will you," Lerial replies with a smile.

Since almost all the senior officers are leaving—except for Valatyr, assuming that Rhamuel has not deceived Lerial—there is no senior officers' meeting. So, after breakfast, Lerial makes his way to the Cigoernean tents. More than half of those that had filled the area south of the main house have been struck and carted off, presumably to some form of storage, and the tents serving Lerial's forces now stand quite separate from those that remained to shelter Ascaar's now-departing battalion.

"Ser . . ." ventures Kusyl, "word is that the arms-commander—"

"Is leaving with Subcommander Ascaar's battalion," finishes Lerial.

"We'll have to see if that's true, but why don't you mount up Twenty-third Company in case they need some maneuvers exercise."

"Yes, ser."

Lerial strongly doubts that such "maneuvers" will be necessary, but . . . anything is possible. Rather than walk back to the house and have to summon an ostler or stableboy to saddle and bring his gelding, he borrows a horse and saddle from the few spares they have brought and joins Kusyl as the company forms up, reining up a few yards away.

"You don't think they'll double-cross us, do you, ser?"

"No. But it's better to be prepared." Lerial glances to the east, where rankers with carts are clearing the toppled stones from the breach in the wall and others appear to be digging around the base of the wall, as if to ready the foundation for reinforcement before masons rebuild the damaged section.

Lerial and Kusyl continue to wait and watch as Ascaar's first battalion forms up. Then, Lerial sees a dark-haired figure that can only be Rhamuel ride around the north side of the country home and rein up beside Ascaar. After a time, the arms-commander rides back to the main entrance, where he dismounts and hands the reins of his mount to an Afritan Guard and then walks through the main entrance.

A tenth of a glass or so passes, and then the column begins to move, riding toward the north entrance and the river road. Lerial continues to watch, but then sees an Afritan ranker riding toward him.

The ranker reins up several yards from Lerial. "Overcaptain Lerial, ser?"

"Yes?"

"I have a message for you, ser." The ranker holds up a folded sheet, apparently sealed at the edge.

Lerial checks his shields, but they are firm.

Kusyl eases his mount toward the Afritan Guard. "I'll give it to him." He takes the extended envelope and rides the few yards to Lerial, handing him the sealed sheet.

Lerial takes it.

Kusyl looks to the guard. "He has it."

"I'm supposed to wait until he reads it, ser."

After using his order-senses to check the seal and the paper, and finding no chaos, Lerial breaks the seal and reads the few unsigned lines of Hamorian script.

> You're likely to have an eventful ride, especially if any of the arms-commander's personal guards "vanish." My condolences.

Lerial has no doubts who wrote it, but the words tell him who is more likely to be trusted and why Rhamuel has staged the withdrawal from Lubana in the way that he has. He looks up. "I've read it. Convey my thanks."

"Yes, ser." The Afritan turns his mount and rides back north.

"Ser?" offers Kusyl.

"Some friendly advice. We should be wary of any of the arms-commander's personal guard that attempt to . . . shall we say . . . reach Swartheld before we do."

Kusyl's expression says more than the unspoken expletive that he is doubtless thinking.

"Exactly," replies Lerial. "You can take the company on a tour of the hunting park, then return."

"Yes, ser."

Lerial continues to watch, still mounted, until it is clear that all of Ascaar's battalion has indeed left Lubana.

A glass later, once it is clear that the only forces that remain at Lubana are the battalion under Majer Chorazt, Lerial's companies, and the arms-commander's personal squad, Lerial rides back to the country house, past a company of rankers striking the remaining Afritan tents, since the single battalion is clearly quartered in the permanent barracks at Lubana. Once back in his chambers, he seats himself at the desk and begins to compose the necessary dispatch to his sire. He takes his time in composing the text. Almost a glass later, he reads over what he has written.

> Ser—
>
> As you had thought, the Heldyans did attack at various points around Luba, including Lubana, the walled grounds surrounding Duke Atroyan's country house south of Luba itself. The attack began early on the tenth twoday of winter, with more than ten flatboats landing south of the duke's hunting park, slightly more than a kay south of Lubana . . .

He nods at the pedestrian description of the first landing and then the beginning of the attack on the east wall, then concentrates on the next words.

. . . with our archers on the narrow pediment of the wall, a Heldyan white wizard began to throw chaos-bolts at them in order to stop them from loosing more shafts into the boats that held the Heldyan archers supporting the attackers. Some of those bolts were diverted, and steam shrouded the riverbank. The Heldyans tried an attack with an earth-magus, but after one section of wall collapsed, there was a tremendous explosion of steam and water amid the Heldyan flatboats. When it cleared, only three boats remained, and they departed immediately.

That allowed us to take two companies to the Luba trading piers in time to repulse an armed attack on the town. More than two-thirds of the attackers died, and we managed to capture roughly one hundred prisoners, whom we turned over to the arms-commander. All in all, we lost ten rankers in the fighting and suffered twenty-two wounded. Of the wounded, despite all efforts at healing, four more succumbed to their injuries, and the remaining wounded are accompanying this dispatch to Ensenla.

While a battalion of Afritan Guards remains at Luba, the other three battalions are moving north, one to Shaelt and two to Swartheld, perhaps because Duke Khesyn appears to be building up forces at Estheld.

The reason why I and the remaining Mirror Lancers are not immediately returning is that Arms-Commander Rhamuel has requested that we escort him to Swartheld to receive the personal thanks of Duke Atroyan. Under the circumstances, it seems wisest to accede to that request.

I do not know if word has reached Cigoerne, but Duke Atroyan's eldest son, Traeyen, died of a violent flux last fall, and Natroyor, the present heir, has not enjoyed excessively robust health. As a result of these events, Arms-Commander Rhamuel is, of course, most protective of the duke and his family, as I feel we should also be, and for that reason as well, believe I should take into account the desires of Arms-Commander Rhamuel. Then, too,

> perhaps I might even have an opportunity to again see the duke's eldest child, the Lady Kyedra, when I am in Swartheld, and it would certainly be good for me to see the duke and the rest of his family as well.
>
> We will, of course, return to Cigoerne as expeditiously as possible once we have paid our respects to the duke and met any other obligations, although I am unaware of any such at present.

Lerial reads the dispatch once more. Then, finally, he signs it and waits for the ink to dry before he seals it.

XVI

Lerial is awake and out of his quarters early on sevenday morning, making certain that the one wagon is properly prepared for the wounded men who cannot ride and that all the other wounded are ready, as well as the half squad of Mirror Lancers he has detailed from Eleventh Company to accompany them. He has already arranged for the Afritan Guard squad promised by Arms-Commander Rhamuel to meet the Mirror Lancer party at daybreak.

After inspecting the Mirror Lancers returning to Cigoerne, Lerial then hands the dispatch he has so carefully crafted to Gherst, who will be the acting squad leader for the lancers returning to Ensenla. "This needs to get to the duke as soon as you can do so once you have reached Ensenla."

"Yes, ser."

Lerial extends a second sealed sheet to Gherst. "These are your orders that declare you are to report immediately, directly, and in person to Duke Kiedron upon your return to Cigoerne and that you are not to be assigned or to undertake any other duties, save those that would preserve your squad or facilitate your return, until you have so reported."

"Yes, ser." Gherst slips the sheet into his riding jacket.

Another sheet appears in Lerial's hand. He smiles as he extends it. "Here is a backup copy of those orders."

"I'd be hoping I won't need those, ser." Gherst smiles in return.

"That makes two of us." Lerial steps back and watches as the acting squad leader mounts and rides toward the front of the small column that is pointed toward the western gate of Lubana. He continues to watch as the riders and the single wagon move out.

Then he inspects his three companies and has them stand down and wait for the arrival of Arms-Commander Rhamuel, Subcommander Valatyr, and the squad of Afritan Guards that will accompany them. Lerial joins Fheldar and the two undercaptains at the head of Eighth Company.

"Ser, doesn't it seem strange that we're the ones escorting the Afritan arms-commander back to Swartheld?" Strauxyn looks to Lerial.

"I'd worry a lot more," replies Lerial, "if we were escorting Commander Sammyl . . . or the head of whatever group represents the merchanters in Afrit. All of the fighting commanders I've met seem to respect Rhamuel."

"And Commander Sammyl isn't a fighting commander?" asks Kusyl dryly.

"Let's just say that he reminds me of a certain former majer in the Mirror Lancers," replies Lerial. "That may not be a fair comparison," *probably not to Phortyn,* "but it's what comes to mind."

While Strauxyn looks puzzled, Kusyl doesn't even try to conceal a wince before saying, "That bad, ser?"

"It might not be, but I think we can trust the Afritan Guard far more than the merchanters and traders of Swartheld."

"Same's true in Cigoerne," adds Fheldar. "Maybe not so bad as in Afrit, but golds are the only thing merchanters respect."

Lerial does not comment, because his experience with traders is limited, although what little he has observed tends to make him agree.

An Afritan Guard undercaptain rides toward them, reining up short of the four. "Overcaptain Lerial?"

Lerial nods. "You are?"

"Norstaan, undercaptain, Afritan Guard. The arms-commander will be here in less than a third of a glass."

"We're ready. Once we see him, we'll mount up."

"Ah . . ."

"There's no sense in tiring mounts and making officers and rankers impatient, Undercaptain. We'll be ready to go before he reaches us."

"That isn't customary . . ."

Lerial looks at the fresh-faced undercaptain, recalling that he was even younger when he first wore the single bars, and smiles. "It's customary for the Mirror Lancers, and we're escorting him at his request. If he has any difficulty with our practices, I'm most certain he'll let me know. Don't you think so, Undercaptain? If he does, I'll explain that it was my decision." Lerial pauses, then goes on, "I'd suggest that your scouts or outriders lead the way, followed by half your squad, then the Mirror Lancers, with your other half squad bringing up the rear. That way, any bystanders and those in the hamlets and towns through which we pass will be reassured that the Afritan Guards have the situation well in hand."

"I had thought . . ." Norstaan stops. "I will present that to the arms-commander and leave the decision to him."

"We'll certainly abide by his decision once he knows of our recommendation," replies Lerial politely.

The Afritan undercaptain turns his mount and rides back in the direction of the stables west of the country house.

Kusyl looks to Lerial. "Took him a moment."

"I'll be interested to see what the arms-commander's personal squad looks like." *And whether they're combat veterans or a parade-polish squad.*

Before that long, and certainly less than a third of a glass, Lerial sees a squad riding toward them and immediately calls out, "Companies mount! Full order!" Then he concentrates on the approaching riders. At the head of the squad escorting the arms-commander is an Afritan trooper bearing a crimson banner trimmed with a gold border and a gold device of some sort in the middle of the long triangular field. As the squad nears, Lerial sees the arms-commander riding beside Norstaan, who is gesturing in an animated fashion. Behind them rides Valatyr, although Lerial cannot see him clearly.

Lerial refrains from sighing. *It looks like Norstaan didn't get it at all.* Then he smiles as Rhamuel says something, and the young undercaptain seems to wilt in the saddle. In moments, the young officer moves away from Rhamuel, then rides forward to Lerial, stopping less than two yards away. "Overcaptain, ser, the arms-commander is agreeable to your plan for the riding order."

Lerial smiles pleasantly. "Thank you, Undercaptain Norstaan. I appreciate the confirmation."

"My apologies for my excessive concern, ser."

"No apology is necessary. I'm certain that the arms-commander understands your concerns."

Norstaan does not speak for several moments, then finally says, "With your permission, ser, the arms-commander has suggested that I might best serve, at least initially, with the half squad in the rear guard."

"You have my permission, Undercaptain."

Norstaan inclines his head, then turns and rides toward the ten Afritan Guards making their way toward the wagons and the rear of the column.

Rhamuel and Valatyr, followed by the other ten Afritan Guards, slow their mounts to a halt short of Lerial and the head of the column.

Lerial surveys the squad, noting that, while the uniforms are spotless, the squad consists of both younger and older rankers, and one ranker decidedly . . . hefty.

"Good morning, Overcaptain," says Rhamuel cheerfully.

"Good morning, ser. Might I introduce my officers?" asks Lerial, easing his gelding back slightly.

Rhamuel nods.

"At the end away from me is senior squad leader and acting undercaptain Fheldar. Then Undercaptain Strauxyn and Undercaptain Kusyl. Undercaptains, Arms-Commander Rhamuel and Subcommander Valatyr."

"Sers . . ." murmur the three, inclining their heads.

"To your companies," Lerial says quietly.

Two Afritan outriders take a position at the head of the column, with the remaining squad members forming up two abreast behind Rhamuel, with the banner bearer directly behind the arms-commander. Valatyr takes a position to the arms-commander's left, leaving the position on the right to Lerial, who eases the gelding into place. Once the Afritan Guards are in place behind the senior officers, Lerial looks to Rhamuel.

The arms-commander nods.

"Column! Forward!" Lerial orders.

The sun is just above the east bank of the river when Lerial and the others ride out through the north gate of Lubana. Lerial has not spoken since giving the order to move out, deciding to leave any initiation of conversation to Rhamuel.

They are still south of the piers at Luba when Rhamuel says, "Young Norstaan is not used to gentle suggestions, Overcaptain. I had to point out a few things to him."

"You are the arms-commander," replies Lerial, "and I offered what I thought was the best arrangement as a suggestion."

"It is the best arrangement, and I would have suggested something similar if you had not."

"Which you gently pointed out to him, and then assigned him to the rear guard."

"He needed to be reminded that you are not only his superior in rank, but far more than that in terms of actual power."

"I would suggest . . . only suggest, that we rotate the rear-guard officer among my three and the undercaptain."

Rhamuel nods. "I agree . . . but Norstaan's first rotation there should be a bit longer." He grins. "He needs a bit of time to think."

From his words and his reactions, more time may not be that helpful. "We were all inexperienced once. Some of us still aren't as experienced as we need to be."

"No one is as experienced as they need to be unless they've stopped trying to do better," replies Rhamuel.

Lerial can't argue with that. He just smiles.

"I notice that all your officers appear to be former rankers. Is that so?"

"It is. Kusyl will likely be promoted to captain when we return to Cigoerne."

"Is that true of all junior officers?" Rhamuel's voice contains more than a modicum of doubt.

"Not of all. I'd say that about two in three junior officers have experience as rankers. About one in three would appear to come from backgrounds similar to Undercaptain Norstaan."

"What would you say his background might be?"

"It's only a guess, but I'd say he comes from a well-off family, most likely is the third or fourth son of a merchanter, or the second son of a successful senior officer."

Valatyr laughs softly.

Even Rhamuel smiles before he asks, "How did you decide that?"

"He acts exactly the way I felt before Majer Altyrn decided to set me straight."

"And your father let him?"

For a moment, Lerial is puzzled, because there is no real curiosity behind Rhamuel's words, but then he understands that the answer is not for the arms-commander. "Let him? He was the one who decided it was necessary. I saw my parents and my brother and sister only once in more than a year."

"Your point is made, Arms-Commander," says Valatyr dryly. "But you can't make it that way with those who need to understand it. Even faced with proof in person, they'll deny what they see."

"Perhaps. We'll see." Rhamuel turns toward Lerial. "Has your family told you much about Swartheld?"

"Not that much. Only that Cigoerne is far, far more modest than Swartheld, and that the grandest dwellings in the duchy are less than those of merchanters who are considered only well-off."

Rhamuel laughs again, more humorously. "That's a bit of an overstatement. The only truly grand thing about Swartheld is the harbor. It is truly magnificent . . ."

As the arms-commander begins to talk about Swartheld, the column reaches the paved section of the river road adjoining the Luba piers where Lerial and the Mirror Lancers had repulsed the last Heldyan attack. Lerial can see that no attempt has been made to replace the shattered paving stones or to clean away the black streaks from the stone.

Nor do any of the people on the side of the road pay much attention to the passing riders.

XVII

The ride on sevenday is long and warm enough, with spring only two days away, that Lerial would not wish to make such a ride in full summer. As he had surmised when he had surveyed the north of Luba, the road turns away from the river and climbs into rugged and dry hills that extend northward for almost twenty kays before descending into rolling grasslands, separated from the Swarth River by sandy hills. The road then takes a track along the top of a ridge for another ten kays before swinging back east toward the river . . . and the small town of Haal, which appears in the distance late in the afternoon.

"That is the first truly green land we've seen all day," observes Lerial to Rhamuel as they ride along the dusty road as it gradually descends into the clearly fertile lands to the north of them. "There isn't much south of Luba, either." *Not until south of Ensenla, anyway.*

"Luba and the area around it do not truly represent the best of Afrit. See the trees here, the olives that have prospered for years, and the apricots, farther to the west, there?" Rhamuel gestures.

"I see them," replies Lerial. "I also saw the same lushness in Guasyra. It is a lovely town, but that is a small area."

"It was settled by people from Haal and Shaelt, and they have made it a garden as well."

"But why are the lands so barren south of Guasyra?"

"The marshes there are so sandy that trying to turn the land fertile is not possible. Where there is soil that might be fertile, those places are too far from water, and where there is water . . ." Rhamuel shrugs. "Because Cigoerne is so far south and beyond the wasting lands, no one had thought that one could do what your grandmere envisioned."

Lerial realizes that Rhamuel has just offered the longest set of statements since they rode out early that morning. "She envisioned a great deal, but you must have thought of things such as that, especially the way you just described the best lands of Afrit."

"I would like to say that I have. I have a few times, but an arms-commander must concentrate on what makes the Afritan Guard strong."

"Everything from supplies to weapons, and what all the other duchies may be doing?" prompts Lerial.

"To begin with."

"What other orchards are there around Haal?"

"Farther to the north, there are date palms, but they require clean water. Once men thought they would thrive in the south, because they like sandy ground, but the date palms die if they are planted too near the salt marshes. The dates from near Shaelt are the best."

"We don't get many dates in Cigoerne. Usually those we do get are dried and not fresh."

"We'll have to have you eat real dates, then," says Rhamuel with a light laugh. "And some good vintages. The grapes from the hills southwest of Swartheld produce a wonderful red wine."

"What about white wines?"

"Ah . . . you would like Ascatyl. It comes from the small white grapes on the higher hills."

"And too much Ascatyl," adds Valatyr from where he rides on the other side of Rhamuel, "will have you liking everything . . . until you wake the next morning."

"That's true of everything in excess," says Rhamuel mildly, "assuming you wake up. That doesn't always happen in parts of Swartheld."

"People doing things to excess in Cigoerne usually do wake up." Lerial pauses. "That used to be true. I'm not so certain it always does now. Cigoerne has grown so much."

"That's one difference between towns and cities," comments Valatyr. "Cigoerne's likely a city now."

"A very small one," replies Lerial.

"How big compared to Luba?" asks Valatyr.

"At least twice as large, perhaps three times."

"It's grown that much?" Rhamuel is clearly surprised.

"It's grown rapidly in the past few years. It was larger every time I rode there from Ensenla."

"Rode there from Ensenla?" asks Valatyr.

"I've been posted to Ensenla for most of the past five years," explains Lerial.

"Five years?" For a long moment, Valatyr says nothing. "Oh . . ." He looks to Rhamuel.

"Yes, I knew that," replies the arms-commander. "The overcaptain likely has more combat experience than any officer now in the Afritan Guard. More successful combat experience."

"And more mistakes," adds Lerial dryly. He cannot but wonder why Rhamuel did not mention that Lerial had been the one to destroy the Afritan battalion years ago . . . and then has admitted to Valatyr that he knew all along. *Because Valatyr had also observed what had happened to the Heldyans attacking the east wall? But if Valatyr had observed . . .* Lerial wants to shake his head at the already-complex politics in the Afritan Guard, politics that he knows will only get messier the longer he is in Afrit. Yet he also knows he had no real choice but to accept Rhamuel's offer. *And perhaps Rhamuel had no real choice but to offer.* That, too, is a frightening and all-too-real possibility.

"Experience is always paid for in mistakes," counters Rhamuel.

"If you're fortunate, someone else's," suggests Valatyr.

"No, that doesn't count as experience." Rhamuel shakes his head. "Profiting from someone else's mistakes, especially when you're young, gives you the feeling that you won't make mistakes . . . and that's sometimes even worse."

"You know, ser," says Valatyr with a smile, "you could give any man pause."

"Some men, but not those who need that pause. Words never affect them."

That statement gives Lerial pause, if for a moment, as he realizes just how true it is.

"There is a pleasant way station at Haal," Rhamuel says cheerfully.

"It will be crowded, but it has held a full battalion," interjects Valatyr.

As they ride closer to Haal, Lerial can see a network of smaller canals, presumably fed by larger canals from the river. The olive trees are stout and well tended, and the mud-brick cottages between the orchards also in good condition, although some of the roofs could use a rethatching. *But where do they get the thatching?* He hasn't seen either long-stemmed wild grasses or wheat-corn fields. Then he smiles. *Water reeds. There's no shortage of those this close to the river.*

"You can see the way station now," announces Valatyr.

As at Guasyra, the way station is located south of the town, and when they approach it, Lerial can see that the simple plaster-covered mud-brick walls three yards high form a square some two hundred yards on a side. In the center of the square are two long buildings, one clearly a stable, the other a two-story barracks.

The main gates, manned by two Afritan Guards, are less than twenty yards west of the road and do not look to have been closed in years, not from the way they sag to the packed clay of the courtyard, observes Lerial as he rides past them.

"The officers' quarters are on the north end," Valatyr explains. "So is the officers' mess. Very small."

"There's a mess staff here?" asks Lerial.

"No," replies Rhamuel, "but there are supplies here for companies to use, and one of the rankers in my personal squad is an excellent cook. You might have noticed him. He does enjoy his own cooking."

Lerial can't help but smile as he recalls the hefty ranker.

"He can do wonders with very little," adds Rhamuel. "You'll see." With that, he nods and turns his mount toward the officers' end of the barracks building.

Once Lerial has accompanied his men to the stables and he is well away from the arms-commander, he draws his undercaptains aside. "We need to keep a close watch on the gates. I want someone watching at all times. Let me know if anyone saddles up and departs the way station."

"You want to let them go, ser?" asks Fheldar.

"No, but we don't want anyone harmed, either. We are guests."

"Leave that to us, ser." Kusyl smiles.

"If . . . if you can find someone sneaking out and you can detain them, let me know immediately. You can't hurt them."

"No, ser. We won't."

Lerial nods slowly. *Are you certain this is wise?* He shakes his head. *Is anything wise?*

"We'll be very careful, ser," adds Strauxyn.

"We'll need to be very careful about everything from here on." Lerial feels that he cannot emphasize that too much, then realizes the absurdity of his words and goes on, grinning wryly as he does, "Even when we're doing something that's exceedingly risky."

"But necessary," says Kusyl.

Lerial doesn't contradict the seasoned undercaptain.

More than two glasses later, Rhamuel, Valatyr, Lerial, the three undercaptains, and Fheldar are seated around the oblong mess table, finishing a meal of noodles and mutton slices in a spicy but tasty brown sauce, accompanied by warm crusty loaves of freshly baked bread. The only beverage is a watery ale that Lerial finds barely drinkable.

"Arms-Commander, ser?" asks Kusyl. "Begging your pardon, ser . . ."

Lerial wants to wince, knowing that the older squad leader, while diplomatic and deferential, will not hesitate to ask a direct question on delicate subjects.

". . . but how did you get to be arms-commander . . . besides, again begging your pardon, ser, being the duke's brother?"

Rhamuel laughs. "I can see why it would never be a good idea to have Cigoerne as an enemy again." A smile follows his words. "Being named arms-commander was easy. My sire, when he was duke, declared my older brother would succeed him, and that I would learn enough to be arms-commander—or that I would be exiled to Lydiar or dropped on the desert isle of Recluce. Like your overcaptain, I started lower than an undercaptain, as a provisional officer trainee. I did make captain before my brother became duke and installed me as arms-commander. I listened to senior officers and followed their advice. I learned whose words were valuable and whose were . . . less valuable. I made a number of mistakes, one of which ended up getting me wounded and captured by Duke Kiedron. I learned enough from that to decide that fighting Cigoerne and its Mirror Lancers was less than wise. Another episode, while I was laid low by a particularly nasty flux, reinforced that decision. Does that answer your question?"

"Yes, ser. Thank you, ser."

"Good. Now, let me ask you one. Why do you think you and Overcaptain Lerial were sent to Afrit?"

Kusyl looks to Lerial.

Lerial nods.

"Yes, ser. The overcaptain is the best commander the duke has. I know that, and so do Fheldar and Strauxyn, and the duke knows we know that."

"So why do you think the duke sent his best commander, and his son, to help Afrit?"

"Because Duke Khesyn is a bastard, ser."

Rhamuel bursts into laughter and laughs for several long moments. Then he shakes his head. "Oh . . . oh . . ." He turns to Valatyr. "I would that . . ." He breaks off and looks at Norstaan. "Would you have said that, Undercaptain?"

"Ah . . . ser . . ." The undercaptain swallows. "No, ser."

Rhamuel shakes his head again, this time ruefully, before turning and looking down the table at Kusyl. "Thank you." He pauses. "Were you in Verdheln, Undercaptain?"

"Yes, ser. Squad leader, acting undercaptain."

"Serving under Lord Lerial?"

"No, ser. He was undercaptain of Second Company, and I was acting undercaptain of Fourth Company. Those were Verdyn Lancers, not Mirror Lancers, ser. Majer Altyrn was commanding."

"How many companies did the majer command?"

"Six, ser."

"How many Meroweyan companies were there?"

"Eight battalions, the majer said."

Rhamuel looks to Norstaan. "I won't put you on the spot." His eyes go to Valatyr. "What would you gather from what Undercaptain Kusyl said, Subcommander?"

"Might I ask one more question of the undercaptain, ser?"

Rhamuel nods.

"How experienced were the Verdyn Lancers?"

"They'd never held a blade when we got there." Kusyl smiles. "The majer, the overcaptain—he was a green undercaptain, barely seventeen—and two of us squad leaders trained them for less than a season before Duke Casseon attacked."

Valatyr offers a tight smile. "I'd draw the conclusion you're asking for, ser . . . that it is unwise to underestimate the Mirror Lancers."

"What part of the training did you do?" Rhamuel asks Lerial.

"Blade training. That's the only skill I really knew then. I had to learn about maneuvers, supplies, scouting, as fast as I could."

Valatyr glances at Kusyl. "How good a blade is he?"

"Then . . . he was one of the best. Now . . ." Kusyl shakes his head. "I wouldn't want to be in the same sparring ring."

"Might I ask how good a blade your brother is?" asks Rhamuel.

"I couldn't say," replies Lerial. "We were close to evenly matched when I became an undercaptain." *That's stretching matters, but . . .* "We've never sparred since then. We seldom even see each other. He's posted to Sudstrym, and I've spent most of my time at Ensenla or along the north border."

Rhamuel frowns slightly. "It's later than I thought. If you wouldn't mind leaving the mess to the subcommander and me . . . we need to go over a few things . . ."

"By your leave, ser?" Lerial stands, followed by all the undercaptains and Fheldar.

Rhamuel nods.

Lerial gestures for Norstaan to lead the way from the small mess, and, after a moment, the dark-haired and fresh-faced undercaptain does so, stepping into the short and narrow hallway. Lerial lags slightly, then pauses at the door to the courtyard, holding the door ajar.

"If you'd all check on the men and mounts," Lerial says. "I need to check some other matters. I'll meet you outside the stable in half a glass or so."

"Yes, ser."

Lerial waits until the undercaptains are well away and half swallowed by the late twilight gloom before he raises a concealment, and then slips back into the hallway, closing the door loudly. He eases his way back toward the mess.

". . . all gone," says Valatyr, whom Lerial can sense moving back to the mess table and seating himself. "Might I ask what that was all about?"

"Didn't you see it?" Rhamuel's voice contains a trace of irritation.

"That Lord Lerial is extraordinarily accomplished and talented? We knew that already."

"No. His undercaptains. They're all seasoned veterans. They're not afraid to speak their minds, if deferentially . . . and they respect him absolutely. What does that tell you?"

"Besides the fact that he'd turn most of our battalions into raw meat?" Valatyr is silent for several moments. "He was candid about his shortcomings as a green undercaptain."

"And?"

"He's unlikely to have an excessive opinion of his own abilities, and his officers know that as well."

"It will be interesting to see how he manages Swartheld," muses Rhamuel.

"Because it's far less direct than a battlefield?" Valatyr laughs. "Deadly as young Lerial may be, I'd wager that Maesoryk will have him charmed and bewildered in less than a glass."

Maesoryk—you need to keep that name in mind.

"He well may . . . but the first glass is not what counts. It's the last glass. The empress won the last glass against my sire."

"And your brother has never forgotten that."

"No. But that last glass may be our saving in the end."

"Ser?"

There is no response, but Lerial's senses give him the impression that Rhamuel has shaken his head. Then, after a moment, the arms-commander speaks again. "Who should we invite to dinner in Shaelt? Those that Lord Lerial should meet?"

"Is Graemaald still willing . . ."

"He will host it and invite anyone we wish. Even on less than a day's notice."

"I thought you might ask that. I have a list here." Valatyr extends a sheet. "You can add others, of course."

"You haven't listed Vonacht."

"He's been stipended off."

"Exactly. That's why he needs to be there. Also, Kenkram, and, if possible, Shalaara."

"Shalaara? That could be awkward . . ."

"She's a woman, and she's powerful and wealthy. We don't have many, and he needs to see that there are some in Afrit."

Lerial listens intently as the two mention other names, although not a single name is familiar to him.

Then, abruptly, the arms-commander yawns. "I need to get some sleep. Even rest would be helpful. It will be a long ride tomorrow." Rhamuel rises.

So does Valatyr.

Lerial slips to the part of the corridor past the archway to the mess, where he waits for the other two to leave. Then he waits before leaving the lower level, still holding a concealment and pondering what he has overheard.

XVIII

Well before dawn on eightday morning, a quiet rap on the door of the small and narrow room that passes for an officer's quarters awakens Lerial.

"Ser?"

Lerial bolts upright and walks to the door, finally focusing his order-senses on the single figure out in the hall outside. "Yes?"

"Undercaptain Kusyl thinks you'd best join him outside the stables, ser."

"I'll be right there."

Lerial yanks on his uniform and boots, then stops and belts on his sabre, the cupridium-plated iron blade that Altyrn claimed had come from one of his ancestors, and hurries down the outside steps from the second level to the courtyard and then across to the stables, glad for his order-sensing abilities, given the darkness cloaking the way station. Even before he leaves the barracks building, he can sense a single figure outside the stable.

The ranker steps forward as Lerial nears the stable door, barely ajar. "Undercaptain Kusyl is inside, ser."

"Thank you." Lerial slips through the door and into the stable, where Kusyl and three rankers stand under the one small lamp. Between them is an Afritan ranker, his black-gloved hands bound before him.

"We found this fellow with a dispatch pouch trying to take a mount out," says Kusyl. "We thought you ought to see him, ser." As Lerial steps closer to the undercaptain, Kusyl murmurs, "Still have men watching, ser,"

Lerial can't help but feel the trace of a wry smile. *Kusyl trusts the Afritans—or some of them—less than you do.* He nods and studies the captive.

The Afritan ranker is not young, but neither is he old, perhaps three or four years older than Lerial, with a narrow face hardened by experience. He has lank blond hair, and a mole or scar on one cheek. Lerial does not recognize him, but that is not surprising, since he wears a regular Afritan Guard uniform and not the slightly dressier version worn by Rhamuel's personal squad. That suggests he is a member of the permanent cadre at the way station . . . except for the black leather gloves. *Could he be a decoy? Or just a contact so that whoever is the spy in Rhamuel's squad can pass off information.*

"What's your name?" asks Lerial pleasantly.

"I only answer to Squad Leader Phoraan or Afritan Guard officers, ser."

How can you get him to reveal something . . . Lerial smiles. "I think we can manage that. Put a rope around his waist. Tightly."

"You can't do that. I'm not under your command."

"You're absolutely right," returns Lerial as he watches one of the rankers slip a rope around the midsection of the Afritan. "And I'm about to return you to a superior officer. I wouldn't think of doing anything else." He turns to Kusyl. "Do you have the dispatch pouch?"

"Yes, ser." The undercaptain holds up a black leather case.

"What do you think about this ranker?" Lerial asks in a low voice.

"He's not a ranker . . . or not just one. His belt knife isn't what most rankers wear. It's too good, more like a bravo's. Doesn't carry himself like a ranker, either."

"Not the way he answered me." Lerial, sensing something like chaos, turns and draws his sabre. He sees that one of the Afritan ranker's hands is free, but the other holds a shimmering blade unlike the dark iron weapons usually used by Afritan Guards. That blade flashes toward the ranker with the rope, who, most sensibly, drops it and jumps back.

In that moment, Lerial steps forward, and a small bolt of chaos flares toward him. Unthinkingly, Lerial parries the chaos with his blade, even before it reaches his shields.

In the momentary light of that flare, Lerial can see the surprise on the false ranker's face, although that doesn't stop the man from beginning a thrust against Lerial.

Lerial instinctively parries the thrust, moving into an attack.

The other gives ground, then suddenly jumps back. Another blast of chaos follows, a small one, aimed at the leather dispatch case in Kusyl's left hand. A gout of fire envelops the undercaptain's hand and forearm.

"Get your hand and arm in cold water! Now!" snaps Lerial, his eyes back on the mage or spy or whatever he may be, slipping the other's blade, then launching a counter.

The Afritan parries the counter, his blade ending up to one side.

Lerial takes advantage of the error and slips a quick thrust to the other's shoulder, then recovers to parry a possible counterthrust, even as he senses a darkness at the tip of his blade, a darkness that turns golden red and immediately fades.

A look of horror crosses the face of the false ranker. He tries to lift his blade, then shudders and topples forward. His blade leaves his hand as he strikes the packed earth of the stable floor face-first. An ugly black-silver miasma, one that Lerial senses, but does not see, issues from the inert form.

The three Mirror Lancer rankers stand as if frozen.

Lerial glances around and sees Kusyl a good ten yards away with his left hand and lower forearm in a bucket. He turns to the three rankers. "Watch the door." Then he walks swiftly toward the undercaptain.

"It's not too bad."

"Leave it there for a bit," Lerial says, extending his order-senses to the undercaptain's hand and arm. From what he can sense, there is only a faint residue of wound chaos, if that, surrounding Kusyl's hand, and none on his forearm, although his jacket sleeve is charred. "How does your hand feel?"

"The stinging's stopped. Good thing I was wearing gloves."

"Very good." Lerial pauses. "Take it out of the water for just a moment. Tell me how it feels."

"Wet."

"No pain? No stinging?"

Kusyl frowns. "No."

"Good. We need to see the arms-commander." Lerial returns to the body and picks up the blade from the stable floor, examining it in the dim light. It is indeed cupridium, but slightly longer and narrower than a sabre, and the

tip is sharpened for a good ten digits on both edges, although the remainder of the blade is one-edged. He has never seen a blade like it, but its purpose is clear enough. *Bastard assassin's weapon.*

"Two of you carry the body. The arms-commander needs to see it now."

Kusyl gestures with his right hand. "Maermyn, Dekkyr . . ."

In less than a tenth of a glass, the four have crossed the courtyard and made their way to the second level.

Two guards stand outside the door to the larger corner chambers that Rhamuel occupies. One looks from Lerial to Kusyl, and then to the two rankers lugging the body wearing the uniform of an Afritan Guard. "Ser . . . he's not to be disturbed."

"I'm afraid he'll have to be," Lerial says politely. "This can't wait."

The two guards exchange glances. One mouths a single word. Lerial thinks it might be "undercaptain." Finally, the shorter one raps on the door. There is no response. His lips tighten and he raps harder.

Muffled words come from inside.

"Lord Lerial with something urgent, ser. He insists."

After several moments, the door opens, but slightly.

Lerial can barely see Rhamuel's eyes. "We need to show you something and then talk."

The door opens a fraction wider. Rhamuel looks as though he might object, then asks, "Why might this be urgent?" His voice is hoarse.

"You'll see."

Rhamuel sighs, then steps back and opens the door. His eyes widen as he sees the two rankers carrying the uniformed body.

"Put it inside on the floor away from the door. Face up." Lerial gestures, then turns to Rhamuel. "I'll explain in a moment. You won't like the explanation."

Rhamuel steps farther from the door. He is barefoot and wearing an undertunic and trousers, only partly buttoned.

Once the body lies on the floor of Rhamuel's chamber, an oblong space three times the size of the small room where Lerial had slept, Lerial nods to the two rankers. "Wait outside with Undercaptain Kusyl."

"Yes, ser."

Lerial closes the door.

When the door closes, Rhamuel looks at Lerial. "I'm waiting."

"We have a dead ranker who isn't a ranker at all. He was at least a minor wizard. Perhaps I'm overly cautious, ser, but when rankers who are not dispatch riders—or even if they are—try to slip out at third glass of the morning with a dispatch case, alone, without escorts, I tend to ask why. So do my men. And when such a ranker refuses even his name, I get more suspicious. And when he turns out to be a wizard with a cupridium blade that isn't of Mirror Lancer or Afritan Guard forging, that's worse." He goes on to explain what else happened in the stable. "The worst part is that I have no idea what was in the dispatch case. I didn't expect a wizard . . . or one that would use chaos to destroy the case."

Rhamuel takes the single candleholder from the bedside table and carries it over to the body. He looks carefully, then straightens and shakes his head. "I've never seen him."

"Neither have I. Nor have I seen a blade like this." Lerial extends the blade carefully, presenting the hilt to Rhamuel.

The arms-commander lifts it. "Lighter than it looks. What's so important about it?" He returns the weapon to Lerial.

"It's difficult for a chaos-wizard to handle an iron blade, and the more powerful the wizard, the harder it is. That's why Magi'i who used weapons once all bore cupridium blades. They're almost impossible to forge because they require a strong ordermage and a skilled swordsmith. There are still a number in Cigoerne, but this isn't like any weapon I've ever seen. It's an assassin's blade, but made for a wizard who's an assassin, and it wasn't forged in Cigoerne. There can't be many of those."

"If he is a wizard . . ." Rhamuel shakes his head. "How did he die? I only see a blot of red on his shoulder."

"I put an iron-cored blade into his shoulder. That killed him. It likely unbalanced the order and chaos in his body." That isn't entirely accurate, Lerial knows, but it's close enough for the circumstances.

"I noticed Undercaptain Kusyl appeared somewhat . . . charred."

"He was holding the dispatch case when the wizard threw a small chaos-bolt and burned it."

"He didn't use chaos on you? He burned a case and let you take him down with a blade?"

"I can parry a small chaos-bolt with the blade," Lerial says blandly, even as he marvels at what happened. "He was less successful with me."

"Considerably less." Rhamuel's voice is dry. "None of this makes sense. Perhaps the way-station undercaptain can enlighten us." He walks to the door and opens it slightly. "Send for Undercaptain Foerris. I want him here immediately."

"Yes, ser."

Rhamuel closes the door and walks to the narrow table desk, where he lifts a striker and, after several attempts, lights the lamp there. He sets the striker back on a brass plate that serves as its holder, then looks at Lerial. "What exactly did he say?"

"I asked him his name, and he replied that he answered only to Squad Leader Phoraan or Afritan officers."

"I can't imagine a ranker responding like that."

"Neither could I," replies Lerial.

"Did he know who you are?"

"He obviously knew I wasn't an Afritan officer, but more than that . . . I don't think so. He looked very surprised when I parried his firebolt. That was when he jumped back and used a small firebolt on the dispatch case."

"What color was it?"

"Black."

"Are you sure?"

"I'm certain. Why?"

"All Afritan Guard dispatch cases are crimson with a black slash."

For several moments, neither speaks.

"Undercaptain Foerris is here, ser."

"Have him come in." Rhamuel's voice is cool.

The door opens, and an officer somewhat shorter than Lerial enters. Foerris is neither fresh-faced nor a grizzled veteran, but an undercaptain only a few years older than Lerial, slightly round-faced and soft in the middle, most likely a younger son of a prosperous merchant. His eyes widen as he beholds the body on the floor. "He broke in here?"

"No," replies Rhamuel. "He attacked Overcaptain Lerial when the overcaptain asked him why he was taking a mount and trying to leave the way station. Is he one of yours?"

"Yes, ser. That's Yussyl. I don't understand . . ."

"What do you know about him?" asks Rhamuel.

"He came with the replacements three eightdays ago. He did his duties with all the others. I talked to him once or twice. He's better spoken . . . he was . . . than many rankers, but it takes all kinds, and we don't ask about their past." After a pause, Foerris ventures, "Might I ask . . . ser?"

"He tried to sneak out of the way station less than a glass ago, and when Overcaptain Lerial's men asked why he was leaving in the middle of the night, he tried to escape. He attacked the overcaptain. The overcaptain had to kill him." Rhamuel looks at the undercaptain. "Can you explain any of this?"

Foerris swallows. "No, ser."

"Find out everything you can about him from his squad and the others. I'll expect a report before we leave."

"Yes, ser."

Once the clearly shaken undercaptain has left, Rhamuel turns back to Lerial. "Why would anyone send a wizard assassin here? No one even knew you were coming to Afrit then . . ."

"But they knew you'd pass through here."

"It would have had to have been planned almost a season ago . . . Three eightdays ago, but why a wizard assassin . . . and why did he just try to leave, rather than kill someone?"

"He must have had a reason," muses Lerial.

An urgent pounding on the door halts the conversation.

"Arms-Commander, ser!"

Lerial recognizes Norstaan's voice . . . and the near-panic in it. He can also sense that there is no one else with the undercaptain, except for the two guards and the Mirror Lancers who were already outside.

"What is it?"

"Someone's killed Subcommander Valatyr!"

"Frig!"

That is the first expletive Lerial recalls hearing from Rhamuel.

"Come in and tell me. Now!"

Norstaan enters, then lurches to a stop as he sees the body on the floor. He looks from Rhamuel to Lerial and then back to the arms-commander.

"He attacked the Mirror Lancers," declares Rhamuel. "We'll talk about that later. What happened to Subcommander Valatyr?"

"His neck was slashed . . . but . . . his sword hand was burned. His blade was on the floor." Norstaan shakes his head.

"The subcommander was an outstanding blade, then, wasn't he?" asks Lerial.

Both Norstaan and Rhamuel nod.

"The assassin had to know that. He probably tried to kill Valatyr just with a blade, and when that didn't work, he likely tried a firebolt. The subcommander probably parried the firebolt, but some of it ran down the blade and burned his hand. That distracted him just enough. The assassin was very good with a blade from what little I saw."

"How did you find out that the subcommander had been killed?" demands Rhamuel.

"I heard people in the courtyard and saw lights near the stable . . . and the stable door was open, but no one could tell me anything . . . The overcaptain wasn't in his quarters. I didn't want to bother you, sir. So I went to the subcommander's room. I called for him, but he didn't answer. I tried the door. It wasn't bolted, and when I opened it . . . I saw him lying on the floor. I thought he might have fallen at first. Then I saw the blood. He was cold. I ran up here."

"Set guards around his room. Don't have anyone else enter," orders Rhamuel. "We'll be there in a few moments."

Norstaan looks at the body.

"He's likely the one who killed the subcommander. Overcaptain Lerial tried to stop him from leaving the way station. He attacked the overcaptain. The overcaptain killed him in trying to capture him. Go and post those guards."

"Yes, ser."

Norstaan does not so much leave as flee.

Once he and Rhamuel are alone, Lerial says slowly, "I think you have your answer. Valatyr was your closest and most trustworthy advisor, wasn't he? You were never the target. He was."

After several moments, Rhamuel shakes his head. "It makes sense. Too much sense. It was all planned in advance. Whoever did it had no idea you'd be returning with me." A grim smile crosses his lips. "You had men watching for someone leaving, didn't you?"

"I did. I thought someone might try to get word of my presence to Swartheld before we reached the city. I didn't think that would be good for either of us." *But it was mostly for self-protection.* Rhamuel may guess that, Lerial knows, but what he has said is true, nonetheless.

"We know a little more because you stopped the assassin," says Rhamuel, almost testily, "but not much."

"I didn't know he had that much chaos in him. A shoulder wound wouldn't have killed a normal assassin. And you know that whoever sent him has golds and is well placed. Otherwise, they couldn't have gotten him into the replacements with the right uniform and training."

"That limits the possibilities to a mere score," replies the arms-commander dryly.

"Whoever it is has also lost a valuable assassin. One that valuable might be missed, and that could tell you more about who hired him."

"True. We can think about this more later. We need to see to the subcommander." Rhamuel sits on the edge of his bed and pulls on his boots, then rises. "Are you going to keep carrying both blades?"

"You ought to keep the assassin's blade . . . and not show it to anyone yet."

Rhamuel nods. "Put it on the desk. It will be safe enough here with guards in place."

If it's not, that will reveal something else . . . even worse. But Lerial only nods and lays the assassin's blade on the table desk.

As he follows Rhamuel from the chamber, another thought occurs to him: the fact that his sabre—the one Altyrn said had come from one of his forebears—was forged so that it could be used to parry small chaos-bolts. *But any iron blade can if the user is quick enough . . . except . . .* Lerial nods. The blade had been created for and used by someone who was of the Magi'i and likely someone who could wield chaos. He wonders if Altyrn had realized that, but that is something Lerial will never know.

XIX

At roughly third glass on threeday afternoon, Lerial, Rhamuel, and their forces are riding north on the river road, just past the stone marker indicating that Shaelt is less than a kay away, although the plots of land to the west of the road are modest and close together, each with a small mud-brick house and its grove of olive or lemon trees, if not both, suggesting that they are close indeed to Shaelt proper. He has also seen the best-designed canals since he entered Afrit, with well-maintained water gates, and even stone-walled channels and bridges immediately off the Swarth River.

Although Rhamuel and Lerial have discussed Valatyr's assassination over the two-day ride and reviewed what they both observed, they have been able to ascertain no more than they did when they left Haal. "Yussyl's" few possessions gave no clue as to his past, or his real name, again suggesting that the assassination was well planned and not a last-moment plot. They have little evidence, except the blade, and a sketch made of the assassin's face soon after his death. That was fortunate, because his body was already discomposing into ash, as a result of the excess of chaos he had carried, Lerial suspects. While Rhamuel may have some surmises, based on what he knows of Swartheld, he has not shared those with Lerial, and all Lerial can do is watch carefully, make certain his shields are strong at all times, and bide his time.

He cannot help but worry about the fact that Rhamuel's enemies have mages, that such mages are costly, and that someone was willing to risk such a valuable agent to kill the subcommander. Valatyr's body has been packed in salt and tightly wrapped, then placed in one of the wagons for a return to Swartheld to his family. Those arrangements delayed their departure from Haal, but the weather has favored them, and they are approaching Shaelt close to when Rhamuel had originally predicted.

"We'll be quartered at the Afritan Guard post on the north side of Shaelt," Rhamuel says. "You'll get a good look at the city as we pass through. You'll have a better chance tomorrow."

"You're intending we stay here for a day? Or longer?"

"Just a day. I would that it were otherwise. Staying at least a day is a necessity, for a number of reasons."

Lerial waits, hoping that Rhamuel will explain more without his having to ask.

After several moments, the arms-commander smiles and adds, "My brother does not travel that much these days. I must stand in for him at times, and this is one of those."

"So far I've not . . ." Lerial smiles wryly. He had been about to say that he had not had to stand in for either his father or his brother, but why else had his presence in Verdheln been required? Or his posting to Ensenla, where his father had previously spent much time commanding companies and patrols?

"There will be more requirements like that for you in the years ahead," predicts Rhamuel.

"You're likely right."

Ahead is a small square, with a pedestal in the middle. Rising from the pedestal is a statue of a man holding a long blade in the air, presumably in triumph. Just before Lerial, some hundred yards south of the square, he can see that the packed dirt and clay of the road ends, and a wider stone-paved way leads on to the square.

"This is the south river market square. Most growers from the south sell here, I'm told," says Rhamuel.

"And the statue?"

"My great-grandsire. He paid to pave the square and the road from the south market square to the river-pier market square."

"Did you know him?"

"He died when I was little more than an infant. Atroyan claims to recall him. I don't."

"That's a rather war-like pose," observes Lerial as they enter the small square. Carts and stalls are lined up, not quite haphazardly, on the east side of the square just a few yards from the river wall. Most of the peddlers and those looking at wares keep glancing at the Mirror Lancers, but slowly seem to return to the business of bargaining.

"There wasn't much real fighting then. Khesyn's grandsire was still struggling to gain control of Heldya, and was struggling to unite the followers of the God of the Balance and the believers in the Chaos Demons, when I doubt he believed in either, and no one ever heard much from the Meroweyans." Rhamuel offers a wry smile. "Back then, I imagine everyone thought of Cyador as distant and mighty."

"As opposed to having its heirs close and possibly troublesome?" asks Lerial lightly.

"Let's just say independent, at least."

To the north of the southern market square, the paved river road widens into an avenue bordering the river and an equally solid-looking river wall whose capstones stand a good five yards above the present water level. While there are horses, carts, and wagons on the river road, all of them immediately pull to one side or the other when they catch sight of the arms-commander's banner.

Lerial would never have thought of the need for that. *But then, in Cigoerne, no one would think of not moving from the road for the Lancers.* "Has the river ever overtopped the wall?"

Rhamuel shakes his head. "Not here. That can't happen. With the marshes to the south and lower ground on the eastern bank some ten kays to the north, even if it did rise that much, it would flood places where no one lives . . . or the oxbow lakes in Heldya."

Lerial can see that a significant rise in the water level is unlikely most times, especially given the width of the Swarth, and if what Rhamuel says is correct, it would appear that Shaelt is safe from flooding. He wonders about Luba, however.

As Lerial rides along the river road, he looks westward, past the shops and crafters' buildings, but all he can see are the roofs of dwellings, shops, and factorages, stretching seemingly to the horizon. Several hundred yards ahead are can see two low redstone towers, likely indicating what must be the trading piers off the main market square.

"I hadn't realized just how large Shaelt is," he finally says.

"It's good-sized compared to most places in Hamor, but very modest compared to Swartheld."

The main market square is impressive, a stone-paved area more than half a kay on a side, filled with large carts and small ones, and stalls on wheels. Two- and three-story factorages line the edges of the square on all sides but the river side, where two piers each extend fifty yards into the river, and two half piers extend three times that parallel to the river wall, one north of the piers out into the water, and one the same distance to the south. There are fifteen flatboats tied to the piers, and Lerial estimates that they could hold more than fifty without doubling up.

And Shaelt is modest compared to Swartheld. Lerial wants to shake his head. *Against this, what can you and three companies do? Is this why Rhamuel wants you to come to Swartheld?* He also notices that very few of those shopping, bargaining, or trading in the main square give more than a passing glance to the riders and the wagons, as if armed troopers are an everyday occurrence.

Although factorages and shops line the west side of the river road for another half kay or so north of the market square, after that there are several blocks of modest two-story dwellings, if almost wall-to-wall, before those give way to much smaller dwellings. There is a certain odor, certainly not as objectionable as that he experienced in the northern quarter of Luba, but it is less than pleasant and possibly more obvious because there is almost no wind, except for an occasional light and vagrant breeze off the river.

Ahead, a good kay away, is a redstone-walled fortification that looks to be a good half kay on a side, with walls that tower a good eight yards above the flat surface of the low bluff on which it stands, a bluff that is in turn a good five yards above the level of the river road where it nears the fort and the stone-paved causeway leading from the river road west up through a sloping cut in the bluff.

Lerial studies the walls as they continue to ride past increasingly meaner dwellings, and finally says, "Quite an impressive post. I imagine there are few anywhere in Hamor that compare."

"The Afritan Guard's Harbor Post in Swartheld is considerably larger, and South Post somewhat so," replies Rhamuel. "I know of no others." After a pause, he adds. "I haven't visited Merowey or Heldya. So my observations likely mean little. There are no Heldyan posts this large visible from our side of the river."

As they turn and ride up the causeway to the massive iron-bound timber gates, drawn back at present, Lerial can see stains on the gate timbers, especially below the heavy iron straps and braces. He also notes that the mortar joins in places in the walls could use repointing. Two Afritan Guards are posted on each side of the entrance, under a short roof that is there to protect them from the sun. Lerial can see that one's head turns from the arms-commander's banner to the Mirror Lancers following the Afritan Guards and back to the banner. The area inside the gates is paved and open, a space several hundred yards on a side. Lerial notes that more than a few of the paving stones are cracked, some severely. Directly ahead is a square two-level building of the same redstone.

Rhamuel gestures. "That's the headquarters building. The rear holds the officers' quarters. The guest quarters are behind that, and the main barracks are along the north wall with the stables on the west wall. All the workshops supporting are along the south wall. You'll be staying in the guest quarters with me. Since one of Ascaar's battalions is still at Lubana, there will be plenty of space in the main barracks and stables for your Lancers."

"What about Subcommander Klassyn? Is he normally posted here?" Lerial is unclear about exactly which senior officers are where.

"He should be on a sailing galley back to Swartheld," says Rhamuel dryly. "After what happened at Luba, he'll need to deal with a great deal of resupply, without as many golds as he'll claim he needs."

Not so many golds? That sounds like Atroyan is having tariff shortfalls, but Lerial does not comment.

As they ride past the headquarters' building, the guest quarters come into view, a gray stone building of two levels with a pillared portico shielding the east entrance. The wide roofed porch surrounds the entire second level, with a low pillared and railed wall as well, clearly designed to catch any possible breeze from whatever direction it might blow. The windows on the lower level are barely more than slits, but those on the upper level are far wider.

Even before they near the small two-story palace that Rhamuel has termed the guest quarters, Lerial sees a familiar figure—Ascaar—standing before the pillars of the entry portico.

"Column halt!" Lerial orders.

"Welcome to Shaelt Post!" Ascaar steps forward. "Your quarters are ready, Arms-Commander, Lord Lerial. We also have made the west end of the barracks ready for the Mirror Lancers."

"Thank you," replies Rhamuel warmly.

"We do appreciate it," adds Lerial. "It has been a long ride."

Rhamuel rides forward, gesturing for Lerial to accompany him, then reins up just short of the steps to the guest quarters. "Subcommander, I hope Lord Lerial and I will have the pleasure of your company at dinner here."

"I'd be very pleased, ser."

"Good. Half past sixth glass." Rhamuel nods, then dismounts.

"I'll be seeing to my men, ser," Lerial says.

Rhamuel nods to that as well.

Only after making sure that his men are indeed settled and that there are messing arrangements, and that the stables and barracks are suitable, does Lerial actually enter the Shaelt Post guest quarters, where he is escorted to the second level by an Afritan ranker. There he finds himself with three spacious rooms—a sitting room with a writing desk, a bedchamber holding a bedstead and mattress wide enough for three, flanked by two bedside tables with polished brass lamps, a large dresser, and an armoire . . . and a small bathing room. All the wooden furniture is of polished dark golden oak, carved with designs depicting river lilies.

He has barely looked around when there is a knock on the door.

"Yes?"

"It's Ascaar. Might I come in?"

"Of course." Lerial walks to the sitting room door and opens it.

Ascaar steps inside, but does not speak until Lerial closes the door. "How did you manage arriving with the arms-commander?"

"I didn't. It was his idea."

"He's never done something like that before."

"You'd know that better than I would. He told me he wanted me to meet the duke and receive thanks from him personally." Lerial offers a crooked smile. "It likely has more to do with who I am than what I did."

"Because you're who you are, you had no choice."

"That's the way I saw it."

"I didn't see Valatyr."

"You did . . . in a way. In the first wagon, packed in salt and wrapped in linen. Someone sent an assassin after him in Haal. The assassin had been planted there as a ranker replacement for almost half a season. We caught him trying to escape . . . and then Norstaan found Valatyr's body. The assassin was a minor chaos-wizard who was also skilled with a blade."

"Why Valatyr? Why not the arms-commander?" Ascaar frowns, then nods. "Take out someone close to him. Someone he relies on. Much easier."

Lerial cannot help but note Ascaar's description of Valatyr as someone Rhamuel relied on, not as someone he trusted. *Keep that in mind.* "Has anything like this happened before?"

"I don't think so. If it has, I don't know about it. What about the assassin?"

"My men caught him as he was trying to escape. He attacked me. He had so much chaos in his system that the iron in my blade killed him. I was trying just to wound him."

Ascaar frowns. "A chaos-wizard assassin? Can't say as I like that."

"Not given that . . ." Lerial pauses. "I could be wrong, but I'm getting the impression that, outside of the arms-commander, Valatyr had a better grasp of tactics and strategy than anyone above the battalion-commander level."

"You put that so delicately."

"I could be mistaken," Lerial admits. "I only know what I saw at Luba."

"Many would wish you were, but wishes don't fill the pot."

"No . . . they don't." Again, Lerial is getting the feeling that Ascaar comes from a less exalted background than any of the other commanders and subcommanders—at least those Lerial has met so far. *That doesn't mean he's either more or less trustworthy.* All the same, it does suggest he may be more able, because to rise to a battalion commander with a background unlike that of most other officers suggests that greater ability in at least some areas is likely.

"If you'll excuse me," Ascaar says, "I need to report to the arms-commander. He has some additional duties for me."

"I trust they won't be too onerous."

Ascaar only raises his eyebrows.

After the subcommander leaves, Lerial goes to find his officers, now that he has given them some time to finish the details of settling their companies. He finds Strauxyn near the stables.

"Ser . . . we've got some mounts that need reshoeing."

"Do they have a farrier?"

"Yes, ser, but he's not from the Afritan Guard. They have to pay him as well."

"How much?" asks Lerial, knowing that he will have to pay whatever the cost.

"A silver a mount, plus the cost of the shoes."

Lerial winces.

"Yes, ser."

"Arrange for it, but it will have to be done early tomorrow."

Strauxyn nods.

Lerial sends for Fheldar and Kusyl, and in less than a fraction of a glass, both join him and Strauxyn.

"I need you and some men you can trust to see what you can find out about Subcommander Ascaar and anything else about Shaelt and the post. Quietly, of course. We'll be here another day, probably not longer."

After going over other company needs, Lerial dismisses the three and heads back to his spacious rooms to clean up for dinner. He is both looking forward to it and worried about what he may learn . . . or that he may learn nothing.

At half past sixth glass Ascaar and Lerial join Rhamuel in the small private dining room of the guest quarters. Lerial would like to make an indirect inquiry about Ascaar's additional duties, but that is not possible, because Rhamuel appears just before Ascaar does and ushers them into the dining room.

As soon as the three are seated at one end of a table that could easily hold ten, Rhamuel says, "I can't provide something as elaborate as Ascatyl, but both the red wine and the lager are good. The white . . ." The arms-commander shakes his head.

After Rhamuel pours himself a goblet of red wine, Lerial and Ascaar fill their beakers with lager.

"To uneventful travels," offers Rhamuel, lifting his goblet.

"To uneventful travels."

After the toast, Rhamuel smiles. "I've had my cook prepare a recipe from Cyador. Beef Fyrad."

"I must admit that I've never had it," Lerial says.

"Excellent," replies Rhamuel. "Then you can't tell whether it's authentic, only whether it's tasty."

"I'm certain it will be excellent," replies Lerial.

A hint of a smile crosses Ascaar's face, but he does not speak.

"By the way," Lerial says, "some of my mounts need reshoeing, but I was led to understand that the farrier here in the post . . ."

Ascaar snorts. "Cantayl is a barefoot relative of Kenkram, and that's the way it's been for years."

Lerial lifts his eyebrows in puzzlement, hoping that will spur some further explanation. He also thinks he's heard the name Kenkram before, but he doesn't recall where.

"Kenkram is a merchanter and an advocate who also trades in water shares," explains Rhamuel. "He's very wealthy as a result."

Water shares? They trade in access to the river? "Water shares?"

"Those who built the main canals offer shares of their profits. By selling shares, they can extend and repair the canals. Also, at times, those who own shares . . . they fall on hard times and need more golds than the shares bring in."

Is everything in Afrit for sale in one way or another? Lerial does not voice the thought, but just nods. "I see."

"Everything is about golds," Ascaar says blandly, although the slight wave of chaos around the subcommander suggests to Lerial that Ascaar feels anything but bland.

"Better about golds than the edge of a blade," replies Rhamuel. "That is often the alternative. At least, it appears to be in Heldya." He looks up as two rankers appear, each with a platter.

Beef Fyrad turns out to be slices of beef browned and then baked in a flaky pastry crust, apparently in a hot oven, with a dark mushroom sauce or gravy over the pastry. On the other platter are two other items, on one side the thinnest strips of potatoes and on the other early yellow beans, sautéed and sprinkled with what look to be crushed nuts.

Lerial waits until Rhamuel takes a bite, then follows. He has to admit that the beef is excellent. But then, so are the potatoes and beans, as well as the dark bread that arrived in a basket.

"Are you certain you haven't had this? Perhaps under another name?" asks Rhamuel, with a smile that could only be called sardonically mischievous.

"If I did, I had it when I was too young to remember it or its name," replies Lerial. "It is quite good, and I'd certainly not mind having it again."

"I'm glad I can show you some of your heritage that you haven't experienced."

"I wish that I could do the same for you."

"You're young. You may yet," replies Rhamuel lightly.

"Then I'll have to be most careful."

"I doubt that you've ever been otherwise."

"With that I'll have to disagree. I've just been fortunate to have had good senior officers and the additional fortune to escape what could have been folly."

"That's true of most senior officers who've fought and survived," adds Ascaar dryly.

"So true." Rhamuel turns back to Lerial. "Matters have been . . . disrupted by Valatyr's death. Because of that, I've had to turn to Subcommander Ascaar. I had already planned a dinner here in Shaelt tomorrow evening so that you could meet some of the more influential merchanters and a few others, but I wasn't certain it would be possible. That is why I didn't mention it until now, when I just learned that Ascaar has been most successful."

Lerial doubts some of that, but merely says, "I understand." That is true. "And I appreciate both your efforts."

"Merchanter Graemaald has been kind enough to offer his villa, and we will leave here just after fifth glass tomorrow. His villa is west of the city and offers a view of Shaelt and the river. If you squint, you can even see the eastern shore . . ."

For the rest of the comparatively short meal, Rhamuel talks pleasantries and offers a few tidbits about Shaelt.

". . . great-great-great-grandsire wanted to build a canal to the valley some twenty kays to the west . . . died before more than two kays were finished, and his son sold the canal and lands to merchanters to raise the golds for an expedition to seize Estheld . . . expedition failed . . . canal turned to irrigation and didn't fail . . .

". . . fort here was then a way station . . . but Atoryl wanted his consort to accompany him . . . felt she needed better quarters . . . build this very building for her . . . and she still refused to come . . ."

". . . almonds here said to be the best in Hamor . . ."

When he returns to his quarters, Lerial thinks over the dinner, and the comments Rhamuel has made, but the one that sticks in his thoughts is the idea that, somehow, Lerial might yet show the arms-commander some of his heritage.

Was he referring to Amaira? But she's his legacy, not his heritage.

It's clear that everyone in Afrit has an agenda, including Rhamuel. While Lerial suspects that at least one part of Rhamuel's agenda is to keep the duke from doing something truly stupid, he obviously has powerful enemies . . . especially if someone has the golds and skills to have Valatyr assassinated. *And who knows what else will surface once it becomes known that you are in Afrit?*

XX

Rhamuel, Lerial, and Ascaar ride out of the gates of Shaelt Post slightly after fifth glass on fourday. With a damp clean cloth and a bit of order, Lerial has managed to return the uniform he wears to a semblance of being freshly washed and pressed. With them are a half squad from one of Ascaar's battalions and two rankers from the arms-commander's personal squad. They ride north on the river road for less than half a kay before turning westward on a wide boulevard. For a moment, Lerial thinks that the two sides of the boulevard—the one for riders, wagons, and coaches headed west, and the other for those headed east—are two separate roads too close together, rather than two halves of the boulevard separated by a wide park-like central median, complete with trees, bushes, and occasional flower beds. For the first few hundred yards, more elaborate shops with stonework facings line the boulevard, but those give way to dwellings, all with front courtyards set behind low stone walls roughly a yard and a half high, just tall enough that only a rider or someone in a coach could see over them easily.

"This is quite an elaborate boulevard," Lerial says.

"It leads into the area where the wealthier merchanters and landowners reside," replies Rhamuel. "I thought I'd take advantage of Graemaald's hospitality. It will also give you a better idea of what to expect in Swartheld."

"This may sound simpleminded," says Lerial, "but is there any real difference between a wealthy landowner and a wealthy merchanter?"

Rhamuel laughs. "The landowners certainly think so. They claim the merchanters come and go, just like the goods they trade for."

"And the land remains," adds Ascaar. "Often overgrazed, overharvested, and near useless, but it remains . . . with what little soil has not blown away."

"Bad landowners and inept merchants aren't that much different." Rhamuel smiles sardonically. "They both end up poor and blaming someone else."

"While an ineffective Guard officer just ends up disabled or dead," comments Ascaar.

And unfortunate or bad rulers end up even worse. "I think you answered my question." Lerial clears his throat. "What can you tell me about Merchanter Graemaald?"

"He is both a landowner and a merchanter," replies Rhamuel. "He invented a device that separates the seeds from the cotton bolls. He didn't tell anyone. Not until he bought a vast holding of land that was somewhat salty, and the rights to water from the local river. He planted cotton, and is now the largest cotton factor in Afrit."

Lerial wonders exactly why such a wealthy factor might feel himself beholden to the arms-commander. *Unless . . .* "Does he supply the cloth for the Guard uniforms?"

"He does, but there are others who would feel that they should also be able to sell their cloth to the Guard."

Will all of the merchanters at this dinner be looking for similar advantages? Most likely, Lerial suspects.

The large dwellings become larger as the boulevard rises gradually, Then, after another kay or so, Rhamuel gestures. "There."

The iron-grille gates on the north side of the boulevard—set into two redstone posts—are drawn back. Two guards, wearing white livery with brown leather belts, scabbards, and boots, stand in front of the gatehouse. A stone-paved lane, flanked on both sides by a trimmed juniper hedge slightly more than a yard in height, leads from the gates through a park-like setting, although Lerial does not see either gardens or flower beds. On a rise at the end of the lane stands a three-level redstone dwelling with two wings angled back from the circular main section. Lerial estimates the distance from the end of one wing to the end of the other at more than a hundred yards.

Six of the Afritan Guard rankers remain at the gatehouse, while the other four trail the arms-commander and the two officers as they ride up the stone lane. Two more liveried guards are posted at the base of the steps up to the columned entry portico, and four stableboys stand ready to lead away mounts. Rhamuel dismounts first, followed by Lerial, then Ascaar.

A burly man in shimmering white trousers and an overtunic belted in gold, with shimmering white boots, hurries forward to greet the arms-commander as Rhamuel reaches the shade at the top of the steps. "Arms-Commander! Welcome to Maaldyn!"

"Thank you. For the welcome and especially for hosting this dinner." Rhamuel's words are warm, as is his smile, and both are practiced, Lerial can sense. "Might I introduce you to Lord Lerial, not only the son of Duke Kiedron, but a quite accomplished overcaptain in the Mirror Lancers?"

Graemaald inclines his head, then says, "It is a pleasure to meet you, Lord Lerial. A pleasure indeed. Come, I must show you to the terrace. Many of the guests are already here. They are anxious to meet you both."

Lerial notices that Graemaald does not even look in Ascaar's direction, but Rhamuel has also noticed, for he immediately says, "And this is Subcommander Ascaar, a senior battalion commander in the Afritan Guard."

"Subcommander! Welcome!" With that, and a gesture for them to follow, Graemaald turns and walks swiftly along the center of the columns and through the open double doors into a vaulted entry hall a good ten yards wide and almost as deep, then straight back along a wide corridor floored in large shimmering white tiles. The walls are plastered in a shade of off-white that holds the faintest greenish hue.

Lerial looks into the chambers they pass, for the doors are all open. He sees a lady's study, which adjoins a ladies' salon. On the other side of the wide hall is a spacious library, and a study that adjoins it. Then there is what appears to be a receiving room, with a large dining chamber beyond, but

Graemaald does not lead them through that archway, but through an open set of double doors out into a walled courtyard garden, filled with blooms and greenery, that stretches some twenty-five yards on aside. The archway at the rear of the courtyard leads out into an immense semicircular and roofed terrace that stretches from the outside of one wing to the outside of the other. A long table is set in the middle with white linen and shimmering cutlery, tall candelabra, crystal goblets and beakers, and porcelain chargers at each place setting.

"Refreshments before dinner are on the east side," explains the merchanter, leading the way. "Where you can see almost all of Shaelt and the river."

Three men are grouped farthest from the edge of the terrace, talking, although Lerial can see that one is positioned to see whoever may enter the terrace.

"A welcoming group," Graemaald murmurs sardonically, before raising his voice. "I see you wish to greet the arms-commander and his guests. You all know the esteemed Arms-Commander Rhamuel, by name and position, if not by face. The officer in the Mirror Lancer greens is Lord Lerial of Cigoerne, and overcaptain of Mirror Lancers, and the Afritan officer is Ascaar, subcommander and senior battalion commander. These distinguished merchanters are, in turn, Kenkram, Poellyn, and Dhelamyn. I will let them provide more on themselves, or not, as they please."

Lerial nods politely, then finds the merchanter identified as Kenkram stepping toward him.

Kenkram is a squarish man of middling height with unruly wiry reddish gray hair surmounting a round and slightly pockmarked face, with incongruously cheerful blue eyes. "So you're the one."

The one what? "If you mean the one senior Mirror Lancer officer to enter Afrit in years, yes, I'm the one. Other than that . . ." Lerial shrugs.

"You're also the youngest undercaptain in Hamor to command in battle. At least the youngest to command, win, and survive."

How does he know that? "I wouldn't know. And neither my father nor I knew that I'd be in battle then. He needed to send a son to show good faith."

Kenkram grins, showing a mouth full of enormous white teeth. "You've been an active Lancer officer ever since. Why?"

"Why not? That way I can be useful, and he can devote more time to Cigoerne."

"Is all of your family that practical?"

Lerial shrugs again. "I'd say so. My mother and my aunt are healers, and my aunt is the head of the Hall of Healing in Cigoerne."

"She's the one who saved the arms-commander, isn't she? That why you're here?"

"No. The duke made a polite request for some Mirror Lancers to assist him in dealing with Duke Khesyn. My father decided I'd be the one to lead them."

"Practical," declares Kenkram.

"Speaking of practical, what do you merchant?"

"Rope and cordage, when I'm not otherwise engaged."

"That's an area of my education that I have to say has been neglected." Belatedly, Lerial remembers that Kenkram is an advocate and merchants water shares.

"There are two kinds of rope. The dryland ropes we make from hemp plants. Hemp will grow almost anywhere, provided there's enough water. The cordage for ships, the best cordage for hawsers and rigging, that comes from falana—the false banana plants."

"They don't grow here, do they?"

"No. We—the family—have some lands on the western edge of Afrit, where the rains come in off the Eastern Ocean. They're near, really below, an old volcano. We draw all the ship ropes and cordage there. We've got a deep-water pier, and that makes it simple."

"Why do you need two kinds of rope?"

"The hemp rope draws water inside, and you can't tell if it's rotten until it breaks. It's less costly, and some shipowners still want the hemp ropes, and they'll tar them with bitumen to keep the inside dry." Kenkram shakes his head, and Lerial notices that not a frizzy hair on his scalp so much as moves.

"What about river traders? For their boats and ships, I mean?" Lerial finds he is interested, despite the almost offhand explanations of the merchant.

The merchanter snorts. "Hemp. They want cheap. If a line or sheet breaks, the shore isn't that far away."

"I understand you also are merchanter in water shares . . ."

"One cannot grow anything without water, but that is not really merchanting." Kenkram shrugs. "There is so much more about rope than most realize . . ."

After learning more about rope than he had ever thought about, and perhaps more than he needs to know, and then about making glass from Poellyn, Lerial finally slips away, realizing that he had never discovered what Dhelamyn merchants or produces. With a rueful smile, he moves toward the edge of the terrace when a server approaches him.

"Ser, what would you like to drink?"

"A pale lager," replies Lerial.

"Pale golden or the ice white, ser?"

"The least bitter."

"That would be the pale golden. Just a moment, ser."

Lerial barely has time to turn to the east toward the river and look over the stone filigreed balustrade, just over waist high, when the server returns.

"Pale golden, ser."

"Thank you." Lerial takes the crystal beaker, on which is cut the initial "G," and lets his order-senses range over the lager. He detects no chaos and takes a small sip. The lager is good, but not so good as that of Rhamuel, or even the darker lager he recalls from his time at Kinaar with Majer Altyrn and Maeroja.

From where he stands, Lerial studies Shaelt, obviously built on a long and gently sloping incline above the river—or the land has been shaped into that over the years—with the more elaborate dwellings higher on the slope. He can barely see the end of the two piers, since his view of the inner sections are blocked by the dwellings below Graemaald's villa and the warehouses and factorages just to the west of the river road.

A tall woman with shimmering black hair appears at Lerial's side. "Good evening, Lord Lerial."

Lerial turns and appraises her. The filmy shimmersilk head scarf she has allowed largely to slip is so sheer that it conceals nothing. She is slender and almost as tall as he is, although some of that height is doubtless from the high-heeled black boots she wears. The fine lines radiating from the corners of her black eyes and the slight creases in her forehead suggest that she is likely near the age of his aunt or mother. She embodies neither excessive order nor any chaos, and an amused smile plays across her lips. "Good evening," he returns after a brief pause.

"I'm Shalaara. The woman merchanter that Rhamuel trots out when he wants to prove that there are women of wealth and power in Afrit. Always when his brother isn't around, of course."

"To that, I'd have to say that I'm Lerial, the younger son of Duke Kiedron, and the one for whom Rhamuel hosts a dinner to prove that there are other younger sons who have a nodding acquaintance with arms." As she smiles at his words, an expression somewhere between amused and sardonic, he adds, "And why might he have to prove that there are powerful women merchanters to a mere second son in the smallest duchy in Hamor?"

"A *mere* second son? There are many who would kill their firstborn son for that position . . . or failing that, kill the daughters of any rivals to consort their daughter to you."

"Then they haven't seen Cigoerne," Lerial replies with a laugh. "The duke's palace is less than half the size of Graemaald's."

"What of yours?"

"I have two rooms there, and a single room at my post in Ensenla." Lerial can see that, unlike many of the men who have appeared on the terrace, who clearly enjoy excessively the benefits of fine food and wine or lager, Shalaara is trim and muscular . . . and, for all that, likely more dangerous. "What kind of merchanting do you engage in?"

"What kind might you think?"

"I haven't the faintest idea, only that you must be very good at it, and likely are excellent with accounts."

Her laugh is soft and throaty, and reminds Lerial of what a mountain cat of the Westhorns might sound like, not that he has ever seen one, let alone heard one.

"You may be right about the ledgers. I began by trading in foodstuffs. There are ways to keep food good for long periods, special ways of drying, salting . . . and . . . other ways."

"Order infusion?"

She shakes her head. "There's too much free chaos around those who need food preserved for longer times. But . . . that is an interesting question. You're Magi'i, aren't you?"

"By birth."

"More than that. I'd judge, but we won't dwell on it." She pauses. "You asked why Rhamuel asked me. He didn't say. Neither did Graemaald. Graemaald wasn't pleased, and he made clear he was doing it as a favor to Rhamuel, hoping I wouldn't come. Of course, I had to then, if only to disappoint that overblown cotton factor."

"You said you began in foodstuffs. That implies quite a bit more."

"I can see why Rhamuel wants you to meet a few people . . . or have them meet you."

"Flatboats, schooners . . . or transport . . . or is it warehouses?" asks Lerial with a smile.

"Both, actually. Who told you?"

"No one. You avoided the question. I guessed—and it was a guess—you wouldn't want to deal with perishables, and since it would be hard to take a commanding position in dealing with another commodity . . . Anyway, that was the idea . . ." Lerial shrugs.

Shalaara laughs again. "You need to talk to a few others. I wish you well, Lord Lerial."

Lerial almost shakes his head as she moves away.

"Overcaptain . . . ?"

At the sound of Ascaar's voice, Lerial turns. With the subcommander is another older officer, also in uniform.

"I'd like you to meet Commander Vonacht."

Vonacht's hair is snow-white, in contrast to his black eyes and weathered and tanned face. He nods to Lerial. "Overcaptain . . . and Lord, I understand."

"Lord only by birth, not accomplishments, Commander."

"You can get away with that for only a few more years."

"Longer, I hope," Lerial replies with a smile. "You were chief of staff, perhaps?"

"Demons, no. Just a senior battalion commander. That was enough. From what I've heard, you've already commanded in more battles than I did in all the time I was in the Guard."

"Fought, perhaps. Not commanded. Majer Altyrn commanded in Verdheln."

"I told you he doesn't like taking credit for what others do," adds Ascaar.

"Good thing you're already a lord, then, and from Cigoerne." The dry edge to Vonacht's voice suggests why Rhamuel had wanted the older commander at the dinner.

Lerial glances around, noticing that there are a good twenty people on the terrace, most with beakers or goblets in their hands. "I'm surprised that so many were able to come on such short notice."

"Few would turn down an opportunity to see the arms-commander," replies Vonacht, "or be seen in his company."

"Or be able to claim that?" asks Lerial.

"That as well."

"Is that because the duke and his family do not visit here often?'

"It has been years since that happened."

"No one talks much about his consort," Lerial ventures.

"That's because she's seen less than he is," says Ascaar. "She comes from the Aenian Clan—"

"Aenian House," corrects Vonacht. "Her father is Aenslem, the head of the Merchanting Council in Swartheld."

"She's said to be charming in private, but terrified in large groups," adds Ascaar.

"Quite charming, I might add, and quiet, but far from terrified," offers a heavyset merchanter attired in a pale lavender overtunic trimmed in deep green. "Lord Lerial, I'm Mesphaes, a shameless factor in wines and other spirits, with a claim on having the best distilleries in Afrit, if not in all Hamor. If I might have a word with you . . ."

Lerial looks to see Vonacht, but the stipended commander winks, grins, and eases away, drawing Ascaar with him.

"You might," Lerial say amiably, "if you'll first tell me a bit about the lady. I don't even know her name."

"Haesychya," replies Mesphaes. "She is fair and slender, with hair the color of pale strawberry wine. Other than that, I can say little, because she reputedly also says very little, except in the privacy of the palace and among family and close friends. That is a trait that runs in the House of Aenian."

"Thank you . . . and what did you have in mind?"

"The possibility of a letter of introduction to a factor of influence in Cigoerne."

Lerial offers an embarrassed smile. "I could offer you a letter of introduction to my father, but not to a factor of influence. I was never trained in trading and factoring, and I've been away from Cigoerne most of the last six years."

"One would think . . ." Mesphaes shakes his head ruefully. "Without trade and tariffs, a land cannot long survive."

Lerial nods. "I agree. So does my father, but we remain slightly removed from the affairs of trade. So long as traders and merchanters pay their tariffs and obey the laws, the duke and his ministers do not become involved. Disputes go to a justicer. Although the duke may review a decision, seldom is a justicer's finding overturned."

For several long moments, Mesphaes is silent.

Lerial keeps a pleasant expression on his face, but does not speak.

Finally, the merchanter shakes his head once more. "Even without an introduction, it appears as though I should look into the possibility of opening a factorage in Cigoerne."

"You are in spirits." Lerial pauses. "You might inquire of the widow of Majer Altyrn about the possibility of purchasing some of the dark lager they brew in Teilyn. I've not had anything like it—not so far—here in Afrit."

A smile crosses the merchanter's face. "Is she attractive?"

"Very. But as a lady long consorted to a man she adored and most recently widowed, I doubt her inclinations will be romantic. The lager, however, is likely to prove profitable."

"Have you other . . . information?"

"There are a number of factoring houses in Cigoerne. Most I know little of, but I would be most wary of Myrapol House." Now that Veraan has taken over running the factoring house founded by his late mother, Lerial isn't about to recommend it.

"Oh?"

"It's quite successful, but . . . I question some of the basis of that success." There is something else about Myrapol . . . but Lerial cannot remember what that might be.

Mesphaes nods. "I appreciate that information."

"Still trying to get the first opportunities, Mesphaes?" The new speaker is an angular man a good half a head shorter than Lerial.

"Why would I do otherwise, Khaythor?" The spirits merchanter turns to Lerial. "Khaythor is renowned for his wit and his ability to procure and mill any kind of timber known to man. Well, except camma wood. That's too dangerous for a mill."

"Too dangerous to grow. We thin those whenever we see one."

Dangerous to grow . . . ? Abruptly, Lerial recalls what Altyrn had said and how the elders of Verdheln used cammabark to blast away dirt and rock for roads . . . and how they'd used it against the Meroweyans at Faerwest. "What about lorken?"

"In smaller quantities," admits Khaythor, with a smile that includes not just his lips, but his whole face and light green eyes. "Are there any stocks in Cigoerne?"

"If there are, they would only be known to the people of the Verd."

"That's too bad. One can scarcely make a profit when timber is eightdays by wagon from a river or the ocean."

Lerial loses track of Mephaes's response, because he hears two men somewhere behind him talking in comparatively low voices, and he is straining to catch the words.

". . . you know Aenian House has an advantage . . ."

". . . not if they don't use it. Alaphyn is far better positioned to deal with the Austrans . . ."

". . . what about the Nordlans?"

While Lerial recognizes the fact that the duke's consort is from Aenian House, he cannot decipher anything close to the specifics of what he hears in passing.

". . . always about transport, Mesphaes," Khaythor continues. "It doesn't matter if you have the goods, not if you can't get them to those who want them cheaply . . ."

"But you have to obtain them with better quality or lower costs, don't you?" asks Lerial amiably.

"Transport is just part of the cost."

"Ah . . . here's Lord Lerial!" Two more merchanters join the group. The speaker wears a white linen jacket over a pale green shirt, rather than the muslin overtunic favored by many of the merchanters, and he looks directly at Lerial. "Corsonnyl—not so much a merchanter as a builder of fine structures."

"A merchanter of buildings and dwellings by any other name," adds the shorter man with him, clad in a dark blue overtunic. "And I'm Sosostryn . . . and proud to claim to be just a merchanter of fine fowl. Any kind, any time."

A merchanter of fowl? Does he raise them by the scores? Lerial nods. "I'm pleased to meet you both. What sort of buildings?"

"Any kind. I built this villa for Graemaald . . ."

Lerial listens as Corsonnyl declaims on the stones in Graemaald's villa and how the stones employed, the purpose of a structure, and the location all must be considered in order to create the best possible building.

A set of chimes brings the time of refreshments to a close, and in moments Lerial finds himself seated at the long table, with Rhamuel at the head, Graemaald to the left of the arms-commander and Lerial to the right. On Lerial's right is an older man, with thick gray hair, introduced to Lerial by Rhamuel as Fhastal, a merchanter of note, both in Shaelt and in Swartheld. Once several toasts have been offered, the first to Rhamuel, the second to Lerial, and the third in appreciation of all those who came on such short notice, Fhastal turns to Lerial.

"Have you been adequately introduced, or merely inundated?"

"Adequately introduced and occasionally inundated."

"That is the nature of such dinners. One attempts to overwhelm with spirits, conversation, excellent fare, the obvious known, and the insignificant otherwise unknown, in an effort to gain an advantage that may never be used, but which will be remembered and held in case of necessity or mere opportunity."

"Then," replies Lerial with a laugh, "what obvious known and intriguing insignificant unknown will you present?"

"The obvious to all but you"—Fhastal smiles—"is that I trade in golds, silvers, and coppers. I provide letters of credit based on those, and take an interest in the resources of those who need ready credit or ready golds."

"Then at times, you must have found yourself with interests in or in possession of almost every form of merchanting . . . and learned something, if not much, about each. That, in turn, since you are here, obviously enabled you to become even more astute."

"Some might say so, but in the merchanting of golds, one single misstep can destroy one, just as a single grave misstep can destroy a ruler."

"Or a commander in battle," adds Rhamuel.

"Precisely."

"And your insignificant but intriguing unknown?"

"That I once purchased some jewelry from your grandmere, and paid more than anyone thought I should have."

"Was it worth it?"

Fhastal smiles once more. "I did not profit from the trade, but I more than profited from the knowledge."

"And what might have been the profit from that knowledge?" Lerial asks lightly.

"Let me just say that I was one trader in golds and credits when I made that purchase. Now . . ." He shrugs.

Lerial looks pointedly at Graemaald.

The cotton merchant pauses, then replies. "He holds the largest countinghouse in Hamor, by any reckoning."

That explains why Fhastal is seated where he is . . . or at least one reason. "That suggests that you maintain interests in far more than golds and credit."

"I must confess that I do have some such interests. Now . . . what about a known obvious and an insignificant unknown in return?"

"The known obvious is that I am the second son of the duke of Cigoerne and an overcaptain in the Mirror Lancers. An insignificant unknown? I spent a summer and more digging irrigation trenches on the lands of Majer Altyrn."

"I will accept that, gratefully," replies Fhastal with a smile more like the grin of a satisfied mountain cat, "although I would not term it insignificant."

"I only returned in kind."

Graemaald stiffens slightly at Lerial's words, while Rhamuel shows the slightest hint of a nod.

Fhastal laughs, if almost softly.

When the laughter ends, Lerial says, "Tell me what others know. In how many towns and cities are your countinghouses . . . those sorts of matters."

"That I can do . . . willingly. There are large houses in Swartheld and Shaelt, and smaller ones in Luba and Guasyra. The main house is in Shaelt. We have very small houses in Dolari, Kysha, Nubyat, and, of course, Cigoerne . . ."

Fhastal has a countinghouse in Cigoerne. That, Lerial had not known, but he had no reason to know. He nods, thinking. *Might that be how Emerya has sent letters to Rhamuel all these years?*

"Those houses outside Afrit . . . would it not be risky for them to hold much in the way of golds or silvers?"

"Not so long as the countinghouses from Merowey and Heldya operate in Afrit," returns Fhastal.

That also makes a sort of sense to Lerial. "And family . . . they are involved?"

"Both daughters and two of my sons."

"Daughters . . ." murmurs Graemaald.

"There are some transactions better suited to women, dear friend," replies Fhastal, although the gentleness of the phrase "dear friend" suggests courtesy rather than friendship, it seems to Lerial.

After more talk of the countinghouses, Rhamuel clears his throat and looks at Lerial. "Perhaps you could enlighten Graemaald and Fhastal on what Cigoerne is like these days."

"I'd be more than happy to do so, but you must realize you'll be seeing it through the eyes of a Lancer officer and not a merchanter."

"That will be far better than no eyes or a faded memory."

Lerial doubts Rhamuel's memory has faded in the least, but he nods and begins. "As I told the arms-commander earlier, Cigoerne has grown greatly in the past five years . . ."

By the time the dinner is finally over, and Lerial, Ascaar, and Rhamuel are riding back to the post, Lerial can only hope he did not reveal anything he will regret, because his head is swimming with details and partly remembered faces and conversations.

And what you'll likely face in Swartheld will be far worse.

XXI

Once they reach Shaelt Post, just before they dismount, Lerial turns to Ascaar. "If you have a moment later . . . there are some details."

Ascaar nods, although there is a hint of a smile in his eyes. "Half a glass in your quarters? They're better than mine."

"That would be fine."

Lerial meets briefly with Fheldar and his officers, but all is as well as can be expected, and he makes his way to his quarters, thinking about several things. First, there is the question about why not a single person at the dinner mentioned the battles at Luba. Nor did anyone mention the assassination of Valatyr. The second might be because neither Lerial nor Rhamuel mentioned it . . . but Lerial has to wonder. As for the first, the impact on all the merchanters in Afrit would have been enormous had the Heldyans succeeded in gaining a foothold on the west side of the river . . . and no one had said anything.

Lerial is still puzzling over the strangeness of what was not mentioned at the dinner when he hears a knock. He checks his shields and renews them, then moves to the door and opens it.

Ascaar stands there holding a pitcher of lager and two beakers. "I thought you might like something to drink. It's not nearly what the arms-commander can offer, but it's not bad."

"It's very welcome . . . and I am thirsty." Lerial closes the door behind Ascaar and walks over to stand by one of the two armchairs.

The subcommander sets the beakers and pitcher on the low table between the chairs, turns one chair so that the chairs almost face, and settles himself. Lerial checks the pitcher and beakers with his order-senses, then fills both beakers two-thirds full, before sitting and gesturing to Ascaar to take a beaker.

The subcommander does, taking a swallow. Then he looks at Lerial. "Details . . . or what you heard or didn't hear at the dinner? Or something else."

"All that." Lerial drinks some of the lager. "This is better than you said." He sets the beaker on the low table. "On the ride back from Graemaald's villa, I finally realized what bothered me about the dinner, something I couldn't put my finger on at the time."

Ascaar tilts his head, but doesn't speak, clearly waiting for Lerial to explain.

"We fought a series of battles only an eightday ago, and if we'd failed all Afrit would be in danger. But no one said a thing. At least, not that I heard. Did you hear anything—besides from the commander, I mean?"

Ascaar offers an amused smile. "I wouldn't have, except from him. That happened almost two eightdays ago. For a wealthy merchanter to talk about something more than an eightday old would suggest that he was not well informed and could hurt him. They all have fast river schooner-galleys. They need information quickly. I'm certain they've all talked about it in private. Some have likely already changed their goods or what they do as a result. But talk about it? Not likely with other merchanters around. I'm sure Graemaald had words in private with the arms-commander."

Lerial has not even thought of that . . . but it also explains why there are no large towns or cities in Afrit that are not on the river or very close to it. The river is not only the major source of water for much of what is grown, but it's also the fastest means of travel, especially downstream.

Ascaar goes on. "I asked the same question years ago. Everyone laughed." He snorts. "All the undercaptains from merchanter families sneered."

"Thank you." Lerial nods. "That answers one question, but not another. No one mentioned Valatyr."

"They wouldn't have. Not in a public setting. There's a different reason for that. If they let it be known they knew . . ."

"Oh . . . the only way they could have found out is by revealing that they have an informant in the Afritan Guard on their payroll."

"Exactly. And commenting on the death of even a high-ranking subcommander isn't worth possibly compromising an informant whose information would be worth golds . . ."

"Rather than momentary prestige," finishes Lerial.

"You picked that up quickly."

"I hope I'm not too slow. I just hadn't thought of it that way." Lerial pauses, then goes on. "I assume you mentioned Valatyr's death to Commander Vonacht. I'd be most interested in hearing what he might have said."

"You didn't mention it to anyone?"

"I thought it would be taken badly, except to Vonacht. Was I wrong?" asks Lerial.

Ascaar shakes his head. "Especially the way it happened." He pauses. "It did happen that way, didn't it?"

"Except for one thing. I had men posted to watch for anyone leaving at odd times."

Ascaar offers a sardonic grin. "For a young overcaptain and a junior heir who looks so honest, you don't trust people much."

"I trust based on the way I see people. That's why I trust you." Lerial can only hope he is seeing Ascaar correctly.

"Vonacht wasn't surprised. Valatyr has a good idea which merchanters provide better supplies at a more reasonable cost, and Subcommander Klassyn has been listening to Valatyr."

"That's enough to risk losing a chaos-handling assassin?" Lerial has strong doubts about that, cutthroat as the merchanters of Afrit appear to be.

"No." Ascaar grins sardonically. "It's a good cover for whatever the real reason might be. That's why Vonacht has heard it, and another reason why none of them talked about it."

"Why do you think he was killed, really?"

"What I said earlier. It's clear the arms-commander relied on Valatyr.

Commander Sammyl's loyalties are to the duke and those who support the duke. Klassyn knows supplies and logistics. He never was much good at tactics and strategy."

"He knows supplies . . . or he knows the suppliers?" asks Lerial warily.

"That's a good question. I don't know . . . not for certain . . . but you can't know anything about supplies without knowing the suppliers."

"Which gives two possible reasons for Valatyr's death, and neither is likely to be the right one."

"That's the way I'd see it."

Lerial takes a deep swallow of the lager. It's more bitter than he'd thought. Or maybe other things make it taste that way. "What did you think of Valatyr?"

"When he was a battalion commander, he was firm and direct. Let you know where you stood and what he thought. He changed some of the river patrol schedules." Ascaar grins again. "Didn't catch that many more Heldyan raiders, but he did catch a few flatboats that never paid tariffs anywhere."

"Is anything in Afrit simple?"

"That's another reason why I stayed in the Guard. Two or three merchanters asked if I'd be interested in shaping up their private forces."

"Do they all have private companies of guards?"

Ascaar shakes his head. "Only the biggest. Aenian House, Fhastal, Maesoryk, maybe Jhosef. And especially Mesphaes . . . he has to. Everyone would steal spirits if they weren't guarded."

By the time they finish the lager and Ascaar leaves, Lerial has a headache . . . and not from the lager.

XXII

By seventh glass on fiveday morning, Lerial is once more riding beside Rhamuel on the river road, this time several kays north of Shaelt, under high gray clouds.

"How did you enjoy the dinner?" asks the arms-commander.

"The fare was excellent," adds Lerial. This is doubtless true, given Rhamuel's position and taste, but Lerial does not even remember much of anything but the taste of the lager, and the fact that the main dish was some form of beef wrapped in flaky pastry, similar to beef Fyrad, if with a creamy basil sauce, rather than a beef mushroom sauce.

"And the lager?"

"Yours is better," replies Lerial with a smile.

"Thank you. And the company?"

"I learned a great deal about cordage, stonework, glassblowing, and, of course, countinghouses." *And about the power and influence of Aenian House.* "I doubt the last was in the slightest accidental or coincidental. What else should I know about Fhastal, especially that which I'm not likely to find out from anyone but you?"

"First, if you'd indulge me, tell me your impressions of him."

"Besides the fact that he's powerful and dangerous? Or that he reveals nothing that he does not wish to? He mostly likely thinks out the implications of what he does much farther than almost anyone else. I doubt he forgets anything, but he mostly likely knows what grudges to forgive, and what never to forgive."

"That's a fair summary. He's also consorted to Haesychya's sister."

Rhamuel's response tells Lerial two things. First, that even more than he has anticipated the inner workings of everything in Swartheld are deeply connected. Second, that Rhamuel either knows almost everything that Lerial was told, or that he believes that Lerial knows more than he does, since Lerial had not known the name of Atroyan's consort until Mesphaes mentioned it. Then, too, perhaps Emerya had told him, and he had forgotten. Even so, neither of the latter two possibilities is exactly encouraging. "And?"

"He's skilled and powerful enough that he always acts within the law and customary practices."

"Customary practices can provide great leeway," Lerial ventures dryly.

"I should have said that he does not engage in any practice, however customary, that is against the law."

"I suspect you wanted to see if I would remark upon that difference," banters Lerial.

"It's always interesting to hear how people respond to what is said, and whether they actually listen." Rhamuel pauses, then adds, "Some hear what they want to. Some hear every word and then fail to understand. Some hear nothing."

"And some hear every word and wonder if that is what the speaker meant."

Rhamuel nods. "Or if that speaker said anything at all beyond mere words. At times, that is necessary."

"Rather than uttering no words at all?"

"There are times when silence is regarded as either agreement or disagreement. At some of such times it is unwise to allow either assumption to prevail."

"You didn't want to leave Drusyn in Lubana, did you?"

"You didn't post anyone to watch for riders leaving in the middle of the night while we were in Shaelt. Why not?" counters Rhamuel.

"After the dinner last night, and the size of Shaelt Post, I didn't see any point in it." Lerial turns to the arms-commander and waits. As he does, he realizes that there are circles under Rhamuel's eyes. *But the dinner ended early, and he retired immediately after we returned to the post. Did he remain awake . . . worrying?*

"I felt Subcommander Drusyn and his battalions would serve better if they were positioned to defend Swartheld."

"And so would the merchanters of Swartheld."

"Naturally."

They ride for another tenth of a glass before Lerial speaks again. "Would you tell me more about Haesychya? Besides the fact that she is either retiring, cautious, or shy, if not all three?"

"She is the daughter of Aenslem. Although you probably know this or soon would have learned it, he is the head of Aenian House. Aenian House owns the largest fleet of merchant vessels, both river and deepwater, in Hamor, and ports some of those vessels out of other lands, not only in Hamor, but in Candar, Austra, and Nordla."

"You and your brother do not wish to be far from merchant power."

"It's not a matter of wishing, Lerial. Their tariffs support a considerable proportion of the Afritan Guard."

"And with countinghouses and ships established elsewhere, they hold out the possibility of moving their operations elsewhere if the duke should pursue . . . policies or tariffs greatly to their dislike?"

"Surely, that doesn't surprise you?"

"No. But some of that possibility has to be a bluff. Such a move, no matter how well planned, would entail near-ruinous costs."

"Substantial, but not near-ruinous. And all the Aenian House vessels are well armed."

"So they could effectively blockade Swartheld? That does sound ruinous . . . for Aenian House, I mean."

"Oh . . . that wouldn't happen. Enough merchanters from other lands would occasionally vanish, without a trace, that there would be less trade. Duke Khesyn would look the other way if certain brigands used the river to prey only on Afritan traders."

"All of this has been so delicately intimated?"

"Not even that. Merely understood."

And merchanters from other lands would be reluctant to establish houses in Afrit against such odds. "You have not told me much about your brother's consort."

"Ah, yes. Haesychya. She is slender and fair. She is a most devoted mother, as well as a faithful and devoted consort. She does not speak Cyadoran, but then, neither does the duke, at least not well enough that he trusts himself to do so in any public place."

Lerial nods, waiting, a habit he has found serves him well.

"She is fond of reading, particularly of history. She does not care for verse, although I did learn to like verse, at least in Cyadoran, when I was in Cigoerne. I may be the only one in the family who does, since it is regarded as an . . . effeminate pastime by many in Swartheld."

"That is interesting, since some of the most powerful emperors of Cyador were fond of verse, and a few even wrote it."

"Ah . . . but Cyador's time has passed. At least, that is what many merchanters will say. Certainly, Duke Khesyn has also said that."

"I don't suppose that he has suggested that any form of alliance with Cigoerne would merely weaken a duchy in Hamor."

"Not in so many words."

"What about Natroyor? He's only . . . is it three years younger than Kyedra?"

"That's about right."

"So he's around eighteen?"

Rhamuel nods. "He looks a bit younger, although he is handsome enough."

"Does he look like Kyedra at all?"

"They look like brother and sister. Kyedra is as tall as he is, and he's not quite as tall as I am."

"I'm guessing that their mother is tall, then."

"She is. Kyedra takes after her in that."

"Is Haesychya older or younger than her sister? The one consorted to Fhastal?"

"She's younger. By several years."

"How large a ministry does the duke have?"

"Ministry?" Rhamuel actually seems puzzled.

"Advisors? Counselors? Those who act as justicers?"

"Oh . . . matters are held more closely here. The duke only has three principal ministers, certainly not enough to comprise a ministry. Cyphret is minister for merchanting, Vaencyr for justice, and Dohaan for roads, harbors, and waterways. As senior minister, Cyphret keeps the master ledger of all the duke's revenues and expenditures."

"And you're in command of the Afritan Guard." Lerial wonders how many of the three ministers are related to the more powerful merchanters, but decides that question should wait, since asking it will reveal more than he wishes and gain him little.

"I did say that matters are held more closely."

"I understand. Afrit is far older than Cigoerne."

"And far different from Cyador."

For now. Lerial cannot help but think of the words that the majer had left for him . . . and the magnitude of the task implied by those words.

"You look doubtful," observes Rhamuel.

"Not doubtful at all. Thoughtful. I have much to learn and trust that I can come to understand what is necessary before making too many mistakes."

"In Afrit, there isn't much space for mistakes."

"I'm getting that impression," Lerial replies dryly. When Rhamuel does not immediately reply, Lerial adds, "Since we have a long ride yet, perhaps you could tell me more about Swartheld."

"Where does one begin?" muses the arms-commander. "Well . . . the harbor dominates the city. That is why there is a city there. It's one of the finest natural harbors in Hamor, perhaps in the world. The piers are all of stone, and the water is deep enough so that the largest of merchant vessels can tie up to any of the piers. There are seldom less than a score of vessels in port at any one time, and usually a ship from every continent in the world. There is black wool from Montgren, and the best salted herring from Spidlar . . ."

Lerial listens carefully as they ride along the dusty river road. Occasionally, he looks eastward, across the Swarth River, to Heldya, wondering just what Duke Khesyn has in mind in dealing with Afrit . . . and Cigoerne. And what, if anything, he can do about it.

XXIII

By the second glass of the afternoon on oneday, it is more than clear to Lerial that they are on the southern outskirts of Swartheld. Not only has the river widened, but there is a large expanse of water to the north, suggesting the mouth of the river and the harbor beyond. In addition, there are almost no open lands or fields of any size between hamlets bordering the river. Less than a kay ahead, on a short point extending out into the river, or perhaps the point is at the edge of where harbor and river meet, Lerial sees a rundown stone building, almost an abandoned fort or the like.

"Is that an old fort?" He points.

"Very old. It was a river patrol station, because it's where the river enters the bay, but there are so many mudbars there now that it was abandoned well before my grandsire was born. Beyond that is the bay, and the harbor proper is well to the northwest. That's where the water is deeper."

As they ride across the base of the point, Lerial studies the bay. Beyond the point the edge of the harbor angles west-northwest, although he can see that some distance ahead, it appears to turn back toward the north. After riding another half kay or so, Lerial spies a three-story structure on the left side of the river road, opposite a large stone pier, with a row of warehouses farther north. The road now runs parallel to the bay, with a gentle slope of some fifty yards between the east shoulder and water's edge. Just a handful of yards ahead on the west side of the road are small dwellings, little more than huts, with only a few yards of open ground between them.

"Is this part of Swartheld?" he asks Rhamuel.

"How can it not be? There's never been an official border. As the city has grown to include outlying hamlets, those hamlets have just become known as districts of the city."

"How many people are there in Swartheld?"

"Years ago there were well over fifty thousand. Now, with all the outlying districts, who knows? There could be over a hundred thousand. I've suggested to the duke an enumeration might be helpful, especially if the enumeration listed the occupation of the residents."

"You might find a few more crafters and factors who owe tariffs . . . perhaps?"

"That would be useful, I'd think," replies Rhamuel. "But the duke keeps his own counsel on such matters."

"I can imagine that more than a few merchanters and factors are willing to advise him on the matter . . . especially on how all of Afrit benefits from lower tariffs." *Or other branches of merchanters that are not known.*

"Do I hear a slight note of cynicism, Lord Lerial?"

"Most likely more than a slight note."

"Why might that be?" Rhamuel smiles.

"Too often I've overheard protestation of factors and traders clad in fine cloth how the slightest increase in tariffs will render them poverty-struck. When the quality of their garments is noted, they then declare that they will not be able to keep all those who work for them."

"With the implication that tariffs will fall on the poorest, of course," adds Rhamuel. "Unhappily, that is often true. Rather than pay higher tariffs from their profits, they will discharge some poor teamster's assistant and then complain about those very same tariffs that help maintain the harbors and canals and roads that benefit them more than anyone."

"What does the duke say about that?"

"Very little. Nor can I to him. And not often."

Rhamuel's words are another indication to Lerial that the arms-commander treads a narrow path in dealing with his brother and the influence of the wealthy merchanters of Swartheld . . . and possibly even the duke's consort.

Although the structures ahead look imposing, Lerial finds those immediately nearer him on the west side of the river road cramped-looking and mean. There are small wooden docks set intermittently at the edge of the water, often amid the straggly reeds, with barely enough space for a boat to reach open water, and bare clay depressions in the slope down to the river, suggesting that small boats are regularly dragged down or hauled up from the water.

The cots soon give way to small shops. One is even boarded up and looks to have been unused for seasons, if not years. After riding another few hundred yards, Lerial sees warehouses and factorages, solid and cared-for, but worn and certainly not new. The stone river piers are older than they had looked from a distance, with weathered bollards, although the larger stone factorage or warehouse opposite them looks to have been recently built, perhaps within the year.

Lerial turns his thoughts from the buildings and asks, "What arrangements will be necessary for my lancers?"

"They will be quartered at the headquarters post of the Afritan Guard in Swartheld. It is less than half a kay from the palace. I did sent word by river to expect a battalion for quartering. I did not specify what battalion. Had I mentioned three companies, that would have aroused immediate speculation. As for you and me . . . that is up to the duke, once he receives word of your arrival . . . although it is likely that he already has, since Fhastal and others who attended the dinner in Shaelt have fast river schooners, and any would like to gain slight favor with the duke."

From Rhamuel's tone, matter-of-fact and slightly amused, it is clear that he fully expects exactly such a reaction from some of the merchanters.

And he will determine who did so and keep that in mind. Lerial decides not to comment on that and goes on, "The location of the Guard headquarters is convenient for you, then."

"It's been suggested that it is too convenient, but the duke prefers it that way, as do I. Most of the Guard troopers are quartered at the South Post or the Harbor Post. We'll be riding by the South Post in a bit less than a glass."

The southern Guard post is a glass away? And we're already in Swartheld? "How far is the southern post from the palace?"

"Two kays, give or take a few hundred yards. The Guard headquarters is north along the bay and east from the palace."

"And how far north is the Harbor Post?"

"Closer to two kays from headquarters."

Lerial's calculations based on Rhamuel's estimations suggest that Swartheld stretches at least ten kays along the river, enough to swallow Cigoerne four times over . . . and possibly more if it extends a greater distance than a kay west from the Swarth River.

Almost imperceptibly, the buildings along the river, whether shops or dwellings, become closer together, and there are more that are larger. On the right of the road ahead is a walled structure, and just south of it is a line of warehouses and two piers extending out into the calm waters of the bay.

"Is that the South Post?"

"It is. Drusyn's there with his battalions. The others are at the Harbor Post."

From what Lerial can tell, the South Post is easily three times the size of Mirror Lancer headquarters. *And it's just one of three posts here.*

A good kay west-northwest of the South Post, as they ride through a modest square, Rhamuel points to the northwest.

"There. You can see the palace on that hill."

The palace is not so much on the hill, from what Lerial can see before the warehouses on the far side of the square block his view, as occupying the entire hill, with massive walls around it, and terraced gardens leading upward to a square structure with towers on each corner.

"Rather larger than my sire's," Lerial says blandly, knowing his words are an extreme understatement.

"Somewhat larger than necessary, but it was expanded by our great-grandsire, in an effort to show power."

"The larger the dwelling, the more powerful . . . ?"

"That . . . and also what is traded. Those who have great ships, like Aenslem, or trade in metals, like Fhastal, are considered higher. Those who trade in more common goods . . ."

"Like produce or timber? They're looked down upon?"

"Usually not to their faces . . . but they know."

Lerial cannot say that such a differentiation makes sense to him, but it must to the Afritans. As they continue along the river road, he also notes that many of the streets and lanes leading off the road are narrow and anything but straight. Most of the dwellings and other structures are of brick, all with red tile roofs. Many of the tiles are cracked, and the bricks are often worn, not to mention stained with soot. In more than a few places, Lerial can pick out where bricks have been replaced. A slight brownish haze hangs over the city, and the air holds the mixed odors of cooking oil, grease, and a mixture of less appetizing smells, from rotten fish to mold, and other scents that Lerial has no interest in even contemplating.

"Now you can see the headquarters Guard post, with the walls just slightly back from the shore road there beyond the Guard Square."

The Guard Square is comparatively modest, a mere hundred yards on a side, with only handfuls of carts and peddlers scattered here and there.

"The hawkers are more numerous when there are more troopers quartered here. There will be more tomorrow . . . assuming your men have even a few coppers apiece."

"They do have that," *and more given their share of the spoils from the fallen Heldyans,* "although they may not last given the temptations of a true city."

Beyond the square rise the walls of the Afritan Guard post, a good seven yards high, even though the post itself cannot be much larger than the Mirror Lancer headquarters in Cigoerne. The gates are only partly open as the combined forces near, but after the guards sight the arms-commander's banner, they swing full open, and a series of horn calls echoes from somewhere on the wall above the gates.

Lerial can smell a miasma—and slight odor—of age permeating the entry courtyard, faint but definitely there as he rides past the gates. A half squad of Afritan Guards barely finishes forming up in front of the central building in the middle of the courtyard before Rhamuel and Lerial rein up. An Afritan captain, hardly much older than Lerial, then hurries forward.

"Arms-Commander, ser, you have a dispatch from the duke." The officer reaches up and extends the missive.

"Thank you, Captain." Rhamuel opens the sealed missive and unfolds it. An amused smile appears and then vanishes. He looks to Lerial. "The duke would earnestly hope that you and I would immediately take up residence at the palace for the duration of your stay. You can, of course, bring a half squad of your lancers, as you see fit. That might be . . . interesting."

"A half squad. I can arrange that."

"I need to send a messenger to notify Valatyr's family and to set up the memorial for him. Shall we say . . . half a glass?"

Lerial nods.

"Good." Rhamuel turns back to the captain. "Lord Lerial's three companies are the ones that will need quarters. It turns out that he did not need to bring a full battalion. Once he's free, you can brief him on what is available."

"Yes, ser."

Lerial immediately summons Fheldar, Strauxyn, and Kusyl and addresses them. "My presence has been requested at the duke's palace. I'm allowed a personal guard of a half squad."

Fheldar and Strauxyn exchange glances.

Then Strauxyn clears his throat. "Begging your pardon, ser, and yours, Undercaptain Kusyl, but your men have more experience around palaces than ours."

"Not at a palace like Duke Atroyan's, but I take your point. If you two agree . . ."

Both Strauxyn and Fheldar nod.

"I'd recommend Second Squad, under Polidaar," Kusyl says. "He's got a good head and is well-mannered but affable."

"Good. If you'd pass that on to him, I'll hear from the captain on billeting and stabling arrangements." While Lerial has not met Squad Leader Polidaar, except in passing and in inspections, Kusyl knows his men well. He always has.

Lerial then rides forward to meet with the waiting Afritan Guard captain.

Slightly more than a glass later, Lerial and his half squad of Mirror Lancers and Rhamuel and his personal squad ride back out through the gates of Swartheld Post, or Afritan Guard headquarters, depending apparently on who was speaking about the post, riding generally southwest, as far as Lerial can determine, through streets that, while able to accommodate two wagons side by side, he would have considered far too narrow for Cigoerne, let alone a city the size of Swartheld. While the faintly unpleasant odor that surrounded the Afritan Guard headquarters slowly fades as they leave the post behind, it appears that the haze has thickened slightly by the time Lerial and Rhamuel emerge from the taller buildings bordering the wide paved avenue that circles the hill dominated by the walled palace of the Duke of Afrit.

While the main gates, those on the east side of the hill, are not closed, they are guarded by four men in bright crimson uniforms and only open into a small walled courtyard, at the end of which is a set of iron-barred gates, closed and guarded by more guards in bright crimson livery. A separate guard beside the main gate studies Lerial—or his uniform—and then runs across the courtyard toward the second gates.

"Those who guard the palace aren't under your command?" asks Lerial.

"No. They're the duke's personal guard. Seldom is the arms-commander of the Afritan Guard so closely related to the duke."

"Often related . . . but not closely?"

"Everything in Afrit is related," replied Rhamuel. "As you will see."

As they ride across the courtyard toward the second set of gates, more guards in crimson appear and flank the way. Other guards open the gates, and a horn fanfare fills the space.

"That's for you," announces Rhamuel. "It's the one they use for important visitors. I don't merit a fanfare."

"More likely that you're here often enough that they decided not to play it for you," suggests Lerial.

"I'm not here *that* often. This time will be interesting."

"Do you have rooms at the headquarters?"

"I do, but those are for times I'm required there. I have a modest dwelling on the hill to the west of the palace."

"Where those of more than modest means and rank also dwell?"

"More than modest second sons, mainly. Had the duke not requested your presence here, I would have turned my dwelling over to you."

That surprises Lerial, although he can sense none of the chaos a blatant untruth often creates. "I appreciate that."

"It would be the least I could do."

Two of the palace guards appear on the far side of the gates. Beyond the gates is a larger courtyard, far larger, a good two hundred yards wide and a hundred deep, beyond which rises the palace, a redstone edifice of four levels, almost the width of the courtyard, and appearing to extend even farther than that to the west.

Rhamuel gestures to the pair of guards. "We follow them to a position below the receiving balcony."

"The duke will receive us there?"

Rhamuel shakes his head. "You'll get an initial welcome from Dafaal. He's the duke's personal scrivener and aide. He welcomes all visitors to the palace and escorts them to their quarters before they meet with Atroyan."

"What about my men?"

"They'll be quartered in chambers on the other side of the corridor from you. That's the usual arrangement for the few truly important visitors."

Just another indication of the size of the palace.

Once they rein up below the second-level balcony, less than two yards above Lerial's head, a white-haired man, attired largely in black, but with a crimson scarf around his neck, steps out onto the narrow balcony. He smiles and begins to speak with a deep and resonant voice at odds with his almost frail appearance.

"On behalf of His Mightiness the Duke Atroyan of Afrit, I bid you welcome, Lord Lerial of Cigoerne. On behalf of the duke, I extend all privileges and graces for the duration of your stay. Both the arms-commander and I remain at your service."

Lerial can sense a certain surprise in Rhamuel at the last phrase, but says nothing, although he has the feeling that Rhamuel may not be totally pleased at being placed in Lerial's service, so to speak. Then, sensing that some reply is required, Lerial inclines his head, then responds. "I deeply appreciate the warmth and hospitality offered by the duke and look forward to closer relations between Afrit and Cigoerne."

The briefest frown appears on Dafaal's brow, then vanishes, as if Lerial had not been expected to offer anything substantive in reply. "I will meet you at the palace stables, Lord Lerial. I'm certain that Arms-Commander Rhamuel can show you the way." Dafaal smiles, then retreats.

"Pompous old bastard," murmurs Rhamuel. "Good-hearted, though." He raises his voice as he continues. "It's shorter if we ride past the entrance. It's actually the rear entrance, but the front one is never open except for the handful of formal balls my brother holds here in the winter and early spring." Rhamuel urges his mount forward and to the left.

Lerial follows, saying, "I take it that he has a summer retreat, then? Besides Lubana?"

"He hasn't been to Lubana in years. He and Haesychya prefer his villa at Lake Reomer. They usually depart by the middle of spring, earlier if the weather is hot, but no later than the first eightday of summer."

But will they this year? With the threats posed by Khesyn? Lerial knows that question will have to wait.

The inner courtyard, at least in the area to the east of the palace, is almost empty except for two men cleaning the windows of the palace and those in the combined forces of Rhamuel and Lerial. Even when they ride around the south end of the palace and under an arched stone bridge that offers access to the terraced gardens stepped down the hillside away from the palace, Lerial sees only two stableboys and an older man, presumably an ostler, standing before the building on the southwestern part of the inner courtyard, away from the palace proper.

"The household stables," notes Rhamuel.

Lerial glances from the stables to his right, observing that a narrower structure extends perhaps another hundred yards from the broader section that held the receiving balcony, then again widens into another broader section that faces westward. "It's almost two palaces connected by a third."

"You could say that," admits Rhamuel, reining up before the main stable door. "It all looks the same once you're inside. Large rooms and small ones, all off seemingly endless hallways. Far too much crimson and gilt." The arms-commander dismounts. "I'm off to brief the duke. We'll all likely have dinner together, but one never knows." He glances toward the palace. "Here comes Dafaal."

Lerial dismounts quickly. "Until later, then."

Rhamuel nods, then hands the reins of his mount to one of the stableboys.

"Lord Lerial, ser . . ." offers the ostler who steps forward.

"Thank you." Lerial hands the reins of the gelding to him.

"Essen, Moertyn, you two accompany the overcaptain, and bring his gear," orders Polidaar, from behind Lerial. "The rest of you take care of the mounts and gear."

"Yes, Squad Leader."

Lerial waits several moments until the elderly Dafaal reaches him, then nods politely.

"I'll escort you to your chambers, Lord Lerial. Then, after you have washed up, in say a glass, I will send an escort to take you to see the duke. Once he has received you, there will be refreshments in the family salon, and then a small dinner—just you, the family, and the arms-commander. On threeday evening, there will be a dinner, and another . . . function . . . on fourday. There may be others, as well, but the duke has not yet informed me of such."

"I appreciate the notice of what he has scheduled."

"Now, if you will come with me . . ."

Two Mirror Lancers accompany Lerial, following behind him and Dafaal.

Just before they reach a door at the courtyard level of what Lerial thinks of as the east palace, Dafaal speaks again. "I must admit I never thought we would see an heir of Cigoerne here in Swartheld."

"I never thought I would be here," admits Lerial, "but given the invitation, I thought it was best for all concerned that I accept."

"There are some who, shall we say, might have some reservations about the . . . appropriateness of your appearance."

"I do hope that the duke is not one of those with reservations."

"Stars, no. He was most surprised that your father dispatched you to the aid of the arms-commander, but that is certainly no secret."

"Although . . ." prompts Lerial, just to see if he can gain any further information.

"Although?" Dafaal chuckles. "I doubt that he had any reservations about his appreciation. He has always felt that Duke Khesyn is a threat to the peace of all Hamor. Ever since Khesyn dredged the harbor at Estheld and built the deepwater piers there." Dafaal goes through the door that a palace guard has opened and into a rather narrow corridor. "This isn't the most well-appointed part of the palace, but it's the quickest and easiest way to get to your chambers. Also, they're doing work on the east side where the larger staircase is. We wouldn't want to run into workmen carrying those heavy barrels. We'll just take the back staircase here . . ."

"Work?"

"Refurbishing some rooms beneath the family quarters. It should have been done years ago." The elderly functionary starts up the narrow steps.

"When did Khesyn improve the harbor at Estheld?" After speaking, Lerial notes that the plastered staircase walls could use another coat of wash or the like.

"A good six years ago. It was right after Duke Casseon lost Verdheln. You had something to do with that, as I recall."

"Only a small part. Most of that was Majer Altyrn's doing." Lerial pauses. "I don't know that you have heard. He died just before I set out for Luba."

"Everyone says that he was a most effective commander. I never had the pleasure of meeting him."

"He was quite a person as well. They're not always the same."

"No. You're quite right about that." Dafaal's breathing becomes more labored, with hints of wheezing.

Lerial decides against saying more until they emerge from the staircase on the third level.

"Ah," declares Dafaal after taking several deep breaths. "Those stairs get steeper every year. Your quarters are to the left at the end."

The door to which Dafaal leads Lerial is less than fifteen yards away, at the end of a corridor stretching more than a hundred yards back to the north. The chambers awaiting Lerial consist of a sitting room—a corner chamber with windows on both outside walls—holding a circular table that could be used as a desk or for a meal, and four chairs, as well as two armchairs and a settee. The sleeping chamber is immediately to the north, with a bathing chamber and jakes beyond it. All the furnishings are of a whitish wood that Lerial has not seen before and are upholstered in crimson, if with cream trim that tends to vanish against the white wood.

"I hope these are to your satisfaction," offers Dafaal.

"They are more than satisfactory, and I appreciate your concern."

"There is warm water in the tub and a steaming kettle if you need it. I'll send a footman to bring you to the receiving room in about a glass." The functionary pauses, then adds, "The six chambers across the hall are for your men. There are two beds in each, and a communal bathing room at the end. They can bring up water from the kitchen or the courtyard."

"Thank you."

Lerial waits until Dafaal departs, then looks to the two lancers. "If one of you would watch the door, the other can check out the quarters to see if they'll do."

"Yes, ser," replies Essen. "Let me bring in your gear."

Moertyn nods, then says, "Checking the quarters won't take long. We can each look in turn, see if one of us misses something."

"Good thought," says Lerial.

Once he has his gear, including a semiclean uniform, he closes the door and moves to the sleeping chamber, where he unpacks the kit bag. By the time he dabs away the worst of the soil on his uniforms and hangs them on the pegs in the armoire, the bathwater is barely lukewarm, but still welcome. So is a good shave.

Once he dresses, he looks in the full-length mirror on the interior wall of the bedchamber. The uniform is at least presentable, but his hair is longer than he prefers, and close to unruly, since the longer it gets, the wirier it is.

Because all of his cleaning up has taken longer than he thought, he doubts he has much time before he is summoned, but when he hears the lancers across the hall he steps out of the sitting room and approaches Polidaar.

"How are the quarters?"

The squad leader grins. "Good enough that I told the men not to say anything to the other lancers. Good beds, even with linens, and no sign of vermin."

"Once in a while, we do get fortunate."

"Do you want an escort to dinner, ser?"

"I doubt I'll need it, but I'll let you know if I do. Did you find out about messing for you and your rankers?"

"Yes, ser. We get fed in the palace guard mess. Fifth glass. Anyone on duty can get rations there until eighth glass."

After finishing arrangements with the squad leader, Lerial waits less than a tenth of a glass before a young palace guard appears. "Lord Lerial, ser."

Before stepping out into the hall, Lerial reinforces his shields, ensuring that they are tightly linked to the iron of his belt knife.

The escort leads him back along the long north-south corridor and then to the right and up a marble staircase to the fourth level, along a wide but short hallway to a double set of doors. They halt in front of the golden wooden doors, where a guard is posted.

"Lord Lerial to see the duke," announces the guard who has escorted Lerial.

The duty guard turns and raps on the door, announcing, "Lord Lerial."

"Have him come in."

The guard opens the door and Lerial steps inside. The receiving room is not enormous, as Lerial had half expected, but neither is it small, a chamber some six yards wide and perhaps ten yards in length, the last yard and a half a dais raised perhaps two thirds of a yard, in the middle of which is an overlarge chair, not exactly a throne, constructed of the white wood oiled or tinted into a rich gold, with a seat upholstered in brilliant crimson. The walls are of while marble tiles shot with gold, with half pillars of the golden-tinted wood at regular intervals. The floor is of black marble tile, and scuffed in more than a few places, Lerial notes. A second look tells him that there are hairline cracks in the marble of the walls and the floor. Light comes from brass wall lamps and two narrow skylights. Stationed on each side of the chair where Atroyan sits are two tall palace guards, each holding a halberd, its base resting on the marble tiles, with a highly polished and visibly sharp blade.

Lerial walks forward until he is within two yards of Atroyan. He stops and inclines his head politely. "Duke Atroyan."

Atroyan is not as Lerial remembers him. The one time Lerial had seen the duke had been in Cigoerne when Lerial was a child. Then Atroyan had seemed tall and lean, with dark brown hair and eyes. The man who sits on the throne-like chair, wearing black trousers and a gold and crimson jacket over a white shirt, has dark gray hair with but a few streaks of brown. His brown eyes are sunken, and his shoulders are stooped. His smile is warm, and his eyes light up as he looks over his visitor.

"Lerial . . . such a change from the last time, except for the unruly red hair. You look every bit the officer my brother has portrayed." Even Atroyan's voice is slightly raspy.

Was it that way when he came to Cigoerne? Although Lerial cannot be absolutely certain, he recalls Atroyan's voice then being more like Rhamuel's, warm and full. "I would hope so, ser, since I have served as such for the last six years."

Atroyan does not laugh, but does smile, almost tentatively, then nods almost brusquely. "Rather effectively, I hear. This last time, I understand, most effectively against the hordes raised by that mongrel Khesyn."

"We did the best we could, ser, as did Subcommander Ascaar and Subcommander Drusyn and their officers and men."

"So I heard. So I heard. And that is good. Very good." After a long pause, Atroyan asks, "Your family is well, I trust?"

"The last I heard, all were well, but that was almost half a season ago."

"Does your father still command the Lancers?"

"He remains in overall command, ser. He has left most of the daily patrolling that he once did to Lephi and me."

"Wise man. Fortunate man, too." A brighter smile crosses the duke's face, although his right eye twitches several times. "I should formally welcome you to Afrit and Swartheld . . . and I do. We must talk more in a less formal setting. You'll have refreshments and then dinner with the family tonight, I would hope."

"I'd be honored and delighted, ser."

"Excellent! Excellent. Half past fifth glass in the family salon." Atroyan nods once more. "I will see you then."

"Thank you, ser. I look forward to that." Lerial inclines his head politely once more. He does not intend to back out of the chamber, but neither does he wish to immediately turn his back on the duke. He compromises by taking two steps backward, inclining his head once more, and then turning and walking to the door—which opens as he nears it, suggesting that the outer door guard, or someone, has been watching.

Since it is just after fourth glass, Lerial has more than a little time, and not that much to do, before he is expected at the duke's family salon . . . wherever that may be. Once the receiving room door is closed, he turns to his escort. "If you don't mind, I'd appreciate a tour of the palace, not anywhere private, just so that I have a general idea where most places are that I might have to be."

"Ah . . . yes, ser."

"I'm supposed to meet the duke at the family salon later. Could you take us there, or reasonably close?"

"Yes, ser. As I can, ser."

The one area it is clear he will not tour is the southeastern section of the fourth level, which is blocked off with heavy barrels. Lerial approaches the stacked barrels, all of which appear to be recently coopered, so recently that there is still an odd woody odor, something like a cross between cork and cinnamon. But the wood of neither tree is suitable for making barrels.

Maybe that's incense to mute the smells of the ongoing work. Beyond the barrels, stacked two deep, he sees two palace guards, and beyond them a carpenter working on a crown molding.

Lerial nods and turns away, following his guide.

Just walking around the third and fourth levels of the palace takes more than a glass, but Lerial has a far better idea of the layout of the massive palace. The duke's family quarters appear to comprise essentially the southern half of the "east palace's" fourth level. Beyond that, Lerial gains the impression that a great many chambers, just on the two upper levels, are essentially empty or at best, used only occasionally, and in places there is a certain odor of mustiness. Even so, the time it takes just to walk around two levels emphasizes just how large the palace is. Certainly, all the chambers on all three levels of his father's palace in Cigoerne would easily fit just within one of the upper levels of Swartheld palace.

By the time he approaches the family salon, a few moments before the appointed time, Lerial has spent more than enough time walking along corridors seemingly populated only by a palace guard or two or a servant hurrying one way or another.

He enters the family salon, past yet another guard, through a recessed archway. As soon as he steps into the chamber, he can see that it is far more cheerful than what else he has seen of the palace. The walls are plaster painted the palest shade of rose, and the far end has a set of double glass-paned doors that open onto a terrace facing the bay. There is a large oval carpet with a design of interwoven foliage and flowers in shades of rose and soft brown. Where the carpet does not cover the floor, the wood is also a polished light brown, as is the wood from which the furniture is made. All the chairs and settees are upholstered in rose, and there are two sideboards, on which are crystal goblets and beakers, and a number of crystal pitchers as well, with what appear to be red and white wines, as well as light and dark lager.

"Lord Lerial, welcome." The greeting comes from the single person in the room, a slender woman with blond hair carrying a tint of rose, rather than the strawberry Mesphaes had mentioned. She does not wear a head scarf, but then, the palace is her home. Her eyes are a surprising black. Despite the fact that she must be at least the age of his mother, Lerial can see no hint of gray in her hair.

"Lady Haesychya . . . Thank you." Lerial inclines his head. "And please, no 'Lord.'"

"Then . . . no 'Lady,' either."

"As you wish," Lerial replies as warmly and gently as he can.

"Having heard of your exploits, I had forgotten how young you are. I suspect Kyedra has as well."

Not wanting to address that, since any response he can immediately think of would be unsuitable, Lerial merely smiles and says, "I had not expected to find you here alone."

"Oh . . . I'm not. Kyedra and Natroyor are out on the terrace. Atroyan will be here shortly. He's always had difficulty in arriving on time for family affairs, even for refreshments or dinner." She turns as a young woman steps through the open terrace doors. "Here comes Kyedra."

Lerial inclines his head in greeting, taking in the young woman with the black hair and eyes, and the slightly olive skin. She is a digit or two shorter than her mother, but with slightly larger bones, Lerial thinks, making her somewhat more muscular, if still trim. Her nose is straight, if slightly stronger than he recalls, as is her chin, but her skin is clear and unblemished. Her face is a gentle oval, and she is pleasant to look at, if not a raving beauty. *But neither are you the handsomest fellow to ride into town.*

"You might remember Lerial from your time in Cigoerne."

At that comment, Kyedra smiles, if slightly ruefully, but the expression transforms her face almost into radiance. "I must say I don't recall much except your kindness . . . and, well, your hair. I wasn't all that happy."

"You did get a bit tart when I didn't describe my grandmere to your satisfaction." Lerial grins.

Kyedra drops her eyes. "I hoped you wouldn't remember that."

"That's all right. I avoided answering some of your questions."

"Not exactly. You just didn't finish some sentences."

Lerial laughs. "That's true."

"What, might I ask, is true?" asks Natroyor as he slips past his sister and stops, inclining his head in greeting to Lerial. The heir is actually a touch shorter than his sister, and more slightly built, with a narrower face, framed by straight dark brown hair. His eyes are a muddy brown, and there is a slight darkness under them.

Lerial immediately tries to sense the presence of chaos or wound chaos. He cannot, but he does gain the impression that the heir carries less order strength than he should. "That I left some sentences unfinished the last time your sister and I spoke."

Natroyor does smile, and the expression is nearly identical to that of his father. "Welcome. I've heard about you. You must tell me how you've managed so much on the battlefield."

"He will," says Haesychya quickly, "but not at the moment. We'll not be talking of fighting and war now or at dinner."

"Why not?" asks Natroyor. "We're fighting one now, and so is Cigoerne."

Lerial detects a certain sulkiness in the young man's words, but that is overshadowed by the chaotic feelings from his mother, although Haesychya's face remains almost serene, and she says nothing. Since she does not speak, Lerial does. "Because your mother expressed a preference, and I intend to honor it."

Natroyor looks stunned, if but for a moment.

Before the young man can speak, Lerial turns back to Kyedra. "You never met my sister, as I recall, nor my cousin Amaira."

"I never had that privilege."

"I'm not sure it would have been a privilege to meet Ryalah then," Lerial replies, "since she was only two. Even Amaira would only have been four."

"I didn't meet your brother, either. They said he was ill with a flux."

"You'd never know that now," replies Lerial. "He's also an overcaptain in the Mirror Lancers, in charge of the post at Sudstrym."

"Which of you is better with a blade?" demands Natroyor.

"The answer would likely depend on which of us you asked . . . but I believe we were talking about family. Have you ever accompanied your uncles on hunting trips or elsewhere?"

"Just to Lake Reomer and a few other places. Mostly with Uncle Mykel and his friend Oestyn . . ."

The mention of Oestyn's name, whoever he may be, and the flutter of chaos from Haesychya suggests certain . . . aspects of Mykel's inclinations.

". . . They say that since I'm the only heir, I must be careful. You and your bother are lucky to have each other."

"We still have to be careful. None of us ever commands Lancers in the same place at the same time. That includes my father."

"You see," says Haesychya gently, "there are similar rules in other duchies."

"I'm late . . . again!" calls Atroyan from the archway to the salon. "Or rather, we're late." He gestures to Rhamuel.

"Not terribly," replies Haesychya. "We've been having a pleasant talk with Lerial."

"Except he won't talk about real things," murmurs Natroyor, in such a low voice that Lerial doubts anyone hears his words other than Kyedra and himself.

With Natroyor's words, Lerial cannot help but think about the times the silver mists of death have washed across him. *You only think you want to hear about them.*

"He's seen a great deal," says Rhamuel warmly, before turning to Kyedra. "You're more beautiful every time I see you."

Lerial can almost sense what Rhamuel has not said, that he wishes he could see his own daughter.

"Uncle Rham . . . you're impossible," banters Kyedra.

"No. Merely difficult. Unlike Lerial, who is neither impossible nor difficult . . . just inscrutable."

"Pour yourself some wine, Rham," orders Atroyan as he fills his goblet with a generous amount of the dark red wine, before looking at Lerial. "You don't have anything to drink."

"Which lager would you recommend?"

"If you like the bitters, the dark. If you don't, the light."

"Definitely the light," suggests Rhamuel.

Lerial moves to the sideboard and looks to Haesychya and then Kyedra. "Might I pour something for either of you?"

"No, thank you," replies Atroyan's consort. "While I like either wine or lager, neither likes me."

"The light lager, if you would." Kyedra smiles and adds, "Just half a beaker, please."

Lerial pours two half beakers of the light lager, a pale golden shade. The last thing he needs is to drink too much, especially inadvertently. He checks the beverages for chaos, but senses none, and then hands one beaker to Kyedra, waiting until she takes a sip before he does the same. He has to admit that the lager is excellent, possibly even better than that of the majer. "Excellent lager."

"My father would have no other," says Natroyor proudly.

"You have outstanding taste," says Lerial to Atroyan, "I imagine the wines are just as superb."

"The Reoman red—that's what I have—is indeed," replies the duke. "The Halyn white . . . it is merely good."

Rhamuel makes a face. "That might be an exaggeration, on both counts. The Halyn white is as good a white as the Reoman is a red."

Haesychya offers the smallest of headshakes, accompanied by a fondly rueful expression that vanishes immediately.

"What have you been telling my son?" asks Atroyan.

"Only about family . . . well, really, just about my sister Ryalah and my cousin Amaira, and a bit about my older brother Lephi."

"Do you two look alike?" asks Haesychya.

"Most brothers share some likeness. I suppose we do, but he got the blond hair from our mother, and I got the freckles."

"Is your father red-haired, then?" asks Natroyor. "It must come from somewhere."

"From my grandmere and my aunt. They both had red hair."

Natroyor looks at Rhamuel, almost dubiously.

The arms-commander nods. "They both do . . . did."

"There were many redheads in Cyador, according to the history," interjects Kyedra.

"There are still quite a few in Cigoerne," replies Lerial. *Among the Magi'i, anyway.*

"What do you think Duke Khesyn will do?" asks Atroyan abruptly as he settles into one of the armchairs and motions for Lerial to take the one facing him.

The question startles Lerial, especially after Haesychya's insistence on not speaking about fighting and war. *Maybe that's because she knew what her consort would want to talk about.* "I'm not certain anyone can say what he will do," Lerial says cautiously as he seats himself. "At the least, I think he will continue attacks of some sort, if only raids, on both Afrit and Cigoerne."

Rhamuel nods as he takes an adjoining chair, while Haesychya and Kyedra share the settee.

"You don't think he will launch an all-out attack?"

"Sooner or later, I think that is likely, ser." Lerial smiles wryly. "I have no idea when sooner or later might be." He wonders why Rhamuel has not spoken, but assumes that the brothers have already spoken about that.

"Neither does anyone else, I fear," responds the duke. "It makes matters less certain than a throw of the bones." He turns to Haesychya. "What do you think, my dear?"

"He will attack until he is stopped. That is his nature."

"Why do you think that, Mother?" asks Kyedra.

The very fact that she asks the question suggests to Lerial that such matters are not normally discussed in the family salon.

"Khesyn wants to rule all of Hamor. Afrit is the greatest bar to that. He also dislikes Cigoerne because he blames Duke Kiedron for the loss of his niece."

"The loss of his niece?" asks Lerial. "That is something I've not heard."

"She fled his palace years and years ago, only a short time after Cigoerne . . . was . . . established. Word reached the duke that she had taken refuge with relatives in Amaershyn, but she and her sister attempted to flee once more before his men arrived. Somehow, the sister died, but the favored niece found a boat and paddled into the river. She headed for Cigoerne. The

Heldyans gave chase. The Cyadoran fireship destroyed them, and days later the duke's men found her ruined boat and some of her garments on a mudbar."

Lerial manages only to nod, hoping he has concealed the shock at what Haesychya has revealed. *Was that niece Maeroja?* How could it not be? Yet . . . will he ever know?

"If she was so favored . . . ?" Kyedra frowns, then goes on, "Or was it because she was perhaps too favored?"

Rhamuel hides an amused smile.

Haesychya's expression turns cold for a moment. "We will not guess about such matters. What is of import is that Khesyn wishes to destroy both Duke Kiedron and your father, and all those related to either. I suggest we need not discuss that aspect of matters more."

"As you wish, my dear," replies Atroyan almost affably. "I will ask Lerial his opinion of the Heldyan armsmen, however."

"From what I have seen," Lerial says, "those we have fought in the south, and those who attacked Luba, are likely not the very best of his armsmen. Those who attacked Luba were better than some of those who have harassed Cigoerne, some of whom are from the nomad clans far to the south or from eastern Atla."

"But your father only sent three companies," interjects Natroyor, an interjection so smooth that Lerial has no doubts it was planned, since it is not a question Atroyan would wish to ask himself.

"It is not just the quality of armsmen that Heldya sends against us," replies Lerial. "It is the number. The length of the west bank of the River Swarth that we must defend is almost as long as that which Afrit must defend, and we have far fewer people . . . and, I must admit, we are less prosperous. The Heldyans, if not intercepted immediately, lay waste to hamlets and individual dwellings and cots. Even with the companies we have posted along the river, we are often outnumbered. Fortunately, our men are better trained."

"As I recall," begins Atroyan, fingering his chin as if trying to remember something, "you are what, twenty-two?"

Lerial nods.

"Yet you were sent out as an undercaptain more than six years ago, and you have commanded lancers since then. Is that not so?"

"Yes, ser."

For just a moment, Kyedra's mouth opens, then quickly closes.

"How many men have you killed?" asks Natroyor.

This interruption was clearly not planned, because the heir's mother and father both turn toward him. Even Rhamuel frowns.

Lerial lets the silence draw out for just a moment. "I have no idea. I was sixteen when I killed a Meroweyan raider who attacked me. I fought in pitched battles for two full seasons, generally near or at the front of my company. We fought two small battles or skirmishes at Luba."

"He was at the front there, too," adds Rhamuel.

"Were you . . . wounded?" murmurs Kyedra.

"Not here, and not enough not to recover in Verdheln," Lerial replies lightly.

"The way you say that . . ." ventures Haesychya. "You were seriously wounded, were you not?"

"Without the healers, I would have died in Verdheln." That is true, but not in the way Lerial hopes they will take it.

"Does that satisfy you, Natroyor?" Haesychya's voice is like ice.

"I just wanted to know." Natroyor's reply holds a hint of both sulkiness and defiance.

"Now you do," declares the duke with a heartiness that sounds a trifle forced. "It is about time to have dinner," he announces, if after a glance from his consort. "And we will not talk further about war, or Heldya. Dinner should be for more pleasant topics." His eyes fix on Natroyor. Then he stands.

As Lerial rises, he thinks about the strangeness of the conversation, staged to reveal some things, and yet obviously not totally controlled. All of it reminds him, again, of how careful he needs to be in what he reveals and what he does not.

Following Atroyan's gesture, Lerial walks with the duke across the hallway to the family dining chamber, not all that larger than the salon in the ducal palace in Cigoerne. The duke sits at the head of the table, with Lerial at his right, and Rhamuel at his left. Kyedra is seated beside her uncle, while Natroyor sits beside Lerial. Haesychya sits at the end of the family table, facing her consort. A pleasant smile is on her thin lips, but the chaotic turmoil behind her expression suggests more than a little strain.

Is Natroyor that frail? Or do they worry that he is? Then again, Lerial realizes, Atroyan himself does not appear all that hale and hearty, either. While Rhamuel is healthy, he has no sons, and his only child is Amaira, whose existence may not be known . . . and if known, certainly cannot be accepted. Lerial has heard no word about Mykel, except that he has no consort and no heirs . . . and Haesychya's reaction to the name of his friend.

The other thing is that Haesychya has not been nearly so silent as Lerial has expected, as if he is not quite an outsider. As for Kyedra, she is more perceptive than she lets on . . . and he does like her smile.

The dinner conversation, it is clear, will be light and polite. After the crosscurrents in the salon, Lerial is more than ready for lighter subjects.

XXIV

When he wakes soon after dawn on twoday, Lerial does not rise immediately, but lies in the moderately comfortable bed big enough for three people—or a couple and several children—thinking over the conversations during refreshments and dinner the evening before. The conversation at dinner had been almost exactly as Atroyan had declared, with discussions of several poets that Lerial has never heard of, let alone read; a mock debate between Rhamuel and Atroyan over the merits of their favorite vintages—the hilltop white called Halyn against the Reoman red; and more than a little speculation about what sort of weather the spring and summer to come might bring, along with Haesychya's observation that the spring was already unseasonably warm.

After just that meeting with the duke and his immediate family, Lerial can understand his aunt's concerns about Afrit. Atroyan does not seem all that strong, and Lerial's own impressions of Natroyor are not particularly favorable, and the youth seems constitutionally even weaker than his father. Rhamuel seems to be the most able male of the lot, but the arms-commander seems almost indifferent to the idea of ruling.

Is he just that good at concealing his feelings . . . or is he truly indifferent? Lerial suspects the former, but cannot dismiss the latter.

After washing up, shaving, and dressing, Lerial leaves his rooms and goes to the family dining room for breakfast. There, Rhamuel is seated alone. The arms-commander gestures to the chair across from him.

"Will anyone else be joining us?"

"No. The duke and his immediate family always have breakfast alone in the breakfast room."

"You're not included?"

Rhamuel shakes his head. "Immediate family only. That's a custom of Aenian House. Or so Haesychya informed me many years ago. Fhastal doesn't know anything about it."

Why would Fhastal . . . oh . . . he's consorted to Haesychya's older sister.

The arms-commander sips a mixture of greenberry juice and lager.

Wondering how anyone could drink such a mixture, Lerial merely pours himself a light lager. "I can see family only. That's the case in Cigoerne, but family means all family in residence."

"My brother is very firm about acceding to his consort on that."

And other matters, I'd wager.

"Besides, I'm here so seldom that it's not an issue."

The more reason it should be. But Lerial just nods and takes another swallow of lager. He *is* thirsty. Within moments, or so it seems, a server appears with a large platter of egg toast and ham strips, accompanied by a generous loaf of dark bread, rare indeed in Cigoerne. He takes several bites before speaking. "Can you tell me any more about the dinner this evening?"

"It will be small. There will be between ten and fifteen men, all important in Swartheld. Mostly merchanters, except for the duke and you and me. The official purpose will be to convey to them how decisively we defeated the Heldyans at Luba. Even though they all know it, and knew it within less than a day."

"We did," says Lerial, "but . . ."

Rhamuel raises his eyebrows and tilts his head. "But?"

"All the survivors took the flatboats downstream, and I'd wager they're all at Estheld . . . or somewhere close."

"I won't take that wager . . . and I won't point out that nine out of ten Heldyans who fought Ascaar and Drusyn's battalions survived, while perhaps two out of ten of those who fought you did."

"So . . . how many battalions do you think Khesyn has massed across the river?"

"Fifteen battalions."

Seventy-five fairly well-trained companies. "Assuming he does attack Swartheld, just how will he get them across the river?"

"The same way he did at Luba. He'll most likely launch the flatboats upstream and use the current to cross. If I were trying to do that, I'd ground them in the shallow water off the point of the old river fort. The first attackers would get wet enough, but they could pull the boats farther in. The later attackers could walk from boat to boat."

"Is that why Drusyn's battalions are at South Post?"

"I told Commander Nythalt and the duke that we needed to protect the harbor from both ends."

"I imagine that's true enough," replies Lerial evenly. "I heard that Commander Nythalt has seven battalions. Are they all at the Harbor Post?"

"Six are there. One is at South Post, with Subcommander Drusyn's battalions."

"So . . . if that's likely . . . ?"

"Why don't I put men there? The place is a ruin, and Khesyn could wait eightdays . . . or longer. If I rebuild there, it costs golds the duke doesn't have, and then Khesyn might just attack the harbor directly. The currents might even carry the flatboats that far anyway. South Post is only a bit more than two kays away, and the river watch will give us time to alert Drusyn."

There is something Rhamuel isn't saying. After a moment, Lerial realizes what that is. Rhamuel cannot allow Khesyn's forces to attack the harbor proper, at least not first, and he cannot position his forces to make the harbor and the merchanting areas a more favorable target. "You want him to land at the point."

"Of course. He can do less damage there."

"But he can also establish a stronger position there."

"There are advantages and disadvantages to every position."

Lerial nods. That was the way the majer thought. "Did you ever talk with Majer Altyrn?"

"Regrettably, I did not. I was younger and more arrogant." Rhamuel smiles. "You are less so than most successful young commanders, but you will also see what I came to see. The majer had to have done that also."

"I would hope to learn from what I could have done better." *As if your failures already have not cost too many lives.*

A hint of a frown flickers across the arms-commander's face.

"You never did say what the unofficial and real reason for the dinner was."

"What do you think?"

"To show the possibility that hostilities between Cigoerne and Afrit have come to an end and that trade will be better . . . or that Afrit can now devote itself to dealing with Heldya without worrying about Cigoerne."

"That's close enough. It won't even be stated. Your presence will imply it." Rhamuel swallows the last of his lager and greenberry. "I'll be leaving shortly. You can certainly wander through the palace. Well . . . except for the part Dafaal insists on refurbishing. That's taken forever, but I suppose it's because my brother insists they only work in the middle of the day. Or you can accompany me back to Swartheld Post."

"I'd thought to check on my companies there."

"I'll meet you at the stables. You can return to the palace when you want. I'll assign half a squad as an escort for your return. It will take some time for people—and the palace guard—to get used to seeing Mirror Lancers here in Swartheld." The arms-commander eases back his chair and stands.

So does Lerial. "I appreciate that."

"It's the least I can do. You've come all the way here."

As he watches the arms-commander leave, Lerial ponders the clear sincerity behind Rhamuel's words, a sincerity that concerns him more than a glib tone would have. He reaches down and lifts his beaker, finishing the lager before returning to his quarters and immediately finding Polidaar.

"Ser?"

"We're headed back to Swartheld Post with the arms-commander. We'll likely be there all morning and some of the afternoon. I want you and your men to study the city as we ride through it. They need to look at everything. What do they see that's the same as in Cigoerne? What's not?" Lerial grins. "And not just the women."

Polidaar tries to hide a smile, but does not succeed. "Yes, ser. Are you looking for something?"

Lerial shakes his head. "No. Not exactly. Call it a feeling. But I don't know enough even to point out what might tell us something." He shrugs. "Then, I might be too cautious, and what you and they see might tell me that. Anyway, ten more pair of eyes can't hurt."

"No, ser."

Polidaar has the squad at the stables quickly enough that they can saddle and lead out their mounts—and Lerial's—in time not to delay Rhamuel.

Lerial rides beside the arms-commander as they leave the inner courtyard and then the smaller outer one. Once they are on the paved road around the palace's outer walls, Rhamuel turns south, seemingly away from Guard headquarters, rather than east or north.

At Lerial's quizzical look, the arms-commander says, "It's quicker this way. One block down this street and we'll reach the old merchants' way. It's wider. It also goes straight—mostly—to headquarters."

Lerial studies the dwellings bordering the street, not so narrow as some of the ways they took the day before, but still not all that wide. He cannot help but wonder why Rhamuel had taken a longer way then. He pushes that aside for the moment and concentrates on his surroundings. For all their ornate stone facings and their two and three levels and red tile roofs, the dwellings are narrow for their height, perhaps as little as ten yards across and barely separated from their neighbors, with tiny front courtyards behind iron gates. At the same time, those dwellings extend more than three times their width back from the street and may have larger walled rear courtyards beyond that.

Who would live here? Since he can see no one outside, and filmy curtains cloak the inside of the windows, there is no way to tell, except that whoever does inhabit the large dwellings cannot be poor.

As Rhamuel has said, at the end of the single long block is a wider street, perhaps almost expansive enough to be called an avenue. The arms-commander turns his mount left, toward the water, and Lerial and the lancers and guards follow. There are no dwellings of any sort, just shops and cafés. Every few doors, or so it seems to Lerial, there is a café with an awning out over small tables and chairs at which a few people are eating . . . or drinking. He looks back over his shoulder for a moment and discovers that the shops extend for at least a block or two uphill as well.

Most of those at the cafés are men, but one is frequented by women alone, all wearing their filmy head scarves, if loosely enough to sip whatever may be in their tumblers or goblets. One café has both men and head-scarfed women. The number of empty tables suggests that there will be more patrons later in the day, and a great deal more by evening, Lerial suspects. The shops and cafés continue for three long blocks, but by the fourth block shops and smaller factorages have replaced the cafés, except for one, its lonely and slightly tattered orange awning extended above empty chairs and tables. By then Lerial can see the walls of Swartheld Post ahead.

Before long, they turn onto the bay road and then ride into the post.

After they dismount at the Afritan Guard headquarters, Lerial turns to

Rhamuel. "I don't want to go behind your back. I'd like two of my officers to ride to the palace and then back with your escort so that they have a better idea of Swartheld. If you're amenable, we could take a longer route."

Rhamuel nods, with the hint of a smile, before he replies. "That would be a good idea. It wouldn't hurt to have people see more of you and your men, either. I'll mention that to the squad leader."

"Thank you."

"If I don't see you before then, I'll see you at the duke's reception before dinner. It's at sixth glass in the west wing of the palace. Until then." With a smile Rhamuel turns and hands his mount's reins to a guard, then walks toward the door of the headquarters building.

Lerial is about to ask Polidaar to send someone to find his officers when he sees the three walking toward him. Instead, he says, "You can have the men stand down and stable their mounts."

"Yes, ser."

"Overcaptain, ser!" calls out Fheldar.

"All's well, I trust." Lerial hands the reins of his gelding to the nearest ranker and moves to join the three.

"Yes, ser."

Strauxyn and Kusyl nod in agreement with Fheldar.

Lerial draws the three aside, waiting until Polidaar has the half squad moving toward the stables, then asks, "What have you to report?" He looks to Fheldar.

"Eighth Company is all accounted for. No illnesses, and no trouble with mounts . . ."

Lerial listens.

Once he has gone over the routine matters with Fheldar, Strauxyn, and Kusyl, and is satisfied that all is as it should be—or at least as close to that as possible in Swartheld—Lerial clears his throat. "There is one other thing. The arms-commander has told me that there are possibly fifteen Heldyan battalions across the river."

"Frig . . ." mutters Kusyl, "begging your pardon, ser."

Lerial offers a crooked smile. "I feel the same way. So does the arms-commander. But we don't know Swartheld at all. So . . . the next thing we're going to do is to inspect Swartheld Post. Then, after that, two of you will accompany me and the two half squads that will escort us around parts of Swartheld and back to the palace. I think we should be able to do this every day for the next two or three days, and I'll rotate who accompanies me, because I want one of you here all the time."

"That makes sense," says Strauxyn. "Who do you want today?"

"Kusyl and Fheldar."

All three nod.

"Now . . . let's see about inspecting the post."

By the time the four of them have finished their informal inspection of Swartheld headquarters two glasses have passed, and Lerial gathers the three into an empty study in the main headquarters building, where they sit around a dusty table desk. He looks at Fheldar. "What do you think?"

"It's clean enough. Nothing's coming apart. I don't think you could close the main gates all the way, either."

"Wouldn't matter if you had to," adds Kusyl. "Not for long. They had to bring in provisions just to feed us. Really isn't a working post. Just a headquarters post."

To keep Rhamuel away from the palace?

"Ah . . ." Strauxyn clears his throat. "The armory is stocked. We didn't go there because it was locked, but I talked to one of the undercaptains this morning. I saw him with one of their blades. They're longer than ours. It looked new-forged. I asked. All the spare blades and weapons for the entire Afritan Guard are stored here."

That makes all too much sense . . . unfortunately. "Under the watchful eyes of the arms-commander or his trusted majer or captains."

"That smells, too," declares Kusyl. "Another thing . . . they've got blade-training circles, but they haven't been used, maybe in years."

"Not a fighting post." Fheldar shakes his head.

"In a way, that makes sense," Lerial says. "It's in the middle of the city. That's why most of the Afritan Guard is posted on the north or south side of Swartheld. We'll see what the Harbor Post looks like in a bit . . ."

Outside of more details that confirm the impressions of all four, the discussion that follows adds little to Lerial's understanding and concerns.

Less than three glasses after riding out with Rhamuel, Lerial sends word to Polidaar and Jhacub, the squad leader whom Rhamuel has assigned to head the Afritan Guards serving as the day's escort for Lerial.

When they both arrive, Lerial addresses Jhacub. "We haven't seen much of the city. Could we take a longer route back to the palace, perhaps riding by the harbor, the Harbor Post, and the trading area?"

The squad leader grins. "Yes, ser. The arms-commander said you'd be doing that. He said to escort you wherever you needed to go."

"I hope that won't inconvenience you or the men. It might add quite some time."

"No, ser. It's a good change." Jhacub pauses. "That'll likely take a glass. Maybe longer. The men wouldn't mind that. Is that satisfactory, ser?"

More than satisfactory. "That will be fine." Lerial mounts, as do Kusyl and Fheldar.

From the gates of the post, Jhacub guides Lerial and the others northwest along the road that parallels the shore. There are several cafés west of the road, but none are apparently open, and their awnings are rolled up.

"Those open in the late afternoon?" Lerial gestures.

"They do. They'll be pleased that your men are posted here. There used to be more than the two companies that took care of the post and headquarters."

"When did that change?"

"Five years ago . . . it was after . . . well . . ." Jhacub looks embarrassed.

"After the Afritan Guard lost an entire battalion in an ill-advised attack on Cigoerne, you mean?"

"Ah . . . yes, ser."

"Did anyone say why?"

"I don't know, ser. I was just a ranker then. No one said anything to us."

"What about this part of Swartheld?"

"It's not what it used to be, ser."

Lerial can see that. A number of the small buildings look to be empty, with shuttered doors and windows, with the wooden sidewalks in front of them sagging. "Because there are fewer guards posted here?"

"I don't think that's the only thing, ser." After several moments, Jhacub adds, "In another kay we'll enter the merchanting area. That's after where the shore road joins the boulevard from the palace."

After riding past almost a half score more blocks of less-than-well-maintained buildings and a few dilapidated dwellings, Lerial notices that the upkeep of the structures on the west side of the road improves notably and that there are solid if short stone and timber piers extending into the bay. Several have boats tied there.

Three blocks later the shore road merges into a wide stone-paved boulevard.

"That's what they call the palace boulevard," says the squad leader. "It goes right to the circular road around the palace."

The best avenue or street you've seen, and it runs straight from the merchanting houses to the palace.

A block later the boulevard begins a wide curve more toward the north, again following the shoreline of the bay.

"This is where the merchanting area and the harbor begin," offers Jhacub.

The merchanting quarter opposite the main piers definitely represents wealth. The shore road and the palace boulevard have combined into a paved avenue wide enough for three large wagons side by side. Even the sidewalks are of stone, not of wooden planks or brick. All of the buildings have glazed windows and heavy shutters.

"Do you happen to know which one of the buildings holds Aenian House?" Lerial asks Jhacub.

"Yes, ser. You can't miss it. See the big three-story one in the next block, with the redstone front and the banners flying from those false towers?"

"I do. Is that it?" Lerial has no trouble picking out the merchanting house. Even from more than a block away, it dominates the other merchanters' buildings, none of which are modest.

As the combined squad rides north on the avenue that also serves as the river road, past the first of the enormous stone piers, each of which extends more than two hundred yards out into the harbor, Lerial takes in the buildings one by one. The first in the block holding Aenian House is older, of gray stone and less than fifteen yards across the front. Chiseled into the stone are the words FINE SPIRITS. Above those words the stone is smooth and recessed, as if a name had been chiseled away. Lerial wonders if Mesphaes has taken over an older merchanting house, of if the building is owned by a competitor who also replaced someone. The next building is of yellow-brown brick, and is twice the size of the spirits building, but without identification, as if to indicate that none is needed. The redstone-fronted House of Aenian is not identified as such, although there is a stone medallion in the middle of the third level, between two windows, consisting of an ornate script "A" encircled by a wreath of leaves, possibly olive leaves, Lerial thinks. A paved lane wide enough for the largest of wagons leads along the west side of the Aenian building, between it and the unidentified structure. The building to the east of Aenian House is also of yellow-brown brick, but with redstone window frames, and is perhaps a third larger than the spirits building and is the last building on the block.

Lerial turns his attention to the piers. He counts almost a score of vessels tied up at the various piers, ranging from a large schooner to an enormous broad-beamed, three-masted square-rigger. He thinks there may be some smaller ships at the piers farther north, but, if so, they are lost behind the nearer ships.

"The harbor fort's up there, ser," announces Jhacub, pointing ahead, partway up the slope of a gentle bluff that extends almost a kay out into the bay and forms a huge natural breakwater on the north end of the harbor. It is also at the end of a wide paved road off the avenue that appears to revert to what Lerial now thinks of as the shore road. That shore road does not go out around the point of the bluff, but northwest across its base.

Lerial turns to Jhacub. "Does the shore road continue beyond the bluff?"

"Yes, ser. It goes all the way to Baiet."

"How far is that?"

"I wouldn't know exactly, sir. Two or three days' ride, I hear. Small cove. Fishermen mostly. They port there, but sell their catch here."

"Do you know why?"

"They say the fishing's better there, but the selling's better here."

They continue to ride along the paved avenue, where the larger merchanting houses have given way to more modest factorages—modest by comparison, since most are built of the yellow-brown brick and are considerably larger than any in Cigoerne, reflects Lerial. It does strike him that all the roofs are of the red tile and he says so.

"Yes, ser. After the Great Fire, the duke's great-grandsire made it a law. That's what they say."

"That makes sense." *Too much sense.*

"Yes, ser. Hasn't been a large fire since."

The Harbor Post is the largest walled fortification that Lerial has ever seen, not counting Lubana, which really isn't a post, with walls extending a half kay in each direction, and iron-bound gates inset between stout redstone towers. With its hillside location, Lerial doubts that even Khesyn's fifteen battalions could take it.

But then, they wouldn't have to. If they took the harbor, they'd just have to surround it and wait.

"Do you want to look into the post?"

Lerial shakes his head. "We're just trying to get a better idea of where everything is. We can turn around and head back toward the palace. Can we take the avenue back?"

"Yes, ser. It's the best way."

Jhacub's assessment of the route proves most accurate. The palace boulevard is paved and smooth. Well-appointed if smaller factorages and shops, as well as occasional cafés, line it for perhaps a kay, then give way to modest but neatly maintained single-level dwellings.

About a kay and a half southwest from the harbor piers on the boulevard, Lerial notes another wide avenue joining the boulevard. "Where does that go?"

"To merchanters' hill. Well . . . that's what they call it. It's where all the wealthiest merchanters have their villas."

Lerial looks back more intently. There are indeed several large structures on the hillside.

"You can't see most of them," adds the squad leader. "They planted the tall trees for shade. There's a good breeze off the ocean that high, too."

Lerial nods without speaking.

The rest of the ride to the palace takes them past more modest dwellings, except for the last few hundred yards, which are crowded with small shops and a number of cafés. At that moment, Lerial realizes that he has not seen anything resembling an inn—anywhere. He turns to Jhacub again. "I haven't seen any inns. Are there any?"

"Yes, sir. There's plenty, just not where we've been. Law says that no inn can be on the shore road or any main avenue, like the palace road or the old merchants' way."

"Don't tell me. Another whim of a former duke?"

"Couldn't say, ser. Just know that's the law. Always been that way."

Because of the duke . . . or the merchanters? Another question for which he would like an answer, and there are getting to be far too many of those, Lerial feels.

Before all that long, Lerial is reining up outside the palace stable—the one assigned to him and his men. Before dismounting he turns to the Afritan squad leader. "Thank you for the tour, Jhacub. I appreciate all for the information, and if you would, please convey my thanks and appreciation to your men as well."

"Yes, ser." Jhacub pauses meaningfully.

"Yes? You have a question? Ask. After all those I've asked you . . ."

"I was just thinking, ser. You speak Hamorian. You speak better than most officers, the way the arms-commander does. But you're from Cigoerne."

"My grandmere and my father insisted that all his children would speak perfect Hamorian as well as Cyadoran. That's why. It's necessary. Many"—*most*—"people in Cigoerne don't speak Cyadoran."

"Hadn't thought of that, ser. Thank you, ser."

"Thank you, again, Jhacub."

"My pleasure, ser."

Lerial dismounts, then watches the half squad of Afritan Guards ride back toward the outer courtyard. By half past third glass, Lerial is back in his quarters—if after refreshing his shields before entering and checking the room for errant chaos, of which he finds no sign. Once there he removes the road dust from his uniform and washes up. Then he steps out into the corridor to find Polidaar waiting.

"Ser . . . will you . . ."

"No escort. I won't be leaving the palace. But I would appreciate someone watching my door. I wouldn't want to return to any surprises."

"We can do that, ser."

As he leaves his rooms, Lerial has a specific initial destination in mind: the duke's library, also on the third level but on the north end of the west wing of the palace. He would like to see if there is a code of laws or something similar there. Once more, as he walks the seemingly endless hallways, he sees servants and palace guards here and there, but far fewer than he would expect in an edifice the size of the palace.

A palace guard is seated at a table desk outside the library. He looks at Lerial warily for a moment, then nods abruptly. "Lord Lerial?"

"The same. I just wanted to look at the library, if I might."

"Yes, ser."

"Thank you." Lerial nods politely, then steps past the table and opens the door, stepping into the library and closing the door behind himself. For a moment, he just stands there, surveying the room.

The duke's library is an oblong chamber some ten yards by seven, with an alcove at one end that holds a table desk. Comfortable-looking leather armchairs are located here and there, sometimes alone, and in one place with a low table separating a pair. Two walls are filled with wooden shelves from a third of a yard off the floor almost to the ceiling, some three yards up.

Lerial counts the volumes on one section of shelving, then estimates how many similar lengths there are in the library and mentally calculates. *Some twenty-five hundred volumes.* That's certainly the largest collection of books he has ever seen in one place, although Emerya has assured him that there had been more than ten thousand in the great library in the Palace of Light.

Are they in any order? He begins to inspect the volumes on the shelves, discovering that while the area on the shelves in front of the books has been dusted, as have the tops of the pages, there is considerable dust behind each of the first score of books he removes from the shelves to inspect and see the subject, since most of the spines do not have a title. After a time, more than a glass, he does discover that one area holds histories, and another observations on nature, a third books on philosophy, and a rather larger section dealing with maps and map folios, with some that must be several hundred years old. While there are some volumes on practical healing, there is nothing on the use of order to heal. Nor can he find any section that deals with law, or even a single volume that does. But then, it would take him several more glasses, if not longer, just to take a quick look inside every volume in the library.

Abruptly, he hears voices, and he quickly raises a concealment, then moves toward the alcove.

Two figures step into the library.

"I don't see anyone . . ." murmurs the woman, Kyedra, Lerial belatedly identifies from her voice, since his order-senses are not nearly so sharp as his vision.

"The guard said he was somewhere here . . ."

". . . what can he do but look . . . besides, he seems pleasant enough . . . and good-looking."

"Except for that awful red hair." Natroyor's scorn is withering

". . . quiet. He'll hear you . . . unruly . . . sometimes, yours is, too . . ."

Lerial gathers that he is obviously meant to hear some of what he does, although it is also clear that Kyedra and Natroyor have differing motives . . . or at least differing approaches. He steps into the alcove and then drops the concealment before stepping out, holding the last volume he has inspected—*Natural Remedies of Afrit.* "You were looking for me? I'm sorry. I was reading this."

"What is it?" asks Kyedra, stepping toward him.

"A book on natural remedies. I wondered if there might be anything that would help with field healing." Lerial smiles. "What can I do for you?"

"Actually," replies Kyedra, "Father realized that he had not provided the details for this evening. He asked us to convey to you that the reception before the dinner will be in the west public hall beginning at sixth glass, and he would hope you would meet him at his study a tenth of a glass before that . . ."

"That is most kind of you. Your uncle had told me about the time of the reception, but not that I was to meet your father before then."

"He wouldn't have known that," says Natroyor blandly.

Lerial can sense Kyedra stiffen, but she manages a pleasant expression and says, "They're so busy that they don't always tell each other everything."

"Especially now, I imagine," returns Lerial.

"Is it true that you've really killed hundreds of men?" asks Natroyor.

"I might have killed a score or more with my sabre," replies Lerial, "but the forces under my command have killed thousands, not hundreds."

"Your sire has let you be in the thick of battle? He really has?"

"It's better that I am than he is."

"Your brother hasn't been in battles as dangerous as those you've been in, has he?" asks Kyedra.

Lerial understands what she wants him to say, but the plain truth she wishes for her brother's sake will undermine Lephi . . . and possibly Cigoerne. "You put me in a delicate position, Lady. I have no idea what dangers he's faced. He's certainly led his companies against Heldyan raiders for years, and men under his command have died in front of and beside him. He's been fortunate not to have been one of them, as I have been. My father, my brother, and I have all led Mirror Lancers in skirmishes and battles." Lerial doubts Lephi has ever been in a battle, but the rest in certainly absolutely true, although, thankfully, it has been years since his father has done so.

"But there are three of you."

"That's true, but we've never fought at the same time or in the same place." That . . . he can acknowledge.

"You see," Kyedra says to her brother. "That's why Uncle Rham can be arms-commander, and you cannot."

"I don't have to like it," replies Natroyor.

"No, you don't," says Lerial, "but you do have to do the best you can do at the tasks your father needs done. Some of those tasks, now, may just be to learn all you can about what he does, how he does it, and why."

"It's so tedious . . ."

"Learning the basics is tedious," replies Lerial, "even in the Mirror Lancers, but without mastering the basics, excellence isn't possible. Most people don't have the will to keep at it, and that's why so few are truly good at anything."

"I suppose you're the exception." Natroyor's reply is just short of a sneer.

"I was black and blue almost all the time for almost two years when I was learning blade skills. That was after more than four years of even more basic training with wooden wands. I suppose there must be exceptions, but I don't know of any." Lerial smiles. "Thank you for conveying your father's message. If I'm to meet him, I should be getting ready." He inclines his head. "I look forward to seeing you soon."

"You're kind," replies Kyedra, but Natroyor barely nods.

"Not kind. Truthful." Lerial looks directly at Kyedra, if but for an instant. "Until then."

Lerial turns and leaves the library, moving quickly away from the guard, but looking back occasionally until the guard turns his head. Then at the moment when he can see no one else around, he raises a concealment and waits.

Because the two do not appear immediately, he wonders what they might be discussing, but when they appear, walking past the guard without nodding, both are silent. Lerial remains motionless until they pass him, hidden in his concealment, then moves to follow them, walking as quietly as he can.

". . . almost rude . . . the way he took his leave . . ." Natroyor snorts.

"You were insolent, and you know it. He was quite restrained. From what Uncle Rham says, he might be the best commander in all Hamor."

"It doesn't excuse his behavior. I am the heir."

"He's an heir also. Have you thought about that?"

"He's second in line. He'll never be duke."

"You never know. You were second once."

"That's different."

Kyedra is silent for a time as the two walk along the corridor back to the east wing of the palace.

"You like him, don't you?" asks Natroyor abruptly, then continues, "That doesn't matter. You'll have to consort his older brother. Or Khesyn's grandson. They're the heirs. If anyone asks at all. Father won't let you consort a younger son. Neither will Mother. Or Grandpapa Aenslem. Besides, you don't even know if he likes you."

"Do you like being cruel, Natroyor?" Kyedra's voice is low, but not gentle.

"You'll see what I like. You will."

Kyedra remains silent as the two continue toward the east wing.

Since neither is talking, Lerial slips away as they take the main marble staircase up to the fourth level and then drops the concealment before making his way back to his quarters, not that he needs that much time to ready himself, but he has not had a chance to talk to Polidaar.

The squad leader appears as Lerial nears his quarters. "Ser?"

"Nothing's amiss, is it?"

"No, ser."

"Good. We need to talk." Lerial opens the door to his sitting room and motions for Polidaar to join him.

The comparatively young squad leader is hesitant, but then steps inside.

Lerial closes the door and takes a seat, gesturing to one of the chairs. He can see that Polidaar has seldom been in such quarters, perhaps only these quarters and only to inspect them . . . and possibly he is worried that he may receive some critical words. Once the squad leader sits, only on the front of the chair, Lerial smiles warmly, then asks, "Have you had a chance to talk to your men about what they've seen and what they think about Swartheld?"

"Yes, ser."

Lerial nods and waits.

"Well . . . ah . . . they all think it's not that clean a place. That's excepting the fancy merchanting part of the palace road." The squad leader offers a lopsided grin. "I know you said . . . about the women . . . but they've never seen a place with so few women on the streets, and all of them are . . . well dressed."

Completely covered, you mean . . . or more so than in Cigoerne? "I have to say I noticed that as well. What else."

"The Afritan Guards aren't as well disciplined, either, and they talk . . . when they think no one's listening . . . maybe because they don't realize most of our rankers speak Hamorian. And . . . well . . . what they say about their officers . . . ah . . . you wouldn't like it, ser."

"They can say what they want, just so long as our rankers don't . . . or our officers don't give our men reason to speak that way."

"No, ser . . . I mean, yes, sir . . ."

"Go on."

"It's just little things. One of the men saw a peddler whipping a boy so hard his back was bloody. Everyone just turned away. No dogs, either. I like dogs, ser. Grew up and used them for keeping the herd in line. You see dogs in any hamlet in Cigoerne . . . and in the city. I haven't seen a one here in Swartheld. And the people. They'd give us a look and they just turn away. Not like they were afraid. Like they just didn't care. Even the children."

After Polidaar leaves, Lerial walks to the window, thinking. *The people pay no attention to the Afritan Guard. . . . . or us . . . and no dogs in Swartheld? What does that all mean . . . if anything? And is what the Guard rankers have said about their officers the way it was in Cyador before the end? Or worse, for all Polidaar is denying, do they talk that way about Lancer officers now?* There certainly have been some, like Veraan, who was forced out and is now a trader, or Captain Dechund, who was a traitor. Even Majer Phortyn . . . *But they were only a few. Still . . .* He shakes his head.

Then there is what little he has overheard between Kyedra and her brother. The more he sees and hears of Natroyor, the more appalled he is that the spoiled youth is the heir to the duchy. Lerial has had his problems with Lephi, but Lephi is without faults compared to Natroyor. As for Kyedra . . . *She seems smarter and far nicer than her brother. She has a smile that lights up her face . . .* He frowns. *Does she agree with what Natroyor said about your hair?* That shouldn't bother him, but it does, at least a little.

He has to admit that he's more impressed with Kyedra and her mother than with either Atroyan or Natroyor. *But you haven't seen enough yet . . .* He smiles wryly. He has seen and heard enough about Natroyor, but he needs to reserve judgment on the duke. Anyone who's managed to hold power for so many years with all the merchanter scheming has to have more abilities that he's revealed.

Lerial washes up and uses a damp cloth to freshen up his uniform as well as he can . . . then frowns. Surely, he can get his uniforms cleaned . . . but no one has even mentioned that. *It's probably assumed.*

He shakes his head, walks to the door, and looks to the duty guard. "If you'd pass on to the squad leader . . . have him find out what we need to do to get our uniforms cleaned."

"Yes, ser."

"Thank you."

After waiting a bit more, Lerial sets out for the duke's study. He arrives promptly and is immediately ushered in.

Atroyan, wearing what Lerial thinks must be the formal crimson uniform of the Afritan Guard, rises from behind the wide—and empty—table desk. He frowns. "No dress uniform?"

"I didn't anticipate coming to Swartheld, ser. Then, it was rather late to send for a dress uniform."

"Well . . . no one will be able to tell for certain." The duke straightens. "We should go. Oh . . . before I forget. There is another function tomorrow evening. You'll get a formal invitation later. Seventh glass. Now . . . how are you finding Swartheld?" He walks to the study door.

"Besides rather larger than Cigoerne? There are a number of differences. You have an excellent deepwater harbor and a much more extensive merchanting quarter. The palace is enormous. Your consort is most gracious, and you've certainly been welcoming. My men are well housed and well fed." Lerial almost says something about what else he could ask for, but catches himself. He still wonders about the "other function."

"Good. Good."

"Might I ask who will be attending the reception and dinner?"

"Oh . . . I told you it would be the most important merchanters, and, of course, my brother the arms-commander."

"You did, ser, but since I am not from Afrit and know almost nothing about Swartheld, I have no idea who the most important merchanters might be."

"So you wouldn't. So you wouldn't. Let's see. The most important is Aenslem. He's the head of the Merchanting Council, not to mention Haesychya's father. Then there's Maesoryk; he has most of the kilns in Afrit, the good ones, everything from fine porcelain to . . . well . . . chamber pots. I think you may have met Mesphaes . . . no?"

"I met him in Shaelt."

"He's one of the few who's not from Swartheld, but since Rhamuel said he'd be at his place here, nothing to compare to his villa in Shaelt, I hear, I thought he should be present . . ."

Rhamuel must have arranged that . . .

". . . and then there's Alaphyn . . . he's mostly a shipper, not so many vessels as Aenslem, but more than anyone else. As a matter of fact, there's not really anyone else . . . and, I almost forgot, there's Lhugar. He has the largest interest in the ironworks at Luba . . ."

Lerial nods and listens to other names he hopes he can remember while they walk down the main staircase of the east wing of the palace.

When they near the reception room, Atroyan says, "Get a glass or beaker of what you want first. You likely won't have a chance later, not without appearing rude, or having to accept whatever someone thrusts at you."

There are already several men in the reception room; the only two Lerial recognizes are Rhamuel and Mesphaes. Like his brother, Rhamuel wears a dress uniform without rank insignia. Neither the arms-commander nor the spirits merchanter moves toward the duke or Lerial. The two other men in the room, attired in formal overtunics, one of a deep blue, the other of a muted maroon, immediately turn to face Atroyan, nodding and even bowing slightly. "Duke Atroyan . . ."

At the two approach, Lerial has the feeling that he is a bit underdressed for the occasion. *But who would have thought . . .* Except his mother had hinted at it. Still, the thought of packing a dress uniform off to battle . . .

"Merchanter Lhugar, Merchanter Nahaan . . . might I present you to Lord Lerial? He's not only the younger heir to Cigoerne, but a most effective commander of Mirror Lancers who did us the signal honor of wiping out a battalion or so of Heldyan invaders and driving even more back to Heldya. At Luba, you know."

Both merchanters nod.

Then Nahaan smiles apologetically, and without a word Atroyan walks toward the sideboard serving wine, Nahaan at his elbow.

"What will you be drinking, Lord Lerial?" asks Lhugar.

"Pale lager." Lerial notes that the merchanter's hands are empty. "Will you join me?"

"Naturally."

Once Lerial has a pale lager and Lhugar a very dark brew, the two stand before an open window, through which blows a slight, but welcome, breeze.

"You're in ironworks, if I heard the duke correctly."

"More accurately, *we're* in ironworks. The ducal family has a four-tenths interest in the ironworks my family and his own and that we operate."

"Oh . . . I didn't know that."

"Most people don't, but it's no secret."

In a fashion, that makes sense, Lerial thinks, especially in a land of merchanters, which Afrit certainly is. "You just smelt and process the iron into lengths and plates, then, and sell it to others?"

"We do pig iron, plates, and rods. The only finished things we sell are nails. Everyone needs nails."

"You don't have any iron-mages, then?"

Lhugar smiles and shakes his head. "There's no need, unless you want black iron, and not many do. Besides, mages are rare in Afrit. Always have been. There's not much sense in spending golds to make something almost no one wants. Your sire likely has more iron-mages than all the rest of Hamor." He pauses. "I'd wager you don't arm your lancers with black-iron blades."

"You're right about that," Lerial replies lightly. "I don't know that anyone else does, either."

"Cupridium's another thing. Can your iron-mages work it?"

Why is he interested in cupridium? It's really only useful for weapons for chaos-mages and white wizards . . . or for blocking chaos-fire . . . or the chaos-lances that we can't even build anymore. "I suppose they could. It takes so much effort to make it, though, that it's seldom used anymore. Might I ask . . . ?"

"There are always those who are interested. Your father got quite a few golds for what he sold when he dismantled that old fireship. Quite a few. Probably more than he collected in tariffs for years. If people want something, it never hurts to see if it's available." Lhugar pauses as another merchanter approaches, then says, "If ever . . . I can get a good price for it."

"I'll keep that in mind."

"Lord Lerial, Khamyst." The newly arrived merchanter wears an overtunic of a green so dark it verges on black.

"I'm pleased to meet you, Khamyst." Even repeating the man's name doesn't recall anything for Lerial.

"The duke won't have mentioned me, and you'd have no reason to know who I am."

Lerial smiles as winningly as he can. "Then you must give me one."

"Well said. I will. I'm the one everyone needs and everyone wants to forget. We're the ones who handle rendering and tallow and candles and hides and leather. We do it well away from Swartheld so that no one suffers."

"And you do it well and are paid well," suggests Lerial.

"Well enough to belong to the Merchanting Council."

Lerial nods, not sure exactly what he should say.

"Most people think of tallow for poor folk's candles, but a lot of what we render goes to Lhugar's plate mills."

Lerial has no idea what Khamyst means, and it must show, because the merchanter grins and adds, "It keeps the rollers from seizing up."

Lhugar has rolling mills? Lerial had thought the only mills like that had been lost with the fall of Cyador.

"Have to admit, Lhugar stole the idea—well, his grandsire did—from Cyador. Not fancy, the way those were, but somehow they got it to work."

"Trying to corner Lord Lerial, are you, Khamyst?" asks yet another merchanter, holding a full goblet of a dark red wine.

Lerial realizes that he has not even taken a sip of his lager, and does so, before looking to the pudgy and short blond man likely not more than a handful of years older than Lerial himself. "He's been most polite, and you are?"

"Haensyn."

"Haensyn represents the House of Haen . . ." begins Khamyst.

". . . since his mother is not properly a merchanter," murmurs Lhugar.

Lerial only hopes he can keep everything straight in his mind, but smiles and nods once more.

Before that long, but not before Lerial has exchanged pleasantries with three other merchanters, a set of chimes rings, presumably to announce the time for the dinner itself. As the merchanters move toward the dining room, Rhamuel appears, seemingly out of nowhere, although Lerial has not seen him except at the beginning of the reception, talking to Mesphaes. "How did your ride through Swartheld go?"

"Through a small portion of Swartheld," Lerial replies with a laugh. "It was useful to learn where things are. I do have a question, though."

"Yes?"

"How did your great-grandsire come up with the idea of requiring tile roofs for every dwelling and building in Swartheld?"

"Fires," replies Rhamuel. "So we were told when we were boys. After the merchanting quarter burned down—that's why all the buildings there are so well planned and the avenue is wider and paved—after that, he issued the law. Every new building had to have a tile roof, and all factorages and shops that didn't already have tile roofs had to reroof with tile in two years. Houses had from five to ten years, depending on where they were."

"It sounds like he thought it out."

"He did, but not that way. He'd borrowed golds to pay the Guard because he'd kept tariffs low to please the merchants. After the fire, he couldn't depend on tariffs to repay the golds. So he issued the law."

"He borrowed the golds from the merchanters who made the tiles?"

"No, but he could tariff the tiles, and the law made it certain that the tariffs were sufficient to cover the payments." Rhamuel shakes his head. "After the merchanters recovered, he did raise all tariffs. He died within the year, but our grandsire only reduced the tariffs a pittance."

"And Maesoryk is still benefiting from the law?"

"So is everyone else," replies Rhamuel almost sardonically as they enter the dining room. "Swartheld hasn't had any large fires since." He nods toward the table. "You're on his right."

"And you're on the left?"

"Always." After a moment, Rhamuel murmurs, "Aenslem will be beside you, and Maesoryk across from you."

Lerial stands behind his chair until everyone is in position. Then Atroyan seats himself, followed by everyone else. Lerial notes that Lhugar is beside Aenslem, and another merchanter Lerial has not seen before, a heavy-lidded but narrow-faced man with thinning brown hair whose strands droop across a high forehead, is beside Maesoryk.

Once everyone has a full goblet or crystal beaker, Atroyan clears his throat. He does not stand, but lifts his goblet. "I'd like to thank you all for coming, and for doing so with little notice. On the other hand, it may be the only time in your lives where you can have dinner with not only a duke, but two younger sons to duchies . . . and, no offense to either, but I'd prefer they remain younger sons." He pauses to allow a few chuckles to subside. "I'm always mindful of what makes a land strong, particularly Afrit, and that's the skill and devotion of those who pay the tariffs to support the harbor and the river patrols, and the Afritan Guard. My brother, of course, is particularly glad for the support of the latter." Another pause allows more chuckles. "I'm glad for all the support, and for your tireless efforts, not only to amass golds, but to continue to use some of it to pay your tariffs . . . so that we can put an end to the attempts by a certain duke to the east to impoverish it all. And, of course, we're also here to commend the arms-commander and Lord

Lerial for their success in defeating the Heldyans at Luba . . . which they accomplished most effectively." Atroyan smiles broadly. "With that . . . well . . . enjoy the fare and the company." He sips from his goblet, then lowers it.

Lerial slowly looks down the table. He has the feeling that he is missing something or someone. *Fhastal!* At the dinner at Shaelt, Rhamuel had introduced him as one of the foremost merchanters in either Shaelt or Swartheld.

The servers place small plates before each diner, on which thinly sliced strips of ham alternate with slivers of what must be an orangish fruit or vegetable.

"Ham and loquats," murmurs someone.

Lerial watches for a moment and notes the other diners wrapping the thin ham slices around the fruit. He does the same . . . and finds the semi-sweet taste intriguing, and not unpleasant. In fact, he finds that he has finished the entire plate.

"Lord Lerial," Maesoryk offers warmly, but not obsequiously or loudly, "it is a pleasure to meet you. It's good to know that Cigoerne understands the dangers posed by Duke Khesyn . . . and that Afrit and Cigoerne can stand against him." The merchanter's smile is modest, but seemingly open, and his warm brown eyes match his mouth.

"It's very much in Cigoerne's interest that Afrit prevail in any struggle with Heldya," replies Lerial. "My father has been quite clear about that."

"He's always shown he has good sense. So did the empress. I regret that I never met her and that I was absent from Swartheld during the brief time your father was here. But then, we were both rather young then." He laughs jovially. "Enjoy your youth. It departs more quickly than you'll ever have thought possible."

In some ways, it already has. "I appreciate your thoughts on that. I'd like to say more . . . but I'm afraid that, if I do, I'll reveal too much that I don't know."

From beside Lerial, Aenslem guffaws, then says, "How do you like that, Maesoryk?"

"He says it better than I could have when I was his age . . . and certainly better than I can now."

"If I pretend to believe that," replies Aenslem in a genially rough voice, "will you give me a better break on the next consignment of amphorae?"

"I'll pretend to."

Lerial cannot help but smile, as does Rhamuel, if ironically. Atroyan maintains a pleasant expression, not quite a smile.

"Well then, I'll pretend to give you a break on shipping that gray clay you want from Atla."

"For what you charge, you should be shipping it from Nordla or Spidlar."

Despite the genial bantering, Lerial can sense the undercurrents that are anything but friendly.

"So what do you think of them all now, Lord Lerial?" asks Lhugar dryly.

"We're all friends. It's all in jest," replies Maesoryk in his warm and winning voice. "How else dare we make our points?"

There's some truth in that. "Better with friendly barbed words than barbed iron," Lerial comments, dryly, adding after the slightest pause, "or chaos and blades." The only one who reacts is the merchanter he does not know, who shakes his head, just slightly and almost sadly.

"Jhosef doesn't much care for chaos. It curdles his milk, his cheeses," says Atroyan.

"And everything else," adds Jhosef. "Taints beef and mutton, too. Don't care much for the tainted."

For just an instant, Lerial thinks, the corners of Aenslem's mouth almost curl into a sneer, while a faint hint of an ironic smile appears momentarily on Rhamuel's lips.

From the comments, Lerial has gained the impression that practically all types of goods produced or traded in Swartheld, and many services, such as shipping, are controlled by one or two family trading houses. The only merchanting house in Cigoerne to compare with that, so far as Lerial knows, is Myrapol . . . and Veraan would certainly fit in with those around the table.

"Chaos is bad for almost anything in trade," Maesoryk points out.

Even Aenslem nods to that. Rhamuel offers an enigmatic smile.

"Here comes dinner," announces Atroyan.

Each diner is served half a small game hen, deeply browned, so that the skin is crispy, garnished with sliced honeyed pearapples, and accompanied with what Lerial guesses must be truffled rice, but a kind he has never seen before.

"Pearapples, no less," declares Jhosef. "How did you come by those at this time of year?"

Atroyan grins and looks to Aenslem. "I have my sources. They know some traders from Merowey who infuse the pearapples with a honey liqueur that preserves them."

"Quite good," declares Jhosef.

Lerial thinks so as well, although his first bite of the unfamiliar rice is small, because he does not know what to expect, but he finds it tasty, although a touch saltier than he would ideally like. He is happy to eat and listen as the others talk about how to keep chaos out of goods, ships, warehouses, and the like.

"You've not said much, Lord Lerial," says Maesoryk after a time.

"It's more interesting to listen. Besides, what little I know deals with weapons and battle. Those are scarcely suited to such a meal, or those attending."

"Will you follow the path of the duke's brother and become the arms-commander of Cigoerne?" asks Maesoryk.

"That is a position my father holds. So long as he is duke that is his decision. When my brother becomes duke, and we both hope that is not any time soon, it will be his decision."

"You're sounding more like a merchanter than a man of arms," comments Maesoryk.

"That might be because the best of both know when not to exceed their knowledge," adds Aenslem in his deep rough voice. "Or to reveal what is not to their advantage. Tell me, Maesoryk, how much profit do you make on each amphora or each roof tile. Surely you know, down to the last portion of a copper."

"Your point is well taken." Maesoryk laughs genially. "Enough, or I wouldn't be here. The same is true of all of us, save the three at the head of the table."

"And we would not be here without the success of the merchanters in our respective duchies," adds Lerial.

"That makes an excellent point to change the conversation to a subject I'd appreciate," declares Atroyan, raising his voice and looking down the table. "Since we have Mesphaes here, and we seldom do, I'd like his opinion on the best wines."

"Best, Your Grace, is often a matter of debate, and I will be pleased to give you my opinions in a moment." The spirits merchant smiles. "I would say first, that more of the honored merchanters here at the table prefer red wines to white, and that the two red wines that most prefer are the better vintages of the Reoman or the Chalbec. The two whites that are most preferred are the Halyn and the Vhanyt. Personally, I prefer the cask-aged Reoman and the reserve Vhanyt."

"You didn't express a preference for the Reoman or the Vhanyt," Atroyan points out.

"My preference is for the Reoman with beef and mutton, and the Vhanyt with fish and fowl. Because I do not like to switch from red to white, or the other way, I prefer to begin my evening refreshment with whichever fits the meal. I will, of course, take either of my favorites over a noticeably inferior vintage . . . if I have the choice. If I don't, I will enjoy the best of what is available."

Lerial cannot but note that Mesphaes has picked Atroyan's favorite red . . . and not the white apparently favored by Rhamuel.

"What about the Cyandran white?" asks Lhugar.

"Or the amber Noorn?" suggests Jhosef.

"That's a wine so perfumed with peach that it's what merchanters' press-gangs prefer," declares Aenslem.

"They add sleeping draughts to it in low inns and taverns so as to drug unsuspecting young men and press them into ship's crews," explains Rhamuel quietly in response to Lerial's raised eyebrows.

"Good Noorn is too dear for that," counters Jhosef.

"What about the golden Chelios?" asks someone farther down the table.

While Lerial does not exactly relax, he is far more comfortable as the discussion of the various vintages proceeds, and trusts that the rest of the dinner will continue in the same pleasant but only marginally informative fashion.

XXV

On threeday morning, before leaving for breakfast, Lerial turns over his most soiled uniforms to one of the palace staff, a youth barely grown, and proceeds to the family dining room, where he breakfasts by himself, since Rhamuel is nowhere to be found. Because the arms-commander was thoughtful enough to leave five of his personal squad, they serve as escorts when Lerial and his half squad set out for the headquarters post once more, taking a circuitous route heading southwest of the palace and then circling back to the shore road before riding north to Afritan Guard headquarters.

Although Lerial is getting a better feel for Swartheld each day, he cannot say that increasing familiarity is leading to a greater appreciation of the city, for all of what is for sale. He is reminded of the array of what is indeed for sale when, on one of the less-frequented streets, they ride past a building that displays open windows with both men and women in filmy garments that leave almost nothing to the imagination, and some of those "men" and "women" look to be barely out of childhood. Lerial cannot repress a shudder.

Everything, indeed, is for sale.

Once Lerial reaches Swartheld Post, he inquires, almost offhandedly, as to whether the arms-commander has arrived, only to learn that Rhamuel arrived early and soon departed for the Harbor Post. Lerial needs little time with his officers—less than a glass—and is soon ready for another and longer exploratory ride around the city before returning to the palace. He thinks about taking a very long route back to the palace, one that winds up the merchanters' road and back, but decides that would serve no purpose but to satisfy his own curiosity, and might well create problems without improving his understanding and knowledge of Swartheld. Instead, he decides on taking the shore road north.

As he and his combined squad ride out of the old post and head north, Lerial can see that one of the cafés that had been closed in the morning on previous days is now open. He turns and looks back, grinning, at Strauxyn, who rides beside Fheldar. "I see you've encouraged one of the cafés to stay open."

"Yes, ser. They have good pastries. We didn't see any harm in sending a ranker or two over and suggesting they might earn a little more if they opened earlier."

"And you're giving the men breaks to enjoy those pastries."

"Yes, ser. They can't go alone, though."

"Good thought."

"The permanent cadre at the post are enjoying that, too, ser," adds Jhacub.

Just beyond the open café, Lerial notices a modest cloth factorage, but he does not see any shimmersilk on display. *Too dear?* The prices he had overheard his father, Altyrn, and Maeroja mentioning to him years earlier suggest that few cloth merchants might carry the shimmersilk. *Or perhaps they simply fear displaying it?*

When they pass the harbor piers, Lerial cannot help but notice that there are less than half a score of ships tied there, the fewest he has seen in the days since he arrived in Swartheld. Not only that, but several of those at the piers appear to be making preparations to cast off. Is it because the masters of the departed vessels have seen something, either at Estheld or on the river? Or something else? That possibility concerns him. *You need to keep watch on that.*

That part of the shore road that runs northwest across the base of the broad point or peninsula on which the harbor fort is located affords a gentle slope, one that is not too taxing on mounts and one that would not be that difficult for wagons. Beyond the point, the road swings closer to the shore, but is a good two hundred yards back from the water and a good five yards higher.

After riding another kay and seeing nothing of great interest, just small plots of land and cots, pastures, and scattered small woodlots, Lerial is about to order a return to Swartheld proper when he sees what looks to be a small harbor in the distance to the north, possibly five kays or more away, with buildings and a mound of some sort behind them. Smoke rises from one of the structures. "I thought there weren't any harbors between here and Baiet."

"There aren't, ser," replies Jhacub.

"What's that up there in the distance with the pier?"

"That's the tileworks . . . well, I guess they make more than tiles there."

"Do you know which merchanter?"

"No, ser."

Lerial would be willing to wager that the owner is Maesoryk, but he supposes it doesn't make any difference where Maesoryk's kilns are located, except it makes sense that they're near where there's clay and a river or the shore. Shipping by water is far cheaper, especially for heavy goods that aren't that high in value for their weight.

When Lerial finally returns to the palace, after circling to the west once past the road to the merchanters' hill and taking in another, more modest area of Swartheld, where there are a profusion of small shops producing various kinds of cotton and muslin cloth, among other goods, it is slightly past third glass of the afternoon. Once back in his rooms, he finds not only clean uniforms carefully hung in the armoire in the bedroom, but an envelope on the writing desk. On the outside are two lines in ornate script:

Lord Lerial of Cigoerne,
Overcaptain, Mirror Lancers

Lerial opens it and reads the same ornate script on a simple heavy white card.

In honor of your presence,
and in celebration of the success of both
Afrit and Cigoerne at Luba,
Atroyan, Duke of Afrit,
would hope you would join him at a ball
this evening at seventh glass
in the Crimson Ballroom.

Why hadn't Atroyan told him that the "other function" was a ball? Why such comparatively short notice? *Because he doesn't want you in Swartheld any longer . . . or to prove that he can put together something this ornate so quickly? Or to put you in the embarrassing position of being underdressed once more?*

The last possibility seems unlikely, only because Lerial cannot see how that would benefit Atroyan, but the duke has to be more devious than he appears. Otherwise, how could he have survived, surrounded by merchanters such as those Lerial has already met?

By late afternoon, Lerial has walked more of the palace halls, visited the library once more, and found no trace of anything that resembles a legal codex. He has been standing at the west window, looking toward the west wing of the palace, for a good fifth of a glass when there is a knock on his door.

Who could that be? He checks his shields, then walks to the door and opens it.

Rhamuel stands in the corridor. "Would you like to have an early dinner with me? I've arranged something in the family dining room. It's not elaborate, but it's likely to be a long evening. Mykel and Oestyn are already there. I thought you might like to meet them in a less formal setting."

Lerial has his doubts about whether any setting in which he finds himself in Swartheld is likely to be less formal. He smiles. "I'd appreciate that. Now?"

Rhamuel nods. "Then we'll have time to attire ourselves more suitably."

"More suitably in my case is merely a clean uniform."

"The ladies may find that more appealing than excessive gilt. Shall we go?"

Lerial nods and steps out into the hallway, closing the door behind himself. As they begin to walk, he says slowly, "I have to admit that I've been to all of a handful of balls in my entire life, and that I know only the basics of dancing . . . and none of the protocols or customs of an Afritan ball. Am I supposed to arrive early, on time, or slightly late? With whom am I supposed to dance? In what order?"

Rhamuel smiles. "You obviously know enough to ask the right questions."

"Well?"

"You shouldn't be early, but only slightly late, and you should arrive before the duke. No one dances until he and Haesychya do. Then, since you're the second most important person there, you should ask her for the second dance . . . while I dance with my niece, and then we switch partners. If you had a consort, of course, Atroyan would dance with her, but since there is no one of suitable rank he will watch the second and third dances. He may reclaim Haesychya from me during the third dance. After that, you may dance with whom you please, but without obviously favoring any man's consort."

"What about Natroyor? Who will he dance with and when?"

"There's no one here appropriate for him in the first three dances. After that he can dance with whomever he wishes. There will certainly be some unconsorted young women."

"What about those unconsorted young women? How do I tell the difference?"

"How do you tell in Cigoerne?"

"Their head scarves are edged in silver."

"That's no different here."

"And I presume no more than two dances in a row with the same partner, unless that partner is one's own consort."

"You see . . . you know how it works." Rhamuel pauses. "I understand that you rode through other parts of Swartheld today."

"We rode past the harbor and a ways north . . ."

"The duty rankers at Harbor Post reported seeing you."

"It seemed to me that there weren't many ships tied at the harbor piers. Several still in port were casting off, and I didn't see any others coming in."

"Sometimes that happens."

"But if it doesn't change . . ."

"You think that it means Khesyn is up to something?" asks the arms-commander almost rhetorically. "I've thought of that, but he may just be spreading rumors to scare off ships.That can prove costly. If they think there is likely to be war, outland merchanters won't port in Estheld or Dolari, either."

"Speaking of merchanters," ventures Lerial, "I have a question about the dinner last night."

"Only one?"

"Several, but one in particular struck me. In Shaelt, you introduced me to Fhastal, as one of the most important merchanters in Afrit . . ."

"But he wasn't at table last night. You wish to know why?"

"It might be useful," replies Lerial dryly.

"There are two reasons. First, he is a Kaordist. Second, he and Aenslem cannot stand each other."

"But you said . . . Fhastal's consorted to his daughter."

"That doesn't matter. His daughters are consorted to the two most powerful men in Afrit, besides himself."

How can it not matter? And a Kaordist? A follower of the dual god/goddess? "Is his dislike so strong because of Fhastal's belief?"

"Partly, I suppose. Aenslem says that order and chaos just are, and to make a deity out of them is just foolish. For your information, he doesn't believe in the Rational Stars, either."

"If belief is only one reason . . ."

"The other is that Fhastal has advanced credit to several merchanters in difficulty at a time when, had they failed, Aenslem could have purchased their merchanting houses for a fraction of their worth."

"But his daughter would benefit."

Rhamuel shrugs. "I don't pretend to understand."

"He can't have only advanced credit to those whom Aenslem wanted to buy or take over."

"No . . . Fhastal has a few more—I wouldn't call them enemies—but those less charitably inclined."

"Who else might be foremost? Perhaps Maesoryk?"

"Why do you think that?"

"From his position at the table, he must be one of the more powerful and wealthy merchanters. He'd have the golds to do the same thing."

"Thanks true. He's certainly one of those who doesn't view Fhastal as favorably as he might. He wanted to buy some timberlands west of Baiet from an old landholding family. They were heavily in debt to a counting-house out of Estheld. Why there, I never knew. Shalaara got wind of it somehow and advanced golds so they could pay off the debts. No one else would, and she had to borrow the golds she advanced from Fhastal. Maesoryk must have wanted the lands badly. The family had already had a few spot fires, possibly camma trees, since the lands weren't that well managed, but Maesoryk ended up buying the lands anyway. It cost him more, and he's not forgiven either Shalaara or Fhastal."

"Why did she do it? Were they friends?"

Rhamuel shakes his head. "More golds. They got a quarter more than they would have, so I heard, and she got a fifth of that plus the usury charges refunded."

In a way, Lerial has to admire Shalaara, even as he reminds himself that trusting any of the Afritan merchanters is chancy . . . and dangerous . . . as witness what happened to Valatyr . . . although he still has no idea which merchanter had hired the assassin . . . or why, except possibly to weaken Rhamuel. "Why did Maesoryk want the lands? Do you know? I thought he was into kilns and ceramics and tiles. Or did he need to provide for a younger son . . . or heir?"

"He's never said, except that he thought they'd pay off in time. It couldn't be for a younger son. He only has one. Three daughters, though. Maybe he worked out something on transport with Alaphyn. Those two are close."

"So . . . one way or another, Fhastal's credit has cost both Aenslem and Maesoryk golds, and likely resulted in Fhastal getting some of the smaller merchanting houses anyway because they couldn't pay him?"

"He wins either way. He either gets the usury or whatever they put up to get the golds."

"That suggests that he's as wealthy as Aenslem."

"He may be wealthier. He's not as powerful. Too many people dislike him."

Lerial nods. "Thank you. I see." What he doesn't see is why Rhamuel maintains a close relationship with Fhastal, or one that seems close. *Keeping close to a potential enemy of the duke . . . or cultivating an ally not close to Atroyan and Aenslem . . . just in case?* He does have one other question. "How does Aenslem feel about Jhosef?"

Rhamuel laughs softly and sardonically. "Not at all. Neither does Atroyan."

"But why . . . ?"

"Favor at table results in lower prices for the palace. Jhosef knows the feelings, but wants the position. He'll be here this evening, although you'll only see a brief encounter between him and Aenslem. Fhastal will be also, but he and Aenslem may not even meet. If they do meet . . ."

"It will be most cordial and polite." *Because neither will give the other the satisfaction of being upset or giving way to poor manners.*

"Everything will be polite and cordial this evening." Rhamuel stops outside the open door to the dining room. "There will only be the four of us eating." Then he leads the way inside.

Two men stand near a serving sideboard on which are arrayed several platters with food, although Lerial cannot see what that might be from the other side of the chamber.

"Mykel . . . this is Lord Lerial. Lerial, my younger brother Mykel."

For some reason, Lerial has pictured Mykel as slight, almost feminine, but the youngest of the three brothers is barrel-chested and broad-shouldered, with an open smile and the same warm brown eyes and hair as Rhamuel. He is perhaps a digit or so taller than his older brother, and definitely taller than the duke. His face is smooth-shaven and youthful, suggesting he is one of those men who look youthful until they suddenly age, although Lerial doubts Mykel is more than fifteen years older than Lerial himself, at the most. He also carries more of the black of order than most people, almost enough that he might have some slight order-handling skills.

Mykel inclines his head and says, "I'm very pleased to meet you. Rham has spoken of you most favorably, particularly of your prowess with arms." He shakes his head self-deprecatingly. "Much to our sire's regret, and that of my brothers, I have proved less than adept with any form of weapon."

"But he is most skilled with a paintbrush," says Rhamuel. "The fellow with him is Oestyn, the youngest son of merchanter Jhosef, whom you met the other night . . ."

"The largest merchanter in dairy and cheese and related goods?"

"The very same," replies Oestyn. "The uncoroneted deity of all things caprine and bovine, and, of course, dried mutton, the staple of the crafter and peasant. He is a great supporter of what he calls natural." Oestyn is slightly shorter than any of the others, and more slender, if muscular, with bright green eyes and short but curly blond hair.

"We have wine and lager, and the food on the sideboard," announces Mykel, "thanks to Rham's persuasiveness with the palace cooks. And some excellent provisions from Oestyn's sire."

Oestyn murmurs something into Mykel's ear.

"As the honored guest, Lord Lerial, perhaps you would begin," Mykel goes on.

"'Lerial,' please, except where required by custom and ceremony." Lerial cannot say what prompts his qualification, other than perhaps Oestyn's description of his father, and he quickly adds, "Certainly not here." He takes one of the large plates stacked at one end of the sideboard and moves toward the platters. He pauses, looking at the platters. He recognizes the rice as the same kind that had been truffled at the dinner the night before, but it has been prepared with mushrooms and a butter sauce. There are also new green beans with slivered almonds, and slices of fowl with a tannish sauce. He does not recognize the last dish—some sort of shredded meat with a pale green sauce.

His hesitation must have been noted, because Oestyn says, "The last dish is shredded pork with green saffron. It's an Atlan dish and very spicy."

Lerial serves himself a small portion, then adds more of the rice, after which he pours himself a beaker of light lager. When he turns back to the table, he sees that four places have been set, two on each side of one end of the table. He lets Rhamuel take a seat, and then sits across from him, leaving Mykel to sit beside him, and Oestyn, who sits down last, beside Rhamuel.

"No toasts, no formality," says Rhamuel.

Mykel nods.

"I hadn't heard that you were here in Swartheld at present," Lerial says, looking to Mykel.

"Not for long. We'll be leaving for Lake Reomer early tomorrow morning," Mykel replies. "We're staying because Oestyn likes the music at the balls. So do I, but that's because he's taught me about it."

"Music was not to be studied in the palace, not by sons, at least, and since Father had no daughters . . . there was little music," explains Rhamuel.

"And not verse, either?" suggests Lerial after taking a swallow of the lager.

"Verse was worse," declares Mykel. "As bad as marionettes and puppetry." A certain irony infuses his last phrase.

"Yet," says Oestyn with knowing smile,

"When words spoken come from the soul,
All praise to the man who is whole."

"That's from Maorym," says Mykel. "He's one of the best poets in Afrit, indeed in all Hamor. The lines of his that I like best are these:

"Fair words, like trees, must seek receptive ground,
For logic's chill is worse than stony ground."

"But then, Father wouldn't have understood that, would he?" With the question, Mykel looks not to Rhamuel, but to Oestyn.

"From what you've said . . ." demurs Oestyn gently.

"Did you study verse and the great poets of Cyador?" Mykel asks Lerial.

"My father is not the greatest enthusiast of verse," replies Lerial, *and that is an understatement,* "but I have read some of the old Cyadoran verse." Rather than say more, Lerial takes a small bite of the Atlan pork, followed by some of the rice.

"Can you quote any?"

His mouth full, Lerial shakes his head.

"That's too bad. I'd hoped . . ."

"Some of us have been trained in skills that allow others the liberty of writing and enjoying verse," Rhamuel says dryly.

"What else have you studied?" presses Mykel.

Lerial finishes what he is eating, then takes a swallow of the lager before replying, since the Atlan pork is not so much spicy as throat-searing and nose-burning, small as the mouthful he took had been. Finally, he speaks. "History, geography, practical mathematics, grammar and logic, the basics of engineering. Later on, with Majer Altyrn, I learned about strategy, tactics, and maps . . . And . . . of course, blades."

"The education of an officer," says Oestyn blandly.

"You should be glad of it," Rhamuel responds. "He kept Luba from suffering great destruction."

"No great loss," sniffs Mykel.

Oestyn nods, if only slightly.

Lerial understands that the purpose of the dinner is not just to make sure he is fed. Even so, he is hungry, and he takes a bite of the more succulent fowl, a far larger bite, and far more to his taste, he discovers.

"Perhaps not to the builders of poetic epics," says Rhamuel, "but that damage would have resulted in reduced tariffs . . . and you know how the duke would have felt about that."

The duke? Very interesting. Rhamuel's choice of words in what is almost a family dinner is most suggestive.

"He'd use it to cut my stipend. You don't have to remind me, Rham."

"Sometimes, I do." The arms-commander's words are gentle.

"You'd think verse and painting were an offense against the laws."

"Just a privilege allowed by the laws," Lerial finds himself saying, "and made possible by those who defend them."

"Lerial . . . you sound like my brother here. No wonder he likes you."

"We share many similarities." Lerial makes his words both light and wry.

Oestyn smiles, but Lerial finds the expression both defensive and somehow predatory.

"Are you here to court my niece?" asks Mykel.

"Not that I know of," replies Lerial. "I was invited by your brother, and according to his invitation, it was because I rendered some assistance to Afrit against Duke Khesyn."

"The barbarian of Heldya," sniffs Oestyn. "He pursues anything with a head scarf, especially those close to him or his favorite merchanters, and if his pursuit is not successful, then those merchanters fall out of favor . . . and sometimes permanently out of sight. Some men can be so . . ."

"Uncultured?" suggests Lerial.

"Precisely," agrees Oestyn.

"Khesyn wouldn't know a verse if it paraded before him wearing nothing but a head scarf," adds Mykel.

"Especially if it wore nothing but a head scarf," corrects Oestyn.

"I understand you also paint," Lerial says, trying not to hurry, but definitely wanting to change the subject.

"Mykel is quite adept with pastels," says Rhamuel. "He did a beautiful portrait of Kyedra."

"It was one of my best," admits Mykel. "I don't do many portraits. I prefer landscapes. There's a beautiful scene at the lake . . ."

Less than a third of a glass later, Rhamuel clears his throat and rises. "I'm glad we could get together, but I have several matters to attend to before tonight's entertainment, and I believe Lerial does as well."

"Unfortunately, I do." Lerial stands. "I do appreciate the chance to meet both of you. I assume you will be at the ball."

"We will be," replies Mykel. "Oestyn and I wouldn't wish to displease our brother the duke."

"Then I'm sure we will see each other there." Lerial inclines his head politely, then leaves with Rhamuel.

Neither man speaks until they are well away from the dining room.

"I thought you should hear what Mykel has to say in less formal circumstances."

Lerial isn't quite sure what to say, but finally manages, "He's not quite what I'd thought. After meeting everyone else, I'd expected someone . . . less robust-looking."

"Oh . . . for all his love of painting and verse, he's an excellent rider, and he's swum across Lake Reomer any number of times. He could be good with a blade. He's actually rather accomplished with a staff, but he says blades make him ill."

They might at that. Lerial just nods and says, "I've heard that edged weapons, even knives, can do that to some people."

"It's a good thing you and I don't have that problem." Rhamuel stops at the foot of the staircase. "I'll see you tonight. I do have to check and see if there are any dispatches."

"Until then."

Lerial makes his way back to his quarters at a measured pace, thinking. He is more than a little confused by Mykel. While he can understand Mykel's inclinations, he wonders why the youngest brother is so outspoken, when both Rhamuel and Atroyan are so much more cautious in their language. *Does he really feel that way . . . or is it a way of removing himself from any consideration as a successor to Atroyan?* And then there was the remark about puppetry, offhand, and yet said ironically. *Because he feels his father made him feel like a marionette on strings?* One thing continues to remain true, and that is that nothing in Swartheld is quite what it seems to be, or that what it seems to be is far from all that it is.

Once he is back at his rooms, he immediately checks with Polidaar, but there are no messages or problems. So, after washing up and donning one of his newly cleaned uniforms, Lerial departs from his quarters. He takes a narrow staircase in the middle of the palace, well away from the duke's personal quarters, to head up to the fourth level, which, for some reason, is where the Crimson Ballroom is located, on the southwest end of the west wing of the palace. As he walks up the steps, he raises a concealment, only after letting his order-senses let him know when no one is near the stairway door. Then he continues to the west wing, where he positions himself outside the vaulted arch leading into the ballroom. From what he can tell, it is about a third before seventh glass when he arrives. There are already a number of people in the ballroom. That, he can sense. He can also hear the musicians playing, but a slow melody unsuited to dancing.

A couple arrives, and they are greeted by Dafaal, at least, from the voice and posture, Lerial believes that to be the functionary.

"Minister Cyphret . . . welcome to the ball."

Behind them is another couple, and several others are walking toward the ballroom from the top of the grand staircase. Others seem to be standing around the top of the staircase. Lerial eases along the side of the corridor back toward the staircase, where he takes up a position behind one of the ornate stone balustrades that curve away from the top of the steps and all the way around the balcony overlooking the staircase. From there he hopes to overhear what at least some of the people might say.

". . . ridiculous . . . climbing three flights of steps to a ballroom . . ."

". . . there's more of a breeze up here . . . cooler . . ."

". . . nuisance . . . don't care if he owes something to the young heir of Cigoerne . . ."

". . . yes, dear . . . you look wonderful . . . and we're only a bit early. I'm only a subcommander, and that means I mustn't be late . . ."

Lerial wonders who the officer is, because his voice is unfamiliar . . . but then with close to ten battalions in and around Swartheld, there have to be at least several senior officers that he has not met.

". . . said to be young and ruthless in battle . . ."

". . . so bad about that in dealing with that barbarian from Heldya?"

He can also sense that the women all wear ankle-length dresses or gowns, the first time he has seen that in Swartheld, but it would have been the same in Cigoerne.

". . . just like the duke . . . ball with little notice . . . have to come . . ."

". . . you like being invited . . . don't complain . . . be far worse if you weren't . . ."

While Lerial has hoped to glean at least some passing information, he only hears what he had already half expected to hear, and at just slightly before seventh glass, he slips to the side of the corridor almost in a corner and drops the concealment, then follows a white-haired couple—something he can see since the woman has let her head scarf drop into a filmy shawl.

Once Dafaal ushers the older pair into the ballroom, he turns to Lerial. "If you would wait just a moment, ser," says Dafaal. "You and the duke must be announced."

"Whatever is necessary," replies Lerial.

A young-faced but gray-haired man with a younger woman approaches.

"Minister Dohaan, Lady . . ." offers Dafaal before Lerial can step back, "since you are both here, might I present you to Lord Lerial."

Dohaan? Oh . . . the minister for roads and harbors.

"A pleasure to meet you, Lord Lerial." Dohaan smiles politely and inclines his head.

His consort merely inclines her head, letting the head scarf slip off her black hair and around her shoulders, permissible inside and at a ball.

"And I'm pleased to meet the minister responsible for highways and harbors, especially since we have no harbors whatsoever . . . and to see you, Lady."

As Dohaan and his consort pass, Dafaal looks back along the corridor, then smiles. "Here comes the duke."

Lerial catches sight of Atroyan and Haesychya, flanked by a pair of palace guards. Atroyan wears a crimson dress uniform, trimmed in gold, but one somewhat different from the one he had worn the evening before. Haesychya wears a silver-streaked deep purple silk that flows yet suggests a still-youthful figure. Her head scarf is not even over her hair, but is draped loosely around her neck. Behind them are Natroyor and Kyedra.

"You'll be announced first. Just walk to the dais that holds the musicians," says Dafaal, then turn and wait for the duke and his lady.

"And once he's there, he starts the dancing?"

"More or less," interjects Rhamuel, who has approached from the staircase, rather than from the side corridor used by Atroyan and Haesychya.

Atroyan smiles pleasantly as he nears, then looks to Dafaal.

"All is ready, ser."

"Then we should proceed."

Dafaal steps into the chamber and waits for a moment. The musicians stop playing. Then a hornist steps forward and plays a short fanfare.

"The honorable Lord Lerial, overcaptain of the Mirror Lancers of Cigoerne."

As he enters the Crimson Ballroom, Lerial is aware that most, but not all, of those gathered have turned in his direction. He walks deliberately, trying not to hurry, but not to be unduly and solemnly slow. His eyes take in the musicians on the dais, most of whom appear to be holding largely stringed instruments ranging from violin to cello, with the exception of two horns and a flute. When he reaches a spot below the dais, he stops and turns.

The hornist plays a second fanfare, longer and more elaborate.

"His Excellency Atroyan, Duke of Afrit, and the Lady Haesychya."

Lerial watches as Atroyan and Haesychya enter the ballroom. Kyedra, with Rhamuel on her right and Natroyor on her left, follows, several yards behind. Lerial takes the time to study the duke thoroughly with his order-senses. Then he nods. Like his youngest brother, the duke is not order/chaos-balanced, but just faintly weighted toward order. *Not so much overweighted to order, as underweighted in chaos.*

Once the duke and Haesychya and those following him join Lerial, the couples in the middle of the ballroom move to the sides. Atroyan gestures to the musicians, and they begin to play, a melody with an almost stately rhythm. The couple moves, if not gracefully, with a certain ease around the ballroom, making three circuits and coming to a halt in front of the musicians. The music ends.

As instructed by Rhamuel, Lerial eases toward Haesychya. "If I might have the honor of the next dance . . ." His words are ambiguous because he does not know whether he should be asking Atroyan or his consort.

"She'll be more than pleased," declares Atroyan.

"I'd be honored." Haesychya's voice is low, but firm, and Lerial catches a glimpse of iron in the momentary glance she levels at the duke.

As the music starts again, Lerial takes Haesychya's hand, noticing that

Rhamuel has appeared from somewhere with Kyedra. "I trust you will pardon any missteps I might make, but I've danced less than a handful of times over the past five years." He has no real idea what the dance might be, but follows the movements of others.

"Then you won't have made a habit of stepping on your partner's feet."

Lerial finds himself surprised by the warmth and gentle humor in those words. "That's true, and I'll try not to begin such a habit."

After a few moments of feeling awkward, Lerial suddenly realizes that dancing is much like sparring, in that he only has to let himself sense the flow of order around Haesychya and respond to that flow.

"For a man so young," Haesychya says after several moments, "you reveal less than most."

"You mean that most young men reveal everything, and I'm somewhat less open than that."

"You're open enough. That openness reveals surprisingly little."

"Perhaps because there's little more to reveal." Lerial keeps his words light, almost sardonic.

"I have my doubts about that, Lord Lerial."

"Please . . . no titles . . . even if it is in public . . . or half public. How did you meet Atroyan?"

"It wasn't a matter of meeting." Her words are cool.

"I see." *Just as whoever you consort, assuming you survive to consort, will not be a matter of meeting.*

"I think you do."

"How could I not? I apologize for the thoughtlessness of the question."

"It must be the dancing. That's the first time I've heard, or heard of, a thoughtless comment from you. Perhaps I should keep you dancing and ask you questions."

"You can ask any question you like."

"What do you think of Kyedra?"

"I scarcely know her. I like what I've seen, and especially what I've heard."

"And my consort?"

Lerial smiles. "I've seen more of him, and yet I've seen less. He seems to be a man walking a narrow path whose greatest abilities are those best left unseen."

Haesychya laughs so softly that Lerial can barely hear her. After a moment, she shakes her head. "I fear you are wasted as the second heir, necessary as you are as the real arms-commander of Cigoerne."

"I'm not the arms-commander. In time, perhaps, but not now."

"I might better have said the champion of Cigoerne. Do not argue with that."

"Since that is a command, I shall obey." Lerial keeps his voice light.

"You mistake me, Lerial. I never command."

"Then I accede to your wishes. Certainly, you have wishes?"

"Don't we all?"

"What else do you wish for?"

"That the ceaseless fighting would end."

"It will end only when Hamor is one land . . . and then it will resume intermittently with other lands."

"Are you a prophet?"

"I've been tutored in history, and that is one of its lessons."

"Yet you don't claim to be a historian."

"I don't know enough to claim that."

"You noticed that Mykel is not able to bear weapons, not those with blades . . ."

Lerial avoids the trap by saying, "That is what he has told me. I have no reason to doubt that."

"Why not? It is clear you have no aversion to doubting . . . when necessary."

"I am most certain that his stance on weapons has been put to the test. Rhamuel has informed me that Mykel is most adept with a staff. That suggests that he is not averse to violence, or even killing, only to edged weapons."

"A staff . . ." Haesychya gives the tiniest of headshakes.

"Hardly the weapon of a ducal legacy, you fear."

"I know . . . sadly."

Why is she bringing this up? "A lance is little more than a longer staff with a point."

"If I'm not mistaken, Mirror Lancer officers do not carry lances."

"Not any longer. The Emperor Lorn did. So did the Emperor Alyiakal. The lesson might be that we should," Lerial keeps his tone light.

"Times change."

"They do."

"Are you always so agreeable?"

"In public I do my best not to be disagreeable. In private, I try harder. I don't always succeed."

Before Lerial knows it, the dance is ending, and Haesychya turns to him. "For someone who has seldom danced, you're excellent."

"Thank you, but it's only because you're an excellent dancer. I just followed what you wished to do."

A faint smile crosses Haesychya's face. "Wise man. Would that more understood that." She inclines her head. "Thank you. I did enjoy that."

"Perhaps later?"

"Perhaps, but now . . ."

"I should see to Kyedra."

Haesychya nods.

Lerial inclines his head. "My thanks for the dance, Lady."

Haesychya does not reply, except by inclining her head in return.

Lerial steps back, then turns to where Kyedra stands beside Rhamuel, the arms-commander almost guarding his niece, or so it seems. Lerial can well imagine Rhamuel doing the same with Amaira . . . and he swallows.

Studying Kyedra as he steps toward her, Lerial sees that she is also wearing a gown of flowing silk, of a color he can only describe as an intense pale green with the slightest hint of golden lime, trimmed, of course, in silver, with a matching silver-trimmed head scarf. He cannot imagine a color that would look any better on her, although there must be some. He can also sense the strength of the black order within her, far the deepest of all of her family.

"Might I have the honor of the dance?" Lerial smiles as warmly as he can.

"You might, Lord Lerial."

"Thank you, Lady Kyedra." His words are gentle, if with just a touch of humor.

"I'm not . . ."

"And neither am I. 'Lerial,' please."

"Then you might . . . Lerial."

"Thank you, Kyedra."

The music begins, and Rhamuel is already dancing with Haesychya before Lerial takes Kyedra's hand, or rather barely more than her fingertips. For several steps, he is hesitant, until he can adjust to her reactions to the music, a piece just slightly faster than the previous one.

"Have you been to many balls?"

"Every one since I turned eighteen. Father only allowed me two a year after I was sixteen."

"I doubt if I've been to as many in my entire life as you were between sixteen and eighteen."

"That is not the greatest of losses."

Several couples away, Lerial sees Mykel dancing with a much older woman.

"Who might that be with your Uncle Mykel?"

"That's Nelyani. She's Maesoryk's consort. Properly speaking, he ought to be dancing with the consort of the head of the Merchanting Council. That would have been Grandmother, but . . ."

"She's . . . no longer with you?"

"She never was. Not with me. She died having Uncle Mykel."

"Thank you. I'd wondered about that." Lerial pauses, then asks, "Your grandfather never took another consort?"

"No."

The reply is so cold and short than Lerial immediately says, "I'm sorry. I did not mean to pry."

"It's not you. Some other time, if you would, we might talk about it."

"You dance well . . . far better than I."

"I don't notice you having any trouble, and you haven't stepped on my shoes the way Uncle Rham did."

"That's because I'm following the hints you give."

For a moment, Kyedra stiffens.

"I mean, if I start to go the wrong way, you move away. So I just stay with you."

"You can sense that?" There is a hint of surprise in her voice.

"If I pay attention, and I'm trying very hard to do that."

A smile crosses her face, and Lerial can't help but smile back. He says, "You have a lovely smile."

"I suppose you tell all the women that."

Lerial manages not to frown as he considers the question. "No. I've only told my cousin that."

"You actually thought about it. I'm flattered. Or were you thinking about who else you said that to and whether I'd find out?"

"I haven't told anyone that they have a lovely smile except Amaira."

"Why not?"

"Because I'm particular, I suppose."

"What about women who did and you didn't tell?"

"Majer Altyrn's consort has a lovely smile, but she's almost old enough to be my mother."

"And you're comparing me to her?"

Lerial grins, then says slowly, "Well . . . there are some similarities . . ."

Kyedra laughs. "I like that."

As the music comes to an end, Lerial guides her back to where Rhamuel and Haesychya stand, then inclines his head. "Thank you."

"Thank you." There is just the slightest emphasis on the word "you."

Mykel steps up to take Kyedra's hand, and Lerial moves away.

For the next glass or so, Lerial dances with a number of women, ranging in age from unconsorted girls to dowagers with white hair, making certain to dance only once with each, and being careful to limit his comments to pleasantries. He sees both Oestyn and Mykel dancing with a number of women, but notes that neither Atroyan nor Rhamuel—nor Haesychya—dance that often.

Then, Lerial notices Dafaal moving across the ballroom to Rhamuel. The functionary leans toward the arms-commander and says something. Rhamuel nods, and the two walk toward the ballroom entry. Lerial cannot determine what happens next because of the swirl of dancers, but he doesn't like what he has seen.

He puts on a smile and asks the bored-looking consort of a merchanter, who is talking to another merchanter, to dance. The brunette immediately smiles and inclines her head. Her consort barely glances in her direction as Lerial leads her out into the dancers.

Two dances pass before Rhamuel returns, and Lerial immediately makes his way to join the arms-commander.

"You have a worried look," Lerial says.

"The piers at Estheld are crowded with merchanters. This afternoon until just before sunset a number set sail, all heading northwest out of the bay."

"That doesn't make sense. You don't have any ports or places they could land to the northwest, do you?"

"Only Baiet, and if Khesyn were going to attack Swartheld, there's little point in landing more than fifty kays northwest and then march back."

"Do you think he's going to attack Nubyat and try to take over Merowey?"

"That would be a problem for us both," Rhamuel points out.

"We don't want to support Casseon, and we don't want Khesyn surrounding us on all borders. I assume that's what you mean."

Rhamuel nods.

"Where are the flatboats?"

"We don't know. They left Luba. We all saw them leave Luba. They're not at Estheld, not now, anyway."

"Could they be upstream somewhere south of Swartheld?"

"It's possible. It's also possible that all those troopers are being loaded onto the merchanters. All we can do is watch . . . and wait."

"You didn't tell the duke."

"I'll tell him after the ball is over, in the family quarters, when everyone is gone. Otherwise . . ." Rhamuel shakes his head.

Atroyan will tell too many people? Or his reaction will be public and unpleasant? "You can't do anything now, anyway, can you?"

"Nothing that we should. I have sent word to cancel all leaves and passes until further notice. Your men are all at headquarters, and you're here. So enjoy what's left of the ball." Rhamuel smiles.

Lerial can sense that the smile is forced, but he nods. "I think it's time to ask your niece for another dance."

"That's a very good idea."

Lerial waits until the music dies, then approaches the dais, where Kyedra stands, talking to Oestyn and Mykel. "If you would . . ."

"I would like that." Kyedra turns to Mykel, beside her. "If you wouldn't mind."

"I can't compete with Lerial," replies Mykel with a broad smile. "Nor would I wish to."

Lerial takes her hand, and as the music begins, he takes a step, then slips into following her rhythms.

"You did wait a while."

Lerial can see the glint in her eyes and replies, "I was instructed not to inflict my presence upon you or your mother too often."

"Too little is as bad as too often. For that, you should pay."

"Oh?"

"You must dance the next one with Mother, and then again with me."

"I can do that."

"Can?"

"I can dance with your mother and would enjoy dancing with you after that."

Kyedra offers a shy smile, but does not look directly at Lerial.

As they continue to dance, he finds even the shy smile charming, especially the warmth beneath it.

"You didn't dance with any unconsorted girls, did you?"

"Only once with any one."

"Why not more often?"

"It didn't seem . . . appropriate."

"Do you care what other people think?"

"It all depends on what they think and why. Sometimes, they have good reasons. Sometimes, they don't. And sometimes, even when they have the worst of reasons, you can cause even worse problems by not considering why they think the way they do."

"You sound like Mother."

"Not like your father?"

"No . . . my mother . . . but we shouldn't talk about that."

"Thank you." Lerial's words are low, but warm, trying to convey that he understands what she has revealed by the way in which she has changed the subject.

"You understand, don't you?"

Lerial is afraid he does. "People always think that men are the wisest. Often men should listen to their sisters, aunts, mothers, or consorts . . . and have the wisdom to know whom to heed and to what degree. Not that they shouldn't listen to men as well, but they should be skeptical."

"Why should they be more skeptical of men?" There is a hint of amusement in Kyedra's voice.

"Anyone who has power needs to be skeptical, but a sister, a consort, or a daughter is more likely to have a man's interest at heart."

"Because his successes or failures will affect her more?"

"Isn't that true?" Lerial asks gently.

"From what little I have seen, I fear so."

"And you dislike being a hostage to any man's weaknesses?"

"Or his strengths," Kyedra replies firmly, if quietly. "Do you think that is awful?"

"No." Lerial struggles for a moment, trying to think who it is that Kyedra reminds him of. *Emerya!* They're not the same, but there is a definite similarity. "Your mother is a strong person, in a quiet way."

"She has to be."

"Both quiet and strong?"

Lerial can feel and sense Kyedra's nod, although she does not speak.

"I haven't seen your brother . . ."

"He's taking advantage of his position and that he can go anywhere in the palace."

"Isn't that a little dangerous?"

"Not for him," replies Kyedra dryly. "He does have enough sense—or cunning—to offer to show the palace to women who are already consorted and whose consorts don't seem to care. They're the men who have other interests."

As the music of the dance dies away, Lerial guides Kyedra back to the edge of the dais, where Rhamuel stands. Lerial glances at the arms-commander, who gives a small shake of his head, then turns to Kyedra. "Thank you. I enjoyed the dance."

She only smiles and inclines her head.

Lerial turns to Haesychya, who has been standing between Rhamuel and Atroyan. "If I might have the next dance?"

Like her daughter, Haesychya merely smiles and nods, belatedly murmuring, "Of course, Lord Lerial."

Neither speaks for several moments, and Lerial finally says, once they are out of earshot of Kyedra and Atroyan, "You have a lovely daughter, you know?"

"Lovely? That is a word men use when they don't know what else to say."

For an instant, Lerial is taken aback and can say nothing. "Perhaps I should have said that she has a lovely smile and that she is quite perceptive and very good-looking."

"Perhaps you should have."

Lerial thinks there is a hint of amusement in her words, but he is anything but certain about that. "As are you, Lady."

"Flattery, yet."

"Truth . . . and you and I both know it."

"As far as the duke is concerned, you're the wrong brother, you know?"

"I've known that for years."

"Is he as charming as you are?"

"Since I don't consider myself charming, he's likely more so." That is certainly true, because, so far as Lerial is concerned, charm embodies a certain elegant dishonesty, and he tries, not always successfully, he fears, to avoid dishonesty. He has some doubts about his brother on that count.

Haesychya is silent for several moments, and from the change in the patterns of order around her, Lerial has the feeling that he has surprised her, at least slightly.

"You have a sister, I understand," he says after some silence. "I would guess that you share some attributes, and not others."

"That is true."

"But neither of you says more than is necessary?" he prods lightly.

"Oh, no," Haesychya says with an amused lilt in her voice. "Sophrosynia speaks often and most cheerfully. She has to, you know. Fhastal is most sober."

"I'd wager that for all her cheer, she says not one word that is not exactly what she meant, and that most of her words reveal nothing."

"For someone who has not met her, that assumes much."

Lerial laughs lightly. "Then you must tell me that I am wrong, for I wouldn't want to hang on to a mistaken notion."

"Ser . . ." After the single word, she shakes her head and laughs as well, if also quietly. After a silence, she says, "You should leave Swartheld soon. It would be for the best."

"I was commanded, in effect, by the duke to remain until after the ball."

"He could do no less."

"Then I will make plans to depart soon and when it seems appropriate." Even as he says those words, Lerial wonders if uttering them is wise.

"There is such a thing as . . ."

"Overstaying one's welcome? I worry greatly about that, Lady."

"Then we are agreed."

"We are." *In principle, at least.*

When Lerial turns from Haesychya at the end of the dance, Kyedra actually steps forward into his arms, but Lerial can sense a certain dismay from Atroyan, as well as observe a fleeting frown. Haesychya's face reveals nothing.

"What did Mother say? She looked rather stern."

"Besides suggesting that it is likely that I will be leaving soon?"

"She said that?"

"In effect." Lerial does not wish to lie, but neither does he wish to depict Haesychya as unduly harsh, concerned as she is for her daughter. "I had not meant to come to Swartheld at all, but your father's invitation was not to be refused, and I cannot overstay my welcome. That would be good for no one."

"You're right. One must consider these things."

"One certainly must," Lerial banters. "We must, must we not? Oh, the tragedy of being born into a ducal line, the endless responsibility, the unending stream of polite phrases concealing murderous thoughts . . . or terminal boredom with continued trivialities, punctuated with occasional unforeseen disasters, and family fallings-out that must be concealed at all costs . . . while smiling so often that one risks snaring bugs with one's teeth . . ."

For an instant, Kyedra stiffens, and Lerial worries that he may have gone too far, but then he realizes that he must have gotten the tone just right, because the stiffness is the result of her trying to contain her laughter. Finally, she looks at him. "You've been so sweet, so polite, and with only a hint of not being absolutely proper . . . I didn't expect . . ."

"Mostly . . . I am proper . . . mostly."

"I'm glad it's not all the time."

"And you're proper all the time . . . in public."

"I'm to be proper all the time, anywhere."

"Is that the dictum from your mother?"

"She doesn't have to say anything. She just has to look."

"I'm familiar with that."

Kyedra doesn't say anything for a time, and Lerial just enjoys dancing with her, realizing that it has been almost two years since he last danced, and that was at the year-turn ball at the palace, but he has no recollection of those with whom he danced, except Ryalah and Amaira.

"What are you thinking?" Kyedra finally asks.

"That it's been years since I danced, and the only ones I remember dancing with are my sister and cousin."

"You're the only one I've danced with who isn't either an older merchanter or officer who's consorted . . . or my uncles."

"Then I am fortunate indeed."

"You are." The slight hint of a smile softens the arch tone of the words.

When the dance ends, Lerial asks, "Might I have the last dance?"

"You may. It won't be long now. Dafaal will announce the last dance, and Father and Mother will dance it together. It's a very short dance. Father believes endings should be quick."

After relinquishing Kyedra, Lerial glances toward Haesychya, who offers the slightest of headshakes, to which Lerial responds with a smile and a nod. He turns away and moves to a sideboard, where he takes a beaker of lager and sips it, watching and waiting.

When Lerial finally sees Dafaal stepping up onto the dais he makes his way to Kyedra.

Atroyan looks at the pair, then glances at his consort. In turn, she bends forward and murmurs something, and the duke nods, if clearly reluctantly.

Once they have moved away from the dais, letting the duke and his consort dance away from them, Lerial looks to Kyedra.

"Father says that I am not to become attached to you. At least, not now."

"That has many meanings."

"I'm sure you have thought of them all."

"And you haven't?"

Kyedra's smile turns mischievous. "I might have missed one or two."

"There are only so many heirs in Hamor."

"What if I don't want to consort an heir?"

"Then I imagine you'll have to settle for an old and very wealthy merchanter," replies Lerial.

Kyedra grimaces.

"Unless, of course, Khesyn poisons his consort, or Casseon needs another one."

"You don't mention Cigoerne," she banters back.

"My mother is most healthy, and as a healer, with my aunt the head healer watching over her, she is unlikely to suffer any strange maladies." Lerial tilts his head. "There might be a tall barbarian among the Tourlegyn clans of Atla, one who worships the Chaos Demons most assiduously."

"You're terrible."

"Just exploring the possibilities."

Lerial realizes that the duke and Haesychya are approaching the dais, and that Dafaal is stepping out in front of the musicians. "The last dance is *very* short."

"I did tell you Father believed in swift endings."

When the music ends, Dafaal announces, "The duke bids you all good evening."

After the last dance, Lerial looks around to see if he can find Rhamuel, but the arms-commander is nowhere to be seen. *There's nothing you can do in the middle of the night.*

"Who are you looking for?" asks Kyedra as Lerial escorts her toward her parents.

"Your uncle Rhamuel."

"He never stays to the end."

"And your brother?"

Kyedra shrugs. "I cannot speak for him."

"Then I should escort you back to your quarters."

"That would be most gracious," interjects Haesychya, her voice pleasant, but not especially warm.

Given that permission, Lerial begins to walk with Kyedra and her parents back to the family quarters, where he hopes Rhamuel is waiting. He cannot help but notice that Mykel and Oestyn have vanished as well.

"Too bad your brother couldn't have come," observes Atroyan, looking back at Lerial. "Is he much like you?"

"I'm not the best one to answer that. Brothers can be very alike, but they're still very different people." *As you should know.*

"We'll have to see about a visit . . . or perhaps we could send Kyedra to Cigoerne before too long."

"All things in their time, dear," says Haesychya warmly. "That is what you always say. You do need to see this dreadful situation with Khesyn resolved before anyone goes anywhere, don't you think?"

"Would that I didn't." Atroyan shakes his head.

"He is an awful man," Haesychya adds. "He's likely worse than Casseon, and you know what I think of him."

"I do indeed," says the duke.

When they reach the guards posted at the double doors, Kyedra turns to Lerial. "I'm glad you walked back with us."

"So am I."

She smiles again, then turns and enters the quarters under Haesychya's watchful eyes, for Atroyan has already preceded his consort and daughter.

Lerial nods to Haesychya, then turns and makes his way down to his own rooms, where one lancer remains on duty.

"Keep an ear out for anything strange. Wake me if there's anything like that."

"Yes, ser."

Lerial hopes that there isn't, but the thought of almost no ships at Swartheld and scores at Estheld still preys on his mind.

XXVI

Lerial awakes abruptly in the darkness before dawn, shuddering. He sits up in the wide bed. What had wakened him? The air in the bedchamber is warm, almost too warm, yet his hands and feet are cold. Could it have been thunder? He walks to the window and pulls back the heavy hangings, but all he can see are a few lamps in the courtyard . . . and the stars overhead, bright and clear in the dark sky. *Definitely not a storm, at least not one close to Swartheld.*

While he returns to his bed, he finds he cannot sleep, and he tries to recall the feelings—or the dreams—that awakened him. All he can recall is a vague sense of ice that burned like fire . . . perhaps fire that froze like ice. *But why would you dream about that?*

Finally, when the sky begins to gray, he rises, washes up, and dresses. Then he looks at the armoire, wondering whether he should pack, in order to be ready to leave Swartheld. Certainly, Haesychya has made it clear that he should be leaving, and the duke has as much as said that Lephi would have been more welcome.

He shakes his head. To leave without at least meeting with Atroyan and thanking him for his kindness would be unwise and could cause more problems for his father and Lephi. He can't help thinking that Kyedra is better than Lephi deserves, and, given the way both Khesyn and Casseon feel, Kyedra is most likely to be the only young woman from a ducal lineage in Hamor available to either Lephi or Lerial.

He snorts softly as he thinks about how the majer and Maeroja had discouraged any entanglement between him and Rojana. Yet . . . Maeroja had talked more than once about the absolute certainty of the majer's feelings. And how had the majer known Lerial would need the iron-cored cupridium sabre? And then there had been Altyrn's emphasis not so much on the need to re-create Cyador but to carry on the best of its heritage and tradition.

Before he leaves the sitting room for breakfast, he goes to the windows on the south side and looks eastward, toward the bay. While he cannot see the harbor, there are no rivercraft headed north toward the harbor piers. For that matter, on the small section of the bay he can view, he can see no vessels at all.

Lerial wonders if anyone will even be at the family dining room, but Rhamuel is already there and eating. He waves Lerial to the place across from him.

"You're up early," Lerial observes.

"So are you."

"Did you talk to the duke last night? About the merchanters?" Lerial slides into the chair, and a server sets a pitcher of lager and a beaker before him, then immediately withdraws.

"I did. He wasn't pleased." Rhamuel takes a swallow of his greenberry-and-lager breakfast beverage, then adds, "He thinks we should know more."

"Have you heard any more this morning?"

"I've sent a river patrol galley to see."

Lerial frowns.

"It's misty or foggy on the east side of the bay," Rhamuel explains.

"The sky is clear. So is the bay. Well . . . the south part is."

Rhamuel smiles indulgently. "We often have fog over the bay and around the harbor with clear skies above. This morning, the west side of the bay is clear, but there's a misty fog around Estheld. It's rare when the fog doesn't cover the entire southern end of the bay, but it does happen every once in a while."

"And the harbor here is clear."

"I said it was."

Lerial manages a shrug. He hates even an implied correction. "I'm not that familiar with fog. It just seems strange to me."

Rhamuel says nothing as the server returns with a platter for Lerial. On it are two slices of egg toast, some thin mutton strips, an orange cut into quarters, and a small loaf of dark bread. The server also sets down a small pitcher of what looks to be a berry syrup. Again, he leaves the private dining room quickly.

"You danced quite a few times with Kyedra."

"Four. I danced twice with Haesychya. She turned me down when I asked her a third time."

"She never dances more than twice with anyone besides Atroyan, and only twice with those of position or great wealth."

"I should feel flattered, since I have little enough of either. Haesychya made it quite clear that I was the wrong brother. So did the duke."

"What did you expect? You're not the heir." Rhamuel's dark eyes fix on Lerial. "What do you think of Kyedra?"

"I like her. She's intelligent and capable."

"Compared to who?"

"She appears to take after her mother in many ways, but I'd say that she has some of the same family traits that you do."

Rhamuel smiles. "I don't think you answered the question."

"I didn't answer the one you didn't ask." Lerial pours the berry syrup over the egg toast and takes a large bite. "I would say that it's a pity she can't be Atroyan's heir. Or yours."

"That sort of talk would incense the Merchanting Council, you know?"

"I have no doubt that it would, but, from what I've heard, Cyad might well be standing if my grandmere had ruled, rather than my grandsire."

Rhamuel smiles. "And matters would be little different if your aunt ruled instead of your father?"

"They'd be different, but I think Cigoerne would still be strong."

"Neither you nor I can change what is." Rhamuel's smile is slightly sad, and he starts to push back his chair, only to stop as he sees Dafaal enter the private dining chamber.

"Oh . . . I didn't expect to see you here, Lord Lerial."

"Nor I you." Lerial smiles politely. "Since you have found me, however, I won't have to go looking for you."

"How might I help you?"

"I suspect that it is time I made preparations to leave Swartheld and return to Cigoerne," Lerial says pleasantly.

"When it is appropriate, I would think so, Lord Lerial."

"Last night, the duke suggested that I should consider it."

The white-haired functionary frowns. "He has not mentioned that to me, and I am certain that he would."

"Then perhaps I should talk to him."

"You . . . Ah, yes, in time, you should." Dafaal looks to Rhamuel. "It is really a matter for both the duke and the arms-commander. I just facilitate what the duke wishes to be done."

Rhamuel raises his eyebrows. "He was fine last night."

"He's likely fine today," replies Dafaal. "But he says he's not seeing anyone this morning. That is why I sought you out. There are certain matters . . ."

Rhamuel rises and turns to Lerial. "I'll see what I can find out. I won't be long."

In moments, Lerial is left alone in the family dining room, looking down at a half-eaten platter of egg toast and mutton strips. *You might as well finish breakfast.* So he does, but then continues to think about matters, deciding, for better or worse, to head for Afritan Guard headquarters immediately after breakfast and to have his forces ready to move out on short notice.

He sips the lager and is still sipping it when Rhamuel returns. He stands as the arms-commander enters the room, but waits for Rhamuel to speak.

"He's physically fine. I asked Haesychya also. She agrees. He just insists on being alone and thinking things over."

"I take it that this isn't unusual?"

"It's not frequent, but not unusual. He does have . . . these moods. I did ask about your departure."

"And?"

"He would like to have you at a family dinner tonight."

"Then we'd leave tomorrow?"

"Tomorrow or sixday. He wants to think that over, too."

Wonderful! Now you're stuck in Swartheld for another day—or longer—by the whims of a moody duke!

"Last night he sounded like he'd be happy the sooner we departed."

"That was last night. I'm sure Haesychya had something to say."

"She was the one who said I was the wrong brother," replies Lerial dryly.

"You might consider that there is more than one meaning to that phrase."

Rhamuel's words are quiet but firm. "She respects you. She doesn't respect many."

That doesn't totally surprise Lerial, but what concerns him is that Haesychya has to cloak her own words in double meanings. Or is she using the ambiguity to convey different meanings to different people? And for what purpose? "I'm surprised that she indicated that."

"She danced with you twice, and she let Kyedra dance with you four times. She also told me that you were far more impressive than almost all men she'd met who were twice your age."

Another comment with multiple possible meanings. Lerial nods, then says, "I'm still worried about what Khesyn has in mind."

"So am I. I've also sent word to all commanders to have their forces ready to move out on a glass's notice."

"I'd thought about that with my companies."

"That would be good."

"Is there anything else I should know?"

"You know as much as I do at the moment. If I hear anything back while you're at headquarters, I'll let you know." Rhamuel pauses, then adds, "Refreshments in the family salon at sixth glass, and dinner will follow."

The two leave the dining room, and Lerial returns to his quarters to inform Polidaar, where he informs the squad that the entire half squad should accompany him to headquarters. If anything is about to happen, he doesn't want any company shorthanded. Interestingly enough, Rhamuel has detailed only two Afritan Guards as escorts.

Because the townspeople are getting used to us being here . . . or because he feels he needs more protection? That's the question Lerial ponders as he rides into the old Swartheld Post.

As has been the case for the past few days, Kusyl, Strauxyn, and Fheldar are waiting for him, although none say anything as he dismounts in front of the still half-empty ancient stables. He draws them aside. "We may be seeing some problems in the next day or so. Kusyl, I'd like to take all of Twenty-third Company on a tour this morning. Strauxyn, Fheldar, I'd like your companies ready to ride out at any time. Mounts saddled, but stabled for now. There's something . . ." Lerial almost shakes his head. There isn't that much he can point to, except a strange bank of fog and no ships to speak of in the harbor.

"Ser? Are we in danger?" asks Kusyl bluntly.

"Not from Duke Atroyan or the arms-commander, but I'm worried that Duke Khesyn may be on the verge of attacking. The harbor is empty, and it's never been this empty. We know most of Khesyn's forces are near Estheld. I'm concerned about what he may do."

"Why don't we just leave?" asks Fheldar.

"If necessary, we will. But the duke has said we'll be able to leave by sixday, and I'd rather not create problems if we don't have to." Lerial knows he is stretching what Rhamuel has told him, but the last thing he wants to convey to his company leaders is the ambivalence and instability of the duke. That will serve no one well.

"Ser . . ." ventures Kusyl, "this is smelling like old fish. Again."

Lerial manages a laugh. "You're surprised? Do we ever get any assignments that don't?"

His words and tone get resigned and sardonic expressions from the three.

"Our task is to deal with those fish. Again." He grins. "Kusyl, how long before you can have your men out and ready to ride?"

"Third of a glass. Maybe less."

"Do it."

"Yes, ser."

"Fheldar, Strauxyn, wait until Twenty-third is out of the courtyard. Then do what you need to do to have your men ready to ride out, if necessary." After a moment, Lerial adds, "Or to defend the post, if that seems wiser."

"Yes, ser."

It is indeed less than a glass later when Lerial and Twenty-third Company, escorted by a rather nervous Jhacub and a half squad of Afritan Guards, ride out through the post gates, headed north along the shore road.

"Ser . . . might I ask why you and the arms-commander have everyone in readiness?" asks Jhacub, riding on Lerial's left, while Kusyl rides on his right.

"Because we don't like what we're seeing, or not seeing. The number of ships in the harbor has dwindled, and there have been far too many merchanters porting in Estheld. We don't know where ten Heldyan battalions are." *Except we really don't know where any of them are.*

"I see, ser."

Jhacub's tone suggests that he doesn't see at all, but Lerial doesn't answer.

When they reach a point where Lerial can see the harbor, he immediately scans the piers that had held more than a score of vessels three days earlier. Now they are four, and two look to be preparing to cast off. *Is a storm coming?* He looks eastward across the bay toward Estheld, but he can only see a foggy mist that shrouds the shore. There are gaps in the mist or fog, as if the morning sun is burning it off, but those gaps are not wide enough or deep enough for him to make out either Estheld or the piers, although, given the distance, he doubts that he could discern much in any case. Other than the area around Estheld, he can see no signs of clouds or fog anywhere else.

No matter what Rhamuel has said, the fog around Estheld bothers him.

"Have you ever seen the harbor this empty, Jhacub?"

"No, ser."

"Look across the bay to Estheld. Can you tell me why the only place that has any fog at all is there?"

"No, ser."

"Smellier and deader fish," murmurs Kusyl under his breath, but just loud enough that Lerial can hear his words.

Lerial turns his eyes upon the merchanters' buildings facing the harbor. They do not look abandoned, although there are not nearly so many people or wagons on the street or sidewalks as he has seen before. Still . . . that is most likely because there are so few ships in the harbor. When they ride past the side road leading up to the Harbor Post of the Afritan Guard, Lerial studies the gates and walls, but can discern no difference in the gate sentries. Nor does he see anyone posted on the lookout tower facing the harbor.

"We'll ride across the point." Lerial hopes that, once north of the short peninsula, he will be able to see any ships that may have left Estheld earlier, although he has doubts that most masters would set to sea through a fog. He glances at the Afritan squad leader. Jhacub looks as much puzzled as worried.

There is no fog immediately north of the point, either at sea or over the shore, but as Twenty-third Company reaches that section of the road that affords a clear view along the shore to the northwest, Lerial immediately sees another band of fog and mist that begins some distance to the northwest, just along the shore of the bay, possibly four kays or so ahead. The mist or fog is thick enough that Lerial cannot even make out Maesoryk's tile factorage and kilns, or the long pier there. The fog appears to be less than two kays wide, half over the water, and half on land.

That can't be natural, and no matter what Rhamuel says, neither is that fog shrouding Estheld.

Due north, to the east and north of the isolated band of fog, Lerial sees a merchanter, all sails set, moving almost due east as if headed for a port farther east, Dolari or Sanclar, or perhaps even Atla.

But why so far north? Because he can't pick up the winds as well closer to land?

Lerial looks at the band of fog and the clear air around it. Then he turns to Kusyl. "What do you think of that fog up there?"

"I'm not a sailor, ser, but I never saw anything like that."

"What do you think, Jhacub?"

"No, ser. I haven't seen anything like that."

"We'll keep riding." Lerial leans toward Kusyl and says in a lower voice. "I may order you to ready arms."

"Yes, ser."

They continue riding for close to a half glass when Lerial begins to sense an imbalance in order and chaos forces ahead, although he cannot see anything but fog and mist, which now appear more like a wall with a clearly defined border that is less than a kay away.

"Never seen anything like that, ser," says Kusyl.

Lerial looks to Jhacub.

"No, ser. That's no fog I've ever seen."

Lerial can order-sense shapes at the long pier, most likely ships, with the form of deep-sea vessels, suggesting very much what he fears—that Khesyn has used merchant vessels to transport troopers to the pier. But he cannot be certain, and he needs to have a better idea of what they might be facing. "We need to get closer. Keep riding."

As he probes beyond the mist and fog, he can sense men forming up as only trained troopers would, and beginning to move southward. There must be at least a battalion forming up, since he can make out three separate formations and others moving into position. He immediately renews and strengthens his shields. While he can sense chaos-shields, the blurring effect means that he cannot tell how many wizards there might be or exactly where they are.

"There are armsmen in that fog," he says quietly to Kusyl.

"Can you tell how many, ser?" asks Kusyl.

"At least a battalion. Likely more." Lerial glances toward the mist, less than three hundred yards away, although he doesn't think all of the shorter distance is because he and his men have covered it. The mist is also creeping toward them.. *No sense in coming closer.* "Company halt!"

Jhacub glances from Kusyl to Lerial and back to the undercaptain, but does not speak. Neither does Kusyl.

Lerial can sense horses being walked from one of the vessels down the long pier toward the shore. *How long have they been transporting men and mounts?* While he doesn't know that much about shipping horses, he does know that even the largest merchanters can carry only fifty to a hundred mounts. *Maybe a few more if they're only going short distances.* But still . . . to come up with enough mounts for a single battalion would require five or six ships, or a number of trips by fewer vessels.

Then out of the mist marches a shield wall, with pikemen immediately behind, the iron-tipped points of their pikes extending two to three yards in front of the shieldmen. Then comes a line of armsmen, with a smaller shields on one arm, and long blades. Behind them are archers.

"Ready arms! Now!"

"Arms ready!"

"Jhacub! Send two of your men to headquarters! Tell the arms-commander we've got several battalions of Heldyans here! They must have come by merchant ships, and they've got chaos-wizards who created the fog." Lerial turns. "Kusyl! Send one man with them. He's to tell the other two companies to be ready to ride upon further word."

"Yes, ser!"

"Yes, ser!" Jhacub replies after Kusyl.

From out of the mist comes a midsized chaos-bolt, arching over the advancing Heldyans in their tan or light-brown uniforms.

With a triple fine-line order-coil, Lerial almost instinctively redirects the bolt back across the shield and pike front so that the chaos-fire turns close to fifty Heldyans into grayish ash . . . and the inevitable silvered death mist sweeps over Lerial. That has barely passed him when two more chaos-bolts flare directly toward him.

This time, he uses a stronger order-coil and merges the two and sends them back toward the nearest chaos-blurred shield. The shield shudders—that Lerial can sense—and then collapses as a pillar of fire rises above the mist. Another set of firebolts—this time three—streaks toward him and Twenty-third Company.

How many strong chaos-wizards do they have? Even as he merges and redirects the three toward another shielded Heldyan wizard, and senses that shield collapse and another pillar of fire rise, Lerial has strong doubts as to how long he can keep throwing back chaos-bolts.

There are no more chaos-bolts, but more shieldmen and pikemen appear, with more archers, and shafts begin to fly.

Lerial manages to throw up quick wide shields, but doing that will soon exhaust him. Expansive shields have always been difficult and tiring for him. He can also sense more Heldyans arriving, at least a company of Heldyan heavy cavalry, with long blades and round shields . . . if they're the typical Heldyan cavalry, not that he has ever seen them except at a distance, but the majer had been clear on that.

He waits until the road and the shoulders on both sides are filled with Heldyans before he concentrates on order-chaos-separating small sections of ground almost under the feet of the front lines. As the deadly pattern of power crisscrosses the front line of the Heldyans, Lerial calls out, "Kusyl—there are at least three battalions forming up. Maybe more, and I can't handle both the archers and the chaos-mages. Withdraw now!"

"Twenty-third Company! Withdraw now!"

The lancers execute a swift turn and ride back south, away from the Heldyan force. Lerial keeps looking over his shoulder, but all he sees is a narrow wasteland of blackened earth, ashes and bodies, possibly close to a battalion of fallen Heldyans. He can also see that the fog and mist is beginning to dissipate, most likely because the Heldyans see no point in maintaining it now that Afrit knows that they have landed a considerable force.

Lerial hates to be forced into a withdrawal, but his men are badly outnumbered, and so is he. *And it's not even your land you're defending.* But that thought bothers him, because, in a way, defending Afrit is defending Cigoerne. From what he has just experienced, for Cigoerne to face Heldya alone would be insane.

As they ride south along the shore road toward Swartheld, Lerial keeps looking back, but there is no pursuit. He has to squint to do even that, given the headache he has and the flashes of light across his eyes. *Just from that short skirmish?* Except, he realizes, he's never had to deal with that many strong mages before. Nor has he tried to merge and return such powerful chaos-bolts so quickly . . . and then undertake even a limited line of order-chaos separation . . . and having to separate order and chaos from dirt is far harder than with wood or other materials. *Except for iron!*

By the time they have covered another two kays, enough of the mist has dispersed that Lerial can make out, if vaguely, that there are at least three deep-sea vessels, and possibly more, tied up at the long pier. *Even if there are five or six, they can't have unloaded all those troopers in just one trip.*

Ahead of them, Lerial hears a sound, a booming echo, and he looks toward the point, where thick gray and black smoke rises from the far side, billowing skyward. "Jhacub, where is that from?"

"That . . . that looks to be near the Harbor Post . . ." stammers the Afritan squad leader.

Now that he thinks of it, Lerial realizes, it couldn't be anything else. He massages his aching forehead, wondering what could have caused such an explosion and fire . . . and how extensive the damage and loss of life might be.

When he reaches the highest point on the road across the point, he again looks back, but sees no sign of pursuit. What he does see are more merchanters sailing toward the tileworks pier from the northwest. *Frig!* Then he looks to the southeast where he can finally see the upper levels of the Harbor Post. From what he can tell, only one section of the post has been damaged, but that part, perhaps a fifth of the entire structure, is little more than a heap of rubble.

"Jhacub! What part of the post was destroyed? What was there?"

"Those were the barracks, ser . . . and the mess hall and kitchen. Might have gotten part of the headquarters building. It's hard to tell from here."

If someone wanted to blow up the mess hall, why did it happen so late, after all the rankers had eaten? Destroying the barracks makes sense, because, although it is a working day, with six battalions there, there will be significant casualties. *But why not at night, when everyone would be there?*

"We'll ride straight to the Afritan Guard headquarters," Lerial declares. Harsh as that likely sounds to Jhacub, there is little his single company can do that those surviving cannot do as well . . . and he needs to find Rhamuel and let him know of the scope of the invasion from the north, although he doubts that is the only point of attack. They also need to work out what sort of defenses and strategy are possible and practical with what is left of the Afritan Guard.

When they pass the road leading to the Harbor Post, Lerial sees rankers leading some mounts outside the gates, and a large wagon team entering the post's gates. He turns to Jhacub. "Send one of your men to inform whoever the senior officer is about the Heldyan forces to the north."

"Yes, ser."

Lerial watches as the Afritan Guard gallops toward the damaged post, then turns his attention to the merchanting section they are approaching. Not surprisingly, several of the large merchanting buildings are already shuttered and closed, and workers at the others are in the process of doing the same. There are only a few people on the streets, and most of them are moving swiftly.

Even before Lerial reaches the entry to the headquarters building, Dhallyn, the captain who had met them when they had first arrived in Swartheld, is hurrying out. "Lord Lerial! There have been two explosions here in Swartheld! Do you know what they are?"

Two? "I only know of one. Part of the Harbor Post is damaged, maybe a third of it. We didn't stop to investigate, not with at least four battalions of Heldyans some five or six kays north of the point. Where's the arms-commander?" Lerial glances past Dhallyn to see Strauxyn and Fheldar moving toward him at close to a run.

"He'd already left for the palace when we got word from you. The duke needed him immediately."

"Was that before or after you got my message about the Heldyans?"

"After, ser. I already sent a guard to the palace to inform the arms-commander."

"Good." Lerial pauses, then asks, "Does anyone know why the duke wanted the arms-commander?"

"No. The message was brought by a palace courier," replies Dhallyn. "That was all the messenger said."

"Not by an Afritan Guard? Is that usual."

Dhallyn looks puzzled. "Of course. Well . . . maybe half the time. Both bring the arms-commander messages."

"Did the arms-commander say anything?"

"No, ser. He just shook his head." The captain pauses. "You don't know about the second explosion?"

"It had to be somewhere south of the Harbor Post, because we were coming back and were just north of the point when the explosion there happened, and we didn't hear anything."

Lerial is wondering exactly what he should do next when two Afritan Guards in the uniforms of Rhamuel's personal company ride through the gates. Their mounts' muzzles are flecked with foam.

"Part of the palace blew up! Where's Lord Lerial? We have—" The ranker in the lead sees Lerial and turns his mount toward the overcaptain, riding around Twenty-third Company and reining up facing Lerial. "Lord Lerial, ser. Part of the palace exploded. The arms-commander is hurt, but he's alive, and he can talk. He wants you there, ser. Undercaptain Norstaan sent word to Commander Nythalt and Commander Sammyl, but we've heard nothing from them."

"Commander Nythalt is at the Harbor Post?"

"Yes, ser."

"Part of it exploded. What about Commander Sammyl?"

"He was at the South Post."

Lerial turns to Dhallyn. "I'll take Twenty-third Company to the palace. I'd recommend your sending a company as well. The palace guard will need help in keeping order." He turns in the saddle. "Kusyl, we need to head out. Strauxyn, Fheldar, stand by. Should anyone attempt to attack here, you're to defend. You're not to leave the post here without my orders . . . or Kusyl's, should anything happen to me."

"Yes, ser."

Because Dhallyn looks slightly dazed, Lerial adds, "You'd best stand by for anything, Captain, and it might not hurt to start getting barracks ready, because some of those battalions may need quarters." Lerial isn't about to suggest that a captain whose functions have been largely logistics head out to fight, not when the Harbor Post is nearer and still has sizable ready forces, from what he saw, and when the headquarters post has only a few companies, most likely not all that well trained in combat.

"Yes, ser."

Lerial nods and then turns his gelding.

"On the overcaptain!" orders Kusyl. "Arms ready!"

As they ride out through the gates once more, Lerial turns to the undercaptain. "You don't have to say it. It's far worse than eightday-old fish."

"Yes, ser."

Once again, Lerial sees fewer people on the streets, but there is not the urgency in their steps that he beheld near the merchanter section of the city. *Because they don't know about what has happened? Or don't think it affects them?*

That is all too possible, sadly, if the people only think that there has been damage to the palace.

XXVII

Because of the narrowness of the streets and the route Lerial has taken from the north, as he nears the palace, he cannot make out any damage—at least not on that part extending above the walls that he can see. He does see that the outer east gate to the palace is closed, but the two Afritan Guards ride forward, and the gates open so quickly that Lerial does not even have to slow his mount. Although he does not look back, even with his still-aching head, he has enough perception left with his order-senses to know that the gates close behind Twenty-third Company as quickly as they opened. The same pattern occurs when they near the inner gates.

As soon as Lerial rides into the inner courtyard, his mouth drops open. The entire southeast corner of the palace appears to be a heap of rubble, and there are stones piled up around the lowest level, almost halfway to the second level, as if a giant hand had knocked off the false tower from the southwest corner and much of the stones and masonry from the fourth level and dropped them around the lower corner of the building. There are palace guards and Afritan Guards swarming over the rubble.

As Lerial rides closer, he can see that what have been destroyed by the explosion are the third and fourth levels, although he would certainly not trust the lower levels to sustain the remaining weight above them. Strangely, the rest of the palace appears intact. But why?

The family quarters and the duke's study and receiving rooms. Before he can even think about that, his concentration is interrupted by a bellowing yell.

"Lord Lerial! Overcaptain! Here!"

Lerial turns in the saddle to see Undercaptain Norstaan waving from the door of a small stone building built against the east wall of the inner courtyard. Lerial immediately rides to where the undercaptain waits. Even before he reins up, Norstaan begins talking.

"The arms-commander is inside, ser. We think he was thrown through the window of the duke's study. He was sprawled on the stones, but he'd landed on some heavy draperies and a settee. He can't move his legs, and there are welts all over his body. He says he'll be all right, but he has to be in great pain. I've sent for a healer, but no one has found him. Without one . . . I don't . . . I don't know . . . You're the only one . . ." Norstaan looks pleadingly up at Lerial.

After immediately checking his shields, Lerial dismounts and hands the reins to the nearest ranker. He looks to Kusyl. "Keep anyone else away from here." Then he follows the undercaptain through the door and into a small chamber.

Rhamuel lies on his back on two table desks pushed together. A jacket or tunic has been rolled up and placed under his neck. His face is slightly contorted, but his eyes focus on Lerial, although he does not move his head. Two Afritan Guards are stationed on each side of the tables, clearly to make sure Rhamuel does not fall.

Lerial immediately lets his order-sense range over the arms-commander. The diffuse chaos across his upper body indicates a large amount of bruising, most of which will not become apparent for several days, but not life-threatening by itself. There is a clear break in the main bone in his left leg halfway between ankle and knee, and more deep bruises on his legs. There is also a band of chaos across Rhamuel's lower back. Lerial turns to Norstaan. "Did a heavy block of stone hit his lower back?"

"There were a lot of masonry stones over him, ser. He was half buried."

Frig!

"What can you feel?" Lerial asks Rhamuel.

"Everything above my waist hurts. There's pain everywhere lower . . ."

"Can you move your fingers?"

"Yes."

"Toes?"

"I don't . . . know . . . can't feel . . . except pain."

"What about your left leg?"

"What's wrong with me?" demands Rhamuel.

"You're badly bruised and battered over most of your body. You've got a broken bone in your left leg, and your lower back is hurt. That might be very bad. We can set and splint the leg. That can wait a little bit."

"Wait?"

Lerial ignores Rhamuel's question, instead concentrating on the chaos-knot in the arms-commander's lower back. He cannot tell exactly what is wrong, but he has the feeling that there is little he can do except to reduce the amount of chaos. Bit by bit, he does, until he has the sense that to remove more would not be a good idea for either Rhamuel or himself. When he shifts his weight from one boot to the other, he feels light-headed. He steps back, carefully. His falling on the injured commander is the last thing either of them needs.

"What did you do? The pain's less."

"What I could." Lerial stands there for a moment, taking a deep breath.

"I can't move my toes . . ."

"We need to splint that leg. Otherwise, what happens with your toes won't matter." Lerial is well aware that it will matter, but he doesn't want to talk about that aspect of Rhamuel's injuries . . . not yet. "What about the others in the palace?"

Rhamuel gestures with his right forearm and hand. "Everyone out except Lord Lerial."

Lerial looks at Norstaan. "I'm going to need straight strong narrow pieces of wood and long strips of cloth, canvas if you can find any. Clear spirits or strong ale . . . ." When he finishes, he adds, "The sooner the better."

After the others leave, Lerial steps closer to the table.

Rhamuel looks up at Lerial. "Atroyan's dead. He was when I got to his study. His throat was slashed. I heard something so loud it shook me and the palace. Everything started to collapse . . . I grabbed the settee and used it like a shield to go through the window as the stones were falling . . . didn't time it quite right . . ."

"What about the rest of the family?"

"I don't know. I went straight to Atroyan's study."

"You have another problem," Lerial says. "We were scouting to the north and discovered that the Heldyans have landed at least four battalions at the pier at Maesoryk's tileworks there. They had chaos-wizards who created the fog. We managed to destroy maybe a battalion of Heldyans, but they had three or four more left and at least three more strong chaos-wizards. I only had a company with me. I couldn't do any more, and we had to withdraw. On the way back we saw part of the Harbor Post explode, maybe a third. There wasn't anything we could do. So we headed back here, but I sent a messenger to the Harbor Post to let the senior officer know about the Heldyans. Then I got word about you and the palace."

"What about the South Post?"

"I don't know. I'll have Norstaan draft some orders and send word. Sammyl's there, isn't he?"

"Yes. What about sending Drusyn's battalions north . . ."

"That would be fine . . . if the Heldyans haven't attacked elsewhere. We still need to take care of you. I need to see how they're coming." Keeping an eye on Rhamuel, Lerial goes to the door and tells the two Afritan Guards, "You can come back."

While waiting for Norstaan to return with what he needs, Lerial steps out into the courtyard. Nothing has changed, and palace guards and rankers are still looking through the rubble. Bodies covered with blankets lie in a line on the stone pavement in front of the east entrance to the palace. Lerial walks to his mount and grabs the water bottle, from which he takes slow swallows, hoping that the watered lager will help his light-headedness and the flashes that have returned to plague his vision.

Norstaan hurries from the southwest corner of the courtyard toward Lerial. "We should have everything in a few moments, ser."

"Good. You never told me what happened."

"I don't know, ser. Not really. I heard that the duke wanted the arms-commander and had sent a messenger. When he entered the courtyard, I came out to see him, but he barely stopped, just long enough to tell me that we'd talk after he met with the duke. He left his mount with one of the rankers and hurried to the east entrance. I went back to looking at the duty rosters. A little later, there was an explosion, and everything shook. I ran out. The palace was pretty near like it is now, but some stone blocks were still falling."

Lerial nods. "I've talked to the arms-commander. Have some men look through the undamaged part of the palace to see if they can find out about the duke and his family—"

"Ser . . . we already did. The arms-commander ordered it. They're not anywhere in the safe parts of the palace. Neither is Councilor Dafaal. Lady Haesychya and her daughter are likely safe. They left early because her father is ailing. They should be at Aenslem's villa. We couldn't find any trace of Lord Natroyor. Lord Mykel departed for Lake Reomer early this morning with his . . . friend."

Lerial finds himself letting out a deep breath at the news about Haesychya and Kyedra. After a moment, he says, "You need to send a messenger to Aenslem's villa, if you haven't already. It's cold, but the lady needs to know that the duke is dead, and that the heir is missing in the rubble. Tell them to stay there because the city is facing Heldyan attack."

"Yes, ser."

"Draft an order to Commander Nythalt, or the senior officer in command at Harbor Post. Order him to set up a line of defense to assure that the Heldyan forces to the north of Swartheld do not take the city. Tell him he'll need to consider earthworks because the Heldyans have chaos-wizards. We'll have the arms-commander sign it, and you'll take it to the Harbor Post."

"But . . . what will I tell them?"

"That an explosion blew up part of the palace. That the duke is buried in the rubble and likely dead. That the arms-commander was injured and has a broken leg, but as arms-commander and possible heir, his commands stand. We'll also need to send orders to Commander Sammyl at South Post. He needs to report here to assist the arms-commander, and Subcommander Drusyn needs to take whatever steps are necessary, if he hasn't already, to repulse any Heldyan troops that may attack from the south." At Norstaan's questioning look, Lerial adds, "I'm certain they have standing orders to that effect," *at least they should,* "but with the explosions and rumors that are going to circulate, a set of written orders, confirmed by a live officer or squad leader who can confirm that the arms-commander, although wounded, is alive and alert, will help settle officers and men."

"Yes, ser."

Lerial can see several troopers and a man in green headed toward them. "I didn't know there was a palace healer. Is he the one you mentioned?"

"Yes, ser. He can't do order-healing, but he's good with other kinds of healing, cleaning and stitching wounds, setting bones . . ."

"Good."

As the healer approaches, Lerial sees that he is a trim square-faced man with graying brown hair. The healer also manifests a strong order-presence, if not as much as a true order-healer.

"Jaermyd, ser."

"It's good you're here. I'd like your help . . . or perhaps it might be better to say that I'll help you in setting the arms-commander's broken leg."

"Is that all . . ."

Lerial shakes his head. "He's got welts everywhere. Much of his body will be bruised, but some of the bruises are so deep that they won't show up for a day or so . . ."

"I heard you were a field healer, but that . . ."

"I can do some order-healing. Not so much as the best . . ." Lerial pauses. "His lower back is damaged. He doesn't have any feeling there. There's a knot of wound chaos there . . . but we still need to set and splint the leg so it will heal."

Jaermyd nods. "Maybe ought to brace his back first. Otherwise . . ."

"We might damage it more?"

"He might. Even the best bonesetting's painful."

You should have remembered that. "You're right."

"Begging your pardon, ser." Kusyl clears his throat and steps forward. "Thought you might like these." He extends several biscuits.

"Thank you." Lerial takes the biscuits and immediately eats one, then the other, before taking another swallow from his now nearly empty water bottle. Then he turns to Jaermyd. "We need to do this." *Before everything else gets worse and while you can.*

Lerial and Jaermyd fashion a brace, using wood and canvas, to keep Rhamuel's lower back as immobilized as possible, since there is little else that they can do, not that Lerial knows of, anyway. Then Lerial lets Jaermyd take the lead in setting Rhamuel's leg, but does at one time stop the older healer. "Wait. There's some wound chaos . . ."

Throughout both procedures, Rhamuel is silent, except for breathing heavily, but his forehead is damp by the time the two finish.

"Are you two done?" the arms-commander finally asks, his voice ragged.

Lerial forces a smile. "For now. Don't move for a bit."

"How could I, the way you've trussed me up?"

"That's the point," replies Lerial. "I'll be back in a moment." Then he leaves the chamber with Jaermyd. He says nothing until they are outside and well away from the doorway. "Thank you. You have more experience in setting bones."

"You would have done just fine, ser." The healer pauses. "You can sense wound chaos inside a body?"

Lerial nods. "There was a touch of it at the end of the spot where the bone broke. I thought it might heal better with a little order. I'm just glad the bones didn't break the skin."

"You know . . . ser . . . ?"

"That he may never walk again? Or that he may not survive for that long? I know both are possible. It is also possible that he will live many years, even if he cannot walk." *But Afrit and Cigoerne both need him alive and alert for as long as possible, and many years would be for the best, especially if Natroyor is still alive. Or Mykel, for that matter.*

"I will wish for the best."

"You'll have to do more than that, I fear, Jaermyd. You're going to have to take care of him. I have this feeling I'm going to be needed elsewhere in Swartheld. I'll need you to stand by near here. He'll need to be moved to somewhere in the west wing of the palace where he can be guarded and where he can recover."

"There are others . . ."

"You can tend to them, but don't go far. Rhamuel is not only arms-commander of Afrit; he may also be the duke, or acting in place of the heir until he can be found."

"Oh . . ."

"Exactly. Now . . . I need to talk to him." Lerial pauses. "Thank you."

Jaermyd looks down for a moment, then replies, "It's what I do. I will do my best."

"That's all I ask." With that, Lerial nods and then turns and walks back into the small room.

"Am I supposed to lie here while all Afrit falls apart?" Rhamuel demands.

"No, but you're going to be mostly on your back for a while. We can tilt you, so long as your back is stiff. That's why you're bound so tightly . . ." Lerial is amazed that Rhamuel can talk so coherently with all his injuries. "In a bit, Jaermyd and Norstaan will have you moved to somewhere in the west part of the palace."

"You're not telling me everything."

"I don't know everything. I've told you all I know about the Heldyans. We haven't had any word—"

"Ser . . ." Norstaan peers into the small room.

"Do you have the orders? And a pen and ink?"

"Yes, ser."

"What orders?" demands Rhamuel.

"The ones we talked about. You can read them. If you don't like them, we'll change them, but we need to get them out to Sammyl and whoever's in command at the Harbor Post."

"*We* need to get them out?"

"*You* need to decide the orders. We need to get them where they go." Lerial hands the first order to Rhamuel.

Rhamuel has to squint to read the words, but he finally looks up. "It sounds like me. Not you. That's better."

"I had Norstaan write them. I thought he might know how you write."

"He drafts most orders."

"Here's the second order."

Rhamuel's hands are shaking by the time he lowers the second sheet. "Good. Your ideas?"

"What I thought should be done. Can you sign them?"

"I'll see."

"I brought a writing board," Norstaan volunteers.

"Good."

With Norstaan holding the inkwell, and the two troopers holding the writing board, Rhamuel manages to sign both orders . . . and add words to the effect that his seal was not available.

"There." The arms-commander takes a shallow breath.

Lerial hands the signed orders to Norstaan. "You'll need to send those out as soon as you can."

"The messengers are ready, with escorts."

"Good. What about copies?"

"I wrote one of each, ser. They're not as neat."

"They'll have to do."

As Lerial watches Norstaan leave the chamber, he wonders what he has forgotten or overlooked and turns to Rhamuel. "What else needs to be done?"

"Besides appointing you arms-commander?" Rhamuel's voice is both wry and dryly raspy.

"Getting you a little lager or something to drink." Lerial turns to one of the Afritan Guards.

"I'll see what we can do, ser."

"I'd like to know what's happening. Lying here and worrying . . ."

"I'm certain we'll hear before long." *Whether we'll like what we hear is another matter.* "I doubt that the force to the north has reached the Harbor Post yet. They may not have even begun an advance. There were more merchanters heading for the tileworks pier."

"Four battalions and they're sending more?"

"They might be sending more horses," Lerial points out. "There might be more than four battalions. That was what we could see." *Not that I actually saw that much.*

Before long, one of the Afritan Guards approaches Lerial. "Ser, there's a messenger here from South Post. He insists on seeing the duke."

Lerial walks out into the courtyard, where another Afritan Guard stands, with two others mounted behind him. "You have a message for the duke?"

The guard looks puzzled as he takes in Lerial.

"I'm Lord Lerial, overcaptain in the Mirror Lancers."

"I'm supposed to deliver the message to the duke. If he is not here, then the arms-commander. No one else, ser."

"Come with me, then." Lerial doesn't even consider objecting.

"Ser . . . ?"

"Look at the palace. The part that was destroyed included the duke's quarters and study. The arms-commander is resting inside this building. He was injured."

Once the messenger enters, Lerial says, "There's a messenger here from South Post."

The courier steps forward, extending a rolled sheet.

"Give the dispatch to Lord Lerial. He can read it to me."

Lerial takes the dispatch, breaks the seal, and scans the single sheet quickly, taking in the important points. Then he says, "It's from Commander Sammyl. The Heldyans have landed about twenty companies on South Point, as you had said they would. Drusyn has them surrounded. He can't attack without losing too many men because they have at least two chaos-wizards there. Sammyl is requesting more forces to enable Drusyn to advance. He doesn't say whether the Heldyans are still landing forces. Now . . . I'll read it word for word."

"I suppose you must."

Lerial skips the salutation and begins, " 'The battalions stationed at South Post are engaged in a holding action against superior Heldyan forces in a battle at South Point. Sometime before dawn, Heldyan flatboats began to land on the river side of South Point . . .' " When he finishes, he asks, "Do you want me to read it again?"

"No." Rhamuel turns his head very slightly toward the courier. "Thank you. You may go. You can stand by for a reply."

"Yes, ser."

"What do you think?" Rhamuel asks Lerial once everyone else has left the small room.

"It's hard to know what to do. We don't know how many battalions of those remaining at the Harbor Post are able to fight. We don't know what else might be happening, either, or whether anything has happened to Haesychya, Kyedra, or Mykel. What about Natroyor?"

"I don't know. He usually sleeps late . . ."

"We'll have to assume the worst, then."

"Send out scouts to see where the Heldyans are," insists Rhamuel. "And if they're trying to land at the harbor. And have someone find out who's in charge at the Harbor Post and how many men are able to fight."

"I can do that. We need to move you—carefully—to the west end of the palace."

"I should be at headquarters."

"You shouldn't travel that far . . . and you certainly can't ride."

"Not yet."

Looking at Rhamuel, Lerial has his doubts as to whether the arms-commander will ever ride again.

Slightly less than a glass later, with the messengers and couriers on their way, and Rhamuel moved to a large guest bedchamber on the third level of the west wing of the palace, Lerial is still worrying. He glances at the arms-commander, eyes closed and lying in the large bed, his back supported not only by the brace, but by a flat and wide frame, once a cabinet door, padded with quilts and slightly inclined. At the near silence, Lerial stiffens, but then sees Rhamuel's chest rising and falling.

What should you do now? Go and support Drusyn? What if the Heldyan attack from the north presents the greater danger? Why hasn't Nythalt or whoever is in charge reported back to the arms-commander?

He feels he needs to do *something*, but he recalls all too clearly his father's advice about the folly of action for the sake of action—and the majer's cautions about the uselessness of needless sacrifice.

None of that makes him feel any better.

XXVIII

Just before fourth glass of the afternoon, Norstaan hurries into the study adjoining the bedchamber where Rhamuel is resting. At least, Lerial hopes he is resting.

"Have the men found any more survivors . . . or bodies?"

"Ah . . . yes, ser. Several more servants . . . and . . . the heir."

"Lord Natroyor?"

"Yes, ser. His skull was crushed by stone blocks. It was even hard to see it was him."

Meaning that there's likely no way to tell if his throat had been cut as well. "What about that functionary . . . Dafaal?"

"No, ser. There's no sign of him, but there's no way to get to most of the third level. That must have been where the explosion was."

Where all the repairs were going on! Lerial nods. The only question is whether Dafaal was part of the plot, or whether someone used Dafaal's insisted-upon repairs as a way to smuggle whatever exploded into the palace. Certainly, Lerial himself had seen plenty of barrels. Who knew what might have been in some of them?

A guard raps on the study door and then peers in. "Commander Sammyl has just arrived, and he's on his way here."

"Thank you. Have him come here."

"Yes, ser."

Once the outer door closes, Lerial says, "I'd like to hear what he has to say." He would not only like to hear, but would like to know why Sammyl hasn't sent any reports on what has been happening in the battle around South Point. The scouts Norstaan has sent have only been able to determine that the Heldyans have continued to land flatboats and troopers, that Drusyn appears to have contained the attackers, if temporarily, and that the Heldyans have chaos-mages who have occasionally sent chaos-bolts against the defenders. Matters to the north of Swartheld appear clearer, but not necessarily better. The short dispatch from Subcommander Dhresyl stated that he was in command because the explosion at the Harbor Post killed Commander Nythalt and Subcommander Klassyn, as well as other subcommanders, and that the remaining four battalions had managed to repulse an initial attack from the north. *And Haesychya and Kyedra are safe at Aenslem's villa.*

After some time, and food, Lerial only feels a dull aching in his skull, rather than the intense throbbing pain he had felt earlier. He has considered moving to support the Afritan Guard, but Rhamuel has suggested he wait until matters become clearer. *Except . . . you've likely been waiting too long.*

Moments later, the outer door opens, and Sammyl steps through. "I'm surprised to see you here, Overcaptain."

"Oh? Why might that be?" replies Lerial.

"With attacks in the north and south . . . one might even accuse you of . . . excessive discretion."

"That's always possible when people make erroneous assumptions, Commander."

"Erroneous?"

"Such as believing the Mirror Lancers have not fought."

"Perhaps I should have suggested that remaining in the field might have shown less excessive discretion . . ."

"Perhaps you should have, but then, after we stopped the first advance from the north, with but a single company, had we remained and been obliterated by four chaos-wizards and four more battalions, who would have been able to report on the matter . . . or come back here and coordinate communications once the southeast part of the palace was destroyed and the arms-commander injured?" Lerial smiles. "Now . . . I'm certain that the arms-commander wishes to hear your report." He turns and gestures toward the door to the bedchamber.

"Why wasn't I summoned sooner?"

"You were. Undercaptain Norstaan sent a squad, and the squad leader delivered the dispatch to your hands."

"That was after midday."

"There was the small matter of fighting a battle with the Heldyans, riding almost ten kays back to Swartheld, while informing Subcommander Dhresyl about the Heldyans, then coming to the palace to heal the arms-commander after discovering it had suffered an explosion. You might consider, Commander, that I have no authority to issue commands over the Afritan Guard. I sent a messenger to the Harbor Post immediately, and as soon as the arms-commander received your report, he replied. That was as soon as he was able."

Sammyl lowers his voice. "How badly is he injured?"

"They had to move stone blocks to move him from the rubble. His left leg is broken, but the bone has been set, and it should heal properly. His entire body is bruised . . . and he has little feeling in his legs. His mind and voice are unimpaired."

The commander nods abruptly. "I apologize. You must understand . . ."

"I understand. The Heldyan attack, the lack of communications, the likely death of the duke, the fact that Natroyor is missing and likely dead in the rubble, and that no one knows for certain where Lord Mykel might be . . ."

"Did you . . . heal . . . ?" Sammyl looks toward the bedchamber.

"I did what I could. I *think* he will largely recover. He may not ride or walk unaided again, but that is too early to tell."

"Without you . . . ?"

"Without Lord Lerial," interjects Norstaan, who has been so quiet that it has skipped Lerial's mind that the undercaptain is in the chamber, "the arms-commander would not recover. You also would not have received orders and information as soon as you did."

"I see."

Lerial is afraid that Sammyl is seeing more than is there. "You need to talk to the arms-commander. Alone." He walks to the doorway to the bedchamber and looks at Rhamuel, who is frowning. "Commander Sammyl is here."

Sammyl does not look at either Lerial or Norstaan as he enters the bedchamber and closes the door behind him.

"I'm sorry, ser," Norstaan says, "but he wasn't seeing what really happened."

Sammyl has always wanted to see things his way. At least, that's what Lerial has observed so far. "He needs to talk to the arms-commander. He doesn't want to believe that matters were as bad as they were here." Yet Lerial knows he likely could have managed matters better. He should have had messengers sent even sooner than he did. *Should you have just gone to support Drusyn immediately?* But that would have left Rhamuel without any senior officer to convey his orders. *You didn't worry about that at Luba . . .* But there were others able to do that.

Lerial pushes away the competing thoughts. *It's too late now. You did what you did.*

Shortly, the bedchamber door opens. Sammyl gestures for Lerial.

Lerial enters and closes the door.

Sammyl inclines his head slightly. "I was not aware that the arms-commander literally had no even field-grade officers present. I can certainly see why you felt constrained to remain here, Overcaptain."

"That was one of the reasons I had the arms-commander request your presence," Lerial replies. "Now that you're here, you can provide that support and a more experienced viewpoint."

"With that in hand," Rhamuel says, his voice raspy, but conveying a certain dryness, "can we get on with deciding how best to handle the Heldyans?"

Lerial looks at the arms-commander. The circles under Rhamuel's eyes are even darker, and Lerial immediately extends the slightest order-probe. He cannot sense any more wound chaos than before . . . and can only hope that Rhamuel's condition will not worsen. Yet he knows of nothing else he can do. He wishes Emerya were closer. In addition to her healing abilities, she has other talents, besides undetectable concealment, he is certain. In any event, she is likely the only one in all Hamor who could do more for Rhamuel. But . . . he cannot do anything about that at the moment. "What is the situation near South Post?"

"So far, Drusyn is managing to hold the Heldyans to the area of South Point, but there are more flatboats landing every glass. They have close to four battalions there now, and at least one, and possibly two chaos-wizards there . . ." Sammy goes on to provide more detail, before ending, "It's likely that they'll attack early tomorrow. I would judge that the Heldyan force to the north will attempt to attack as well, so that we are engaged in two battles at once."

"You've seen the force to the north, and you've heard Commander Sammyl's summation of the situation," says Rhamuel, wincing as he lifts his left hand. "Where do you think you and your men could be the most effective?"

"That's a bit of a guess. From what I've seen and from what you've reported, the force to the north is the stronger, but they're taking their time, likely so that they can mass overwhelming numbers. I'd like to see what we could do at South Point early tomorrow. If we can weaken that force enough . . ."

Sammyl nods.

"Either way, even if I have to support the Harbor Post on sixday, that will help Drusyn and buy some time."

"To what end?" asks Sammyl.

"The more time we have, the more likely we are to prevail. It's still spring. They can't feed all those men by foraging, not in the north and not in the middle of a city. That means shipping food, and that takes more time. Let them attack, and give ground slowly. They'll take more casualties that way."

"This sounds familiar," observes Rhamuel.

"If either of you has a better idea," replies Lerial, "I'm certainly open to it." *Anything that doesn't require Mirror Lancers doing something suicidal.*

"You have some abilities in handling chaos yourself," Sammyl says blandly.

"Some," admits Lerial. "I can't create chaos-bolts and throw them, but I can often redirect what is thrown at us. That's if I'm not outnumbered by chaos-wizards." He isn't about to mention the use of order-chaos unlocking. That remains a last resort. He still recalls the times doing that has come too close to killing him and everyone around him. As it was, with the comparatively small unlocking he had done on the north shore road, he'd been lightheaded for more than a glass.

"That's why you think you can be more effective at South Point," says Rhamuel.

"If they have fewer chaos-wizards there . . . and if . . . well . . . it *might* be possible to use their own chaos against them and remove one or both of them. It can't hurt to try. That way . . ."

"That way Drusyn would only have to worry about weapons and not wizards," concludes Sammyl.

"That would be the plan," says Lerial.

Left unsaid is the understanding that, in battles, seldom will matters go as planned.

Almost a glass later, after the three have agreed on the general approach for fiveday and sixday, and some of the supporting details, Sammyl leaves, promising to return shortly. While Rhamuel rests, Lerial sits down at the table desk in the sitting room and begins to draft a dispatch.

When he finally finishes it, he reads over the words once more.

Ser—

This may be the first word you receive of the Heldyan attack on Swartheld. The Afritan Guard is fighting two invasion forces, as well as extensive treachery. This treachery included an explosion which destroyed part of the ducal palace in Swartheld and killed the duke and his son, the heir presumptive. This has left Rhamuel, the arms-commander and the brother of the duke, as the heir apparent. He was injured as well, and has severe damage to his lower back and legs. Despite the injury, he is fully alert and in command. Given matters here in Swartheld, a more complete recovery on his part is beyond my limited abilities as a healer, and I would suggest that a more experienced healer, if at all possible, the healer who made certain he recovered from his previous injury, be escorted to Swartheld, by watercraft, in order to assure that Afrit will have its most capable duke in the best possible health for as long as possible. I would not make this suggestion did I not feel that its implementation would be of the greatest possible benefit for both Cigoerne and Afrit.

After reading it over, he signs it with his name and rank. Next, he addresses the sheet that will become the envelope.

Kiedron
Duke of Cigoerne
Of the Rational Stars

Then he summons Norstaan.

When the undercaptain appears, Lerial says, "I understand you have often arranged for dispatches to reach places expeditiously, sometimes not always through the usual . . . manner." This is totally a guess on Lerial's part, but given what he has seen so far in Afrit, *someone* has to have done that for Rhamuel.

Norstaan frowns, pauses. "Ser . . ."

"I need a dispatch sent." Lerial extends the sheet. "I need this dispatch sent, and it needs to get to its destination swiftly. Go ahead and read it." He extends the envelope sheet. "And here is to whom it will go eventually."

Norstaan's eyes widen.

"Just read the dispatch first. Then you can ask questions."

When Norstaan finishes, he looks at Lerial, his expression half-quizzical, half-hopeful.

"The dispatch you have," Lerial explains, "will be enclosed, sealed, within a dispatch to Majer Jhalet, the commander of the Mirror Lancers in Cigoerne. Can you arrange for this, even with the chaos around us?"

"Yes, ser. Do you think . . ."

"I don't know. I only know two things in this regard. The first is that Rhamuel is likely to be the next duke and his health is paramount for the sake of Afrit. The second is that the healer in question is the only one in all Hamor who might be able to do more than I have."

"Ser . . . I can get it to Subcommander Ascaar in Shaelt . . . but to go farther south . . ."

"Then do so. His men, or Major Chorazt's in Luba, should be able to get the dispatch to the Lancer post in Ensenla, and the lancers there can get it to Cigoerne." *You can only hope that this will work. Even so, it took you almost two eightdays to cover that distance. A fast courier* ***might*** *do it in half that time.*

"Yes, ser. Will the duke . . . ?"

"I don't know. But I have to ask."

"Yes, ser." Norstaan nods. "I'll get the dispatch to Subcommander Ascaar. Both dispatches, I mean."

"Good. I'll have the package ready in less than a glass." Lerial pauses, then adds, "I'd appreciate it if you didn't tell the arms-commander. I wouldn't want to get his hopes up."

"Yes, ser. I understand."

You just hope Father and Emerya will understand as well. A second thought crosses his mind. *The majer would.*

XXIX

Just after dawn on fiveday morning, Lerial and his three companies leave the headquarters post and begin the ride south along the shore road toward South Post and South Point. The latest reports from Subcommander Dhresyl indicate that the Heldyans have moved to a point some three kays north of the Harbor Post, but show no signs of an imminent attack on Swartheld, and that more merchanters have ported at the tileworks, although scouts report those vessels to be carrying mounts.

The more Lerial thinks about the situation, the angrier he finds himself getting. Afrit, as a land, is wealthier than either Cigoerne or Heldya, and it has more people. Its merchants are richer, and yet they have watched Duke Khesyn build up forces and done little. The only mages or wizards in Afrit appear to be a handful controlled by the merchanters. So now, Lerial and his Lancers have to find a way to counter as many as a half-score, if not more, wizards, because Atroyan was too weak to control his own merchanters. If Lerial fails, Afrit will be weakened, perhaps enough to fall, and then, sooner or later, Cigoerne. To top it all off, someone among the merchanters, or perhaps more than one, is a traitor and has created explosions designed to leave Afrit leaderless and crippled. Lerial also can't help but wonder just what the traitor had used. Cammabark is certainly the most likely possibility, although there are other explosive powders, but none of the others are as easy to obtain . . . and thus, cammabark is the hardest to trace.

As Lerial and his forces approach South Post, across the bay to the east, the sky above the gray eastern shore and the buildings beyond it is beginning to brighten when an Afritan Guard undercaptain, flanked by two rankers and followed by two others, rides toward the Mirror Lancer force.

"Lord Lerial!" calls out the undercaptain. "We're here to escort you."

Lerial motions for the undercaptain to join him on the left. Kusyl rides on his right.

"Subcommander Drusyn has his command post in a warehouse on the shore road a half kay west of the Heldyan perimeter. He'd like to meet with you there, ser."

"We can do that," Lerial acknowledges. "Tell me what you know about their forces."

"It's hard to tell, ser. They've been using the stones of the old fort to build walls. If we try to get close, they throw that chaos-fire at us. They must have five battalions there."

"How many mounted?"

"Not many. Two or three companies at the most, and they arrived late yesterday after the Heldyans turned some of their flatboats into a pier of sorts."

That makes sense. "Did they try to land more men during the night?"

"Not that we could see."

"Have you lost many men?"

"Not too many, ser. The subcommander's had us stay behind walls and houses. If they leave the open places, we can cut them down, but we can't attack much because of their chaos-bolts."

Although Lerial asks more questions, he doesn't learn much more than there is a temporary stalemate of sorts before they rein up outside an oblong three-story stone warehouse and factorage, with a simple name on the sign over the narrow entrance—Whyppel. The upper windows are closed with salt-bleached gray shutters. Across the shore road from the warehouse and factorage is a stone pier. Unsurprisingly, there are no boats or vessels tied there.

Lerial dismounts and turns to Kusyl. "Have the men stand down, but ready to mount when I return."

"Yes, ser."

Then Lerial, shields ready, walks into the factorage, where he sees Drusyn standing over a counter on which maps are spread.

The subcommander straightens. "Good to see you, Overcaptain. Especially with what's facing us."

Lerial halts and looks at the maps for a moment, then asks, "Have they landed more men since last evening?"

"One flatboat's worth . . . for now. They'll tow more boats upstream. Then it will start all over again."

"How successful have you been in trying to burn their temporary pier?"

Drusyn shakes his head. "We've tried fire arrows, but they have men wetting it down all the time. I've posted archers to the south along the river. They've had some success in targeting flatboats with armsmen, but the last few flatboats before dark yesterday came with shields. They can't have that many, though. So once they offload, they push back into the current and angle for the east shore. They've got a galley out there, and they tow the empty boat to the shore. Whether they just use a wagon to take the shields back to the next boat or tow that boat back upstream I couldn't say."

"It sounds like your archers are slowing their reinforcements."

"Slowing, but that won't help if we can't attack and wipe out a good portion of the men they've already landed."

"Before they land more."

The subcommander nods.

"Do you know how many chaos-wizards they have?"

"More than one. Might be three. I don't think it's as many as four."

Lerial asks more questions, letting Drusyn reply, until he has a better idea of where the Heldyans are and how Drusyn's forces are deployed. Finally, he steps back from the counter.

"What do you plan?" asks the subcommander.

"To see what we can do to remove the chaos-wizards and allow your men to attack without that distraction. How?" Lerial shrugs. "That will depend on them."

"What do you need from us?"

"Just follow up and attack if we're successful in dealing with the wizards. We don't have enough rankers to be effective in a hand-to-hand situation where we can't charge." This isn't quite true, but the last thing Lerial wants to do is to lose large numbers of rankers in hand-to-hand fighting, especially in Afrit.

"I can see that. I've already informed all the officers not to be surprised if you and the Mirror Lancers arrived at some point."

"Thank you."

"Might I ask . . ."

"Why we're here?" Lerial offers a wry smile. "We'd rather fight Heldya alongside Afrit now than fight Heldya alone several years from now."

Drusyn stiffens, almost as if Lerial has offered an insult. Then he swallows.

Before the subcommander can reply, possibly with words he and Lerial both might regret later, Lerial adds, "It would be the same if you were aiding us in repulsing an attack on Cigoerne. Right now, Duke Khesyn has more armsmen than both Cigoerne and Afrit combined. We need to work together."

"I can see that," manages Drusyn, if stiffly.

"And you're hampered because you don't have many chaos-mages." *Except those employed by traitorous merchanters.* "I can usually handle a few of them . . . and that, hopefully, will allow your men to do what mine cannot."

Drusyn nods. "I had not thought in that fashion."

"We will never have the number of armsmen that Afrit or Heldya has," Lerial adds. He hopes he has mollified the subcommander at least to some degree. *You should have been more careful with your words.* "And we had best do what we can before there are even more Heldyans occupying South Point."

"I wish you well."

"Thank you." Lerial offers as warm a smile as he can before turning and leaving the warehouse. *Don't any of them, besides Rhamuel, see how weakened the merchanters have made Afrit?*

Once outside the warehouse, Lerial gathers his officers and Fheldar, briefing them on the general positions of the Heldyans. When he finishes, he adds, "In effect, we have to play the target to flush out the chaos-mages." *And you hope you're able to deal with them.*

"Ser . . ." ventures Strauxyn.

"You're wondering why we're doing this?" Lerial shakes his head. "There's the small matter of something like seventy-five Heldyan companies. If we can help Afrit destroy them, then we won't be fighting off a hundred companies outside of Cigoerne in five years . . . all by ourselves. And it certainly won't hurt to have the arms-commander's gratitude, since he is apparently the duke's sole heir." Lerial grins sardonically and turns to Kusyl. "And yes, it stinks worse than anything we've been stuck with yet." *So far.* For Lerial has doubts that they have seen anything close to the worst of the mess that Afrit has become. "We need to head out. I'd like to see what we're facing before the Heldyans land even more men. We'll lead with Eighth Company. Kusyl, you and Twenty-third Company bring up the rear. Keep an eye out. For all we know there might be Heldyans in position to attack from behind."

"Yes, ser."

Lerial waits until the companies are in riding order, three abreast, rather than in double files, and then gives the command. "Companies! Forward!"

As they ride toward South Point, less than a kay away, Lerial extends his order-chaos senses, focusing on trying to locate concentrations of chaos or more "orderly" points. He finds two clear swirls of chaos and one muted diffuse area of chaos, the kind of diffusion that suggests a chaos-shield and a more talented chaos-mage. There are no obvious signs of an ordermage. The two points of chaos are, from what he can tell, about a hundred yards back of the rough stone barricades thrown up by the Heldyans and about a hundred yards apart, barricades now visible less than five hundred yards ahead in the middle of the wide curve that the shore road takes around the point to where it parallels the Swarth River and becomes the river road.

Looking down one of the angled streets, little more than two hundred yards ahead, and probably only the same distance from the Heldyan barricades, Lerial sees horses tethered in a warehouse loading yard, with several Afritan Guards watching them, yet he does not see any Afritan troops along the shore road ahead. That suggests the chaos-wizards have already been lobbing chaos-bolts . . . or that the Afritan company officers are being cautious, based on what had happened on fourday.

At the next corner, out of view of anyone on the point, stands an Afritan captain, who gestures, motioning for the lancers to move to the side of the road.

"To the right at the corner!" Lerial orders.

Once the companies are clear of the shore road, Lerial rides back to the captain. "I take it that they have mages throwing firebolts?"

"Yes, ser. Every time we've tried to advance, they've sent chaos-fire against us."

Then this might might be the best place to begin. "Can you tell where it's coming from?"

"Not exactly, ser, but you see that low spot in the stones, right above that big crack in the long block?"

It takes Lerial a moment to locate the cracked block. "The one with the edge of the old fort above it?"

"Yes, ser. The chaos-bolts seem to come from behind there."

Lerial concentrates again, nodding as he locates the well of chaos behind the line of stone. He continues to study the rough stone barricade until he locates an area where the stones are lower, seemingly low enough for a mount to clear easily. There is a slight depression behind the stones, but not one that is particularly deep or wide. "We'll see what we can do. If we do manage to put a stop to the chaos-bolts and break their line, I trust you'll be able to take advantage of that."

"Yes, ser."

"Good." Lerial turns the gelding and rides back to the head of the Mirror Lancer column, where he again gathers his officers and begins to explain. "What we have to do is breach the Heldyan defenses and remove at least some of the chaos-wizards. That means we'll be a target, but unless we look like we're making a serious attack, the wizards won't reveal themselves. We'll take the back lanes until we get as close as we can. For the first attack, I'll lead Eighth Company. Eleventh and Twenty-third Company will stand ready to follow up, or to relieve Eighth Company, as necessary. After that, we'll see." *If there is an "after that."*

The three nod. Not a one looks particularly pleased.

Lerial can't blame them. He isn't pleased himself. "Same as before—Eighth Company in the fore, then Eleventh Company."

Lerial leads Eighth Company along the narrow lane. His order-senses indicate that, some hundred yards ahead, it will intersect a slightly wider street that in turn angles back to the shore or river road. Where it does, they will have gotten as close as they can to their point of attack without being exposed to chaos-fire. Even so, the low point on the stone barricade is still some fifty yards from where they will leave the side street to cross the shore road and attack. Lerial's plan is based on a swift attack that will keep the Heldyan wizards from immediately coordinating their response so that he can deal with the wizards separately.

Once they reach the end of the side street nearest their target, Lerial signals a halt, orders a re-formation to a five-man front, and again uses his order-senses to study the Heldyan positions. Nothing has changed—except that the sun is low above the ruined buildings of the river fort. There is a slight haze above the river so that the low light is not blinding, but it is likely to be distracting. On the other hand, if Lerial waits, more shielded flatboats are likely to land at the temporary Heldyan pier . . . and possibly more wizards.

Lerial concentrates on the nearest chaos-focus, then gestures to Fheldar. "Eighth Company! Forward!"

Clearly, Lerial's attack takes the Heldyans by surprise, because there is no reaction until the leading lancers are within twenty yards of the stone barricade. Then a few scattered arrows fly in Lerial's direction, but his personal shields deflect them.

Whhssst!

An arrow of chaos sizzles directly toward the leading five riders, moving so quickly that Lerial, much as he is expecting chaos from somewhere, barely can muster a twin five-line pattern deflection toward the Heldyan armsmen behind the stone barricade. His forced reaction results in an off-center line of deflected fire that only strikes perhaps half of the line, the rest slamming into the stones themselves.

A second chaos-bolt follows swiftly, but is not quite so powerful, and Lerial manages to redirect the fire across the defenders directly before the Mirror Lancers.

The first lancers are within a few yards of the stone barricade when

Lerial can sense mounting chaos, not just from the wizard who has twice loosed chaos, but also from the other unshielded wizard. Lerial immediately begins creating a triple ten-line return pattern.

Two chaos-bolts merge and flare toward Lerial, one of the most powerful bolts he's felt since he has arrived in Afrit, but the thirty lines of patterned order *twist* the chaos back at the nearer chaos-wizard. A pillar of reddish white geysers skyward, and silver mists flow over Lerial, evidence of the deaths of the wizard's guards and the wizard.

Lerial is staggered, and unsettled from that reaction, when another chaos-blast, far weaker, arches toward him. Instinctively, he order-parries it and returns it.

A smaller wave of chaos rises.

Lerial reins up, not wanting to charge across another fifty yards or so of open ground to reach what was likely the inner wall around the old fort, once likely more than two yards high, but now more like a yard and a half or a yard and a cubit high in most places. Most of the Heldyans who survived the redirected chaos and the Mirror Lancer charge are either behind that higher wall or scrambling back to reach it.

The third chaos-wizard has vanished—at least from Lerial's order-senses. *Because you're getting tired? Or does he have a different kind of shield. You can't have stunned or killed him. He wasn't even near the others.*

He looks back across the shore road, where he sees a score or more of the Afritan Guards moving out—far too slowly—and heading toward the now-undefended stone barricade. Then, belatedly, he turns and surveys the river. He swallows as he sees several more flatboats, separated by close to thirty yards, and headed toward the temporary pier. All three flatboats have shield walls on the shoreward side.

What can you do?

Without drawing on a white wizard's chaos, he can't use chaos against the men on the boats, and without knowing where the last chaos-mage is, he can't use order-chaos separation effectively because, unless he uses it near the mage, the mage's shields are likely strong enough to withstand the destruction. *Unless you push matters, and then you'll end up destroying the Heldyans, the mage, your own men, and a chunk of Swartheld . . . and yourself . . . and the mage might still survive.* And he can't do much more with order-diversion because he is getting too tired to focus accurately.

Even in those brief moments of thought, he sees yet another flatboat, shielded on the shoreward side, moving in behind the first three, all angling toward the makeshift pier on the point.

At that moment, he wants to slam his palm into his forehead. *The frigging pier, of course!* While he knows he is stretching his reach and his abilities, the last thing he wants is to allow even more Heldyans to land, or land easily, particularly any more wizards or mages.

As carefully as he can, despite his blurring vision and aching head, he extends his senses to the middle of the covered flatboats that serve as the makeshift pier, then begins just a small order-chaos separation of the planks in the bottom of one of the flatboats . . . as well as a tiny order-chaos separation in the leading flatboat.

Chaos and steam erupt from the middle of the pier, then race in both directions, with flame and more steam. Squinting to try to make out whether the destruction he has wreaked has been adequate to accomplish his goal, Lerial finds himself even more light-headed . . . and weaving back and forth in the saddle.

"Ser?"

Fheldar's voice seems all too far away, so far that Lerial can barely hear him.

"Send a messenger to the subcommander . . . that we've destroyed the pier and a flatboat . . . that . . . will make . . . landing reinforcements . . . more difficult." As he speaks, Lerial is aware that each word requires more effort. "Archers . . . need . . . to target men wading . . . ashore . . ."

Why so hard to speak . . . ?

And then there is just blackness . . .

XXX

Lerial wakes stretched on a pallet lying in a large room that smells of wood . . . and more wood. His head is throbbing and his vision blurry, when what he can see is not blocked by sharp flashes of light. A young Mirror Lancer ranker sits beside him on a stool.

"Here's some lager, ser," says the ranker, whose name Lerial cannot remember, although he knows it . . . and knows he does.

Lerial slowly gathers himself into a sitting position, takes the water bottle, and begins to drink the lager. The first sips are hard because his mouth is so dry. After several sips, and then somewhat larger swallows, the throbbing drops from being excruciating to merely exceedingly painful.

"What time is it?"

"Second glass of the afternoon, ser."

"Did everyone get clear?"

"Yes, ser. Squad Leader Fheldar had us take care of the Heldyans who remained, then withdrew." The ranker's lips turn almost sardonic.

Lerial wonders about that, and is about to ask when he realizes that, for some reason, his hip, the part right under his knife, feels warm, almost as if it were sunburned. That thought leaves his mind as he sees Fheldar walk through the doorway of the lumber or timber factorage, or cabinetry shop.

"Good to see that you're still with us, ser." The senior squad leader gestures to the ranker, who backs away. Then Fheldar continues, "Begging your pardon, ser . . . but . . . if you won't think of yourself . . . would you think about what would happen if I have to report to Duke Kiedron that you got yourself killed in Afrit? Or who would defend Cigoerne against that bastard Khesyn?"

"I *thought* I was being careful, Fheldar. I misjudged. How many men did we lose?"

"Six dead, eight wounded. One likely won't make it." Fheldar's mouth twists into a disgusted expression. "Ser . . ."

"What is it?"

"The Heldyans retook everything we cleared out. Less than a company of the Afritans advanced, and then they withdrew after a single blast of chaos. Just a little blast, and it didn't even come close."

"Was there more chaos-fire after that?"

"No, ser. And the Afritans didn't even try another advance."

"At least the Heldyans couldn't land any more mounted forces." Lerial pauses. "Could they?"

"No, ser. But they did get another company of foot ashore. The Afritan archers picked off a few of them wading in from deeper water."

Lerial takes another, deeper, swallow of the lager.

Fheldar extends a small loaf of bread. "Didn't have any biscuits. Thought you might need something to eat."

"Thank you." Lerial has no doubts that he does, especially before meeting with whoever is in charge of the Afritan forces—which he intends to do. "I just hope the Heldyans don't come to know my weaknesses as well as you do."

"What you do takes a lot of food. I've never seen a fat mage or wizard, and you all eat a lot."

"Would you find out who the majer in charge of the battalion that didn't follow up is . . . and where he is?"

"Yes, ser. I can do that."

It is a good half glass later when Lerial meets with Majer Fhaet at an empty shop that once likely held a coppersmith or tinsmith. Fhaet is a slightly rotund and fresh-faced blond officer.

"Overcaptain Lerial . . . How gracious of you to let me know of your presence."

"I was perhaps too interested in stopping the Heldyans from overrunning you. I had hoped that the captain I had informed would relay my intentions."

"That is scarcely the usual procedure, for a captain to order a majer."

These aren't usual times. "You're absolutely correct, Majer, but might I ask why, once it became obvious that we had cleared out the Heldyans, your men didn't follow up?"

The majer does not meet Lerial's eyes. "As I indicated, you never told me what you were doing, ser."

"I told the captain of the company nearest to us." *As well as Subcommander Drusyn.* But Lerial does not mention Drusyn, since that would only make Drusyn look bad, and matters with Drusyn are already touchy. Besides, Lerial has to admit, he should have talked matters over with the majer first. *You really should have.* Once again, his desire to resolve the situation before it worsened led him into acting, rather than talking, and his inexperience in dealing with fragmented and regimented command structures has complicated matters even further.

"I didn't know that, ser . . . and the other captains said there was too much chaos-fire."

Your other captains are idiots, then. Lerial manages not to blurt out those words. He also ignores the implication that the majer overruled the one captain and pulled his company back, while refusing to let the others advance. Instead, he massages his forehead, and then the back of his neck. "The area on the other side of the stone barricades was cleared. All they had to do was advance to the stones and use them for cover. The chaos-fire isn't very effective against stone."

"I listen to my captains, ser."

Much as Lerial wants to strangle the majer, he nods. "Obviously, you do." He smiles politely. "I will make sure you know the next time we have to clear out the Heldyans." He pauses and adds. "For a second time. Good afternoon." He does not wait for a response, but turns and leaves Fhaet.

"What did the majer say?" asks Strauxyn as Lerial walks toward his gelding.

"His captains felt it was too dangerous to advance, and he listens to his captains." Lerial mounts, then looks at Fheldar, Strauxyn, and Kusyl. "We can't do anything more this afternoon." ***You*** *can't anyway, and there's no sense in risking Mirror Lancers when the Afritan officers won't risk their own men.* "There's obviously some confusion among the Afritan senior field officers. So I need to go talk to Subcommander Drusyn."

A third of a glass later, after Lerial and the Mirror Lancers have made their way along back streets to the shore road and then back to Drusyn's temporary headquarters, Lerial walks slowly into the factorage.

"I didn't expect you back so soon. You've taken care of the chaos-mages?" Drusyn smiles warily.

"Two out of three, and we managed to destroy the temporary pier and two flatboats. After we had accomplished that, unfortunately some of that chaos came back and stunned me. Then there was a communications problem. Although we had cleared all the Heldyans from their forward line, and the last chaos-wizard was unable to attack, only one Afritan Guard captain followed up, and the battalion majer called back everyone." Lerial shrugs. "So I didn't feel like sacrificing my men without support . . . and the Heldyans have reoccupied their former lines."

"Majer Fhaet reported that he did not have clear orders and that there was too much chaos flying."

Already? Fhaet must have sent an urgent message with a fast horse and rider, Lerial realizes. That tempers his reply. "The majer is partly correct. I did not make our maneuvers clear to all your officers, but only to the captain of the nearest company. The majer is perhaps excessively cautious, since after I was stunned, there was only one single small chaos-bolt launched."

"You did not return to the fight, later, then?"

"Subcommander . . ." Lerial takes a slow deep breath. "My head is splitting. I can barely see. The effect of trying to redirect chaos leaves few marks—unless one fails, and then there are no marks at all, just a pile of ashes. Attempting something that would have turned me into ashes would scarcely benefit either Afrit or Cigoerne. We did destroy a good battalion's worth of Heldyans, the pier and two flatboats. Perhaps I've missed something, but I haven't seen either much effort or much in the way of results from the Afritan Guard so far."

"We do not have your skills."

"That is true, but it is your land and your city." Before Drusyn can say more, Lerial continues, knowing he has once again antagonized the subcommander. *But you're hurting and angry, and if it weren't so critical in terms of stopping the Heldyans quickly, you wouldn't even be here. Either in Afrit or Swartheld . . . or talking to Drusyn.* "Tomorrow, weather permitting, we will attack again, with the goal of removing the last chaos-wizard here. If we are successful, you and your men will be totally responsible for dealing with the Heldyan armsmen."

"While you take another half day to . . . recover?" Drusyn doesn't conceal the edge to his voice.

"No. So that the Mirror Lancers and I can ride north, hopefully before the four or more chaos-wizards that are moving toward the Harbor Post inflict too much damage on Subcommander Dhresyl's forces—those remaining after the traitor-caused explosion that killed Commander Nythalt and injured or killed more than two battalions of Afritan Guards. You might not have heard, but I was with Twenty-third Company when we were the ones to discover the forces landing north of Swartheld at the tileworks. We managed to destroy a battalion of them, perhaps more, before they mustered four chaos-wizards and three more battalions, but that was enough to delay them a day or more."

Drusyn's mouth almost opens. He is silent for several moments. Then he says quietly, "You did not mention any of that."

Even though his head is still pounding, if slightly more dully, Lerial offers a wry smile. "No. That's another thing I forgot to mention, but I didn't know you didn't know. I'm not in your chain of command." What Lerial feels he cannot mention is that he would have felt rather strange telling Norstaan and Rhamuel what to put in the arms-commander's orders to his senior officers, and in all the confusion following the explosion at the palace and Rhamuel's injuries, Lerial wonders what else he should have written or had conveyed . . . and whether conveying in writing what he did would have been a good idea in the first place—if he'd even have thought of it . . . which he hadn't.

"I hadn't thought about that," Drusyn admits. He takes a deep breath. "I'm sorry."

"So am I," replies Lerial. "I trust you can see that I'm not trying to avoid things or leave you in an impossible situation, but the arms-commander felt that if the Mirror Lancers and I could act quickly here and remove the worst threats, then you could contain and handle the Heldyans, while everyone else tries to stop the larger force to the north."

"That makes sense . . ."

"But we didn't spell it out. Part of that was because of the arms-commander's injuries. Now that Commander Sammyl is there, communications should improve." *Not that you're at all convinced of that.*

"How badly is he injured?"

"He's bruised all over, and his left leg is broken. He has no feeling in his legs and cannot move them. He's well in control of himself," *at least when we left,* "and is using the undamaged west part of the palace as his headquarters."

"But . . . he is likely the heir . . . and if he is so damaged . . ."

"He may recover. Sometimes people do." *Most don't, but that problem can wait.* "But, if we don't stop the Heldyans, it won't matter who will succeed who as duke."

"Not everyone is likely to feel that way," Drusyn points out.

"Those who are more concerned about who rules might be the best ones to look at in search of the traitor who blew up the palace . . . and the Harbor Post." *And spreading that idea might put a damper on some of the maneuvering for power among the merchanters.*

"You really don't think . . . ?"

"Who else? The only people who have the resources to do that are merchanters. Most likely whoever set it up corrupted someone in the palace and an officer in the Afritan Guard. In turn, they might have been promised great gains by Duke Khesyn if he is successful in conquering Afrit. Even if he is not, he's weakened Afrit, and it costs him little."

"You don't have a high opinion of our merchanters, do you?"

Do you, really? "Not your merchanters . . . any merchanters, including those in Cigoerne. Merchanters are necessary. Most necessary, but trusting them blindly is unwise."

"Then how would you trust them?"

"Only when they profit by our success," replies Lerial dryly. After a moment, he goes on. "Perhaps we should plan out what will happen tomorrow morning so that there is no confusion as there was today."

Drusyn nods.

As he moves toward the counter on which the maps are spread, Lerial can only hope he has mitigated the impact of his earlier words.

XXXI

After spending more than a glass working out details of what Lerial and the Mirror Lancers—and Drusyn's Afritan Guards—would do on sixday, Lerial and the Lancers withdraw to South Post, where Drusyn has arranged for quarters and rations. For the rest of the day, through dinner, and even when he is falling asleep in a room in the officers' quarters, the same thought keeps running through Lerial's mind. *You have to find a way to deal with that last chaos-wizard. Otherwise, Drusyn and his idiot majers will sit here until they lose.* That thought is still there, stronger than ever, when he wakes and dresses on sixday, but he pushes it aside and gets on with readying himself and the three companies.

By slightly before seventh glass, they leave South Post. When they reach the factorage that serves as Subcommander Drusyn's command center, Lerial dismounts and makes his way inside.

"Good morning, Overcaptain," says Drusyn cheerfully.

"The same to you. Has anything changed at South Point?"

"Not so far. The Heldyans haven't landed any more men." The subcommander frowns. "I did receive a dispatch from the arms-commander. They're still bringing in men and mounts at the tileworks."

"That's good and bad. Good because they may not attack as soon as we feared, and bad . . ." Lerial shakes his head.

"Because they'll have a massive force there when they do."

After a moment, Lerial asks, "You have three battalions here?"

Drusyn nods. "Aerlyt's Fourth Battalion is on the south side, and Fhaet's Third is to the north and east of the point. Majer Knaak has Fifth in reserve, back slightly and between them." He gestures to the maps on the counters. "I can show you."

Lerial follows the subcommander to the counter.

"Third is here, Fourth here, and Fifth there." Drusyn looks up.

"Have you given the majers written orders?" Lerial asks cautiously.

"No. Do you think that's necessary?"

"I'd appreciate that. When there's conflict and confusion, there are some officers who have a tendency to forget orders that they question."

"I presume you're referring to Majer Fhaet."

"I apparently haven't made the best impression on him," Lerial says dryly, suspecting that his words are a massive understatement. "I'd prefer there not be any more confusion."

"I can understand that. I'll write up a brief order to all three majers and dispatch them by courier immediately."

"Thank you. I appreciate it."

"I appreciate your taking on chaos-mages." Drusyn actually smiles, if for a moment.

Once Lerial leaves the subcommander, he decides to proceed deliberately, even as he worries about what the Heldyans on South Point may be doing. First, he moves the three companies to a back street out of sight of the attackers, but within easy striking distance, then takes three rankers with him to visit each of the battalion commanders, beginning with the reserve battalion.

His eyes study the high thin gray clouds, which will probably burn off by midmorning, but which will mean that the Mirror Lancers will not be riding into the sun. The air is still, damp, and heavy. The streets are deserted, although Lerial can sense people watching through the cracks in shuttered windows, and the echoes from the gelding's hoofs on the stone pavement sound hollow. He sees a single smudge-gray cat sitting on a sand barrel. The cat looks back at Lerial evenly, and so regally that he smiles.

Once Lerial turns onto Spinners' Lane, he has no trouble locating the Fifth Battalion command post, since the horses outside a café ahead are the only sign of any activity.

Lerial has barely reined up when Majer Knaak hurries off a narrow porch where he is meeting with his captains to see Lerial. "Good morning, Overcaptain. Amazing what you did yesterday." He shakes his head. "Too bad we couldn't take advantage of it."

Lerial dismounts, ties the gelding to the end of the hitching rail, then turns to the majer. "There was a bit of confusion. That's why I'm here. We're going to try to remove the last of the chaos-mages to make matters easier. But it would be best if . . ." Lerial goes on to explain what he and Drusyn have planned.

When Lerial finishes, Knaak, a short man with black and gray hair, nods approvingly. "That sounds good to me. You know we're in reserve, though."

"I know, but I thought you should hear it from me."

"Appreciate it." Knaak offers a warm and open smile. "We wish you the best, and we'll be ready if we're needed."

From there, Lerial makes his way to the Rusty Nail, a tavern one block off the river road on the south side of the point, less than a hundred yards from where Majer Aerlyt has positioned Fourth Battalion. While Aerlyt does not come out to meet Lerial, a junior squad leader does and escorts Lerial into a small side room, most likely a plaques or gaming room.

Aerlyt rises from the table and smiles. He is silver-haired and easily the oldest Afritan Guard officer that Lerial has met, at least so far. He listens intently as Lerial explains, then says, "I wish I'd known what you were doing yesterday. We were slow to react, and then Fhaet sent word that we weren't to attack."

That sleazy worm. Lerial still manages an apologetic smile. "That was my fault. I thought Subcommander Drusyn had informed you, and he thought I had." Lerial isn't going to go so far as to admit just how much he had fouled up matters, but it is becoming more clear that he had overlooked far too much. "So we planned today's attack together, and I thought it best to check with each battalion commander before beginning our attack."

"It helps when everyone's clear on who will do what." Aerlyt smiles. "We'll be ready, Overcaptain."

"Thank you."

The last stop is the empty tinsmith's shop. There are no officers around, except for Fhaet himself, and he barely looks up as Lerial enters the front area of the shop.

"Good morning, Majer," Lerial offers pleasantly.

"Good morning, Overcaptain."

"I just wanted to stop by before we begin our attack so that you would know what we're doing, and how your battalion is expected to follow up."

Fhaet smiles politely, but scarcely pleasantly. "I understand what you're doing, Overcaptain. I've read the subcommander's orders, and I'm a good Afritan officer."

Lerial doesn't like Fhaet's tone, or the way he is responding, but doesn't wish to push. "We'll be starting our attack shortly. I just thought you should know so that you can follow up if we're successful."

"We'll do what is necessary, Overcaptain."

"I'm sure that you will. I appreciate that."

"I won't keep you, Overcaptain."

"Nor I you, Majer."

As he leaves the former tinsmith's shop and rides back toward the Mirror Lancers, Lerial cannot help but wonder exactly why Fhaet is so politely unpleasant. *What does he have against you? Or Cigoerne?*

"Everyone's ready, ser," Fheldar announces when Lerial reins up on the side street, just out of sight of South Point.

"Good. It's going to be a few moments."

As he did on fiveday, Lerial uses his eyes and order-senses to survey the Heldyan positions. It is clear that they have built up the initial stone barricades to the point where it will be difficult for a mount to clear them, unlike before—another reminder of the costs of his haste and sloppiness and Fhaet's anger and/or incompetence. Still . . . there is an area some thirty yards to the north of the center of the barricade where perhaps the tiniest bit of order-chaos separation could create an opening wide enough for the Mirror Lancers, provided that Lerial can deal with the remaining chaos-mage. Except . . . his senses reveal that there are now two chaos focal points, one most likely the diffuse and shielded mage who survived the attack on five-day, the other a more open and less-shielded and likely younger white wizard.

But Drusyn reported that the Heldyans didn't land any more men. Lerial frowns. The combination of more armsmen behind the first line of the rough stone wall, the increased height of that barricade, and, now, another mage suggests all too strongly that either Drusyn is lying or that he is relying on Fhaet, who is either failing to report or sending false or incomplete reports. Lerial can only hope it is the second possibility, but even that doesn't reflect all that well on Drusyn. He forces himself to study the entire South Point area once more, slowly and methodically.

Finally, he nods.

"Ser?" asks Fheldar.

"Apparently, Majer Fhaet failed to notice or to notify the subcommander that the Heldyans did manage to land a few more troopers. I'd judge another two companies, possibly three. Pass the word that we'll attack with two companies, Eighth and Eleventh. Undercaptain Kusyl is to reinforce us where necessary."

"Yes, ser."

A tenth of a glass passes before Lerial receives word that all companies are ready. He strengthens his shields, then orders, "Mirror Lancers! Forward!"

Unlike on fiveday, Lerial's forces have barely cleared the side street and begun to move toward the stone barricade when the first firebolt arches almost lazily from somewhere behind the stone barricade but forward of the old walls of the fort proper. It is not aimed at Lerial, however, but at the rear squad of Eleventh Company—the most distant part of the formation from Lerial.

Because it is a small chaos-bolt, Lerial uses a twin five-line order-pattern to redirect the chaos back down behind the front stone barricade along where he intends to attack.

Another chaos-bolt arches higher and seems aimed farther back, toward Twenty-third Company, but Lerial intercepts it as well and angles it into the Heldyan troopers to the south of those who perished from the first firebolt.

Abruptly, a shielded column of Heldyan foot rises and charges out of the north end of the stone barricade, as far from Lerial and his lancers as possible, clearly heading for Third Battalion, while avoiding the Mirror Lancers. Leading, as well as flanking the south side of the column, are shieldmen and pikemen, enough so that Lerial wishes that he had ordered his men armed with their lances. Without them, charging the column would result in far too many deaths and injuries.

Frig! "Mirror Lancers! Halt!" Lerial immediately creates the smallest amount of order-chaos separation in one of the shields in the middle of the column roughly two ranks back from the front.

Chaos erupts, but not nearly so much as Lerial would have thought—if only for a moment, as the remainder of that chaos is gathered and arrowed straight toward him. Lerial parries and redirects the chaos he has created back toward the chaos-wizard who has been throwing the firebolts, if while trying to keep track of the stronger and more concealed chaos-mage.

Sun-white chaos flares where the first wizard had been, then flashes toward Lerial like lightning, so quickly that he has no time to react, but his shields throw the chaos back toward the remaining Heldyan chaos-mage, who in turn boosts more chaos and returns the chaos to Lerial.

On the third pass, Lerial is ready and uses a triple ten-line pattern to focus all that chaos into a narrow lightning-like spear back at the chaos-mage.

WHHHSTT!

The entire front wall of the old fort explodes into a seething wall of sun-white heat, tinged with golden red, so bright that Lerial cannot even see for several moments thereafter.

When he can see, he finds his hands are shaking, not quite uncontrollably.

Only the last squad or so of the Heldyan column remains, and those survivors scramble back toward the remnants of the old fort.

It takes Lerial two hands to grasp his water bottle, uncork it, and take a swallow . . . then another. He looks around . . . and has to swallow hard. Four men in the front rank of Eighth Company, the two at each end of the rank, are charred corpses. So are their mounts, the result of Lerial's shields, wide enough to protect him and those on each side, and quick enough to keep the chaos from passing the front rank. One of those rankers had been Vominen, the Verdyn lancer and scout who had left the Verdyn Lancers to join Eighth Company . . . and Lerial.

For several moments, Lerial just remains in his saddle. He swallows again, then forces himself to study the area before him. Still no one is moving. It is as if the rapid series of chaos-battles has frozen the Heldyans in place.

Lerial uses his order-chaos senses to seek out any signs that might remain of concentrated order or chaos. There are none.

"Mirror Lancers! Hold position!" He turns to Fheldar. "Send messengers to Third and Fourth Battalions that the chaos-wizards have been removed. They can handle the Heldyans from here on." *We've already lost enough men dealing with the results of Afritan weakness and incompetence.* Even as he thinks that, he knows the losses will continue . . . and will likely get worse. But he needs to save his men for what only he and the Mirror Lancers can do.

He watches what remains of the barricades and the fort, takes another swallow of the watered lager, forcing it down, trying to ignore the stench of burned flesh . . . and waits for the Heldyan advance. Then he eats one of the hard biscuits he has brought, and swallows more watered lager.

Less than a tenth of a glass later, a Mirror Lancer rides toward Lerial and reins up.

"Ser . . . Undercaptain Kusyl wants you to know the Afritan battalion on the south and east side of the point is moving, but not the one to the north and west."

Somehow, Lerial isn't surprised. "Fheldar, hold the company here. If the Heldyans try an attack, charge them. Otherwise, just maintain the position here."

"Yes, ser."

Lerial raises the sabre he has not even been aware of drawing. "If the Afritans begin to advance, don't get in their way. If they don't, be ready." He shrugs. "For what, I don't know." *Yet.*

Lerial hates galloping down city streets. It's hard on the mount, and it's not all that pleasant for the rider. And, there's always the possibility of running into or over someone darting out of a side lane or alleyway. Nonetheless, he urges the gelding into a gallop toward where he thinks Majer Fhaet will be. Two rankers, dispatched by Fheldar, follow closely.

Holding his shields close to his body, because that takes less effort, Lerial turns the gelding back toward the empty tinsmith's shop on the side street where he had met Fhaet earlier. Fhaet is outside, mounted and flanked by several Afritan rankers. He is gesturing at the same captain who had followed Lerial's lead the day before and then pulled back.

". . . follow my orders, Captain . . ." Lerial overhears as he nears the pair. He can see that Fhaet is red in the face.

"I notice that the other battalion is advancing, Majer," Lerial says loudly as he reins up facing the majer and escorts or guards.

"I don't answer to you, Lord and Overcaptain. You're not my lord, and I've the discretion not to follow orders if it would endanger my men." Fhaet's face turns redder.

The captain eases his mount away from the majer, then gestures to the two rankers, saying in a low voice, "This is between superiors."

Fhaet glares at the captain and opens his mouth.

"Enough!" snaps Lerial. "You have verbal and written orders to attack. Are you going to order that attack?"

"No. You're not the one who can order me around. You're a foreign nobody."

Lerial is the one whose mouth almost drops open. Instead, he smiles, lifting his sabre slightly. "Is that your final answer? That you won't obey the orders issued by the arms-commander of Afrit and Subcommander Drusyn?"

"You wrote those orders for him." Fhaet offers a crooked smile. "Everyone knows that."

How do they know that? Lerial doesn't pursue that. Instead he rides toward Fhaet.

The majer's eyes barely have time to widen before Lerial's blade slashes across his throat. Lerial turns to the wide-eyed captain. "Since the majer was unwilling to carry out his orders, Captain, will you allow me to lead Third Battalion against the Heldyan invaders?"

The captain straightens. "Yes, ser!"

"Then we'd better get to it. The Heldyans tried to attack from the north side of the point, beyond the edge of the first line of defense. I suggest we attack there, since your men won't have to climb over the barricade."

"You lead, and we'll follow, ser."

"First, you have to get me where the battalion is," Lerial says dryly.

"Just one street over, ser."

The captain is as direct and accurate as the majer had failed to be, and in what seems moments, he and Lerial are at the head of a column of Afritan foot that stretches back more than a long block. The two Mirror Lancer rankers are drawn up directly behind Lerial.

Lerial surveys the formation. "A five-man front might be better."

"Yes, ser! Five men front!"

Once the column is re-formed, Lerial does not wait. "Third Battalion! Forward!" Lerial uses order to boost his voice, then urges the gelding forward at a quick walk, letting the front rank of the Afritan foot take the lead once they have emerged from the side street and crossed the shore road. Surprisingly, Third Battalion does not lag the Afritan Fourth Battalion by all that much, perhaps because Lerial's chaos-war had inflicted far more damage on the north end of the stone barricade, where there are few Heldyans remaining.

By circling slightly to the north, Lerial avoids marching the Afritan Guards through either Eighth or Eleventh Company . . . and while scattered Heldyan shields and bodies remain from what had been a shielded column, the Afritans meet little resistance until they reach what remains of the walls of the old fort. Once there, Lerial lets the Afritans storm over the low rubble that is all that remains of the west wall, and takes a position just short of the wall.

The Afritan captain details four rankers to remain with Lerial and the pair of Mirror Lancers, then urges his company into the old fort proper. The other four companies follow.

A glass later, the slaughter is over, and there are less than a hundred Heldyan survivors, mostly wounded. The only person who has felt Lerial's sabre was Majer Fhaet. Before long, the captain returns.

"Now what, ser?"

"Are you the senior captain?"

"Yes, ser."

"Then you're in command until Subcommander Drusyn relieves you or promotes you. I'd suggest that you and Majer Aerlyt keep a force here for a time. I'd also suggest that you write up what occurred between me and Majer Fhaet as accurately as possible. Make two copies, one for the subcommander. Keep the other. And I'd suggest you write it immediately, before someone hints you write it in a way that shades matters one way or another."

"But . . ."

Lerial smiles sadly. "Five people saw what happened. Usually two have trouble hushing something up. Tell what happened as it happened."

"Yes, ser."

"I need to talk to Majer Aerlyt. Have you seen him?"

"He's at the south entrance to the old fort."

"Good. Thank you, Captain. I appreciate your doing your duty well and effectively."

"Thank you, ser."

Lerial inclines his head, then rides, followed by the rankers, to the south end of the fort, where Aerlyt rides to meet him.

The older majer reins up beside Lerial and gestures toward the bodies in Heldyan bluish-gray and black, then shakes his head. "Stars, what a waste of armsmen."

"It wouldn't have been a waste if it kept us from reinforcing the battalions in the north," Lerial points out. "Or if they had defeated and scattered all the battalions from South Post. If they prevail in the north and conquer Afrit, all this will be forgotten. It's only a waste when you're defeated."

"You're cynical for one so young."

Lerial shakes his head. "Perhaps for one so young, but not for one responsible for so much death."

Aerlyt appears likely to say something, but then, after a moment of looking at Lerial, he merely nods, then says, "Is there anything else you need from us?"

"Just keep any other Heldyans from landing and hold the South Point until you get other orders from Subcommander Drusyn. We need to report what happened to him and then move north to deal with the other Heldyan force."

"We wish you well, Overcaptain."

"Thank you." Lerial nods and turns the gelding.

By the time he returns to the Mirror Lancers, all three companies are in traveling formation, with Eighth Company in the lead and Twenty-third bringing up the rear. But Fheldar, Strauxyn, and Kusyl are at the head of the column, waiting for his orders . . . and most likely his report, reflects Lerial.

"Ser . . . ?" ventures Strauxyn.

"Why did I lead the Afritan Third Battalion? Because their majer was unable to, and I wanted to make certain they attacked so that we wouldn't have to do this all over again a third time."

"That frigging majer, again," mutters someone.

"We won't have trouble with him again," Lerial says mildly. *With the reason we won't, we likely will, and that's what you'll have to explain to Drusyn . . . and Sammyl . . . and Rhamuel.* He almost sighs. "We need to get moving."

"Yes, ser."

Less than a fifth of a glass later, Lerial is walking into the former factorage that serves as Drusyn's command post.

Drusyn hurries toward Lerial, then stops.

"Your battalions hold South Point. Most of the Heldyans are dead. There might be a hundred survivors, most of them wounded."

"You're hard on your enemies," observes Drusyn.

"This time, your men did much of it, once we removed the two chaos-wizards and perhaps a company or two of Heldyans protecting them. We did have one major problem." Lerial does not smile at his own pun.

"Yes?"

"Majer Fhaet refused to attack, even after all the chaos-wizards had been removed."

Drusyn frowns. "You said that my battalions held South Point."

Lerial nods.

"But if . . ."

"I told him to follow your written orders. He refused. I asked him why. He declared that he didn't have to obey a foreign officer he outranked. I asked him why he didn't follow his own commander's orders. He said he didn't have to follow orders written by a foreign officer." Lerial shrugs tiredly. "So I cut him down for insubordination and led his battalion myself."

Drusyn's mouth drops open. "You . . ."

"I don't know about you, Subcommander, but in a war, I believe that the objective is to win as quickly and as decisively as possible, when possible. When it is not possible, the objective is to force as many casualties on the enemy as you are able to do with the smallest possible loss of life, before withdrawing and doing the same thing until you can defeat and destroy the enemy. Sitting around South Point only would have tied up more than three battalions when the arms-commander may need every battalion he can muster in the north. Sitting there neither inflicted losses, nor would it have destroyed the attackers."

Drusyn says nothing, clearly appalled.

"Oh . . . and by the way, he apparently forgot, did not notice, or did notice and failed to inform you that the Heldyans landed another three companies—and another chaos-wizard—sometime late yesterday or during the night. That didn't make anything any easier for anyone. You can take your pick on whether that was incompetence, willful neglect, or treason." Lerial inclines his head politely. "You now have three battalions free to move to support the Harbor Post. I will so inform Commander Sammyl and the arms-commander."

"You're not exactly . . ." Drusyn shakes his head.

"I tend to forget to be politic when facing treason or incompetence, Subcommander, especially when I'm risking my life and the lives of my men to defend another land from an invasion also enabled by treason. Under such circumstances, you might feel less inclined to be politic as well." Lerial softens his voice. "Except, unhappily, you can't afford to be less than politic, and I understand that. So feel free to blame me for whatever's necessary."

"For the sake of all of us," Drusyn says evenly, "try to be a bit more politic in dealing with Sammyl."

"I will . . . and thank you."

As he leaves the subcommander, Lerial knows that Drusyn is right, but that doesn't make him feel any better, not given the scale of incompetence and outright treason he's already encountered. That thought engenders another, one even more stark in some ways—*Was that the way it was in Cyador at the end?*

From the hints he received from Altyrn, both when the majer had been training him, and in the last letter Maejora had delivered, he fears that it was . . . and that is not the heritage that Altyrn wanted Lerial to remember . . . or continue.

And he still has to report to Sammyl and Rhamuel. At the thought of Rhamuel, he can only hope that Norstaan has been successful in getting his dispatch on its way.

XXXII

Third glass is ringing out across Swartheld when the Mirror Lancers enter the Afritan Guard headquarters post. It takes almost a glass to get everything settled before Lerial can again ride out, this time to the palace, accompanied by a squad from Eleventh Company, so that he can report to Sammyl and Rhamuel. Although the latest reports indicate that Heldyans continue to build up their forces less than three kays north of the Harbor Post, they have not yet begun to attack. For his part, Lerial can only hope that Rhamuel remains strong enough to function as arms-commander . . . and that Subcommander Dhresyl is successfully reorganizing and commanding the Afritan Guards from the Harbor Post.

What strikes Lerial as he rides toward the palace is that the streets and ways are only slightly less crowded than they have been in the past. *Doesn't anyone know how close the Heldyans are?* Or is that because Swartheld has never been attacked so no one really believes it will happen? He would like to know what the people he rides past on the streets really think. *But now is not the time to ask . . . as if you even had that time.*

On the other hand, a full squad of Afritan Guards is posted at the outer gates to the palace and nearly as many at the gates to the inner courtyard. None attempt to stop Lerial and his squad, although there are only two Afritan rankers leading the way. Once inside the courtyard, Lerial and his squad ride around the rubble—now roughly stacked piles of stone that have been set against the lower walls of the palace—to the stables. By the time Lerial is dismounting, an Afritan ranker is hurrying toward him.

"Is something the matter?" *More the matter, you should be asking.*

"No, ser. Both Commander Sammyl and the arms-commander left word with the duty squad that you were to be escorted to see them immediately whenever you arrived."

That doesn't exactly reassure Lerial, although he can hope that the mention of Rhamuel in those orders is encouraging. He walks swiftly across the courtyard behind the ranker, into the part of the palace connecting the two sections, and eventually up two flights of stairs and to the rooms serving Rhamuel. Outside the doorway to the sitting room is a pair of rankers.

In the sitting room, Commander Sammyl is seated at a desk, maps on one side, and papers on the other. At Lerial's entrance, he immediately rises, a slight frown on his face.

"Is he awake?" asks Lerial.

"He doesn't sleep that much, and he wants to know everything."

"Then I should tell you both at the same time," replies Lerial.

"He'd appreciate that. There are a few questions . . ." Sammyl walks to the half-open door. "Lord Lerial is here."

"You two come in. No one else." Rhamuel's voice is strong, if slightly raspy.

Lerial follows the commander, then closes the door.

Rhamuel is propped up in the bed at a slight angle, but he immediately looks at Lerial. "I hope *you* have good news."

"The good news is that the Afritan Guard holds South Point—"

"We know that," says Sammyl almost blandly. "We don't know much more than that, except . . ." He pauses and looks to Rhamuel.

"Subcommander Drusyn forwarded Captain Grusart's report on your confrontation with Majer Fhaet. It's not pleasant reading."

"I imagine not." Lerial doesn't know what else to say, but he is somewhat surprised at the calmness in Rhamuel's voice. He is also astounded that both Grusart's report and that of Drusyn are already in Rhamuel's hands, except, if Rhamuel and Sammyl have that report and don't know the details of the battles . . . *Then Drusyn didn't wait to write his own report, except likely a few lines saying that the Afritans held the point. Did you upset them both that much?*

"Drusyn intimates that you might have been more politic," Rhamuel goes on. "According to what Grusart wrote, Fhaet was an arrogant and condescending idiot. What would you say to those comments?"

"They're both right . . . and I'm not so certain that Fhaet was an idiot. I do wonder whether he was paid to try to slow down the attacks on the Heldyans."

"Why do you say that?"

"Because there's been treason or betrayal, if you want to call it that, in more than a few places. Someone in the Afritan Guard, and that someone had to be a captain or of higher rank, enabled the placement of cammabark or something similar in the Harbor Post. Someone trusted had to have planted explosives in the palace."

"Unhappily, I have to agree with you," says Rhamuel.

"One rumor suggests a Cigoernean officer," adds Sammyl.

"That would have been rather difficult," Lerial says dryly, "since no Mirror Lancer has ever brought more than himself or a kit bag into the palace, and no Mirror Lancer has ever set foot in Harbor Post." After a moment, he adds, "There were a number of barrels on the third level of the palace, though. Has anyone found Dafaal . . . or his body?"

"No," replies Sammyl. "That was my question, but it could easily have been someone working on the repairs."

"That would mean an even larger plot," Lerial says.

Sammyl nods, almost reluctantly, it seems to Lerial.

"We can't do much about the explosion right now. What happened at South Point?" demands Rhamuel.

"As we agreed, the Mirror Lancers and I immediately rode to meet with Subcommander Drusyn . . ." Lerial proceeds to relate the entire story, including his own failure to inform the battalion majers on fiveday.

When he finishes, Sammyl frowns, then asks, "You did tell Subcommander Drusyn exactly what you planned yesterday—before you took action?"

"Yes, ser. I told him. And I told Captain Grusart. I didn't tell any of the three majers."

"And you told Fhaet again this morning . . . and he received written orders from Drusyn?"

"I told Fhaet this morning. Subcommander Drusyn said he would send written orders. I never saw the orders, but all three majers confirmed that they received orders, and the other two indicated that they were aware of the attack. Fhaet said that he had received orders and that he was a good Afritan Guard officer. Because of the problems yesterday, I just indicated that we would be attacking and looked forward to his support if we were successful in removing the chaos-mages. He repeated that he was a good officer, or words to that effect."

"What about the other two majers?"

"Both of them were receptive and cooperative, and Major Aerlyt's forces moved on the Heldyans almost immediately after receiving word that we had removed the Heldyan mages."

Sammyl nods again. "That's one less Heldyan force to face."

"Draft orders to Drusyn to move his forces to support Dhresyl," declares Rhamuel, looking toward the door. "I want Lerial to see if he can discover more about what's wrong with me."

"Yes, ser."

"And close the door."

As Sammyl leaves, Lerial asks, "How do you feel?"

"How would you feel in overgrown swaddling clothes?" demands Rhamuel, who waits until the bedchamber door is closed before asking, "How long will I be like this?"

"The honest answer is that I don't know. The fact that you're awake and alert and feel some pain is a good sign, I think." *If Emerya were only here now. If the dispatch . . . if Father . . . if . . . if . . .* But the dispatch had likely not even reached Ascar yet.

"You think?"

"I'm not a master healer," Lerial points out. "Hold still, and let me—"

"What else am I going to do besides hold still?" interrupts Rhamuel.

Lerial ignores the question and concentrates on trying to sense all Rhamuel's injuries.

While there is still a knot of wound chaos just above the end of Rhamuel's backbone, Lerial can detect nothing else—except for the lighter and diffuse chaos of bruises almost everywhere. Finally, he steps back. "You're in better shape than I thought you'd be."

"This is better shape? I can't move my legs. At least I'm not pissing myself."

"You're not? That's good." *Very good.* "How does your back feel?"

"The part just below my waist . . . Let's just say it hurts more than I want to dwell on. Below my ass, I can't feel anything." Rhamuel looks at Lerial. "Don't tell me everything will get better, either."

"It looks like you will get better. Whether you'll be as hale and hearty as you were . . . that's less likely."

"So I'll be a weakling arms-commander or duke?"

"That's a matter of judgment and will, not physical strength, and you know that more than anyone," replies Lerial, not quite tartly.

"You sound just like your aunt. Do you know that?"

"I don't think she'd agree." Since there is little more he can say about Rhamuel's condition at the moment, Lerial asks, "Have you any word on the rest of the family?"

"Haesychya and Kyedra are safe with Aenslem. They found Natroyor's body in the rubble, but I think I told you that. Atroyan's, too."

Actually, Norstaan had told Lerial of Natroyor's death, but Lerial nods.

"Both Norstaan and Sammyl saw the slash in his throat. I told them to say nothing, but . . ."

"That will out, sooner or later," suggests Lerial.

"Later is better, I think. There's no word on Mykel. I sent couriers to Lake Reomer, with word for him to remain there."

"He didn't go unescorted, did he?"

"He had a half squad of palace guards, and Oestyn had two personal guards supplied by his father."

"That's all?" asks Lerial.

"That was what my brother deemed appropriate. They were well provisioned. Jhosef always provides for their . . . journeys."

"You're still worried, aren't you?"

"After all this, wouldn't you be? This was well planned, and if Aenslem hadn't gotten ill, most likely Haesychya and Kyedra would be laid out with Atroyan and Natroyor."

"And you as well." Lerial has to wonder about Aenslem's "illness," but perhaps the merchanter had truly been ill, and Lerial cannot see what Aenslem would gain by Atroyan's death, or the death of his grandson. Still, it's something to keep in mind. "Who would gain from all this?"

"Offhand, I can't say. It could be Khesyn or Heldyan merchanters . . . or someone with a grudge against my brother."

"Or someone who made an arrangement with Khesyn." Lerial frowns. "It has to be someone with golds and resources. An unhappy merchanter."

"Where do we start looking? Except for Aenslem and Fhastal, they're all unhappy about something." Rhamuel looks up at the knock on the door. "Yes?"

"There's a dispatch from Subcommander Dhresyl, ser."

"Bring it in."

Sammyl immediately opens the door and, dispatch in hand, walks to the bedside.

Rhamuel takes the dispatch and reads it. Then he looks up. "Dhresyl thinks the Heldyans will attack in force tomorrow. Certainly no later than on eightday." His eyes go to Sammyl. "Is there any other information?"

"No, ser. No signs of any other Heldyan forces. Not so far."

Rhamuel looks to Lerial. "Do you think there will be others?"

"It's always possible, but given the size of the two forces . . ."

"You think it's unlikely. What about you, Sammyl?"

"I couldn't say, ser. Who would have thought they'd attack Swartheld itself?"

Except that's the logical place to attack, and Luba was likely half a feint.

"For now, at least, we need to get Drusyn's battalions to join Dhresyl's forces," Rhamuel goes on.

Sammyl clears his throat. "Ah . . . ser . . ."

"You think you should be with the subcommanders?" asks Rhamuel.

"I am the chief of staff . . ."

"And that's why I need you here, now. That does raise a question. Who do you think should be in overall field command—Dhresyl or Drusyn?"

"Drusyn is senior . . ."

"But you think Dhresyl is a better field commander."

"Yes, ser." Sammyl frowns. "I don't know that, but he has a wider view."

"Then you need to write up another dispatch appointing him as acting commander, with a copy to Drusyn. Immediately."

"Yes, ser." Sammyl does not move, but looks pointedly at Lerial.

"Lord Lerial," asks Rhamuel, his voice almost formal, for all the hints of raspiness in it, "can we again count on your support?"

"We will be happy to support Afrit, especially in dealing with Heldyan mages and wizards. I fear any other use of a mere three companies would merely waste men."

"In the dispatch to Dhresyl, also make that point about the use of the Mirror Lancers."

"Yes, ser."

"Now . . . go draft all those orders so that all the battalion commanders—and Dhresyl—know what they're doing and who's in charge."

Sammyl nods. "Yes, ser."

"And don't look so glum. I happen to need someone who knows all the commanders and battalions and everything else. And that means you. If I weren't confined to this frigging bed, it would be different. But I am, and you're stuck here, Sammyl."

"I just had thought . . . ser . . ."

"You saw how much better things were once Overcaptain Lerial got you here to take over. Do you think I want to go back to that chaos mess?"

"No, ser."

"Good. Now . . . if you would get those orders drafted . . ."

"Yes, ser." Sammyl actually smiles, if briefly, before he turns and leaves.

Even so, Lerial can see that Rhamuel doesn't want Sammyl in the field. *Because he's not that good a strategist and field commander? Or for some other reason?*

"Can you actually handle four chaos-wizards?" asks Rhamuel.

"Not all at once. Possibly only one at a time." Lerial pauses, thinking of the power he had sensed when he had withdrawn from the forces south of the tileworks. "And . . . possibly . . . one of them might be strong enough to destroy me."

"Then don't confront one that strong. Use your abilities on the others. Even the strongest chaos-mage can't remain in Afrit if we can defeat all the Heldyan armsmen around him."

"I've thought of that," Lerial admits.

"Think some more about other ways, if necessary."

Rhamuel's firm words convey something close to desperation . . . and the unspoken point that Afrit has no chaos-mages worthy of the name . . . and that raises yet another question. *Why not?* And another. *If not, why has Khesyn not known and not invaded sooner?* Lerial has the definite feeling that, if he ever discovers the answer, he won't like it.

"I will, but I'd better leave. We need to make some preparations, and I need to move the companies to the Harbor Post."

"Then go. But be as careful as you can."

"I will." Lerial appreciates the thought, but he has his doubts. Somehow . . . Nonetheless, he manages a smile.

As he walks from the bedchamber, he is already thinking about what will be necessary. The first thing that crosses his mind is that he needs to make certain all the Mirror Lancer companies are carrying lances, especially after what he has seen so far about the Heldyan companies and their tactics. Then there is the problem of feeling out Subcommander Dhresyl . . . and his thoughts and tactics . . . and the ever-present feeling that he has overlooked or missed something very obvious . . . and that such an omission will prove deadly.

XXXIII

By half past sixth glass of sixday evening, Lerial and his three companies of Mirror Lancers are as settled as they can be into a single battered barracks in the southeast corner of the Harbor Post. After reaching the post and reporting to acting Commander Dhresyl, and asking for and receiving a sheaf of blank paper, Lerial almost immediately departs with Kusyl, Strauxyn, a squad from Eighth Company, and an Afritan scout familiar with the deployment of the Heldyan forces.

They only ride about a kay before turning west on a dirt lane. Less than two hundred yards from the shore road, the scout reins up. "You can see how they're set up from here, ser. They've lined up companies from the shore to the hill over there." The scout points. "The hamlet—that's where their headquarters are. Leastwise, that's where everyone rides to."

The hamlet is a rough clumping of perhaps a score of cots on the west side of the shore road, set on a flat to the north of a small creek that flows under a bridge crossing the shore road and into the bay. Surprisingly, there are few reeds or marsh grasses where the creek joins the bay. Recently turned fields, now covered with rows of tents, extend more than a kay west of the road before giving way to a sparsely grassed slope rising to a long ridge that roughly parallels the shoreline. Almost due west, and just a shade north of the hamlet, there is a dip in the ridge that would afford an easier passage than riding over the ridge. Lerial can see men and mounts posted there, as well as lookouts on the ridge on both sides of the low point. He takes out one of the sheets of paper and uses a grease marker to sketch the Heldyan camp and the brook and other key features of the terrain.

"What's beyond the ridge? Can we ride far enough that way to get a glimpse of the land there?"

"Yes, ser. Not much there. Ground's not too rough, but not much grass and more than a few thornbushes, the low prickly kind."

As they ride westward along the higher ground on the south side of the creek, Lerial studies the west end of the fields, trying to memorize them so that he can add them to his map. A low grassy swale separates the fields from the gradual slope of the ridge, which is sandier and less grassy than Lerial had originally thought. The swale is almost, but not quite, a natural moat, but Lerial doesn't see that it would be that much of a barrier to the lancers, especially if they could surprise the Heldyans. On the other hand, the slope up from the creek to the north flat is steeper than it first looked, although the creek is also narrower, no more than a yard across and likely less than a half yard deep, from what Lerial can see.

After half a kay or so, the scout again reins up where the lane turns to the southwest to parallel the swale. Lerial can see that the creek flows northward in the center of the swale until it reaches a point some hundred yards northwest of him where it turns, almost abruptly, to the east and toward the bay. Absently, he wonders when the creek was diverted

"You can just see part of the back of the ridge from here," says the scout. "You want to go farther?"

Lerial doesn't answer, but studies the back of the ridge, taking out his crude map and sketching in more details. The part he can see has what might pass for a forest, a mixture of dryland pines and tree cactuses that seems to stretch almost a kay, perhaps a third of a kay south of the low point in the ridge and two-thirds of a kay north.

"Is there a trail through that low point?"

"No, ser. Maybe a footpath, but it's steep between the first ridge and the second one back."

"How do you get around those trees?" asks Lerial, thinking about Dhresyl's comments about scouts.

"There's a trail just below the top of the next ridge. Must go a good five kays before it runs into the shore road. Wouldn't want to ride the last kay though. Heldyans have patrols there."

"Where does it go to the south?"

"There's another lane off the shore road."

"Good." Lerial nods. "You can show us that on the way back. I think I've seen enough."

"Yes, ser."

Lerial can sense a certain puzzlement from the scout, but that's fine with him. The fewer people who can guess exactly what he is thinking, the better.

A glass later, Lerial is meeting with acting commander Dhresyl and Drusyn in a tiny room adjoining a small chamber off the south end of what had been the auxiliary troopers' mess hall. The larger of the two small chambers clearly serves as both headquarters and the senior officers' mess since the destruction of the headquarters and main messing buildings.

Dhresyl is scarcely imposing physically—stoop-shouldered and slight of build, with short shaggy brown hair and a receding hairline—but his eyes are an intense hazel-yellow that reminds Lerial of a predatory vulcrow, and his voice is firm, but somehow mellow as he continues his briefing. "... been rotating battalions holding the hills overlooking shore road a mille to the north ... saw no sense in having everyone out there when we can be there in less than a glass ..."

"How far between your battalions and their advance forces?" asks Drusyn.

Lerial refrains from commenting, allowing Dhresyl to answer the question.

"About a kay and a half. They're set up in that hamlet. It's so small it doesn't have a name. They're keeping something like two battalions in reserve at the tileworks. Might be three."

"And they've made no advances south of the hamlet?" presses Drusyn.

"No. Not a one."

"Have they sent scouts or small forces south and west as though they might make an encircling move?" asks Lerial.

"I've worried about that. I've kept more than a company, squads and single scouts, patrolling to the west, and even to the north. I wanted to see if they'd invested Baiet. They haven't. Not as of yesterday."

"And you think that they'll attack tomorrow because they built large cookfires today?" Drusyn's voice is skeptical.

"Tomorrow or the next day. You don't want to be fixing warm meals when you're on the march. They also haven't landed any more men and mounts in the last two days, and there aren't any merchanters tied up at the tileworks pier."

"Did your scouts find out anything about the merchanters porting there?"

Dhresyl shakes his head. "For the most part, the scouts couldn't get that close. Those few they could spy had canvas over their names and ports and flew no colors."

"So they were likely hired and possibly not even from Hamor," says Drusyn.

"Hired, but some might be from Hamor," suggests Lerial. "If all names were covered, how could we tell?"

"Sailors talk, sooner or later," replies Dhresyl. "If they were Hamorian, someone would find out. If they're outlanders, with their names covered and no colors, even if they ported here later and talked in the inns or taverns, if they spoke other than Hamorian, who would understand?"

"Why would outlanders do that?"

"For golds and a chance to ruin Afritan traders at the same time," Dhresyl points out.

Lerial understands that. *And you should have thought about sailors talking. You've listened to lancers talking often enough.* Is his slowness because he's tired and the last days have been long? He can only hope that is the reason.

After several more questions from Drusyn, more about billeting and messing, there is little more to be discussed, and Lerial and Drusyn leave the temporary headquarters. Once outside, he glances at the evening sky. It is clear, with no sign of rain. Even his order-senses suggest that the next few days will be fair . . . and that also suggests Dhresyl is correct about the coming attack.

"Do you know why Commander Sammyl and the arms-commander decided to put Dhresyl in overall command?" asks Drusyn in a low voice once they are well away from Dhresyl and the mess chamber.

"No, I don't. They didn't ask me. I hope you don't take offense, but they shouldn't have. I've seen your battalions fight, and they've been effective both times," *when Fhaet didn't get in the way,* "but I know nothing about any of the other subcommanders besides you and Ascaar."

"I can see that, but Dhresyl . . ."

"He's junior to you and doesn't have any more experience?" says Lerial gently.

"That's . . . the best way of putting it."

"I have no idea on what they made their decision," Lerial says, and that is certainly truthful.

"Well . . . we'll see how well he does in the days ahead." Drusyn's voice holds a certain forced cheer.

"That's true for all of us," replies Lerial. "Speaking of the days ahead, I need to meet with my captains and pass on what Dhresyl told us."

"Me, too." With a nod, Drusyn turns toward the northwest corner of the Harbor Post, walking steadily toward the tents that shelter his battalions.

Lerial turns toward the small barracks.

Over the next tenth of a glass, he gathers Fheldar, Strauxyn, and Kusyl into the cramped narrow space that barely holds a bunk, a table desk, and the four of them. He relays all that he has learned from Dhresyl, then asks, "Have any of you heard anything?"

Strauxyn shakes his head.

"I had my squad leaders nose around," says Kusyl. "What they heard seems pretty much like you heard from the subcommander. There was one thing, though. We saw lots of chaos when we ran into the Heldyans up north. No one here has seen any. The Afritan battalions don't even have anyone who passes for a hedge wizard, begging your pardon, ser. The Afritans have to know they're facing chaos . . . and there are no mages."

"I've asked about that," Lerial replies. "I've been told that mages are rare in Afrit. The few that there are work for the wealthy merchanters."

"They can't spare them to defend Afrit?" asks Kusyl. "Doesn't seem that bright to me."

Fheldar nods.

That raises another question that Lerial does not ask. *If the Heldyans have mages and have had them for a time, and the Afritans don't, then why have they waited so long to attack Afrit?* Or is it just because it has taken Khesyn this long to unite his land and raise enough armsmen? Lerial has another thought. *Have all the attacks on Cigoerne been just a way of giving the Heldyans experience and training to deal with Afrit?* He finally says, "I can't answer that, not really, but I'd guess that Khesyn has been planning this for a very long time, and he didn't want to attack Afrit until he was certain that he wouldn't have trouble with the Tourlegyn nomads and all their clans. From what I know, that's the only thing that makes any sense." *And even that doesn't make that much sense.*

"Doesn't matter, one way or another," says Kusyl. "They got mages and wizards, and the Afritans want the overcaptain and us to deal with them."

"And if we don't here," adds Lerial, "we'll end up doing it again outside Cigoerne before long."

Kusyl offers a patently false long and doleful face. "More summer-old dead fish."

Even Lerial has to smile, if only for a moment.

After the three leave, he hopes he is not making a mistake by not telling the undercaptains the fundamental problem created by Dhresyl's and Rhamuel's defensive strategy . . . and the reason for his scouting trip. *If we wait until they hit us with four chaos-mages or more . . .* He shakes his head, recalling how he and Twenty-third Company had been forced to withdraw from even the initial invasion force. *And if they've added more mages . . . You definitely need to talk to Dhresyl . . . early tomorrow.*

Somehow he needs to persuade the commander to allow him to do what he has in mind. Whether he can or not, he will have to do it, or risk death or an ignominious retreat in a huge pitched battle. But persuading Dhresyl would be better. *Much better.*

XXXIV

Lerial is up before dawn on sevenday, finishing sketching out a clearer version of the map of the Heldyan camp he had made the night before. Then, before he heads to the senior officers' mess for breakfast, Lerial walks across the large courtyard to the east side, where he studies the ruins of the main mess hall and the headquarters building some fifty yards west of the mess. He frowns. Although the undercaptains he encountered the night before insisted that the explosions began in the mess-hall kitchens, Lerial cannot see how that explosion could possibly have destroyed the headquarters building. With a nod, he turns and makes his way to the makeshift officers' mess. Since there is a vacant chair beside Dhresyl, in fact, several on each side, Lerial takes the one to the commander's right.

"Good morning, Overcaptain."

"Good morning, ser. Are there any reports yet?"

"Only that there were no cookfires this morning. The Heldyans haven't formed up . . . or hadn't less than a fifth of a glass ago."

"Speaking of fires, do you know what caused the explosion here?"

"It had to be cammabark. I'd guess it was brought into the post in barrels, labeled as flour or something else, and put in the kitchen near the ovens so the heat would dry it out . . . and then it would have only taken a single flame, maybe even just a candle beside a barrel . . ."

"It couldn't have been labeled as flour," muses Lerial.

Both wait as a ranker places platters in front of them, containing some form of eggs, cheese and thin slivers of what Lerial hopes is ham.

"Lager, if you have it?" Lerial requests.

"Yes, ser."

Once the ranker has moved away, Dhresyl asks, "Why don't you think the barrels were labeled as flour?"

"Flour dust can explode. The cooks would know that. They'd only keep what they needed." Lerial pauses. "Most cooks wouldn't keep anything close to the ovens unless they were going to use it soon."

"There's not much else that comes in barrels—mutton, some dried beef, pickled root vegetables, dried fruit, but we only get a few barrels of that—too costly, you know."

The ranker returns with Lerial's lager, then departs. Lerial takes a swallow, sets down the beaker, and says, "The headquarters building couldn't have been that badly damaged from an explosion in the kitchens."

"No . . . and that's troubling. Both Commander Nythalt and Subcommander Mhorig were there, and, of course, Cythern and Varndyr, for the morning commanders' meeting. I should have been, but the scouts were briefing me on the fog and the fact that they insisted merchanters were porting north at the tileworks. That was so unusual that I took some time to arrange for another scouting party. That made me late. I was just leaving the front gates when everything exploded."

"So who else was missing, from the battalion commanders, I mean, besides you?"

"Subcommander Shaerthyn. He had violent flux."

How convenient.

Before Lerial can say more, Dhresyl goes on, "He's so ill that his consort fears he may not live. I visited him yesterday. He's in great pain. There's some thought he was poisoned."

"Poisoned? How? Does anyone know?"

"He and his consort went to a consorting ceremony last threeday evening. I remember thinking that threeday was an odd day for that . . ."

Lerial agrees. Almost all consortings are on sixday or sevenday. He takes another bite of the egg, cheese, and ham. It's hot and passable.

". . . and he sent word that he was ill the next morning. He's been worse every day."

"Is Commander Shaerthyn considered a good field commander?"

Dhresyl takes a swallow of greenberry juice and nods. "Perhaps not as good as Ascaar, but good. Certainly better than I am."

Dhresyl's last words surprise Lerial, but he manages to reply, "You're being modest, I'm sure."

"I wouldn't call myself a poor field commander, but outstanding?" Dhresyl shakes his head. "I'm better with logistics."

"And now you find yourself in command?"

"I'd relinquish command to Ascaar, if he were here, but he's not."

Almost the entire command structure wiped out, with the known most effective field commander poisoned, the duke and his family largely wiped out, and the only two survivors are Rhamuel through quick action and luck and Dhresyl through sheer chance. Lerial is staggered by the apparent combination of advance planning and treachery behind the Heldyan invasion.

Dhresyl takes another swallow of greenberry. "Not much we can do about what's already happened. I've asked Commander Sammyl to send for Subcommander Ascaar and his battalions."

"He only has one at Shaelt. The other is still at Luba," Lerial says.

"Another battalion will help, but Ascaar will help more. Right now, Drusyn is the only battalion commander with any experience at all . . ."

Again, Lerial hears the implications behind Dhresyl's words.

". . . and you have more battle experience than any commander in all of Afrit."

"What do you plan for today?" Lerial asks, afraid that another officer will intrude before he can get to the point he needs to make, although he has not pushed, because he is trying to make the matter come up in the course of conversation.

"If they attack, reinforce the battalions in position south of them." Dhresyl raises his eyebrows. "The way you ask that . . . Do you have another idea?"

So much for indirection and subtlety. "I was thinking about an attack from the west."

"Any attack in force from there would leave too few battalions between them and the city."

"I wasn't thinking about an attack in force," Lerial replies. "Just one strong enough that they couldn't afford to ignore it."

Dhresyl frowns.

"That would give them pause, perhaps more," Lerial suggests.

"You think that will delay them?"

"If we can surprise them even a little, we might cause them unanticipated losses. Or, as you say, it might delay them. I think it's worth the effort, and we might be able to do some damage with an attack from a direction that they don't expect."

"What sort of attack?"

"Mounted, with lances. The Mirror Lancers aren't a large enough force by themselves, though, for enough of an effect."

"I couldn't divert more than a battalion, and there are only a few trained in lances."

Lerial can sense that Dhresyl believes that little support will cause Lerial to reconsider his recommendation. "That should do it, I would think."

After a momentary pause, Dhresyl replies, "It would have to be one of Drusyn's or Majer Paelwyr's Fourteenth."

"I've not met Majer Paelwyr." Lerial keeps his voice even.

"He's one of the more junior majers. Good head on his shoulders. He asks questions at the right time—before things happen. Then he follows orders."

"Then I'll leave the choice to you, ser."

"Paelwyr, I think. His battalion is all that remains of Subcommander Varndyr's command. Varndyr had the Thirteenth and Fourteen Battalions. What little that was left of the Thirteenth was transferred to the Twelfth." Dhresyl smiles professionally. "If you want to brief your officers, you have less than half a glass before the senior officers' meeting. That's assuming the Heldyans don't attack first."

"Thank you, ser."

Dhresyl shakes his head. "I suspect I'll be thanking you."

Lerial quickly finishes what remains of his breakfast and lager, departing as several majers enter the mess.

Fheldar and the two undercaptains are waiting outside his quarters' door.

"You left early this morning, ser," offers Kusyl.

"I needed to talk to Commander Dhresyl. He's given his approval for a surprise attack . . ." Lerial goes on to describe what he has in mind and what little he knows about Majer Paelwyr and Fourteenth Battalion.

He makes it back to the mess room with a few moments to spare. He isn't even the last one to arrive. Drusyn is, if but a few steps behind Lerial. Dhresyl gestures to the empty chairs flanking him. Lerial takes the one on the left, since he properly isn't actually in the Afritan command structure. While Drusyn is seating himself, Lerial studies the officers around the long table. Except for the three at the end, all six are majers, one of whom must be Paelwyr, whom he has not met. Considering that there should be ten, the way Lerial figures, that means that something like four battalions, or close to it, have been lost. It also means that there were close to ten battalions originally at the Harbor Post.

Dhresyl clears his throat, then begins. "As of a few moments ago, the Heldyans were not in any formation resembling an attack. Perhaps they're following the Kaordist doctrine of not fighting on sevenday." The commander smiles, an expression that is ironic, given that the Heldyans are largely followers of the God of the Balance, thanks at least in part to Khesyn's sire's brutal campaigns against the chaos animists. "That is the good news. On the other hand, our best estimates are that the Heldyans have between twelve and fifteen battalions. We think four are mounted. The others are most likely either heavy foot or archers.

"I have requested that, if possible, Subcommander Ascaar be allowed to add his forces to ours. Even if that is possible, we won't see them for an eightday. All of you have heard that Duke Atroyan was killed in the palace explosion. Arms-Commander Rhamuel was injured, but is still able, and Commander Sammyl is assisting him. Overcaptain Lerial of Cigoerne, here on my left, has joined our forces with his contingent of Mirror Lancers. If we do not see an immediate attack by the Heldyans this morning, then he and the Mirror Lancers will lead a diversionary attack on the Heldyans. He will be accompanied and supported by Majer Paelwyr and Fourteenth Battalion." Dhresyl inclines his head toward the left side of the table.

A majer nods slightly in response. The sandy-haired Paelwyr is the youngest-looking Afritan majer Lerial has encountered and is most likely only five or six years older than Lerial himself. Dhresyl's choice doesn't exactly surprise Lerial.

"Diversionary attack?" asks Drusyn politely.

"I'm sure Overcaptain Lerial can explain far better than I," replies Dhresyl.

"We'll attack from where the Heldyans are not expecting any attack," says Lerial. "That will allow us to inflict more casualties than would merely waiting for their attack. There is also a good chance that it will delay or change their plans."

Drusyn does not conceal his frown.

"A surprise attack against an enemy in a place where there aren't emplacements has a better chance of succeeding. Also, it will aid in keeping their chaos-wizards spread out in the future, and that will reduce the impact of chaos-firebolts when they attack."

"It will also allow the rest of us to observe how they react, which could prove most useful," adds Dhresyl. "Are there any other matters? No? Then the briefing is over."

Lerial can see that Dhresyl doesn't like meetings, and, for the most part, that's fine with him. He has barely risen when Paelwyr moves to join him.

"Overcaptain, ser, since Fourteenth Battalion is assigned to your command, I wanted to say that we're fully under your orders and command."

For today's attack. "Thank you for the forthrightness, Majer. How soon will Fourteenth Battalion be ready to ride out—with lances?"

"Less than half a glass, ser. The commander told me about the lances. I've had to borrow a few from Tenth Battalion. Some of ours were damaged by the explosion."

"That should do. If you'll come with me, I'll go over the plan with you and my undercaptains. Would you like me to include your company officers?" Lerial doesn't want Paelwyr to think that he wants to command Fourteenth Battalion directly, although he would like the Afritan captains to hear the plan firsthand and, in turn, see their reactions and hear any thoughts they might have.

"If you would, ser."

Lerial glances around, but all the other officers have left. "Then have them here as soon as you can."

"Yes, ser."

Lerial barely manages to retrieve his hand-drawn map and his company leaders before Paelwyr returns with his company officers. While they are gathering around the end of the long table, Lerial lays the small map on the wooden surface.

Then, with Paelwyr standing beside him, Lerial looks over Fheldar, his two undercaptains, and the five Afritan company officers. "Contrary to what some may think, this is not a gallant suicide attack. It's supposed to be a swift jab to the Heldyan western flank to put them off-balance, and, if we're successful, to inflict significant casualties before they can bring all their forces against us."

"Might I ask why?" asks Paelwyr almost matter-of-factly, clearly wanting more explanation for his officers.

"There are two reasons. First, an attack from the west will suggest we have more forces than we do, and that will make them more cautious. Second, the more casualties we can inflict before we engage in a huge battle, the better the odds for us when that happens."

"If this is successful, then you'll try again?"

"That depends on how successful and what the Heldyans do."

Paelwyr offers a broad smile. "We'll be pleased to be part of anything like that."

Lerial points to the map. "Here's where they are. They've posted at least a company in that low dip. Rather than attack there, we'll take the trail to the west past the scrub forest, and then attack from the northwest . . ." He goes on to detail what he has in mind. When he finishes, he looks to Paelwyr. "Do you have any questions, Majer?"

"How do you want us to handle any chaos-fire?"

"We have some defenses against that. If those defenses fail, you'll get an order to withdraw. If possible, we'll withdraw by heading south along the grassy swale . . . the same way we've planned to complete the attack—except sooner. If that is not possible, then I'd recommend heading due west, right over the ridge. The slope isn't that steep, and you shouldn't have to fight your way out. You would if you head for the dip in the ridge." Lerial pauses, then adds, "One other thing. Even if the Heldyans we attack break and scatter, you're not to pursue more than fifty to a hundred yards. If you do, you'll find yourselves surrounded, and, as I said earlier, this attack is not a gallant suicide charge. The idea is to disrupt and kill them, then withdraw without getting many of our men hurt or killed. Is that clear?"

"Yes, ser."

Lerial then answers several questions about command terms and what type of front he wants before there are no other inquiries, and he ends the briefing.

A third of a glass later, under a sun barely above the waters of the bay, and obscured partly by a haze that suggests a hot spring day, Lerial leads his combined force out through the gates of the Harbor Post and south, seemingly away from the Heldyans—but only for slightly more than half a kay before turning west on a narrow field lane, one beyond the sight of even any Heldyan lookouts on the rises around their encampment. The narrow lane makes progress slower than Lerial would prefer, and almost a glass passes before they have crossed the brook and two ridges and are headed north along the trail described by the Afritan scout.

Lerial is glad that the trail is hidden from the Heldyans, because his force is strung out for almost a kay on the trail, although he can order-sense his surroundings almost two kays away in the more open grounds away from cities and buildings, and there are only a few Heldyan scouts, and those are a good kay away, along the western perimeter of the Heldyan encampment. It is well past eighth glass when the combined forces reach a point north and west of the Heldyans and Lerial reforms the companies before they begin to circle more to the north around the area of pines and thornbushes that Lerial had noticed the day before.

Lerial, at the head of Eighth Company, still cannot sense any chaos-mages until he is less than half a kay from the Heldyan perimeter, just over the top of the ridge overlooking the western end of the Heldyan encampment. There he calls a halt while using his senses to get a better understanding of where the Heldyans are located. There are four chaos-mages, but three of the four are strong enough that they carry the diffuse shields that make discovering their location, except in very general terms, almost impossible. The Heldyans have mustered close to three battalions behind the low earth embankments they have created overlooking the creek.

After several long moments, Lerial decides that his original attack plan will not work in the way he had hoped, and he sends for Majer Paelwyr.

"Yes, ser?" Paelwyr reins up.

"We're going to have to change the plan of attack slightly, Majer. The Heldyans still have most of their forces in tents and quarters. There are likely about three to four battalions in ready positions, along the southern perimeter at the end of the flat ground overlooking the creek. We can do far more damage—and leave more quickly—if we charge down the western perimeter, behind their lines, until we reach the southern lines, and then swing east. We can cut through the defenders and make for the shore road. From what I can tell, there's only a company of mounted armsmen stationed at the east end of the hamlet, and they're well north of the southern defenders."

"You lead, and we'll follow, ser. I'll pass the changes on to the company officers."

"We'll wait until you can."

The one problem with Lerial's plan is that they will not be able to move down the east side of the slope at more than a fast walk, not until they reach the grassy swale, but that is a distance of less than two hundred yards, and even if the Heldyans notice them immediately, it will take some time for them to react, since there are far fewer defenders on the far west and north sides of the encampment.

Once Lerial is satisfied that Paelwyr has passed on the change to the Afritan companies, he turns to Fheldar. "Five-man front! Lances tight!" He waits as Fheldar and the undercaptains relay the orders, then adds, "Forward! Fast walk!"

All of Eighth Company is over the crest of the ridge and headed down, less than fifty yards from the grass of the swale, before Lerial can see any movement among the defenders, and he and the first ranks are at the swale before shields start forming.

"Charge!" Lerial raises his sabre, then drops it, letting the first rank sweep past him, since he is not carrying a lance, and then keeps pace with the second rank.

In moments, or so it seems, Eighth Company has smashed through the thin line of surprised defenders and turned south against the troopers manning the perimeter. By now loud clangings and horn signals are coming from everywhere in the Heldyan camp, along with shouted orders, and groups of armed Heldyans taking defensive positions almost randomly.

A single chaos-bolt arches from somewhere to Lerial's left toward Eighth Company, and Lerial immediately redirects it to a line of defenders on the south perimeter that has already pivoted to bring shields and pikes against the Mirror Lancers. The chaos-flame slashes through a score of shieldmen and pikemen.

Almost instantly, two lines of brilliant chaos-fire sear toward Lerial, almost as if the Heldyan mages had sent up the first chaos-bolt as a way to locate him. *Which they probably did.* He manages to deflect and redirect both bolts into more defenders, but the attack is so swift that he cannot redirect that force back at the mages.

Even before the next wave of chaos comes, though, he is forming a multiline order pattern that returns that chaos to the Heldyan mages. Fast as he has been, the Heldyan mages are just as swift—and add more chaos—to send that power again at Lerial. That return redirection gives Lerial a better feel, and his return of that massive chaos slams into one of the concealed chaos focuses.

WHHHSASSTTT!!

A pillar of brilliant reddish-white energy flares skyward, momentarily as bright as the white morning sun, so powerful that Lerial can barely sense the accompanying silver-gray death mist flowing out from the chaos, especially since some of that energy slams back at his shields, likely the effort of one of the surviving mages. A searing surge of heat burns at his hip, then fades.

"To the left!" roars Fheldar, for which Lerial is grateful, struggling as he is to deal with the Heldyan chaos-mages.

Lerial strengthens his shields, which have faded, and barely manages another redirection of chaos into the Heldyans ahead, just before the lances of Eighth Company rip into the remainder of those defenders. *You should have sent that back at the mages.*

With that thought, he immediately struggles to create a massive diversion pattern, suspecting that he will see more chaos focused on him. He almost does not finish the thought or the pattern before another intense blast of fused chaos strikes at him—one line from not quite directly behind him and another from ahead of him and slightly to his left. Sensing that the control must come from the wizard ahead, Lerial narrows the redirected chaos into a point.

Whhhsstt!!

The resulting chaos pillar is far narrower, but rises much higher than the previous one . . . and the silver mist is fainter.

Lerial sways in the saddle, realizing that he is most light-headed . . . and unlikely to survive another chaos-blast. Although he does not immediately sense a chaos buildup, he looks forward to the shore road, still almost half a kay away, then again tries to sense the concentrations of chaos. He can find only two, both somewhat diminished, at least for the moment. *Did you manage to take out two?*

Still concentrating on staying in the saddle, he sees that the shore road is nearing, so much closer that he wonders if he has lost awareness for a time . . . or is it that he is so exhausted that even trying to sense chaos takes so much longer than he realizes?

As the Heldyans in front of Eighth Company scatter, Lerial calls out, "Battalions! Forward and withdraw!" The command is possibly unnecessary, but he knows he cannot parry, redirect, or even shield much more chaos. He also worries that he will not be able to issue commands for much longer, and he wants his force away from the Heldyans before the enemy mages recover enough to throw more chaos.

As the gelding reaches the road, and Lerial turns onto it, heading southeast and back toward the Harbor Post, Lerial remains so unsteady that it takes most of his concentration just to keep riding, but he does sense that, behind them, the Heldyans have rushed to reinforce the gap in their defenses, but that they do not keep pursuing. *Thank the Rational Stars for that.*

Finally, after the entire force is clear and has slowed to a fast walk, with Paelwyr's last company several hundred yards from the nearest Heldyan defenders, Lerial manages to fumble out his water bottle and take several swallows of watered lager.

He is still light-headed, with flashes of light and accompanying daggers of pain across his eyes, when he and the first ranks rein up in the courtyard of the Harbor Post. After a longer swallow that empties the water bottle, he lowers it, corks it, and turns to Fheldar. "Did you tell me how many we lost? If you did, I didn't hear."

"No, ser. I thought I'd wait until I could check again."

Lerial almost asks, "Why not?," but manages not to utter the words. "Let's find out." He can only hope that the casualties are not too high. He also wishes he'd taken some bread from the mess and stuffed it in his saddlebags. That would have helped with the light-headedness.

He isn't certain just how much time passes before Fheldar rides back to report, but doubts it could be much more than a tenth of a glass.

"Eighth Company, three killed, two missing, and likely dead, eight wounded, two seriously. Eleventh Company, six dead, eleven wounded. Twenty-third Company, four dead, seven wounded. Fourteenth Battalion is still determining their casualties, but Majer Paelwyr does not think that they were especially high, except possibly with his Fifth Company."

"Thank you." *Why would the last company have higher casualties . . . unless they lagged too far behind?* "Dismiss the men to quarters, the wounded to the healers. I'll see them shortly. Once the officers are through with their companies, and I hear more, I'll meet with them. If you'd convey to Majer Paelwyr that I'd like to meet with him in the senior officers' mess when he's available . . ."

"Yes, ser."

Lerial rides slowly to the stables, untouched by the earlier explosions, where he dismounts and turns the gelding over to an ostler, patting his mount on the shoulder before he walks back toward the makeshift senior officers' mess. Once there, even though it is not mealtime, he asks for lager, bread, and cheese. The sole ranker on duty does not question him.

Then he eats and drinks, deliberately. After a third of a glass, he begins to feel some strength returning, and the throbbing in his head and eyes begins to diminish. At the sound of a door opening, he turns his head to see Majer Paelwyr step into the mess.

"You requested to see me, Overcaptain?"

Lerial gestures to the table. "I did. I apologize for leaving, but . . . there was no help for it." He pauses only for a moment, not enough for Paelwyr to say anything, before going on. "How did your battalion fare?"

Paelwyr drops into the chair across the long table from Lerial. "Our casualties were light. Very light, given that we rode right through the Heldyan encampment. How did you manage that, ser?"

"Surprise. I doubt that anyone expected an attack like that. We were inside their lines before they could react."

"You *knew* where their lines were thin before you ever saw the encampment."

"I scouted it out yesterday. People seldom change their lines when they haven't been attacked." All of that is true and allows Lerial to avoid answering Paelwyr's implied question. "What were your casualties? I'll need to report them to the commander."

"Twenty-nine killed or missing, forty wounded, most only slightly."

Lerial nods. "That's good for what you accomplished. We likely created a battalion's worth of casualties. You obviously kept your men in an effective tight formation."

"Not quite as tight as I would have liked."

"That tight under those conditions was admirable."

"Will we be doing something like that again, ser?"

"Not like that. We may be called on to undertake another diversionary attack, but it will have to be different if we are."

"Is there anything else, ser?"

"Not for now. If that changes, I'll let you know."

"By your leave . . . then . . . ?"

"Of course." Lerial watches as Paelwyr rises and then leaves the mess. Once he is alone, he takes a swallow of the lager, then sets the beaker down. He worries about the thrust of Paelwyr's questions, and hopes he has defused at least some of the majer's suspicions.

"Overcaptain, ser?"

Lerial looks up to see a junior squad leader standing at the end of the mess table. "Yes?"

"Commander Dhresyl wanted you and Subcommander Drusyn to know that Subcommander Ascaar is fighting off four battalions of Heldyans at Shaelt."

"Thank you." Lerial can't say he is surprised.

"The commander would like to meet with you both as soon as Subcommander Drusyn arrives."

"I'll wait here for Subcommander Drusyn."

"Yes, ser." The squad leader nods and then hurries out.

Lerial takes another swallow of lager, realizing that the beaker is almost empty and that he has eaten the entire small loaf of bread and the wedge of cheese.

"Would you like more, ser?" asks the mess ranker.

"Please."

Lerial has only drunk several swallows from the second beaker of lager when Drusyn walks into the senior officers' mess.

"I hear you did some damage to the Heldyans . . ." begins the subcommander.

"Both of you in here, if you would!" calls Dhresyl from the small chamber adjoining the mess.

Lerial rises from the table, taking the beaker with him, and joins Drusyn in entering the smaller room, where Dhresyl sits behind a table desk. The commander looks askance at the half beaker of lager that Lerial carries.

"It's been a long morning . . . day." Lerial takes one of the straight-backed chairs before the desk and sits down.

Drusyn takes the other chair.

"What sort of damage did you inflict on the Heldyans?"

"We cost them at least a battalion, possibly two," replies Lerial.

"You don't know the enemy casualties?" The commander frowns.

"It wouldn't have been wise to remain close enough to count." Lerial takes another swallow of lager. "We rode inside the western perimeter of their encampment and then along the southern edge. Along the way, we took out as many as we could without stopping or slowing."

"They didn't pursue?"

"Not beyond their own lines."

"What about their pikes and shields?"

"They're not nearly as effective if you attack them from the side or from behind . . . and if your riders have lances." Lerial's tone is dry.

"I see. What about your casualties?"

"The Mirror Lancers lost fifteen men and suffered twenty-six wounded. Fourteenth Battalion lost twenty-nine and had forty wounded."

"A hundred or so casualties from a diversionary attack?" Dhresyl's eyebrows lift.

"A diversionary attack that removed over a battalion of Heldyans." *And likely two chaos-mages.*

"It is rather difficult to kill a large number of enemy armsmen without losing some troopers," Drusyn adds dryly.

After he leaves Drusyn and Dhresyl, Lerial makes his way to the officers' quarters, where he gathers Fheldar, Strauxyn, and Kusyl and briefs them on the situation Ascaar is facing.

"Doesn't surprise you, does it, ser?" asks Fheldar.

"I would have been surprised if there hadn't been another attack somewhere, and an attack on Ascaar makes sense." *And the fact that Khesyn knows where all Rhamuel's forces are makes another kind of sense.*

"Do you think the Heldyans will attack somewhere else?" Strauxyn looks intently at Lerial.

"You can never tell, but I would doubt it. All these attacks are designed to destroy the Afritan Guard. So far as I know, there aren't any large Guard forces anywhere else besides where the last four attacks have been. There's more likely to be an attack somewhere else in Swartheld than in any other town or city."

"Begging your pardon, ser," begins Kusyl, "but what did the commander really want?"

Lerial can't help smiling faintly, since he has not mentioned that Dhresyl wanted anything, but Kusyl has been in the Lancers far longer than Lerial—long enough to be skeptical of senior officers and to know that they often want far more than seems reasonable. "To know why our casualties were so high."

"We ought to bring him along next time," says Strauxyn.

"Wouldn't do any good," drawls Kusyl. "Have to be able to see what you're looking at."

Fheldar offers the smallest of headshakes, then asks, "What's next, ser?"

"That depends on the Heldyans. I'd be happy if they just don't attack today."

"When do you think they will?"

"If they're smart, and they've generally been effective, they'll attack tomorrow. Plan on that. If they don't, the men will get another day to recover." *And you'll start worrying about what else they've caused to go wrong somewhere else.* Lerial manages a smile. "That's all for now."

After he leaves them and begins to walk to his small room, where he hopes he can take a nap or at least rest, his mind is already considering the possibilities of what the days ahead will bring.

XXXV

Lerial awakens early on eightday, feeling the heavy stillness of the air even at dawn. When he looks outside, the sky is darker than usual for dawn, and he can discern a thick haze overhead. At least his headache has finally vanished, and there are no flashes across his eyes. He washes, shaves, and dresses quickly, then makes his way to the duty officer stationed in the small chamber off the senior officers' mess.

The captain on duty looks toward the door as Lerial enters, then straightens. "Ser?"

"Do you have any reports on the Heldyans?"

"Ah . . ." The captain yawns. "Sorry, ser. It's been a long watch. The last word came in about half a glass ago. The scouts report some movement in the center of the encampment. No companies appear to be forming up. They weren't then, that is."

"Do we have any word from the arms-commander?"

"Nothing since yesterday."

"No messages or dispatches for me?"

"No, ser. No dispatches since yesterday afternoon."

"Thank you." Lerial turns and walks back into the mess.

One of the servers hurries over. "Ser . . . ah . . ."

"Nothing's ready, I take it."

"Not yet, ser."

"I'll have a lager while I wait." Lerial settles into one of the chairs at the long table, worrying. *Why haven't there been any dispatches from Rhamuel? Has he taken a turn for the worse?* Yet at the same time, he knows that whether Rhamuel survives or perishes is, at least at the moment, secondary to the need to defeat and destroy the Heldyans and remove them from Afrit. *Destroying would be better, especially if Rhamuel does not survive.* Lerial just hopes that the arms-commander survives . . . and that his father and Emerya will agree to her coming to Swartheld . . . if she will even consider it. Even crippled, Rhamuel would be a far better duke than Atroyan had been, and Lerial shudders to think of Afrit under Mykel, if he has even survived . . . or one of the merchanters, since Kyedra would never be allowed to rule. *Then, they might consort her to the son of whatever merchanter took over so that they could claim the line would continue.* That thought also disturbs him, even as he considers that he scarcely knows her. He directs his thoughts back to the likely battle ahead.

He is still pondering over what role or task the Mirror Lancers might best accomplish in the face of the certain oncoming Heldyan attack when the server reappears with a beaker of lager and a platter with cheesed scrambled eggs and a still-steaming small loaf of bread.

"The cook thought you might need this now, ser."

"Thank you . . . and thank him. I appreciate it."

Lerial eats the eggs and bread—all of it—quickly, draining the beaker as well, then stands as he starts to head out to meet with his officers.

"Ser?" A junior squad leader hurries toward him. "There is a senior officers' meeting at half before seventh glass. Commander Dhresyl would appreciate meeting with you immediately before that."

"Did he say how much before?"

"No, ser."

"I'll plan to be there," Lerial gestures toward the door to Dhresyl's makeshift study, still only occupied by the duty officer, "a tenth of a glass before the meeting. If he needs more time than that, I'll be meeting with my officers." Lerial pauses briefly, then asks, "Did the commander say anything about the meeting?"

"No, ser."

"Thank you."

The squad leader turns and leaves the mess. Lerial follows him out but turns toward the junior officers' quarters. In less than a tenth of a glass, he has gathered Strauxyn, Fheldar, and Kusyl together in a corner outside the stables, where he briefs them on what he knows, finishing up with the message from Dhresyl. "I have no idea what he wants, but it's likely he wants to know what we intend to do if the Heldyans attack. I'd like your thoughts on that."

"Keep us out of the front lines," suggests Strauxyn. "It'd be a mess."

"Rankers will get so jammed together that we won't be able to use lances," adds Fheldar.

"We'd have more effect by circling and attacking their rear," says Kusyl.

"That'd also keep their wizards from frying a lot of the Afritans." He pauses. "Not that some of them couldn't use frying."

"Oh?" Lerial looks to the older undercaptain.

"Some of the majers and younger captains act like some mages, begging your pardon, ser, excepting they don't have talent at either leading or arms, from the way the old undercaptains look at them when they don't think anyone's watching."

Lerial manages not to grin. "Let's just let them do us a service by blunting the Heldyan attack."

Fheldar nods. Strauxyn looks puzzled for a moment, but only a moment.

Kusyl grins. "Sounds like a good idea to me. They need to do some of the hard work."

"Some more of the productive hard work," Lerial says. "They've already taken significant losses, but South Point was the only place in Swartheld where they managed to damage the Heldyans." He pauses. "That's unfair. What happened here also reveals the sort of attack we could expect if Cigoerne has to deal with Khesyn . . . and that knowledge isn't costing us anywhere near what it's cost Afrit."

"Shows what a total bastard Khesyn is," Kusyl comments. "He deserves some of his own poison."

"That may be, but first we need to deal with the armsmen outside Swartheld." *If we can.* "I'd like you to think over how you think we could be most effective while I meet with Commander Dhresyl."

After leaving the three, Lerial walks quickly back to the senior officers' mess and then to the door of the small study, now occupied just by Dhresyl, who motions for him to enter . . . and for him to close the door. Lerial does and then takes the chair across the table desk from the commander. "You requested my presence, ser."

"You're always so polite. You remind me of the arms-commander."

"How is he? Do you know?"

"According to Commander Sammyl's dispatch yesterday, he's alert and very much in command."

Lerial nods and waits, not that he totally trusts what Sammyl might write.

"I'm convinced that the Heldyans will begin their march on Swartheld today, later this morning. What I need to know is where you believe you and the Mirror Lancers would be most effective." Dhresyl's tone is even, not quite bland.

"I couldn't say until I know what you plan as a defense or a counter," replies Lerial.

"I've already positioned Ninth and Tenth Battalion behind earthworks across the road and to the east on the south side of the stream, even with First and Seventeenth Battalion. They're the ones on the south side of the stream opposite the Heldyans' south perimeter."

"You don't think they'll cross the stream and attack uphill?"

Dhresyl shakes his head, then says, "Not unless I move First and Seventeenth Battalion. Once the Heldyans commit to an attack, assuming they take the road, First and Seventeenth can either move north—if the Heldyans don't maintain their perimeter—hold against remaining forces, or move to support Ninth and Tenth . . . whatever's necessary. Drusyn's battalions will take position at the fork between the road to the post and the shore road . . . so that the Heldyans cannot move east off the shore road and flank our positions . . ."

Lerial listens as the commander continues to detail what he has in mind.

When Dhresyl finishes, he looks to Lerial, inquiringly.

"I think the Mirror Lancers should initially remain out of the immediate line of battle, but forward enough so that we can move quickly where we can do the most good."

"If . . ." Dhresyl does not finish his statement.

"If we hadn't already killed so many, it might sound like we had reservations about fighting. Is that what you meant, Commander? Putting the Mirror Lancers where they can't move destroys our effectiveness. Just let us do what we do best, and you won't regret it." Lerial knows that is a dangerous promise, but getting his men and himself in the middle of a massive melee would be even more deadly—and a total waste of men and mounts.

"Still . . ."

Lerial says nothing.

"What do you have in mind?"

"Destroying as many Heldyans as possible so that Khesyn cannot attack again any time soon."

"I can't fault that, but how . . . ?"

"By attacking where they're not expecting it. That's all I can say at the moment. Once you finish briefing the senior officers, I'd like to take a squad and study the situation while the Mirror Lancers ready themselves."

"That might be useful."

"I'm certain it will be," Lerial returns. "That way we'll know where to move and attack when the time comes." He hopes that reminder that the Mirror Lancers will indeed attack penetrates Dhresyl's skepticism.

"We might as well move into the mess for the briefing," says the commander as he rises.

Lerial stands and follows. Subcommander Drusyn is already there, as are several majers that Lerial does not recognize. By the time all the battalion commanders have arrived, in addition to Drusyn, Dhresyl, and Lerial, there are ten majers and one captain around the long table. Lerial recognizes only four—Paelwyr, Knaak, Aerlyt, and Captain Grusart, who is clearly replacing Majer Fhaet, whose loss, so far as Lerial is concerned, is a benefit to the Afritan Guard.

Dhresyl clears his throat loudly. "All of you know the general plan of battle from the orders you've received or from what I have informed you of personally. The latest scouting reports indicate that the Heldyans appear to be preparing to attack . . ." The commander goes on to give more details about what he expects from each battalion and then finishes by saying, "Overcaptain Lerial's forces will not be part of the initial order of battle, but will act independently and in coordination with the Afritan Guard."

Lerial notices a momentary frown from Drusyn and a faint smile that quickly vanishes from Paelwyr. Aerlyt nods almost sagely. The other majers offer no immediate reaction, almost as if that is what they have expected.

"Do you have any questions?" asks Dhresyl.

"How long will it take the Heldyans to move once they're formed up?"

Dhresyl looks to Lerial. "Overcaptain . . . you've seen the Heldyans in that situation. What would you say?"

"I've seen them turn an entire battalion with pikes and a shield wall in less than a tenth of a glass, and they can move forward at a trot, holding a shield wall. With the size of their forces, it will likely take them longer to initially form up, but they maneuver quickly."

"How many mounted battalions do they have?"

"The scouts have reported that they have five, possibly six," replies Dhresyl.

"What arms do they bear?" asks Lerial. *You should have asked that earlier. Much earlier.*

"The scouts couldn't tell, except that they had round shields."

"Heavy cavalry, most likely, not lancers, then."

After several more questions, Dhresyl simply stands. "Time to form up and be ready to move out."

Lerial leaves quickly. Less than a tenth of a glass later, after giving brief and more general instructions than he would have liked to his company commanders, he is riding down the paved road from the Harbor Post toward the shore road with a single squad from Twenty-third Company . . . and Kusyl. At the last lane short of the shore road, he turns northward because he doesn't want to interfere with the Afritan battalions and because he wants to determine if the lane is suitable for what he has in mind for his forces. After passing two cots and several sheds, the lane narrows into a wide path that will just hold two mounts comfortably, three if crowded. The ground between the path and the shore is rocky, with intermittent patches of grass, and slopes downward both toward the bay and to the north, although there is a small ridge about a half kay ahead. The ground between where he rides and the ridge rises enough that he can no longer see either the shore road or the Heldyan encampment, and there are two Afritan scouts reined up a hundred yards or so short of the section of the rise toward which Lerial leads the squad.

Farther from the Heldyans than you'd like, but it might do. "This way." He turns the gelding toward the north end of the low ridge, trying to see and sense the most level way through the rocky pasture.

"If this is as I think it is," Lerial says to Kusyl, "you'll be leading the Lancer forces back this way."

"What if the Heldyans want to take the rise here?" asks Kusyl.

"I'm thinking that they might, especially if there's only a small force visible."

"Do you think they'll expect what we're going to try?" asks Kusyl.

"They won't put the cavalry in the front. They'll want to use the road, if they can, before they try to flank Dhresyl. We haven't fought their heavy cavalry before. So it's likely they'll think we will charge directly, especially if we make it look good." Lerial can't see any other way that the Heldyans can bring their cavalry to bear effectively. *You just hope that they do what seems right. But then, usually an attacker with overwhelming forces doesn't try to be too innovative.*

Lerial continues to study the ground, as well as try to sense what lies over the rise and to the northwest. So far as he can tell, the Heldyans have not yet left their encampment, but he can feel a great number of men moving. He can also sense the two Afritan scouts watching as he and Kusyl and the squad ride east of them toward the slightly lower northern end of the rise. Once they reach a point where Lerial can survey the shore road some two hundred yards to the west and little more than twenty yards lower, he reins up and looks to the north and northwest.

All the Heldyan tents have been struck, and apparently stacked in neat bundles west of the hamlet. The organization and neatness worries Lerial as much as the number of battalions that appear to be formed up and ready to move, especially since he doubts that the Afritan Guards would be nearly so organized were they in Heldya.

Lerial turns to Kusyl. "I've seen enough. Take as many men as you need and get back to the post. Bring the companies the same way we came."

"Yes, ser."

Once Kusyl leaves, Lerial returns to studying the Heldyans. So far as he can sense, there are only two chaos-focuses among the Heldyan forces, and both remain within the encampment, but south of the cots of the hamlet that is either unnamed or whose name is unknown to Dhresyl and the Afritan Guard. *Another worrisome sign?* Lerial pushes that thought aside and continues to watch as the Heldyan formations tighten into disciplined oblongs. After a time, he turns in the saddle and looks toward the Harbor Post, where Drusyn's battalions are riding out toward the shore road, taking positions that will allow them to support either the Ninth or Tenth Battalion or to move north toward the position Lerial has taken.

Almost half a glass passes before the Mirror Lancers arrive and take positions on the east side of the hill, out of direct sight of the Heldyans. Then Lerial meets with Fheldar, Kusyl, and Strauxyn once again.

"We're going to stay put here until we see how things are going," he begins. "I'm judging that the Heldyans will bring up their cavalry to take this rise first, so that they can flank the Afritans . . . or keep Drusyn's battalions from flanking them. By being out here, we're in a strong position because we're uphill, but I suspect that they'll think that we don't have enough forces to hold the ridge." Lerial grins raggedly. "And they're right. We don't. But that's not what I have in mind . . ." He goes on to explain.

Once he has finished, the companies move into the tight formation Lerial wants, all out of easy sight except for the First Squad of Eighth Company. Then the company officers dispatch scouts . . . and Lerial waits and watches.

He feels as though time is dragging, yet he knows less than a glass has passed when he sees one of Strauxyn's scouts riding swiftly toward him.

The scout reins up. "Ser . . . there are two mounted battalions moving down the shore road . . . and there's more dust behind them."

"Are they lancers or heavy mounted cavalry?" Lerial doesn't totally trust Dhresyl's scouts.

"Heavy cavalry, ser. Round shields and long blades."

"Good. Thank you. Take a position just at the end of the rise. Halfway down. Let me know if you see anything else that might be unexpected. If you don't see anything like that, once the Heldyans are close enough for archers, rejoin your company."

"Yes, ser."

Before long, Lerial can see the Heldyan main force beginning to move. Half appear to be moving to take the road; the other half, led by a shield wall, are marching due south down the slope to the creek, and presumably up it toward Ninth and Tenth Battalion, contrary to what Dhresyl has expected. The total mass of armsmen moving forward must comprise close to ten battalions—and that doesn't include the mounted companies or any archers. *Khesyn must have been transporting troopers for more than a week . . . and kept it up over the last few days.* Just the number of trips and the presumed cost of transport must have been staggering. *Except the trip is fairly short.* Still . . .

Horn signals from the direction of the Harbor Post suggest that Dhresyl is already bringing up reinforcements, although Lerial cannot see past Drusyn's forces to determine where Dhresyl is sending the reserve battalions.

The lead Heldyan battalion moves off the shore road to take that part of the western side of the rise that offers the most gradual approach to Lerial and First Squad.

"Eighth Company! On First Squad," Lerial orders.

"Eighth Company! Forward!" Even before the order is completely out of Fheldar's mouth, the remainder of Eighth Company moves forward and rejoins First Squad. Eleventh and Twenty-third Companies also move forward, so that Eleventh Company is flanking Eighth on the right, if slightly back, and Twenty-third on the left, also back.

The Heldyan advance quickens, and the second Heldyan battalion speeds up even more, but does not take the slope but moves along the road, as if to cut off any possibility of the Mirror Lancers riding down to the road and withdrawing. Lerial doesn't even have to use order-senses to see that the third mounted Heldyan battalion is swinging more to the east, so that the three will eventually form a solid line, designed to sweep over the small Mirror Lancer force and then flank Dhresyl's main body.

Lerial glances south. Drusyn's forces remain planted firmly in place. *Good!* Then he looks back at the lancers, checking their spacing—each company set in a tight ten-man front, essentially almost a square. His eyes go back to the advancing Heldyan mounted battalions. Forcing himself to be patient, he waits . . . and waits . . . until the lead riders are barely more than fifty yards from the front rank of Eighth Company.

"Mirror Lancers! Charge!" Lerial drops back into the middle of the first rank as Eighth Company levels its lances and heads downhill directly toward the middle of the Heldyan cavalry. He hopes that they are far enough from the main forces that the Heldyan mages will not immediately direct their attention to what is happening on the flank.

Lerial hears a command he does not understand—except that its meaning is clear, because the Heldyans immediately raise and brace their shields, angling them so that they can try to slide the lances rather than take a full direct impact. When he is less than ten yards from the wide line of Heldyan cavalry, he shouts a single-word order. "Flank!" Then he turns the gelding at an angle left . . . and downhill, while raising order-shields wide enough to cover himself and two riders on each side.

When his shields sweep aside two Heldyans, Lerial manages not to be unhorsed by the impact pressure, but is forced to shrink the shields so that they barely cover himself and the gelding. Even so, the front ranks of Eighth Company shear across the southwestern corner of the Heldyan cavalry and keep moving toward the rear of the other cavalry battalion, still on the shore road.

Behind him, Lerial can sense that Eleventh and Twenty-third Companies have managed to rip at an angle across more ranks of the Heldyans and then close up, so that the Mirror Lancers are now a tight wedge charging into the side and rear of the second Heldyan cavalry battalion. Lerial urges the gelding forward, aiming for a slight gap between ranks, possibly a break between companies.

He can feel the pressure as he rides into that gap, and then fragments of silver mists as Eighth Company and the rest of the Mirror Lancers follow, cutting down Heldyan cavalrymen as they aim through the cavalry and toward the middle of the encampment that still holds the Heldyan reserves . . .

and at least two chaos-mages or wizards. Lerial knows all too well that not all of those death mists are from Heldyans. He hopes that moving quickly will keep the losses to his own men from being too great. *But what else can you do?*

From seemingly nowhere, a long blade slashes toward Lerial. He slides the heavier blade and backcuts as he passes, feeling that he has struck well, but not looking back, concentrating on where Eighth Company needs to go.

"Eighth Company! South on me!" He turns the gelding slightly, so that he is angling toward the westernmost point of the rear of the Heldyan reserves . . . or those that are mustered and actually moving toward the fighting.

Abruptly, a wave of chaos-flame flashes toward Eighth Company—and Lerial, who has been waiting for this, redirects it across the rear ranks of the Heldyan reserve foot battalions. Another more powerful chaos blast follows, and Lerial does the same.

Sensing what is likely to come next, he is already creating a multiorder line diversion and redirection pattern even before a line of brilliant gold chaos-fire sears directly at him.

The diversion sends it back at the chaos-mage. While the wizard's shields hold, the chaos flares in all directions from him, incinerating likely well more than a company of Heldyan foot. Lerial is readying another diversion when the other mage strikes, this time with a probe that Lerial recognizes—an attempt to separate order and chaos right before Eighth Company.

Lerial clamps shields over the probe for a moment, then tries to locate the other mage, but can only find the diffuse sense of a shield. The other mage's effort to shield himself breaks off the order-chaos separation effort, but the first mage sends more chaos at Lerial.

Again, Lerial redirects it—this time into the rear of the main body that has just engaged Dhresyl's forces.

Then both mages aim chaos at Lerial. He manages another diversion, but some of the chaos evades his pattern and strikes his shields, leaving his hip burning. *Burning? Of course. The knife's the anchor.* Sweat oozes from all over his body and dribbles down from his visor cap across his forehead, as well as down his neck in back. He can also sense that another Heldyan heavy cavalry force has turned from the shore road and gallops toward the Mirror Lancer rear.

You're running out of time and space.

He is also breathing heavily, and his arms ache.

Yet another chaos-bolt flares toward him, and redirecting it is an effort . . . But more Heldyan foot are turned to ashes . . . and silver death mists flow.

You're going to have to use order-chaos separation on at least one of those mages. He'd prefer aiming at the stronger one, but Lerial still cannot locate him precisely. *Except . . . if they're coordinating those attacks . . . they can't be that far apart . . . and besides, it should be easier just a bit away from their shields.*

He senses the slightly weaker mage ahead of him and to the south. Guessing that the stronger one must be more to his left, he begins to create a circle of order-chaos separation, trying to focus the flow of destruction to the south. A chaos-bolt splashes against his shields, and the burning pain from his hip is agonizing as he concentrates on the separation.

He can feel one of the mages trying to throw a shield around the order-chaos separation, followed by another shield from the other.

Too late, you slimy bastards!

A circular wall of silvered-golden-white sears skyward, so intense that Lerial can see nothing. Vain as he knows it must be, he extends his shields across the front of Eighth Company.

. . . and then . . . he feels them shredding and crumpling, with spears of red-dark chaos and black-silver order flaring toward him, bolts of power that jerk him back in the saddle and then slam him forward into an even darker blackness.

XXXVI

Lerial finds himself lying on a bed or a pallet. His entire body is painfully hot, as if he'd been sunburned all over, and his back is damp from hot sweat. The spot on his hip is especially painful. His eyes open, but he can see only darkness, and he can order-sense nothing. *Is this death?* His second thought is, *Neither Father nor the majer would approve of what you did.*

He blinks several times, and the blackness lifts slightly, enough that he can see that he is not in darkness, just in a dim chamber. While the darkness lifts, he also realizes that his head is throbbing and he feels sore across his chest and upper arms, as if they are bruised. He is only wearing smallclothes, as if his uniform has been removed. There is a faint light, perhaps a small lamp, to his left.

"Ser?" asks an unfamiliar voice.

"Yes . . ." Lerial's mouth is so dry that he can barely get the single word out.

"You need to drink as much as you can." A man in a Mirror Lancer uniform moves to stand beside the bed.

Lerial turns his head slightly, but does not immediately recognize the ranker. *You should. You should know them all.* He squints, trying to place the man, younger than most, but not all, of the men. *He's not in Eighth Company.* Lerial tries to moisten his lips, but his tongue is dry, and his mouth feels like it has been stuffed with hot wool.

"This will help, ser." The ranker lifts a mug from somewhere. "It's not water. It's lager with a little water. Undercaptain Kusyl insisted on it."

"You're . . . Twenty-third . . . Company . . . ?"

"Yes, ser."

At least he's not in Eighth or Eleventh. Lerial tries to sit up, but he is so sore and stiff that the ranker has to set the mug on the side table and help him into a sitting position against some scratchy pillows of some sort.

He hands Lerial the mug. Lerial drinks . . . and is surprised to find himself drinking and drinking. Finally, as he shifts his body to set the empty mug on the table, the pain on the side of his hip shoots up his side, so sharp that he almost drops the mug before easing it onto the small square table. Then he looks down to find a damp compress on his hip.

"There was a bad burn or blister there, ser."

"What about my knife?"

The ranker looks puzzled. "Your knife, ser?"

"The blister was under my knife and sheath, wasn't it?"

"I don't know, ser. I just came on duty."

"What glass is it?"

"Sometime past seventh glass, ser."

"You're a field healer, then?"

"I've been working at it, ser. I'm not like you, ser."

Lerial manages a smile. "You're more likely to survive to practice healing, then." As he looks at the young ranker, he wouldn't be surprised if the man had some order-healing talent. *But how can you tell now?*

"Will you be all right for a moment, ser? I need to send word to Undercaptain Kusyl."

"Go ahead."

When the ranker opens the door, Lerial can see that the corridor outside is as dim as where he lies. He doesn't recognize the chamber, but it looks like a junior officer's space. He tries to think things through. Whatever happened, the Afritans had not been routed, or he wouldn't be where he is, but had the Heldyans held their position, or withdrawn, or had Dhresyl been able to take advantage of what Lerial and the Mirror Lancers have done . . . whatever it happened to have been?

In less than a tenth of a glass, Kusyl steps into the small room, followed by the ranker Lerial does not know.

"Ser . . . it's good to see you're awake."

"It's good to be here. I wasn't sure I would be." Lerial moistens his lips, damp but chapped, he realizes, then asks, "How many did we lose?" He fears the answer.

"More than you'd like, ser, but a lot less than most of the Afritan companies."

"That doesn't tell me much, Kusyl."

"Fifty men dead, fifteen wounded. We only lost five men and the wounded in the fighting. The rest . . . that chaos-fire . . . some of it flared back across us. You did . . . something . . . it protected most of us, but not the men in the outer files of Eleventh and Twenty-third Company. It didn't totally protect you, either."

"I feel like the sun blistered me."

"You were blistered, ser. Not by the sun. The front of your uniform was partly charred, and some of your hair . . ."

"I take it that it's more unruly than ever . . . what's left?"

"Yes, ser."

"What about the Heldyans?"

"We won. If you can call it that. The Afritan Guard lost more than a third of their men, maybe half killed, half wounded, The Heldyans . . . I don't know. I'd judge that a battalion or two of theirs survived. There are some things you ought to know before the commander shows up. Fheldar threw himself in front of you, ser. Squad Leader Dhoraat, grabbed your reins . . . and followed your orders. He led Eighth Company through the gap in the western hill and then south. By the time we re-formed . . . well, the

Afritans had matters mostly in hand," Kusyl says dryly. "They should have. We . . . you, really, ser, took out almost five battalions, maybe more, and that pretty much left the rest of them disorganized." The undercaptain grins. "Majer Paelwyr drove his battalion right through the gaps we made and cut down the battalion guarding their commanders. Most of them didn't survive, I heard." The grin fades.

"What else?"

"Subcommander Drusyn was killed."

That surprises Lerial, given that Drusyn has avoided leading from the front. "How did that happen?"

"No one I've talked to knows. If they do, they aren't saying. Majer Paelwyr . . . he was the one who told me. He came to see about you, less than a glass ago."

"What did he say?"

"He just said it was strange. The commander said anyone could get killed in battle." Kusyl turns to the ranker. "Erekstone . . . I'll call you when we're done."

Erekstone inclines his head. "Yes, ser. I'll be outside."

Kusyl waits until the door is closed. "We brought you here because it was closer. It's the older junior officer's quarters. After I heard from Paelwyr, I brought in some of the men as guards as well, and decided it'd be better if you stayed here. The Afritan company officers like what you did. The ones with sense, anyway."

"Paelwyr must have indicated something . . ."

"All he said was that we'd done well putting you here. That was all he had to say."

Lerial has never been certain about Drusyn, and where the subcommander's loyalties really lay, but it's more than clear that, regardless of the outcome of the battle, matters in Afrit are far from settled. "What about the Subcommander Ascaar and what happened in Shaelt? Do you know?"

"No, ser. We haven't heard anything."

Lerial suddenly feels drowsy . . . or exhausted, and his eyes are too heavy to keep open. Much as he wants to know more, much as he tries to open his mouth to ask about whether anyone has heard about the arms-commander, all he can do is yawn . . . and try to keep his eyes open . . . except he cannot.

XXXVII

When he wakes again in the dawn of oneday, Lerial starts to rise . . . and realizes that while his headache is now only a dull ache, his chest and upper arms are stiff and very, very sore . . . and the blistering burn on his hip is both painful and itchy. He also can barely order-sense, just a blurry feel for a pair of Lancers guarding the door of the small chamber. *Better than last night, anyway.*

Slowly, very slowly, he sits up.

In the dim light filtering through the closed shutters he can see his uniform laid out across a chair. He frowns. Hadn't Kusyl said something about his uniform being charred?

A pitcher and a bowl are set on the narrow table desk, along with a small towel and soap and his personal gear. He stands and moves to the table desk, where he washes up and shaves, very carefully, given that his face is still warm, and tender, and the mirror reveals that his skin remains reddened. The ends of the hair on his sideburns, what is left of them, are frizzy, and he uses the razor to trim the flame-crisped ends away, as well as he can.

Next he eases into the uniform. Even sitting and bending to pull on his boots is painful. When he touches the knife sheath, he is surprised to find, although the leather has darkened almost to black, it is still flexible and the tooled "L" is now silver. *Using order . . . or are the silver and black a reminder of all the deaths?* He does have to move the sheath farther back on his belt so that it doesn't rub against the dressing over the blistered spot on his hip . . . which is still tender and painful.

Once he is dressed, except for his visor cap, he sits there for a moment, his eyes surveying the room. On one of the two shelves designed to hold clothes he sees another uniform, but the shade is wrong. When he stands and walks over to the shelves, he can see that the front of the shirt and the trousers are a dark brown, and the fabric gives and crumbles in places as he fingers it. Sitting on the shelf is his cap. The fabric around the Lancer device also looks charred. *It will have to do for now.*

"Ser? Are you all right?" calls one of the lancers acting as a guard.

"I'm doing well enough to get along. If one of you wouldn't mind sending for the undercaptains, I'd like to talk to them."

"Yes, ser."

Lerial sits down on the edge of the bed to wait, but he doesn't wait long before there is a rap on the door.

"Ser? It's Kusyl. Strauxyn's with me."

"Come on in."

Kusyl enters, followed by Strauxyn, who closes the door.

"You look better this morning," offers the older undercaptain.

"I'd hate to think I'd look worse," Lerial replies dryly. "What else has happened since then? Oh . . . I've lost track of time. What glass . . . ?"

"A bit past half after sixth glass," says Strauxyn.

"Not much new. Then, they don't tell undercaptains much," adds Kusyl. "There is one thing. Last night . . . there was a healer who said the arms-commander had sent him." The undercaptain shakes his head. "Didn't feel right. I said you had your own healer. He made some fuss about coming all the way from the palace."

"What did he do then?"

"He kept insisting, and the more he insisted, the more it seemed wrong. Then . . . he left, all huffy. I tried to find Commander Dhresyl, but he wasn't around. Then the healer wasn't around, either."

Despite the heat of his face, Lerial feels a chill go down his spine. "What did he look like?"

"Thin fellow. Black hair."

Lerial thinks back. The only healer in the palace had been Jaermyd, and he was more square-faced and gray-haired. *And Norstaan had said there were few true healers in Swartheld.* "You did right. There's no black-haired healer at the palace. Was this before or after I woke up?"

"Before, ser. Maybe half a glass."

"How would anyone from the palace even have known by then," muses Lerial. "Maybe they could have. When did you get me here, and when did Commander Dhresyl find out about me?"

"He didn't get back to the post until almost second glass of the afternoon."

Lerial shakes his head. There's really no way to tell, not with what he knows so far, but it's clear that someone seems out to remove any officer with any ability. *Will they remove Dhresyl as well . . . or do they intend that he remain in command?* All that raises even more questions.

"Before I make any decisions, I need to see Commander Dhresyl . . ."

"We'll escort you. The post isn't exactly organized," says Kusyl.

"Not in any way you could see," adds Strauxyn. "Almost makes you wonder how they managed to beat the Heldyans."

"Are we sure they did?" asks Lerial, almost sardonically.

"They did." Kusyl snorts. "Bodies everywhere. Think they did it to get any coins the Heldyans had."

Lerial manages not to wince. *Is everything in Afrit about coins?* "We might as well head out."

When they leave the officers' quarters and emerge into the wide courtyard of the post, Lerial is flanked by the undercaptains. They are bombarded by the cacophony, a mixture of moans, groans, horses and wagons moving, other sounds, all punctuated by occasional orders and a vague feeling of death, although Lerial cannot sense the silver-gray mists. *That might be for the best right now.*

"Quieter now," says Kusyl. "Last night . . ." He shakes his head.

The three walk quickly to the senior officers' mess. When Lerial enters the chamber, the odors of overcooked meat and burned cheese strike him, almost turning his stomach. He hasn't even considered that it is breakfast time. The second thing is how the four majers in the mess look at the three of them, but do not quite meet his eyes, before looking away.

Lerial crosses the end of the room, avoiding the lower end of the long table, and opens the door to the small chamber off the mess.

"What is it?" Dhresyl looks up, clearly irritated, as Lerial steps inside. Lerial glances back at the undercaptains.

"We'll wait, ser," says Kusyl.

Lerial closes the door and then takes the chair across the desk from Kusyl.

"That healer must have done you some good," offers Dhresyl. "But, you still look like shit." Lerial is surprised that the commander is that blunt, but it's a sign of just how tired the man is.

"Where did you find him?"

"I didn't. I was having enough trouble just trying to straighten out the battalions and arrange for the Heldyan prisoners. He said the arms-commander had sent him. I figured any healer might help."

From Dhresyl's appearance, harried look, and reaction, Lerial doubts that the false healer was the commander's doing. "Are there any Heldyan forces unaccounted for?"

"It depends on what you mean. We've gathered up close to a thousand captives, mostly wounded. Some likely won't make it. It's been a mess. We're not equipped for taking prisoners. The damage to the post makes it worst, but we can't leave them loose. Heldya's too close. One mounted group—almost a battalion—turned north right after whatever it was you did. By the time we could do anything about it, they'd boarded the merchanters at the tileworks pier and sailed off. They made for Estheld. They did leave almost three hundred decent mounts behind."

"What about Afritan Guard casualties?"

"They're heavy. We've lost another two battalions, maybe more, what with deaths and wounds." Dhresyl looks sadly at Lerial. "That's nothing compared to the Heldyans. I'd judge there are more than six thousand bodies out there. More than half were your doing."

"Would you have it the other way?" asks Lerial.

Dhresyl shakes his head.

"Have you heard from the arms-commander or Commander Sammyl? What about Ascaar?"

"Nothing yet this morning . . . or yesterday."

"I heard Drusyn was killed."

"Barbed arrow through the throat."

Lerial frowns.

"My thought exactly. The Heldyans don't use barbed arrows, and neither do we. It might have been poisoned as well, but they didn't need that. He bled to death in moments. There were several fired. Two rankers in his personal guard also died, early this morning, apparently from the poison. They were wounded as well by barbed arrows."

"Who . . . ?"

"Whoever doesn't want Afrit to have any effective commanders left alive. That's all I can say. We'd have lost everything if you weren't here."

"They tried for me last night," Lerial says.

This time Dhresyl is the one to frown. Finally, he asks, "The healer?"

"My men didn't let him near me. His description doesn't match the only healer at the palace."

"Starshit . . ." Dhresyl shakes his head again, almost despondently. Then he looks up. "How did they know?"

"They didn't. They just didn't trust his looks. They felt better leaving me to one of our field healers."

"You're fortunate."

Fortunate to have good and loyal undercaptains. "I am." After a moment, Lerial asks, "Do we have any Heldyan majers or subcommanders who are prisoners?"

"I've been asking that already. Right now, we've only found one majer. He's got a broken leg and some broken fingers. There might be others, but . . ."

"With a thousand wounded . . . it may take a while . . ."

"Especially if they don't want anyone to know."

"I'd like to talk to the majer."

"Would you mind if I listened in?"

"Not at all." At this point, Lerial is inclined to believe that Dhresyl isn't a part of the plot, although any form of treachery is beginning to appear possible in Afrit.

The commander stands. "He's in a guarded chamber on the other side of the kitchens. It's not far."

Both Kusyl and Strauxyn follow the two as they walk through the kitchens. The guarded chamber turns out to be a windowless storeroom off a back corridor. Two Afritan rankers are posted outside the door.

"Sers, you want to talk to him?" asks the broader ranker.

Lerial wonders if the stocky and muscular man might have once been a loader capable of hoisting large flour barrels and the like.

Dhresyl nods.

The guard slides the timber out from the iron brackets that appear to have been bolted in place in the last few glasses, given the wood chips and scraps on the stone floor, then opens the door. The undercaptains and guards remain outside as Lerial and Dhresyl enter.

The Heldyan majer lies on a straw pallet, his back against the wall of the storeroom, a rough splint around his right leg. He glares at Dhresyl, but his eyes widen as he takes in Lerial's uniform.

"What heavy cavalry battalion did you command, majer?" Lerial asks evenly.

"That's something I'll keep to myself." The officer replies in Hamorian, but with an accent that is so thick that Lerial has to concentrate to understand his words.

"You can do that. It doesn't matter. Most of your men are either dead or prisoners. It was a well-planned invasion, though. Very costly to Duke Khesyn in the end."

"You didn't have to slaughter my rankers."

"You didn't have to invade Afrit," replies Dhresyl mildly.

"You didn't have to invite it."

"Invite it?" asks Dhresyl.

"All you Afritans care about is golds. You sell yourselves to the highest bidder."

"So you come from a merchanter family yourself, then?" suggests Lerial.

"Keep that to myself."

"You know the terms . . . better than a mere majer would," Lerial pursues.

"A strong land doesn't have to bribe its men to fight."

"That's a strange comment," muses Lerial. "Especially since it appears that we've beaten you on all three attempts."

"Can't see why Cigoerne supports fat Afritan traders . . ."

Because they're less of a danger than Heldyan traders and a ruthless duke. Lerial just smiles.

"You won't . . . get away with this," mutters the wounded majer. "You think we're all that the duke has . . . you're wrong."

"Were we wrong at Luba? Or South Point? Or here?"

"Anyone can be lucky a few times. Especially against . . ." The majer breaks off his words, shaking his head.

"Against what?"

The Heldyan officer offers a ragged smile, but does not speak.

"A few times?" presses Lerial. "What happened to your battalion?"

The majer does not answer, but tightens his lips.

"Even if Duke Khesyn can scrape together another ten battalions, what difference will that make?" Lerial tries to look honestly puzzled.

"Wouldn't you like to know."

"It won't make any difference. He's sent almost twenty against us . . . and how many of you do you think are still alive?"

The majer does not answer, his expression between a glower and a smirk.

"There might be two Heldyan battalions remaining, mostly of wounded men. Three at the outside."

". . . butchers . . ."

"You were trying to do the same," Dhresyl points out.

"You'll see . . . you will." The majer turns his head to the wall.

Neither Lerial nor Dhresyl can get another word out of the Heldyan officer, and after another tenth of a glass, they leave. Lerial knows that he didn't handle the majer that well. But he is tired . . . and sore . . . and he has the feeling that whatever Khesyn has planned isn't over yet, even though it would seem as though it should be.

He says nothing as they walk back to the space serving as the commander's study, again shadowed by Kusyl and Strauxyn.

Once they are alone with the door closed, Dhresyl looks at Lerial. "Your officers are rather protective."

It's a good thing they are. "They're very good . . . and very loyal."

"I can see that." Dhresyl purses his lips, then shakes his head. "I don't think the majer was bluffing."

"I don't think so, either. Do we have any word on whether there are merchanters moored or anchored off Estheld?"

"We don't." Dhresyl frowns. "You think Khesyn will try another attack?

"He just might. You might want to find out about the merchanters. In the meantime, I'll be moving the Mirror Lancers back to the Afritan Guard headquarters. That will give you more space to deal with any Heldyan prisoners and to begin repairs to the post."

"After what you've been through . . . do you think . . ."

"I'm certainly well enough to ride for a glass, and you don't need to worry about the additional burden of another three companies. Oh . . . and if that false healer shows up again . . . you might want to hold him and try to find out who hired him."

"He won't show his face."

"Most likely not . . . but you never know. We'll be leaving as soon as we can."

"That might take some doing."

"We'll manage." Lerial smiles politely. "Until later." *Whenever that may be.* He turns and opens the door.

XXXVIII

As Dhresyl has predicted, it takes Lerial and the Mirror Lancers almost two glasses to get themselves out through the gates of Harbor Post and just on the paved road down to the shore road that will take them to Afritan Guard headquarters. Much of that delay is caused by the need to ready the wagons for the wounded, since Lerial is not about to leave them at the Harbor Post. Lerial himself rides at the head of Eighth Company, with the First Squad leader Dhoraat.

Once Lerial can see—since he still cannot order-sense more than a few yards away—that Twenty-third Company is away from the post, he looks to Dhoraat, the First Squad leader. "I haven't had a chance to thank you for getting me out of the mess I created. I do appreciate it. So will my family."

"I couldn't do any less, ser. Any of the men would have done it. I was just the closest."

"That may be, but you did do it, and if it had been anyone else, I'd thank them as well. But it wasn't. It was you, and I'm most grateful."

Dhoraat inclines his head slightly, then asks, as if not wanting to dwell on his own acts, "Do you think the Heldyans will attack again?"

"They will if they can. I'm hoping that Commander Sammyl and the arms-commander may know more." *And I'd really like to know if Ascaar was able to defeat or at least repulse the attackers at Shaelt.* Lerial glances ahead along the right side of the road, where he can see scores of bodies in the gray-blue colors of Heldya. Already, the flies, especially the red flies, are beginning to circle the corpses, but Lerial does not see any burial details . . . or anything that looks like a pyre. With as many deaths as Dhresyl has reported, something needs to be done . . . and fairly quickly. *Another suggestion for Sammyl . . . or Rhamuel . . . assuming Rhamuel hasn't taken a turn for the worse.* Both to the south of the stream and to the north of where he rides, he can also see figures searching the bodies of the fallen, most likely locals seeking anything of value overlooked by the Afritan Guards who have doubtless already looted the fallen.

Although Lerial cannot see more than glimpses of the site of yesterday's battle, those few patches of ground he can see through the scattered trees and above a low stone wall and the shoulder of the shore road are little more than blackened ground. Thin wisps of grayish white smoke drift upward from the site of Lerial's use of order-chaos separation, soon lost in the thin high haze of a spring day that already seems more like a day in early summer.

Several companies of Afritan Guards are posted at the east end of the hamlet where the Heldyans had encamped, some still mounted, others on foot. Lerial doubts they will find much of use, except for the neatly bundled tents. *But you could be wrong.* He also puzzles over the Heldyan majer's cryptic references and half statements. *Against whom?* But if the majer is suggesting that Khesyn did not send his best troops . . . why wouldn't Khesyn? Why would he send less than the best? *It doesn't make sense.* Yet Lerial could sense a hint of truth . . . or at least that the majer believes what he almost said was true.

At the end of the road down from the Harbor Post, Lerial leads the lancers south on the shore road, back toward Swartheld, and for all his musing, he cannot come up with a reason why Khesyn would not have sent his best troopers.

Even before Lerial reaches the north end of the harbor, and the beginning of the merchanting district, he sees people walking the streets, going about whatever they are doing as if there had not been a massive battle less than four kays to the north. There are even a few vessels tied up at the piers, if far fewer than there had been an eightday before. All of the merchanting buildings appear open and unshuttered, and Lerial cannot help but recall the scathing observations of the wounded Heldyan majer. Even the small cloth factorage near the Afritan Guard headquarters is open.

The troopers guarding the gates at headquarters look surprised, if only briefly, as they see Lerial and the Mirror Lancers approaching.

Captain Dhallyn, again, is the first officer to come out to meet Lerial once he reins up outside the headquarters building. "Overcaptain, ser . . . ah . . ."

"We'll be here for a time, I suspect. Harbor Post was getting overcrowded, what with Heldyan prisoners and the companies from South Post. I'll be leaving in a few moments with one squad to head to the palace to meet with Commander Sammyl and the arms-commander. How is he? Do you know? We haven't heard anything."

"Undercaptain Norstaan sent word yesterday that the arms-commander was doing well, but that he's likely not leaving the palace for a time yet."

Meaning that he still can't walk or ride, most likely. "Have you heard any word about Subcommander Ascaar?"

"No, ser. Only that he had engaged the Heldyans at Shaelt."

Once Lerial is convinced that nothing is amiss at the headquarters, he immediately leaves the post, accompanied by the Fourth Squad from Eighth Company—the one that has suffered the fewest losses out of all three companies. Again, on the way to the palace, he notices that very little is different from when he had first arrived in Swartheld. *You'd think that there might be some change when there was a battle less than ten kays north of here, especially after an explosion at the palace.*

The one thing that has changed is that there are more Afritan Guards stationed at both the inner and the outer gates to the palace. As Lerial turns to ride to the stables, he notices a platform built of stones, obviously from the rubble of the damaged section of the palace, and the hint of soot and ashes on top of the stones. *A private memorial to Atroyan and Natroyor?*

Something was probably necessary, given the heat. Still, Lerial worries. Also, Dhallyn must have dispatched a messenger immediately, because Lerial has barely reined up outside the inside west entrance to the palace when Norstaan hurries to meet him.

"Good morning, ser."

"Good morning, Norstaan. Are Commander Sammyl and the arms-commander in the same chambers as before?"

"Yes, ser. They're expecting you."

"I take it Captain Dhallyn sent a messenger."

Norstaan looks puzzled for a moment. "No, ser. Commander Dhresyl did. He told the commander that you were returning to Afritan Guard headquarters."

Lerial nods. *You should have thought of that. Dhresyl wouldn't want Sammyl surprised.* He dismounts and hands the gelding's reins to the ranker beside Fhuraan, the squad leader. "I need to see them."

"Yes, ser. The commander thought you would. Will you and your squad be staying at the palace?"

"I think that's unlikely, but I won't know until after I meet with the arms-commander. They could use a bite to eat and water for the mounts."

"We'll take care of it, ser."

"Thank you."

"Oh . . . do you know if that dispatch reached Subcommander Ascaar?"

"No, ser. Might be a day or two . . ."

Lerial nods.

Norstaan gestures, and an Afritan Guard ranker walks toward them. "Seilyn will escort you, ser."

Fhuraan gestures, in turn, and two older rankers immediately dismount and join Lerial.

Norstaan blinks, but says nothing.

"Everyone will feel better this way," Lerial says blandly. *Especially you, since you can't hold shields for more than a moment or so.*

"Ser . . . it was Commander Sammyl's order that everyone have an escort."

"And I do." Lerial smiles. "Shall we go?"

The Afritan trooper leads the way, and the two lancers flank Lerial. When they reach the guards outside the sitting room, all three remain in the corridor as Lerial enters.

"How is the arms-commander?" asks Lerial, looking at Sammyl, who has stood as Lerial enters the sitting room.

"Tired of being confined to a bed or a star-fired chair!" comes Rhamuel's voice from where he is seated at a table desk in the corner of the sitting room, one that has been added to the chamber.

Lerial turns. "How are you feeling?"

"I'd feel better if my leg hurt."

"So would I," admits Lerial, walking toward Rhamuel and studying him. From his limited order-senses, the arms-commander seems to be better. Even the knot of chaos at the end of his backbone seems smaller . . . but not that much smaller. There is no trace of wound chaos around the break in his leg.

"You look worse for the wear," Rhamuel observes.

"The last few days have been hard." Lerial pauses. "I noticed a stone platform . . ."

"We had to have a memorial for Atroyan and Natroyor . . . It's been five days. I sent word to Haesychya, but she declined, saying that her father needed her. He's still not well."

"You didn't attend?"

"I did. Norstaan found an old sedan chair, and they carted me down. I had all the officers I could find witness the memorial, but I've held off sending out any proclamations yet."

Lerial isn't certain of the wisdom of that, but then, refraining from making public pronouncements while the Heldyans are still attacking might be for the best. "Have you heard anything from Ascaar?"

Sammyl shakes his head.

"That's not good."

"His second dispatch said that there were three Heldyan battalions—all foot."

"Were they well trained?" asks Lerial. "Or did Ascaar say?"

"He did say that they weren't the best of Khesyn's forces, but the numbers made it difficult. He didn't say much more, except that he had the better position, if he could hold it."

"We can't do anything about that yet," says Rhamuel.

"Did you send a healer to the Harbor Post last night?"

Immediate puzzled looks cross both men's faces.

"No, why?" asks Rhamuel.

"One showed up, claiming the palace sent him, then vanished when my men tried to question him." Lerial watches Sammyl closely, with both eyes and order-senses, but the commander seems as disconcerted as Rhamuel.

"Trying to get to you, then?" asks the arms-commander.

"It would seem so. I was still unconscious then."

"Unconscious?" asks Sammyl.

"The last part of the battle was harder than I'd thought it would be." *And that's an understatement.*

Rhamuel shakes his head. "It just keeps getting worse." He offers a brief and sardonic smile. "Dwelling on that won't resolve it. Tell us what happened in the north—as you saw it, and how you ended up unconscious."

The way the arms-commander has phrased his inquiry tells Lerial that Rhamuel has his doubts about whatever Dhresyl has already reported.

"The Mirror Lancers and I made the first attack on sevenday . . ." Lerial describes what he and the Lancers did on both days. The only matter about which he is less than forthcoming is how he dealt with the chaos-wizards, merely saying that he was able to turn their chaos back on them and continuing, "I wasn't completely successful, because some of it came back at me and part of the Mirror Lancers. The blow knocked me out, and I lost one officer and fifty men, with fifteen wounded. My squad leaders and undercaptains had to finish the fight."

"Commander Dhresyl indicated you and your men defeated three battalions," says Sammyl.

"More like five, according to my officers and several of the commander's majers. That doesn't count the battalion or so on sevenday."

"That sounds about right," interjects Rhamuel before Sammyl can speak. "Is there anything else we should know?"

"Commander Dhresyl has close to a thousand prisoners. Most are wounded. One mounted battalion managed to withdraw to a merchanter at the tileworks and had set sail. They left almost three hundred mounts. Commander Dhresyl and I questioned a wounded Heldyan majer. He was most adamant that we would pay for the way we slaughtered Khesyn's troops . . . and that Khesyn had more than enough battalions in reserve to do so."

"How could he after . . . ?" Sammyl does not say more.

"After what we've been through, anything is possible," suggests Rhamuel. "Khesyn has been planning this for a long time."

Lerial notices that neither man mentions the amount of treason that has occurred, but that's not something he wants to bring up before Sammyl. Instead, he says, "I would recommend getting a scouting report as to how many merchanters might be tied up or anchored off Estheld, and if anyone has seen more flatboats on the river. Khesyn would need ships or boats or both to get enough men here. If there aren't many merchanters, we might have some time before the next attack."

"If there even is one," comments Sammyl.

"Do you think that, if he has that many more armsmen, they are already attacking Shaelt?" Rhamuel's tone is almost matter-of-fact.

"I doubt it. I would judge that the attack on Shaelt is to keep you from moving more of your forces to defend Swartheld."

"Commander," says Rhamuel, "I'd appreciate it if you'd make arrangements to find out about boats and merchanters right now."

Sammyl stiffens. "Yes, ser."

Rhamuel smiles indulgently. "I'm not plotting or planning to replace you. I am worried that Khesyn might try another attack. If there aren't any ships to speak of at Estheld and no sign of flatboats on the river, we can rest easier . . . at least for a little while. That would be good to know."

Sammyl nods, then leaves.

Once the door closes, Lerial says, "He's worried."

"*He's* worried? After all the treachery . . . and the assassination of Subcommander Drusyn . . ." Rhamuel shakes his head.

"Any word on Mykel?"

"Not a thing, but I wouldn't expect anything for another day at the soonest, possibly two or three days if they made good time."

And even longer if something untoward has occurred. "Are Haesychya and Kyedra back in the palace?"

"They're still at Aenslem's. I didn't think we all should be together." Rhamuel offers a sardonic smile. "I know. That blade cuts both ways, but since daughters cannot succeed as duke . . . who ever heard of a duchess?"

"There have been empresses . . ."

"Your grandmere was the only one who actually ruled, I believe." Rhamuel laughs softly. "If she had been the ruler earlier, we might not even be here together. You'd be in Cyad worrying about things that no one will worry about again for centuries . . . and I'd likely be dead."

"Have you heard from Maesoryk?"

"Should I have?"

"I can't believe that the Heldyans landed at his tileworks without his involvement." There is something else about Maesoryk, but Lerial cannot remember what it might be, just a vague feeling that something else ties Maesoryk to the treachery. *You're too tired to think as clearly as you should.*

"Neither can I. But I haven't heard."

"Has anyone seen Dafaal?"

"You didn't hear? The palace guards found his body in the lower cellars. He'd been garroted. They also found fuses and a striker."

"He was either part of the plot . . . or someone wants you to think he was."

"Right now, there's no way to tell. He wasn't part of the memorial. He's not family, and that had to be family only . . . or . . ."

Lerial understands. If Dafaal had been included, then Rhamuel can't claim the memorial was family and private. "Dafaal could have been part of the plot, and whoever was in charge wants to remove all links . . ."

"I fear that is the most likely. We won't ever know for certain, I suspect."

"What other merchanters have you heard from?"

"Fhastal. He's pledged whatever golds I need, for Afritan Guard pay, rebuilding, whatever. Aenslem, although he's not well . . . flux is hanging on . . ."

It is the second time Lerial has heard about Aenslem's illness, and that disturbs him.

". . . Mesphaes and Lhugar, of course, and Jhosef, but he would toady up to whoever is in power . . ."

"Not . . . Alaphyn?" Lerial has to struggle for the merchanter's name.

"You think he might have been with Maesoryk?"

"It took a number of merchant vessels to carry those troopers from Estheld, and we can be fairly sure Aenslem's ships weren't involved."

"Frig . . . should have thought about that. Those two have always been close."

"Those two? Alaphyn and Maesoryk?"

Rhamuel nods.

Although they discuss more about the merchanters over the next third of a glass or so, in the end, Lerial does not discover anything new, and he forces himself to sit down and wait for Sammyl to return. He hopes it won't be too long before the commander can discover what is happening in Estheld . . . and whether there are more merchant ships gathering there.

Another attack is all we need.

XXXIX

By fourth glass of the afternoon, Lerial is ready to pace around the outer sitting room, despite feeling still tired, although he can order-sense a bit farther away. Rhamuel is resting in the bedchamber. While Sammyl has sent out scouts to see what can be determined about the harbor at Estheld, he has cautioned Lerial that it may take several glasses, or possibly until twoday morning. In the meantime, he has departed to meet with Dhresyl and to see the situation at the Harbor Post for himself.

So Lerial sits behind the table desk, thinking, and waiting for either the scouting reports or for Norstaan to return, since the undercaptain has been summoned to the courtyard for some reason. *What if Khesyn is readying another attack? Why would he do that? Especially after losing so many men?* Lerial knows he is missing something . . . and just hopes he can recall that in time. *Maybe by tomorrow . . .*

He looks up as the outer door opens and Norstaan steps into the sitting room, accompanied by a youth wearing a riding jacket that looks to be a uniform of sorts, along with a soft felt hat of the kind worn by merchanter guards, and a broad leather belt. The blade at the youth's waist looks to be slightly shorter than a sabre, the kind claimed to be more effective in dealing with ruffians at close range. That is the rationale, Lerial knows, although he has his doubts about the greater effectiveness of a shorter blade, suspecting that it is a tacit acknowledgment that merchanter guards should not bear longer weapons than the Afritan Guard . . . or the Mirror Lancers.

Those thoughts vanish as he sees the smile on Norstaan's face and belatedly recognizes Kyedra. He bolts to his feet. "What are you doing here?"

"Grandpapa is ill. He may be dying. Mother sent me."

"Alone? Why did you have to come?"

Kyedra shakes her head impatiently. "Of course not. I had two palace guards and two of Grandpapa's guards. I wore men's riding trousers and a guard's jacket—an Aenian House jacket. Besides, no one thinks a woman in man's clothing without a head scarf could be anything but a youth. I came so that you'd know it wasn't a ruse or a trap . . . after all the . . . after everything . . ."

"And you can handle that blade?"

"I can. Uncle Rham saw to that." She looks directly at Lerial. "Mother wants you to tend to Grandpapa."

"I can see what I can do." Lerial refrains from frowning, because he has never mentioned anything about his being able to heal to Haesychya. *Rhamuel must have told her.*

"See?"

"Look at him, Lady," Norstaan says, his voice barely above a murmur.

For the first time, Kyedra studies Lerial. Then she asks, "What happened?"

"I got caught in the backlash of a huge chaos-explosion."

"It destroyed more than three battalions of Heldyan troops," Norstaan says. "Commander Dhresyl doubts we would have prevailed otherwise."

Lerial looks to Norstaan. "I don't think we should wake the arms-commander." *For a number of reasons.* "There's nothing else the Mirror Lancers can do today, and my squad should certainly provide enough protection for Lady Kyedra. If Commander Sammyl should return before the arms-commander wakes . . ." Lerial ponders what he should say.

"Ser?"

"I will most likely be returning to Guard headquarters before I come back to the palace. So you can tell him that something's come up, and I needed to return to my men." *That will be true so far as it goes.*

"Yes, ser." A trace of a smile lurks around Norstaan's lips.

"When the arms-commander wakes, you can tell him exactly what happened—alone."

"Yes, ser." With the words, Norstaan offers a vigorous nod.

Lerial turns to Kyedra. "We'd best go."

Between Kyedra's two guards and the two Mirror Lancers, and one Afritan Guard, the seven make quite a procession down to the stables. At least, that's the thought Lerial has.

Once Lerial and Fourth Squad leave the palace, the two Aenian House guards take the lead, with Lerial and Kyedra directly behind, followed by Fhuraan and his squad. Lerial studies the people and riders and wagons moving on the circular road around the palace, but no one gives them more than a casual glance.

"Can you do anything?" When Kyedra finally speaks again, her voice is low. "I'm sorry. Mother and I had hoped . . ."

"I can likely sense what might be the problem. Perhaps more."

"Have you heard more about Natroyor?"

Hasn't anyone told her or Haesychya? "I asked your uncle about Mykel. He hasn't heard anything."

"Lord . . . I mean Lerial, you didn't answer my question."

"No, I didn't."

"He's dead, too, isn't he?"

"I'm sorry. Rhamuel told me he was crushed when the palace collapsed. He was likely asleep."

There is low moment of silence that drags out . . . and out.

Finally, there is only the slightest catch, a small roughness in Kyedra's voice as she asks, "Why? Why does someone want us all dead?"

"Why do you think that?"

"I could answer that simply. That's not what you meant, was it?"

Lerial cannot help but smile slightly at Kyedra's response. "Perhaps the better question would be who in Afrit has the most to gain from the death of the duke and all his heirs, as well as from the death of all of his best commanders."

"All of his best commanders?"

"Of his best commanders, only your uncle and Subcommander Ascaar are still alive or able to command. The explosions at the Harbor Post, a poisoning, and an assassination have accounted for the rest. The senior remaining commander freely admits he is the least qualified commander for battles, and wishes that Ascaar were in command—except Ascaar is tied up fighting more Heldyans in Shaelt."

"What about you?"

"Someone sent a false healer last night, supposedly from the palace. I was unconscious, but my officers wouldn't let him see me."

"There have to be traitors within the Afritan Guard. How else would they know?"

"There might be another way," Lerial admits, "but I can't think of it. I think there have to be more than one or two." After several moments of silence, he asks, "What can you tell me about what ails your grandfather?"

"He's hot, but not burning up. His stomach aches all the time, and his head hurts."

That could be almost anything. "He's not coughing or sneezing?"

"No. It's not like a cold or consumption."

"We'll just have to see."

After riding little more than a half kay on the boulevard that leads to the merchanting quarter opposite the harbor, they reach the wide road that heads westward up a gentle grade. The first several villas that they pass are modest, perhaps not even half the size of the palace in Cigoerne, but the next several are larger. After riding another half kay, the Aenian House guards turn up a paved lane. Thirty yards off the road is a pair of sturdy ironwork gates not quite three yards tall, which open as the two guards approach. Lerial and Kyedra ride through. Lerial can hear . . . and sense . . . when the gates closes behind the last riders in the squad. He thinks his order-sensing has increased slightly over the course of the day, but knows that could be wistful thinking.

While the grounds and gardens surrounding the redstone villa are shaded, the sprawling two-level structure is set on a low rise away from the trees and extends more than a hundred yards across the front. Lerial wonders about the lack of trees until they ride up to the main entrance, where, despite the seeming stillness of the day, he feels a cooler breeze coming from the north.

The entrance is on the east side of the villa, positioned so that it is shaded by the villa and the columns flanking the stone steps. The two Aenian house guards rein up at the north end of the wide steps, so that Lerial and Kyedra are opposite the middle of the steps when they halt.

"Ser . . ." murmurs Fhuraan, "I'd prefer you be accompanied."

Much as he dislikes the idea, Lerial has to admit that the squad leader is right. He turns to look at Fhuraan. "For both the lady and me. She is likely in just as much danger."

"Four men, then."

Kyedra looks to Lerial as if to protest, then nods, almost sadly.

Lerial dismounts quickly, handing the gelding's reins to a ranker who rides forward, then offers a hand to Kyedra.

She takes it, but places no pressure on him when she dismounts, her voice almost inaudible as she murmurs. "I don't need the aid, but I appreciate the courtesy."

He replies in an equally low voice. "I know that, but I'd hate to seem like a boor for not offering, especially in front of your grandfather's retainers."

She lifts her eyebrows as if to question.

"Anyone Rhamuel has trained to use a blade scarcely *needs* any help." He smiles, but does not move until four rankers dismount and flank them. Only then does he nod toward the redstone steps.

The breeze is even stronger when they reach the stone terrace that fans out from the double doors of the main entrance. "He built this here, oriented in this direction, just for the prevailing winds, didn't he?"

Kyedra gives Lerial a curious glance, but does not reply. Lerial does not press her.

After looking at Kyedra, the two guards open the doors, barely looking at Lerial or the rankers. Immediately beyond the doors is a circular vaulted entry hall, some fifteen yards across. The domed ceiling is an off-white, as are the walls. The floor is of interlocking white tiles, but the masonry grout is black, rather than the customary white or off-white. The hall itself has four archways, one for the entry, and each of the others opening to a wide hallway extending the length of each wing of the villa. Rising on both sides of the west archway are two curved staircases that lead to what looks to be an upper hall. The only furnishings in the entry hall are four identical sideboard cabinets of a golden wood, each one more than three yards long and curved to fit against the wall and placed equidistant from the archways flanking it. Each cabinet has a raised back, on which is carved a scene, although in the dim light, Lerial cannot make out the details.

Kyedra motions to the hall to the right, the one leading to the north wing. "Grandpapa is in his study."

The corridor is also tiled in the black-grouted white tile, with the same off-white plaster walls. Lerial feels the breeze blowing in his face as they walk past door after door. Those few that are open reveal a library, a salon, a lady's study, and what looks to be a children's study.

"Is that where your mother had her lessons?"

"When she was older. I've had lessons there, too. Usually in the summer."

"I imagine it's much cooler here in the summer than in the palace."

"Much cooler."

Lerial guesses that the north wing is for family common spaces and studies, the west wing for entertaining, and the south wing for personal chambers.

Near the end of the corridor, Kyedra points to a half-open door on the left. "There's the study." She looks pointedly at the rankers behind them, then at Lerial.

"Just one inside," Lerial murmurs. He would prefer none, but he has no real shields, and he knows he is physically still weary, if not close to exhausted.

The four rankers exchange glances before one, the broadest and oldest, steps forward. "Ser."

Lerial nods.

Kyedra frowns, but does not voice a complaint before she eases the door open and steps inside, announcing, "I've brought Lord Lerial."

Lerial and the lancer follow her. The study is not excessively large, some ten yards long and perhaps five wide, containing a wide table desk at one end, with four large cabinets against the wall behind it on each side of the large desk chair. The merchanter lies on a long leather couch set between two bookcases at the north end of the study. At each end of the couch is a small end table. Haesychya rises from a leather armchair facing the couch. The matching chair is empty, and only a pitcher and two mugs sit on the table between the armchairs. The wide windows on the west wall are open, and with the open door, there is a pleasant flow of air through the study.

Within moments of entering the study, Lerial can sense the chaos radiating from Aenslem's gut. He can also sense chaos in the tumbler on the side table nearest Aenslem.

"What's in the tumbler?" The words come out more sharply than Lerial intends.

"Tonic . . ." gasps the merchanter.

"That's his tonic," says Haesychya.

Lerial walks to the side table and lets his order-senses study the tumbler . . . and the small corked jug behind it. Both exude chaos, far stronger than he has originally sensed. He turns to Aenslem and leans down. "Pardon me, ser." Lerial lets his fingertips brush the merchanter's hot and damp forehead and then hover near his chest and the abdomen below. There is a definite similarity between the chaos in the tumbler and jug, and that emanating from Aenslem.

"What is it?"

"There's something in your tonic. It's not doing you any good." Lerial doesn't want to claim that Aenslem is being poisoned, although that is his surmise. It is just possible that some would-be healer has concocted some potion that is poisonous out of the best intentions.

"You're saying he's being poisoned?" Haesychya looks hard at Lerial.

"But . . . no one . . ." protests Aenslem, still gasping.

"I can't say that." *For many reasons.* "I can say that whatever is in the tumbler and jug is causing him some distress."

"How can you tell?"

"It's the same kind of chaos." Lerial regrets his words immediately. *Doing things when you're tired means you're not as a careful as you should be.*

"Besides being a field healer, you can sense chaos?" asks Haesychya.

"That's what allows me to be a field healer," Lerial replies.

"Then do something," says Haesychya, in a tone that combines plea and demand.

"I'm not a full-fledged healer." *And not anywhere close to full strength.* "I'll do what I can." He bends over Aenslem again, feeling chaos even in the merchanter's breath. He extends his fingertips and says, once more, "Pardon me." He lets the smallest amount of order flow from him, directing it to Aenslem's lungs and stomach. Then he straightens and waits. He feels just a touch of light-headedness, but he can sense an immediate reduction in the chaos in Aenslem, suggesting most strongly that the merchanter has been poisoned, because if the problem were an illness the chaos would be far more diffuse than it is.

"Well?" asks Haesychya.

"He likely has been poisoned. I may be able to do a little more." Lerial again bends and extends his fingertips to the base of Aenslem's neck, willing more order into the merchanter.

As he straightens, Lerial can feel the study spin around him, and he immediately drops into the vacant leather armchair and lowers his head. He feels as though, if he moves at all, he will topple into darkness.

"What . . ." Haesychya glances around the study.

"He's injured, Lady," blurts one of the rankers by the door. "He had to be carried from his mount last night."

Haesychya looks to Kyedra. "Did you know this?"

"He seemed all right on the ride here."

Haesychya looks to the ranker. "Injured? How?"

"Saving us, Lady. He . . . he used order to shield us from chaos."

Kyedra's mouth opens, but she does not speak.

"Lager would help, Lady."

"Kyedra . . . you stay here. I'll get it myself." Haesychya turns and hurries from the study, almost at a run.

Kyedra eases over to stand by Lerial. "I'm sorry . . . I didn't realize."

Even through his light-headedness and his feeling that the study is spinning around him, Lerial can hear the concern in Kyedra's voice. Somehow . . . that helps, if not physically.

"Realize what, girl?" While Aenslem's voice is raspy, it is clearly stronger, although Lerial cannot sense either order or chaos.

"That he was so weak."

"Exhausted," declares Aenslem. "Healing takes strength . . . like fighting."

Lerial says nothing, fearing that even trying to speak will start the room spinning around him . . . or send him back into darkness. He can hear Aenslem and Kyedra speaking, but the words make little sense.

After time, how long he does not know, Haesychya is kneeling beside the chair, holding a goblet. "I took this from an untapped cask. That's why it took longer. I got one that had dust on it."

Lerial understands. He manages a faint smile before taking a small swallow of the lager. His hands are shaking so much that Haesychya helps him hold the goblet for the first swallows. He slowly drinks, and by the time he is halfway through the goblet he feels steadier. At least, the room has stopped spinning around him, and his hands are no longer shaking. He takes another swallow, realizing, rather belatedly, that careful as he had tried to be, he had used too much order. *Because your physical strength exceeded the amount of order you required from your body?* Yet another thing he needs to consider.

He takes yet another swallow from the goblet, finishing the lager, and looks up.

"Would you like some more?" Haesychya is sitting in the other chair, with a pitcher on the side table, and Kyedra has pulled a straight-backed chair over beside her mother.

"Yes, please. Perhaps some bread . . ."

Haesychya rises, glancing at her daughter. Kyedra immediately leaves the study.

As Haesychya refills the goblet, Lerial looks to the merchanter, whose brow is no longer damp with sweat. "Are you feeling better?" *Let's hope so . . . after this.* The moment he thinks that, he feels ashamed of himself. Aenslem didn't exactly choose to be poisoned.

"Quite a bit. Not up to myself . . . but much better."

Lerial then looks to Haesychya, who has reseated herself. "No more of any tonics. Just bread and soup for the next few days . . . and lager. If he starts to get worse . . . let me know."

"It's a wonder . . . what you did . . ."

"No." Lerial wants to shake his head, but stops himself. "Just fortune. Some poisons . . . what I could do wouldn't have helped . . . but those are the kinds that are slower-acting and must be given continually in small doses." He lifts the goblet and takes another swallow, realizing for the first time just how good the lager tastes.

"You're an expert on poisons, too?"

"Hardly. That's something I've picked up from some reading and from listening. Some plants and foods are actually like that. Not many, or we'd all have trouble."

At that moment, Kyedra hurries back into the study, carrying two loaves of bread, one white and one dark. She stops just short of Lerial.

He takes the dark bread, breaks off a chunk, and slowly eats it. After several mouthfuls, most of the light-headedness is gone, but that might have been from the lager he'd drunk earlier. He also discovers he has regained the tiniest bit of order-sensing. *That's hopeful.*

"I'm so sorry," Kyedra says. "I didn't think about what healing might do. I was so worried about Grandpapa."

"I understand," Lerial replies, offering what he hopes is an understanding smile.

"Don't you think you should stay here?" asks Haesychya. "You're not in the best of health at the moment."

"I'm not, but I need to be closer to the Mirror Lancers. I hope what I did will continue to help you," Lerial says to Aenslem before turning and offering a wry expression to Haesychya. "You might suggest to your father that the lager you gave me will do him far better than any tonic."

"I'm . . . not much for lager . . . more a wine man," says Aenslem slowly, "but I'd hate to waste your effort, Lerial."

"Then don't," says Haesychya, her voice so curt that she is almost snapping at her father. "Drink the lager. Otherwise you might not ever drink your wines again."

"Women . . . daughters . . ." Aenslem offers a tired smile.

Lerial walks over to the merchanter, close enough that order-sensing is not a strain. The chaos in Aenslem's gut is definitely weaker than before. *Considerably weaker.* He nods. "You are doing better."

"Stay with your grandfather," Haesychya says to her daughter, her words an iron order. "I'll escort Lerial out."

"Yes, Mother."

Once Lerial and Haesychya are outside the study, escorted once more by the Lancer rankers, she asks, her voice barely above a murmur, "He's better, isn't he?"

"He is. There's still some chaos there, but it seems to be fading. I'd keep him on bread you've seen baked and lager for a while." Lerial does not mention the obvious again: that someone should look into whoever provided the "tonic"—or who might have adulterated it, since Aenslem had acted as though it was something he took regularly.

"You will take care of yourself, will you not?"

"As I can, Lady."

"Please do. For all our sakes."

"You also need to take care . . . after everything." He realizes his sympathy is belated, but better later than not at all.

"You're kind."

There is little enough Lerial can say to that. So he nods. "Thank you."

When he leaves Haesychya at the double doors to the villa, he is surprised that it is only twilight. *But then, it is midspring.*

As he rides out through the iron gates on his way back to the palace, Lerial wonders why, among other things, if Kyedra had not known about Natroyor's death, Haesychya never asked anything about her son. *Had Rhamuel already let her know? But it that were so, why hadn't anyone told Kyedra?*

And you thought your family kept things close!

XL

Lerial does not wake on twoday morning until full light spreads across Swartheld, although there is no direct light coming through the shutters of the senior officer's chamber he occupies at Afritan Guard headquarters. He feels far better than when he had dropped onto the bunk the night before, although he can order-sense only out into the hallway outside his door. Still . . . after what had happened at Aenslem's villa . . .

He wonders if Rhamuel has received any information from Ascaar, since Sammyl had not returned when Lerial had left the palace on oneday evening and there had been no dispatches from Shaelt. The lack of dispatches bothers Lerial. Ascaar isn't the sort who would neglect to report, whether he did well . . . or poorly. *Unless he's dead or severely wounded.*

Lerial washes, shaves, and dresses quickly, and his stomach reminds him that he needs to eat. The two rankers outside Lerial's door stiffen as he steps out into the hallway. He can read the question on their minds and lips. He smiles. "Yes. I'm feeling much better this morning." *Not enough to handle much in the way of order and chaos, but enough not to fall over with minor healing.* At that thought, he wonders how Aenslem is doing, but pushes that away.

You did what you could, and likely more than you should have. Except . . . He almost shakes his head, before realizing that the rankers will misinterpret the gesture. "I'm ready for something to eat."

Dhoraat, Kusyl, and Strauxyn are waiting at the mess. All look intently at him.

"I'm fine. Really."

Kusyl raises his eyebrows. "Begging your pardon, ser . . ."

"Did I have to try to heal Aenslem? Yes. If the most powerful merchanter in Afrit died because I refused to try to save him, we'd be in almost as bad a shape as if we'd lost the last battle." Lerial pauses. "Maybe not quite that bad, but close." He manages a grin. "I need to eat. You can sit down and ask any questions while I do. And no, there isn't any word on what happened at Shaelt." Lerial takes a seat near one end of the table. "That's why I'll have to head out to the palace once I eat."

Immediately, two Afritan Guard servers appear, one with a beaker and a pitcher, the other with a platter that he sets before Lerial. On the platter are two large slices of egg toast covered in berry syrup, along with ham rashers on the side, and a quarter of a ripe melon, its interior a pale shade of green, a type that Lerial has not seen. He tries not to eat too quickly, but he finishes the first piece of egg toast in about three bites, along with a deep swallow of lager.

"What about the Heldyans?" asks Kusyl.

"They may have more troopers in reserve. It's possible they'll try another attack. Commander Sammyl's sent scouts out to see what's happening in Estheld."

"More troopers, ser?" asks Dhoraat.

"I'm guessing that Khesyn made some sort of agreement with the Tourlegyn clan leaders. That's why so many of the Heldyan troopers fought to the death. They weren't Heldyans, but Tourlegyns . . ."

In between mouthfuls, Lerial answers more questions. After he finishes, while Strauxyn readies a squad to accompany Lerial to the palace, Lerial immediately walks to the section of the barracks holding the Mirror Lancer wounded.

"Ser?" asks Kusyl. "Do you think . . . ?"

"I'm stronger today, and I need to see to the men." Fortunately, of the twelve wounded, Lerial finds wound chaos in only two, and in both cases, it is minor, and something with which he can deal without even feeling light-headed. He tries not to think about the three who died when he was unable to even take care of himself.

From the barracks he then walks to the headquarters building, where he seeks out Captain Dhallyn.

"What can I do for you, ser?" Dhallyn stands from behind the duty desk and smiles warmly.

"I'm curious. Do you keep records of dispatch riders . . . when they leave for where or when they arrive from where?"

"Yes, ser. Failure to do so would get any officer on duty in great trouble."

"Would you mind if I looked at the records for the past few days?"

"No . . . why?"

"We haven't heard anything from Shaelt."

"I don't recall any dispatch riders from the south, but we can check. There are two records. One at the gates, and the one here. Every morning the duty officer has to check both to make certain they agree. I can't recall when they haven't." Dhallyn turns and lifts a leather-bound folder, attached to a bracket on the wall with a thin chain, then opens it. He studies it and says, "Just four riders since sixday. Three from Harbor Post, one from the palace." He holds the book so that Lerial can read the entries . . . which are exactly as Dhallyn has described them.

"Thank you."

Dhallyn frowns.

Before the captain can speak, Lerial goes on, "It struck me that there are several reasons why we haven't heard. The first is that Subcommander Ascaar has been defeated or killed. I have my doubts about that. The second is that whatever dispatch was sent did not reach the arms-commander. That leaves open where it went astray. The only thing we can check here is whether there were any dispatch riders from the south."

"They might have gone straight to the palace."

Lerial smiles. "That's where I'll make the next inquiry."

"They keep the dispatch record at the guardhouse at the outer gate."

"Thank you."

A third of a glass later, Lerial, accompanied by Second Squad from Eleventh Company, rides out from Afritan Guard headquarters toward the palace, through streets that look much as they have almost every day since he has arrived in Swartheld—with little sign that a war is ongoing.

Once at the palace, Lerial reins up opposite the small gatehouse just inside the outer gates to the palace. "I'd like to talk to the duty officer or squad leader."

In moments, an older burly squad leader appears.

"If you don't mind, Squad Leader, I'd like to see the book that shows the arrival and departures of couriers over the past three days."

"Ah . . . ser . . ."

"I'm not asking what was in the dispatches, if there were any. I'm asking where they came from." Lerial looks hard at the squad leader.

"Yes, ser. One moment, ser." Several moments pass before the burly squad leader returns. "Ser, we've had eight couriers in the last three days. One came from Lake Reomer. Six came from the Harbor Post, and one from the South Post."

"None from farther south?" Lerial decides against demanding the book, given how promptly the squad leader has responded.

"No, ser."

"Thank you very much, Squad Leader. I appreciate such good record-keeping. So will Commander Sammyl."

While the squad leader looks slightly puzzled, he replies, "My pleasure, ser."

After he rides to the stables and dismounts, two rankers accompany him into the palace and to the chambers still occupied by Rhamuel. The arms-commander is alone in the outer chamber, although two Afritan Guards are posted in the corridor outside, where Lerial's rankers stop.

When Lerial enters, Rhamuel looks up from where he sits behind his table desk perusing a stack of papers. "You look considerably better than you did last night. I also received a note from Haesychya, informing me that her father is much improved this morning. She is more hopeful than she has been in several days."

"I just hope there won't be a recurrence."

"Don't we all. Oh . . . there's also something for you, although I don't think it's from her." Rhamuel holds up an envelope.

Lerial crosses the room, takes it, looking at the outside, with the near-perfect calligraphy:

Lord Lerial
Overcaptain
Mirror Lancers of Cigoerne

Kyedra? While he has not expected anything from her, he hopes that whatever is within the envelope is favorable.

"You look like that envelope might contain poison," says Rhamuel dryly. "What did you say to her?"

"To who?"

"It has to be Kyedra. It's not Haesychya's hand."

"Not too much. I was more concerned about Aenslem. Then . . . well . . . I told you what happened."

"Apparently not everything. Not if you're getting a note."

Lerial opens the envelope. Inside is a card, on the front cover of which is a stylized "K" within an oval, clearly hand-drawn most precisely. He looks at the section of the card beneath and begins to read.

> Dear Lerial—
> I would like to ask your forgiveness for my failure to appreciate your risking your life in order to save Grandpapa. He is much, much better this morning, and we have no doubts that would not be so had it not been for your efforts. I cannot express what that means, especially to me, and I would hope that you will indeed forgive my lack of grace and understanding.

His eyes widen as he reads the line above her signature—"With great appreciation." What exactly does "great appreciation" mean? Does it mean anything at all, especially given that Haesychya had to have read every word? *But . . . is that a form of manipulation? Or another way of pleading for you to keep supporting Afrit?* He shakes his head. *The more you learn in Afrit, the less you know.* At least, that's the way it feels.

"You look rather pensive," observes Rhamuel.

"Kyedra offers . . ." Lerial breaks off his words and hands the card to Rhamuel. "I'm hard-pressed as to what it means. Is it just what it says, or more . . . or less?"

"You may be trying to read too much into it."

"In Afrit? Where nothing is quite what it seems, and few indeed are to be trusted except to find ways to make more golds?"

"You judge Afrit harshly," Rhamuel says mildly.

"I think not. Not in a land where an attempt has been made to assassinate every senior officer with any degree of competence, where at least one merchanter has betrayed both the duke and his arms-commander, and where a trusted advisor was likely involved in the plot to kill the duke and his family." Lerial pauses. "And that is only what I know." *And not all of that, even.*

"You have a point . . . but Kyedra is not that devious."

Lerial sees no reason to say more on the subject of Afritan deviousness. "Have you heard from Ascaar?"

"Not directly," replies Rhamuel dryly. "I did get a dispatch from Fhastal, and a shorter one from Mesphaes, congratulating me on my decision to leave Ascaar in Shaelt, given his handling and destruction of more than three Heldyan battalions. Even if they were largely Tourlegyn warriors."

"Then one of his officers mislaid the dispatches," suggests Lerial, "since it would be unlikely that could happen here."

"Why do you say that?" says Rhamuel.

"Because I checked with the squad leader in charge of the dispatch records. There haven't been any riders coming in from the south." He frowns. "Ascaar wouldn't send dispatches to the Harbor Post, but either to headquarters or the palace, and there's no record of a courier from the south coming to either place."

"So there aren't any . . . or they went to the Harbor Post?"

"I'm inclined to think . . ." Lerial stops as Sammyl steps into the outer chamber, then turns and asks, "What did you discover from Commander Dhresyl?"

"I asked him about the level of troops you both faced. He said that they fought fiercely, to the death in many cases." Sammyl frowns. "That was not the case at Luba, as I recall."

Lerial manages to keep his mouth in place. "Were many of them Tourlegyn?"

"I asked the same question," replies the commander. "It appears, and I say appears, because most of them were not taken captive, and many of the bodies had already been dropped into pits, but it appears that a great number were."

"So . . . Khesyn is using them to solve two problems at once," says Rhamuel. "Save many of his own troops while whittling down our forces . . . and reducing the future difficulties he may have with the Tourlegyns . . . who are known to have many offspring."

"That might mean . . ." Lerial pauses, then turns back to Sammyl. "What have your scouts discovered?"

"More than ten merchanters moored or anchored off Estheld . . ."

"No fog or mist?"

"No. The scouts didn't report any."

"Good." *That means that there aren't that many mages there . . . or that Khesyn wants us to think that there aren't.* "Are any of the ships readying to set sail?"

"It doesn't appear that way. There was one more ship coming in under reefed sail, and there was another too far off shore to determine where it was headed."

"I'd suggest posting a battalion at the tileworks . . . if you haven't already." *For more than one reason.*

"I've already dispatched Fourteenth Battalion," Sammyl declares.

Paelwyr's battalion? Lerial finds that interesting, possibly disturbing. *But then, you're finding everything disturbing these days.* "Has anyone seen Maesoryk?"

"We haven't been looking," Sammyl says. "He's either a traitor or dead."

"Why do you think that?" asks Rhamuel.

Why is he asking that? To see Sammyl's reaction? Lerial manages a puzzled expression.

"Because, if he weren't, he'd be begging to see you or the duke, claiming that the Heldyans invaded his property. At the very least, he'd have sent some sort of whining letter."

Lerial has to agree with that, and yet . . . *given the arrogance of Afritan merchanters . . .* who could tell for certain how they might react? "Does anyone know whether he's still in Swartheld? Maybe you should send a company to see if he is?"

Sammyl and Rhamuel exchange glances.

"I take it that isn't done?"

"It hasn't been," says Rhamuel. "Maybe this time we should." He looks to Sammyl.

"I'll arrange for it, ser."

"What about the other merchanters? Have any said anything?" asks Lerial.

"Alaphyn wants to know what we intend to do to reassure all the traders that Swartheld is safe for trade," says Rhamuel. "He sent a brief note late yesterday."

"Anyone else?"

"Fhastal has informed me that it's likely Khesyn has seized his countinghouses in Estheld, Dolari, and Heldya. He has suggested that I seize the countinghouse of Effram in return. There are two, one here in Swartheld and one in Shaelt. He has also suggested that I keep watch on a Cigoernean merchanting factorage in Swartheld."

"Which one?" asks Lerial.

"Myrapol House. It has factorages in Amaershyn, Heldya, Dolari, Estheld . . . and Shaelt and Swartheld." Rhamuel looks to Lerial. "What do you know about it?"

Lerial takes a deep breath, then says, "Enough to say that Myrapol bears watching."

"It sounds like you know more than that."

"The house was founded by the consort of a magus who survived the voyage from Cyad. She brought a great array of jewelry, which she sold surreptitiously to gain the golds to build the first factorages. Her death was suspicious. Her son was a Mirror Lancer junior officer likely involved in a plot against Duke Kiedron, but that could never be proved, although he was dismissed from the Lancers. His father is the titular head of Myrapol, but he's the one running it now." There was something else about Veraan, but Lerial cannot remember exactly what it was.

"The father is a magus, then?"

"He is."

"You don't trust him, I take it?" asks Rhamuel rhetorically.

"I don't trust either of them."

"Very interesting." Abruptly, Rhamuel asks Lerial, "When will I walk again?"

"You may not. If you do, you will regain some feeling in your legs . . . possibly within a season. If you don't, it's unlikely that you will."

Rhamuel nods, if in a manner conveying a certain resignation. "That's what Jaermyd said as well. He also said that, without what you did, I might have had even less feeling below my waist." He looks to Sammyl. "What are your thoughts about taking over the countinghouses of Effram?"

"Take temporary possession of them, but leave everything as it is until matters are settled, one way or another, with Heldya. If Khesyn does not restore Fhastal's countinghouses, then turn Effram's over to Fhastal."

"Have you heard anything about Mykel?" Lerial isn't quite sure why he is asking, except that the gate squad leader had mentioned a courier from Lake Reomer, which was where Mykel had been headed.

"He never reached the lake," replies Rhamuel. "Neither did Oestyn. There's no sign of either. I've sent out men to search for signs of them along the way they took."

"I'm sorry."

"You had nothing to do with whatever happened."

"No . . . but I can be sorry for everything that has happened to you and your family."

Rhamuel shakes his head. "You represent Cigoerne. We have not always seen eye-to-eye. Yet you and your family have supported me and mine more than most in Afrit. Sometimes . . . I find the world strange." He forces a smile. "There's not much you can do here at the palace. I'll let you know if anything happens."

"Then I think I'll ride over to Aenslem's and see how he is doing. I still worry about him."

Rhamuel raises his eyebrows, but only says, "Haesychya will appreciate that. Aenslem might . . . also."

In less than a half glass, Lerial and his squad are outside the iron gates of Aenslem's villa. The guards look suspiciously at Lerial and the Mirror Lancer squad.

"I'm Overcaptain Lerial, and I'm also a healer. I was the one who helped Merchanter Aenslem last night. You can ask him or Lady Haesychya. We'll wait."

Despite what Lerial has said, he and the lancers do have to wait almost a tenth of a glass before a guard comes running back down the lane and talks quietly to the head guard. After several moments, the head guard looks up.

"I'm sorry for the delay, ser. I didn't know. With everything that's happened . . ."

"I understand. You're doing your duty."

The guards open just one of the iron gates and watch as Lerial and Second Squad ride through.

While Lerial hopes that Kyedra might be the one to meet him at the entrance to the villa, Haesychya is the one waiting after he dismounts and walks up the steps to the double doors. "Thank you for coming. I'm glad you did." She gestures toward the entry hall.

Lerial accompanies her into the coolness of the villa. "How is he?"

"Much better . . . but . . ."

"But not so much as you'd like?"

"He's still pale to my eyes."

"He may be for several days. I'll see."

Haesychya smiles gently as she walks through the archway into the north corridor. "I can see you hoped to see someone else. She's playing plaques with her grandfather. He insisted on it."

"That's still a fair improvement. It's not a strain on him?"

Haesychya shakes her head. "He's just not . . . maybe I worry too much."

All Lerial can say is, "I'll have to see."

"How are you doing?"

"Much better. How are *you* doing?"

"As I can. I doubt you're back to full strength."

Her words tell Lerial not to say more, even indirectly, about her loss of her consort and son. "Physically . . . I'm much, much better. In order-chaos terms, it will take a little longer."

As close as he is to Haesychya, Lerial can sense, even without trying, a certain sense of chaotic feeling. *About her losses? Or about you? About Kyedra?* His lips twist into a wry smile. That makes sense, given that he's possibly saved her father, yet is the "wrong brother." *Then, it's more likely she's not even thinking about you. She's got far greater problems and losses.*

As he steps into the study behind Haesychya, Lerial sees that Aenslem is now seated in one of the leather armchairs with the side table before him. Across the table from the merchanter sits Kyedra in a straight-backed chair. Both hold plaques in their hands, and there are small piles of plaques set facedown on each side of the small table. Kyedra looks up and toward the door. Then she smiles warmly as her eyes take in Lerial. Once again, Lerial is amazed at how her smile transforms her from an attractive young woman to a beautiful one, and he can't help but return the smile.

"I didn't know you'd be coming again," Kyedra says, rising from the chair.

"I thought it wise. I wasn't at my best yesterday afternoon, and I worried that I might have missed something."

Aenslem chuckles. "Missed *something*, Lord Lerial?"

Lerial hopes he is not flushing too obviously as he replies. "Even Rhamuel thought I should come."

"That boy worries too much."

"He worries when he should," says Haesychya quietly. "Now you let Lerial look at you. You're not as strong as you think you are."

"Haven't been for years, according to you, daughter."

Lerial walks over beside Aenslem, all too conscious that Kyedra's eyes are on him. He lets his order-senses range over the merchanter. While there is clearly less wound/poison chaos within the merchanter, there is still a pocket of more defined chaos lower in Aenslem's abdomen. "There's still something there. You'll have to pardon me once more." He extends his fingertips to the side of Aenslem's throat, barely touching the skin, and directs a thin line of order down through the merchanter to the chaos.

He can feel some, if not all, of the chaos, dissipate, but he immediately stops as he senses the possibility of light-headedness.

"That feels better," the merchanter admits.

"It's not all gone," Lerial says, "but that's all I can do today. The rest of that may vanish on its own. If I can, I'll check on you tomorrow."

"If . . . ?" Haesychya looks at Lerial.

"It appears that Duke Khesyn may not be done with his assaults on Afrit."

"After all the killing . . . destruction . . ." Haesychya shakes her head. "I'm forgetting my hospitality. Let me bring you some lager."

"That would be good," Lerial admits.

"What have you heard about Khesyn?" demands Aenslem. "No one tells me anything." The merchanter offers a mock glare at his granddaughter.

"Grandpapa . . ."

"He used Tourlegyn warriors in many of the battalions he sent against us, and it appears as though he is once more gathering more merchant vessels in Estheld. We're likely down to the equivalent of perhaps six battalions after all the death and casualties."

"I told Atroyan he needed warships." Aenslem snorts.

"It's hard to build warships without larger tariffs," Lerial says cautiously.

"I'd pay 'em . . . so long as everyone else did. Maesoryk . . . never thought much of him . . . thought less of his father . . . he kept saying we didn't need warships."

"That's interesting. The Heldyans used the pier at his tileworks to land their largest force."

"That . . ." Redness suffuses Aenslem's face, as if he is so angry he cannot express himself.

"Grandpapa!"

With Kyedra's anguished cry, Aenslem exhales abruptly, then begins to cough. After several moments, he stops coughing and wipes spittle off his face with a large cloth. "Sorry . . . just . . . never thought much of him." He looks at Lerial. "Did you kill the bastard?"

"No one's been able to find him. Commander Sammyl thought he was either dead or a traitor, since he's never appeared or sent word."

"Death'd be too good for him."

"Grandpapa." This time Kyedra's voice carries the iron of her mother's.

"All right, Granddaughter."

"Anyway," Lerial adds quickly, "Sammyl's sent out sail-galleys to scout out Estheld's harbor. Even a few days' respite would help. And we've sent a battalion to hold the tileworks pier. That would make landing easier."

"Then they'll sail to Baiet and march down the shore road. You couldn't afford to send your battalions that far from Swartheld."

That makes far too much sense.

"What will you do, then?" asks Kyedra.

"Whatever we can that's necessary."

Aenslem nods.

At that moment, Haesychya returns, followed by a serving girl carrying a tray with a large pitcher and four beakers, as well as a small platter of biscuits.

Lerial notices that the serving girl, rather beautiful and well formed, glances toward Aenslem, and then looks away immediately when Kyedra looks toward her.

"Everyone could use a biscuit . . . or two." With the last two words Haesychya looks at Lerial.

"I wouldn't think of not following your suggestion." Lerial grins as he finishes speaking.

"Good idea," says Aenslem.

Lerial does enjoy both the lager and the biscuits, and in the end, he has three, in between answering several questions about the Mirror Lancers. He does notice that, if but for a moment, Aenslem's eyes follow the serving girl when she slips away after a gesture from Haesychya.

He has barely finished the last sip of the lager when Haesychya looks to Kyedra and says, "Why don't you walk Lerial to the front terrace?"

Kyedra stiffens, if but for a moment, then rises and turns to Lerial.

Lerial stands and addresses Aenslem. "If I can, I'll be here sometime tomorrow." Then he turns to Haesychya. "Thank you for the lager and biscuits. They were excellent."

"You're more than welcome." Haesychya inclines her head.

Lerial returns the gesture, then follows Kyedra from the study. He waits until they are several yards from the study door before speaking. "I got your note this morning. You were kind to write, and you have an elegant hand."

"Mother would not have it any other way." Kyedra does not look at Lerial. "You're not what I expected."

"Might I ask what you mean by that?"

"You may." There is a long pause, although she still does not look at him. "First, I thought you were just like . . . my brother, in a way, except older, more polished. Stronger, of course. Then . . . I heard about everything you've done . . . how many have died because of that . . . and I couldn't understand . . . you seemed to care . . . but all the deaths . . ."

Lerial waits, not quite holding his breath.

"You risked your life to protect your men, didn't you? You could have protected yourself without almost dying. Isn't that so?"

"How can I answer that, Lady? If I say yes to either, it sounds boastful."

"You could say no."

Lerial thinks he detects a hint of mischievousness in her voice. "I'd rather not lie, especially to you."

"Most men do."

"I'd prefer not to be most men."

"That's what I mean. Mother says you're older than your years in some ways, and younger in others."

"Definitely younger in understanding women." Lerial offers a wry smile.

"That's also what she said."

She also said I was the wrong brother. "I think your mother knows a great deal, a very great deal."

"She doesn't know everything."

"None of us do." Lerial cannot help but recall how little he understood what his parents—or Majer Altyrn—knew . . . until after Verdheln.

"Will you come tomorrow?"

"If I can. I promised . . . and I don't think your grandpapa is as well as either of us would like."

"You're sounding like a healer, now."

Lerial laughs softly. "I suppose I am."

"I like that, too."

When they reach the double doors, Kyedra stops. After a moment, she says, "You will take care."

"As I can, Lady . . . Kyedra . . . and thank you." Lerial realizes he may have stepped toward too much familiarity in using her name, yet "Lady" is too formal. He offers a smile and inclines his head. "Until tomorrow."

"Until tomorrow."

He turns and walks to where a ranker holds the reins to the gelding. He mounts and looks back to the doors where Kyedra still stands. He has the feeling that Kyedra's eyes are on him until he rides past the hedgerow flanking the lane near the gates. *Or is that just wistful thinking?*

But you're still the wrong brother.

XLI

By the time Lerial finishes breakfast at the mess on threeday, he is feeling physically close to full strength. Even the burn on his hip has subsided to a healing, but intermittently annoying, itch. He can also order-sense more than a hundred yards, perhaps farther, although it is difficult to tell within the walls of the Afritan Guard headquarters. He had not returned to the palace on threeday after leaving Kyedra, but had spent the remainder of the day with his officers and men, going over equipment and weapons, and seeing to repairs, while also making arrangements for reshoeing a number of mounts, including some of the twenty they had received as replacements from those abandoned by the Heldyans. He eats quickly, meets for a short time with Strauxyn, Kusyl, and Dhoraat, then leaves for the palace with Third Squad from Twenty-third Company as his escort.

As on threeday, the streets are busy with wagons, coaches, peddlers, and various pedestrians, all of them seemingly going about their day, as if unaware of the carnage that had occurred little more than ten kays away. At the palace, by comparison, the gates remain heavily guarded, although the Afritan officers no longer insist on an escort for Lerial, and only a single Lancer ranker accompanies him as he walks to the west wing to meet with Rhamuel—and Sammyl, if the commander happens to be there.

Both Sammyl and Rhamuel are in the sitting room, with Sammyl standing by the open window and Rhamuel at the table desk.

"Good morning," offers Lerial.

"The same to you," replies the arms-commander. "You didn't come back here yesterday. Why not?"

"I had some matters to go over with my officers and men. I thought you'd know where I was."

"How is Aenslem? I'm assuming he's better, since I heard nothing from Haesychya."

"He appeared much better yesterday afternoon. There was still some wound or poison chaos in his system."

"Poison? You didn't mention that he'd been poisoned," declares Sammyl.

"Oh . . . I thought I had. Someone put something in his tonic. I don't think it was accidental, but I haven't pressed him on who might have done something or how."

"You might . . . if you see him again." Rhamuel frowns. "Perhaps you should visit him after we finish here."

"If there's nothing pressing."

"How is my niece?"

"She is in much better spirits."

"I imagine. A handsome heir and officer visiting might cheer her up."

Handsome? When she thinks you have unruly hair? "Have you heard from Ascaar?"

"We finally received a dispatch this morning." Rhamuel smiles. "He managed to defeat three Heldyan battalions. Most were Tourlegyn warriors. About half a battalion managed to escape downstream on the flatboats they used. He did lose more than a full company in deaths and casualties." The smile vanishes. "He sent this dispatch with three rankers on one of Fhastal's river galleys, because it appeared that his first dispatch might not have arrived in Swartheld. That was because, a day after the battle, a certain Captain Jontarl had vanished, leaving behind certain indications suggesting that."

"What do you know about Jontarl?"

"Other than he is a nephew of Merchanter Jhosef . . . not a great deal."

"Isn't Oestyn related to Jhosef?" asks Lerial.

"His youngest son, but you knew that already, didn't you?"

"I thought I recalled something like that," replies Lerial blandly. "Remember, all these families and names are new to me." *Not that this one was, but questions make better points sometimes, even rhetorical questions.*

"I doubt you forget much. Your point is taken, however."

"Unfortunately, there's much to it," adds Sammyl, scowling. "But since he's *merely* a nephew, and no proof that Jhosef was involved, there's little we can do."

"Not directly," murmurs Rhamuel. "Not at the moment."

The quiet iron in the arms-commander's voice reminds Lerial that displeasing Rhamuel, crippled as he may turn out to be, is most unwise.

Rhamuel smiles, an expression similar to Kyedra's, and the room is suddenly less oppressive. "Ascaar also indicated that he had sent on your message . . ."

Lerial notes the briefly puzzled look on Sammyl's face, but does not intend to explain. ". . . and enclosed a dispatch to you. It originally went to Luba, and Majer Chorazt forwarded it to Ascaar at Shaelt. In turn . . ." Rhamuel extends the still-sealed missive to Lerial.

Lerial takes it and studies the outside, which merely bears his name and rank, with the words "Mirror Lancers of Cigoerne" beneath. Then he takes his belt knife, the one that had burned him—and shows no signs of it—and slits the envelope. He immediately checks the signature and seal: both of Major Jhalet.

Why from Majer Jhalet? Why not from Father? Because he doesn't want anyone to know you're related if the dispatch should fall into the wrong hands? Lerial nods and—and then begins to read.

> Overcaptain Lerial—
>
> We have heard from the wounded you dispatched back to Cigoerne, as well as from a number of traders, that you and the

Afritan Guard were successful in repulsing the Heldyan attack on Luba. We also understand that you have been requested to attend the duke of Afrit to receive his thanks, and trust that, once you have accomplished whatever is necessary, you and your companies will be returning to Cigoerne as soon as practicable.

It has also come to the duke's attention, and to that of Overcaptain Lephi, that there has not been a single Heldyan incursion or attack along the entire river bordering Heldya for the past three eightdays. This is so unprecedented that the duke requested that I so inform you.

We trust that this information will prove useful. The duke and the Mirror Lancers look forward to your speedy return.

After a moment, Lerial hands the dispatch to Rhamuel. "You should read this."

Rhamuel does. "Would you mind if Sammyl . . . ?"

"Not at all."

The commander reads the dispatch and then returns it to Lerial. "Khesyn must have pulled every Heldyan armsman from everywhere."

"It looks that way," admits Rhamuel.

"What have your scouts discovered?" asks Lerial.

"Two more merchanters have ported at Estheld. None have left. There may be more happening than that, but our sailing galley had to withdraw when the Heldyans sent out three of their sail-galleys armed with archers."

"Were the merchanters preparing to sail?"

"It didn't appear that way. Not then."

"That reminds me," Lerial says. "I mentioned the merchanters to Aenslem, and that you'd garrisoned the tileworks. He pointed out that the Heldyans could easily land at Baiet and march to Swartheld."

"They could," admits Rhamuel.

"It'd take two or three days," replies Sammyl.

"But we don't have enough battalions left to garrison Baiet," says Rhamuel, "not and leave enough to defend Swartheld—and it would take us two days to get them there even if we did. Besides, there's nowhere else that they could go besides here. We're better off fighting closer to Swartheld."

Except that means more deaths and even possible defeat if Khesyn can raise another force as large as the first. "Can you keep a close watch on the ships?"

"As well as we can," says Sammyl. "I'd guess it will be a few days. The merchanters didn't start gathering again until yesterday, or late oneday at the earliest."

"Let's hope so." *Because you won't be able to do much any sooner.* "Oh . . . what about Maesoryk?"

"His villa is empty," reports Sammyl. "Only a handful of retainers are there. They said he had repaired to his hill villa for the summer."

"Summer?" Lerial frowns. "It isn't even midspring." Then he nods. "So that, if we defeat Khesyn, he can claim he wasn't even around when all this happened, and that he had no idea about any of it."

Rhamuel nods. "And there won't even be any proof that he was involved."

Lerial understands all too well. Even as duke, with no direct proof, Rhamuel would face immense difficulties in trying to hold Maesoryk responsible. Most likely, any retainer who could link him to the putative mislabeled barrels of cammabark has vanished, one way or another. He takes a slow deep breath, trying not to think about how hamstrung the dukes of Afrit have been. "I suppose I should pay another visit to Aenslem."

"It wouldn't hurt," says Rhamuel. "You might press a bit about that tonic . . ."

"I'll see what I can do."

Lerial makes his way back to the stables and Third Squad, and they set out for Aenslem's villa under a sky that is only slightly hazy, the white-hot sun burning down on them with an intensity that is more like midsummer in Cigoerne, again reminding Lerial why he definitely would rather not be in Swartheld in full summer. Yet . . .

He pushes that thought away.

When they reach the iron gates, this time Aenslem's guards admit them without difficulty, but the gates close quickly behind Third Squad, a quickness that comes from long practice. *Long practice and mistrust of anyone not known . . . and perhaps some known all too well.* When they reach the entrance to the villa, a single retainer, not a guard, waits by the steps.

"Lord Lerial, there are refreshments for your men and water for your horses in the rear courtyard."

"Thank you."

"It is Master Aenslem's pleasure."

Lerial dismounts and walks quickly up the steps, to the double doors, where a guard opens one for him. He is more than a little surprised to see Kyedra standing just inside the double doors. "I didn't expect to see you."

"Why not?" Kyedra's tone is practical and matter-of-fact. "We're perfectly safe here at Grandpapa's. It appears it's safer here than in the palace. His guards are well trained. Uncle Rham even said so."

"Every one of them is trustworthy?" asks Lerial.

"You doubt me?"

"I've led many men for a few years. There are usually a few one has to watch or have watched. I doubt that is any different here." *Especially with what you've learned about the merchanters of Afrit.*

Kyedra frowns.

"I mean it. Think it over."

After a moment, Kyedra nods . . . and that also surprises Lerial.

"You're right. There is one. Well . . . he may not be here now. He did special duties for Grandpapa. That's all Grandpapa would say. Sometimes, the way he looked at me scared me. So did the black gloves he always wore. I never saw him without them."

Black gloves? Lerial has an almost sinking feeling. "What was his name? What did he look like?"

"I never knew his name. I didn't see him that much, but the few times I did he kept watching me."

"His looks?"

"You are persistent. He was perhaps five years older than you, but he looked much older. He had a narrow face. Pinched really. He had floppy blond hair that looked dirty, and a dark mole on one cheek. Maybe it was a scar. He was thin. He always had a long blade at his side. Why are you asking?"

"I might have met him once."

"When?"

"On the way to Swartheld. How is your grandfather?"

"You don't want to talk about that man, do you?"

"Not until I know more. I'll need to talk to your grandfather. How is he?"

"Much better. He's beating me at plaques again."

Lerial wonders if that is because plaques don't matter than much to Kyedra.

"You have that look on your face."

"What look?"

"It's not a look, except your head tilts just a bit . . . as if you're thinking."

"I was. I was wondering whether you really care that much about winning at plaques."

"I wouldn't let even Grandpapa win."

Lerial smiles. "That's not the same thing."

"I suppose not. Does that answer the question you didn't ask?"

"With an answer you didn't really give?"

Kyedra laughs, then smiles ruefully. "We had better get you to see him." She turns and looks at him, then starts toward the north archway.

Lerial immediately takes two quick steps to catch up. "How are you and your mother doing?"

"As we can." Kyedra looks sideways at him. "Thank you for asking."

Later than you should have. "All of this has to have been hard on you both."

"Did your grandmere talk about it?"

For an instant, Lerial is disconcerted, before he makes the connection. "Not to me. I don't know if she talked to my parents or my aunt."

"Your aunt. Uncle Rham once said she was special. I think he still might be in love with her. What . . . I shouldn't ask."

"She never consorted. I think I might have mentioned that she's the head of healing in Cigoerne."

"That's sad."

Lerial nods, wishing he could say more, but knowing it is not his place to do so, especially if that knowledge could jeopardize Rhamuel's position as duke. *But it is interesting that Kyedra thinks Rhamuel might still love Emerya.*

When they enter the study, Lerial can tell even before he nears Aenslem that there is still some residual wound/poison chaos within the merchanter, but that it has diminished.

"So . . . am I better, Overcaptain and healer of sorts?" demands Aenslem in a gruffly cheerful voice from where he sits at the desk at the end of the study, surrounded by papers.

"You can answer that more accurately than I."

"Better, but there's still a touch of discomfort."

"You'd recover without my doing more, but a little additional order will speed that up." Lerial walks to the side of Aenslem's chair. "Pardon me." He touches Aenslem's neck gently, directing a slight bit of order to the remaining chaos, immediately feeling it dissipate.

"It's gone. That feels better."

"You might still feel uncomfortable from time to time for a few days." Lerial clears his throat. "Now . . . about that tonic . . ."

"Did Rhamuel put you up to asking?"

"As a matter of fact, he did. I also have my own reasons for asking."

"Which are?"

"I'd like to know whom to watch out for."

"It's my own fault," says Aenslem. "The tonic was recommended by Alaphyn. I take everything he says with a cask of salt. First I fed it to a sickly hound. The hound recovered. Then, I offered it to others—retainers—in small doses. Everyone prospered. I took it for a good half season, and when I ran out, I asked Alaphyn where he got it. He said it came from Cigoerne, and I could order it through Myrapol House . . ."

Myrapol House? Majer Jhalet had mentioned a connection . . . Could Veraan . . .

". . . I did, and tested it again. The third jug . . . I did not . . ." Aenslem shakes his head.

"Could someone here . . . in the villa?"

"No. I kept it in a locked cabinet for that reason . . . and took certain . . . other precautions. No one has touched it beside me. The jugs were all sealed . . ."

How can they live like this, where no one can trust anyone? Yet the way in which Aenslem has answered Lerial's questions is worrisome, perhaps because the words are likely truthful, but not complete.

Aenslem laughs gruffly. "Do you have any more questions from Rhamuel . . . or should I say the duke?"

"No. I do have one of my own. You had a man serving you who wore black gloves—"

"One moment." Aenslem clears his throat loudly and holds up his hand to stop Lerial from continuing. "Lord Lerial and I need to talk. Alone."

"As you wish." Haesychya gestures to Kyedra. "Let us know when you want more lager . . . or anything else."

"Daughters . . ." Aenslem shakes his head, but says nothing else, watching as the study door closes. Then he looks at Lerial. "Are you the one?"

"The one what?"

"The one who killed Willem."

"If Willem is the black-gloved, chaos-using assassin who killed Subcommander Valatyr, yes. He tried to kill me and two of my men rather than be taken captive."

Aenslem nods. "I'm not surprised. You seem to be at the heart of everything. He didn't know who you were, then?"

"He knew I was a Mirror Lancer overcaptain. Nothing more. He didn't give me a chance to say much more before he attacked me. I tried just to wound him, but there was too much chaos in his system."

"That really wasn't your question, was it?"

"No. Why Valatyr? He seemed to be quite competent, and I can't believe you're part of all the other assassinations of senior officers."

"I'm not. I wasn't. Valatyr was in Maesoryk's wallet. I didn't know why. I did know that he accepted hundreds of golds. It could have been more. When that many golds change hands, it's not good. I'd heard rumors, hints, that Valatyr would be a far better chief of staff than Sammyl. I've never cared much for Sammyl, but he was loyal to a fault, especially to Atroyan. Wrong, at times, but loyal."

Possibly for preferring Dhresyl over Drusyn as well . . . although . . . "Why didn't you just send Willem after Maesoryk?"

"It wouldn't have worked. Maesoryk has two chaos-mages near him all the time, and when they're not, he's heavily guarded or someplace where success would be unlikely . . . and too obvious."

"Like the palace?"

Aenslem nods.

"Why are you telling me this?"

"You should know. That's so you don't make matters worse. After what Maesoryk seems to have done, can you say that removing Valatyr was wrong?"

"Why not tell Rhamuel?"

"That hasn't worked in the past." Aenslem's voice is not only raspy, but dry. "Even if he had listened, he would have asked for proof, and I couldn't have given it without revealing too much. You must have seen that Rhamuel and I are not exactly close."

While Lerial's mind isn't exactly reeling, he feels appalled at the currents and crosscurrents, schemes and counterschemes that run beneath the seemingly placid surface of Afritan merchanter society. He also understands that there are no witnesses to their conversation, and no real proof. For him to accuse Aenslem would indeed make matters worse—not to mention creating a rift between Cigoerne and Afrit. *And it would accomplish nothing.*

"I think you're beginning to understand," observes the merchanter.

"I doubt I understand near enough. I feel like I'm standing in a camma tree grove with a forest fire raging toward me." At his own words, he starts . . . and then swallows, remembering just what he had forgotten about Maesoryk. "Frig! Frig! Frig!"

"What is it?"

"Cammabark. That's why Maesoryk wanted those forest lands so filled with camma trees that most others didn't. That's most likely where the cammabark in the palace and at the Harbor Post came from."

Aenslem frowns. "I can't believe . . . even Maesoryk . . ."

"A merchanter, Shalaara, I think it was, borrowed golds from Fhastal to keep some forest lands infested with camma trees from falling into Maesoryk's hands through debts a family owed. But he bought the lands anyway, paying much more for them. Shalaara got a profit from it, and Maesoryk was furious. Rhamuel told me that as a reason why Maesoryk dislikes Fhastal."

"I remember that . . . we all thought it was about the golds . . . and Maesoryk being forced to pay more for what he felt was rightly his."

"Maybe that was what you were supposed to think." *Hidden right out in the open.*

Aenslem nods again, almost reluctantly, it seems to Lerial, then asks, "Do you have any more questions?"

Lerial shakes his head.

"I have one for you. Why are you still here, risking yourself?"

"Because, if Afrit falls, so will Cigoerne."

"So you're the sacrificial goat to save Cigoerne?"

Lerial does not reply for a moment, thinking about what Altyrn had written him. "More to save the best of Cyador that remains in Cigoerne, I think."

"That's a strange answer."

Only if you're a merchanter, thinking golds are both means and ends. "It's the only one I can give."

"You can invite my daughter and granddaughter back in, if you wish."

"I should be going. The Heldyans may already be preparing their next attack, and I'd like to know what Sammyl and his scouts have discovered."

Aenslem nods. "I won't keep you. You do have my thanks and gratitude for saving my life. I don't forget."

Either good or evil. "Thank you. I'm glad I could do what I could."

"So am I . . . and so is my daughter. Whether she'll say so . . . that's another question."

Lerial isn't about to comment on that. He just says, "Good day," and leaves the study.

Kyedra is the first to see him, and she emerges from the salon that is behind the next door in the long corridor. "You're leaving?"

"I'm certain he needs to get back to the palace," says Haesychya from the salon door.

"I'll walk you to the door, then," says Kyedra, not looking in her mother's direction.

"I'd appreciate that," Lerial says immediately.

Neither speaks until they are several yards from Haesychya.

"You won't tell me what you talked about?"

"No. That's up to your grandfather. If he wants to tell you, he will."

"You're as bad as he is."

Lerial's initial reaction is to deny the charge . . . but, unhappily, he realizes Kyedra is right, if not in the way she meant. "No. In some ways, I'm worse. I've certainly killed more men than he has, and the men under me have certainly killed more than those under him."

Kyedra offers a puzzled look before her mouth opens, then closes. Finally, she says, "That was a strange way of answering."

"No. Just accurate, and it might be best to leave it at that. I don't want you to have illusions."

"About either of you, I presume." Her tone is cool.

"You know your grandfather. You scarcely know me. I'm more worried about any illusions you might have about me."

"Most men would rather women have illusions." Kyedra stops well short of the double doors that lead out onto the entry terrace.

"I'm not most men."

"I believe you mentioned that before." Kyedra softens her words at the end, with a slight smile as well. "You seem very determined I not have illusions about you. Why?"

"That's a long story."

"I can stand here as long as necessary." She glances around the entry hall of the villa.

Lerial smiles. "I think I mentioned Majer Altyrn to you . . ."

"You said his consort had a lovely smile."

"He was a great man. I don't think many understood how great. She was great in a different way. They were very much in love, and despite many difficulties and very different backgrounds, they never argued, although they shared feelings that, from what I saw, had to have been very different in the past. I got the sense that they got on so well because neither had any illusions about either life or each other . . ."

"You're verging on the presumptuous, you know?"

"I didn't mean to. What I was trying to say was that I think that many troubles between people come from illusions that they hold."

"Perhaps. But you have no illusions about Duke Khesyn. He is ruthless and bloody. That lack of illusion doesn't mean Afrit or Cigoerne will ever get on with him."

"The lack of illusion means that we know that."

"I think that might undermine your point."

Lerial shakes his head in a mock-serious fashion. "I should not debate with you."

"You respect the majer a great deal, don't you?"

"I did. I still do. I probably respect him even more after what I've seen and been through in the last season."

"You should tell him that."

"I can't. He died just before I left for Afrit."

"Oh . . . I'm sorry. I didn't mean . . ."

"I never told you. You wouldn't have known." Lerial pauses, then says gently, "I should get back to the palace to see if Sammyl has discovered anything more about what Khesyn may be doing." Lerial regrets having to leave, but he also worries about what may be happening in Estheld . . . or elsewhere in Heldya.

"I suppose you should. I shouldn't be keeping you."

"You will send word if your grandfather doesn't improve?"

"We will."

"Good." Lerial smiles, hoping Kyedra will smile back, then turns when she just nods.

She does not come out onto the entry terrace to watch as he departs.

When Lerial returns to the palace and the sitting room, both Sammyl and Rhamuel are still there, each behind a table desk. Neither looks particularly pleased.

"How is Aenslem?"

"It appears as though he is largely recovered. It's likely he was poisoned . . ." Lerial goes on to explain what Aenslem had said about the tonic. He does not mention Veraan or anything about Myrapol House, except what Aenslem has said.

"Trusting Alaphyn . . . about anything . . ." Rhamuel shakes his head.

"What is happening in Estheld?" Lerial asks.

"Two more merchanters have arrived," replies Sammyl. "So far as we can tell, none have left, and none appear ready to cast off. There's no sign of flatboats on the river."

"Not yet." Rhamuel's voice is dry and ironic, with a foreboding tone.

"All we can do is prepare and wait," says Sammyl. "What else can we do?"

What else can we do? Lerial is still pondering that question later that night as he lies in the bunk in the senior officer's quarters at Afritan Guard headquarters, trying to go to sleep.

XLII

Lerial wakes up on fourday, his thoughts on Veraan and Myrapol House. Had Veraan's father Apollyn actually created a chaos-based poison for the tainted tonic . . . or had Veraan just used a fast-acting tincture of some sort? And why would he have done that? Lerial can certainly understand why Alaphyn would have wanted Aenslem to order the deadly tonic directly from Myrapol House, but why would Veraan have agreed to it? *For golds?* The sum would have to have been quite significant. *Or perhaps, in an odd way,*

Veraan felt that the death of an Afritan merchanter would not hurt Cigoerne . . . or more likely, would reduce rivals to Myrapol House.

And then there was Maesoryk . . . who had to have been involved in the explosions and the invasion landings at his tileworks, but with no proof . . . except indirectly . . .

Lerial bolts upright in his bunk, recalling what Aenslem had said the afternoon before about Maesoryk—two *chaos-mages around him all the time.* "Of course," he murmurs to himself, "the fog . . . the unnatural chaos-caused fog." The fog that had enabled the ships to land had to have been created by a mage on land—at the tileworks. And there had been at least four mages when Lerial and Twenty-third Company had first faced the invaders. *That was how they knew they'd be covered.* Two mages from Maesoryk and those with the Heldyans. Except . . . again, the fact that the fog had been created on land wasn't definitive proof of Maesoryk's involvement or guilt. Even if Maesoryk should return to Swartheld without his mages, that would not constitute real proof.

Lerial shakes his head. Then he tries order-sensing, and is pleased to discover that he is finally much stronger, if not back to full strength. He is still thinking things over when he walks to the mess.

By half past seventh glass, he has eaten, met with his officers and Dhoraat, and is on his way to the palace under a blustery gray sky, accompanied by Fourth Squad from Eighth Company. They have barely covered half a kay before rain begins to fall—in large droplets that are almost warm. By the time Lerial has turned his gelding over to one of the palace stableboys, the air in the courtyard and likely across Swartheld is a mixture of moisture, mist, and fog . . . and the rain keeps failing.

For several moments, he stands under the edge of the stable roof, letting his order-senses range through the clouds, wondering if there will be strong thunderstorms that he can turn to his advantage—which would take much less effort than order-chaos separation. Yet he cannot sense the vortices of order and chaos that distinguish thunderstorms, just much milder flows and the heaviness of moisture.

He hurries across the courtyard in the rain, accompanied by two rankers, and makes his way to the west wing of the palace and Rhamuel's sitting room. There he finds Norstaan, Sammyl, and Rhamuel.

"What have the scouts reported?" asks Lerial.

"The merchanters were prepared to load armsmen. It's hard to tell." Rhamuel looks to the closed window and the heavy droplets beating against it and the misty fog beginning to rise off the warm stone of the city's buildings and streets. "But they cast off without doing so, from what the scouts saw before the rain closed in."

"With rain and strong seas, they wouldn't remain in Estheld," adds Sammyl.

"If the storm dies down by midday," asks Lerial, "how long before the merchanters could port?"

"Late afternoon, if the winds didn't carry them too far east."

"You had something in mind?" Rhamuel asks Lerial.

"I was thinking about asking for a fast sailing galley that could get me close to the harbor at Estheld late this afternoon. That's if the storm does die down."

"I don't know . . . The sea might still be high by then." Rhamuel frowns. "What do you have in mind?'

"I need to find out where those armsmen are, and how many they'll be loading." All that is true, but Lerial isn't about to mention what else he has in mind. *If it's even possible . . . What else can you do? You're outnumbered and on the defense . . . and if they bring another five battalions or more . . .*

"How do you expect to learn that offshore in fog and mist?"

"It's likely to be easier in the mist. I'd like to know just how many troopers Khesyn is sending."

"Do we know he's sending any?" asks Sammyl.

"Not really," admits Lerial. "That's what I'd like to find out . . . before they land at Baiet or somewhere closer."

"That wouldn't hurt," says Sammyl. "But can you get closer than the scouts did? Close enough to learn that?"

"I've got a good chance at that."

"Then I'll send word to the Harbor Post. The sail-galleys leave from the small pier there. Don't try to go if the galley master says it's too dangerous. We can't afford to lose anyone else at this point."

"I won't." Lerial has no intention of drowning. "How many battalions do you have that can fight?"

"Right now?" Sammyl shakes his head. "Three at the most. That doesn't include Ascaar, but he has less than three full companies left after the last attack, and it would take him at least three days to get here, and at that speed, they wouldn't be in the best shape to fight. I've already sent orders for him to join us at deliberate speed."

"Including your Mirror Lancers and his companies," Rhamuel says, "that's four battalions. If you're as effective as before . . ."

"We might . . . just might . . . defeat Khesyn again. Is that what you think?" asks Lerial.

"It's better than the alternative."

None of the three mentions the difficulties Afrit will face with only what likely would remain after such a battle.

By the second glass of the afternoon, the rain has diminished to intermittent showers, but showers driven by strong winds, and Lerial, wearing a borrowed oiled leather waterproof, rides with his squad from the palace to the Harbor Post. He leaves the squad under cover and walks with one of the seamen assigned to the galleys down a tunnel corridor that opens onto a boatyard above the pier.

He has barely stepped out of the tunnel when another Afritan Guard, wearing an oilskin jacket, moves toward him.

"Squad Leader Elphred, ser. Commander Dhresyl assigned me to your reconnaissance voyage."

"You're the galley master?"

"Yes, ser."

Lerial looks toward the shore end of the Harbor Post pier and then to the far end, where waves break over the stone, normally a good three to four yards above the surface of the water, swirling around the bollards, leaving them momentarily protruding from white-foamed waters. To his left and farther down the slope is the shallow-draft sailing galley, still in its launch cradle, clearly dragged farther up from the turbulent waves pounding the pier.

"Ser, there's no way we can go out in this weather," declares Elphred. "We'd get swamped before we got half a kay."

"That's clear enough," replies Lerial. "Once the weather subsides, I will need the galley."

"Yes, ser. We'll stand by." The squad leader gestures to the crew, who begin to winch the cradle even farther up the launching ramp.

"Thank you."

In turn, Lerial uses his order-senses on the clouds. The actual storm center is too far away for him to sense, but it is clearly strong enough to create the winds that drive the waves against the piers. He is certainly not a sailor, but it stands to reason that if he cannot get out of Swartheld Harbor, it is most unlikely that any of Khesyn's merchanters will be able to return to Estheld and load the armsmen. *If that's even what Khesyn has in mind.* Lerial pauses. *But what else could he be planning?*

He hurries out of the rain that is already beginning to diminish, although the waves have shown no sign of that yet, back through the tunnel toward the makeshift headquarters of the post. The intermittent rain has flowed off his borrowed oilskin jacket and dampened his trousers, not quite all the way through. By the time he has seated himself in the small chamber that serves as Dhresyl's study, he hopes they will dry some before he ventures forth again.

"I understand you're going to take the sail-galley to look at Estheld," offers Dhresyl. "Isn't that likely to expose you unduly?"

"So long as I don't have to worry about high waves, I think we'll be able to manage. I'd be interested to know how matters are coming here. The last time we talked, I wasn't in the best of condition and you were busy trying to hold everything together."

"We're using the more able of the Heldyan prisoners to clear the rubble here in the post and we've begun some limited repairs. We've recovered as many weapons as we could from the areas where we fought, and we have the armorers repairing those that can be used. I've combined some companies and battalions so that those we have are closer to full strength . . ."

Lerial listens, intently and carefully.

When Dhresyl finally finishes, he just says, ". . . and that's where we stand." He does not ask anything about Lerial and the Mirror Lancers.

Lerial does not volunteer anything and politely takes his leave. While he waits to see if the weather and waves will moderate, he considers what Dhresyl has said and wonders why the commander's words have left him vaguely disturbed. Certainly, everything Dhresyl is undertaking makes sense . . .

Then, after almost a glass of pondering and stewing, Lerial realizes what has troubled him. Everything that Dhresyl had said related to organization and logistics. There had not been a single word about what the commander might do if the Heldyans attacked again, or what preparations or plans he had made.

By the sixth glass of the afternoon, the winds out of the north are dying down and the waves are subsiding, but are still too rough for the sail-galleys to set out, not that doing so would help Lerial much, since the Harbor Post lookouts have informed Lerial that it appears likely that none of the merchanters that left Estheld to ride out the rough weather at sea have yet returned . . . or are even in sight.

Given that information, the fact that the waves are likely to remain high for at least several glasses more, and that a night voyage would be dangerous without allowing Lerial to accomplish much of what he has in mind, Lerial gathers his squad for the ride back to Afritan Guard headquarters. When they finally set out, the air is damp and cooler, and little remains of the clouds that had brought the earlier downpour. The high winds have dropped off to a stiff breeze, but the waves crashing against the piers of the main harbor are still high and strong enough that there seems to be more foam than water.

So much for using the mist and fog to get close to Estheld without being seen.

Lerial looks from the harbor toward the merchanter buildings, all shuttered tight for the night, wondering if any of the merchanters really care all that much about Afrit, or Swartheld, except as a base from which they can make more golds.

XLIII

Fiveday morning dawns bright and clear, and Lerial is at the palace shortly after seventh glass, again meeting with Sammyl and Rhamuel.

"The merchanters put to sea before the storm hit," Sammyl reports. "Now that the weather has calmed, they're all returning. There wasn't any great damage to the piers here, and there likely wasn't much to the piers at Estheld."

"How long will it take to load the first ships?" asks Lerial, shifting his weight in the uncomfortable straight-backed chair.

"Most of today, I'd say. That's if they're not carrying cargo. Could be days if they're loading cargo," ventures Sammyl.

"The only cargo will be weapons and mounts," declares Rhamuel, his forearms resting on the wooden surface of the table desk.

"If they're headed to Baiet, they'll want to cast off by second or third glass at the latest. That's if they want to port before dark."

"Then I need to be going," says Lerial. "I need to get very close to Estheld." *The city of Heldya would be better, but it's hundreds of kays away over hostile ground, not water, and we don't have time for that.*

"You're planning what . . ." begins Sammyl, his voice dropping off at the look from the arms-commander.

"I think we can trust Overcaptain Lerial to act in both our interests and his," Rhamuel says firmly.

Lerial can tell that Sammyl wants to know what he has in mind. For that reason alone, he doesn't want to say much, in part because he has no idea if he can do what he has in mind. "The more I know, the more we'll know what to do . . . and when."

"We have sent scouts in other sail-galleys . . ."

Lerial smiles and rises. "For that I'm very grateful. I'll let you know what I've found out when I return."

Sammyl looks as though he wants to say something, but then just nods, as though he has decided against it.

"We'll look forward to your report," says Rhamuel.

Fhuraan and Fourth Squad from Eighth Company are waiting in the palace courtyard when Lerial reaches the stables.

"You've already got the squad mounted?" asks Lerial.

"I didn't think you'd be long this morning, ser."

The squad, with Fhuraan and Lerial immediately behind two outriders, takes the wide merchant avenue from the ring road around the palace along the base of the merchanters' hill, where Kyedra remains with her mother and grandfather, then past the harbor. Lerial is surprised to see a good ten merchanters tied up at the piers, and crews and loaders very busily carrying goods on board the vessels.

Lerial frowns. *The last time the Heldyans invaded, the harbor was empty. Why is it different now?* He looks at the piers. All the goods are going *on* the ships. He nods. That, unfortunately, makes sense. It is also suggestive of the lack of confidence at least some of the merchanters have in Rhamuel and the Afritan Guard. But then, it could be that they are simply coppering their bets, sending goods out just in case matters do turn out badly for Swartheld.

As they ride up the road toward the Harbor Post, Lerial sees that groups of Heldyan prisoners, under guard, are still engaged in burying the dead from the fighting that ended almost an eightday ago. *So many dead . . . or such lack of organization?* Given that Dhresyl seems stronger on logistics than battle planning and anticipation, Lerial would wager on the former. *And for what?* And the fighting and the deaths are far from over, no matter who triumphs.

"Ser? You're going to take a sail-galley out, aren't you?"

For a moment, Lerial wonders how Fhuraan knows that, since he has not mentioned that specifically, but then realizes that the squad leaders must talk among themselves, and there was no secret about the fact that he'd tried to take one the day before. "Yes."

"I'd feel better if you'd take Toeryn with you. He comes from a river family, and knows boats . . . and he's good with weapons."

"That's a good idea." Lerial grins. "I wish I'd thought of it."

"I wish I had, ser," admits Fhuraan. "Dhoraat suggested it."

"I'm glad you two came up with it."

When Lerial arrives at the stables at Harbor Post, he and Toeryn, a wiry ranker half a head shorter than Lerial, dismount, leave the squad, cross the southern end of the courtyard, and walk down the tunnel corridor to the boatyard and the pier. Lerial carries a water bottle filled with slightly watered lager. After they walk from the dimness of the tunnel into the bright early-morning sunlight, Lerial has to look around before he sees any of the Afritan Guards. Then, from the far side of the boatyard, Elphred hurries toward them.

"Overcaptain, ser! No one told us you were coming so early."

"You're right about that, galley master. I didn't. That's my fault. How soon can you be ready to set out?"

"Might be a half glass, ser."

"Oh, this is Toeryn. He'll be accompanying us. Unlike me, he has some experience on the water."

"Just two of you, ser . . . that won't be a problem. If you'll excuse me . . ."

"Of course."

Lerial watches as the sailing galley is released from its cradle and then moved alongside the stone pier. It is a narrow double-ended craft some ten yards long and slightly less than two wide, with benches for twelve oarsmen, a steering oar at the end that is presumably the stern, and a single mast, which is raised and stepped after the galley is tied in place beside the pier. Lerial is conscious of how small the craft is, given the expanse of water between him and Estheld. *And how shallow a draft it has, most likely only about a yard.*

After a time, Elphred walks from the pier to where Lerial waits, trying to stay out of the men's way as they prepare. "You wouldn't be minding, ser, if you were in the bow, and your ranker in the stern with me."

"It's your vessel, Elphred. That would be fine with me. How long will it take for us to get to Estheld?"

"There's not much wind. Might be three glasses. Or we could row the whole way . . ."

"But you'd prefer to save the men in case we have to depart quickly?"

"Yes, ser."

"Unless matters change, you can use the sail."

"Yes, ser. We're ready for you, then."

"There is one thing you need to tell your men. I may have to place a concealment over the galley when we get close to Estheld. That means that the Heldyans won't be able to see us. It also means that we'll be surrounded by darkness deeper than the blackest night. I'll be able to direct the vessel, but . . . no one else will be able to see. I hope it's not necessary, but it could be."

"Yes, ser. I'll tell them."

Lerial waits for Elphred to brief his crew before he and Toeryn board the sail-galley. When the galley pulls away from the pier, propelled by twelve oarsmen, Lerial is seated on a narrow bench just aft of the bow, his knees tucked under the triangle of polished wood that extends a half yard back from the stem, a spray shield too small for much protection and not wide enough for much motion for his legs and knees. He puts the water bottle between his boots.

Once the sail-galley is well away from the shore and the sail is unfurled and catching some of the light breeze, the rowers ship their oars, and Lerial turns his attention to the Swartheld harbor, where the loading of the merchanters tied there continues at a steady pace. As closely as he looks, he cannot see a single vessel that appears to be unloading. He does note that five of the vessels each fly a dull maroon ensign. When a light gust of wind strikes the merchanter closest to him, he gets a glimpse of what looks to be a green key in the center of the maroon field.

There is only a slight chop to the water in the bay, and Lerial is glad for the limited protection from the sun provided by his visor cap as the sail-galley moves slowly eastward across the wide bay toward Estheld. After perhaps another half glass, Lerial can begin to make out the shapes of the nearer buildings on shore. What surprises him is that Estheld is really not that large a city, perhaps only a large town, even if it has more piers than does Swartheld. There is also something about the piers . . . something that he should recognize . . . but cannot.

After another third of a glass, Elphred moves down the center of the sail-galley bending his way around the mast until he is within a yard of Lerial. "How do you want to approach Estheld, ser?"

"What are the possibilities?"

"With this wind—it's picked up a bit—we could sail directly east from here. We'd be almost a kay offshore. They might not come after us, and we could tack enough to get back to catch the river current that would give us enough speed that they couldn't catch us. Or . . . we could head for the shoreline and try to creep in. That could cause a problem because we'd lose some of the wind, and we'd have to row back to catch the current."

"Could you use the sail to get closer offshore once we near the harbor . . . if we sail due east?"

"We can, but when we've done that before, they send out their fast galleys."

"We'll have to chance that. I'll need to be about half a kay offshore." *Maybe closer.* After a moment, he asks. "Elphred . . . there seems to be something different about the piers at Estheld, but I don't know enough to determine what it is."

"They're cheap. They're all timber. Most of them were built five-six years ago. A real storm, or a few years, and most of them will fall apart, if you ask me. It's not the best place for a harbor, either. Deep enough, but too open to the northwesters that hit in the winter."

Of course! They were built to last only a few years, possibly even for the invasion of Afrit. *And after that, Swartheld would serve Heldya and a conquered Afrit.* "Thank you. I knew there was something. Is there anything else I should know? Things so obvious to you that someone like me wouldn't even think of?"

"They've got their warehouses too close together, and they're all timber. You build like that, and you get too much spoilage, especially in a wet spell. They did put a set of piers near the river, though, just at the edge of where you lose the current. Makes it easy for their flatboats to dock and tie up there.

Means more than two kays by wagon to the nearest deepwater pier, but you don't risk losing the flatboats either."

After Elphred retreats to the stern, where he alternates as steersman with another Afritan, Lerial again concentrates on studying the merchanters, if only for a short time, because he is still too far away to see or sense the details he needs to know.

Almost another glass passes before the sail-galley reaches a point due north of the westernmost dwellings and buildings of Estheld, but still west of the harbor piers. Elphred turns the sail-galley more to the southeast, and two of the men adjust the sail, angling it to the wind. The galley picks up a bit more speed, or so it seems to Lerial, from the light spray coming up over the bow.

Before long, Lerial can begin to sense more details of Estheld, rather than see them, because the large merchanters at the piers block much of his view of the warehouses and other buildings along the waterfront. The first, and most obvious, discovery is that there are two chaos-mages there, one clearly aboard a large merchanter tied at the end of the westernmost pier, the other somewhere ashore. At the same time, he still cannot tell much about what or who might be loading aboard the merchanters, although he can sense cold iron on the nearest vessel, a likely hint of weapons, but certainly not anything conclusive.

"Ser! There are two fast galleys headed our way . . . over there to the south. They're twenty-oar boats."

Lerial looks to where Elphred is pointing, and, unhappily, there are indeed two galleys moving toward them, each twice the size of the Afritan sail-galley. Knowing how much more difficult it is to use order or chaos over water—and the fact that he'll need every bit of strength he has to deal with the real Heldyan problem—Lerial doesn't even consider using order-chaos separation. *Not yet, anyway.* And since no chaos-mage is supplying chaos, that limits his choices. "We need to get closer. I'm going to conceal us. After everything goes black, turn more to port, and then keep moving on that heading. But have the men ready to row when I give the word."

"Yes, ser."

Lerial can sense a certain fatalism in Elphred's voice, and while he'd like to reassure the galley master, he has his own doubts, especially since he's trying to keep in mind his father's advice about avoiding suicidal efforts. He raises the concealment . . . and listens to the murmurs from the Afritan crew, if only for a moment.

". . . frigging . . . black . . ."

". . . told us . . ."

". . . said we'd be in less danger . . ."

". . . mages . . . always danger . . ."

Lerial keeps the concealment as close to the sail-galley as possible while gauging the shift in heading and trying to determine if Elphred's new course is widening the gap between them and the galleys while also trying to sense everything in the Estheld harbor.

The Heldyan galleys appear not to have changed course, while the Afritan sail-galley nears the piers, passing less than a hundred yards from yet another merchanter anchored off the harbor proper. Lerial can sense no troopers on the decks, suggesting that the merchanter is waiting for a berth at one of the piers.

Now Lerial can sense armsmen on one of the piers, shuffling up a gangplank and onto the main deck of a vessel. He shifts his sensing to another vessel, whose decks are crowded with men, that is preparing to cast off. After another tenth of a glass, from what Lerial can tell, there are indeed thousands of troopers in and around the Estheld harbor, either already on vessels, boarding them, or waiting to board them.

What can you do? What will stop all of them?

After several moments, the answer strikes him: *Fire . . . fire everywhere.* But how can he accomplish that without totally exhausting himself long before he has created a wide-enough conflagration? *Will small bits of order-chaos separation all across the merchanters and the warehouses near the harbor do that? But how can you do even that without exhausting yourself?* The only way for that to work is for the sail-galley to get much, much closer.

Even so, Lerial has his doubts about how much destruction he can cause. *But any delay and anything that reduces the number of armsmen headed to Afrit is far better than fighting them in Afrit.* He checks the position of the Heldyan galleys, but they have slowed, as if they are trying to determine where the sail-galley has gone. Next he tries to calculate how close they are to the outermost pier, and he thinks that they are less than half a kay away. He doesn't want to be too close to the piers, but he also doesn't want to have to strain too much.

So he sits in the bow, order-sensing and waiting, before realizing that one of the Heldyan galleys has shifted its course and is directly behind the sail-galley, if a good third of a kay back. How could that be, with the concealment? *Following your wake, of course.*

"Where are we, ser?" calls out Elphred.

"Less than half a kay north of the middle of the piers. Hold this course for just a bit."

"Aye, ser." Elphred definitely sounds worried and unhappy.

Behind them, the Heldyan galley is closing.

Lerial knows he can no longer put off doing something, either escaping or acting. The first question is where he should begin . . . on the ships at the piers . . . or on the shore. He swallows and concentrates on the fully loaded merchanter, creating a spaced line of order-chaos separations beginning just above the waterline on one side of the ship and angling them up and across the ship. Then he concentrates on the outermost vessel at the next pier, followed by the largest vessel at the westernmost pier. As he continues to place his separations, sweat begins to well up all over his body and ooze from under his visor cap down the sides of his forehead. Almost absently, he blots it away with the back of his sleeve.

He can sense a slight hint of light-headedness and decides to drop the concealment. As he does, he orders, "Turn west!"

For an instant, the return of full sunlight blinds him, and his eyes water. When he can make out things clearly again, he sees that most of the ships at the piers are aflame, but there are no fires ashore, although he can sense men and mounts moving in all directions.

He concentrates on focusing on the largest structure along the harbor front, setting three different order-separations. A line of pain feels like it has split his head, and he massages his forehead, then forces himself to uncork the bottle of lager and take several swallows.

". . . the frig is he doing . . . ?"

". . . need to get out of here!"

Lerial is vaguely aware that several men are resetting the sail, while the others have unshipped their oars and are beginning to row. He glances back, his mouth opening as he realizes that the one fast galley is less than fifty yards behind them.

"Frig . . ." While he hates to spend the effort on something as small as the fast galley, he and the sail-galley won't be around to do much of anything else if he doesn't deal with it. He immediately concentrates on creating a tiny order-chaos separation right above the waterline at the galley's bow, wincing at the jolt of fire that shivers through his skull as he does.

The entire bow of the pursuing galley explodes and a rush of flame sweeps back along the narrow vessel. Then water floods into the open stem of the craft, and it noses down and comes to a stop.

Lerial looks back toward the shore and concentrates on another set of order-chaos separations, this time dealing with more waterfront structures. Each separation is more painful than the last, and Lerial has to pause longer between each, occasionally taking another swallow of lager.

One ship, already flaming, abruptly explodes, and fragments of chaos and burning debris spray everywhere.

A chaos-mage, trying to hold shields against the heat and flames?

Fires now rage along all the piers, including parts of the piers themselves, and most of the buildings along the waterfront are now in flames, with thickening clouds of smoke billowing skyward.

Lerial realizes that he has done nothing about the merchanter anchored away from the piers. He concentrates once more—and the pain is so intense he cannot even move or see for several moments. When he can finally see, he has no order-sensing ability, but when he looks back, he can see flames across the midsection of the anchored merchanter, and before that long there are explosions, and the ship sags in the midsection, then begins to take on water. He looks toward the piers. So far as he can tell, every vessel at the piers has either vanished or appears to be in flames or sinking, if not both.

Lerial leans forward and closes his eyes for several moments, resting his head on the spray shield, then looks up once more. Clouds of black and gray smoke continue to rise skyward from the flames that seemingly fill the southern horizon, and the black-silvered mists of death flow out in all directions from the conflagration.

"Ser?" calls out Elphred.

"Head back to Swartheld . . . any way you can. I don't think I can do much more." *More like nothing.*

". . . much more . . . ?" murmurs someone.

"It looks clear, ser. The other fast galley headed back south."

"Good," murmurs Lerial. He slumps over the spray shield of the sail-galley, the sea and sky spinning slowly around him, his guts churning, and his eyes burning, light flashes searing through closed eyes. Despite the wind from the north, he can smell smoke and all manner of acrid odors . . . and he can imagine, if not sense, the silver-black death mists flowing out across the burning debris that had once been ships and piers.

At least you didn't pass out this time. After a long moment, a second thought strikes him. *But you barely managed not to.*

XLIV

Just after third glass of the afternoon, Elphred eases the sail-galley alongside the Harbor Post pier. From what Lerial has seen on the last part of the return to Afrit, the merchanters in Swartheld Harbor are continuing to load various cargoes. He wonders exactly what the ships' masters, or owners, will do now that the immediate threat from Heldya has been removed.

Immediate threat? More like any threat for several years, if not longer.

Lerial still has flashes across his vision when he climbs out of the galley and looks back toward Estheld, still marked by towering clouds of gray and black smoke. After a moment, he turns and walks back to the stern of the sail-galley, where he stands beside Toeryn and waits for Elphred to finish giving orders to his crew.

Once the galley master is on the stone pier, Lerial says, "Thank you."

"Yes, ser," replies Elphred. His eyes do not quite meet Lerial's.

"Would you have preferred to have another ten battalions of Heldyans marching down from Baiet in a few days?" asks Lerial quietly. "We have less than three battalions remaining. I am grateful to you and your men." He smiles sadly, because he does understand the galley master's feelings, then turns and walks toward the tunnel, Toeryn beside him. He carries the empty water bottle in his left hand. "We'll need to head to the palace once I give a brief report to Commander Dhresyl. The arms-commander needs to know immediately." *Or as close to immediately as you can manage.*

The cool and the darkness of the tunnel up to the Harbor Post are welcome, but the squad leader waiting at the end of the tunnel is less so.

"Ser, Commander Dhresyl would hope you might spare him a few moments."

Lerial doubts that Dhresyl had been quite so deferential in his wording, but merely says, "Lead the way."

When they reach the senior officers' mess, Lerial hands the water bottle to Toeryn. "If you wouldn't mind, while I talk to the commander . . . I could use some lager."

"Yes, ser."

Lerial walks into the small chamber, closes the door, and settles himself into the chair across from the commander. "You wished to see me?"

Dhresyl does not speak for a moment, his eyes studying Lerial. Finally, he says, almost pensively, "The lookouts report a great deal of smoke and fire around Estheld. Do you think that will delay the Heldyans that much?"

"It might," replies Lerial, "that is, if they can find a way to replace something like fifteen merchanters, all their piers, most of the city of Estheld, and at least several thousand trained armsmen . . . if not more."

The commander frowns. "There's that much damage?"

"It appears that almost everything in Estheld was built of wood. So are ships. Wood burns. There was so much fire, and it spread so quickly, that many could not escape, especially the armsmen already loaded onto the merchanters." Lerial smiles, then stands. "I thought you'd like to know. I need to report to the arms-commander." Without another word Lerial turns and leaves the makeshift study.

Toeryn hurries up as Lerial walks out of the study. "That didn't take long, ser."

"I told the commander what he needed to know."

"Ser . . . I filled the water bottle, but the cook is bringing some bread and cheese and a beaker of lager . . ."

Lerial offers a crooked smile. "That is a very good idea."

"I also persuaded one of the cooks' boys to take a message to Squad Leader Fhuraan, that you'd be there shortly. That way, you can eat while they're readying the horses."

"Thank you." Lerial doesn't need any more urging to sit down at the end of the long mess table. As soon as the lager and the bread and cheese arrive, he takes a long swallow and then begins to eat, slowly and methodically.

Toeryn stands by the door to the mess, his hand on his sabre, the entire time that it takes Lerial to finish what is before him. He is no longer even in the slightest light-headed when he finally stands, but he cannot order-sense, and occasional flashes of light flicker across his eyes. Still, he feels much better as he walks from the mess to the stables, where Fhuraan waits with Fourth Squad.

"We saw smoke," offers the squad leader. "Were you able . . . ?"

"I doubt we'll have to worry about the Heldyans for some time." *The merchanters of Afrit are another question, especially once they're no longer worried about Khesyn.*

Fhuraan studies Lerial. "You'll need guards, I think, even after we get to the palace?"

Lerial nods.

"Begging your pardon, ser, but should you even ride that far?"

"I may not be in the best of condition, but I'm in no danger of collapsing. Thanks to Toeryn, I had some food and lager after we returned. I trust you and the squad did as well."

"Yes, ser."

"Then we'd best head out."

Lerial and Fourth Squad leave Harbor Post almost unnoticed, or so it seems to him, and then ride past what looks to be the last of the Heldyan prisoner burial details. When they come to that section of the road passing the harbor, Lerial notes that the loading of the various merchanters is continuing, unabated. *Do they think that Khesyn will attack because they believe the fires at Estheld aren't that severe? Or because he'll be enraged at an attack on his lands?* Lerial just hopes he is not mistaken in his belief that Khesyn will have his hands more than full with troubles in Heldya for several years to come.

The guards at the palace look at Lerial and the Mirror Lancers and wave them through, and the duty squad leader doesn't even look askance as two lancers flank Lerial when he enters the building, before making his way up to Rhamuel's chambers. The lancers plant themselves outside the sitting room—after looking in to see that only Sammyl and Rhamuel are inside.

"Escorts, yet?" murmurs Sammyl in a voice barely audible.

"They tend to be protective when I'm tired," replies Lerial with a faint smile. "I am a bit tired. It's been a rather long day."

"The lookouts report a great deal of fire and smoke rising from Estheld," says Rhamuel, his words clearly a bland understatement. "I presume you and your lancers had something to do with that."

Lerial doesn't feel like either boasting or demurring. "We did."

"Won't that just enrage Duke Khesyn?" asks Sammyl.

"I'm sure it will," replies Lerial. "He's bound to be enraged by the loss of all the merchanters tied or anchored at Estheld, somewhere around fifteen, not to mention the thousands of armsmen who died or the fact that it appeared that most of the harbor was burning to the ground when we departed. I could be wrong, but I believe he's going to have more serious problems on his hands than trying to invade Afrit again."

"Might I ask how . . . all that happened?" Sammyl doesn't conceal his skepticism.

"A little chaos and order, placed here and there, combined with the fact that Khesyn built everything cheaply, believing that Estheld only had to last until he conquered Afrit and took Swartheld . . . with the encouragement of Maesoryk and a few other well-placed Afritan merchanters, of course."

The commander's skeptical expression gives way to one of puzzlement.

"He built everything of wood, and it was built close together. Seasoned wood burns very quickly, and if there's a great deal of it, it burns hot and faster than people can escape, except into the water, and the water off Estheld, I'm told, is rather deep." After taking in the appalled expression on Sammyl's face, Lerial adds, "I don't like fighting unnecessary battles against unprincipled enemies enabled by even less principled merchanters who are also traitors to their own land, because others have been more successful in amassing golds."

"I believe Lord Lerial has an excellent point, Sammyl," says Rhamuel. "Do you have any problems with what he has said?"

"Ah . . . there may well be traitors, but proving that they have acted in such a fashion might be difficult."

"It might," agrees Rhamuel, "but it's to be preferred over sending an outnumbered Afritan Guard out to fight another battle against fresh Heldyan hordes. Is it not?"

"Yes, ser."

"I do have one question," Lerial adds. "Who bears the cost of the loss of all those merchanters that were destroyed at Estheld?"

"That depends on the contracts between the merchanters and Duke Khesyn. Unless there are special provisions, vessels used for purposes of warfare are not covered by any surety."

"That would mean that the merchanters owning them would bear the losses, then?" asks Lerial.

"Some of them might have asked Khesyn for indemnity. He'd likely have agreed, but he won't pay it. Of course," Rhamuel adds, dryly, "Khesyn might attempt to claim Afrit was the cause of the fires."

"If it comes to that, blame it on the god/goddess of the Kaordists," suggests Lerial tiredly. "There were no ships attacking, and no troopers anywhere around."

While Sammyl again looks appalled, Rhamuel laughs ironically. "It won't come to that. Khesyn will be hard-pressed to maintain his borders against the Tourlegyns, especially when the spoils he most likely promised didn't materialize."

"There's one other item," Lerial says. "On our way out to Estheld, and then on the way back, I noticed several things. First, all the ships in the harbor here were loading goods on board. None were offloading. Second, almost half flew a maroon ensign with a golden key in the center."

"Those had to be Alaphyn's ships . . ." muses Rhamuel.

"It is suggestive," points out Lerial. "Along with Maesoryk . . ." *And possibly Jhosef . . .*

"There's no proof . . ." declares Sammyl. "Without that . . . all the other merchanters will refuse to pay their tariffs if you act against Maesoryk and Alaphyn."

We just might have to see about that, thinks Lerial, if without speaking those words.

"There's no proof, yet." Rhamuel smiles. "It may not even come to that." He looks to Sammyl. "I need a few words with Lord Lerial, about my healing . . . and a few other matters."

"Yes, ser." Before he turns and leaves the sitting room, Sammyl's momentary glance at Lerial is one of a very worried man.

"Jaermyd tells me that my broken leg is healing, not quite so fast as I'd like, obviously."

Lerial considers what Rhamuel has said, then realizes that, for all that has happened, not that much time has passed. "It's been less than two eightdays. You'd probably have felt the pain diminish . . ." Lerial immediately regrets those words.

"If I could feel any pain, you're doubtless right." Rhamuel uses his hands and arms to shift his weight in the wooden armchair behind the table desk. "I'm not going to get the use of my legs back, am I?"

"It's still too soon to tell. If you have no feeling in a season . . . then . . ."

"You aren't putting me off, are you?"

"No . . . Emerya might be able to tell you, but I don't have her skills. Nor do I have her years of knowledge."

"Jaermyd is convinced my injuries would have been fatal without you."

"He's too kind. I'd agree that they'd have been worse, but I suspect you still would have survived."

"He says no . . . that the chaos around the broken bone would have spread, and no one would have known in time."

Lerial had not even thought of that, he realizes.

Rhamuel laughs. "Sometimes, you don't even realize how much the little things you do ending up mattering."

"I imagine that's just as true of you."

"Not quite as much. I do have a few more years of observing people."

"I grant you that. What else did you wish to discuss?" Lerial definitely wants to change the subject.

"Your remaining in Swartheld for a time longer. Cigoerne certainly doesn't need you at the moment. The dispatch from that majer, most likely penned for him by your father, shows that Khesyn doesn't have any armsmen there. The Tourlegyns have lost too many warriors to raid Cigoerne. But . . . matters here are far from settled. They'll get worse once it is known that I am crippled, and there will be muttered demands for a duke who can have offspring."

"You're not that crippled."

"People will say that. That's what matters. I can't, obviously, require you to stay. First, you're not an Afritan. Second, I doubt there's any power left in Afrit that could force you and your lancers to remain. At the same time, I'd appreciate your presence and support until I am officially duke of Afrit."

"Who else could be duke?" asks Lerial. "You're older than Mykel . . . if he's even alive, and you've already pointed out that Kyedra cannot rule in her own name."

"But the lineage runs through her."

"It also runs through you."

"There will always be doubts if I am duke."

"That's absurd. You almost died. You could have."

"It doesn't matter. People will still believe that I had a hand in my brother's death." Rhamuel shakes his head. "I've never wanted to be duke. I've wanted other things . . . but never that."

Even as Lerial wonders what those "other things" might be, he replies bluntly, "You don't have any choice. Neither does Afrit."

"Not now," admits Rhamuel. "That brings up another question. You've been the one in the midst of all the battles. What do you suggest I do with the Afritan Guard . . . and its officers?"

"Keep Sammyl as your chief of staff. Praise him publicly for his firm hand and loyalty in a time of crisis. Promise him something . . . you'd know better than I what is possible and acceptable. Make Commander Dhresyl the one in charge of supplies and logistics, but let him remain a commander. Promote Ascaar to commander and make him the overall field commander. There's a young majer named Paelwyr. Make him a subcommander and a battalion commander. Review all the other majers who need to be promoted to subcommander with Paelwyr and Ascaar. From what I've seen, possibly Majer Aerlyt might be a decent subcommander, but I'd defer to Ascaar on that."

"What about a new arms-commander?"

"You need to remain arms-commander for now, possibly for at least another year. You can do that with Sammyl as your chief of staff."

"You don't trust Sammyl, do you? Why are you recommending him?"

"I don't trust his judgment on military matters. I do trust his loyalty to you. Right now, that's very important."

"It's a pity you're the younger son."

Lerial shakes his head. "Where did those words come from?"

"From what I've seen, and from what Emerya has written. And please don't tell me you don't know we've exchanged letters for years."

Almost . . . almost, Lerial laughs. Finally, he smiles. "I thought that was so, but she never, ever said anything about it to me, or to anyone else that I know of. I suspect Father and Mother know. Probably Grandmere knew."

"By sending that miniature, Emerya told you."

"She confirmed what I already knew."

"We need to talk of that . . . later."

Lerial understands. "How long do you think you'll need me?"

"It's a little early to set dates . . . don't you think? I won't ask you to stay here any longer than necessary . . . but . . . would you be serving Cigoerne's interests by leaving too soon?"

With a rueful smile, Lerial says, "No. You know that."

"I just wanted to make sure you understand that as well."

Lerial finds himself yawning, wondering why, when it's only a bit past fifth glass. "It's time for me to head back to Afritan Guard headquarters."

"Get some rest or sleep," suggests Rhamuel.

"I'd thought of that."

"If you're feeling better tomorrow morning, I'd suggest you go to Aenslem's first. We're going to need his knowledge and advice over the days ahead. I want to be certain he's up to it."

"I can do that."

"If he is, escort him here, and we can go over some matters. Now . . . go and get some food and rest. Don't worry. You can start that tomorrow." Rhamuel spoils the stern words with a grin.

Lerial can't help but smile back before he turns and leaves the sitting room. Outside, he smiles again, cheerfully, at Sammyl. "I think he has a few more things for you to do."

Then he nods to the two rankers, and the three head for the palace stables. He hopes he won't fall asleep before he can brief his own officers. At the same time, he also wonders, not for the first time, if his dispatch has reached Emerya. He shakes his head. It has only been a little more than a eightday.

XLV

Lerial manages to brief his officers and Dhoraat on the events at Estheld, but not about Rhamuel's request, before retiring to his chamber in the officers' quarters at Afritan Guard headquarters and falling asleep well before eighth glass, deeply enough that he does not dream. Then . . . in the darkness, he bolts awake, yet hears nothing. Half sitting up in the bunk, he glances around, but he can see only the vague outline of the room, the doorless armoire, the narrow table desk. He is relieved that he can order-sense, slightly, and only for a short distance, enough to discern no one outside the barred door.

What woke you so suddenly? He shakes his head and lies back down. For a time he listens and order-senses, but the quarters remain still, and there are no loud sounds issuing from the headquarters courtyard outside and below his shuttered window, no wind, no rain or thunder.

How long will you have to stay here? With that question, his mind is filled with all the complications—Rhamuel's health, how the merchanters will react, how to deal with Maesoryk, if he even returns to Swartheld, Jhosef, and Alaphyn . . . or the possible problem with the fact that Aenslem has no sons . . . and that Fhastal has two, both Aenslem's grandsons, but complicated because Aenslem cannot stand Fhastal . . . and the two are the wealthiest and most powerful merchanters in Afrit. He also has to tell his officers and men about Rhamuel's request, something he avoided the night before, because he wanted to think about the matter more before he did.

Then too, he must admit, there is the question of what will happen to Kyedra. Certainly, no one in Afrit, especially not Rhamuel, would want her consorted to any heir in Heldya, and from what Lerial has seen of Casseon's acts, any consorting to anyone in Merowey wouldn't be much better.

She's too good for Lephi . . . and you're the wrong brother.

Finally, he falls back asleep, only to wake at the first glimmer of light through the cracks in the closed shutters. While he feels better than he did on fiveday, his neck and face are still warm and red, doubtless from all the sun he'd endured, something he had not even noticed the day before, and he has a faint headache, although the light-flashes across his eyes have stopped. So, he realizes, has the itching on his hip.

After eating a sizable if not particularly tasty breakfast, he gathers Strauxyn, Kusyl, and Dhoraat together in one of the small conference rooms in the headquarters building.

"This must be serious, ser," says Kusyl, glancing around the chamber before taking a seat opposite Lerial across the circular table that could accommodate six at most.

"It is. You know I met with Arms-Commander Rhamuel early last evening to report on what happened at Estheld. There was one other matter I did not mention." He pauses and looks at Kusyl, who is shaking his head, just slightly, then grins. "It's not quite that bad, Kusyl. The arms-commander has requested that we remain here for a short time, just to make certain something else doesn't happen."

"There aren't more Heldyan armsmen somewhere else, are there?" asks Strauxyn worriedly.

"Not that we know of. The problem he faces is that, right now, everything is up in the air in Swartheld. The Afritan Guard has suffered so many casualties and deaths that it doesn't have a single intact battalion, and the only decent field commander is Subcommander Ascaar. He is on his way here, and I think that he'll be very helpful in straightening out matters."

"The new duke doesn't trust some of his officers?" asks Kusyl.

"It's not a question of trust. All those left are loyal."

"Oh . . ." murmurs Strauxyn. "He wants someone who can lead who knows one end of a lance from the other—until Subcommander Ascaar gets here."

"There's also the problem that several merchanters may have been helping the Heldyans, and one may have a company of private guards and a chaos-mage or two." Lerial has his doubts as to whether Maesoryk's mages have survived, but he has no doubts that the merchanter's private guards are still intact . . . and that no one seems to know where they are.

"Begging your pardon, ser," Kusyl says slowly, "but it seems like trying to leave Afrit is like trying to swim out of a vat of molasses."

Lerial can't help but smile. "I've never tried, but . . ."

"I was pushed into one when I was ten. Starshit near drowned and died before they pulled me out. You don't float and can't swim, and can barely breathe."

"What we face isn't likely to be quite that bad," Lerial replies, "but Cigoerne can't afford to have Afrit fall apart after all this . . . and . . ." He isn't quite sure what to say that is at least most accurate, yet persuasive.

"We're the only ones the new duke is sure of, because all we want is to get out of here with as much skin left as we can keep," says Kusyl.

"That's partly what it comes down to," admits Lerial. "The other part is that we've now got a duke who did his best to keep Afrit from attacking Cigoerne when he was arms-commander, and it would be a good thing to make sure he stays duke."

Strauxyn's face shows puzzlement.

"The only attack in the last five years was ordered by Duke Atroyan when Arms-Commander Rhamuel had such a bad flux they weren't sure he'd recover."

"Star-frigging thing, ser, when we got more interest in Afrit having a good duke than they do." Kusyl shakes his head.

"So you can see why we need to be here a little longer." *Too long, considering we left Cigoerne almost exactly a season ago . . . well . . . a few days short of a season.*

All three men nod, Kusyl offering a sardonically disgusted expression as well.

"It'll be a story you can tell for years," Lerial says.

"The worst thing, ser," adds Kusyl, "is that we'll be telling the truth, and everyone will think we're lying."

"As for today," Lerial goes on, "I need a squad to accompany me to

Merchanter Aenslem's and then to the palace. They'll likely be gone most of the day."

"My second squad hasn't seen that fancy villa," volunteers Kusyl.

"Then they will," replies Lerial.

A third after seventh glass, Lerial and the Second Squad from Twenty-third Company ride out through the headquarters gates and take the shore road to the avenue leading to the merchanter's hill, a route Lerial chooses so that he can observe the harbor. From what he can tell, more than half the merchanter vessels that had been tied at the piers have departed. While Lerial is not absolutely certain, he has the feeling that all of those that have set sail, or most of them, anyway, were ships belonging to Alaphyn.

Was he aboard one of them? That wouldn't have surprised Lerial in the slightest. But then, given the arrogance of at least some of the Afritan merchanters, it wouldn't have surprised Lerial if Alaphyn remained, stoutly proclaiming his allegiance to Rhamuel.

Lerial can maintain only very slight shields, and does so, given what has happened to all too many senior officers . . . and also given his lack of trust, but no one even comes close to the Lancer squad on its way to Aenslem's villa.

Haesychya is the one who meets Lerial in the circular entry hall of the villa.

"I understand we owe you once more." Haesychya's voice is cool.

"Lady, in some ways, we owe you, since we do not have to fight on our lands, and we have suffered far less than you have. Like Afrit, Cigoerne has had to fight off Heldyan depredations for years. Unlike Afrit, we have not faced the magnitude of betrayal and treachery that has been your lot."

"Are all Cigoernean mages as skilled as you are in the ways of destruction?"

"There are some who are skilled in such. There have never been a great number." Lerial looks directly into Haesychya's black eyes. "I would appreciate not being considered one of the black angels."

A momentary look of puzzlement crosses her face. "Black angels?"

"The ones who called down destruction and devastation upon Cyador from the heights of the Westhorns to the depths of the ocean. I am scarcely a mage compared to them."

"But you are a mage."

Lerial shakes his head. "None of the true Magi'i would consider me such. I have mastered a few destructive skills and some healing, but . . . there is much I cannot do and likely never will be able to do."

"My consort wanted to reunite Cigoerne and Afrit, you know? You have made that impossible."

"It was never possible the way in which he wanted to accomplish it."

Haesychya looks away for an instant. Then she meets Lerial's eyes again. "So why are you here this morning?"

"To see that your father is well and continuing to improve."

"I think you will find him much improved." She turns and begins to walk toward the archway to the north corridor. "You know, you're not doing Kyedra any favors by coming here."

"That may be . . . or it may not be, but I am here at Rhamuel's request."

"You would defy your parents' wishes? They will certainly press for her hand for your brother."

Lerial manages a rueful smile. "They have not . . . not yet, and I have found that assuming what others will do, in the absence of evidence of intent, can be most misleading." What Lerial says is not wholly true, he knows, given his mother's wishes, but his father has said nothing.

"The needs of power override intent or emotion. They override love, also, especially young love."

"I will not question you on that, Lady. You have far more experience than I." Again . . . this is true, and Lerial's experience with Rojana would certainly support Haesychya's point, but he does not wish to concede that directly. He wonders what else he can say when he sees a serving girl—the attractive one he has seen before—slipping out the study door. By the slight change in Haesychya's walk and posture, Lerial can tell that she has seen as well . . . and that it is likely that the young woman is more than a mere serving girl.

"Still . . ." Haesychya says, seeming almost to muse, "we have just seen what two younger brothers have done, and few would have believed how events have turned out."

"I would not underestimate the power of younger sisters, either," replies Lerial.

"You have one in mind?"

"I have several," he counters, pausing to allow her to enter Aenslem's study first.

Aenslem is alone in the study, but Lerial still manages to smile and say, "You're looking much better." He moves closer to the merchanter, stopping short of the desk and letting his order-senses range over the older man. He almost nods as he can find no trace of the chaos that would indicate a lingering effect of the poison.

"You worry too much about me, young Lerial."

"I worry less than Rhamuel does. He's the one who asked that I stop and see how you are. He's going to need your counsel and advice."

"He's never asked for it before."

"He wasn't duke before," replies Lerial.

"He hasn't proclaimed the title for himself. Most of Afrit still thinks his brother is."

"He's had a few other things to consider," Lerial points out dryly. "Are you up to riding?"

"A short ride would do me good."

"Are you sure, Father?" asks Haesychya.

"I'm sure. You can accompany us, if you're that worried."

"I'll never set foot back in that prison." Haesychya's words are cool and matter-of-fact. "Never."

" 'Never' is a dangerous word, Daughter," says Aenslem as he rises from the chair behind the table desk.

"When will you be back?" asks Haesychya, as if she has talked about nothing but the weather or a pleasant afternoon.

"When I'm done with Rhamuel. Assuming he'll listen."

"He always listens," replies Haesychya. "He seldom agrees with you."

Aenslem snorts and turns to Lerial. "You can walk with me to the stables."

Lerial addresses Haesychya. "Thank you for everything. I do appreciate your kindness and your insights."

"You are leaving Swartheld soon, then?"

"The arms-commander has asked me to remain for a short time, at least until Subcommander Ascaar arrives in a few days. Perhaps longer, but that is his choice."

"For now," suggests Haesychya.

"For now," Lerial agrees.

Haesychya inclines her head, and Lerial returns the gesture.

Aenslem and Lerial walk toward the entry hall.

"She's worried that Kyedra will become attached to you, as if you don't already know."

"Is that her worry . . . or is it that Kyedra will become attached to a less powerful junior son when she might have more power in consorting his elder brother?"

"For someone your age, you don't miss much."

Lerial laughs. "I think that suggests that I still miss too much."

This time Aenslem laughs.

When he finishes, Lerial asks, "What am I missing?"

"What do you think you're missing?" As they enter the main entry hall, Aenslem heads for the west corridor.

"Besides the fact that Haesychya resents women being subservient to men, when she's more perceptive than most?" *As if that is not often true.*

"You're close enough." Aenslem turns down a small side corridor that leads to a door out into a walk that leads through a walled garden and out into the rear courtyard.

Neither speaks much until they are mounted and well away from the villa. Finally, Lerial ventures, "I didn't realize Haesychya hated the palace so much."

"I gave her and Sophrosynia too much freedom growing up. They thought they were the equal of any man."

"I haven't met Sophrosynia, but Haesychya certainly is."

Aenslem shakes his head. "No. They're both smarter and see more than most men, and most men don't like that. Atroyan certainly didn't. Fhastal doesn't either, but, unlike Atroyan, he listens and weighs what Sophrosynia has to say."

"Some have said you don't much care for Fhastal, but that doesn't sound as though that's the case."

"I don't like him. He's arrogant, and he's cost me more than I want to count. But he's the best at what he does, and he's been good to Sophrosynia. She loves him, and he loves her. But I don't have to like him."

Lerial doesn't know what to say to that, and he is silent for several long moments, thinking.

"I have my likes and dislikes, young Lerial, and I've got more than a few faults. My daughters and Kyedra could list them all, but they're loyal, and they won't. One thing I learned a long time ago was not to judge men—or women—on whether you like them. I'll do business with a man I dislike who's trustworthy, and I won't with a man I like personally but distrust." After a moment Aenslem smiles and adds, "Unless, of course, it's golds in advance, and all the risk is on his part. Even then, I'm wary."

Lerial nods, hoping Aenslem will say more.

After they have ridden a while longer and are on the road leading to the circle around the palace, the merchanter speaks again. "I heard you say that you're remaining at Rhamuel's request. Just how badly is he injured? The plain truth, now. Will he live?"

"He's as likely to live as any of us. He may not walk again, but it's early to say on that."

"What about children? Even if he weren't crippled, he's no longer a young man."

"It's possible, so far as I can tell."

"Possible doesn't mean there'll be an heir."

"That may be, but Afrit needs a duke."

Aenslem nods, cautiously, and Lerial doesn't press.

Less than half a glass later, Lerial and Aenslem walk into the sitting room that has effectively become Rhamuel's study. The arms-commander is looking at a map.

"Rhamuel, I brought someone to see you."

The surprise in the arms-commander's eyes is unfeigned as he catches sight of the merchanter. "Aenslem!"

"It seems I'm up and around sooner than you, Rhamuel."

"It would seem so." Rhamuel gestures to one of the chairs before the table desk.

Aenslem takes one and Lerial the other.

"Where's Sammyl?" asks Lerial.

"Visiting South Point, South Post, and Harbor Post. We both thought his presence would confirm that matters are stable here in Swartheld."

"That will help, but you need to proclaim yourself duke," declares Aenslem.

"I thought it wise to discuss the matter with the head of the Merchanting Council . . . after I was certain that it appeared likely I'd survive long enough for it to matter," says Rhamuel dryly. "Otherwise . . . what would be the point?"

"You've always been practical. I'll grant you that," says Aenslem. "I'll be the same. I'll support you, and so will Fhastal. Maesoryk doesn't matter, if he's even still alive, and Lhugar has to back you. You have Maephaes on your side. Alaphyn won't. He hated your brother, and he doesn't like you any better—"

"He's not in Swartheld. He may not even be in Afrit," Rhamuel says, looking to Lerial.

"Five of his ships loaded cargo on sixday and departed from Swartheld."

"I sent a messenger to his villa here, but there is no one there but a handful of retainers, and they don't know where he and his family are," adds Rhamuel.

"Then that leaves Jhosef," concludes Aenslem, "and he'll do whatever benefits him."

"We have some doubts about Jhosef," says Rhamuel, who goes on to explain about Oestyn and Mykel's disappearance, as well as the missing dispatch and the missing Captain Jontarl.

Aenslem nods when Rhamuel finishes. "Then he won't be here in Swartheld for some time. Put out proclamations. Affirm Atroyan's and Natroyor's deaths in the explosion, declare an eightday of proper mourning, and note that there was a private memorial for them because of the Heldyan attacks on Swartheld. Blame the explosions in the palace and Harbor Post on Duke Khesyn. Don't mention Mykel yet. It's not necessary, because you'd be the heir in any case. There's no point in waiting any longer in letting people know."

"Not after I've consulted with you, but it seemed best not to rush matters."

"Now that you've consulted, don't dither."

"Have I ever?"

"No, but that doesn't mean you wouldn't."

Lerial is quickly seeing why frequent meetings between Aenslem and Rhamuel might not be the wisest course. He turns to Aenslem. "Is there anything else you'd recommend?"

"Wait a few days. Send out letters to all the merchanters—except Alaphyn and Jhosef and Maesoryk—commending them on their levelheadedness and forbearance . . . and then note that there will likely be some changes in the way the duchy is governed as a result of the war with Heldya."

"Do you have suggestions on what those might be?"

"That's your task, not mine. I told your brother to raise tariffs and build a few warships. He didn't. A few warships would have made things almost impossible for Khesyn. I don't like tariffs, but war is even worse for merchanting than tariffs. Listen to young Lerial. He might have a good idea or two." Aenslem stands. "I'll send you a note if I think of anything else. Oh . . . and in a few days, get yourself seen around the city. You can ride in an open coach. Let it be known that's because your leg was broken in the palace explosion. Then get a special saddle made so that you can ride."

Rhamuel nods. "Thank you for coming. I do appreciate it."

"I couldn't do any less."

"I still appreciate it."

Since it is clear that Aenslem will need an escort back to his villa, Lerial has also risen. He looks to Rhamuel. "After we escort Merchanter Aenslem back, I'll be at headquarters, unless you need anything."

"If I do, I'll let you know. Thank you."

Lerial and Aenslem walk back to the stables without talking, except in pleasantries, and they ride to the avenue leading up to Aenslem's villa before the merchanter speaks again.

"He might work out as duke, after all. It'd be better if you could stay here. I understand it can't happen. You've done more than enough." Aenslem shakes his head, and then is silent.

When they reach the villa's stables, Aenslem dismounts, then looks up. "He didn't ask me to come there today, did he?"

"He said he needed to consult with you. I took care of the details."

Aenslem laughs, gruffly, but cheerfully, then shakes his head once more. "Good day, young Lerial."

"Good day, ser."

Lerial turns the gelding. On his way to the villa gates, he does not catch sight of either Kyedra or Haesychya, not that he really expects to, but . . .

XLVI

Lerial spends the remainder of sixday, as well as sevenday morning, on preparations for the Mirror Lancers' departure and return journey to Cigoerne, making certain that the wagons are in good condition, and arranging with Captain Dhallyn to obtain provisions and other supplies when the time comes that they can finally leave. As he sits in the small conference room at Afritan Guard headquarters that he is using as his personal command center, he has to admit, if only to himself, that he has mixed feelings about departing.

Why? Is it just because he feels that what he and the Lancers have accomplished in Afrit has been worthwhile for both Afrit and Cigoerne . . . and has doubts about what of equal worth he can do in Cigoerne? Or the fact that he isn't looking forward to returning to wondering about what Lephi is doing . . . and dealing with the unvoiced comparisons. *Or . . . how much does Kyedra play into your feelings?* More, he suspects, than he had ever thought, possibly because for years he has recalled her as she was when she had visited Cigoerne with her father as a young girl . . . most likely just to make her familiar with Cigoerne in the event she ended up as Lephi's consort. Yet now that he has seen her . . . *she's too good for Lephi . . .*

Lerial can't help shaking his head. *You're still the second son.*

He turns his attention back to the supply lists and logistical requirements, but less than a third of a glass later, a ranker knocks on the conference room door.

"Yes?"

"There's a messenger from Arms-Commander Rhamuel, ser. He would appreciate your coming to the palace at your earliest convenience."

"Thank you." *That doesn't sound good.* "If you'd ask Squad Leader Dhoraat to select a squad to accompany me, I'd appreciate it. I'll be at the stables shortly."

"Yes, ser."

Lerial jots a note to himself to check on grain for mounts. Given that it's late spring, just about as far as possible from most grain harvests, supplies are likely to be short in many places on their return, and he'd prefer to carry more with them, just in case. Then he takes all his papers back to his quarters before making his way to the stables, where Eighth Company's Third Squad and his own gelding are already forming up.

A half glass later, just before the first glass of the afternoon, he and Third Squad rein up outside the palace stables. Lerial does notice that white and black mourning drapes have been hung on the gates and the main entrances. From the stables, he makes his way to the west wing of the palace, but before he can turn toward the sitting room Rhamuel has been using, an Afritan Guard ranker hurries up to him.

"Overcaptain, ser, the duke is now in his receiving study. This way, if you would, ser."

Lerial follows the ranker to another door, still on the second level, but overlooking the west entrance to the palace. Inside the door is an anteroom, with two table desks. A palace guard sits at the table desk set directly facing the door, while Norstaan is seated at the other desk, set well to one side.

"For the moment, Commander Sammyl and I are sharing this one," Norstaan explains. "Go on in. He's expecting you."

Lerial opens the door to the inner chamber and steps into a much larger room. At one end is a circular conference table with six chairs around it, and at the other is a large table desk, behind which Rhamuel is seated, with stacks of papers arrayed around him. In the corner of the study is a chair on wheels, essentially a chair fastened to a frame to which small cart wheels or the like have been attached.

"You've moved, I see."

"Norstaan pointed out that, now that I'm duke, I'll need to see more people at one time, and that I needed a more proper receiving study. The wheeled chair was his idea. One person can push it, and I can even move the wheels sitting in it. For a short distance, anyway. It's a great improvement, even if it does squeak and squeal. Sit down." The pleasant expression on Rhamuel's face vanishes.

"Trouble?" asks Lerial.

Rhamuel nods. "The palace guards I sent looking for Mykel and Oestyn . . ."

"Yes?" replies Lerial cautiously.

"They've found the bodies of some of his escort guards—what's left of them."

"What about Mykel and Oestyn?"

"There's no trace of them." Rhamuel shakes his head. "Ghersen—he's the squad leader I sent—he's very methodical. He stopped at every village and hamlet along the way. He found the inn where they stayed the second night . . . and the innkeeper said that they had left very early, before dawn." Rhamuel offers a sardonic smile. "Neither Mykel nor Oestyn would leave that early. Not willingly, and Ghersen knew that. I imagine he was rough on the innkeeper. He's now convinced that the innkeeper had nothing to do with it—especially since his son was found at the bottom of the well the next morning, and one of the serving maids was missing. The innkeeper said that everyone slept late that morning. Ghersen questioned some locals, and several said that the inn wasn't open until midmorning."

"That sounds like someone put sleeping draughts in the food or lager."

"My thought as well."

"Didn't Oestyn have some personal guards?'

"That thought has also already crossed my mind." Rhamuel shakes his head. "I still have trouble believing Oestyn . . . he was so devoted to Mykel . . ."

"There are two possibilities," Lerial suggests.

"I've thought of both. One is that Jhosef set it all up, using Oestyn, who had no idea of what was happening. The second is that Oestyn has been playing his father's plaques all along. In the end, it doesn't matter at all." Rhamuel takes a deep breath. "Ghersen questioned people all around there, but no one would admit to seeing anything. Maybe they didn't. He went to a little place a good kay off the main road because someone had said something about seeing a strange wagon coming back from a swampy lake in a hill valley where there are stun lizards and mountain cats. When he was going through the hamlet, he saw a little girl in a gray shift, and that made him curious."

"A gray shift?"

"The material seemed to be the same as that used for palace guard undertunics. He questioned and prodded. In the end, one of the villagers led him to the swampy lake. They found some remains. The stun lizards and cats hadn't left too much. Perhaps six or seven, but all were palace guards—except for a young woman."

"The serving maid?"

Rhamuel shrugs. "Most likely. There were still wagon tracks in places—just one wagon."

"Someone familiar with the area. How far is it from Lake Reomer?"

"A short day's ride. It's also a short day's ride from Lake Jhulyn, if in a slightly different direction."

"So what merchanters have summer villas on Lake Jhulyn?" asks Lerial. "Or Lake Reomer?"

"Reomer is the duke's lake. Khamyst, Nahaan, and Jhosef—among others—have villas overlooking Jhulyn. Maesoryk has a much grander villa on his own lake, midway between the two. Jhosef and Maesoryk are not in Swartheld."

"You mentioned Maesoryk wasn't here earlier. What about Alaphyn?"

"We knew his villa here was empty, but he also left word at his factorage that he was removing himself and at family to Dolari."

"In Heldya. That explains all his ships leaving Swartheld last sixday." Lerial pauses, then asks, "You want me to go visit those villas? Is that it?"

"Not yet. Not until Ascaar arrives. I did want you to be able to think things over. Once he arrives, if all goes well, I thought Norstaan could take my personal squad and escort you and one of your companies on a tour of the lakes area."

"A company?"

"It might make matters easier."

"Especially if Afritan Guards aren't used against Afritan merchanters?" Lerial raises his eyebrows.

"There is that." Rhamuel smiles grimly. "I did send out the proclamations that Aenslem suggested . . . and declared official mourning for Atroyan and Natroyor. It will be days before they're posted even everywhere here in Swartheld, and longer before they get to Shaelt and Luba and the more out-of-the-way towns and hamlets."

"Then you're both duke and arms-commander."

"For what it's worth, considering I'm not exactly able to move around much."

"What about Aenslem's suggestions?"

"They're good, but I don't see much point in struggling to get into a coach until most of the people have a chance to learn they have a new duke."

Lerial can see the wisdom in that. "Have you heard anything from His Mightiness Duke Khesyn?"

"No. Do you think we will?"

"Did your father or Atroyan?"

"Very, very seldom."

"Then it's unlikely. What could he say? Accuse you of untoward conduct after he's invaded Afrit? Complain about the destruction of Estheld after he's attacked Luba, Shaelt, and Swartheld?"

For a moment, Rhamuel smiles, then looks at the stacks of papers, as well as a thick ledger. "I have to get ready for a meeting with Cyphret."

"Cyphret?" Lerial frowns, trying to recall where he has heard the name.

"Cyphret is minister for merchanting, and senior minister. He controls the duke's wallet, so to speak. I have no doubt that we are woefully short of golds."

"Can't you seize Alaphyn's villa and assets?"

"That won't likely be enough."

"Aenslem said that you need to raise tariffs."

"I'll have to, but they aren't paid until midfall, and that means I'll have to borrow golds from Fhastal."

"Suggest that he forgo usury as a public duty."

"I might at that." After a pause, Rhamuel says, "There is one other thing."

"Yes?"

"You haven't seen Kyedra lately." The new duke's words are blandly uttered.

"Not since last eightday. Haesychya has quietly kept her out of sight."

"Perhaps you should pay her a call. She may think you don't think much of her because you only talk to her when you go to see Aenslem as a healer."

"Will her mother let me?"

"Whether Haesychya approves of your seeing Kyedra or not, she can't afford to refuse you so long as your behavior isn't untoward, and I doubt that yours ever would be."

"I've been reluctant to impose . . . given . . ." Lerial shakes his head.

"Matters have changed greatly over the past season. More than you've considered." Rhamuel smiles. "Let's just say that I don't want my niece to think badly of you."

"Neither do I," admits Lerial.

Since there is nothing else pressing, at least not until Ascaar arrives, once Lerial leaves the palace, he and his squad head for Aenslem's villa, where the guards admit them without question.

Lerial is just about to enter the villa when Haesychya steps out.

"Why might you be here today?"

"I came to see Kyedra."

"What if she does not wish to see you?"

"Then she can tell me that herself. Or whatever else she may wish."

Haesychya smiles at his last words. "When you say that to a woman, you risk much, Lerial."

Her tone is so humorously ironic that he cannot help but laugh, if softly. "Thank you for the observation, but I'd rather know what a lady I appreciate thinks than have to guess."

"Appreciate . . . an interesting choice of words."

"Not really. Accurate. Appreciation of anyone or anything is the first step to understanding." He smiles. "Then, perhaps understanding should come first. Either way, I think they go hand in hand."

"In that, I would quite agree." Haesychya gestures. "This way. She is in the lady's study she seems to have appropriated." She leads the way into the entry hall.

Lerial follows, then moves beside her.

"I had thought we might not see you again, except at official functions, and that would mean not at all, since there are likely to be none at all for the foreseeable future."

"Proper mourning, you mean?" As he asks the question, Lerial realizes that he has not seen mourning head scarves on either Haesychya or Kyedra. *But then, they don't wear head scarves in the home . . . or family homes.*

"Proper hypocrisy. Only a few care."

"You, Kyedra, and Rhamuel . . . perhaps a very few others," Lerial says.

"You don't."

"How could I care that deeply—honestly? Mourning would only convey respect on my part. I met your consort once, as a child, and twice more here. You cannot mourn, not deeply, someone you do not know. I am far more deeply concerned about what his death has cost you and Kyedra."

Haesychya almost stops short of the north archway, looking at Lerial. "You actually mean that. Why?"

"I've seen enough of you both to have more feelings and understanding about you two."

"I should have asked why you were willing to say that." She keeps walking along the north corridor.

"Because it's true."

She shakes her head ruefully. "'Truth' is a word whose meaning is unique to each person."

"Usually . . . but not always."

Haesychya does not reply but eases open a door on the west side of the corridor. "Dear, you have a caller."

Lerial stands in the doorway with Haesychya, unwilling to enter unless welcomed in some fashion.

For just an instant, Kyedra's eyes widen, in pleasure, Lerial hopes. He inclines his head. "It came to me that with all the aiding of your grandfather and uncle I had not paid you the attention I wished."

"You truly are here to see me, and not Grandpapa?"

"I had no thoughts at all of seeing him. He seemed perfectly healthy yesterday, and I have no doubt I would hear were he not." Lerial takes several steps into the room, hoping her expression is at least a conditional welcome.

"I will leave you two," Haesychya steps out of the study and closes the door behind herself.

For a moment, neither Kyedra nor Lerial speaks.

Finally, Kyedra motions to the armchairs flanking a low table. "We could sit."

Lerial smiles. "We could indeed, Lady."

"That . . ."

". . . sounds too formal? Perhaps, but I would not wish to be presumptuous." *Not after all you have been through.*

"You've been anything but." Kyedra offers a mischievous smile. "Except with your eyes."

"I like it when you smile."

"I believe you've mentioned that before."

"It bears repeating, because you have a most enchanting and radiant smile." Before Kyedra can reply, Lerial adds, "And that is neither presumptuous nor excessively flattering because you do."

"Are you going to insist on putting words in my mouth?"

"My apologies, Kyedra."

"That is much better . . . Lerial. I do like your name. It fits you."

"As does yours you."

" 'Kyedra' sounds harsh."

"I don't think so."

She smiles, fleetingly, before speaking again. "Enough of names. Why are you here?"

"I told you. I wanted to see you. You, not your grandfather or your mother. I've been reluctant to press, given that my presence seemed . . . to your mother . . . less than welcome, except as necessary to heal your grandfather."

"Then why did you press . . . today?"

"Because I wanted to see you, because . . ." He smiles, almost saying, *I think you know,* before realizing just how presumptuous and condescending those words might sound. He swallows. "Because, I wanted you to know just that—that I wanted to see you."

"You know that we do not decide our fates . . . or consorts."

"That is possible, but it cannot hurt to know what we feel."

"It could hurt very much. Look at Uncle Rham. He still loves your aunt."

"You know that?"

"You didn't?"

"Not until I met him." Lerial pauses. "Will you keep something between us? Because if it doesn't turn out, it could hurt him even more."

"You will have to trust my judgment on that. I cannot pledge to something I don't know."

Lerial doesn't hesitate. "I sent a dispatch to my father more than an eightday ago, asking for a healer for your uncle, the same healer that had healed him once before. I suggested that it would be for the best for both Cigoerne and Afrit. I also suggested that she arrive by rivercraft, since that would be faster."

Kyedra's mouth opens.

"Was I wrong?"

She shakes her head, then says, "I would suggest that you have Norstaan pass the word to all pier guards that a healer from Cigoerne may be coming and that he will supply a squad to convey her to the palace if such a healer arrives. Norstaan will keep that confidence, as will I."

"I should have thought of that. He did make the arrangements for sending the dispatch, and I know it got as far as Subcommander Ascaar and that he sent it on."

"Then it is in your father's hands . . . and hers." She looks directly at Lerial. "Thank you. Even if it is not to be, thank you."

Lerial decides not to bring up the possible complications if Emerya does choose to come to Swartheld, although her presence would not likely cause as much of a concern as once it might have—*you hope*—given what the Mirror Lancers have done for Afrit.

Kyedra offers a full smile, the one that transfigures her. "I'm glad you came."

"So am I."

"I want to hear more about you, your sister . . . not about the fighting . . ."

"Only if you'll offer the same . . ."

"But nothing about what may or may not be. Do you understand?" Her voice is firm as she asks the question.

"I do. Too many others can determine the future." Lerial phrases his words that way because he is not willing to accept that others have full control of their fate.

"Start with your sister."

While Lerial wonders about why Kyedra would wish that, he begins, "She was only two when we first met, and she's changed quite a bit since then. Like you, she knows her own mind, and there have been times . . ."

Lerial and Kyedra are still talking nearly a glass later, when there is a knock on the study door.

"You can come in, Mother," says Kyedra with a smile, saying in a lower voice to Lerial, "It can't be anyone else."

The study door opens and Haesychya follows the serving girl bearing a tray into the study. On the tray are two platters, one of butter biscuits and one of small cakes, along with three beakers and a pitcher of pale lager.

Lerial understands fully, but lets Haesychya make the obvious statement.

"I can't let you have all of Lerial's time, Kyedra."

"I'm glad you let me have some of it." Kyedra smiles cheerfully.

So am I, thinks Lerial, knowing that after the refreshments, and casual and polite conversation, it will be time for him to take his leave.

XLVII

After leaving Aenslem's villa late on sevenday afternoon, Lerial rides back to the palace and meets briefly with Norstaan, conveying exactly what Kyedra has suggested.

The undercaptain smiles. "Yes, ser. I'll make sure of that."

"I can't say if the healer is coming, but if she does, I don't think there should be any hindrance to anything she may be able to accomplish in improving the duke's health."

"No, ser. We're agreed on that. Thank you for letting me know . . . and I won't tell him until you want me to."

"Thank you."

"My pleasure, ser."

Lerial returns to Afritan Guard headquarters, where he summons his officers and Dhoraat, whom he has promoted to senior squad leader, to the small conference room,

"I had a meeting earlier today with the duke—he's is now the duke in name as well as in fact. He has requested that we undertake one more task before we leave Afrit—once Subcommander Ascaar arrives in Swartheld."

All three men facing him across the table look dubious, and Lerial cannot blame them.

"You all know that one of the reasons why the Afritans lost so many men, and why Duke Atroyan was killed, was because there were traitors among the Afritan merchanters. It also appears that one or two of these merchanters may have had some part in the disappearance of Lord Mykel, the duke's younger brother . . ." Lerial goes on to explain what Rhamuel has relayed to him and Rhamuel's "request." He finishes by saying, "We could refuse this, but after all the years of poor relations with Afrit, I think having the duke owe us would be better than declaring he is on his own on this, especially since, if he were the one to discipline the traitors, many of the merchanters would view him badly . . . and he cannot afford that much ill will at present."

"More dirty work, if you ask me, ser," declares Kusyl.

"Absolutely, but, all things considered, it's worth doing. It also makes the point that the duke trusts us, and that might just make his merchanters less likely to cheat Duke Kiedron's merchanters as well . . . or not so badly."

Kusyl's sour expression indicates his feeling about merchanters so expressively that Lerial can barely refrain from laughing.

"When will this happen?" asks Strauxyn.

"Not before oneday at the earliest, because Subcommander Ascaar hasn't arrived yet."

"What company are you thinking about?" asks Kusyl.

"Eleventh Company, unless any of you have other suggestions." Lerial looks from Kusyl to Strauxyn, and then to Dhoraat.

"That makes sense," Strauxyn finally says.

Kusyl nods, as does Dhoraat.

"Since there's nothing else . . . right now, that's all."

Lerial notices that Strauxyn and Dhoraat leave quickly, but Kusyl does not, suggesting that the senior undercaptain has something in mind and has arranged the situation with the other two. "What is it, Kusyl?"

"One good thing about this war, ser, for us, anyway. We won't be having to fight Heldyans all the time, and not the Afritans, either. Not while the arms-commander is duke."

"That's true, but it's been hard on the Afritans."

"There was one good thing for them . . . in a way."

"Oh?"

"It got rid of a lot of poor senior officers . . . even some stupid captains. That's what some of the undercaptains who came up from rankers are saying. They had too many officers who never served as rankers."

"That may be, but it cost them a lot of good rankers." Lerial can't help but wonder from what direction the weapons that took out some of the "stupid" captains happened to come. He also realizes what Kusyl is hinting at and smiles. "Yes, you'll be a captain. Officially, I can only recommend, but it will happen."

"Strauxyn, too, begging your pardon, ser."

"Done. What about Dhoraat as an undercaptain?"

"Give him another year as a senior squad leader. He understands."

"Meaning that you've made it clear to him."

"I've been where he is. I know what he needs to know. He knows that, too." Kusyl simply waits after speaking.

"What else are you thinking about, Kusyl?"

"Begging your pardon, ser, but you ought to be arms-commander and in charge of the Mirror Lancers."

"That can't happen now." *If ever, because you can't become arms-commander while Lephi serves in the Mirror Lancers.*

"Yes, ser. I know." Kusyl's voice conveys both understanding and resigned acceptance. "Still be better if it could."

"That's not my decision."

"Yes, ser."

Lerial also understands what Kusyl is not saying, and cannot say—that there is likely going to be a problem, in time, given Lerial's experience, abilities, and accomplishments . . . and Lephi's comparative lack of the same, especially since Lephi will not be the duke for some years to come, barring some unforeseen health problem striking their father. "We'll just have to deal with what the future brings, Kusyl. That's all we can do."

"Sometimes . . . seems like the Rational Stars aren't so rational."

"Sometimes, I've thought the same thing," replies Lerial with a laugh. "Let's go get some food and lager. It's been a long day."

That night, after he climbs into his bunk, Lerial's thoughts go back to his conversation with Kusyl. *Only Kusyl could have dared to bring up what he did . . . and only most likely outside of Cigoerne. But he's right. It's already been a bit of a problem, and it's going to get worse.* The only solution Lerial can see is for him, once he returns to Cigoerne, to remain at posts well away from the palace, perhaps even as far away as in Verdheln . . . or for him to switch duties with Lephi so that Lephi will be closer to the city of Cigoerne itself. *You're going to have to talk that over with Father . . .* And that is not something to which he is looking forward.

Nor is he looking forward to leaving Kyedra, he realizes, even as he knows that, as Altyrn has pointed out, there are great responsibilities involved in being even the junior heir . . . *and the wrong brother.*

Finally, he does drift off to sleep.

XLVIII

Lerial wakes early on eightday, and with no real solutions to the problems awaiting him in leaving Afrit and returning to Cigoerne, spends almost a glass after breakfast and morning muster, both sparring against Kusyl and Strauxyn—left-handed, since neither can match him right-handed—and then giving blade instruction to those picked out by their squad leaders as needing improvement. All that effort requires washing up and a clean uniform. It does not help his mood that much, although he feels slightly more virtuous, since he has not done that much one-on-one bladework since arriving in Afrit.

Then he decides to do something that has flitted in and out of his mind for days. When he steps out of his quarters, he glances around. Seeing no one, he raises a concealment, and then carefully makes his way out of the quarters and across the courtyard and, very slowly, and very carefully, past the guards at the gates, not fully closed, but open only enough for a single horse and rider to pass. He turns north onto the uneven stone walk flanking the wall. When he reaches the narrow lane at the north end of the wall, he steps into it, and sensing no one near, drops the concealment before continuing on past the café, still open, despite it being eightday, and to the cloth factorage that he has ridden past so often in recent days. When he reaches it, he tries the door, and finding it open, steps inside, where the air seems slightly drier, but not at all musty. Bolts of cloth are held in old but clean wooden racks. Before he can really survey the range of cloth on the racks, a voice rises from his left.

"This isn't the café . . . or Madam Kula's place . . . oh . . . I'm sorry, ser." The older woman who had spoken frowns as she steps from behind one of the wooden racks. "You're not a Guard ranker. Not a Guard officer, either."

"No. I'm a Mirror Lancer overcaptain." Lerial keeps his voice pleasant. "I just wanted to see what range of cloth you have."

"Doesn't seem that you'd have need for such."

"Not now, but I once worked for a shimmersilk grower, and I didn't see any of that in the window. Is that because it's so dear?"

"Golds are cheaper than shimmersilk."

A white-haired man eases from behind a counter on which are stacked bolts of what look to be differing cottons. He stops several yards away, but says nothing.

"They always have been, I'm told, at least since the fall of Cyador."

"No one makes shimmersilk in Hamor."

"There's one grower in Cigoerne, but what they produce goes to Candar and Austra."

"They say it comes from moths," offers the woman.

Lerial has a feeling that her words are an invitation for him to reveal ignorance. "Not quite. It comes from the cocoons made by the worms that would turn into moths. Except they boil the cocoons and then tease out the strands for thread." He pauses for an instant, trying to think of what to say to turn the conversation to what he wants to know. "It's difficult, and that's one reason why, I was told, anyway, that shimmersilk is so costly. I doubt that even the duke has many shimmercloth garments . . . or did, anyway."

"Not as though we'd know," says the white-haired man.

"I noticed some places have mourning cloths hanging, and others don't. Is there a reason for that?" asks Lerial, adding, "I'm not from here, and I wondered."

"I couldn't say," replies the woman. "We serve honest tradespeople. Probably years since I gave the palace more than a passing glance."

The older man offers a piercing glance to the woman and asks, genially, "That's quite a blade you sport, ser. It must have seen some use in the past few days."

Lerial offers a polite smile. "Far too much, I fear. I notice most of your cloth is cotton or linen. Do you have much need of wool?"

"In Swartheld?" The man chuckles. "Most folks might have a wool blanket or two, and it's handed down from mother to daughter." After a pause, he asks, "Where was the silkmaker you worked for, if I might ask?"

"In Teilyn, southwest some two days from the city of Cigoerne."

The man nods. "Is there anything in which we might interest you?"

"No, thank you. You've been most indulgent of my curiosity." Lerial inclines his head.

"Glad we could help," grudges the woman. She turns her back as Lerial walks toward the door. He opens it, and seeing that neither she nor the older man who is likely her consort is looking, he raises a concealment shield and closes the door without leaving the factorage. He moves back to where he can listen to anything they might say.

"Mite strange, Shaera, mite strange, especially that bit about mourning the duke," says the older man.

"Paah . . . every duke's like the one before. So long as they don't raise tariffs and leave our granddaughters alone . . . it doesn't much matter. Think that fellow really knew about shimmersilk?"

"He's done more'n hold it. Didn't hesitate to say where the grower was."

"Can't have done much more. Too young to be an officer worked up from a ranker."

"Maybe not, but there's a toughness there . . . not just a rich merchanter's younger brat like so many Guard officers. See how cold his eyes got when I asked about that blade?"

"They say Cigoerne's a tougher place."

"Could be . . ." The older man signs. "Enough chatter. Need to see about that dun cotton . . . see if we can save it . . . or something . . ."

"You save that . . . and I'll make you duke . . ." The woman does not quite cackle as the two move farther back in the factorage.

Lerial makes his way to the front door, drops the concealment, opens the door, and then slips outside, closing the door as gently as he can, before turning and walking briskly back toward the headquarters post.

The rest of the morning and the early afternoon he spends going over equipment and preparing the spare weapons—those recovered from the field and from casualties—and switching out poorer or damaged blades being used by various lancers with better ones, as well as going over details of the forthcoming trip to Lake Jhulyn with Strauxyn and obtaining a map from Dhallyn of the area. He is almost relieved when a messenger arrives in midafternoon, requesting his presence at the palace.

Kusyl sends his First Squad as Lerial's escort, and as they ride through the streets leading to the palace, Lerial does notice a few mourning drapes hung here and there, almost haphazardly, and he wonders whether all the merchanters' buildings near the harbor will hang the drapes, not that he intends to take time to make a special trip to see.

He has barely dismounted outside the palace stables when an officer in an Afritan Guard uniform—Ascaar—hurries across the courtyard to meet him.

Lerial grins. "You made a fast trip from Shaelt."

"Commander Sammyl indicated all deliberate speed, but apparently it wasn't necessary. I heard that you dealt with the Heldyans all by yourself . . . something about turning Estheld into an inferno and destroying ships and men . . ."

"Matters worked out better than I'd hoped. Thankfully," Lerial says. "We didn't see your men riding by Guard headquarters."

"I quartered them at South Post. It was almost empty . . . and that seemed better."

"And you'd rather not deal with Dhresyl?"

"I had that thought. It appears that matters less now." Ascaar glances toward the west wing of the palace. "I wanted to talk to you before we both meet with the duke. I only had a few moments with him. He said the rest could wait until you arrived. I gather he's also still arms-commander as well."

"I told him I thought he should be for a time yet."

"You've told him a few things, I can tell."

"Not just me. Merchanter Aenslem has as well."

"You're the one who's given me more headaches than any old officer needs."

"Me? What did I do?"

"Insisted that I have field command of all Afritan Guard battalions."

"I didn't insist. I suggested."

"Given who you are . . . it's the same thing."

That is indeed a chilling thought. *Just who does he think I am?* That is not a thought on which Lerial wishes to long dwell. "Given Sammyl or Dhresyl, would you want to serve under either in a fight? Would you want anyone else to?"

Ascaar offers a mock groan. "You would ask something like that."

Lerial shrugs. "Better a Lancer officer who won't be here long than an Afritan Guard officer who will."

"We'd better get to the duke's study and find out what he wants to tell us," Ascaar says. "I doubt I want to know."

Lerial almost asks, *What else could happen?*, but realizes even uttering those words is an invitation for another disaster to occur. "What else is new?"

Ascaar shakes his head.

Less than a tenth of a glass later, Lerial and Ascaar are seated before Rhamuel's table desk in the receiving study, the door closed firmly behind them.

"As you both know," Rhamuel says, "we need to clean up a few loose ends here in Afrit. Lerial has taken care of those dealing with Heldya, but the Afritan Guard needs restructuring. We also need quite a number of replacements, who will need training. That will have to be your immediate priority, Commander Ascaar." The duke turns to Lerial. "The matter of my younger brother's disappearance also needs attention, the sooner the better. When can you leave?"

"The first thing in the morning."

"So soon?"

"We started making preparations as soon as you made your request." Lerial smiles. "Some supplies, as well as reimbursement for supplies along the way . . . might be useful."

Rhamuel offers a wry smile. "Draw what you need in travel supplies. You'll have some golds before you leave."

"Thank you, ser."

"I'd best supply you. I wouldn't want you imposing on my people. That wouldn't be good, especially for a new duke."

"What do you expect from us?" Lerial asks bluntly.

"To find Mykel. If you cannot do that, discover what happened to him and why, and deal with those that caused it to happen. If that is not possible, discover all you can about what Jhosef and Maesoryk have had to do with the Heldyan attack on Afrit."

"And if you can't do that," adds Ascaar dryly, "leave the bastards shitless so that they won't make more trouble."

Rhamuel frowns, then abruptly shakes his head with a wry smile. "Becoming a full commander hasn't changed you at all, Ascaar."

"Be a shame if it had, ser."

The duke laughs. "You're right about that." He turns to Lerial. "I would suggest that you personally inform Lady Haesychya of your mission this afternoon."

"Thank you for the suggestion." *And the excuse to visit Aenslem's villa.* "I will do so."

"Good." Rhamuel smiles. "I don't have anything else for you. I do have a long list of matters to take up with Commander Ascaar."

"Then I will take my leave." Lerial smiles and stands.

Before that long, he and Kusyl's First Squad are riding out through the gates and onto the ring road. Lerial does notice more mourning drapes on houses and buildings to the north and west of the palace. *Because it's a more affluent part of Swartheld?* And when they reach Aenslem's villa, there are also drapes on the gates. *But not until Rhamuel proclaimed mourning. That's interesting.*

While he is grateful for the opportunity to see Kyedra again, he worries about doing so. *Is this just a futile hope? Will you make matters worse with Haesychya by appearing again on such a thin pretext?* He is still fretting when he dismounts and walks to the villa.

A retainer greets Lerial at the entry. "Might I inform whoever you're here to see that you are here, Lord Lerial?"

"I'm here to see Lady Haesychya, first, and then Lady Kyedra . . . on a different matter."

"If you would not mind waiting in the entry hall, ser?"

"I'll wait."

Although Lerial doubtless waits only a small fraction of a glass—a very small fraction—it seems as though a good third or half glass has passed before Haesychya appears, coming from the north wing of the Villa.

Lerial inclines his head to her. "Lady."

"I understand that you are here on two separate matters, Lerial. What is the one that concerns me, might I ask?"

"Duke Rhamuel has requested that I travel, with one Mirror Lancer company, escorted by one of his personal squads and Undercaptain Norstaan, to the area of Lake Jhulyn to look into the role certain merchanters may have played in the death of your consort and son and the disappearance of Lord Mykel."

"I'm not interested in vengeance, Lerial."

"Neither am I, Lady. I am interested in discovering anyone who cares so little about Afrit, its Guards, and its ruler that they would kill so many for mere personal gain and drag all the duchies in Hamor into war. If such is the case, they remain a danger to all Afrit, indeed all Hamor. I also don't particularly wish to see them escape the consequences of their actions, because that would set a very poor example for which both Afrit and Cigoerne will pay dearly in years to come."

"That is a rather eloquent statement. It is not exactly direct."

"I'd like to put an end to it all. Emphatically."

A cool smile crosses Haesychya's face. "You just might. Then what?"

"Then . . . whatever will be will be."

"Indeed." Haesychya's smile is enigmatic. "Thank you for informing me. I will not ask what you wish of Kyedra. She is in her study. I'll walk that far with you."

"I appreciate that."

This time the study door is open, and Kyedra stands immediately as she sees Lerial.

Is she surprised to see you? That would seem to be the case, from her reaction, although Lerial wonders what her mother or grandfather may have said that has caused such a reaction. "Might I have some of your time?"

Abruptly, she smiles, that smile that enchants him. "You might. Please . . ."

He steps into the study. He is surprised that Haesychya, after her earlier coolness, closes the door to leave the two alone.

"I didn't expect to see you today, Lerial."

"I didn't expect to be here. But . . . I'm leaving Swartheld . . . just for a few days, perhaps an eightday. Your uncle has asked me to go to the lakes area—"

"To see what happened to Uncle Mykel?"

"I don't know if anyone has told you, but the bodies of some of his guards have been found . . ." Lerial explains briefly.

"Uncle Rham is sending you—"

"And Norstaan."

"He's sending you because he has so few with great ability that he can truly trust. That means Subcommander Ascaar has arrived?"

"He's now Commander Ascaar. He arrived a few glasses ago. I just came from the palace."

Kyedra gestures to the armchairs. "You don't have to leave right now?"

"I don't. I wanted to see you before I left. We'll be leaving very early tomorrow." He waits for her to seat herself before settling into the other chair.

"What if you discover that one of the wealthy merchanters is behind it? What will you do?"

Lerial smiles wryly. "That's a good question, but I can't believe any of them would admit it."

"Then why go to the trouble of riding all that way?"

"Because there might be more to it."

"Do you really think that anyone would be hiding an army at the lakes?"

"That's rather unlikely. I suspect that Rhamuel thinks my presence will cause them to reveal something."

"Of course. You're a healer. Healers sense things. Most merchanters here in Swartheld know you have some abilities that way. If they have anything to hide, they won't want you on their grounds. They won't dare to deny you. So, if they do have something to hide, they'll either conceal it in some place you won't or can't look . . . or they'll try something to kill you . . . poison, rocks or trees falling on you."

"You're cheerful."

"You don't believe they'd do things like that?"

"I believe you. From what I've seen, I definitely do. It saddens me, though."

"Golds are everything to them. Cigoerne's a new duchy. In time, it will be the same there." Kyedra's voice carries a bleak tone.

"There are already some merchanters there like that," Lerial admits. *And some who have already tried to subvert the Mirror Lancers.* He'd just been fortunate enough to discover that plot and foil it. "I'd like to change that, but . . ."

"You don't think Father didn't know . . ." Kyedra's eyes are suddenly bright.

"I'm sorry. I didn't mean to bring up memories."

"He just couldn't do anything."

Lerial nods. "I've seen that."

"That's why Uncle Rham is using you."

"I know that, too."

Kyedra frowns. "Then why are you letting him?"

"Because the stronger he is, the stronger Afrit is. The stronger Afrit is . . . the less danger we both face from Heldya and Merowey" Lerial almost had said, *The stronger Cigoerne is,* but that had not felt right.

"That's not all, is it?"

"No."

"You aren't saying, are you?"

"Right now . . . it's better I don't."

Kyedra looks at him more intently, then offers an enigmatic smile, one much like her mother's, if a touch warmer. "That might be for the best . . . right now."

Lerial has no doubt that she understands his reluctance.

"The early redberries might be ripe by the time you reach the lakes."

"Is that a recommendation for them or a warning against them?" Lerial asks cheerfully.

"Very much for them . . . as long as you don't eat the ones that still have traces of green . . ."

Lerial knows that the remainder of their conversation will be most conventional . . . but he is in no hurry to depart . . . and from what he can sense, Kyedra is also in no hurry for that, either.

XLIX

While Lerial, Strauxyn, and Eleventh Company leave the headquarters gates well before seventh glass, it is closer to eighth glass by the time they have met Norstaan and his squad outside the palace and ride westward on a paved avenue that is barely half the width of the merchanters' avenue. The shops and dwellings close to the palace are neat and well kept, but they exude a feel of age that Lerial can sense as well as see. Farther west, but still within Swartheld, the dwellings are less ancient, but not recently constructed, somewhat larger, and exhibit a differing range of style and size, as if some older buildings had been removed and replaced or rebuilt. In places, it appears that odd additions have been built onto older structures.

"Who lives here?" Lerial asks Norstaan, riding on his left.

"Tradespeople, crafters, some of the more successful artisans, those who do not need a patron or those who have chosen not to rely on one."

"Isn't that chancy?" asks Strauxyn from where he rides on Lerial's left. "An artisan not having a patron when they could?"

"Swartheld is large enough to support quite a number of artisans. There are always some well-off tradesmen who would like to boast of having a painting or a bronze or a small sculpture. The smaller merchanters can easily afford art, but may not wish to limit themselves to a particular artisan. Maintaining a well-known artisan is not cheap."

Another glass passes as they ride through more shops and dwellings, and the farther they are from the river, the poorer both houses and shops become. The amount of poor and modest houses they pass again reminds Lerial, perhaps because of his visit to the cloth factorage, just how little he has come in contact with most of the people his father or Rhamuel rule. *And you've likely seen far more than Rhamuel or Lephi.* But that, he reminds himself, has largely been because of his father's and his aunt's requirements in teaching him healing . . . and working with rankers for years.

The street gradually narrows but remains stone paved. After a time, Lerial can see that the ground is rising and that, several hundred yards ahead, the houses thin abruptly and only extend partway up the dry and sandy hills.

"This is where Swartheld ends, then?" he asks Norstaan.

"Yes, ser."

"What about the road? What is it like beyond the hills?"

"It gets narrower. It is paved all the way to the lakes."

All the way to the lakes? "Is there that much trade this way? How did that happen?"

"There is the date trade, and timber. Besides the duke, there are also quite a few prominent merchanters with villas on the lakes. The road was paved in the time of the present duke's grandsire. That's all I know."

Lerial nods. Looking to his right, he can see that the low hills that define the western border of Swartheld angle to the east as they run northward, which explains why they are closer to the bay near Maesoryk's tileworks.

It is well after noon before Lerial and his force finish crossing the low, dry hills and descend into a wide and flat valley that appears to contain little beside circular palm orchards, at least that is what they seem to be, linked by narrow stone canals, and surrounded by sandy, sparsely grassed flat land.

In one orchard, and then another, Lerial notices figures climbing the tall palms. Finally, he asks, "What are they doing? It's a bit late for pruning any tree, isn't it?"

"I think that must be the second pollination," replies Norstaan. "The first one is usually around the second eightday of spring. The winds aren't strong enough to assure that all the trees are pollinated, and having too many male trees just wastes water."

"How . . . ?" Strauxyn breaks off the question.

"My uncle grows dates. I overheard some of the talk when I was growing up."

Lerial looks westward, but as far as he can see, there are only the date orchards and the sandy grasslands. "How far west do the date orchards go?"

"Another ten kays. Before too long, we'll see the hills that mark the west side of the valley. They're not very high."

"Does any one merchanter own all this?" asks Lerial.

"Most of these belong to the House of Haen, I'm told. Merchanter Jhosef owns the orchards south of the road for the last two kays before the Low Pass. Those are the best lands, because he has the water shares from the river."

"We haven't seen a river," points out Strauxyn.

Norstaan laughs. "You won't. Jhosef built a dam, and all the water from the reservoir goes into the canals, according to who has how many water shares."

"What happens if someone takes or gets too much water?" asks Lerial. "I'd think it would be hard to gauge that."

"All the canals have to have the same width and depth, and there are special gates at the reservoir. One of the growers deepened his channels, years ago. Jhosef kept track of the extra water he took for two years. When it amounted to an entire year's supply, he shut the man's gate and demanded he buy another water share or do without for a year. The man could not afford the share. Many of his trees died. He could not afford to keep growing. Jhosef bought his lands for a fraction of their worth."

Very controlling and very well thought out. Lerial keeps those thoughts to himself, although he wonders into how many other areas Jhosef's fingers and golds reach, particularly since not a single person has mentioned the dates or even produce as a part of what Jhosef controls, almost as if a mere few kays of date orchards are insignificant.

More than a glass later, after the road turns slightly southwest, Lerial catches sight of a line of gray against the reddish-colored low hills . . . or rather between two hills. As they ride closer, he can see that the gray is comprised of stone blocks, and that at the base of what must be a spillway is a stone-lined pond, from which runs a wide stone-lined canal, beside which runs a narrow graveled lane. The dam between the two hills extends hundreds of yards, perhaps a third of a kay, and at one end is a structure that resembles a stone fort.

"That looks like a small Afritan Guard post." Lerial points.

"That's where Jhosef's guards and workers live. They patrol the canals," replies Norstaan.

"How many guards does he have?"

"I couldn't say. I've been told that there are a squad's worth posted there. They don't get paid as much as an Afritan Guard, but, after they serve a year, they can leave with two eightdays' notice. A lot of bravos get their start with the private guards of the wealthier merchanters. A few Afritan Guards have, too, but the smarter ones just start with the Guard and stay."

"Because there's no real hope of advancement?" asks Lerial.

"That . . . and who wants to beat up helpless peasants and landcroppers?" Norstaan shakes his head.

Lerial only nods slowly. The more he sees of the Afritan merchanters, the less he cares for them . . . and he didn't feel that charitably toward them in the beginning.

L

On oneday, Lerial and his forces spend the night at an inn in Pondatyn, a village some ten kays west of the date valley. The inn, which Norstaan simply calls that, apparently has no other name, but clearly caters to large groups of travelers, if infrequently, because there are ample stables and several large floored sheds able to hold all of the rankers with room to spare. They depart early on twoday morning, under the hazy sky that indicates the day will again be hot.

And it's only midspring. While Lerial knows that Afrit is hotter than Cigoerne, he had not realized just how much hotter it is.

For the first few glasses they ride through sparse pine forests that somehow have grown in the rocky and sandy soil and survived, but by noon they have passed though somewhat higher hills and entered an area where there are more trees, some small hamlets, and occasional plots of land that bear low greenery.

"What do they grow here?" Lerial asks Norstaan.

"They have melons . . . and the black-syrup plants . . . a small grain, I think. That is if there is some rain. It does not rain much here. It rains more near Swartheld."

"How far is the inn from where Mykel and Oestyn were taken?"

"The Streamside? We won't reach there until after second glass. Why?"

"I'd like to talk to everyone there."

"They may not wish to talk to you."

"They don't have much choice, I think."

Slightly more than two glasses later, just after they have ridden through a small hamlet, Lerial sees a cluster of buildings on the south side of the road, set in the middle of an area whose grasses barely reach calf high. There is a winding line of green meandering from the hills to the south past the buildings and then under a small stone bridge and to the northeast. He wonders if the stream actually goes anywhere or just ends in some dry valley.

As they approach the Streamside, Lerial can see that it is similar enough to the inn at Pondatyn that it also must be a regular stopping point for large parties of travelers, such as when Atroyan took his family to Lake Reomer, and likely the retainers and guards of those merchanters who frequent the lakes in the summer.

Lerial has barely reined to a halt in front of the main building when a man in gray rushes out through the door and flattens himself on the dusty clay in front of the inn. "Please, honorable sers! I did nothing wrong! I beg you!"

"Is that the innkeeper?" Lerial asks Norstaan.

"I think that's Immar. I've only traveled this road twice. The arms-commander, I mean the duke, did not often visit Lake Reomer."

"Immar!" commands Lerial. "Stand up! Now! Enough groveling."

The innkeeper slowly rises, his eyes going from Norstaan to Lerial and then back to Lerial in puzzlement.

"Duke Rhamuel has sent Lord Lerial to seek the truth," offers the undercaptain.

"We need to talk," Lerial declares.

Behind him, Strauxyn murmurs, "Permission to inspect the inn, ser?"

"Granted."

From behind Lerial comes the command, "First Squad, First File, dismount."

"Once my men look around, you and I, Immar, are going to talk."

"Yes, ser. Yes, ser." The innkeeper continues to glance at Norstaan.

"Lord Lerial is the overcaptain who did the most to defeat the Heldyans. He stands high in the duke's esteem and trust," Norstaan explains. "He is the second son of the duke of Cigoerne."

"The people of the Rational Stars . . ." murmurs the innkeeper in a resigned voice, as if he has lost all hope.

A third of a glass later, Lerial sits across a circular table from the innkeeper in the otherwise deserted public room, except for the pair of Lancers posted by the main door and the second pair by the kitchen door.

"Why did you throw yourself in front of us, Immar?"

"The Afritan Guard . . . the squad leader . . . the one who came searching for the heir . . . he told me we would pay if we were guilty."

"Are you?" asks Lerial, letting his senses range over the innkeeper.

"No, ser. I have lost my only son to this evil. Many will not speak to me. Those from whom I must buy provisions demand silvers in advance. They fear I will not live to pay them."

Lerial doubts the man's distress is feigned. "Perhaps you can tell me what happened on that night when the heir and his friend arrived with their guards."

"I will tell you all I know. All those here will tell you what they know."

"How many were in the party?"

"The same number as there always were, ser. Lord Mykel and his friend, and ten Afritan Guards and two merchanter guards."

"Had any of the Afritan Guards been at the inn before? Did you remember any?"

"No, ser. That was not strange. There was always a different group of Afritan Guards every year. They joked about it when I was not listening. They said that they had thrown lucky bones because they could spend the summer at the lakes."

Lerial looks to Norstaan. The undercaptain nods.

"What about the merchanter guards?"

"I have thought about that, ser. They were different. They were not the guards that had been with Lord Mykel's friend every time in the two years before."

"Was there anything else different about them?"

"I did not see anything different. They were guards. They had blades. They watched. They did not eat when the others did. Neither did two Afritan Guards. That was the way it always was."

"What happened after they ate?"

"The heir and his friend sat here and talked. Then they went upstairs."

"What about the guards?"

"Most of them went to their rooms. One guarded the upstairs, and another guarded the front door. That was the way it always was."

"What about you and your consort?"

"She was tired. She went to bed early. I went upstairs to wait for Jahib. I fell asleep in the chair. When I woke it was light, and she was screaming that Jahib was missing. We began looking everywhere for him. Ottar found him at the bottom of the well."

Although Lerial continues to question the innkeeper for another half glass, he learns little more. Finally, he says, "I'd like to speak to your consort."

"Ser . . . I beg of you. Do not be cruel. Jahib was our only child. She mourns. She will mourn always."

"I do need to speak to her."

"I will find her and bring her here."

"Thank you."

After the innkeeper leaves, Lerial reviews what Immar had said, but he can find no inconsistencies. *We'll see what his consort has to say.*

"Ser . . ." At the sound of the innkeeper's voice, Lerial rises from the small table and turns.

The woman who approaches from the entry hall archway wears a heavy black and white mourning head scarf, swirled around her head so that Lerial can see little except her eyes. She stops short of the table. Lerial gestures for her to sit, and she does. She does not speak, even after Lerial seats himself.

"Your son is dead," he says quietly. "I cannot restore him to you. I would ask your help in finding the sons of other mothers."

The woman still does not speak.

Lerial reaches out, his hand just short of the woman's forehead, then extends the smallest trace of order, along with what he hopes is a feeling of comfort. He lowers his hand.

Her eyes widen, then brighten, as if with unshed tears. After a moment, she says, "You are a magus from the south, are you not?"

"From the south and of the Magi'i," he replies, for he does not consider himself a magus.

"You can tell the truth of my words?"

Lerial smiles, wryly. "I can tell if you do not believe your own words."

"They killed my Jahib. He was but twelve, and they killed him."

"I heard he was found in the well."

"They wanted me to think my son was stupid and careless. My son. He was dutiful and the most careful of boys."

"Who wanted you to think that?"

"Those who killed him."

"Do you know who killed him? Or how? When?"

"Someone with the heir. It could have been no one else."

"How do you know he was killed?"

"His belt was caught in the bucket strap. He never stood that way in lifting water. He always set the bucket on the well wall. The wall is chest high. Immar built it that high so no one would ever fall in."

"Why didn't you know that something had happened to him?"

"I was so . . . tired. I didn't know why. I asked Quiela to make sure that Jahib came upstairs after he swept the kitchen. That was his chore. When I woke the next morning, it was light. I never sleep past dawn."

"Why did you then?"

"Someone must have put something in the lager. We all slept late, except Quiela." Her eyes brighten once more. "The Afritan Guard—the mean one who beat Immar—he told me she was dead. She was a sweet girl. She hurt no one. She was not pretty, but she was so sweet."

"How could anyone have put anything in the lager?" asks Lerial.

"When the heir comes, a guard always watches the kitchen and the food. It is true when a merchanter comes also."

"Were there two men in the kitchen, then?"

She frowns, trying to remember. "No. There was only the merchanter guard."

Lerial wants to nod. "Were you in the kitchen all the time?"

"No. I watched Ottar when he prepared the food. I watched Quiela and helped her serve the food."

"Did the heir drink your lager?"

"The heir always brings casks of his own wine. He drank that. So did his friends. The guards drank our lager."

"Did you or Immar drink any of the wine?"

"The heir offered some to Immar. He always does. Immar does not like wine, but he always drinks some. He would not wish to offend the heir."

"You only drank the lager?"

"That was all. Our water is better than most, but the lager is always clean."

"Did Jahib drink lager?"

"We made him water his lager."

"What about Quiela?"

"She watered her lager. She said it was better that way."

"Did you see anything else strange after you woke up?"

"My head hurt. So did Immar's. So did Ottar's. The front door to the inn was barred. So was the rear door, and the kitchen door."

"Are those the only doors?"

She nods.

"How did anyone get out, then?"

"The shutters on the side window of the public room weren't fastened."

Lerial asks more questions of the innkeeper's consort, but discovers nothing more, and then goes to the kitchen, where he questions Ottar the cook.

"What did you prepare for their dinner?"

"They had a young goat. I made the meat tender, seared it, and then put it in an iron pot with the spices for burhka. I served it all with pearl millet. Between the heir and his friend and their guards, there wasn't much left. Just enough for small portions for the rest of us."

"Everyone ate some of the goat, then?"

"The merchanter guard in the kitchen . . . he ate later, with the rest of us."

"Did you drink much lager?"

Ottar snorts. "Can't last in the kitchen without lager. It's too hot."

"You slept late?"

"Later than anyone, I guess. Immar was shaking me. My head was splitting. Never had a skull-ache like that before."

"How did you find the boy?"

"The bucket is always hung on the post closest to the inn door. Jamara gets real upset if it's not. It wasn't there. When I looked down in the well, I saw something. It took both of us—Immar and me—to pull up the bucket, because Jahib's belt was caught."

"Was he wounded?"

"No, ser. He had a bump on the head. Like maybe he'd fallen and hit it. Don't see how he could have done that. Soon as she saw him, Jamara started screaming that someone had killed him."

"What did you think?"

"Someone bashed him, hooked his belt to the bucket, and lowered him into the well. Maybe they wanted him out of the way, figured he wouldn't drown. Maybe they wanted him dead." Ottar shrugs fatalistically.

Again, more questions bring little more information, and a half glass later, Lerial and Norstaan are sitting at the same small table where Lerial had questioned the innkeeper. Lerial looks at the dark lager in the heavy mug, then order-senses it, and finding no chaos takes a sip. The lager is even more bitter than it looks. He sets the mug down.

"What do you think, ser?" asks Norstaan.

"It wasn't anyone here at the inn. One of Oestyn's guards had to be the one who added sleeping draughts to the lager." Lerial nods to the mug. "This is so bitter you could add anything. The wine might have been adulterated earlier. That's most likely."

"Why?"

"Oestyn and Mykel know wine. Whoever added something had to add it skillfully enough that it didn't affect the taste too much. Or . . . maybe Jhosef sent a new or different vintage, one unfamiliar to the two."

Norstaan nods. "Most inn lager is bitter, and it varies from place to place. Likely enough that the guards wouldn't notice."

"The boy wouldn't be drinking as much, and his parents insisted on watering his lager . . . and the serving girl watered her own lager. The cook drank more lager than anyone, slept later, and woke with his head splitting."

"And they did it here because they could get rid of the bodies fairly close," suggests Norstaan.

"That means someone very familiar with the area."

Like Jhosef. Except that Lerial does not voice that observation.

LI

Because Lerial can see no point in spending another day or even part of one at the Streamside, he and his force set out for Lake Jhulyn early on threeday. He does pay Immar two golds from the small bag with which Rhamuel has entrusted him, for which Immar again practically grovels thanks. *Or relief, more likely,* Lerial suspects.

As they ride away from the inn, Lerial cannot help but wonder whether Emerya will come to Swartheld. *Father has to have received your dispatch by now.* But there is also the question of whether he will even tell Emerya. *Should you have sent a separate dispatch to her?* But doing so would have meant going around his father . . . and that . . .

He shakes his head.

By the third glass of the afternoon they are approaching Merchanter Jhosef's villa, set on the west edge of the lake near its northern tip. Even from over a kay away, the size of Jhosef's grounds and summer villa are impressive, the villa itself a white structure set facing the lake, with lawn running down to a sandy beach. Walls a good three yards high run from fifty yards out into the water up each the side of the lawn past the villa and its outbuildings to a point a half kay higher on the long gentle slope leading down to the lake. The west wall, the one high on the hill, appears to be closer to four yards tall. The road leads to an entry gate in the north wall.

Flanking the gate, inside the walls, are several white stone buildings, and out of those buildings a white stone-paved lane leads due south, passing directly beside stone retaining walls, on the top of which are extensive terraces, before curving south and uphill around the villa, presumably to an uphill entrance on the west side.

Lerial cannot help but wonder why the entry road does not just angle directly across the slope to the entry on the west side of the villa, but then realizes that the existing approach is far more artistic. *Oestyn's idea? Or someone else's earlier?* Lerial cannot imagine it being Jhosef's. As he rides closer to the gates, he continues to study the walls and the grounds, and the paved lanes connecting the gates and all the outbuildings, certainly enough outbuildings to quarter several companies of private guards.

"How do you plan to get in to see the merchanter, ser?" asks Strauxyn, riding on Lerial's left. "Those walls are high and stout."

"First, we'll ask. Then we'll see."

"I can't imagine them defying you, ser," says Norstaan.

Lerial can, unhappily, given all he has witnessed since entering Afrit more than a season before, and especially after seeing the small stone fortress set beside Jhosef's dam and above the water gates. He carries full shields as he rides up toward the stout timbered gates, iron-bound and set into massive stone posts.

"Lord Lerial to see Merchanter Jhosef."

"Merchanter Jhosef is not receiving visitors. He never receives unannounced visitors here."

Lerial can sense . . . something beyond the walls—well beyond—almost a swirl of order and chaos. *A very good shield!* So Jhosef has a strong mage . . . something no one has ever mentioned, not that Lerial is especially surprised. He finds that he is angry. Aenslem had a low-level chaos-mage; Maesoryk had or has two or more. Jhosef has one . . . *And you had to deal with the Heldyans and the traitor mages without any magely support because not a single merchanter would even admit to having mages or white wizards.*

Except, Lerial realizes, he had never asked for such support, nor had he learned about who had any mages, until after most of the Heldyan attacks were over—and neither Atroyan nor Rhamuel had mentioned such a possibility, except in general terms, and none of the merchanters had volunteered their mages. Lerial knows why, or what they would have said—that they could not afford to give up any advantage to other merchanters. And that, too, feeds his anger.

"Then I suggest that you announce us. He will receive us," Lerial states calmly. *One way or another.*

"I think not, ser." Whoever is behind the iron-framed peephole closes it.

"We'll move back," Lerial says to Strauxyn, gesturing. "Around that curve in the lane." He waits as Strauxyn gives the necessary orders, and the entire force withdraws a good quarter kay.

Lerial then concentrates and attempts what he hopes will be two very small order-chaos separations, one on each side of the heavy gates.

Crumppt!

Powdered stone cloaks the gates. Then there is a huge thud, and the paving stones under Lerial's mount's hoofs shudder. As the dust and stone subside, Lerial can see that the gates have toppled forward, leaving a narrow passage between the gateposts and the buildings directly behind them.

"Lances ready!" orders Strauxyn.

"Lances, ready, ser!"

"Forward!"

Lerial holds back slightly, letting the first rank of lancers precede him, although he does strengthen his shields, as well as mentally readies an order-line pattern in case the mage beyond the gates should attempt some sort of attack. A squad of men in white tunics and brown trousers is still forming up in the narrow stone-walled passage behind the entry gates to the villa, but at the sight of the lancers bearing down on them, most drop their pikes and attempt to flee. Those who are not quick enough are cut down. In moments, Twenty-third Company sweeps through the narrow space and up the paved lane. Lerial glances ahead, studying the approach to the villa, still almost half a kay away.

"Deliberate advance!" Lerial orders.

They have covered almost half of that distance at a fast walk when from out of nowhere comes a warm and comforting feeling . . . the sense that everything is fine. Then a voice says, *You don't need that knife among friends . . . just unstrap it . . . you'll feel so much better without it . . . so much better . . .*

Lerial feels his hand going down to his belt, even though he has not willed it to do so.

You're among friends here . . . we all want you to feel welcome . . . your very good friends . . . such good friends. . . .

. . . yes . . . good friends . . . Somewhere . . . Lerial hears people talking, but their words don't seem all that important . . . His hand brushes the highly ordered and tooled leather of the sheath . . . and the comforting words vanish . . . and he can sense a web of twisted order and chaos retreating from

him . . . and that his shields are lowering. He immediately refreshes them, then concentrates on trying to locate the source of that probe . . . that insinuating attack that he has not even anticipated. He cannot determine the exact location of the chaos-mage, only the general feeling that he is near or in the villa proper.

Projecting feelings . . . over that distance? Lerial almost shudders as he rides closer to the villa, a low single-level structure that stretches close to a hundred and fifty yards, end to end. Below the east-facing terraces is a stone retaining wall that extends the length of the terraces, some fifty yards, and well beyond the terraces on both the north and south, and which rises from the west side of the road to the terrace floor. Above that is a waist-high stone balustrade, clearly placed to keep revelers or children or anyone from falling some three yards off the terrace to the road below. From the east side of the road, the lawn stretches down to the water, although there is a hedge maze of some sort in the middle of the lawn. Lerial does not recognize the bushes of the hedge that composes the diversion. A single white stone pier extends some twenty yards out into the water, with several small boats tied to bollards, and one much larger pleasure barge tied at the very end.

When they are less than fifty yards from the north end of the terrace, Lerial sees several figures move up to the balustrade. He almost swallows in amazement because, standing behind the middle of the terrace wall, several yards above an iron-bound door that doubtless blocks a staircase up from the road to the terraces, is Jhosef, flanked by two guards in brown and white uniforms. *After denying us entrance, he can just stand there as if nothing happened?*

"Company! Halt!" Lerial orders, looking up at the merchanter and past the retaining wall to the base of the sculpted and decorative balustrade that defines the end of the terrace. *There's no way to get up there quickly . . . not from here.*

"That's a very good idea, Lord Lerial. It is you, isn't it? Who else would it be? Running errands for whelp Rhamuel again?"

"If you call seeing why you had Mykel killed running an errand," replies Lerial sardonically.

"Killing Mykel? Perish the thought! Why would I ever wish to do that? That's the last thing on my mind. You mistake me, Lord Lerial. I have only the highest interests of Afrit in mind. Killing young Mykel would scarcely further restoring the strength of Afrit, no matter what you younger sons think. Why don't you ride up to the main entrance? From there you can easily enter the villa, and we can discuss what might be the best future for Afrit." With that, Josef steps back, and in moments is out of sight.

For an instant, Lerial is dumbfounded. *Now what?* He had expected either more fighting, or Josef fleeing, or not being at his villa, or even some sort of attempt at a negotiated surrender. *Unless those words are his way of offering such.* Except Lerial trusts the merchanter not at all.

"Ser?" asks Strauxyn.

"Capture and tie up all Jhosef's personal guards, everyone in those gate buildings. Send one squad up to the entrance immediately so that no one escapes, but keep them well back. Norstaan and I and his squad will follow that squad. Once we have the grounds secure, then we'll look into the villa and consider Merchanter Josef's kind invitation." Lerial doesn't keep the sarcasm from the last words.

"Yes, ser! First Squad, forward!"

While Lerial waits for Norstaan and his squad to move up behind First Squad, he makes certain he is maintaining his shields while he uses his order-senses to determine what pitfalls may lie farther along the approach road or on the terrace above. He can sense no other living beings in either place. There are more than a few people inside the villa, but how many are unarmed retainers, how many are armed guards, and where exactly the chaos-mage might be he cannot tell, except that he is somewhere nearby. Nor is there any indication of whether Mykel or Oestyn are even in the villa, but there is no way for him to pick them from the others within.

Before long, Lerial and Norstaan ride at the head of the Afritan squad, immediately behind First Squad. They encounter no one along the sweeping and gently rising stone-paved lane that curves around the south end of the villa, past low gardens and private terraces outside several rooms. Before long they rein up short of a columned portico in the middle of the west side of the villa. Lerial still sees no one. Nor can he sense exactly where the chaos mage might be, other than in the villa, somewhere near the entrance, he feels, although he cannot be certain.

As Lerial and the two squads wait for Strauxyn and the remainder of Twenty-third Company to secure the grounds, Lerial continues to check his shields and use his eyes and order-senses, wondering whether he is being too cautious. Except there are the "small" problems that, first, despite the fact that Lerial *knows* Josef has to be behind whatever happened to Mykel and

Oestyn, he has no proof, and, second, if Mykel is still alive, as Josef has indicated, simply storming into the villa might not be the best approach, especially with a chaos-mage in waiting. On the other hand, not storming the villa, given the mage, might be more than a little dangerous for Lerial personally. Either way, he's not about to take any action until Strauxyn reports that the estate grounds are secure.

As he waits and considers, and reconsiders, no other guards or armsmen attempt to flee from the villa, nor from the outbuildings near the villa, from what he can see and sense. Before that long, Strauxyn returns with two of his three remaining squads, reins up, and reports, "All of the merchanter's guards are taken care of."

"Casualties?" asks Lerial.

"None from our side, ser. We had to kill three more of them, and several others are wounded. That doesn't count a handful or so who fled. Fourth Squad has the others under guard."

Lerial glances at the columned entrance to the villa. Finally, he smiles wryly. "I think I'm going to have to take Josef's invitation."

"Ser . . . after . . . ?" Strauxyn breaks off before he can say more, but the concern is written across his face.

"We broke the gates to enter, but once we entered, the merchanter himself has not opposed us. Besides, we don't know what has happened to the heir. I will take half a squad as personal support, and Undercaptain Norstaan should accompany us." *We just might need an Afritan officer as a witness.* "Have another squad ready to follow immediately, just in case."

"You're certain, ser? You don't want to have the Lancers go in first?"

"That wouldn't be wise," replies Lerial. "First, there's a chaos-mage somewhere. If he's hostile and attacks, without me there, that's sentencing the lead rankers to certain death. I'd prefer not to lose any more Lancers in Afrit than we already have. Second, it's not polite to honor an invitation with a Lancer squad preceding the invitee."

Strauxyn nods reluctantly. After a moment, so does Norstaan, if with a slightly puzzled expression.

"First Squad, then, sir?" asks Strauxyn.

Lerial nods.

"First Squad! First ten men! Dismount!"

Lerial waits until the rankers are in position with their sabres out before he dismounts. He does not draw his own sabre, that cupridium-plated, iron-cored weapon that has served him so well for so many years, but his hand rests on its hilt. Then, he walks toward the door, abruptly halting and stepping back as he senses the faintest hint of chaos somewhere ahead to his left.

After a moment, Lerial takes another step, then opens the door, stepping inside past another short line of columns, with Norstaan immediately behind him, and the Lancers behind Norstaan. Lerial holds his shields wide enough to protect them. No one approaches as he leads the way past the columns into the hexagonal entry hall, but he gains a feeling that the chaos-mage is close . . . perhaps even at the other side of the hall, a space a good fifteen yards across, floored with alternating tiles of shimmering white and lustrous golden brown. Lerial advances just far enough into the hall that Norstaan and the ten Lancers are fully clear of the columns and directly behind him before he halts and sends out the slimmest probe of pure order.

A flash of light flares, and when it fades, Jhosef stands on the other side of the entry hall. Beside him stands Mykel. "You see? Mykel is quite alive." He turns his head toward the heir. "Aren't you, Mykel?"

"Of course, I'm alive. Why would I not be?"

With Mykel's words, words that are somehow slightly stilted and flat, comes a sense of peace, of cool reassurance . . . and the thought that *we're all reasonable men . . . we can work this out . . . we all have the same goal in mind.*

Lerial almost finds himself agreeing, but catches himself. *The same kind of attack as before.* "Where is Oestyn?" he asks quickly, the first words that come to his mouth, as he uses his order-senses to try to locate the chaos mage. He can also sense that the Lancers behind him have been slowed somehow.

"Oestyn is fine," replies Mykel, his voice still just slightly flat.

Lerial can see that Mykel is not even looking at him, although the heir is facing him directly.

"Come here, Oestyn." Jhosef motions, and Oestyn walks out of the side hall stiffly, almost as though he does not wish to step forward.

Like a marionette. Manipulated somehow by the chaos-mage? As his eyes flick from Jhosef to Mykel and then to Oestyn, Lerial realizes that there is little emotion shown on the faces of the two younger men. Lerial extends a quick order probe, but Mykel and Oestyn are alive, if surrounded by a reddish silver order-chaos web . . . and something else within them, especially within Oestyn. *Something like that mage tried on me, as well as some sort of drug or potion . . . it has to be.*

Lerial finally says, "Now that I'm here, what exactly did you want to discuss?"

"I told you," replies Jhosef. "The future of Afrit. Who will be heir after Rhamuel's short time of ruling."

"It won't be short, and he can still have children."

"He's crippled. No one will believe that he can sire heirs. You know that. So does all of Afrit, and all of Hamor," Jhosef responds. "Mykel is the only one of the blood whom the merchanters will accept. If anything happens to Mykel, it will be your fault, and all Afrit will turn on you. They'll turn on Cigoerne as well. They'll raze everything in that poor excuse for a capital to the ground, and it all will be your fault. You don't want that on your head, especially not as a younger son."

Lerial cannot believe what he is hearing. *How can he believe that? How can he possibly think that? We've beaten back Merowey and destroyed Khesyn's ability to invade anywhere for a while . . . if not years.* "They'll turn on you. You're the one who kidnapped Mykel. Not me. Not the arms-commander. All I'm asking is for you to release Mykel, and let us take him back to Swartheld and his family."

"What family? A crippled brother, a useless niece, and the worthless sisters who consorted for golds and power?"

Keep him talking . . . until you can find a way to free Mykel . . . "They're still his family, Jhosef."

"They're all worthless. Just like Mykel, a half-grown half-man." Jhosef snorts theatrically. "Except he can learn, unlike the others."

Learn? Lerial wouldn't call it that. "Just because a man isn't suited to bear arms doesn't make him less." *What else can you say?*

"Just leave," replies Jhosef. "I'll keep Mykel safe until you come around. I'm not in the mood for debating."

"Perhaps we should leave," suggests Norstaan, his voice also just slightly flat. "It might be best."

Leave . . . and then what? After all this madness? All this death? Lerial isn't sure that saying anything will work, but withdrawing . . . ?

It would be for the best . . . The cool but reassuring words creep into Lerial's skull.

Lerial knows he has to act, and quickly, or he will stand totally alone in the hall, if indeed he does not already, and he is already having trouble fighting the insidious suggestions from the chaos-mage. He forces the thinnest order-pulse from the immobile Oestyn away from the columns behind Jhosef, Mykel, and Oestyn and toward the far left side of the entry hall, toward . . . something. The probe is stopped by a shield of some sort.

Order and chaos meet, and another flash of light occurs. When it subsides, Lerial sees a slender blond man, attired in brilliant white, except for the scarlet sash and the black leather of his boots. The chaos-mage stands to Lerial's left, almost as far from Lerial as from Jhosef.

"You have not met Maastrik, I believe," declares Jhosef.

"Only in my thoughts," replies Lerial, studying the mage and sensing the strength of the blond wizard's shields, strong enough that Lerial does not have the ability to penetrate them without using order-chaos separation. *And any order-chaos separation strong enough to crush him would pulverize most of the villa and everyone around you.*

The white-clad mage smiles faintly, and inclines his head, as if signifying that he knows what Lerial has just determined.

"Your lack of understanding represents the greatest threat ever posed to Afrit," Jhosef says, breaking the momentary silence. "Anyone who sees the wider picture would conclude the same."

You . . . as the greatest threat? Abruptly, he understands. "To Afrit, or to the most powerful merchanters who in turn control the chaos-mages who influence all that happens in Afrit?"

"Does it matter? Gold controls everything, and we control the gold."

"No," replies Lerial, realizing that, in one sense, it does not matter, although his realization, he suspects, is based on a somewhat different line of reasoning.

"You cannot destroy Maastrik, he has told me, without destroying all those around you. You cannot afford to do that . . . no matter how much you wish to destroy Maastrik . . . or me. You do not wish to destroy Lord Mykel. Nor do I wish that, either. Therefore, the best thing for both of us, and especially those you wish to protect, is for you and your men to depart." Jhosef smiles warmly.

Lerial blocks the overwhelming feeling of warmth and friendliness that surrounds him and smiles in return . . . coldly. "I think you have overlooked something. What if I don't wish to depart?"

"Then we will remain here until Maastrik wears you down, and he will, and then you will depart, in one fashion or another. Or, possibly, you will attempt a foolish attack, and you and your men will watch Mykel perish, and I will rally the merchanters against Cigoerne and to restore Afrit to its former glory."

He's truly mad. With what he now understands, Lerial cannot allow either alternative. He also knows that he cannot hold out forever against the insistent voices projected by the chaos-mage. Even if he can, he cannot let Jhosef and such a deadly chaos-mage escape, and the longer the standoff continues the weaker his position becomes.

What can you do?

"Well?" asks Jhosef.

Lerial can think of only one thing. He can only hope that it will work. He immediately creates three almost minute order-chaos separations in the stone under the white mage's right boot, knowing that the mage's shields will block the direct impact. He also knows that no one can do much of anything but fling out their hands when they feel themselves falling.

The explosion muffled by the mage's shields staggers him, and the white-clad man flails, while pulverized rock and dust flare up around him.

Lerial contracts his shields almost to his body, sprints forward, and attacks through the swirling dust, not with either order or chaos, but with the ancient iron-cored, cupridium-plated blade. While he runs into what feels like a wall, the ancient blade continues onward, slicing into the mage's shoulder.

The unvoiced scream dies, and ugly reddish silver mud-black splotches—not even close to the usual black-silver death mists—spray out from the near-instant ashes that are all that remain of the wizard. Even the shimmering white cloth turns gray and then ashen, before joining the pile of ash so fine that it will sift with any movement anywhere close.

"Kill them all!" screams Jhosef.

For a moment, Lerial does not understand to whom Jhosef is talking, not until a chaos-bolt slams against his shields. He turns toward Jhosef, only to see Mykel half-wreathed in flame from a second chaos-bolt, far weaker than the first. Lerial's eyes turn to the other side of the entry hall, where another mage in white stands, a dark-haired man most likely younger than Lerial.

Lerial immediately attempts an order-pulse against the younger mage's shields, if only to distract him. That pulse, likely aided by some chaos depletion, does just that, and the mage flings another chaos-bolt at Lerial, one that he returns to the attacker with enough force that the younger mage staggers, his shields disintegrating, then turns and runs, heading toward the corridor behind the columns.

Unwilling to let the mage escape, although he is more properly a white wizard, and unable to project significant chaos that distance, Lerial separates the smallest possible section of the fleeing man's belt into order and chaos, because that is all he can do at that moment. A chunk of the man's back explodes. The white wizard pitches forward onto the polished white and brown tiles, his body slowly turning to ash as the chaos consumes it.

Lerial immediately turns to face Jhosef, only to see Oestyn and his father in an embrace—except it is more deadly. Jhosef's arms flail as Oestyn steps back and wrenches the knife from his father's body.

"You . . . you . . ." Jhosef cannot seem to speak more as his hands clutch at his abdomen. Lerial can only see blood everywhere across Jhosef's chest and abdomen, and it is clear enough that Oestyn has struck more than once. Abruptly, Jhosef sags, and then collapses like a marionette whose strings have been cut.

Oestyn turns, the bloody knife in his hand. "I tried so hard . . . I did . . ." Tears are streaming down his face. "It was never . . . never enough. Never . . ." He looks down at Mykel's half-charred form, then lifts the knife again. "I'm . . . sorry, Mykel . . . sorry . . . so sorry." Then the knife clatters on the floor tiles.

Lerial is frozen for a moment before he lunges toward Oestyn, but by the time he crosses the almost ten yards that separate them, even his efforts to use order to stanch the blood from Oestyn's neck are too little and too late . . . and the quick shower of black and silver tells Lerial that Oestyn is dead. Lerial sees that, as Oestyn collapsed, he had reached out and clutched Mykel's hand with both of his.

Lerial slowly straightens, ignoring the blood on his hands . . . *and in those places from where you can never wash it away,*

Belatedly, his shields in place, Lerial immediately searches for yet another concentration of chaos. *If there were two, could there be another?* He can find no sign of another chaos-mage, and he glances toward Norstaan, who looks stunned, if not more than stunned.

The undercaptain shakes his head and asks, "What happened?"

"Didn't you see?"

"You were talking to someone . . . and then there was something like a small chaos-bolt, and you got to him with your blade, and he turned to ashes.

But then someone hit Mykel with chaos . . . I saw everything after that—Oestyn, Jhosef . . . and the heir." Norstaan shivers.

The fact that the dead and vanished wizard had managed to cloud the minds of Norstaan and likely the rankers from First Squad is another chilling reminder to Lerial of just how complex the situation in Afrit was . . . and likely still is. "There were two chaos-mages. I never sensed the second one because the first was so strong he overshadowed the other. The second one was likely his assistant."

"Jhosef . . . he wanted to use Mykel . . . didn't he?"

"Like a puppet, a marionette," Lerial confirmed.

"Who would ever have thought . . . a produce merchanter . . . a frigging produce merchanter . . ."

Strauxyn and several Afritan Guards hurry into the vast entry hall, where the fine particles of dust and ash are slowly settling.

"Ser?" asks the undercaptain, his eyes widening as he takes in the three bodies sprawled on the white and brown tiles and the few metal items and coins scattered amid the ashes that are all that remains of the two chaos-mages.

"Jhosef's chaos-mage attacked. I stopped him, and when I did, his control over Oestyn and Mykel vanished. The moment Jhosef thought we'd be able to rescue Mykel, he ordered the other chaos-mage to kill everyone. We didn't know there was a second mage. He started with Mykel, then me. I stopped him, too, but while I was doing that, Oestyn must have grabbed his father's belt knife, and he stabbed his father so quickly and so deeply that no healer could have saved him, even if I'd wanted to. Then Oestyn slit his own throat." Lerial knows that the first part of his explanation is not true. *But what else could you have done? Or said?* Besides, in a way the chaos-mage had attacked, with his insidiously and false projections.

"Oestyn slit his own throat?"

"He did," Norstaan confirms. "He said he tried, that he was so sorry, and then he just . . . slashed his own neck. Overcaptain Lerial tried to stop the blood, but he couldn't."

After a long silence, Strauxyn clears his throat, once, and again, before he finally speaks. "Now what, ser?"

"We'll stay here this evening," replies Lerial. "I intend to make a thorough search and inventory of the entire estate. We also need to do what we can to prepare the heir's body for return to Swartheld." *As well as deal with a few other matters.* More than a few, Lerial fears.

LII

Two glasses later, Lerial surveys Jhosef's personal study, with a pair of lancers standing guard in the doorway behind him. A windowed door that overlooks the lake to the east is flanked on each side by two wide windows, beyond which is a roofed terrace graced by a circular table and chairs. The table is covered with a brown-bordered linen cloth, tied down as indicated by the fact that the cloth does not move or flutter in the light breeze. The study floor is composed of the same glistening white and brown tiles that appear everywhere throughout the villa, although most of the study tiles are covered by a rich light brown carpet that has a border design of intertwined golden chains. The draperies, tied back with golden ropes, are of velvet the same shade as the rich brown of the carpet.

The north wall of the study consists of a fireplace flanked by goldenwood bookcases that extend only as high as the top of the fireplace mantel, a flat shelf that holds two small busts of Jhosef, one at each end. The entire mantel structure appears to have been sculpted out of a pale tan marble. The fire area is concealed by a decorative bronze screen featuring an image of the villa itself as seen from the east side of the lake. Each bookcase has four large shelves, but only the second shelf from the top contains books. The top of each bookcase and the other three shelves contain an assortment of ornate boxes, each one different from any other, and of a variety of materials and sizes, and include small golden boxes, oblong silver boxes, and even one formed of interlocking triangles of lapis lazuli.

The wide pedestal goldenwood desk set out from the south wall of the study has an inlaid border on the top that matches the carpet design. Bronze lamps on each side of the desktop have mirrors on the outer side, slightly tilted forward, presumably to focus the reflected light on the center of the desk to allow easier reading after dark. The chair pulled back from the desk is upholstered in the same padded brown leather as the two armchairs that face the fireplace.

Something about the study . . . Then Lerial realizes that he stands in the first study he can recall that does not have what amounts to a conference or plaques table within it.

He walks to the desk, admiring the workmanship of the inlay pattern, reflecting on all that he has viewed over the past two glasses, ranging from an extensive subterranean wine cellar in one outbuilding, to the three cells of a dungeon beneath the barracks building, adjoining an armory still containing a considerable assortment of well-maintained weapons. Both the barracks and dungeon have been recently occupied. Surrounding the villa are the varied gardens, several of which can be entered from a handful of the more than a score of luxurious chambers in the south wing of the villa. There is even a small locked chamber that serves as repository for chests of golds and silvers. Finding the key had not been that difficult. It had been one of three concealed in Jhosef's wide leather belt.

Lerial, accompanied by Norstaan, had unlocked the strongbox chamber and viewed the three chests—one for golds, one for silvers, and one for coppers. He hadn't counted the coins, just estimated, and that estimate suggested that the three small chests contained an amount equal to more than five thousand golds.

Thinking over the locked storeroom and all the furnishings, garments, paintings, and other artwork, not to mention the villa and grounds, Lerial shakes his head at the wealth embodied in Jhosef's summer villa. *Perhaps worth more golds than the value of not only the palace but of every merchanter's dwelling and factorage in all Cigoerne . . . and he is not even the wealthiest factor in Afrit . . . and this is just a summer villa.*

At the knock on the study door, Lerial turns. "Yes?"

Two lancers stand there. Between them is a round-faced and balding man of perhaps thirty-five years.

"The seneschal fled, ser. We have the assistant to the seneschal."

"What's your name?" asks Lerial.

"Baniel, ser, honored Lord." The assistant seneschal's bow almost prostrates him, and as he rises his eyes do not quite meet Lerial's.

"Come in. We have a few matters to discuss, Baniel."

The assistant seneschal steps into the study, stopping several yards short of Lerial.

"Was any other member of Merchanter Jhosef's family here beside his son Oestyn?"

"No, ser."

"Why not?"

"They do not come here. I do not know why. Kourast might know, but he fled with the merchanter's personal guards."

"Where was the heir staying while he was here?"

"In one of the guest chambers . . ."

"Was that the one with the iron-braced outside shutters and the door that could be barred only from outside?"

"Yes, ser."

"How often is that chamber used?"

"I could not say, ser. It has not been used often in recent years, but how many times I could not say."

"Were women housed there?"

"I know that happened once. The other times, I do not know. I do not know of any men who stayed there besides the heir."

"Why not?"

"Kourast was in charge of the villa, ser. I was the assistant for the grounds."

Lerial can sense no chaos or evasion with that statement. In fact, he has sensed little of that, except a trace when Baniel talked about not knowing whether those housed in the only barred guest chamber were women.

"What were your duties?"

"I was over those who worked in all of the outbuildings except for the spirits building, the guardhouse, and the gate buildings. The gardens and the orchards, and the grounds themselves. I had nothing to do with the merchanter's grounds guards or personal guards. They reported to Oiden."

"Was Oiden the chaos-mage?"

"Yes, ser."

That doesn't surprise Lerial, either.

Lerial's questions last for another half glass before he asks, "Do you have any questions, Baniel?"

"Are you claiming the villa, honored Lord?" asks Baniel, his voice more obsequious than deferential.

"It's not mine to claim. What happens to the villa and those in it is up to Duke Rhamuel. Your task is to maintain it for whoever will take possession. If anything is missing or damaged, beyond what has already occurred, everyone will suffer, especially you. Is that clear?"

Baniel swallows, not so much at the words, Lerial suspects, but at the tone in which Lerial has delivered them. "Yes, ser."

"You may go. No one is to leave the grounds. That includes you. You are to relay my orders to the rest of the villa and grounds staff immediately."

"Yes, ser." Baniel's bow is deep and obsequious.

"And your bows would be better if you weren't so obviously excessively flattering," Lerial adds dryly.

Baniel stiffens, then swallows again before asking, "By your leave, Lord Lerial?"

"You may go."

Lerial watches as Baniel turns and leaves. He waits several moments, then follows, pausing beside the rankers. "Guard the study." After those words to the pair of lancers, Lerial wraps a concealment around himself and follows the assistant seneschal.

". . . wouldn't want to be the seneschal," murmurs one of the rankers.

Those words remind Lerial just how much more he is certain, the longer he is in Afrit, that he doesn't want to be anyone or anything in the duchy. *And yet every single day brings something that drags out your duty here.*

Some fifty yards down the corridor toward the entry hall, Baniel turns into a narrower side hall and then descends the steps to the cellar level. Lerial continues to follow the assistant seneschal into a narrow hallway to a larger chamber. There, several women and an older man wait.

"Gather everyone you can find," Baniel says in a voice that is firm but not overly loud.

Lerial eases against the wall beside the archway and waits almost a third of a glass as the servants' hall fills.

Finally, Baniel steps forward and speaks. "I met with Lord Lerial. He is the second heir to the duchy of Cigoerne. He is an overcaptain in the Mirror Lancers and a great mage as well. He is the one who defeated the Heldyans and destroyed Merchanter Jhosef and his wizards. You all know how powerful Wizard Maastrik was. Lord Lerial's orders are very simple. We are to remain and to carry on. No one is to leave the grounds. All of us will be punished if anything is damaged or missing."

Baniel may not have known everything about what went on in the villa, Lerial observes, but the man knows more about Lerial himself than Lerial or the lancers had told him, and that suggests, if indirectly, that Jhosef had indeed been deeply involved in the events surrounding the Heldyan invasion.

"What if the armsmen take things?" asks a woman, older from her voice.

"You have not seen the Lord Lerial. He is not that old, but iron would bend sooner than him. His men will touch nothing."

"There are Afritan Guards . . ."

"They have seen the overcaptain. They will likely touch nothing, either. If they remove anything, tell me. I will tell Lord Lerial."

"What will happen after he leaves?"

"Duke Rhamuel will decide."

"When a great Magi'i lord destroys Afritan merchanters . . ." says another voice, "everything we have known will change . . ."

Lerial certainly hopes so.

"We must leave the change to them," declares Baniel. "Do what you always do, and do it well, and we will survive."

Sometimes that is enough, reflects Lerial, *and sometimes it's not.*

Other questions follow, but those deal with who will handle what duties, since some servitors fled with Seneschal Kourast before Lerial's men sealed off the grounds. When it is clear that he will learn little more from listening and observing the servants with his order-senses, Lerial eases out of the lower chamber and makes his way back to the main level, where he drops the concealment.

By then, Strauxyn has gathered up those remaining merchanter guards who had not already been captured or fled. Although Lerial spends more than a glass questioning the five survivors, only one had accompanied the group that had attacked the Streamside and he cannot recall more than waiting outside the inn and then conveying the dead to the swamp and Mykel and Oestyn back to Jhosef's villa.

In the end, Lerial and his men take over one wing of the villa and he sleeps in a modest guest room, if uneasily.

LIII

Although Maesoryk's villa is not located on Lake Jhulyn, the lakes are not that far apart, and the ride north to Lake Leomyn takes slightly more than four glasses. With Lerial's forces is an additional wagon, containing Mykel's body, packed as much as possible in salt. Lerial leaves the arrangements for Jhosef and Oestyn to the villa staff, while all the guards who died at Jhosef's villa are buried in a mass grave on the grounds.

Just after the first glass of the afternoon Norstaan points along the shore of the lake. "You see the large buff-colored building? That's Merchanter Maesoryk's villa."

"Have you been there before?"

"Only once. I've never seen the inside. The arms-commander . . . the duke, I mean, said that it was impressive without being excessively lavish."

"Unlike Jhosef's villa, you mean."

"He didn't compare the two, ser." Norstaan smiles. "He might have had that in mind, though."

As Lerial rides up to the white-painted wrought-iron gates, he can see that Maesoryk's summer villa is markedly different from Jhosef's. The three-story buff stone building is set on a low rise less than fifty yards from the water, facing south, and it appears as if every other chamber facing the lake has its own railed and roofed balcony. The road leading to the gates is graveled, as it has been for the entire way since splitting from the main paved road that runs from Swartheld to Lake Jhulyn and then to Lake Reomer, although the narrow lane beyond the gates leading to the villa and outbuildings is paved. There are only three outbuildings, all comparatively modest, and the grounds are enclosed by a stone wall two yards high topped with another yard of the white iron grillework. The pier out into the lake is far shorter and narrower than the one at Jhosef's villa.

The greatest difference is that the two guards at the gates immediately open them, proclaiming, "Welcome to Sorykan, Lord Lerial."

That welcome in itself, with the quick recognition of Lerial, suggests

Maesoryk has anticipated their arrival . . . or at least the arrival of someone dispatched by Rhamuel. The fact that Maesoryk himself appears at the entry to the villa almost as soon as the Mirror Lancers rein up reinforces Lerial's suspicion, although he can sense no concentrations of order or chaos in or around the villa and its grounds, nor any sign of a shielded mage or wizard.

"Welcome! Welcome! I hadn't expected you, Lord Lerial, of all people, to ride to Lake Leomyn, but when I heard that you had paid a call on Jhosef, I thought you might chance this way." Maesoryk's voice is warm and cheerful, but reminds Lerial of the insinuating feel of Jhosef's mage. He also has more than a few doubts about Maesoryk's just "hearing" of a visit more than fifteen kays away.

"We ended up paying more than a call on Jhosef," Lerial says before dismounting and walking across the paving of the entry portico to meet the merchanter. He gestures for Norstaan to accompany him.

"Do come in and tell me all about it." Maesoryk radiates curiosity. "It must be a fascinating story."

"We might at that," Lerial agrees, silently checking his shields, "although the story is more sordid than fascinating, but then some people do in fact find the sordid more fascinating than honorable accomplishments."

"That is a fascinating observation as well." Maesoryk gestures, then turns. "We can sit on the terrace outside the study."

Lerial and Norstaan follow him through the square entry hall to a wide staircase and up that to the second level. The white walls are almost bare of decoration, except for two identical hangings, one on each side of the staircase,

"Are those your merchanting house crest?" asks Lerial.

"What else would they be? They're a reminder of what makes all this possible."

At the top of the staircase, the merchanter turns to his right, then takes the first door on the left, which leads into a comparatively modest study, one that is seven yards by five, with a small fireplace on the left wall, and a desk set against the wall on the right. Between the two is a plaques table with chairs for six people. Maesoryk eases around the table and out onto the roofed terrace, where four armchairs are set in an arc facing the balcony railing and the lake. The merchanter takes the chair on the end farthest from the door and gestures.

Lerial seats himself at the other end, and Norstaan sits beside Lerial.

"You were going to tell me about Jhosef and your call upon him?" prompts Maesoryk.

"We weren't exactly welcomed," Lerial begins, "and when we finally entered the grounds a company of armed guards attempted to stop us. When we reached the villa, Jhosef was waiting on a high terrace. When I suggested he might have had something to do with the death of Lord Mykel, he said that was the last thing on his mind, or words to that effect, and then he most pleasantly suggested that I join him in the villa to discuss the future of Afrit. He left the terrace, and we proceeded to the main entrance. Undercaptain Norstaan and I entered. In the main entry hall, we were met by Jhosef, Mykel, and Oestyn. Jhosef suggested that Duke Rhamuel's rule would be short and that the only one of his lineage that the merchanters of Afrit would accept as duke would be Mykel. I begged to differ, whereupon a chaos-mage who had concealed himself with wizardry attacked me. I defended myself, and managed to lay a blade on him. Since he was steeped in chaos, that was sufficient to kill him.

"When that happened, young Oestyn appeared from nowhere and stabbed his father in the back. Jhosef ordered a second wizard to kill all of us as he struggled with Oestyn. The young wizard used chaos on Mykel and attempted that on me. He was unsuccessful, but by the time I had dealt with him, Oestyn had killed his father and then slit his own throat."

"I suppose you were the only one to see this?"

"Hardly. Undercaptain Norstaan did, and so did a number of armsmen and some servitors."

"Ah . . . so many witnesses that there is little doubt of what happened." Maesoryk frowns. "Do you know why Jhosef acted as he did?"

"I thought you might have some idea," replies Lerial. "He did say that the merchanters would never accept Rhamuel as duke."

" 'Never' is a dangerous word to bandy about."

"I've thought that as well. But . . . you didn't offer any thought as to why Jhosef did what he did."

"It's obvious that he was deluded enough to believe he could rule Afrit through Mykel. Only a produce merchanter could be that deluded," Maesoryk finishes dryly.

"Were Jhosef's mages acquainted with your mages?"

"I have no chaos-mages."

The fact that Maesoryk's statement comes across without chaos is only an indication that he has none at the moment. "I had heard that you did, and that you lost both of them in supporting Khesyn's invasion of Afrit . . ."

Maesoryk laughs, an open and honest sound. "I see you believe what everyone thinks. I've never had a chaos-mage in my life. I told everyone that I did so that no one would try to kill me . . ."

There is enough chaos around Maesoryk as he speaks that Lerial is fascinated, because it is clear that there is at least some truth behind the merchanter's words, but that chaos, combined with his earlier statement of not presently having chaos mages, is effectively a confirmation that he did in fact have such . . . before Lerial destroyed them. Lerial can almost—*almost*—admire the merchanter's bold-faced effrontery and clever prevarication.

"Do you really think I could live with two mages close by? For them to be useful, they would have to be closer than I'd ever want one . . ." Maesoryk shakes his head. "You said you killed both of Jhosef's mages? And that resulted in Jhosef's and Oestyn's deaths?"

"Since the mages attacked me, I didn't have much choice."

"Still . . . you seem to have allowed some possibly unnecessary deaths, Lord Lerial."

"Unnecessary? I think not. My duty is to do what is best for Cigoerne and for Afrit, and that means what is best for Duke Rhamuel, not merchanters who have committed treason for the sake of golds."

"What a quaint concept of duty. Golds are what support a land."

"Only when they are honestly obtained and used."

"In some cases, honestly is a matter of perspective." Maesoryk smiles. "Would you like a lager, Lord Lerial?"

"Not at the moment."

"You are indeed determined to remain on serious matters, then. Am I suspected of some nefarious deed? Some rancid and revolting plot?"

"Suspected?" rejoins Lerial. "I wouldn't say that." *Involved or implicated, rather.* "But I must say that I hadn't expected you to greet me so cheerfully. Especially after so many Heldyans were able to use the pier at your tileworks to land and begin their attack on Swartheld."

"I cannot be held responsible for where Duke Khesyn landed his armsmen in this reprehensible attack on Afrit. I have suffered great damage, and that tileworks may well be ruined for any future use."

At those words, Lerial realizes that, in all probability, Maesoryk lost little from the damage to the tileworks, but he presses on. "Certainly, if that use was contrary to your wishes, it would seem strange that you never let either the duke or arms-commander know that your tileworks had been occupied by the Heldyans."

"How could I let the duke know when I myself did not know until after the fact?" The merchanter shakes his head. "By the time I knew, the duke was dead, and the arms-commander injured and reported likely to die, and many of the senior officers were also dead."

Rather interesting, since those of us in the midst of the fighting didn't even know that until later.

"So what did you do then?"

"I dispatched a messenger to Subcommander Klassyn, thinking he was the most senior officer left. The messenger told me he gave it to Subcommander Dhresyl, because he was in charge."

"Dhresyl never received such a message."

"I'd venture to say that he did," returns Maesoryk. "He never did care for us, not after he tried to cheat us on tiles we supplied for the Harbor Post several years ago."

Surprisingly, that statement carries a heavy sense of order. *But then, that doesn't change anything, really.* "Do you have your family here often?" asks Lerial, sensing there is little point in continuing the charade.

Even Maesoryk seems disconcerted by the sudden change of topic, for he pauses a long moment before replying.

"Only when I'm here, if then. Not much these days. Nonsoryk is my youngest. He's in Nubyat, rebuilding a tileworks we recently bought. The oldest is Bhalmaes. He's in Luba at present. Well . . . a bit west of there on the new canal where he's just completed our new ceramic works. From there, it's easier to send goods downstream. We'll be able to boat goods to some of the Heldyan river towns as well—Vyada, Thoerne, and some others. We have an arrangement with Kenkram that allows use of the canal for an annual fee, rather than for a levy on each barge or boat . . ."

"No daughters?"

"Just one. Maera. She was recently consorted to Kenkram's eldest. We try to use family ties, you know." The merchanter laughs again.

Lerial studies Maesoryk carefully, noting again the heavy gold chain around the merchanter's neck. After a moment of consideration, he extends his order-senses and creates a variation on one of the patterns he has used in the past, a very small pattern linked to the chain that will slowly remove chaos, and only chaos, over the next glass or so . . . and possibly longer. "Do you believe in the power of order?"

"A man would be a fool to deny either order or chaos."

"That's true." Lerial stands and smiles. "I believe you've answered my questions to the best of your ability, Merchanter Maesoryk. We won't take any more of your time. We do have a long ride back to Swartheld, and Duke Rhamuel will wish to know about Merchanter Jhosef's treachery as soon as possible."

After a brief hesitation, Norstaan rises, unable to conceal a frown.

Maesoryk is more successful in concealing what he feels behind a pleasant smile. "I'm glad that I was able to address your questions."

"So am I," replies Lerial, smiling, if for a different reason. He can already sense what Maesoryk cannot yet feel. He looks to Norstaan. "We should be going." Then his eyes turn to Maesoryk. "We can find our way out." With those words, he leaves the merchanter before Maesoryk can protest.

Lerial says little except for the necessary commands as they leave Maesoryk's grounds and ride back along the lake road that leads toward Lake Jhulyn.

Finally, Norstaan looks at Lerial. "He was lying, you know. Every word was a lie. Why did you let him get away with it?"

"There's no proof . . . He's right. He had great damage to his tileworks. No one will realize that he was likely going to destroy or close the works anyway. Why else would he be opening a new works near Luba and another in Nubyat? Even so, there will be a cloud on his reputation, no matter what he says, and everyone will look askance at him for the rest of his life."

"But we all know that he was in as deep as Jhosef and Alaphyn. How could you let him get away with it, ser?"

Lerial looks at Norstaan. "He won't get away with anything. You'll see. Even Maesoryk won't be able to live with himself." That, of course, is absolutely true, but not in the way that Lerial is implying.

Norstaan offers a puzzled frown.

"Trust me. You'll see. The important thing, now, is to return to Swartheld as quickly as possible." Lerial isn't about to explain.

LIV

Lerial takes his forces back to Jhosef's villa, where they spend fourday night before setting out before dawn on fiveday morning on the return journey to Swartheld. As he rides through the gray before full light, Lerial considers what he has done with Maesoryk, wondering if he has acted too much like the scheming merchanters who have undermined Afrit. Yet, what else could he have done with Maesoryk? The man was a masterful prevaricator and deceiver, so masterful that there is not a decent shed of physical evidence against him. The other merchanters will not be able to complain about Lerial's handling of Jhosef, because Jhosef was killed by his own son while Lerial was under attack—*or thought to be,* he reminds himself—by two chaos-mages. Any physical attack on Maesoryk would only have made relations between Rhamuel and the merchanters even worse, as well as made matters more difficult for Lerial's father.

Self-justification? Lerial laughs silently. It is just that, but it's also absolutely true.

By midafternoon, they reach the Streamside, where Lerial calls for a rest stop while he seeks out the innkeeper and his consort. He does not have to search, because no sooner has he entered the inn than the stocky and graying Immar appears, his eyes moving from Lerial to the door behind him.

"Honored Overcaptain . . ."

"Please summon your consort. I am not here to make life harder for you, but to tell you what I have discovered. I will wait in the public room."

"Yes, ser."

Lerial does not wait long before the innkeeper returns to the public room with his consort, although both come from the kitchen entrance. He gestures to a square table in the middle of the room, then seats himself, waiting for them to do the same before speaking. "A wealthy merchanter was the one who sent the armsmen who kidnapped the heir and his friend. His acts led to his own death and that of the heir and his own son."

"The merchanter . . . Jhosef?" Immar's voice trembles.

"You don't have to worry about him. He is dead. So are the chaos-mages who helped him, and so are most of his armsmen." Lerial shifts his gaze to Jamara. "I cannot bring back your son. I told you that earlier, but I wanted you to know what had happened . . . and that the duke will know that all this evil was done against you as well as the heir." He pauses as he sees a young and clearly new serving girl approaching the table with a mug. Lerial does not refuse the lager that she sets on the table before him. He *is* thirsty. "How much?"

"For you, ser . . ." begins Immar.

Lerial shakes his head. "You have already lost too much. I cannot add to that loss." He takes three coppers from his personal wallet and sets them on the table, then looks at the girl. "Is that what he charges?"

The girl swallows. "Two, ser." Her voice trembles.

Lerial smiles gently. "Take the extra copper for your honesty. The two go in Immar's till."

"Yes, ser." She takes the coppers and retreats quickly.

Lerial turns back to Immar and Jamara. He senses that the lager holds no chaos and takes a small swallow, finding it better than he has expected. "This is a fair lager."

"We've good water," replies Jamara, almost proudly.

"I appreciate that." After a moment, he goes on. "The new duke is a fair and honest man, and I think you will find him so. I have, I know." He reaches for the provisions wallet and takes out five golds, setting them on the table. "One can never replace a child, nor a loved one. But all dukes pay death golds for those who have died in their service. These are the same, for you and your family provided services to the duke for years, and you should have some recognition of your loss beyond mere words." Lerial takes another swallow of the lager, hoping that he is doing the right thing, for he does not wish to insult them . . . and yet there should be some recognition. "One other thing . . . Do you have some paper and a pen and ink I could use?"

"Ah . . . yes, ser." Immar hurries away . . . not touching the golds that lie still on the table.

Lerial takes another swallow two of the lager while he waits for the innkeeper to return. When Immar does, he hands a single sheet to Lerial, and sets the pen and inkpot on the table, well away from the golds.

The paper is thick, but smooth enough for what Lerial has in mind as he begins to write. When he finishes, he reads over the words, set out in as precise a script as he can manage, good, if not quite as elegant as the hand of a true scrivener.

To All Men of Afrit—

Be it known from this day forth, the fourth fiveday of spring, in the year of the death of Duke Atroyan, that Immar the innkeeper has rendered service to Rhamuel, Duke of Afrit, and that he is held in regard by the Duke for that service.

Set forth in the Duke's name.

Lerial,
Emissary of the Duke
Overcaptain

Lerial lays the sheet on the table for the ink to dry, turned and positioned so that the two can see it. "This might help with others who question you. If you like, I can read what I wrote."

Immar shakes his head. "I know my letters, unlike some."

Jamara's eyes are bright as she looks to Lerial.

He eases back the chair and stands. "I need to press on and report to the duke. I likely will not see you again. I can only wish you well."

He turns and leaves the public room, hoping that the less than formal proclamation will reduce the innkeeper's concerns.

Once they leave the inn, by pressing on late on fiveday and beginning before dawn on sixday, they reach Swartheld just before seventh glass on sixday night.

As Lerial rides silently beside Norstaan through the twilit streets of the city, he continues to ponder those concerns that he has thought about over and over on the ride back from the lakes, realizing again that he cannot reveal much of what he has learned to almost anyone, possibly not everything even to Rhamuel, and certainly not to Haesychya or Kyedra. He doesn't mind limiting what he says to Atroyan's widow, but keeping things from Kyedra bothers him, even though he knows that is a foolish feeling, given that he remains the younger brother—the wrong brother.

While he had suspected that the merchanters of the council were far more powerful and influential than merchanters in Cigoerne, until the Heldyan attacks he had not realized that they controlled not only the trade and golds of Afrit, but the majority of the powerful mages.

The Magi'i of Cyador had been different . . . but why? Because they had been forced into a useful and required role? Because they had responsibilities along with power . . . or because the Mirror Lancers often also had officers with order-chaos abilities and equal power in some fashion? Or had there been some other reason? What his experiences in Afrit—and even what he had seen with Veraan, Myrapol House, and Majer Phortyn—have shown him is that, without structure and checks and balances, mages and wizards are far more likely to end up controlled by merchanters and their golds. The result, if Afrit is any example, is societal and personal loss and chaos for everyone beside the merchanters, with the majority, if not all, of the gain going to the most powerful merchanters.

The problem with his realization is that he doesn't see a solution. While he could in fact return to Cigoerne and then lead the Mirror Lancers into Afrit and defeat what remains of the Afritan Guard, that would solve nothing, because, unless Lerial also destroyed all the merchanting houses in Afrit and took their golds, within a few years those same merchanters, or their successors, would effectively own not only everything in Afrit, but everything in Cigoerne as well. And if the merchanting houses were destroyed, then in a few years, both lands, not just Afrit, would again be easy prey for Khesyn and/or Casseon. *Unless the entire way in which merchanting is conducted in Afrit is changed, and you don't have the knowledge or enough trained merchanters who aren't Afritan to do that.*

Lerial shudders at what Veraan and Myrapol House would do in such circumstances. *They'd be worse than Jhosef.* The problem is that Afrit has too much more wealth and too many more people, and Cigoerne too few, although, in time, Lerial knows that will change. *All you can do is buy that time . . . somehow.* Except he has no real idea of how to do that, only the understanding that it is necessary.

According to Kyedra, Atroyan already understood the situation with the merchanters in Afrit, and Rhamuel certainly does . . . and has gone out of his way to cultivate powerful allies among the merchanters. *Could the brothers' concerns about merchanter power have been another factor in creating the alliance of Jhosef, Alaphyn, and Maesoryk with Khesyn?* Lerial would be willing to wager on it . . . and give odds as well, but there's no way to prove that, except indirectly.

Much as he turns matters over in his mind, he has no workable solutions when he and Norstaan lead their men through the gates of the Afritan Guard headquarters around eighth glass that night. Almost another glass passes before the lancers and guards, and their mounts, are settled and Lerial, Strauxyn, and Norstaan sit down in one of the small conference rooms with Kusyl and Dhoraat. Lerial begins with a summary of what happened, and then asks the two who had remained in Swartheld, "Do you have any questions?"

"Begging your pardon, ser," begins Kusyl, "but there wasn't anything you could do about that bastard Maesoryk?"

"What we know about Maesoryk and what I, or anyone else, could prove are two different things. I may be carrying out Duke Rhamuel's wishes, but to attack or use arms against Merchanter Maesoryk, when he was open and welcoming, would have been most unwise, and would have destroyed much of what we have accomplished here." Lerial would like to have emphasized just slightly the words "use arms against," but that, too, would have been unwise, because Norstaan is bound by loyalty and oath to report everything to Rhamuel, and Lerial would not have it any other way.

"And he'll get away with it?"

"Not necessarily," replies Lerial. "He still has to live with himself. Sometimes, that's far harder than it appears. He also will have to live with the knowledge that the duke will not trust him at all, and there are likely options open to the duke that are not open to us."

Kusyl frowns, then abruptly nods. Dhoraat looks puzzled, and that is fine with Lerial, at least until the newly appointed senior squad leader has more experience in his current rank and responsibilities.

"What about what has happened here?" asks Lerial. "What should I know?"

"It's mostly back to the way it was when we arrived," says Kusyl. "We've been sending out squads and looking over everything, like you ordered, sort of city patrols. No one pays us much attention. There are more ships in the harbor now. They've got the Heldyan prisoners working on rebuilding the Harbor Post. We haven't sent anyone to the palace, but the word is that the duke has started rebuilding the damaged part of the palace."

"Any dispatches from Cigoerne? Or from the duke or anyone in the Afritan Guard?"

"No, ser."

"How are the wounded coming?"

"Everyone left looks to recover." Kusyl stops and looks at Lerial directly.

"You're wondering when we'll be able to leave for Cigoerne." Lerial shrugs. "I'll meet with the duke tomorrow and see what we can work out." He's not about to promise anything, especially before talking to Rhamuel, not with more than a few matters unresolved, such as the entire question of what to do with the merchanters so that the same situation doesn't reoccur in a few years, with even worse results. "If there's nothing else . . . that's all for now."

The yawn that Lerial stifles after his last words reminds him of just how tired he really is. He stands and manages to smile. As he walks back toward his quarters, the belated realization strikes him that he has never sent another dispatch to Cigoerne.

Another thing to do tomorrow.

LV

As tired as he is on sixday night, Lerial still has trouble falling asleep, and what sleep he does get is filled with disturbing dreams, most of which he does not recall. The one fragment of a dream he does remember when he wakes at dawn on sevenday is one where Kyedra is telling him that she must either consort his brother Lephi or the son of Merchanter Maesoryk. Lerial does not recall whether the Kyedra of his dreams explained why, but recalling what that explanation might have been is unnecessary. Lerial understands all too well that her mother and grandfather or Rhamuel, if not all three, will choose her consort for either his power or his wealth.

Lerial hurries to the mess to grab something to eat and finds Norstaan there, as if waiting for him.

"Good morning, ser."

"Good morning."

"If you wouldn't mind, ser, I'd prefer to accompany you to the palace this morning so that we could both report to the duke at once."

"I wouldn't mind at all. That way he won't have to listen to two reports, and we're likely to present a fuller picture together." Lerial appreciates Norstaan's deference, since the undercaptain could easily, and justifiably, have reported directly to Rhamuel. Then too, he suspects Norstaan might not want to be the one reporting Mykel's death and the apparent lack of action in dealing with Maesoryk. Either way, a joint appearance and report will be better for all concerned.

"We should eat, though. I'll need to spend a moment with my captains after breakfast, and write a quick dispatch that I'll have to impose on you to have sent, I fear. All that, I hope, won't take long."

"However long it takes, ser."

After eating and then meeting briefly with Dhoraat, Strauxyn, and Kusyl, Lerial immediately writes a brief dispatch to his father, although it is formally addressed to "Kiedron, Duke of Cigoerne." The dispatch is effectively a summary of what has happened with a conclusion stating that he will be remaining in Swartheld for at least several more days to assure that a few more matters are completed. He does not specify what those are.

With Norstaan's assurances that the dispatch will wend its way southward to Cigoerne, since Lerial does not wish to send a full squad, which is what would be necessary, to convey it with Mirror Lancers, Lerial sets off for the palace with Norstaan and his squad, and Kusyl and his first squad from Twenty-third Company escorting the wagon that contains Mykel's body. They enter the palace gates at a third past seventh glass.

Norstaan makes arrangements for guards for the wagon. Lerial leaves Kusyl with his squad, having quietly suggested that the undercaptain find out what he can while waiting for Lerial.

Lerial and Norstaan are climbing the staircase to the second level when Lerial senses someone hurrying after them. He glances back to see Ascaar and waits for the commander. Norstaan eases back down several steps and waits as well.

"Do you have a moment before you meet with the duke?" asks Ascaar.

"Since he hasn't summoned me, I have as many moments as you need." Lerial grins. "What do you have in mind?"

"Just telling you a few things."

"Such as?"

"While you were gone finishing up what I imagine were unpleasant details, I interviewed as many surviving captains and majers as I could." Ascaar raises his eyebrows.

"And?" Lerial doesn't feel like guessing, not after having dealt with both Jhosef and Maesoryk.

"They all believe that Atroyan was an idiot to even think of attacking Cigoerne and that Rhamuel was a genius to ask for your assistance. They'll never say that. It's what they meant. There were phrases like 'I'd never want to face the overcaptain across a battlefield' . . . little things like that." Ascaar's tone is gently sardonic. "A few would follow you to the Rational Stars. I also heard that you executed an insubordinate majer on the spot."

"Not the most diplomatic thing to do. Subcommander Drusyn was less than pleased."

"And then you led his battalion to victory at South Point."

Lerial shakes his head. "That took the Mirror Lancers, his battalion, and Majer Aerlyt's battalion."

"You realize that there's not a single officer left in the Afritan Guard that would willingly attack Cigoerne at this point?"

"That might be an overstatement. In any case, what would be the point? Afrit is far more prosperous, and an attack on Cigoerne would gain little."

"Except new opportunities for merchanters." Ascaar's tone is dry.

Lerial understands exactly what Ascaar is conveying . . . and the fact that the older commander knows the dangers of saying it directly. "Some opportunities cost far more than the most powerful of merchanters understand. Why don't you join us? You should be there when I report to the duke." Lerial knows very well that is exactly what Ascaar wants, but Ascaar's presence will be more than just helpful. It may well be vital in keeping the Afritan merchanters in line, at least as much in line as the duke can do under the conditions with which he is faced.

When the three arrive at the anteroom outside the duke's receiving study, Commander Sammyl looks up from a side desk, then stands with an ironic smile. "I'll tell the duke that you're all here."

In moments, the four are in the duke's receiving study, with Lerial seated in the middle chair facing the desk, flanked by Ascaar and Sammyl, and Norstaan standing to the side.

"I didn't expect you back quite so soon." Rhamuel's voice is quiet.

"I thought you would like to know what happened to your brother . . ."

"He's dead, then? How did it happen?"

Lerial explains, going through events beginning with what he learned from the innkeeper and then all that happened at Jhosef's villa—except for some of the details surrounding how Lerial dealt with the chaos mages. When he finishes, he waits, uneasily, for Rhamuel's reaction.

For a long moment, the duke says nothing. Finally, he speaks. "There wasn't any chance for anyone to do anything?"

"We were more than ten yards away when the first chaos-mage attacked . . . and I was still ten yards away after dealing with the first chaos-mage. Oestyn couldn't act to save Mykel until it was too late, and then he killed himself before we could get closer. One moment Jhosef was talking about how Mykel would be duke, the next about how I should leave, and the moment I said I wasn't about to just depart on his whim, the first chaos-mage attacked me. After that . . ." Lerial spreads his hands in a gesture of helplessness.

"I find one thing . . . strange. Why would Oestyn allow Mykel to be captured . . . but then kill his father?"

"From what I've learned," Lerial replies, "Jhosef changed the merchanter guards accompanying Oestyn, and the wine both Oestyn and Mykel drank at the Streamside had to have been drugged. After that . . . I'm guessing, but based on what Jhosef said and what Oestyn said before he slit his throat, Oestyn didn't know what his father had in mind and tried to protect Mykel."

"That makes a sad kind of sense," Rhamuel says. "I might let it be known that Oestyn was killed trying to protect Mykel."

Sammyl looks surprised and about to object.

"That way, I won't have to seize Jhosef's holdings. Regardless of what he did, that wouldn't be the wisest course. Also, enough people saw what happened that we might as well put the best face on it. If what Oestyn did gets out, and it will, and I seize Jhosef's holdings, people will claim that I ignored Oestyn's efforts for my own personal gain. After what's already happened, we don't need more problems. Shortly, the Merchanting Council will affirm Jhosef's eldest as his heir, and we'll meet. I'll suggest that Jhosef's eldest son cannot afford to allow any suspicion of trying to follow his father's efforts. I'm certain he won't."

"Not any time soon," adds Ascaar.

"That should suffice." After a pause, Rhamuel goes on in a smooth tone, almost devoid of expression. "It's too bad you couldn't do anything about Maesoryk, but, without proof, that made it difficult."

"I don't think Maesoryk is in the best of health," Lerial offers blandly.

"You didn't offer your services as a healer?" Sammyl frowns.

"He didn't ask, and I didn't volunteer. Given that he was likely a conspirator with Jhosef and Alaphyn, and likely others we may never know, I didn't feel I had to go out of my way for him."

"How ill is he?"

"It's a wasting illness. Those are hard to predict." Lerial shrugs. "He might already be dead, or he might live for a few more seasons . . . or even longer." The last is a flat lie, but Lerial is not about to predict Maesoryk's death, because, in his absence, something might have gone wrong with his order manipulation. By claiming the merchanter does have a wasting illness, if his first effort has not worked, Lerial does not destroy his own credibility.

"You don't think so, do you?"

"I think it unlikely, but stranger things have happened."

"Indeed." Rhamuel nods. "We now need to plan for Mykel's memorial and contact the Merchanting Council." He looks to Lerial. "I trust you will remain for the memorial? After that, we can discuss your departure from Swartheld. I realize I am imposing somewhat, but you and your men have traveled hard and fast, and a day or two would rest them and their mounts."

"Of course." What else can Lerial say?

"I would also request that while the commanders and I discuss the details of the memorial you inform Lady Haesychya and Merchanter Aenslem of what happened at the lakes. They would be more inclined to hear it from you than from me, particularly since the lady has no interest in visiting the palace any time soon."

"I would be pleased to undertake that duty." Lerial rises.

"Thank you."

After making his way back down to the stables, Lerial has to wait for a time before Kusyl returns. Then the two mount up and lead the squad out of the palace onto the ring road and then onto the avenue that leads to the merchanters' hill.

"Did you find out anything?" asks Lerial.

"Not much. The duke has replaced a number of retainers in the palace staff. He's ordered a special saddle that will hold his legs so that he can ride again. They've promoted some majers to subcommander."

"Any we know?"

"Aerlyt and Paelwyr. Oh . . . and they made Captain Grusart a majer."

For a moment, Lerial struggles to remember Grusart, then smiles. "Good. Anything else?"

"One of the masons rebuilding the palace found a leather bag with a hundred golds in it."

"And he didn't keep it?"

"He said that if he showed up with so much as one gold in his house, everyone would think he stole it. The duke gave him twenty silvers and a letter saying that he'd earned every one of them through his honesty."

"No one knows whose bag it was?"

"Word is that someone thought it looked like a wallet the old retainer wore at his belt, but no one knows for certain."

A hundred golds? Would that have been enough to buy Dafaal? Or was it cheap at the price as a way to shift blame? Lerial doubts that he or anyone else will ever know.

When they reach Aenslem's villa, the guards immediately open the gates, and shut them just as quickly. Then, at the door to the main entry, Lerial is greeted by a man a good fifteen years older than Lerial himself.

"Lord Lerial, I'm Cathylt. I'm Merchanter Aenslem's ship master. He has requested a few moments of your time. He awaits you in his study."

"Thank you. I take it you were here for other matters?"

"I'm here every day, unless he is at the merchanting building."

"Ship master—the one who keeps track of what ships and cargoes are where?"

"As much as one can . . . yes."

Cathylt walks with Lerial only so far as Aenslem's study, then closes the door as Lerial steps inside.

Lerial lets his order-senses range over the merchanter as he walks toward Aenslem, who has risen to stand by his table desk, but he can detect no wound chaos or other overt injuries or illness. "You asked to see me."

"I did. I'd prefer not to be surprised. Since you seem to create surprises, I thought the best way to avoid that was simply to ask you what you're willing to tell me." Aenslem offers a pleasant smile, then motions to the leather armchairs before walking to the nearest and seating himself.

"You've placed me in a difficult position," Lerial says as he sits. "The duke requested that I inform Lady Haesychya of certain facts, but you are the head of the Merchanting Council, and this is your villa."

"That does present a problem. If you will answer a question or two, I will not press you."

"That depends on the questions, ser."

"Do you intend to take advantage of your abilities and the Mirror Lancers of Cigoerne to invade or dominate Afrit?"

"That thought had never crossed my mind. In the end, I fear, such an attempt now, or any time in the near future, would eventually result in disaster for Cigoerne."

Aenslem frowns. "Why do you say that?"

"The merchanters of Afrit have too many golds and too much experience in using them in ways to undermine simple lancers or even most Cigoernean factors and crafters." That is not all he has learned, but all that he needs to say.

Aenslem laughs, heartily. "Stars! You're wasted as an overcaptain. I suspected that from the beginning." With that, he picks up a small silver bell that rests on the desk and rings it gently.

Lerial can sense a door opening and turns to discover that an entire panel in the south wall of the study has swung out, revealing a space and a circular staircase to a lower level. Stepping into the study is the serving girl he has seen before, who closes the panel behind herself.

"Murara, would you tell my daughter and granddaughter that I'd like to see them here in the study?"

The serving girl who is far more than that, Lerial knows, not only from Kyedra's veiled references, but also from the look that passes between her and Aenslem, nods and departs. Lerial understands that what has just occurred is Aenslem's way of showing a degree of trust in Lerial.

What else does he want? Lerial isn't even ashamed of himself for thinking that, not after a season in Afrit.

A small fraction of a glass passes before the study door opens again and Haesychya and Kyedra enter. Kyedra closes the door more firmly than necessary, and Haesycha moves to the leather couch and sits down.

As Kyedra passes Lerial to also take a seat on the leather couch, she glances at Lerial, not at all happily, and he can sense a feeling almost of betrayal.

"That was my doing," says Aenslem, who has seen the look. "You can ask Cathylt. I left word that whenever Lord Lerial arrived, I was to see him first."

"You could have let us know," rejoins Haesychya coolly.

"I just have. It is my villa, as I recall."

"That's something that's never been in question." Haesychya's tone remains cool.

"We'll discuss that later, Daughter. I will assure you that he was sent to inform you of certain things, and that he has not told me one thing. In fact, the only thing he has said is that he has no intention of returning to Cigoerne in order to gather forces to invade Afrit."

"That's ridiculous," snaps Haesychya. "They couldn't do that."

"Unfortunately you're wrong, Daughter. As a result of the war with Heldya, we now have less than half the forces available to Duke Kiedron." Aenslem turns to Lerial. "Is that not so?"

"We could muster nine full battalions at present. Although there are officially about twelve battalions of Afritan Guards, most are at far less than full complement. Some are battalions in name only. Neither I nor my sire has any such intent, as I told your father. It would be a victory we would not survive."

"That's all you told him?"

"That's all."

"Now that we have settled that matter," Aenslem says gruffly, "I think we all would like to hear what Lerial has to report about his recent journey to the lakes."

Lerial looks straight at Haesychya. "Duke Rhamuel asked that I inform you first. If you wish me to do that without others present, I will do so."

Haesychya offers a faint and cool smile. "You actually would, wouldn't you?"

"Yes."

"There's little point in that. I'd have to tell father and Kyedra what you said, and repeating it might be doubly painful. Go ahead."

"The duke requested I travel to the lakes to see if I could discover what happened to his brother and whether certain merchanters might have been involved . . ." Lerial goes on to relate the story just as he had to Rhamuel, almost word for word.

When he finishes, for several moments, no one says anything. Then

Aenslem clears his throat. "There's no hard proof that Maesoryk did anything, but it's clear he was as guilty as Jhosef or Alaphyn. You couldn't do anything? Wasn't that why Rhamuel sent you to the lakes, rather than one of his Afritan Guard commanders?"

"He never said so, but it doubtless was. The problem is that, just as you know that, so does every merchanter in Afrit. If I'd done anything obvious to Maesoryk, all the merchanters remaining in Afrit would be wondering when Rhamuel might turn on them, because, frankly, not a single one of you is without guilt in doing something against the duke or his predecessor."

Haesychya nods, although she does not speak.

"You have an answer for everything," declares Aenslem. "But Maesoryk will feel he can do anything now."

"He's likely ill. He doesn't know it, but he is. We'll just have to see how matters progress."

"And you have no obligation to heal him. Is that it?" asks Aenslem.

"Do you think I do . . . after everything?" asks Lerial.

The merchanter shakes his head. "I just hope you're right."

"So do I." Although Lerial is fairly certain he is, he hopes that matters "progress" as he has planned.

Haesychya looks to her father for a moment, and something passes between the two before she turns. "I have a few matters to discuss with your grandfather, Kyedra. If you would not mind entertaining Lerial for a few moments before he leaves, we would appreciate that. If you can stay," she adds, looking to Lerial.

"I have some time before I need to return to Afritan Guard headquarters." He turns to Kyedra. "If it would not be an imposition."

"I believe I can manage," returns Kyedra dryly. "At least for a time."

Lerial manages not to wince, but he and Kyedra stand at the same time. Neither speaks as they leave Aenslem's study.

Once they enter the lady's study and Lerial closes the door, he turns to Kyedra. "I'm sorry. I didn't want to offend your grandfather."

"You didn't act that way before."

"No, I didn't, but I didn't go out of my way to upset him, and I felt refusing to see him first would be seen that way."

"Does it matter?"

"Yes. It does. Very much. I hope you know why. And I told the truth. I told him nothing but what he said I did."

"I believe you . . . but . . ."

"Why am I so deferential to him, after all this? Because he's your grandsire." *And he'll have a great say in whom you consort.* He may be hoping against hope, but he cannot help hoping. *You couldn't help that after the first time you saw her smile.*

Suddenly, she smiles. "You could have said that a long time ago."

"I didn't dare."

Her smile vanishes, so abruptly its disappearance is painful to Lerial. "Mother likes you. She won't say it. She won't tell me, either. But she does. I can tell." After another silence, she says, "You can't ask, can you?"

"Not now. You know why."

"Because your father is duke, and your brother will succeed him, and you cannot afford to risk the future of both lands."

"After all that has happened . . . no."

She reaches out and takes his hands. "I can be more forward than you. A little more forward." Then she smiles.

That alone warms him, and he just looks at her.

"Even if . . . even if . . . things . . . don't . . . aren't . . . I'll remember the way you're looking at me. Always."

"I've remembered your smile from the first . . ."

At that moment, there is a rap on the door.

Kyedra lets go of Lerial's hands. "Yes?"

The door opens, and Haesychya stands there. "I don't think we should delay Lerial any longer."

"I suppose not." Kyedra's voice is slightly flat.

"We can both accompany him to the entry hall," says Haesychya, not unkindly.

The three leave the study and walk several steps before Haesychya asks, "Do you know how much longer you will be in Swartheld?"

"Until after Lord Mykel's memorial, at least several more days. The duke has asked me to remain for now."

"Have you heard from Duke Kiedron?"

"Not in more than an eightday. I sent off a dispatch this morning, but it will likely be an eightday before he receives it, possibly longer."

"Might I ask . . . ?" ventures Haesychya.

"I only told him what happened so far as the Heldyans were concerned, and that a noted merchanter had been involved in the murder of Lord Mykel, and that such matters were likely to be resolved in the next eightday or so . . . and that I would not feel free to return until they were to the satisfaction of the duke . . . in the interests of renewed harmony between Afrit and Cigoerne." Lerial had not quite written the last, but had implied it.

"You're very cautious."

"I would prefer to think I'm careful, Lady. Any commitment I make is likely to have to last for a very long time."

"You are that sort," says Haesychya, "and that is good." She stops at the doors from the villa. "We trust it will not be that long before we see you again."

At those words, Kyedra smiles again. So does Lerial, if more cautiously. Then he inclines his head. "I look forward to that."

His smile is broader as he rides away from the villa beside Kusyl at the head of the Mirror Lancer squad.

LVI

Just before midday on an already hot and steamy eightday morning, Lerial is going over details of organizing the return ride to Cigoerne with Strauxyn, Kusyl, and Dhoraat, details that are necessary, but that feel unwelcome to him, when Norstaan rides into the courtyard of Afritan Guards headquarters with half a squad from Rhamuel's personal company.

Lerial hurries over to the undercaptain, wondering why he has come, since there would be no need for him to ride from the palace if Rhamuel wishes to meet with him. "It must be important if you're here."

Norstaan smiles. "I've just received word that the healer you requested is arriving at the river piers just east of South Post. I thought you might wish to join us in welcoming the healer."

Emerya? In Swartheld? Lerial finds it hard to believe. *Could she have sent someone else?* That would be even harder to believe. "I would. Very much." He turns and hurries back to the other three. "I need ten rankers from the duty squad to accompany me to escort a healer from Cigoerne to the palace. Oh . . . and a spare mount."

"Duty squad is my second," declares Kusyl. "Do you want Polidaar as well?"

"That would be good." Lerial realizes he will need the squad leader.

Less than a tenth of a glass later, Norstaan and Lerial are riding south on the shore road at the head of the two half squads.

"The duke doesn't know, does he?" asks Lerial, blotting his face with the back of his sleeve, wondering just how much hotter Swartheld will get, considering that it is barely past midspring.

"You requested that he not be told, and I've made as certain as I can that he does not."

"Thank you. Do you know what kind of rivercraft it is? Or whose?"

"No. We just got a message by fast courier that the healer's boat had passed the southern river piers and should make the piers west of South Point within the glass. They may have landed already, but they'll wait for an escort to the palace."

"I hope we won't make them wait too long," worries Lerial.

"It shouldn't be that long."

Even so, another third of a glass passes before they ride past South Post and turn onto the paved area that stretches from the base of one pier to the other. After a moment, Lerial spies a sail-galley tied up at the southern stone pier. It is half again as large as the one Lerial had taken to deal with Estheld, making it over fifteen yards from stem to stern, and has a small upper deck that extends some five yards forward from the stern. As he reins up at the base of the pier, Lerial can see several people standing on the pier beside the rivercraft.

Lerial dismounts quickly, followed by Norstaan. Leaving their mounts with the rankers, the two stride out the pier toward the sail-galley.

Lerial immediately recognizes the green head scarf of a Cigoernean healer and the pale green blouse and trousers, not to mention the darkness of order that still suffuses his aunt. She must sense him, because she turns from the man with whom she has been talking, possibly the master of the rivercraft, and steps toward hm.

Lerial's mouth almost drops open as he sees her, since her hair is no longer silver and red, but entirely red.

"Not a word, Lerial." She spoils the severity of her tone with a smile. "It's good to see that you're hale . . . and still relatively balanced. I worried about that after the tales that have traveled upriver."

Lerial's second surprise is the figure who steps forward to stand beside Emerya.

Fhastal smiles at Lerial. "I thought it might be best if I accompanied the most noted healer in Cigoerne to Swartheld."

"Just as your rivercraft have carried letters to and from her for years?"

"A mere convenience." Fhastal shrugs. "I gained far more from it than they have."

Lerial doesn't dispute that and nods. "I can see that, but I still appreciate it, and I have no doubts that they have as well. I hope you won't mind, but we do have a duty to get her to the palace—"

"Please, Nephew, do not speak of me as if I am not here." Again, her words are humorous—mostly.

Lerial turns and bows excessively deeply. "Honored Healer and Lady, we apologize for the lack of deference and for only being able to supply a mount rather than a carriage."

Emerya laughs. "I suppose I deserve that."

"So did I," Lerial replies.

"I do have two Lancer kit bags."

"We brought a mount, and not a wagon, but we can put one behind you and one behind me. We'll be heading directly to the palace."

"In a moment," Emerya says, drawing Lerial to one side of the pier, close enough that he can look down at the gentle waves lapping against the stone posts. "Before we go to the palace, I need to know just how bad his injury is."

"His back was crushed at the bottom of his backbone. His leg was broken. It is healing well. He isn't pissing himself, but he cannot move his legs. There was a huge chaos-knot around the lower part of his backbone. I managed to reduce that within a glass or two of the time they got him out of the rubble."

"That soon?"

"Sheer fortune," Lerial declares. "I mean that it was fortune that I arrived at the palace so soon."

"You didn't try to remove all the chaos?"

"No . . . that didn't feel right. I would have . . . it would have taken too much order . . . That was the way I felt."

Emerya nods. "You've always been more than a field healer. What's so unusual is that you still have the feel of both a healer and . . . well, not a chaos-mage, but more like a gray mage."

"Gray mage? I didn't know there were such."

"The Emperor Lorn was probably one. They're rare. Most mages can't continually balance order and chaos. We can talk about that later." She looks directly at Lerial. "Do you expect me to heal him?"

"No. I expect you to do what you can. You know more than I do, and Afrit needs him to rule for years to come, not just a few seasons or a year or two."

"You're suggesting I remain in Swartheld?"

"That isn't my decision. It's yours."

"Not your father's?"

"No. You've given Father more than enough. Mother could take your place at the Hall of Healing, and in time I wouldn't be surprised if Ryalah could . . . or Amaira, if that is your and her choice."

"I left her in Cigoerne . . . obviously."

"That makes sense." *For now.* "He took the miniature and kept it close."

"I know, although his words were veiled. He wrote almost immediately."

Lerial debates whether to tell her what Kyedra has told him, but decides against doing so immediately. Matters might not go as he hopes they will, and if they don't . . . "I'm glad."

While they have been speaking, two of the galley crew have carried two completely full and overstuffed Mirror Lancer kit bags onto the pier. They stand beside them, clearly waiting to carry them to the horses.

"I need to introduce you to Undercaptain Norstaan . . ."

"I heard much about him." Emerya turns.

"Norstaan, this is the healer Emerya. She is head of the Hall of Healing in Cigoerne. She is also my aunt and the one who taught me what healing I know."

Norstaan bows. "Lady Healer."

"Undercaptain, I've heard nothing but good of you."

"Then, Lady, I fear you have not heard everything." Norstaan smiles. "I do believe we should not tarry."

"Then we will not," declares Emerya.

Once the kit bags are tied in place, and they have set off northward on the shore road, Lerial draws his mount closer to his aunt's.

"I do have one confession. I didn't tell the duke I'd asked for you to come."

"I had that feeling. Do you mind telling me why?"

"I didn't know if you would . . . or could, and I didn't want to give him false hopes."

"In more ways than one?"

"That, too."

"We'll just have to see how it goes, then."

Lerial can sense the worry . . . and something more. Yet what else could he have done?

After a time, Emerya says, "I'd forgotten just how large Swartheld is."

"From what I've figured, it stretches more than fifteen kays north and south, and almost five kays, east to west, more in some places. It turned out to be a very good idea to come to Swartheld."

"Besides your successes with the Heldyans?"

"Fhastal told you?"

"I already knew what happened at Luba. He told me that you broke the back of the attackers and the Afritan Guard finished them off . . . and that you did something to destroy the next invasion force."

"I turned Estheld into an inferno when they were loading out for the attack."

"You don't show that much chaos."

"I'm glad."

Emerya nods and says in a low voice, "Later."

It takes two-thirds of a glass to reach the ring road around the palace. As they ride past the gates and the east side of the palace, Lerial can see a number of Afritan Guards working on the wooden framework on the stone platform that will be the base of Mykel's pyre.

"Who died?" murmurs Emerya.

"Lord Mykel," replies Lerial. "He was killed as part of an attempt to replace the duke. He wasn't part of it, but captured by those behind the plot and killed when they realized they had failed."

Emerya adjusts her head scarf and glances up at the southeast corner of the palace, where the masons continue to work at rebuilding the outer wall.

"The plotters also used cammabark to create the explosion that killed Duke Atroyan and his son and injured Duke Rhamuel."

"You do end up in difficult situations, Lerial." Emerya's voice contains sardonic humor. "Or you create them. Your father says it's hard to tell which."

"Majer Altyrn seemed to know." Lerial regrets those words as soon as he speaks them.

"That's why your father sent you to Teilyn. He does understand his own limits, Lerial."

"I'm sorry."

"That's all right. For all the great things you've done, there is still always something to be learned."

Lerial chuckles almost silently. Emerya has always been good at reminding him of such.

Although the Afritan Guards at the stable are clearly puzzled, they say nothing when Lerial and the others rein up, and he tells Polidaar to leave Emerya's kit bags in place for the time being. Then Norstaan and Lerial accompany Emerya across the courtyard and into the palace. While Emerya could let her head scarf drop to her shoulders once she enters the palace, she leaves it in place, even adjusting it to reveal less of her face.

They are still on the main level when a serving woman or maid rushes out of a side corridor and toward them, then bows so deeply to Emerya that Lerial fears she will prostrate herself, before the woman backs away. An older man, a servitor of some sort, behaves the same way after they reach the top of the main staircase and turn toward the duke's receiving study.

"Perhaps I should come to Swartheld more often," murmurs Emerya to Lerial just before they reach the door to the anteroom.

"Perhaps you should." Lerial nods to the guard and opens the door, gesturing for Emerya to enter.

In turn, Norstaan nods for Lerial to follow his aunt, then joins them and closes the door.

Sammyl, alone in the anteroom, looks up from the papers he has on the desk in front of him, then quickly stands. "Ah . . . the duke wasn't expecting you, Lord Lerial."

Lerial can sense that Rhamuel is alone in his study, but he still asks, "Is he in?" His question is not an inquiry.

"I'll tell him . . ."

"No . . . this time, we'll just go in."

Lerial raps and then opens the door without waiting for a response.

Rhamuel, who has been looking out the window into the hazy summer-like sky, jerks his head back toward the door in annoyance. "I said—" His mouth opens as Emerya lets the head scarf slip off her hair and away from her face.

"I heard you might need a healer," Emerya says as softly as Lerial has ever heard her speak.

"I . . . never . . . how . . ." Rhamuel looks at Lerial.

"I asked for the best," Lerial manages to reply almost blandly, although he feels anything but bland, after hearing Emerya's voice and seeing the expression on the duke's face.

"Lerial . . . you are a devious bastard." Rhamuel tries not to smile, although he cannot control the dampness from his eyes. "Why didn't you—"

"I could only ask, and she came faster than a reply would have." Lerial wants to smile in relief—and joy—because he has seen the looks between the two. "Now that I have delivered the best healer in Hamor, I'm going to leave the two of you and wait outside while she determines the state of your health and injuries." He manages not to grin as he steps back, opens the study door, and then leaves, making certain that the door is closed firmly behind him.

Sammyl's face remains almost frozen in puzzlement, while Norstaan is doing his best to hide a wide grin.

"The healer I escorted in to see the duke is the best in Hamor, most likely one of the best in the world. She is also my aunt, and the one who healed him after his ill-advised attack on Cigoerne a number of years ago. I did not know if she would travel to Swartheld when I sent the message asking if Duke Kiedron would allow her to come . . . or if she would choose to. That is why I said nothing, and why I did not even tell the duke."

"She's . . . the one . . . ?" stammers the commander.

The only one, from what you just saw. "Yes."

After a long moment, Lerial says, "While we're waiting, why don't you fill me in on the arrangements for Lord Mykel's memorial?"

More than a glass passes before Emerya opens the study door. "He'd like to see all of you." Then she looks at Lerial, who lets the other officers enter the study while he waits beside her.

"I'll wait out here. It's better that way."

Lerial understands . . . and nods. He enters the study and closes the door, letting his order-senses range over the duke. While he can sense traces of order here and there that had not been present before, he cannot discern any major changes in Rhamuel.

The duke waits until the three senior officers are seated before clearing his throat. "The Lady Healer Emerya has consented to remain here in Swartheld for at least a time as my personal healer. She will also be working to establish a hall of healing somewhere not too far but not too close to the palace. That's something we've lacked for too long. For now, she will have quarters in the palace suitable to her station."

Sammyl frowns, if slightly.

"She is, or was, the high healer in Cigoerne, and she is Duke Kiedron's sister."

Sammyl cannot conceal the surprise on his face. "No one . . . said . . ."

"That's absolutely correct, Commander," Lerial says smoothly. "It was an unfortunate oversight on my part not to inform you and Commander Ascaar, but I was glad to see my aunt, and the duke did not realize I had not informed you."

"What will people say?"

"No one would say a thing if I consorted her," Rhamuel points out. "Dukes often consort the close relatives of other dukes, and after all the aid that Cigoerne has provided . . ." He smiles. "In fact, maybe I should consort her . . . after a proper time of mourning, of course, for my brothers and nephew. In the meantime, why would anyone care so long as matters appear to remain proper?"

"But . . ." Sammyl appears ready to protest.

"Do you think that most of the people of Afrit really care?" asks Ascaar. "All they want from the duke is to keep tariffs low and to be left alone."

Lerial manages to keep from grinning, given that he'd been thinking along the same lines. "The only people who might care are merchanters with eligible daughters that won't get to consort the duke. But how could they complain, at least in public, if the duke consorts the sister of another duke." Before anyone can say more, Lerial adds, "Admittedly, I'm biased, because she is my aunt, but that's balanced by the fact that I do like her, and if she's in Swartheld and I'm in Cigoerne, I won't get to see her."

"What about heirs?" demands Sammyl.

"What about them?" retorts Rhamuel. "I've only been duke a few eightdays, and brothers of a duke aren't allowed to consort and have heirs unless they succeed. Besides, I haven't consorted her. I haven't even asked her. So talk of heirs will have to wait. All I said . . ." He shakes his head. "Never mind. Is there anything else? Good." He looks to Lerial. "I understand the healer needs to talk to you about what you did. You can all go so that I can finish what I'm going to say at Mykel's memorial tomorrow."

"You're going to speak?" asks Sammyl.

"He is . . . was my brother. The memorial is in the palace. Everyone who will be there already knows I broke my leg." Rhamuel gestures.

Lerial immediately rises, nodding to the duke, then turns toward the door. The other three follow him. Norstaan is the last and closes the study door after he leaves.

"We'll leave the anteroom to you and the healer," Sammyl says.

In moments, Lerial and Emerya are alone. She walks to the window and looks out to the west. Not a hint of a breeze comes into the room, even though the window is full open.

Lerial waits.

"I never thought . . . and now . . ."

"And now . . . what?" he finally asks.

"We'll just have to see, won't we?" The enigmatic expression vanishes as she looks directly at her nephew. "Did you do anything besides what you told me on the way to the palace?"

"I added a little more order, trying to reduce the chaos, later on, as I felt he might be able to receive it. That was all."

"I think I can help him a little more. However you did what you did, it worked. He shouldn't be able to feel anything much below his waist, but he does."

"Enough to do most things . . . except for riding and walking?"

Emerya nods.

"What about his leg?"

"It will heal, but it will likely take longer because he can't move the muscles around it."

Lerial takes a deep breath, then faces his aunt.

"What is it?" A worried expression crosses Emerya's face.

"You can't return to Cigoerne."

A bemused smile appears on her face. "You're telling me where I can and can't go? Your father couldn't stop me from coming here, and . . ." Her smile broadens. "But that's not what you meant, was it?"

Lerial shakes his head. "It would be wrong for you to leave him. Even I can see that. And it's not because you'll keep him strong so that he can put Afrit back together, either." Although Lerial knows that Emerya's presence will help Rhamuel in more ways than one.

"I know. Your father was likely most unhappy when he found I had left."

"You didn't tell him?"

"He would have forbidden it. I didn't give him the choice. I'd already made arrangements with Fhastal's people. They told me there was a message from you to your father. They also told me Rhamuel had been injured. I asked Kiedron what was in the message. Then, he had to tell me."

"Because you'd know if he lied."

"He wasn't happy about that, either. He said he'd done enough in risking you. He wasn't about to lose me, too. I didn't argue. I just left. No one saw me."

"A concealment?"

"What else?"

"Does Amaira know?"

"She begged me to go."

Lerial can understand that. Amaira would know why her mother needed to go, and unlike many young people, Amaira feels well beyond herself. But then, even young healers do. *Mostly. You didn't.*

After a moment of silence, he says, "We need to arrange for your quarters."

"That might be for the best."

Lerial understands that she doesn't wish to say more. So he just leads the way to the door.

LVII

After Lerial makes certain that Emerya is settled, and that includes transferring a half squad of lancers to the palace to serve as her personal guards, he returns to Guard headquarters. He doubts that Emerya needs protection from anyone in the palace itself, but he is far less certain about whether there are other merchanters who might pose a threat to her, simply because they would prefer that Rhamuel not be physically strong. He hopes that perhaps Rhamuel will invite him to a private dinner, with Emerya, but such an invitation does not appear. Upon reflection, he suspects that the duke feels that such a "personal" dinner before the memorial might be seen less than favorably, if only by powerful merchanters, since Lerial doubts others in Afrit care that much about the duke's personal habits.

Lerial is still thinking over those matters, along with another, long after he has eaten in the officers' mess at Guard headquarters and returned to his quarters. The other concern is the fact that the merchanters, and even Rhamuel himself, seem unaware of how they are regarded by the everyday people in Afrit, and that sense is reinforced when he thinks about the reaction of his rankers over the years and, more recently, the comments of the couple at the cloth factorage, and even the reaction of Immar the innkeeper. While he certainly understands that Rhamuel needs to remain highly wary of the powerful merchanters, it seems to him that doing a few more things that gain the confidence of the small merchants, crafters, and tradespople would be helpful. That was something his grandmere had been most aware of . . . and one of the reasons why there was a Hall of Healing in Cigoerne, one well away from the palace.

Lerial is still half musing about that on oneday when he and a squad from Eleventh Company ride to the palace for the morning memorial to Mykel. Norstaan, wearing the crimson dress uniform of the Afritan Guard, meets Lerial at the stables almost as soon as Lerial has dismounted.

"Good morning, ser."

"Good morning." Lerial smiles. "What do I need to know about the ceremony?"

"It will begin at eighth glass, but everyone except you, the lady healer, and the duke and his family will be in place before that . . ."

After going over the arrangements, and allowing Lerial to inform his men of their duties, Norstaan adds, "This evening, there will be a family dinner at the palace. You and Lady Emerya are invited, and even the Lady Haesychya will be there."

As Norstaan continues, Lerial follows him into the middle section of the palace, where Emerya waits. She wears a black and white mourning head scarf over her healer's head scarf, arranged so that both show, suggesting both her understanding of the memorial and her position in Swartheld.

"I will leave you two here for a few moments," Norstaan says. "The duke and his family will be here shortly."

Once the undercaptain is out of sight, Lerial asks, "Do you know who in the duke's family is likely to be here? I can't imagine Haesychya will be."

"I haven't talked to him since we left his study yesterday."

"You haven't?"

"Propriety and concern, dear nephew."

"You mean that you're concerned about his propriety?" banters Lerial. His voice is low. "Or . . . I'm sorry."

"I think you understand." Emerya's voice is cool.

Lerial does. Emerya has made the first and dramatic move in coming to Swartheld. Now . . . the question is whether Rhamuel will reciprocate. Lerial knows Rhamuel wants to, but rulers do not and often feel they cannot do what they personally wish. Lerial also doesn't know, not for certain, how strong an influence Sammyl will be. "I hope he has the sense to do what is right for both of you."

"He will do what he thinks is right."

Lerial understands what she means by that as well.

Before long, Lerial sees four figures in dress uniforms approaching: Sammyl, Ascaar, Dhresyl, and Norstaan—the three senior commanders of the Afritan Guard and the duke's personal aide.

Norstaan hurries ahead to meet Lerial and Emerya. "If you two would follow the commanders out, and take your places . . . The duke and his family are on their way."

"We can do that."

After exchanging brief pleasantries with the commanders, Lerial and Emerya follow them along the corridor and out through a doorway on the east side of the palace, taking a position on the north side of the stone platform, with the timber framework holding Mykel's coffin, under which is a mixture of fatwood and huge long-burning hardwood logs. They stand some four yards back and about three yards to the left of where the duke and his family will be, directly in front of the four Mirror Lancers who had taken positions earlier, with Emerya the one closer to the duke's position, an arrangement, Norstaan has declared, that reflects Rhamuel's wishes. An equal distance to the right from where the duke will be are Sammyl, Ascaar, and Dhresyl, representing the Afritan Guard, with four Afritan Guard rankers behind them. On the west side of the stone platform stand the palace retainers. Lerial understands that, for a more public memorial, prominent merchants and others would stand on the east side.

Then they wait . . . and wait . . . for more than a third of a glass before the door from the palace opens once again. Norstaan walks beside Rhamuel, who wears the crimson Afritan Guard dress uniform, although one trouser leg has been slit from thigh to cuff to allow for the cast on his leg, as two palace guards guide the wheeled chair to a point just short of the middle of the north side of the stone platform Immediately behind the duke walk Kyedra and Aenslem, the only other family members present, both attired in black and white.

Lerial manages not to look at Kyedra, although he does use his order-senses to confirm it is indeed Kyedra.

"You're lingering with that order-sensing," murmurs Emerya. "That's a bit too familiar, even if she can't sense it."

Lerial flushes. It's been so long since he has been around other Magi'i that it has slipped his mind that his aunt can certainly sense what he does, at least when they are relatively close.

After several moments of silence, the two palace guards ease Rhamuel's chair forward a yard or so, and he begins to speak.

"We are here to memorialize the life of my brother Mykel and to mourn his death. He was a good man, and he was taken from us far too soon by the greed for golds and the forces of chaos that serve that greed. Those who took him have paid. That is as it should be, but there will be no great revenge against those houses. Mykel would not have wished it, for what he desired most was harmony and prosperity for everyone in Afrit . . ."

Rhamuel does not speak all that long. When he finishes the memorial itself, the palace guards wheel him to the base of the pyre, and Norstaan steps forward with a flaming torch, one that Lerial suspects is significantly longer than that usually employed. He hands the torch to Rhamuel.

"With this torch, the symbol of chaos controlled by order, we return the mortal remains of Lord Mykel to the forces from which he was born that he may live in them and they in him." After the last words, Rhamuel thrusts the long torch into the pyre, and the guards ease him and his chair back from the rapidly growing flames.

Once the pyre is a roaring inferno, the duke passes a few words to the others, and the guards turn his chair and escort him back into the palace with his family. Lerial and Emerya are next, followed by the Mirror Lancers, and then by the commanders. After the mourners leave the courtyard, Lerial knows, they will be replaced by shifts of Afritan Guards until nothing is left on the stone platform but ashes.

Once Lerial and Emerya are inside the palace, she says quietly, "We have some considerable time before the dinner this evening. I would appreciate learning from you the details of what has happened here in Afrit, and just what you have done that your father does not know. I'd also appreciate your letting me know what you do not wish him to learn. Knowing you, those are usually the details you tend to forget to mention."

"I still might forget some of those," replies Lerial, half-humorously.

"Forgetting a few 'inconvenient' facts is fine, if they aren't ones that will cause me trouble if I don't know them."

"I won't skip over that kind." *Mostly, anyway.*

They make their way to Emerya's quarters, on the second level of the west wing of the palace, but on the northwest corner, as far as possible from the duke's sleeping quarters while still remaining on the same floor.

"Definitely the appearance of propriety," Lerial observes as he steps into the sitting room, furnished as a lady's study.

Emerya does not immediately reply, but walks to the window and opens it full wide, standing before it and looking to the north for a long time. Finally, she turns and takes one of the armchairs, more delicate than those in Rhamuel's sitting room and upholstered in a muted dark blue velvet.

Lerial takes the other chair. "Where do you want me to start?"

"I won't say 'at the beginning.' I would like to know how you accomplished so much destruction when you can't draw much natural chaos from anything."

"I seem to have two talents. One is that, while I cannot draw much chaos or create it out of myself, I have become fairly adept at redirecting the chaos others muster, and the larger the amount, the more I can concentrate it into a focused force. That was mostly what I did at Luba. Duke Khesyn sent three or four chaos-wizards. He really didn't intend to land there, I think. He just wanted to kill as many Afritan Guards as he could. Khesyn probably hoped that attack would force Rhamuel to retain forces there, while the Heldyan armsmen went downriver to swell the invasion force he was building at Estheld . . ." Lerial offers a brief summary of the battles around Luba and then the ride to Swartheld, including the dinner at Shaelt and the assassination of Valatyr. "That was the first indication I had that there was something fundamentally wrong in Afrit."

"The first indication . . . after all your patrols?" Emerya's question is probingly ironic.

"I mean, within the very structure of Afrit. I began to listen more carefully and ask a few questions. It didn't take long to discover that there were no mages or wizards available in any fashion to the Afritan Guard. That bothered me a lot, and then that became a real problem when the Heldyans invaded and parts of the Harbor Post and the palace exploded and several commanders died in strange ways . . ." Lerial runs through all the events, including Aenslem's poisoning and Maesoryk's likely connection through the cammabark, and the expedition to Estheld . . . and the results.

"Your summary is missing one very important detail. Just how did you manage all this devastation and destruction? The mages sent against you couldn't have gathered that much chaos. No one could. Not that I know."

"I learned something in Verdyn. I was advised by a very wise nature mage not to use it unless all was otherwise lost . . . and to do so quite sparingly."

"Yes?"

"Apparently, I have two abilities. The first is to create order patterns that can constrain and direct chaos, even large amounts, if I construct the patterns accurately. The second is to break things apart into order and chaos. Even the tiniest bits of things release . . ." Lerial stops as he sees the stunned expression on Emerya's face.

"No one . . . I don't know of any mage . . ."

"Some of the Verdyn mages could. Doing it killed one of them. I liked her." Lerial shakes his head. "Not that way. She was much older than you. I think that was because they didn't have the patterning ability. That's why I have to be very careful. If I get too tired, I can't control the patterns, and doing any separation . . ." He frowns. "Klerryt—he was one of the mage-elders of Verdheln and the one who cautioned me about how dangerous it was. The first time, I almost did kill myself."

"I thought you came back from Verdheln rather subdued, if more within yourself. I wasn't sure. Amaira was convinced you were different. So was Maeroja."

Lerial finds it interesting that Emerya does not mention his mother. "Anyway, that was how it happened. Then, after the fighting was all over, Rhamuel asked me to go to the lakes and look into what happened to Mykel . . ." Lerial finishes his tale with what happened at both lake villas, except he only uses the wasting-illness explanation for Maesoryk.

"It will be interesting to see if Maesoryk survives long."

"We'll just have to see." *As with many things.* "Are you looking forward to dinner?"

"It's likely to tell us both much."

Lerial nods. "If you have no more questions . . ."

"For now. I am supposed to look at the duke at second glass, with his other healer."

"That's Jaermyd. More ordered than most people, but not enough to be an order-healer. He was very good at setting Rhamuel's leg."

Another enigmatic smile crosses Emerya's face. "I'll see you at dinner."

Lerial wonders about that smile for a time, even as he rides back to Afritan Guard headquarters to check with his officers and senior squad leader.

LVIII

Lerial returns to the palace just before fifth glass, making his way first to Rhamuel's receiving study, where he finds Norstaan, but not the duke, not that he has expected to see Rhamuel.

"I neglected to find out where the dinner is . . ." Lerial explains.

"That's right." Norstaan smiles. "I forgot to tell you. The Blue Salon on the third level will be serving as the family dining room for now. There will be refreshments there before dinner is served. Once the repairs and restoration on the east wing are completed that may change. The duke hasn't said."

Most likely because he wants to see how well and how much he recovers. "Thank you."

"My pleasure, ser."

With a smile and a nod, Lerial departs, walking toward the north end of the palace. When he reaches Emerya's quarters, he knocks, then waits until she admits him.

"You're early," she says.

"I finished what I needed to do with the Lancers." As he waits for her to sit down, he notices that Emerya is wearing a pale green blouse, with a darker green vest and trousers that match the vest. Lerial has to admit that his aunt looks more attractive than ever . . . or perhaps he has just not looked at her in that way.

"You have a questioning look," she ventures.

Rather than address exactly what he was thinking, he sits down and says, "When I left here, you had the strangest smile. I kept wondering why."

"You've changed more than you know . . . and that's good."

"Why? Because I admitted Jaermyd was a better bonesetter? He is."

"That's what I meant. He also told me that Rhamuel wouldn't have lived without all you did."

"How is he? Really."

Emerya offers a faint, almost sad smile. "It's early to tell."

"You don't think he'll walk again . . . or only barely, if that?"

"If I had to guess. And if you hadn't been there . . ." She shakes her head.

"I'm sorry. I tried . . ."

"Lerial . . . he should live for many years, and he's still the same man he was, except he can't walk. Not many can say that after having part of a wall fall on them. Now . . . I've told you three times how well you did. Accept it, and don't give me that look that asks for reassurance ever again."

Lerial grins at the vinegar in her last words. "I won't." He doesn't need to mention that part of how long Rhamuel will live depends on whether she decides to stay . . . or feels that she can.

"Do you want to consort his niece?"

"What?"

"Oh . . . even I could sense the longing in your order-probe."

"Even you? How about only you?"

"You didn't answer the question."

"I didn't," Lerial admits. "I want to. I admit it, but . . ."

"You worry about Lephi and your father, and especially your mother. Don't."

"There's also the *small* problem about whether her mother, grandfather, and Rhamuel would agree."

"They all owe you."

"They do, but I've noticed that there's not exactly a great sense of obligation here in Afrit." *Nor of honor, honesty . . . or much of anything but a love of amassing golds.* "Except for Rhamuel, the dukes appear to be constrained greatly by the power of the merchanters."

"You might want to talk to him about what he could do about changing that."

"I've thought about that . . . a great deal, but until . . ."

"Until you finished what had to be done, you didn't want to bring those things up?"

"Not only that, but I knew how they ended up would affect what I could say."

Emerya nods. "I'd say the time has come." She stands. "We can go to the salon and have some refreshments. We don't have to wait until they ring the glass. I have that on good authority."

Good authority? Rhamuel? *What else has been going on that she isn't saying?*

"Leave it at that, for now, Lerial," she says warmly, if with a touch of humor.

Lerial wonders, but does not question, since it's clear she's not about to say more. He rises, and the two leave the study, walking toward the grand staircase up to the third level. As they climb the marble steps, he cannot but help noticing the dust on the top of the balustrade.

When he and Emerya enter the Blue Salon, Lerial is surprised to see a circular table, rather than the usual oblong, placed at one end of the room before the open windows, with a sideboard and servitor immediately to the left, just inside the salon. The only diner already in the salon is Aenslem, and he has a beaker of lager in his hand.

The merchanter walks toward them before stopping, nodding to Lerial, and smiling at Emerya. "Lady . . . I had no idea healers were so beautiful."

"When most people need healers, they're not inclined to notice how we look." Both her words and her smile are gently warm.

"You're looking more rested, Lerial," adds the merchanter. "My daughter and granddaughter will be here shortly, now that they know you two have arrived."

"More likely Lerial," suggests Emerya.

"Both of you," rejoins Aenslem. "Young Lerial has been fulsome in his praise of your healing abilities."

Lerial doesn't recall being fulsome, although he has said that she is the best in Cigoerne, but Aenslem may wish to embellish that for his own purposes. Rather say anything, he has the servitor pour two beakers of lager.

"Lerial might have been complimentary and honest, but I don't recall him ever being fulsome in praise of anything. He tends to be rather understated."

Aenslem laughs. "Is such directness a family trait?"

"No," replies Emerya. "Only Lerial and I seem afflicted with it, one of the few attributes we share." She takes the beaker of lager from Lerial. "Thank you."

"The other being healing. I owe my life to him, you know?"

Lerial takes a small swallow of the lager, good, but still not as good as Altyrn's lager.

"He did mention being of some assistance . . ."

Smiling, the merchanter shakes his head, but does not say more as Haesychya and Kyedra enter the salon. Kyedra still wears a long-sleeved black blouse and trousers, with a black-bordered white vest, but without the head scarf, and her mother is similarly attired. She and her mother immediately walk to meet Emerya, who sets the crystal beaker on the sideboard and turns to face the two.

"Welcome to Swartheld," offers Haesychya. "I have wanted to meet you for so many years."

"I wish it could have been at a less stressful time for you," replies Emerya.

"We all have times of trouble. This is ours." Haesychya's smile is more than polite, but less than effusive.

"Thank you so much for coming," offers Kyedra, the warmth in her tone obvious. "Lerial so hoped you could come and help Uncle Rham."

"He made that rather clear." Emerya's tone is gently humorous. "I am glad I was able to come. At times, what one wishes and desires is not always possible."

Lerial can almost hear the unspoken words—*and one seldom gets a second chance.* Yet he knows she will not stay merely to be Rhamuel's healer . . . and that could make matters even more awkward—again—between Cigoerne and Afrit, especially if Lerial's father feels Rhamuel has acted badly.

Kyedra smiles softly and again says, "Thank you," before turning to Lerial.

"I'm glad you're here," he says, "and glad your mother came."

"I couldn't have come to dinner if she hadn't." Kyedra's voice is barely above a murmur. "She didn't want to come, but she did. Only for me, she said."

Those words send a chill through Lerial because the implication is that he will not be seeing much—or any—of Kyedra before long. He manages not to swallow. "Would you like a lager?"

"Please."

Lerial obtains two beakers of lager, presenting one to Haesychya and the other to Kyedra, before reclaiming the beaker from which he has barely sipped.

"When did you know you were a healer?" Haesychya asks Emerya.

"I was not quite ten . . ."

Lerial returns his full attention to Kyedra, but for several moments neither speaks. Finally, he says, "I don't know what to say."

"You're at a loss for words?" Kyedra smiles, a forced expression, Lerial can tell. "You never are."

"Almost never. This is one of those times." He doesn't want to mention anything about leaving Swartheld, and yet that is uppermost on his mind, with the knowledge that he does not control their fate, and neither does Kyedra.

As they stand there, unspeaking, the door opens, and two palace guards wheel Rhamuel into the salon. The duke still wears the dress uniform.

"Greetings, everyone." Rhamuel's voice is cheerful, and while he looks first and quickly at Emerya, his eyes do not linger on her, but turn to Haesychya. "I'm glad you came. Thank you."

Haesychya does not speak, but nods in reply.

"Because I obviously can't stand and talk," Rhamuel continues cheerfully, "I suggest that we move to the table."

When Lerial and Kyedra reach the table, he sees placards before each setting. Rhamuel is seated facing the window, with Emerya to his right and Haesychya on his left. Aenslem is to Emerya's right, with Kyedra between her grandfather and Lerial and facing her uncle. As he sits down, Lerial takes in the platters and crystal, noting the eggshell-shaded porcelain banded at the edge in crimson and gold, and both crystal beakers and goblets at each place setting.

Once everyone is seated, the guards have left, and the servitors have filled either a goblet or a beaker for each diner, Rhamuel lifts his goblet. "To Mykel."

The others raise their goblets or beakers, then drink.

At that point, Aenslem raises his beaker. "To Cigoerne and Afrit."

There is no third toast, and the servitors begin serving.

Lerial turns to Haesychya and says, barely above a murmur, "I do appreciate your coming this evening."

"Kyedra has asked for very little, Lerial. This is something I could do. There are others that I do not have the power to affect."

"I understand."

"You would. We will not speak more of that this evening." Her voice strengthens. "Has anyone heard anything from that barbarian Khesyn?"

"Not a word or a dispatch," replies Rhamuel, "but I cannot recall one in years. He prefers to make his point with blades. Now that we have replied more emphatically and effectively than he expected, I doubt we will hear anything in either fashion for a time."

The server eases a split fowl breast covered in a thin glaze onto the eggshell-white porcelain plate. Normally, the thought of basil-cumin glazed fowl might have had Lerial's mouth watering, but he is still thinking about Kyedra . . . and having to leave her.

"What does your brother think of the matter?" Haesychya asks Emerya. "Or has he discussed it with you?"

"He was greatly concerned when he heard of the scope of the battles involved. But he was pleased that it turned out as it did. He was saddened by the treachery that claimed so much of your family. He did say that there was no action too base that Khesyn wouldn't attempt if he thought it might succeed."

And none too base for some merchanters, either in Afrit or Cigoerne.

"That would be true, unhappily, for a few merchanters as well," adds Aenslem dryly, a comment that vaguely surprises Lerial. "Have you thought about what to do with the assets Alaphyn left behind?" He looks to Rhamuel.

"What would you suggest?" asks the duke.

"Take them for the duchy, and perhaps a share of Jhosef's as well."

"We can talk that over in a day or so. Perhaps you might mention it . . . to others."

"I can do that."

"It's said that there is some beautiful Cyadoran verse," Haesychya begins, looking at Emerya.

"Very little remains . . ."

Lerial turns to Kyedra and asks dryly, "What pleasantries shall we discuss, being precluded from mentioning all that we would otherwise wish to share? Perhaps whether your grandfather has a summer villa?"

"Or whether your father has one?"

"Alas, few in Cigoerne have such, for we are a poor land compared to the riches possessed by the merchanters of the north."

"Poor in golds, perhaps, but not in bravery and accomplishment," she says in a voice low enough that the conversation of others keeps all but Lerial from hearing her words.

The diners eat and talk in pleasantries, and Lerial looks at Kyedra and talks with her, again in more pleasantries, with a few low asides, as much as he dares, and before long the servers remove the main course and serve each person dessert, almond-filled pastry crescents. Perhaps a third of a glass after the pastry crescents have vanished from most diners' plates, but not Kyedra's, Lerial notes, Haesychya throws a piercing glance at her father, one so direct that Aenslem stops what he is saying to Emerya in midsentence for a moment.

After finishing whatever it might have been, Aenslem clears his throat, then says, "Your Grace . . . this dinner has been a great honor, but the day has been long . . ."

"I understand, Aenslem." Rhamuel turns to Haesychya. "My thanks for your coming. I would not keep you long. I will need just a few moments with your sire, but only a few."

"We can manage," replies Haesychya. "We will take our time going to the coach."

Lerial almost smiles at her words and tone, which convey the sense that if whatever the two are going to discuss takes much longer, she will not be pleased. Lerial wouldn't put it past her to just direct the coach back to the villa if Aenslem takes too much time with the duke. He turns to Kyedra and takes her hand, under the table, squeezing it gently. "Thank you . . . for everything."

Her voice is firm, but low, as she replies, "I am the one who should offer thanks, for what you have done. I will not offer thanks for your departure." She squeezes his hand in return, then slips her fingers from his.

"Nor I."

"Kyedra," offers Haesychya, "we do need to go." She looks at Lerial, almost sadly, and nods. "Good evening, Lerial . . . and thank you, again, for my father's life."

Lerial stands with everyone else, and watches as Emerya departs with the other two women. *Why is she going?* But he really cannot ask. So, after several moments, he walks over to the duke, but before he can say anything, Rhamuel speaks.

"We'll talk in the morning about your departure. I'd thought we might tonight, but it's been a long day, and I need a few moments with Aenslem." Rhamuel shakes his head ruefully. "There's one thing that can't wait, but I'm not getting into merchanter affairs tonight."

"There are a few other things I'd also like to suggest."

Rhamuel looks away, then motions to someone.

Lerial realizes that someone is Emerya, who obviously only spent a few moments with Haesychya and Kyedra before she returned. She moves to Rhamuel's shoulder. The way she touches the duke's shoulder tells Lerial that there is something else he has missed.

"Yes," murmurs Emerya, "but you're the first to know. Official word must wait for mourning to end."

"I could not let her go, or leave her, not again," murmurs Rhamuel, before smiling widely. "She will have the position she long deserved. And now, I need to talk to Aenslem. I'll see you in the morning. Not too early. Say . . . eighth glass."

That is an obvious dismissal, and Lerial inclines his head. "Eighth glass."

As he walks from the chamber, then to the stables, and even as he rides back to Afritan Guard headquarters, he is still pondering how he missed what had occurred between his aunt and Rhamuel, but he is pleased for them, especially for Emerya.

All that doesn't help him, especially since it doesn't seem that there is anything he can do as far as Kyedra is concerned. *You can't ask for her hand, not as the younger brother of the heir, without your father's consent, and she can't consent without Rhamuel's approval and Aenslem's, and Aenslem won't consent unless both Haesychya and Rhamuel agree . . . and Lephi would have a fit.* Except Lerial really doesn't care what Lephi thinks, nor does that matter unless their father agrees with Lephi. And then there is the other small problem that he has three companies of Mirror Lancers, or what is left of them, to look after as well.

He laughs softly. *And all because she smiled . . . and that smile made you look at her more closely.*

He shakes his head and keeps riding, not really hearing the echoes of the gelding's hoofs on the paving stones.

LIX

When Lerial meets with his officers and senior squad leaders on twoday morning, after going over muster reports, Strauxyn asks, "Begging your pardon, ser, but do you know when we'll be leaving?"

"That's one of the things I hope to settle with the duke this morning. Now that he's dealt with his brother's memorial, we should be able to settle things."

"You don't like Swartheld so well?" asks Kusyl jestingly.

"It's all right. It's just . . ." Strauxyn breaks off his words.

"Who is she?" Kusyl grins.

Strauxyn flushes.

Lerial smiles. "It's amazing what women can do."

"Or what men will do for the ones they love," adds Kusyl.

That comment shocks Lerial, because it's not what he'd have expected from the sardonic older undercaptain. *But there's likely so much you don't know, just like Aenslem and Atroyan, and perhaps even Rhamuel, who know so little of those below them.* He pushes aside that sobering thought, as well as the near-continual thoughts about Kyedra, wondering if there is any way he can get his father to agree to letting him ask for Kyedra's hand. *That's assuming Aenslem and Rhamuel—and Haesychya—would agree.* And that is anything but certain.

"Ser . . . there is one thing," ventures Dhoraat.

"Yes?"

"There are some rankers whose terms expire on eightday . . ."

Lerial should have remembered that. All rankers' terms expire on one of ten days in the year—the last day of a season or the eightday of the fifth week of the season. "They can still travel back to Cigoerne with their company. It's not as though we're likely to be fighting, and they can draw pay for the travel time without agreeing to extend their term."

"They know that, ser. There are a couple who want to stay here. They've found positions."

"And lady-friends, I'd wager," adds Kusyl.

"That can happen to any man, anywhere," Lerial replies. "I don't see a problem there. If there aren't too many, I can find a way to cover their back pay."

"Just three that want to stay, ser."

"We can manage that. Anything else?"

"No, ser."

"Then I need to get to the palace to meet with the duke."

Lerial takes only a half squad of rankers as an escort, and he doubts he needs more than two men, but there still is the question of appearances. When he reaches the anteroom outside the duke's study, only Norstaan is there.

"Go right in, ser," says Norstaan. "He's alone. The commander is at South Post this morning."

"Thank you." Not without some trepidation, Lerial steps into the receiving study.

Rhamuel motions for him to take a chair, and Lerial does so, waiting.

"To begin with, I thought you'd like to know that five days ago, Maesoryk died peacefully in his sleep. The local healer could find no trace of chaos or poison."

Lerial manages to avoid taking a deep breath. "I'm not surprised."

"I didn't think you would be. In fact, I think you'd only have been surprised if you had not heard of his death." After a moment, Rhamuel continues, his voice firm and decisive, "I have some other things I'd like to discuss with you, but let's go over what you had in mind first. Save the questions about your departure for last."

Lerial again feels like taking a deep breath. He doesn't. "You need to make some changes in what the merchanters can and cannot do."

"Such as?"

"Powerful order-mages or chaos-mages should serve the duke and/or the Afritan Guard, not the merchanters. Less powerful mages or wizards should only serve merchanters with the knowledge and consent of the duke."

"Why do you think that?" Rhamuel's tone is even, not quite skeptical.

"Most of the treachery your brother faced was made possible by the fact that Duke Khesyn had control of chaos-mages and traitorous Afritan merchanters did also—"

"And the only thing that saved me and Afrit was one powerful magus loaned to me by the grace of the Duke of Cigoerne."

"I'm not a full magus, and never will be."

"Call you a war magus, then, but you were the difference. I'll admit it. I also agree with your recommendation. There is, however, just one small problem with it. How exactly am I going to enforce it?" Rhamuel smiles.

"You make failure to comply treason against Afrit and execute anyone who fails to comply. It won't work otherwise."

"I'd agree with that as well, but the same problem remains. If someone has a powerful mage, how can a duke without mages make them comply?"

Lerial can see the difficulty . . . and he realizes, as he has considered before, just how much tradition and structure had kept the Cyadoran Magi'i and merchanters in their places . . . and that Rhamuel has neither. Nor does he have any mages.

"You see . . ." says the duke, "I've thought about this. So did my brother. But we've never had enough golds to buy mages, and without them, we don't have enough power to raise tariffs to gain the golds to buy their services, let alone their loyalty."

"I can see that."

"I also have another problem. As duke, I'm supposed to produce heirs—sons. What most people do not know is that I was more seriously injured than almost anyone knew in the battle against your father and the Mirror Lancers years ago. It is sheer fortune that I even have a daughter. With Mykel dead, it will become obvious that I can have no heirs. The only living individual who can carry on the family blood is my niece."

"That's not true." Lerial doesn't want to dwell on that. "Besides, Amaira is your daughter, and her mother is the sister of the duke of Cigoerne. You can't get better bloodlines than that. Why not just find her an appropriate consort and make her son heir to Afrit?"

"I thought of that. It won't work."

"Why not?"

"Because Amaira isn't known to either the merchanters or the people of Afrit and because *you* can't consort your cousin."

"I can't? What does that have to do—"

"Whether I like it or not, or whether you do or not, the duke of Afrit must be seen as both wise and powerful or be wise with a powerful backer. I can supply the wisdom, or at least enough of it or the image of it, but no one believes a crippled ruler is powerful, and you are the only individual of ducal lineage in all Hamor that the merchanters absolutely know is powerful and loyal to me . . . at least loyal to me in terms of Afrit."

"But . . . what about Lephi?" Lerial hates to ask that question, but it is one his parents will certainly ask.

"He doesn't have your skills, and even if he did, which he doesn't, the last thing the merchanters would accept is a consorting that puts Cigoerne in a position to control Afrit. You have fought and nearly died, possibly more than once, to save Afrit from the Heldyans. You are of ducal blood, but you are not the principal heir. In addition, and not unimportant, you're halfway to falling in love with Kyedra and she with you."

"I still don't like Kyedra being forced to consort me as if she were a tool."

"We're all tools, Lerial. I was for my brother, and you have been for yours. Your father was for your grandmere until he was old enough and smart enough to rule on his own. Even after that, she supplied the wisdom he had not yet learned. I know. I was there, you might recall."

"I don't recall. I was too young, and they kept me away from you."

"There is one other thing. If you consort her, you'll have to renounce any claim to Cigoerne, you know," Rhamuel says.

Renounce Cigoerne? Everything Grandmere had worked for? All that Father has done? All that you've done? All those you've killed to allow Cigoerne to survive and prosper? "That's asking a great deal, even though you know I never intended to be the heir."

"I know that. Few others do, and fewer still will after all that has happened. If you don't renounce any claim to Cigoerne, the people, especially the merchanters, will not accept Kyedra's son, assuming she will have one, as duke, or her as his regent, should I die before he is of age." Rhamuel laughs ironically. "In my condition, that is likely. Do you want another uprising? Do you want another Maesoryk scheming to turn Afrit over to Khesyn or his heirs? You have to decide what you think is best. No one else can. You can ride back to Cigoerne, and no one will think badly of you. Not after destroying Khesyn's invasion." Rhamuel holds up his hand to stop Lerial from saying anything.

Lerial can see the effort that requires of the duke, and the fact that his hand begins to shake, and Rhamuel has to lower it. *He's not as strong as he seems.*

"You gave your word that you wouldn't reveal Maesoryk's treachery. But how long will that remain hidden once you leave . . . if that is your choice?"

Lerial also knows what Rhamuel has not said. That if he does not consort Kyedra, that will further weaken Rhamuel . . . and Afrit . . . and Cigoerne in turn. And now that Kyedra is the only one carrying the possibility of producing an heir, she cannot consort Lephi, because all the merchanters of Afrit would protest. Paradoxically, he is faced with what he never wanted for Kyedra, for her to be forced into consorting someone, and he is that someone. *What would the majer have said to this? How would he . . . ?*

A slow smile crosses Lerial's face as he realizes that the majer had already known. Why else would he have written that last letter? The one that had said, the words burned into Lerial's memory:

> What I task you with, and it is a task and not a request, is to assure that the heirs of the Malachite Throne do not perish, that they do not stoop to petty bargains for a peace that will not last, and that their heritage will shine on when the City of Light is long forgotten. This does not mean you are to re-create Cyad or Cyador. That time is past. It does mean that what was best of that time should live on through you and what you do.

And what is the best of that time? "Doing what is right and proper."

"What?" asks Rhamuel.

"I will consort Kyedra . . . only if she will have me of her own *free* will."

"It took you long enough," says a too-familiar voice.

Lerial turns and then stands to see Emerya standing in the corner of the study, with Kyedra beside her. Kyedra is smiling, offering that radiance that warms him even when it is not directed at him.

A concealment shield . . . and you didn't even sense it!

His expression must have revealed his thoughts, because Emerya says gently, "There are still some things you don't know about order."

Then he and Kyedra are moving toward each other, and no one else is in the study, not for them.

EPILOGUE

Lerial hands the missive to Kyedra, a missive that they have hoped to receive for more than a season. "You should read this."

She takes it, but he stands at her shoulder and watches as she reads the words set so carefully on the thick parchment.

> My Dear Lerial . . .
> Or should I address you as Arms-Commander of Afrit?
>
> Majer Altyrn always said that you would do great and unexpected deeds, and that I should not be surprised at where your deeds led you. I am surprised. I was also disappointed at first, and that is why this letter, I freely admit, has been so long in coming, but both your mother and Maeroja counseled me that what has happened has turned out for the best . . .

When he had read those words the first time, for a moment, Lerial had been surprised, but now he understands. His mother has always feared that his abilities would outshine his older brother's and cause difficulties for Lephi and incidentally for the future of Cigoerne, but mainly for Lephi. Now those difficulties will not exist. There may be others, but not those.

> . . . I have always hoped for better relations between Afrit and Cigoerne. That was why I dispatched you and your companies to assist Duke Atroyan, as you well know.
>
> In time, once matters have settled slightly, I would hope that we might see you and your consort, either here in Cigoerne or in Swartheld, a possibility I had thought might never be practical in my lifetime. Nor did your mother and I ever entertain the possibility that we might have grandchildren ruling differing lands.
>
> As for your aunt, I can only wish her the best. I have written her as well to tell her that. We will miss her, and Ryalah will

miss Amaira, but they both deserve what happiness they can grasp in an uncertain and changing world.

Lerial nods as he reads those words, his hand resting lightly on Kyedra's shoulder, making it slightly easier for him to sense already the life within Kyedra, although he cannot tell whether the child will be a boy or girl. Either way, he and Rhamuel, and Kyedra—especially Kyedra—will work it out.